UNDOING OF
THREA
DREAMS IN SHADOW

KEEGEN HORST

MILTON & HUGO L.L.C.
4407 Park Ave., Suite 5
Union City, NJ 07087, USA

Website: *www. miltonandhugo.com*
Hotline: *1- 888-778-0033*
Email: *info@miltonandhugo.com*

Ordering Information:
Quantity sales. Special discounts are granted to corporations, associations, and other organizations. For more information on these discounts, please reach out to the publisher using the contact information provided above.

Library of Congress Control Number:		2024913718
ISBN-13:	979-8-89285-198-5	[Paperback Edition]
	979-8-89285-199-2	[Hardback Edition]
	979-8-89285-197-8	[Digital Edition]

Rev. date: 06/17/2024

The Prologue

At the beginning of this world, but after the beginning of time, The One willed for servants. He was the First and is the Final, and so servants were made. The One told His Servants of the world that He wished to make and asked them to contribute. So He gave them powers and each servant gained the ability to Sculpt, and so they each were assigned a domain. The One crafted then the sphere that was to be the world, and the laws that would govern over everything that would be sculpted.

Then the One spoke to His Nine, saying "This place is your canvas to paint and the matter is yours to sculpt. Fill this world with life and things of good." But before the Nine carried out the One's will, the One spoke to Genus, the one who was closest to His will. "As you paint and sculpt, watch over your brother Nath. I made him good, yet darkness is near to entering his heart. Do not allow him to paint with an ill mind." With that the One departed from His Nine, and left to attend to another world. Troubled, Genus went to his siblings and held council about that which the One had told him, yet Nath was not summoned. The Eight agreed that letting Nath join in the work risked too much, so they exiled him. Extremely embittered at this Nath left to reside in a plain that mirrored the world. Nath, now stripped of his domain, took on that of Vengeance and Vindication in replacement of the Charity that had been stolen from him. This was the seed planted by the Sculptors that would sprout into the second most devastating war the world would know.

Now the Eight Sculptors began the work set out for them by the One and began to paint and sculpt the world into its form. Genus, who was the Sculptor of Light, gave color to the world and made the sun, allowing all things to see what is good. Eleanora, who was the Sculptor of Darkness, filled the sky with the stars and the Moon, giving beauty in the pale light. Valoria, who was the Sculptor of Life, filled the land with plants and animals. Bonaventure, who was the Sculptor of Earth, filled the sphere with rock and terrain. Darshon, who was the Sculptor of Fire, gave warmth to the land, and filled creatures with blood. Sasara, who was the Sculptor of Water, filled the world with the oceans, rivers, and lakes, letting the azure coolness of life fill the sphere. Atlas, who was the Sculptor of Lightning, crafted the sky and clouds, and filled things with sound. Finally, Celerious, who was the Sculptor of Air, filled the sphere with wind and all gases.

The Sculptors looked upon everything and knew that something was missing from the world. So, they held council and decided to create a creature based on the One. So, they created the first human. The human was named Aradoth, which means "the first". As the Eight looked upon the human, they realized that while he was in all things like them, Aradoth was missing the one thing that they had, the most important thing. Aradoth did not have Charity within him. Before they could decide what to do, the One returned. He looked over all that had been made and blessed all of it. Then the Eight went to Him and said, "Master, we have filled the world with our works like you have asked, yet the human is not as he should be for there is no Charity within him." The One frowned and asked, "Why is there no Charity in him? Why has Nath withheld giving this precious gift to them? Yet, nine and I left and only eight do I see now. Where is Nath?"

The Eight then explained all that they had done, and the One grew enraged at them. "You have punished one who was innocent for a crime he did not commit! Because of this evil you all have sealed your fates. Each of you shall die far before this world does. But because you have done all things according to my will except this, you will still exist alongside a few of the humans whom I choose. The One then stripped their power into Cores, and bound the Eight to the world which they had named Romevan, which means, "that which is perfect." Nath then entered Romevan, unbeknownst to the Eight, and filled humans with his new domain. As he was about to leave, the One caught him, and said, "You I was about to allow to return to this world and join me in another world. Now you have woven your fate to suffer that of your siblings." And so the One did the same to Nath as he had the Eight. Then, before leaving, the One turned to humans and said to Himself, "I will bless them with Charity myself, so that they may survive and do good in the face of the evils that will assault them." So the One Himself gave men the gift of Charity Himself, filling up all hearts with love. And so ended the creation of Romevan.

Now Aradoth was fruitful with his wife Aradotha, and they filled the world with their offspring. Now Aradoth was beloved by the Eight, and he often walked with them and spoke to them. They taught him many things about the world, form the magic that coursed through the world's veins, to the sciences of nature. Humans made much progress under his guidance, and soon Romevan was filled with magic wonders and technological advancements. Yet no matter how much Aradoth learned, he always wanted more. He was always practicing magic and trying to become stronger and always he researched. Now Nath had been watching all of this, and was filled with envy as he looked upon the works that he had been denied a hand in. Nath decided that he would have works of his own in the world, but all material had been sculpted and used. So, one day Nath snuck into Romevan and stole Aradoth's seven newly sired children, killing Aradotha in the process. Aradoth, who was a hundred years old by this time, returned home to find his children, who were no younger than three, all gone and his wife's bloody corpse upon the floor.

With this crime, Nath had quickened his fate over the others, and sealed the fate many a human. Aradoth swore vengeance upon whomever had killed his beloved wife and stolen his children, and so evil entered his heart and began to cloud it. Aradoth then began to search all over Romevan for his children. Eleanora, who had always pitied Nath and had regretted his exile, spotted him with leave Romevan with the children. So Eleanora went to him in his home of Heshtanarus, which means, "the place of the scorned". Upon entering his palace, she found Nath in the throne room. Six dead bodies of small children lay on the floor, blood gushing from their mouths, while a grotesque, humanoid figure lay next to Nath curled up in a ball. Eleanora looked in horror and asked Nath, "What crime have you committed? You have killed Aradotha, the beloved of Aradoth and kidnapped his children and killed them! Even now Aradoth searches the land for his children, cursing whomever has done this to him." Nath looked upon Eleanora with spite as he said, "I have only collected my due. I was denied my rightful place in the Sculpting. Well now I have sculpted my own work and as you have scorned me, so shall I make is so that your work be scorned also." Nath then pointed to the thing curled up, frightened at his feet saying, "Behold, Malanus the first Heshtisi! He who was once loved shall now be scorned by all."

Pity welled up inside of Eleanora as she looked up the former human child. Pity for both Nath and Malanus. "I must tell Aradoth of this. These are his children whom you have killed in your attempt to change what is. Yet, because I believe that you deserve to have your works in this world, I will not punish you nor will I tell our siblings of this. But I beg you, do not continue to kill. Only evil will come of it." Nath, who then realized the evil that he had done by killing, wept as Eleanora left. He vowed that he would not kill any other humans as he turned them.

When Eleanora returned to Romevan and told Aradoth of what had happened. He became very angry that she nor any of the Eight had done nothing nor attempted to return his child to him. Yet he hid his anger behind tears as he wept. Eleanora took pity upon Aradoth and so showed him a secret art of her domain known as Shadewelding. This allowed one to combine two things by fusing them into one, and to also make them stronger through this process. Yet, Eleanora also revealed to him that it could do something else. One could use Shadewelding in a reverse process to siphon power from a creature and take the power for one's own. Aradoth thanked her with tears in his eyes, saying, "I am humbled that you would teach one such as me this art that is so intimate to you. I only wish I could see my child once more." So, before Eleanora left, she taught Aradoth how to enter Heshtanarus.

Aradoth then went to Heshtanarus and found Nath. Nath, who was warry of Aradoth demanded to know why he was there. Aradoth had looked upon Malanus, and was revolted by the sight of his once beautiful son, yet hid this from his face. Much of the love he once had for his son left, and he swore vengeance upon all the Sculptors for this deformity. Aradoth told Nath that he had forgiven him and understood why he had done all this. Nath was taken in by Aradoth's eloquent tongue, and believe him. Aradoth also told Nath that he wished to help him and further his works. "I wish to make the Eight pay for the slight they have done to you. How can we trust them to rule over this world justly when they punish those who have never committed a crime?"

And so Nath, in return for Aradoth bringing humans to him, taught Aradoth Natharian magic. This magic's source lay in Nath himself, and did was not known to any of the Eight. Thus, Nath and Aradoth began to kidnap people and turn them into Heshtisi. Aradoth though secretly would Shadeweld animals with people to make new breeds of Heshtisi, and he would also wipe the memories of Heshtisi to ensure their loyalty to him. The world then became full of fear as people disappeared, and crime began to become regular for men as their hearts were filled with terror. Perturbed at what was happening, the Eight began to investigate. Yet they could not discover what was the cause of all this fear for many years.

Twenty years it took for the Eight to discover Nath's doings, and over those twenty years Aradoth worked his cunning upon all of them. He began to divide them, and make them distrust one another, and he also began to turn some's sympathies towards Nath and his unjust punishment. Once the Eight finally discovered what Nath had done, they called council and brought Nath to them. Eleanora, who had become a mother figure to the poor Malanus, defended Nath's actions. Then Genus spoke saying, "Nath, have now done evil things for no other reason than to spite us. I will give you one last chance. Stop now, and we shall allow your works to exist. Contiune, and we shall go to war with you, destroying all of your works." Nath simply laughed and mocked Genus saying, "You sit there demanding I stop doing that which I was entitled to. You pronounce my fate with all the authority and grimness of one who is just, just as you did when you unjustly exiled me for no wrong. No, I will not stop and it is I who shall destroy you." And so the War of the Nine was begun.

Genus, Valoria, Celerious and Bonaventure were the only fought against Eleanora, Nathn, Atlas, Sasara, and Darshon. Aradoth laughed as the War of the Nine ensued. While The Nine fought, he secretly went about Romevan and stole the power of many mages, and also took their life force, making him young once more. Heshtisi armies roamed the world as they fought human armies, both being led by the Sculptors. For thousands of years the war raged on, neither side gaining the upper hand. Human heroes arose and fell, and through their valiant efforts, the war changed to Genus's side. Humans began to beat back the hoardes of demons that had invaded their homes, and the ended appeared in sight.

Then, one day Nath was grievously injured in battle by Genus and fled to his palace. As he lay gravely wounded, he called for Aradoth. Aradoth came, and when he say Nath in his weakened state, he knew his plans were almost complete. Nath asked him to heal him, for he knew that Aradoth was the only one who could. Aradoth simply smiled as he plunged his knife deep into Nath's neck, and using Shadewelding, took all of Nath's power for his own. He absorbed all of the power, and as he did, his body was transformed. His legs became bow-bent, and he grew rust colored scales all over his body. Horns grew from his head and his pupils became slits. Aradoth smiled and then using his new power, he cast Charity from himself, and his heart became one filled with nothing but evil. Aradoth then called his allies together and told them of Nath's death, telling them that he had been too late to save him and that Nath had bestowed this power upon him. His allies rallied around their new leader, and he turned the tides of the war in their favor.

As the war raged on, Sasara, Atlas, and Bonaventure were killed, and Aradoth also took their power. Yet he was not able to take all of it, for the majority of their powers resided in their Cores, which were hidden. Aradoth became enraged and decided that once the war was over he would find them. Eleanora though discovered how Aradoth was taking the powers of the Nine, and uncovered his true purpose; to take the world for his own and sculpt it how he wished. Eleanora fled to Genus, telling him how they had all been deceived. They were at this time the last of the Nine.

Now at this time, two humans existed who had made names for themselves as brave heroes and righteous people. They were Threa Elnoreth, and Jethro Markus. Genus and Eleanora took council, and realized that their time was near. So together they gave their powers to Threa, and entrusted the world to her warriors. Soon after, Genus and Eleanora were killed. Aradoth then gleefully cast of his name and took the name Romevan. His victory undeniable, Romevan gathered all of his forces to invade the last stronghold of Ala'Kathar. Threa and Jethro gathered the humans and made a one last stand against the forces of darkness. The Disciples of Threa fought a Romevan many times, but could never defeat him, yet he grew enraged that he could not overtake this one last place of hope.

The Disciples then devised a plan, and a spell to stop Romevan. During the final battle in which Romevan threw all of his strength against them, the Disciples put their plan into action. They cast their spell, and Romevan and all of the Heshtisi were sucked into Heshtanarus and bound there, unable to leave. The world rejoiced as it was freed from the darkness of the War, and in defiance of Romevan, the people renamed the world Threa. Yet when things should have been calm and peaceful, Threa was killed by Malanus, who still retained much of his intrinsic humanity, and so had not been affected by the spell. Jethro was given Threa's powers at her deathbed, and so using them, he and the remaining Disciples fought Malanus. They knew they could not kill him, and so devised another way of imprisoning him. Gathering many mages, they trapped Malanus and as Jethro fought him, they cast a spell to imprison Malanus inside a mask. Yet, as Malanus was imprisoned, the mages helping them had ulterior motives, and cast the spell at Jethro also. Geoffrey, who was a good friend of Jethro, saw the spell and pushed Jethro out of the way sacrificing himself instead. The mages were promptly killed, yet they had no way of freeing Geoffrey, for the spell had been designed only one way.

The two masks then were hidden from the world but placed together in a place only know to Jethro. Jethro Markus continued as a hero, yet also found the secret of immortality, a secret more pure and good than what Romevan had done to achieve immortality. For a thousand years Jethro fought as a hero, doing good and protecting Threa, and watching over the barrier that held the Heshtisi. This time is known as the Bountiful Age, for during these thousand years, men began to recover and re-learn what had been lost during the War of the Nine. Yet after a thousand years, Jethro grew weary. Then, finally he laid down his sword and married, and that is where our tale begins...

Chapter 1

Darkness Enclosing

In 5the village of Ala'Kathar, Jethro Markus, now looking into his thirties, set down his pen upon the polished wooden desk and closed the cured leather book he had been writing in. He leaned back in his chair, stretching his arms. He looked out the window, wondering how long he had been at it. The sun was high in the sky now. Jethro smiled wryly as he gauged the time. He had been hard at work writing before the sun was even up. He had been scolded by Lorelei for getting up so early after going to be well past midnight. *It was time well spent* Jethro thought, *even though I was scolded*. Jethro stood up, his toned muscles flexing as he moved, even though he was getting on in years. He brushed a strand his brown hair with black tips out of his face, although a few gray streaks were appearing. He ran his hand through his hair in a hopeless attempt at trying to fix his unruly hair. He sighed as that one strand above his nose fell back into place. He could never get that strand to disappear. He instead stroked his goatee as he thought about what to do next. His stomach growled in answer.

Well, lunch would be nice but there was something he needed to take care before he went ahead and filled his stomach's demands. Jethro chuckled to himself at his own comedic thoughts as he stood up and grabbed the leather-bound book. He walked over to his polished oak closet and opened it up. Various clothes hung about, and miscellaneous items of small significance were placed on the shelf at the top. Jethro then placed his hand on one of the panels on the back of the closet, and pushed it in. There were some clicking noises behind the wall as the panels in front of him slid into the wall horizontally and a path opened up. "Honey!" Lorelei called, "Lunch is ready!" Jethro smiled as he shouted back, "I'll be right there! I just need to take care of something first."

Jethro walked down the hidden staircase that had appeared, torches on the wall bursting into life as he passed them. At the end of the staircase was a massive storeroom filled with tons of shelves and chests. Various items were stored on the shelves, nothing seeming to be related to another except to one who was as learned in the magical arts as Jethro. Weapons, vials, jewelry, and books, the list kept going for all the items that one could find in this room, yet each item was labeled with explanations for what it was. The labels were a bit of a necessity since the room probably had more cursed items in it than actually useful items.

Jethro walked over to one shelf near the back of the room to a shelf filled with identical books as the one that he held. He went ahead and placed it on the shelf with its brethren. He looked over the shelf. Ten books filled with his memoirs, each one spanning a hundred years and twelve more books filled with his studies about magic, and five more books about his alchemic research. Now that Jethro the Immortal was no longer immortal, he figured he should leave all that he had learned to everyone who he deemed worthy of the knowledge. Jethro smiled as he gave a self-satisfied nod at looking over all the books and turned to leave.

He paused though as his looked over the room, filling him up with bittersweet nostalgia. So many of these items had been obtained with a friend's help, but at the same many more of these items had cost a friend's life. He smiled though as he his gaze fell upon the pedestal against the back of the center of the wall. The pedestal held four swords of separate stands, but only one sword held his gaze. Jethro walked over to the sword, picked up the hand-and-a-half sword. The handle had two garnets inlaid in the hilt, and if one could see the fabric of magic, one would see the intricate spells placed upon those two unseeingly important gems. The blade though was curious. It was split down into two colors, one side pure black, and the other pure white. There was a triangular tip jutting out at the top of the white side, while the black side had an identical formation at the base of the blade. It had been many years since he had needed to wield his sword, Darkest Flame. A sword made for him by the master blacksmith Zechariah Marrobrath the day he had formed the Champions for Threa. Using a secret metal, Zechariah had made all of the Champions' weapons, and his work was still unmatched. This sword could cut through practically anything. Only a few things could stand up to it. Yet for some reason unknown, this metal could not cut through any metal forged into a weapon as cleanly as if that same metal were an iron bar, which the sword could cut through like butter.

Jethro was removed from his stupor of memories though as his stomach growled at him once more. He quickly put the sword down as he left the room and went back upstairs. As he exited, he closed the secret passage and headed to the kitchen. He went through the stone hallway and entered the kitchen. The kitchen had a big rectangular oak table that could seat up to twelve people. Jethro sat down in front of the plate on the table, beef and cheese and some grapes.

"Did you wash your hands?" Lorelei asked without even turning around from her spot in the sink. "Uhhh..." "I swear," Lorelei said exasperated, "you're just as bad as Joseph. He must get it from you. You never know what kind of stuff is on your hands." Jethro just grinned and walked over next to her, plunging his hands into the warm soapy water. "What can I say? I'm incorrigible." Lorelei just gave a small giggle as Jethro sat back down. His wife was a short woman at five foot four. She wore a light purple shirt today with a blue skirt. She had dark black hair that was cut short. She wore two hairpins though that kept her hair tucked behind her ears that were the same bright blue as her eyes.

"I expect you to go and entertain our sons after you're done eating." Lorelei said, "I need to go out and gather herbs for the store." Jethro just smiled as he said, "Gladly. I'm done with the book now anyways." Lorelei sold potions on the side at Jethro's forge in town. It was a strange combination, but they made it work. "That's the last one now, isn't it?" Lorelei asked curiously. "Yep," Jethro replied, "sure is. All my knowledge of the past three thousand years has now been written down. I am now allowed to live my life." Lorelei finished washing and as she dried her hands, she asked, "So, who do you plan on letting read what's in them? You plan on just keeping them in the storage room?" Jethro began to cough as he almost choked on the grape he just swallowed. "You knew about that?" Jethro asked incredulously. "Of course, I did."

Lorelei said, "I'm your wife remember?" Jethro just laughed, "I should have known you would figure it out. When did you find out?"

"As soon as you built it. Now, are you going to answer my question or not?" Jethro finished the last of his meal before he answered. "The information in a lot of those books could prove to be dangerous if I let the wrong person read them. So really, I guess the right kind of person."

"And how will you know that?" Lorelei asked curiously. Jethro just shook his head, "I'm not exactly sure. I guess I'll just know when I know. "Hmph," Lorelei sniffed, "Don't you think you would want more than a feeling with something that dangerous?" Jethro just grinned as he said, "Come now, my instincts are honed from three thousand years, you really think they would steer me wrong in something like this? Whenever it comes to the important things, my instincts are spot on. They did tell me to marry you after all" Lorelei just sighed, "I suppose that's true. But still, you don't want to come up with some sort of trial or something to have them prove their worth? All artifacts of that level of importance always have something like that."

"These books are hardly old enough to be artifacts." Jethro said wryly, "Besides, you would actually be surprised at how many magical artifacts are just lying around. That trial stuff is for fairy tales." Jethro lied, "I know how to judge a person's character. You'll just have to trust me on this." There was a bit of silence before Jethro said mischievously, "Well, if you want me to devise some trials, you could do something for me."

"And what would that be?" Lorelei asked. "Well, the kids are going to be over at their friend's house tonight and the house will be just to ourselves." Jethro answered with a grin. Lorelei just shook her head, "So you want a prize for doing something you should be doing without motivation?" Jethro just kept grinning, "Yeah, pretty much. What do you say?" Lorelei just rolled her eyes as the air next to her became gray and shimmery, but it was no wider than a thumb. Jethro's grin turned into a frown as he saw the air magic appear, and then before he could put two and two together, the air fabric rushed towards his chair, knocking it over. Jethro fell cursing and as he got to his feet, he saw turned to Lorelei. Her mouth was twitching, trying to hold in a smile. "What was that?" Jethro demanded. "An answerer." Lorelei explained as she then burst out laughing." Jethro just shook his head as he muttered sulkily, "A simple no would have sufficed." His wife had the strangest sense of humor sometimes, mostly involving him getting hurt in some way. "Now go find the boys." Lorelei said playfully as she shoved him out of the kitchen with a gust of air. "You know," Jethro said, "It's fitting you're an air mage with how much comes out of your mouth." He then quickly ran out of sight before she could retaliate, "Look who's talking!" Lorelei shot back. Jethro just chuckled to himself as he headed towards the door, when suddenly his sons came running in from outside.

The two boys came rushing up to him. Joseph, his eldest, was six years old. Glasses framed two yellow eyes that always seemed to be glowing with mischief. His raven black hair was the same shade as Lorelei's. Klin, who was younger by a year, had dark brown hair that seemed as hard to keep from being messy as his father's, and Klin's hair was far shorter. His dark brown eyes though revealed the astounding intelligence that he had. Klin was smarter than any of the kids his age, and seemed to be just as smart, or maybe even smarter than kids three years older than him. "Daddy," Joseph said, "Bert is here."

"Really?" Jethro asked surprised, "Did he ask you two to find me?" Klin nodded as he replied, "Yeah. He said that it was very important. But he also muttered something about a stranger, and he needs to go." Jethro frowned as he commanded, "Alright, stay inside and go to your mother. She's in the kitchen." Without seeing if they obeyed, Jethro opened the door and went outside. At the end of the path leading to his house stood his nearest neighbor, and by nearest, he was three hundred yards away. Bert Kalamon was a short, scrawny man who had a wiry way of moving. "Jethro!" Bert nearly shouted as he saw him. "The Village Council just sent me!" Jethro frowned, "What's going on?"

"This strange creature showed up about two hours ago. It's waiting outside the walls, just standing there. Thinking it might be some sort of monster, someone wondered aloud what it might want, and the thing actually answered! It heard he man from a hundred paces away! This thing though, it is asking for you!" Jethro's brow furrowed in thought as he heard all this. "This monster, what does it look like?" Bert gave a shudder as he said, "Evil looking it is, like some monster from the War of the Nine. It had face that had frost floating all around it, and wings of crystalline that were twice as long as its body. It also had this dark blue carapace on it that was framed like armor on its body." Jethro felt his heart stop and forgot how to breathe as his breath caught. "Are you sure that's what it looked like?" Bert nodded, "I saw it with my own two eyes. Do you have any idea what it wants?" Jethro finally got control of his breathing once more and said grimly, "Yeah, I think I know exactly what it wants. Wait here. I need to grab something, then lead me to it."

Bart was maybe a weasel at times, but he was an honest man for the most part, and so Jethro trusted his testimony. Jethro sprinted back inside and rushed back down to his storage room. He went over to a coat rack and grabbed a long blue leather coat. This coat had been made from Densar skin so that only weapons with magical properties could pierce the sturdy coat. This coat had saved him from many a deadly blow. As soon as he had the coat on, he made sure to check that the Spell of Deflection was still in place on it. He often wore the coat open since it was more comfortable, and the spell allowed him to not have to worry about attacks to his center as much. The gray weaves of air were still there. Jethro then walked on over to the pedestal and grabbed his sword. As soon as he had grasped the handle, he barely concentrated at all as he wove the spell, the action having been done so many times, and let go of his sword. The weapon vanished, awaiting in the void till he called on it once more. He was now ready to fight.

Jethro climbed back up the stairs, locked up the closet, and turned around to see Lorelei standing at the doorway to the room and the two boys behind her. "I haven't seen that outfit in sixteen years." Lorelei said with a small smile that did not reach her eyes. "What's going on?" Jethro took a deep breath as he scanned her face. Worry was etched all across it. "Viscious is here." Jethro finally said, "He somehow got free and is at the edge of the village." Lorelei's eyes widened in shock as she exclaimed, "But all of the Heshtisi are imprisoned!"

"I know," Jethro replied, "and that is precisely why I need to look into this. It was my job to keep an eye on the Barrier and Bart saw Viscious with his own eyes, describing him perfectly. He didn't just describe him from one of the paintings, but Viscious in his Battle Form! Very few people remember his true look these days. So, unless Bart is actually a secret ancient historian, an Archeshtisi is here, and I need to know how it is possible." Jethro braced himself for protests form Lorelei, but her face hardened into the resolve he knew her for as she said, "Alright, then I'm coming with you also."

"What? No way are you coming!" Jethro shouted. Lorelei sniffed, "Someone needs to watch your back! If you think I'm going to let you go into battle alone without anyone to help you, then think again!" Jethro struggled to keep his anger in as he noticed Klin and Joseph run away as the shouting began. "You have no experience with enemies like this." Jethro growled, "This one is way above your skill!" Lorelei glared at him as she retorted, "Yet I helped you fight Malanus, who was supposed to be the most powerful of all the Heshtisi."

"And if I remember correctly," Jethro said, "you were barely able to stand for most of that fight. You only lived because he was so focused on me and never engaged the rest of you. Viscious won't make that mistake. Malanus may be the most powerful, but Viscious was the craftiest of them. I know Viscious and his powers. He is the weakest of the eight. I can handle him." Jethro then lowered his voice as it softened, "Besides, I don't want our children to become orphans." Tears began to form at the edge of those beautiful azure eyes as Lorelei whispered, "And I don't want to become a widow." Jethro wrapped her in his arms and squeezed her tight against him. "I know," he said softly, "and I know what I'm asking of you is beyond painful, yet I need you to do it. Viscious only wants me. You know I have to do this. It's my duty as a hero." Lorelei began to sob as she clutched his coat, "I know but that doesn't make it fair." She said in between her sobs, "You have spent three thousand years carrying out that duty. You are supposed to be done with this hero business." Jethro smiled wryly as he responded, "Unfortunately that's the problem with a hero's retirement plan; we never actually get one." Jethro then gently pried his wife off him and wiped the tears from her eyes. He kissed her and smiled, "Now, I need to go. Don't worry too much. I'll be back in time for dinner." Lorelei gave him a weak smile back as she gave a small laugh, "You better. I'm making your favorite soup."

"See, another reason to come back home quickly." Jethro replied as he walked out the door, his stomach feeling sick as he had the distinct feeling of this being a final farewell. As he grabbed the door handle to head outside though, he spotted Klin and Joseph hiding behind the table. "Come one out you two." Jethro said, "Your mother and I are done fighting." The two boys tentatively came on out, looking around to make sure no more loud noises would be happening. "Where are you going?" Klin asked. Jethro started; surprised Klin had figured that out. "Bert and I have to go and do some work in town." Jethro said. "Oooo, can we come?" Joseph asked excitedly. "No," Jethro said firmly, "You boys need to stay here and help out your mother."

"Awww, but dad!" Both boys complained at the same time. "No buts," Jethro said, "I need you both to do as your told, got that?" Klin and Joseph nodded surly before Joseph asked, "What are you wearing? It looks cool!" Jethro allowed himself a smile as he replied, "This is the outfit of a hero." "You're a hero?!" Klin asked with wide eyes. "I want to be a hero too!" Joseph said and proceeded to swing an imaginary sword around. Jethro laughed at their innocence and knelt down next to them, ruffling their hair. The boys let out some indignant protests. "Maybe one day you both will be." Jethro said, "Then you can wear outfits like mine, but first I'll need to make sure you both are men at that point." Jethro looked at his two sons who were grinning and felt a pang of regret and loss. "I may be gone for a while," he said, "so while I'm gone I need you two to listen to your mother, okay? She'll need your help, and I also need you both to try and take care of her for me while I'm gone. Can you do that?" Joseph and Klin looked at each other as a wordless conversation passed between them before giving Jethro a confused nod. "Good," Jethro said and hugged them, "I love you, my sons. Never forget that."

Jethro let go of them, an uneasy feeling in his stomach as he opened the door and pain in his heart and a sense of loss as he closed the door. Bert was tapping his foot impatiently and was looking around with a nervous look. Bert was so caught up in looking around that he did not notice Jethro until he was right next to him. Bert jumped, but recovered quickly before asking, "Ready?" Jethro nodded in affirmation. "Let's go."

The two set off towards the village. As they neared the wall, Jethro could not help but reminisce about how the wall used to be. Once the most impenetrable stronghold in all of Threa, Ala'Kathar was now a village with nary a defense. The original village had been destroyed nine hundred years ago during an uprising. The walls that had once been towering structures at a good three hundred feet high, now barely stood at ten feet. Jethro shook his head as they went through the gate. Ala'Kathar had such poor defenses that it would never survive a true attack. The people only knew this as a home of warriors only in tales. As they entered the Commercial District, a thought occurred to Jethro. "Bert," Jethro asked, "why exactly were you at the edge of the village when you saw the monster?"

"Oh, that." Bert replied, "Well uh, I was heading to the woods to go and collect some mushrooms. Today was my day off." Bert worked as a clerk in the local bank, so that explained some of his answer. Jethro frowned though and asked, "But I thought you hated mushrooms?" Bert nodded hastily, "Oh I do. They were for my wife is all." Jethro frowned even deeper. Bert was speaking to fast and was trying to clench his one fist subtly; something he did when he was lying. Jethro was just about to ask Bert for the truth when they arrived at the Northern Wall. "We're here." Bert said, "Viscious should still be waiting on the other side on the plain right before the woods." Jethro nodded and climbed the stairs up the wall but froze as he got to the top. He turned around and stared at Bert suspiciously. "Hold on," Jethro said, "you just called the monster Viscious. I don't think you ever called it that before." Bert froze where he stood, fear on his face. "How did you know that that creature is the Archeshtisi Viscious." Before Bert could answer a too familiar smooth voice called out, "Greetings Jethro, but my, it has been a while."

Jethro whipped his head to look over the wall and there stood the Archeshtisi Viscious, right below him. Each of the Archeshtisi had been formed to be an opposite to one of the Sculptors. Viscious had been made to oppose Celerious and so specialized in air magic. He used air in a way that he cooled the water molecules in the air to form ice as his favorite style. Viscious was just like how Bert had described. His face was framed like a collar in ice crystals, and his face itself was a pale blue color, with gray eyes peering at him. The wings were folded behind him like a cape, one that shimmered and sparkled in the sun as it was made from ice also. Dark blue carapace covered the chest like armor, and too sparkled and gave off a shimmer, like it was made of precious gems. Vicious also had a blue kilt that while lighter than the carapace, looked like it was made from the same material. In the noon sun, Viscious almost hurt to look at because of how much he shone.

9

"What do you want?" Jethro replied. Viscious feigned offense as he spoke, "What, no hello or how are you doing? It has been a couple hundred years since we last spoke you know, but then again you were always one to get straight to the point." Jethro crossed his arms and raised an eyebrow, "You might want to tell me what you're doing here before I decide to just send you back to Heshtanarus. Which I will find out how you got out by the way." Viscious just shook his head and smiled, "Why, I simply came here to talk to an old friend! I really must find out how you are still alive. A mere human being able to live for this long is no small feat you know. I'm sure you have a lot to talk about." Jethro frowned. So, he wanted to try and discover any secrets that he knew basically. Viscious would always avoid battles as best he could, instead either relying on his speaking skills to try and convince others to not fight him, or just simply assassinating them. "Yeah, I do, but not with you." Jethro said as he summoned his sword. Viscious sighed, "Still has damn righteous as ever. I have a deal to offer you know?"

"Sorry," Jethro retorted, "but I don't make deals with ugly bastards." Viscious's eyebrow twitched in annoyance. If there was one thing that Viscious despised, it was being called ugly. "I have questions that you *will* answer though." Viscious growled, dropping all niceties, "One way or another, I will get answers out of you." Jethro just shrugged, "Guess I'll have to cut out that slimy thing you call a tongue, so I won't have to listen to them." Viscious sneered, "We'll see about that." Daggers made of ice formed in the air next to Viscious and shot towards Jethro. Jethro threw himself over the edge of wall and sliced through the daggers shooting towards him. He hit the ground, rolling and came up on one knee with his sword crossed over his left shoulder. Viscious was now about ten feet away from him. The demon summoned more daggers and threw them at him. Jethro smiled as he casually swept his sword in a circle in front of him, summoning a void wall. At least, that was the plan. The daggers kept coming towards him as no magic flowed from him. Jethro quickly rolled to the side with a curse.

Viscious began to laugh, "What's wrong Jethro? Magic not working? You're not the only one who has learned new things." Jethro opened himself to his Source, but ran into an invisible barrier. *Damn him*, Jethro thought, *he's blocking me using Natharian magic*. Natharian magic's source was Romevan himself, and only those who used it could see the fabrics of that specific type. With a Natharian barrier, Jethro could not break it with a counter spell and so either he broke Viscious's concentration or broke through the barrier with sheer force. If he did the later, it would take too much time and leave him vulnerable for the amount of concentration he would need. He would have to take Viscious head on.

Four more daggers appeared in the air next to Viscious, who stood primly with his arms clasped behind his back. The daggers came at him once again, but this time Jethro charged at them. Viscious's eyes widened in surprise as Jethro ran, deflecting two before falling to his knees and sliding underneath the other two before coming up in front of Viscious with a upwards vertical strike. The air solidified in front of Jethro barley in time to stop the attack, but Jethro shattered the shield, making Viscious stumble. Jethro didn't miss a beat as he changed the attack into a stab. Viscious's claws iced over as he moved them to knock Jethro's sword to the side, barely missing his ribs. Jethro though stopped the stab before it sunk into the ribs, and instead swung up, cutting off Viscious's left arm at the shoulder. Gray blood splattered all over as Viscious screamed in pain and leapt back a good ten feet. Jethro quickly felt for the Weave and was relieved was he was able to touch it. Viscious had always had a very low pain tolerance.

Jethro quickly formed a protective barrier to keep his connection to the Weave safe. Even though he did not know Natharian spells, he could still protect his Connection. Viscious was clutching the stump of his arm and glaring at Jethro. "Looks like you're out of practice." Jethro taunted, "It was far easier to hurt you than I remember. That, or you're in above your head." Viscious snarled at him as his arm began to regrow, "Don't get too cocky now. This fight is far from over. It's not just me you have to worry about." Jethro frowned as Viscious began to laugh and flew up into the air. "Wh-get back down here!" Jethro shouted as he shot a fireball at Viscious. Viscious dodged the fire and retreated about forty feet. Jethro started to chase after him until he heard the clambering of bows and feet behind him. He spun around and saw many villagers that he recognized standing on the wall, bows drawn back and pointing at him. Bill Nardoth, Marth, Cra'son, Jeffrey Mardon, and various others with Bart standing at the head of them. Jethro cursed himself for forgetting about Bert. "Humans are so fickle." Viscious cackled, "You never know when they will betray you. Get him!"

"You heard him," Bert shouted, "Fire!" Jethro cursed as twenty bowstrings were released and the arrows soared towards him. Jethro summoned a void shield around himself and waited for the arrows to hit. He frowned as they continued over him and towards a shocked Viscious who was suddenly a pin cushion. Viscious cursed as half the arrows punctured him, being too surprised to protect himself. Jethro grinned as the villagers released another volley at Viscious. Viscious snarled as he created gusts of wind and scattered the arrows. As the villagers shot once more, Jethro created a void in the path and as Viscious created a gust, the arrows disappeared only to reappear behind the demon as Jethro opened another one. Viscious screamed as Jethro made sure all twenty sliced into him. Viscious removed the arrows though with some air magic, and as he healed his wounds, he cast a look of absolute malice upon them before flying off into the woods, dripping blood. Jethro let out a sigh of relief as Viscious disappeared from sight and the villagers let out a victorious cry.

Jethro turned to the villagers, who were now off the wall and on the field. Bert came running towards him, his bow in hand. "Sorry about all that whole misleading act." Bert said, "We needed him to think we were on his side, otherwise we wouldn't've been able to get the jump on him. Jethro smiled, "No harm done. How long has he had this planned though?"

"A week now." Bert grunted, "That bastard showed up a week ago and threatened to kill our families if we don't do what he wants. Unfortunately for him, he had to reveal that you were *the* Jethro Markus, and none of us wanted to betray a legend." Jethro laughed, "I suppose I'll have to reward you all after this then." Bert looked away, and if he had not just shot Viscious, Jethro would have sworn guilt was on his face for the briefest of moments. Jethro decided though that his eyes were deceiving him, and Bert was just what he looked like right now, embarrassed. Bert then smiled and shouted to the men now next to him, "So, what are we waiting for? Let's go finish off that ugly bastard!" The villagers let out a terrifying roar as they rushed to the woods. "Wait, stop!" Jethro cried, but no one listened to him and kept on running.

"Idiots," Jethro muttered, "they're probably walking right into a trap. Viscious always has a backup plan."

As if on cue, screams of terror and pain came from the woods. "Damn it all." Jethro cursed as he ran into the woods after the foolish villagers. He ran deep into the woods, following the sounds of the screams as they went deeper in. A chill went down his spine though as the screams suddenly stopped. The woods became deadly silent as Jethro readied his sword, and prowled through the woods, following the trampled path of the villagers. Dark memories then started flooding back to him. The last time he had chased an Archeshtisi through the woods had ended with Threa's death. Suddenly, a twig snapped behind him. Jethro whirled around to find Gruntlet leaping at him with a shrill cry. Jethro sidestepped and cleaved its two heads off. The two heads rolled off as the body slumped to the ground. "Viscious must have a squad with him." Jethro muttered, "I bet these are what ambushed the villagers." Jethro then looked back at the body to examine it and was shocked as the body turned into a pile of ashes. "Okay," Jethro said to himself, "I don't remember them doing that before. Things just keep getting better and better today."

Jethro turned to leave the body behind, perturbed at this new mystery, but moving even more cautiously than he had before. His body was taught with nerves and the expectation of a fight around every tree. Finally, the trail ended in a small clearing. Jethro looked around the clearing and saw five bodies lying on the ground. He started to run towards them, but stopped as he noticed that there was no blood near them. There was also no sign of which way the rest of the villagers went. Viscious's laughter then began to echo all around him. "My, my, that was easy." Viscious said oily.

"Come on out you coward." Jethro growled. "I know you killed those three. Did you kill all of them, or just those three?" Viscious began to laugh manically as he asked, "Now who said I killed anyone?" Jethro howled in pain as three arrows pierced him. One in each shoulder and one in his lower ribs. Jethro painful turned around to see the three dead villagers now on their feet, knocked bows pointed at him. Leaves rustled as he spied the rest of the villagers perched in the trees. More Gruntlets emerged from the shadows and surrounded him. "I told you that you can't trust people," Viscious tisked, "not even by their actions, for even actions can lie." Viscious materialized in the air in front of him, his entire form made of black smoke. Viscious gave flashed him a triumphant smile as he landed on the ground next to Jethro, his body becoming solid, yet all that was blue was now shades of gray and what was frost was now smoky. "So, it seems I have you surrounded, with you wounded and no way out."

"It does seem that way." Jethro said as he began to cast a dark spell. He moved the dark fabric into his wounds and placed them right in front of the tips of the arrows. "Will you surrender?" Viscious asked. Jethro prepared himself as he looked up and Viscious and placed more dark fabrics in a sphere around him but did not activate them. "Sorry, but I don't believe I'm done just yet. Want to see why?" Viscious frowned as Jethro activated the fabrics in his wounds, opening voids. The arrows fell in, and it was all Jethro could do to not scream in pain. The villagers released more arrows as the Gruntlets charged him, which is when he activated the rest of the fabrics. A void sphere appeared all around him, and as the arrows went in, they popped back out after a few seconds impaling the Gruntlets in the head. At the same time, Jethro wove fabrics of life into his wounds, a skill he learned from Lorelei, and healed himself.

Jethro dropped the sphere as he charged at Viscious, who swiped at him, his body now once more incased in ice. Jethro blocked the attack, sparks flying as the iced claw meet the mysterious metal of his sword. Jethro quickly countered with a vertical strike, which put Viscious off balance and barely blocked. That one moment was all Jethro needed. He moved to in and began unleashing a flurry of attacks, forcing Viscious to quickly go on the defensive. That was all Jethro allowed him to do. The Archeshtisi's face became contorted with concentration as he tried to avoid being skewered by Jethro. Jethro's blade became a whirlwind of strikes, moving too fast for a normal man to follow. Even an un-Threan creature like Viscious was not able to move fast enough to evade every attack. Soon Viscious was covered in multiple wounds, the gray blood streaking Darkest Flame. While Jethro fought, the traitorous villagers did their best to help Viscious by firing at Jethro, but Jethro simply kept up a small void shield around him that was hard to see, and so every time they fired the arrows were labeled return to sender.

The villagers scrambled about, trying to find a chink in his shield, but it was a hopeless endeavor. The few chinks in the shield were to small for arrows to fit through. Then Jethro grinned as Viscious's hands became entangled as he finally blocked at an attack to his shoulder. "You're not doing so hot." Jethro taunted, "What, you never fought a thousand-year-old swordsman?" Jethro then kicked Viscious in the stomach, sending him rolling, and before the demon could stand back up, Jethro had his sword pressed upon the neck. As he stared down at Viscious, who was glowering at him, Jethro sent out fire fabrics and ignited all of the villagers' bows. He smiled down at Viscious as the villagers yelled in surprise, staring at Jethro in fear. "Looks like your trap failed." Jethro said, "Better luck next time. For now, though, I think I'm going to send you back to Heshtanarus."

Jethro then reached for the Weave to prepare the fabrics to imprison Viscious till he could send him back, when he suddenly his body began to shake. "Wh-what is going on?" Jethro asked as he dropped his sword. His whole body became weak, and his muscles felt like liquid as he dropped to his knees. Viscious got to his feet slowly, obviously in pain as he shouted at the villagers, "Quickly, tie him up! This is your chance!" Two villagers rushed forward with rope from somewhere and tied his hands and feet. "What did you do to me?" Jethro asked weakly. Viscious gave him a malicious smile, "I had those three arrows coated in poison. Don't worry though, it won't kill you. It only drains your strength to the point you cannot stay awake." Bert walked up over to him bent down. "Why Bert?" Jethro asked, "I could have gotten rid of him." Bert grinned, "He never threatened us." Bert answered, "He promised us rewards." Darkness began to creep around him, and as the world faded to black, Jethro's muttered, "I'm sorry Lorelei, looks like I can't keep our promise after all."

The pale moonlight reflected off the marble palace tiles of the Coronus Throne Room. King Gabriel Winters looked over the sprawling city below him. Even though it was well into the night, the city glowed with lights. A gentle breeze blew through his hair, and the smell of the sea was brought with it. This entire week had been full of disasters.

First, he revives reports of the king of Ardaven being visited by a creature, that according to Jethro's tales, seemed like it was Viscious. Viscious! The Archeshtisi of air. Then he hears reports of demons flooding the Empire, yet only in a few places were there tales of death and ruin from where they had been seen. Then, the worst one had been three days ago when his wife became sick. The first day it had only seemed minor; a very low fever and headache. Then it had turned worse the next day, till finally, tonight it had killed her. Gabriel felt his eyes go moist has just thinking about it brought about the pain. Yet only a few drops slid down his cheeks. He was still too dry to produce any real tears yet.

The entire city below mourned Viloria's death with him, and from what he could tell, it was genuine. Viloria had been loved by the entire Empire, and the people knew they would feel her disappearance. Since she had died late afternoon, the funeral would take place tomorrow morning.

Gabriel sighed as the bells rung, announcing the time. It was late and he should be getting to bed. Besides, he needed to check on his daughter. She was taking the death just as hard as he was, maybe even harder. She was only five, and today had been her birthday. Gabriel turned to leave and as he neared the throne, the ruby colored stone on around his neck began to glow. Gabriel frowned as the light slowly grew. The Coronus Stone was inherited by all Coronus rulers, and only glowed when the wearer was using its powers, which he was certainly not doing at the moment. Suddenly the light encompassed him, and the throne room vanished from his sight. Images began to quickly flash before him in a whirlwind of information.

Four young men travelling through a dark tunnel towards an obscured light. The same four at the head of armies. His best friend Joshua next to him as demon-like creatures encircled them. His sister killing Coronus soldiers, and a young woman whom Gabriel knew immediately to be his daughter somehow. Gabriel watched horrified as she launched herself with a bloody sword at a man. He tried to look away as he saw her doing evil things, but he could not move. Then, all the images coalesced into one. The four young men stood together, a sense of brotherhood between them as they stared defiantly at a giant figure cloaked in darkness and radiating power. The image faded to black as glowing red words appeared.

That who was sealed has been freed. He has returned to the world and his goals will be achieved. The Eight must unite. The final battle draws near. All of humanity must fight or embrace the darkness that he holds dear.

The words faded as Gabriel found himself standing back in the throne room. *Wha–what in Threa was that?!* Gabriel thought as he found himself breathing hard. *Did, did I just receive a vison? But can the Stone even do that?* Gabriel thought hard, and yet ever conclusion brought him the same answer. He had received a vision of the future. "That who was sealed." Gabriel muttered. "I wonder who it meant?" The words still burned in his eyes, so he took the time to memorize them, and examined each one. A chill went down his spine though as he remembered the rumors and reports of this week. "No, it can't mean that, can it?" Gabriel thought it over again and again, but each time he had the growing suspicion that his instinct was right. Romevan had somehow broken free and had returned to Threa. Gabriel said a silent prayer to the One that he was wrong, for if he was right, the Sculptors help them all. As Gabriel climbed up the stairs to head to bed, he decided that tomorrow he would take action. It was time to see if those rumors were true.

Chapter 2

Brothers Markus

11 years later

Klin walked through the streets of Ala'Kathar, the setting sun beating down upon him pleasantly. A cool summer breeze blew across his face, ruffling his long and messy brown hair. It was the middle of summer, the seventh month of the year. Genua the thirtieth to be exact. His birthday. Yet for Klin, birthdays were not much a day for celebration. Oh, his mom and brother would try to celebrate with him, but they would be the only ones. He let out a small sigh as the money pouch at his side jingled. It had been another long day of work at the smithy and another day of being forced to accept the meager pay of the Companions. He leaned back, his brown eyes squinting under the force of the faint golden sun. Klin's imagination always leapt and flew away under such beautiful colors, bringing him to a place where things were not so difficult.

He rolled his shoulders as he came back to reality, working out the stiffness from hammering away all day. Nothing like a day to celebrate your coming of age as working under a time crunch. "Hello Klin!" Klin turned to see Mrs. O'Mar and her daughter Mara sweeping dust out of their shop. Klin smiled and waved to her. "Hello Mrs. O'Mar. Is it cleaning day today?" Mrs. O'Mar was a large, stout woman with graying hair. She was one of the most pleasant people to talk with in all of the city. She smiled and nodded, "Indeed it is! You would not believe the amount of dirt and grime people will track into a tailor's store! For Sculptor's sake, you would at least hope they would wash before getting new clothes!" Klin laughed, "Well, I suppose most people need new

18

clothes because of the dirty ones?" She just shook her head vehemently, "Well yes! But clean the ones you have! Proper hygiene means proper mind! Anyway dear, did you just close the shop?" Klin nodded and said a bit wryly, "Yep. Got an order from Marth with a ridiculous time crunch too of course."

Mrs. O'Mar let out a sigh. "Of course, he did. By the way, do you need something dear? You've got a look in your eyes that says you do." Klin grinned back and held out his pouch. "You got me. I need a new skirt for my mom. She'll never buy one for herself, but her old one is falling apart." Mrs. O'Mar gave him a warm smile, "Oh my, aren't you a thoughtful one. We were going to close but come on in! I can get one in under an hour! Come Mara!" Her daughter, who was the same age as Klin went in the shop. Klin followed them, his long brown hair falling over his eyes briefly. He brushed the one long strand aside that went to the bridge of his nose. "Have you ever considered cutting you hair?" O'Mar called back to him. Klin shook his head. "No thanks. My dad wore his this long, and so will I." O'Mar shook her head disapprovingly as she grabbed a selection of fabrics. "Don't worry too much about that mother." Mara said, her own long brown hair swaying as she passed Klin. "I think it looks quite dashing on him." Klin turned bright red and twirled the long strand of his hair. "Uh, thanks." She smiled as she began to gather the tools they needed. "So dear, what color you think?" Klin stoked his chin as he looked over all the colors she had laid out.

"That one. The light blue will go really well with her favorite shirt." Mrs. O'Mar smiled as she and Mara got to work. Klin began to simply browse the pre-made clothes in the shop as he waited. Most of these were way above what he and Joseph could afford. Yet, they were also better made than the really shoddily made clothes they had to wear. Klin was currently wearing a worn out tan shirt, the threads were stretched and ready to come apart soon. His thin pants were barely in better shape. Another month and they would be where the shirt was. What he really wanted though was the one of those coats. Mrs. O'Mar had about five different colored leather coats that came down to the thighs. Perfect for keeping you warm in winter, and most importantly, they looked cool. "There! Finished!" Mara declared proudly. Klin jogged over to the counter as Mara held up the skirt. "Nice! That was about thirty minutes?" He asked. Mrs. O'Mar twirled a needle around her fingers. "Twenty-five to be exact." She said with a smug smile. Klin let out a small chuckle. "How much?"

O'Mar twirled the needle around as she stroked her chin. "Hmm, how about three saphiras?" Klin blinked a few times. "Uh, are you sure? That seems a bit cheap for this quality." Mara gave him a weird smile that he could not determine the meaning of. "Oh, don't worry," she purred, "We love a man who looks after his mother." Klin pulled out the sapphire-colored square coins. "Wow, uh thanks then. You guys are way too nice to us." Mrs. O'Mar simply snorted, "Well I'll be damned if you boys are the only upstanding folk in this city. More people could learn from you and your brother."

"Please don't go making false statements." Klin replied, "Lying is not a good thing. Sure, my brother is great guy, but I'm not."

"But that's not true at all!" Mara protested. "Look at you! Coming in to buy your mother something and on *your* birthday of all days! I bet you haven't bought anything for yourself!" Klin opened his mouth and then closed it. There were plenty of things he could say that would get them to change their mind about him, and one in particular. "Well, thanks. If you guys say it is true, it must be true." Sometimes it was better to let people believe a lie rather than try and show them the truth. Mara wrapped the skirt and placed it in a bag as Klin paid. "Thank you both again." He thanked as he waved goodbye. "Of course, dear." O'Mar replied, "Say hello to your mother for me!"

"Will do!" With that Klin left the store. He was back in the clean streets of Ala'Kathar. His feet gently clacked against the stone road as he began to make his way home. As he walked, he kept an eye out for Joseph. As soon as they had closed the shop, he had run off, saying he had somewhere to be. Klin had a few suspicions on where his older brother had run off to. One, he had run off to get him a birthday present. Two, he was at the bar, or three, he was at a pre-arranged brawl. Unfortunately, out of all three, the fight was probably most likely. He would know for sure when he got home. "Hey, hey! Look who we have here!" Klin let out an internal groan as he stopped. *Herk.* He turned around to see Monastrath.

The man was his age, but that was where the similarities ended. Monastrath was taller and built like a warrior from the north. He wore a shirtless, tight fitting, green shirt to show off his bugling muscles. His arms were as thick as an ox. He had yellow eyes, similar to Joseph's, but they were more sinister and paler, whereas Joseph's were more golden. He had long, straight blonde hair that fell in a tumble about a handsome face that made most women swoon at the sight of him. "Hello Monastrath." Klin greeted through gritted teeth. "What do you want?" Monastrath strutted over and bent down. "Oh, just doing my daily patrols. Just figured I would say hi to my favorite, oh what's the word?" He snapped his fingers. "Ah, that's right!" He exclaimed, "Indentured servant!"

"I think you need a dictionary." Klin retorted. Monastrath's benevolent smile faded as a he crossed his arms and leered. "Oh, and why's that? You implying I'm stupid?" *I don't need to imply anything.* Klin thought, but kept his tongue, instead saying, "Wouldn't dare. Just maybe saying another word would better explain our relationship." Monastrath gave him a nasty smile, "Oh, and what would that be?" Klin knew he was being baited, but damn did he want to just throw out seven different insults. "I don't know." He finally replied, "I'm not smart enough to know that." Monastrath nodded in satisfaction. "Damn right you aren't. You're just some stupid nobody. Now, what do you have in that bag there?" Klin clutched the bag and moved it slightly away from man. "Just a present." Monastrath reached out to grab it. "It's not for me!" Klin said hurriedly, successfully stopping him. "Oh, well then who is it for? Maybe Mara?"

Klin hesitated. If he found out it was for his mom, he might tear it to pieces. "Ohoho!" Monastrath exclaimed, "What do we have here? Could it be Klin has crush on her?" Klin closed gulped as his heart began to beat fast. Monastrath clapped him on the back. "Well why didn't you tell me? Your old pal Monastrath would have helped you out sooner! Let's see, she's near your age. Sixteen, right? Oh, but wait. We have a problem with that." Klin frowned. "What's that?" Monastrath shrugged as he crossed his arms. "Well, you see, she's of age. I'm of age. But you aren't. Speaking of which…maybe I should really make her a woman. Can't have chasing after some child. Once she's met me in bed maybe that will make her see how much of a child you are."

"Keep your mosquito poker away from her!" Klin snapped, dropping the bag and balling up his fists. "And for your information today's my birthday! So, I am of age!" Rage boiled all around him. A fierce glare overcame Monastrath, but it was soon replaced by an evil smile. "Well, if you are of age today, we'll need a proper ceremony! Just for today, I'll allow you to fight me with no repercussions! I'll even overlook that little insult just now. Consider this your birthday present!"

"Bought damn time!" Klin growled as he threw the first punch. Monastrath dodged it easily as punched his jaw. Klin stumbled back, briefly seeing spots. He shook his head and snarled as he threw three more punches. Monastrath dodged all of them, and then kicked Klin in the stomach. He let out a gasp as he doubled over. He forced himself to stand back up, his breathing struggling to return to its normal rhythms. *Come on Klin! You've suffered worse from this asshole! Keep pushing!* He ran forward and tried to kick, but Monastrath just caught it between his arms. Klin smiled and punched him in the nose twice. Monastrath howled and let go. As he stumbled back, Klin closed in and tried to get an uppercut to the jaw. Monastrath though glared at him as he caught his fist. He then forced Klin's fist back and made him punch himself in the face with it. Klin grimaced, and tried to kick, but Monastrath just twisted his arm, forcing Klin around him. Klin yelped as he was forced to his knees, his arm pinned to his back. "Think you might have broken my nose." Monastrath spat. "Let me return the sentiment." Klin howled as Monastrath broke his right arm.

Monastrath let him go, kicking the bag with his mom's present over. "Welcome to manhood Klin. I can officially say you'll never be one now." Monastrath spat on his head and walked away. Cradling his arm, he stumbled over and picked up the bag with his good arm. Lucky for him, he did not have to try and get the skirt back in it. With a wince, he let go of his broken arm and did his best to keep it in the least possible position. Unfortunately for him, the least painful was still incredibly painful. *Herking Heshtanus!* He thought, *This sucks.* Well, at least it was just him hurt. Hopefully, him attacking Monastrath would make the Guardian in training forget about Mara. He would hate to see her bothered by the pig after the kindness she and her mother showed his family.

It took him longer than normal, but he exited the city, passing some more Guardian's at the gate. They made no comment about his arm, just giving him the disdainful glare, he had grown accustomed to from them. "Watch out tonight!" One of jeered, "We got a report that some of them monsters will be attacking then!" Klin turned and gave them a blank stare. "Thanks." He did not even bother asking for an escort. That would just most likely result in some insult and a punch to the face. All because he was a traitor's son. With an angry heart, Klin made his way out into the pastures of Ala'Kathar. After an hour of walking his house came into sight. Despite being so poor, the home he lived in was one of the nicest houses in the entire area. The home was two stories, standing at fifty feet tall and seventy-feet wide. On the west end was a tower that was a few feet taller than the rest of the house. Their home was made from cut stone, with delicate designs carved into the stones on the tower and around the door frame. From animals to flowers and magical symbols, the person who had carved them had been quite the artist.

His mom claimed that it had been his father, but Klin had some doubts about that. He did not remember him well, but he was sure he had never seen him involved in art, but hey, his dad had built the place after all. Back when he was alive. Before everyone called him a traitor. Klin shook his head, pushing aside those thoughts for the moment as he gingerly opened the front door. He let out a soundless gasp of pain and quickly masked his face. "Hey mom, I'm home!" His mom was sitting on the couch, a stack of papers in her hands. Lorelei Markus was a woman in exceptional health for a mother at her age. She had bright, baby-blue eyes and silk black hair that she kept short, yet she still always had a hair pin as she liked to keep her bangs a bit long. Lorelei. She was a short woman, standing at five foot four, but that had never stopped her from being able to intimidate the tallest and most muscular of men.

Lorelei smiled as she set the papers done. "Hello. How was today?" Klin shrugged and gave an internal wince. Okay, bad idea. Don't shrug with a broken arm. "Eh, same old thing." He grunted. "Anyway, I got you something." Lorelei gave a start as he held up the bag and handed it to her. "Oh Klin, why?" She asked sadly, but there was warmth in her eyes as she unwrapped the skirt. He just shrugged. *Ow okay. I'm an idiot.* "You needed something new way more than me." He said aloud. "I figured sooner the better, right?" Lorelei just shook her head and gave him a hug. At that, Klin finally let out a quiet yelp. Lorelei pulled back immediately and narrowed her eyes. "What's hurt?" Klin let out a sigh. "Right arm. It's broken."

"What?!" Lorelei shrieked. "Klin! Who did this to you?"

"No one!" He lied quickly. "I just, uh, well. I fell on my way back." Lorelei gave him a searching look while she began to heal his arm. Klin was able to keep from shuddering as the familiar tingles spread across his arm as his bones were healed. "Come on mom. It's embarrassing enough I broke it, even more from just falling." She finally sighed and shook her head. "I swear, you are so accident prone. Getting all these terrible bruises and scrapes from just walking home! At least it's not from brawling in the streets like your brother." Klin flexed and rotated his arm as she finished. "Speaking of which, where is Joseph?" Lorelei frowned, "I had expected him to come back with you. Don't tell me..." Klin let out a weary sigh and put a hand to his head and leaning back. "Ahh, damn it! I'll be back."

Klin found Joseph back in the city right as the twilight was setting in. As expected, he was at the sparring pit. He could see his brother leaning against the fence. Klin cursed under his breath as he ran over. "Joseph!" His brother turned around, a flash of surprise on his face before grinning at him. "Hey, Klin! You found me!" Klin crossed his arms and glared. "Where else would you be you big buffoon?" His brother stood two inches taller than Klin, who was at an even six feet. Where Klin was thin, Joseph was big. He was not built like Monastrath, but not by much. He had strapping arms, muscled from all their time working the forge. His long, raven black hair was tied back in a ponytail, but a few strands were lose and fell over his face. His golden eyes glowed with a mischievous light from behind his glasses.

Joseph rolled his arms around and stretched. "Sorry, this fight was not planned this time. I swear." Klin let out a sigh as he looked over at the opposite side of the ring and frowned. "Is that Matthew?" Joseph gave a quick nod and bent down, touching his toes. "Yep. Seems he was *really* laying it thick on the insults at June's today." Klin rolled his eyes, "So you were at the bar then before this?" Joseph turned red and mumbled, "No. I was out getting you a present. Mara was though. We ran into each other, and she let me know. So, naturally I had to show this asshole why you don't say such things about my brother."

"You ready Markus?" Matthew jeered. Joseph stretched his neck, "More than you are." Klin tapped Joseph on the shoulder. "Joseph?" His brother began to wave a hand, "Yeah, yeah. I know, I know. I'll go easy." Klin grinned, "Not actually what I was going to say. Kick his ass." Joseph grinned widely as he walked out into the center of the ring. "With pleasure." Matthew waddled up to Joseph, his rolls of fat jiggling as he took up a fighting stance. How that man had a gang amazed Klin. Klin looked over and saw a few of his goons cheering their leader on. Thankfully, the man presiding over the match was Jonathan. He was not fond of either Klin or Joseph, but he *hated* the Mardons. So, Joseph would get fair calls at least. Jonathan held up his hand, and then threw it down. "Fight!" Joseph kept his hands up and close to his head as Matthew tried to throw a punch at his face. The man was far too short and out of shape to do that well though. He stumbled, allowing Joseph to dodge with easy and counter with a quick jab to the side. Matthew stumbled back with a howl and threw a left hook. Joseph swatted it aside and punched him in the side of the head.

Matthew stumbled back and feel on the ground. "Submit?" Joseph asked. Matthew crawled to his feet, sweat pouring down his face. "You wish!" He gasped, "I'm just getting started!" Joseph groaned in annoyance and looked at Klin, who nodded. As Matthew was still getting to his feet, Joseph told him cheerily, "Listen, I'm hungry and want this to end, so no hard feelings?" The man narrowed his eyes, "Wha—" But never get to finish as Joseph punched him in the face and kidney at the same time. The man fell over moaning and did not get back up. "Markus wins!" Jonathan declared. Joseph threw his hands up as Mardon's gang booed him. "Pay up!" Jonathan barked. The men began to grumble as they walked up and handed the money over to Jonathan, before picking up their leader and carrying him home. Jonathan handed the money over to Joseph. "Good job Markus, been wanting to see him put in his place for a bit. And don't worry, I won't say anything to the Guardians about how much was bet, and neither will they I bet. Too humiliating." With that the man walked away. Joseph waved at him while Klin waited, leaning over the fence. "Okay, fess up. How much did you bet?"

Joseph flashed him a grin as he absentmindedly bounced his winnings in his palm. "Three emeraldas." Klin's eyes widened, "Genus that's a lot! We don't even *have* that much money."

"Oh, I know." Joseph replied, "But the rules don't specify you have to pay it that day you know. You can pay it over time." Klin shook his head, "And if you had lost that match?" Joseph let out a derisive snort, "Oh please. You really think that idiot could have won?" Klin let out a small chuckle, "No, I suppose not. Still, try and be a little more prudent next time, okay?" Joseph hopped over the fence in one smooth motion. "Don't worry so much Klin. I'm well aware of where my limits are. Anyway, I needed the money to pay for your present." Klin let out a groan, "You didn't borrow any money, did you? I told you, stuff like this is not important enough to be doing that." Joseph lightly smacked the side of Klin's head. "Didn't I say not to worry about stuff like that? Nah, I did something better. I made an upfront payment and promised I'd have the rest tomorrow." Klin blinked, "Wait, I thought this fight wasn't planned?"

"It wasn't."

"Then how the herk did you plan to pay it back by tomorrow?!" Klin sputtered. Joseph stopped. "Oh, huh. I hadn't thought of that." Klin shook his head but could not help but laugh. "Well, it worked out. Come on you idiot, let's get back home." Joseph beamed, "Agreed. Can't wait to see the look on your face when you get your present."

Klin and Joseph made it back home just as night fell. The cool light from the Light Stones in the lamps hit spread out, letting them see better than oil light. Another thing the Guardians could not mess with in their living situation. Sure, most days they had trouble getting enough food, but hey, at least the house was always well lit and had plenty of heat. "Boys, that you?" Lorelei called from the kitchen. "Yeah. I found Joseph." Klin called back. "Guess what he was doing?" Joseph shot Klin a panicked look mixed with a glare. "Fighting?"

"Yep!" There was a very loud, and dramatic sigh from the kitchen. Joseph rubbed the back of his head as they went to meet their mom. "So, I can explain." Joseph began. Lorelei had just pulled dinner out of the oven. She turned around and gave him a flat stare. "Did they deserve it?" She asked. A big grin grew over Joseph's face. "Hesh yeah they did! They were talking massive shit about Klin! Matthew Mardon was calling him un-manly and—wait you don't want to hear the rest. It was bad." Lorelei crossed her arms and raised an eyebrow. "I have one question then for you. Matthew normally hangs out at June's at this time. So, you were at the bar?" Joseph shook his head vehemently. "No, not at all! Mara was the one who told me, and then Matthew challenged me when I sought him out to give him a piece of my mind!" Lorelei continued to give him a flat stare before cracking a smile. "Well, did you give him a good beating?" Joseph grinned, "You know it mom! Fat lout never stood a chance."

"Well then, shall we eat?" Lorelei said gesturing to the steaming food. Klin smiled, but stopped as he saw what it was. Chendillas. Flat bread wrapped up with meat, cheese, beans, and rice served with a spicy tomato sauce. His favorite kind of food, but also expensive these days. "Mom—" He began. Lorelei gave him a motherly glare, "If I hear one word about the price, I'm going to make you fast for two days, and then give you only bread for the next three days. Today you are of age, so let me celebrate it properly." Klin hesitated, then allowed himself a smile. "Alright. Should we invite Dreas then?" Lorelei shook her head. "No, she already declined. She's not feeling the best tonight she said." Klin nodded as he grabbed a plate, "Alright then. Let's eat!"

After a very pleasant and delicious meal, Klin helped his mother do the dishes while Joseph went and bathed. "So, I hear you two have an order from Marth?" Lorelei asked. Klin nodded, "Yeah, he put in the order yesterday. We don't have much more to do for it, but he wanted ten bowls of silver! Done in three days! He's damn lucky we had enough silver left from our last shipment." Lorelei shook her head. "Did he at least promise to pay well?" Klin cocked his head, "Actually, yeah, he did. Twenty emeraldas." Lorelei let out a low whistle. "Wow. That will be enough to keep us feed for the next three months." Klin nodded.

"Yeah," He grumbled, "But for anyone other than us that would be enough for a year."

"Yes, I know." Lorelei replied wearily, "But we really cannot do anything about it." Klin wanted to push more, but they had had this conversation so often that it was pointless. The Guardians of Ala'Kathar ruled this city. Ever since their dad was condemned a traitor and said to have brought the monsters that would attack the city weekly, the Markus's had been living under an especially oppressive thumb. All prices for their family were raised, and they had half of their wages taken at the end of the day. Math Cra'Son, father of Monastrath, was the leader. "I still don't understand why people put up with them." Klin complained as he dried his hands. Lorelei cast a blast of air at her hands, drying them instantly. "They provide protection against a fearsome foe." She explained calmly, "People will tolerate the lesser evil as long as they see the threat of these monsters as greater."

"Yeah, yeah." Joseph said dismissively as he walked in, "But they're still an evil. Don't think anyone right actually likes that prick Marth." Lorelei let out a giggle. "No, I don't think even his wife does. Anyway, enough of this talk of gloom. Let's give Klin his presents." Klin smiled as he followed his family into the living room. He would be lying to himself if he said he was not actually excited to see what they got him. "I'll go first." Lorelei said. She went into her room and came back holding a book. Klin blinked a few times as he saw it. "Is that what I think it is?" Lorelei smiled and handed to him. "It is. *The Complete History of the Magical Creations and Creatures of Threa.* I know you've been wanting the rest, so here it is." Klin took the book gingerly and could not stop smiling as he hugged his mom. "Thank you!" He exclaimed as he cracked it open and scanned the table of contents. "Whoa! They actually have the full list of the magic beasts from the East! The other one only has the Western ones! This is awesome! Thank you!" Lorelei beamed as she sat on the couch. "You're welcome."

"Well, if you think *that's* cool, wait till you see mine!" Joseph said smugly as he produced the bag he had been carrying on the trip home. Klin took it and rifled through, freezing as he saw what was in it. Two books and a travel alchemist's set, along with various materials for alchemy. "Joseph, this is amazing. How in the world did you get her to sell you this on a *promise*?" Joseph flashed a smirk, "Well I can be very charming you know. Read the what the books are though." Klin frowned as he checked them out. One was *A Beginners Guide to the Theoretics of Elemental Stones*, while the other was *Advanced Alchemy: Beyond Plants*. Klin shook his head and gave his brother a tight hug. "Thank you, Joseph. This…this means a lot." Joseph patted him on the back as they broke apart. "You're welcome bro. So, you going to go try it out?" Klin grinned but looked to his mom. "Go ahead. I'm sure you can sell some tomorrow" She assented with a small smile. "But don't stay up too late. You two have to be at work early in the morning." Klin nodded and ran off towards the tower. Their dad had been a mysterious man, building a tower for astronomy and having an alchemy lab at the top? He had to have been a *very* well-educated soldier to learn about so many things. He cracked open the alchemy book and began to rifle through their store of ingredients.

Hmmm, which one should I try first? He thought. *Oooo, this looks interesting, and I got everything I need for it. Let's try it.* It took him five separate tries, but he successfully was able to get the mixture for a Silence Potion right. He was tempted to try it right then, but he wanted to make another. So, he stayed up till midnight trying out different potion recipes. He made it back to his room and collapsed. Overall, it had definitely been one of the best birthdays he had had.

Chapter 3

The Suffering Servant

"Hey, Klin! Get up!" Joseph gently yelled in his ear. Klin moaned as he rolled out of bed. "Oh crap, did I oversleep?" He asked. Joseph turned on the lamp by his bed. "No. I just figured you'd not be up yet." Klin grunted as he started drowsily finding his clothes. Joseph knew better than to try and talk to him right now, so he left to head downstairs. Klin quickly changed and went downstairs, joining his brother in the kitchen. As quietly as they could, they prepared breakfast and quickly wolfed it down. As soon as they were finished, they left the house and made their way to the city walls. It was still dark out, around five in the morning.

Klin could not help but let out a massive yawn as they walked. Joseph let out of quiet chuckle. "Stay up late playing with potions?" Klin stretched out his arms as they walked, hoping it would help wake him up more. "Yeah. Lost track of time. Got some really cool ones made at least. Should fetch a decent price." Joseph nodded, "Good. Any we can use ourselves?" Klin frowned, "Joseph, you know that we're forbidden to use them." He hissed, "We're lucky we can even sell them." Joseph let out a derisive snort, "Yeah, because the Guardians don't know about our little side business. Just saying." Klin shook his head and sighed as they got to the east gate. Smears of blood stained the walls and grass. "Looks like it was a heavy fight last night." Klin grunted. "Who goes there?!" A guard shouted, leaping out from the shadows, spear leveled at them. "Markus brothers." Klin answered. The man frowned, "What in the blazes are you doing out and about? Don't you know the Sculpting monsters are still out and about?!"

Klin and Joseph exchanged a worried look. "No." Joseph explained, "We never heard the horn." Now it was the guards turn to frown. "Oh. I-I uh suppose it never did blow. Anyway, get on in." He gave a signal as the gate was opened. Before they went in, the guard gave them a nasty smile, "Suppose it wouldn't have mattered to you if you had known anyway. Marth be worse than them monsters for you, ain't that right?" The man laughed hysterically at his own little joke, but Klin and Joseph ignored him as they went on in. "Herking idiot." Joseph muttered, "It's any wonder this city hasn't fallen to those things." Klin nodded in agreement. For eleven years, strange monsters had been assaulting the city of Ala'Kathar. Most people never saw them, as the protocols for an attack were so heavily enforced, but every once in a while, a Guardian would die; their body torn to pieces by claws of a creature unlike anything known in Threa. The king had never bothered to help them and would not unless they suddenly stopped sending him their monthly tithe.

Klin and Joseph walked through the streets, sticking close to the shadows as much as they could. Even though there were hardly any people out and about, they did not want to take the chance of running into anyone who would delay them. They had a lot of work to get done. Their shop was in the heart of Ala'Kathar, which was a decent sized city of seven thousand people. It was one of the three major cities in Ardaven. Their smithy was a small stone building, barely fifty feet wide. No building closer than seventy feet stood near it. Above the door was a worn-down wooden sign bearing a hammer and anvil, the only thing that even hinted at what kind of place this was. The Guardians had forbidden them from actually naming the place. All they had to stick out from other blacksmiths was the quality of their work. Klin fished around his pocket for the key and unlocked the door.

They went in and began their daily routine. Joseph immediately went over and began to get the forges started. While he did that, Klin turned on the Light Stones, illuminating the place. After that, he gathered their tools and placed them where they could easily switch out without moving. He then went to the stone counter at the back of the store and checked the money chest. Everything was still there. Good. He went around the store and quickly took inventory. Various crafted objects decorated the store. Things from swords to silverware were for sale, hanging from walls or sitting on a shelf. Klin grabbed a smithing apron and went out back to check on Jospeh. By now the forge should be ready, or at least close. He heard the sound a hammer hitting metal and found Joseph already working on Marth's order. "There you are!" Joseph cried as he wiped some sweat from his brow. "What took you so long?" Klin gave him smirk as he crossed his arms. "Giving you plenty of time to get the forge going. I'm surprised it's hot enough to work already though."

A mischievous grin swept over his brother's face as he pulled out a Fire Stone. "I may have had some help today." Klin laughed, "You devious genius! How did you get one?" Joseph shook his head and gestured to Klin's tools and forge. "I'll tell you later. We got five of those bowls to make before three." Klin nodded and joined his set to work. He did *not* want to see what Marth would do if they did not have his order ready. Klin and Joseph worked through the morning and into the afternoon, only breaking for water and abstaining from any food. They did not have the time for it. For not only did they have to craft the silver into a bowl, but then had to carve designs onto them. After they had two made and cooled, Klin began to work on the designs. They had got the most difficult designs done the other day, staying late to get them done. Each bowl had a pairing design. So far, they had leaves, deer, and wolves. Klin was finishing the last of the leaves. After he was done with that, he went to work on a fish design as Joseph worked on the final bowl.

Finally, after that they worked together on the flame designs. "Whew, done with an hour to spare too!" Joseph exclaimed. Klin nodded, his stomach clenching and crying out in pain from hunger. "Yeah. Can we eat now?"

"Took the words right out of my mouth." The two placed gathered all the bowls together and placed them on the counter. "Alright, you go buy us some food, I'll watch the shop?" Klin asked. Joseph nodded and took off. Klin let out a small sigh of relief. They had actually done it. Three days would have been more than enough if they were used to having to do anything fancy. They had spent most of yesterday just practicing the designs on iron bowls. The ones that did not look horrendous were now up for sale. Of course, they could have done all that the first day if Marth had not placed the order a minute before they closed for the day. Klin's face curdled at the memory and shook it off. Suddenly, the bell to the shop announced a visitor. Klin looked up, and felt his empty stomach drop at the sight of Monastrath.

"Hey Klin!" He called, "Why aren't you at work on my dad's order?" Klin bit the inside of his mouth and took a deep breath. "We just finished it. We're about to take a lunch break." Monastrath began to walk around browsing. "It's nearly three though. Way past lunch, don't you think?" Klin's mouth twitched slightly, but Monastrath did not see it. "Well. We did not have time to break. Your father's order is top priority." Monastrath spun around and walked up to the counter, leaning against it. "I see your arm is fixed. That bitch healed it, huh?" Klin clenched his fists. *Don't. Don't. Don't.* "Yeah. She did. Anything I can help you with or you just here to keep me from work?" Monastrath clucked his tongue. "Well, well. Someone's still a little feisty. But," He began to chuckle, "I suppose you have entered manhood now. Got to catch up to the rest of us, am I right?" At that moment, Joseph walked in, the smile on his face dropping as he saw who was by Klin. "Oi, what are you doing here?" Joseph snapped. Monastrath spun around and shrugged, "What? I can't browse a place of business?"

"Don't seem to be doing much browsing now do you?" Joseph growled, walking behind the counter and sliding Klin a sandwich. "Besides, it's our lunch break." Monastrath clucked his tongue, "Really now? So rude. You going to let him talk to me like this Klin?" Klin kept his face emotionless and hard as stone. "Knock it off Joseph."

"What? But he—"

"I said knock it off!" He snapped. Joseph took a step back but nodded. "Fine. Sorry." Monastrath nodded in satisfaction. "Apology accepted. Now, I suppose I need to head out and let you eat. I'll be back though. Need an order placed." With that he strut out the door. As soon as he did, Joseph turned to Klin with a big grin. "I was apologizing to you, not him for the record." Klin laughed quietly, "I kind of figured. Anyway, what did you get me?"

"Eh, just a lettuce, cheese, and some salted meat on a stale slab of bread." Klin grimaced as he took a bite. Was not the worst thing he had ever had to eat. "Nice." Klin ate with ravenous intent, trying to stop his stomach from trying to kill him. Once they were done, Joseph shifted about awkwardly. "Alright," Klin sighed, "What do you want to scold me for?" A soft light shone from Joseph's eyes as he crossed his arms. "Why the herk do you still put up with Moanstrath? I know for a herking fact that all your "accidents" are from him. You never stand up for yourself! Why?" Klin tapped his finger on the counter. Was it time for him to finally explain, or would doing even that make things worse. Finally he gave an answer, "I have my reasons."

"Oh, and what in the Eight's Names are those?" Joseph exclaimed, "I'm beginning to think you're a coward who's too scared to do anything that might hurt someone!" Klin swirled towards Joseph, eyes blazing in anger, but he was stopped as the bell over the door rang. Unfortunately, the man who walked in was in no way helpful for his anger. It was Marth Cra'Son. He was shorter than his son, standing around average height. He had a silk with shirt which clung to his skin, barely keeping the muscles from underneath bulging out. He had blonde hair that was kept trim and swept back, and a nicely trimmed beard. He tossed back a black cape with blue trim, the colors of the Guardians. A servant in a plain white cotton tunic followed behind, eyes constantly cast down. "Hello Markuses." Marth greeted with a sneer. "I'm here for my order." Klin nodded to Joseph and went to grab the bowls. "Of course, my lord." Joseph said with thin humility, "We have them. Just finished them barely an hour ago." Klin felt some gratitude for Joseph. Normally Klin did all the talking, but his brother had taken the hint. Now was not a good time for him.

Klin placed all the bowls on the counter in a row. Marth picked each one up and inspected them, one by one. "Hmmm, masterful work. Servant! Pack them up! And you better be careful, or I will have your head! These are worth more than you will ever make in a year! Your payment boys." Marth placed ten emeraladas on the counter. Joseph frowned, "I'm sorry to ask this my lord, but I believe you are missing some of the payment." Marth gave him a distasteful look. "Am I? Are you saying I miscounted?" Joseph shook his head, "Uh, no. But the agreed payment was twenty." Marth gave him a nasty smile, "Yes, for *exquisite* bowls. These are merely masterful." Klin felt his earlier rage hitting a newfound height. He wanted to do something, and he felt like he really did not care what the consequences were. "You pompous ass." Klin growled and snatched five of the silver bowls away. Marth narrowed his eyes. "Carful boy. Those are *mine*. I paid for them." Klin handed three of them to a very confused Joseph. "We haven't taken your payment yet. So, no, they aren't. Masterful and exquisite are merely synonyms, meant to convey the same sentiment. Only reason for using one or the other is stylistics reasons. So, *my lord*, I believe you are missing some of the payment." The servant cautiously looked up and was giving Klin a look of awe and admiration.

Marth crossed his arms, and tilted his head up. "What nonsense is this?!" He asked furiously, "Is this how you worms repay my generosity?! I kept this pathetic shop open out of the kindness of my heart when your worthless father abandoned you! And *then*, I gave it to you two when you were of the age to run it! And now, my repayment is insults and venom! I pray that you reconsider what it is you are doing."

Klin laughed, "Don't act like that all somehow makes up for what you're doing right now! Generous heart? Your heart is as generous as a fox's! A weasel could be kinder than you! Now! Full payment, or I'm going to start breaking them. I don't care if we don't get paid right now. *You*, don't deserve these." Marth's face curdled as his whole face went red. He stood there, shaking in anger before slamming the rest of the payment down. "Fine. Now give them to me!" Klin set the bowls down and motioned for Joseph to do the same. Yet, before Klin or Joseph could pick up the emerald-colored triangles, Marth snatched up all but five. "Hey!" Joseph protested, "What do you think you're doing?!" Marth gave them both a cool look. "Taxes for insults. I believe Klin knows what is promised when he disobeys. However, I'm feeling more generous than a weasel, so consider this the payment." Marth snapped his fingers and walked away. Before he closed the door though, he looked over his shoulder and said, "While I begrudgingly admire the newfound spine Klin, I don't recommend making it any stronger." With that he slammed the door shut.

"ARRRRRGHGHGHH!" Klin screamed and slammed his fists on the counter. "That herking---arrrrggggghhhhh!" Joseph patted him on the shoulder. "Don't stress to much bro, we'll get him one of these days. But holy shit! I've never seen you stand up like that! And what you said!' Joseph laughed and imitated his Klin's voice, "The words are synonyms, and meant to convey the same sentiment. HA! Brilliant!" Klin allowed himself a smile, but he felt a little cold inside after that. "Yeah, guess I went off a little bit, huh?" Joseph chuckled as he took the emeraldas and put them someplace safe. "A bit? You jumped off the entire herking cliff! But...what did he mean about you knowing the whole punishment thing?" Klin suddenly felt like he was freezing and looked away in shame. "I...I can't say." Joseph frowned, "Why not? I don't think Marth wants it as a secret?" Klin shook his head. "No, it's a trap. He's wanting me to take it and I can't."

Joseph furrowed his brow and asked angrily, "Alright, what's so damn important that you can't even tell me?!" Klin clenched his fists. "Well, why can't you just take my word for it?!"

"Well, *maybe* because I think I could help!"

"And why the herk do you think that? Maybe this isn't something you can actually help with!"

"Bullshit!" Joseph yelled, "I'm one hundred percent certain I can!" Klin crossed his arms, "Yeah? Guess what Joseph? You're dead wrong here!" Joseph flinched and took a deep breath, closing his eyes as he did so. "Klin, what's going? For real?" He asked gently. Klin's anger abated, replaced by deep, deep guilt as he cast his head down, no longer having the strength to look Joseph in the eye. "I'm sorry. I really can't tell. I-it will put you guys in a lot of danger." Suddenly, Klin felt Joseph's hand on his shoulder. He gave him a gentle, but firm squeeze. "Alright. I'll accept that for now. But remember, mom and I are always here for you." Klin patted his hand. "I know." *It's the only reason I've gone this long.* He thought.

Suddenly the bell announced the arrival of another customer. Joseph let out an annoyed sigh and muttered, "I swear to Genus, if it's another Guardian I might break some bones." But it was not. Instead, an old woman with a walking cane shuffled in. The woman wore a multicolored shawl with a hood that was lowered, revealing a dark, wrinkled face that shone with wisdom. The elderly woman's name was Dreas O'Loole, and she was the oldest woman in Ala'Kathar, if not the world. Her white hair was short, but it was still healthy despite being such a clean white, which made Klin suspect that white had been her natural hair color. Klin and Joseph thought blinked in surprise as she came in. "Dreas," Klin greeted, "Hello. Uh, what can we do for you?" Dreas shuffled around, looking at all the different things for sale. "I need some new jewelry." She said simply. "Figured you boys might have some on hand." Klin and Joseph frowned and Joseph went over to help her. "Dreas, you know you could just order one from us? You don't have to settle for anything pre-made." Dreas let out a snort. "I know that young man! Maybe I don't have anything in particular in mind and just want to enjoy the pleasure of shopping! Thought about that?" Joseph rubbed the back of his head sheepishly, "Sorry Dreas." The old woman gave him a satisfied nod.

Klin could not help but crack a smile. Dreas was basically their grandmother. They had known her even before their dad had disappeared. When their father had been deemed a traitor, Klin and Joseph had been forbidden from attending school and learning any sort of self-defense. Dreas, who seemed to have endless knowledge, had taken up their education. Many a day in their childhood had been spent cozily in her cottage as she carefully instructed them. Albeit, she could be quite harsh, but Klin and Joseph loved her. "How are you feeling?" Klin asked, "Mom said you were sick yesterday." Dreas gave him a mischievous look, "Oh much better. I came down with a mysterious illness called hatredofsocializing. Seems like it is gone now." Klin laughed and walked over, pulling down a box of necklaces for her. "Glad you are feeling better now." Dreas patted his cheek. "Thank you dear." She studied the necklaces and grabbed one of them. "Hmm, such irony." Klin frowned, "Uh, why?"

Dreas picked up one of the necklaces and held it up. It was nothing too terribly fancy. The most striking feature was that the symbols for Light and Dark were fused together, their respective colors of gold and purple shining off the metal. "Oh nothing. Just seems like this must be hereditary." Dreas replied with a smirk. Klin and Joseph exchanged a look. "Okay. What?" Joseph asked incredulously. Dreas shook her head. "Oh, must I say it in such an obvious way? I thought you boys were smart." Joseph shook his head with a grin. "Nah. Just Klin." Klin rolled his eyes but turned his attention back to Dreas, and pondered her words. It seemed very unlikely she was referring to either Lorelei or their Uncle, so that just left…"Dad." Klin frowned, "Dreas. What are you going on about? I thought you barely knew our dad?"

"Since when have I ever implied that?" Dreas cackled. "Anyway, how much for the necklace?"

"One topaza." Joseph answered, "But, you can't just stop there! Explain!"

"No." Dreas sated as she paid, "I think this is not the place to discuss such things. Come by after work." Klin was about to protest, but at that moment yet another customer entered into the store. Joseph let out a weary sigh. "Sheesh, we're busy today it seems." The brothers frowned as a young woman walked in. They had never seen her before, and they at least recognized the people they did not know by name in this city. She was short, standing around five foot four, but she walked with a lithe grace and powerful steps. The woman was somewhat stocky, but nothing like Mrs. O'Mar. Her legs and arms were well muscled, but not large. She had blonde hair that fell just a little below the neck, while the left side of her bangs hanged freely. The woman had sky-blue eyes that examined them with a mix of mischief and judgement, as if she was appraising their moral character, and if found lacking, there would be a pretty brutal insult from her mouth.

The woman had katana strapped to her side, but she was not really dressed like a warrior. She wore a white shirt with a red and black jacket, a pink skirt, and buckled boots. The woman walked straight up to them. As she got closer, Klin could see that she had dried mud, and various stains on her clothes and skin. The glossy black sheathe of her weapon though remained pristine. "Hello ma'am, how can we help you?" Joseph asked. She untied the blue cloth that kept the sheathe tied to her waist and placed the katana on the counter, her head barely above it. "I'd like to see if you two could make a sword better than this." She explained. Klin frowned as he took reached out. "May I?" The woman rolled her eyes, "If I didn't want you touching it, I wouldn't have put it up there would I?" Klin's eye twitched a bit. "I was just being polite." He said sharply. Rather than getting angry, the woman gave him a grin. Klin shook his head and unsheathed the sword. "Damn!" Joseph whistled. The blade was made from no metal they had ever seen. It had a steel coloration, but had a silver glow to it. The blade was heavier than expected too, making Klin feel a little awkward wielding the thing. "What is this metal?" Klin asked admiringly.

"Don't know." The woman shrugged, "Was hoping you two could help." Klin frowned and was about to put it down but froze. A little girl was on the counter, starting at him. He blinked a few times, and just like that, she was gone. Cautiously, he set the katana back down. "Sorry, never even heard of a metal like this. Might be able to figure out what it is, but we'd have to take off a decent amount of the blade, and I'm sure you don't want that." The woman gave him a look of admiration and surprise. "Heh, you are the first one to not just automatically try to take a sample." She chuckled, "Thanks for that."

"Uh, sure." Klin replied. How many blacksmiths had she visited before them? And who was she? Joseph reached out for the sword, "Hey, can I hold it?" He asked excitedly. Klin gestured with a small flourish, making his brother grin. "So, anyway ma'am, where are you from?" Klin inquired. The woman shifted a little, "Uh, private." Klin frowned, "Okay. Well, why did you come here? You're obviously not from around here." The woman raised her eyebrow at him. "This how you always deal with strange women?" Klin let out a snort. "That's assuming we even get them. I don't know if you know this, but Ala'Kathar is not exactly known for having many visitors. We get merchants wanting to trade and the king's taxers. That's it." The woman crossed her arms. "Are you serious? This is one of Ardavens best cities!" Klin shook his head, "*Was.* Not anymore."

Suddenly, Joseph let out a yelp as the katana clattered against the stone counter. "Joseph!" Klin snapped, "Careful!" Joseph shook his hand, flecks of blood flying in through the air. "Sorry." He mumbled sheepishly, "Cut myself." Klin sighed and checked over the sword real quick and let out a sigh of relief. Good, nothing looked damaged. "Sorry about that." Klin apologized, "My brother is normally more careful than this." The woman shrugged, "Eh, not big deal. You two done with my sword then?" Klin looked at Joseph who nodded. As the woman retied her sword around her waist, he caught a sly smile and look in her eyes. Klin frowned, feeling like whatever Joseph had just done had been exactly what she wanted. "By the way," she asked, "you two would not happen to know where a Dreas O'Loole lives, would you?" Before Klin could ask why, his brother blurted out. "Oh yeah! She actually is right behind you!" The woman spun around to see Dreas studying here while Klin smacked his brother on the head. "Joseph!" Klin hissed, "We don't know what she wants with her!" Joseph turned very, very bright red. "Oops." Dreas just grinned at all three of them. "Oh, it is okay Klin. I think this stranger is trustworthy." That elicited a frown from all three in the room. "What makes you say that?" The woman asked. "I mean, I had this whole speech prepared about how I wasn't going to do anything shitty, but you are right."

Dreas tapped her forehead. "Call it the elderly's instincts. What's your name dear?"

"Celeste." Celeste replied and then turned to Klin and Joseph. "Celeste Coal. Klin and Joseph looked at one another and then shrugged. "I'm Klin Markus." Klin introduced, "And this is my brother, Joseph." Celeste nodded, and then hesitated. "Wait, Markus? Like, as in Jethro Markus; the Immortal Hero's last name?" Joseph nodded, "Yeah, but we aren't related to him." Dreas let out a snort, that was both derisive and a stifled laugh, producing an overall strange sound. "Later boys." Dreas said, stopping their question before they could ask it. "Now, Celeste? How about you come over to my place for some tea, along with these two? I have a feeling all three of you have will learn something that may be to your benefit." The three exchanged a confused look but nodded. "Alright, sounds good. Let us just close shop first." Joseph said. Dreas nodded. "Celeste and I will stay outside and wait." With that, the two set about closing up the store. "So, what do you make of all this?" Joseph asked. Klin shook his head as he locked up their money. "I don't know. Dreas obviously is hinting at something about our dad, but why weren't we told the truth then? As for Celeste, I don't know. She seems nice I guess, but she's hiding a lot. I can tell." Joseph nodded. "Yeah. My thoughts exactly. Hey, did you see anything…weird when holding the sword?"

Klin looked up, "Weird how?"

"Like, maybe seeing a litter girl? Who was for sure from the East?"

Klin frowned, "Wait is that why…" He trailed off though as he saw Monastrath staring at him through the window, tapping his wrist.

"Uh, Klin?" Joseph asked. Klin jumped, making Joseph give him a worried look. "Hey, are you okay bro?" Klin nodded, "Yeah, sorry just remembered I have to go take care of something important after this. Joseph shook his head as he grunted, "And you call me the forgetful one. Well, let's go. Sooner you get that taken care of, sooner we can figure out what's going on with Dreas." Klin nodded, a pit settling in his stomach. "Yeah."

Once they were done, Klin tossed Joseph the key. "I'm going to head out the back door," he explained, "It'll be faster for me. Just explain to them. I'll meet you guys at Dreas's." Joseph shrugged, "Alright. See you there." With that, Klin slipped out the back door, and found Monastrath standing there. "Hey Klin." He growled, "I heard what happened with my dad earlier. You got some nerve insulting your superior like that." Klin crossed his arms. "If you're here to collect the 'debt' your father already took care of that, as I'm sure he gleefully explained." Monastrath narrowed his eyes, "Well, the dog is starting to bite back today. Come on, just for that alone you added more to your debt." Klin took a deep breath and forced himself to bow his head as he followed Monastrath. The man led him to an alleyway, where in the middle, his two lackeys stood with idiotic grins. Klin grimaced as he saw the leather whip. He had messed up big today. Both were shorter than Monastarth, but just as well built. The one Klin considered uglier was Draco, an idiot who was already starting to go bald, despite being only seventeen. The other one, Cenn, had more brains than either Monastrath or Draco, but chose not to use them.

"Alright, let's see." Monastrath said, "For talking back to my dad, myself, and then fighting me *and* threatening my dad, you get…twenty punches and thirty lashes." Klin moved to take his shirt off, but was stopped as Draco punched him in the face. Klin stumbled back, rolling his jaw. "One." Draco cackled. Cenn leapt up and threw three punches to his stomach. "That's four!" Draco then kicked him in the shit, forcing him to the ground before he threw a hook to Klin's face. Klin's head was whipped back, throwing him on his side. "Get up!" Draco sneered. Klin's ears were ringing, but he forced himself to stand up. He looked his abusers in the eye definatly. "Get that look out of your eyes!" Cenn snarled as he unleashed five punches to the face. Klin stayed standing, but it was difficult. His face was starting to get bloodied now. "Ten." Cenn smirked, "Draco?" Draco laughed menacingly as he ran up and unleashed ten punches to Klin's stomach. Klin gasped, struggling for air as he was doubled over. "That's twenty boss!" Moanstrath nodded, "Good, now take his shirt off." As Klin was stripped, he closed his eyes, bracing himself, and resolved not to let out any cry of pain.

At the first lash, he stayed quiet. The second, he grunted internally, at the third he let out a small grunt. After that, he could not help but cry out in pain as his flesh was stripped from his back. The alley echoed with his screams as lash after lash ripped scraps of flesh off and covered his back in blood. The air stung against his open wounds, and each additional lash added more pain than he thought he could take. Yet, he stayed conscious through the ordeal, refusing to curl up and cry, even though that was what he wanted to do most. Finally, it stopped. After a minute, and some very deep, heavy breathing, Klin forced himself to look up. Draco and Cenn were staring at him in horror. Even Monastarth had unease in his eyes. "Uh, boss?" Draco asked tentatively. "What?" Monastrath snapped. Draco rubbed his hands and wet his mouth. "Do uh, do you think we went overboard?" Monastrath shot him an evil glare, but when he turned back to Klin, it was replaced by heavy guilt. Monastrath threw down the whip, punching Klin in the face. "This is your fault!" He snarled, "I won! I won this! Yet somehow, I didn't! I know this is your fault!" Monastrath pulled back his hand, preparing to throw another. Klin closed his eyes. He could not take anymore.

"That's enough!" Joseph snarled. Klin looked up to see Joseph, Celeste, and Dreas standing at the end of the alley. Monastrath spun back to Klin. "You told them?!" He snarled. Klin shook his head weakly. "No. I know what—" He was cut off as he was kicked in the face. "I SAID ENOUGH!" Joseph roared. His scream echoed, reverberating against the walls, making Draco and Cenn flinch. "Do anything else to him, and I'll return it to you tenfold!" Celeste exclaimed. Moanstrath crossed his arms, "And just who are you sweetie? Obviously you aren't from around here, or you wouldn't be making such threats." Suddenly, Dreas began to shuffle forward. "And you, you old hag what—"

"Quiet!" Dreas snapped, "Unless you want me to show you why your father has forbidden anyone to ever harm me. You are already on thin ice Mona, carrying out a punishment such as this without the authority too!" Monastrath flinched and growled, "Don't. Call me that. Besides, I do have the authority! I'm a Guardian!" Dreas raised an eyebrow, still advancing towards him. "Oh? Since when did membership become hereditary. Your father may be the leader, but that does not make you a prince! Even under your own unjust laws, what you have just done is illegal! I wonder what your father would think of this? Afterall, he is all about appearances and authority." Monastrath paled and clenched his fists. "Why, you little hag!" He moved to punch, but then faster than should be possible for one of her age, Dreas spun her cane and stabbed him in the stomach before twirling it around to hit both sides of the head. Monastrath crumbled to the ground unconscious. Klin then watched as golden lines, almost like fabric threads, spread out from Dreas. They formed a silhouette around her, and she began to glow with a golden light. Draco and Cenn took one look at her before they turned and ran. The light faded, as well as the golden threads. "Klin! Are you okay?" Joseph exclaimed as he rushed to his side. Klin coughed, spitting out some blood. "Yaeagh." He gurgled. His nose was probably broken. "How...how long were you guys there?" Celeste shook her head. "We saw the whole thing."

Joseph nodded, shooting Dreas a glare. "Yeah, but Dreas refused to let us help. Said we had to watch." Dreas walked up to Klin and pulled out a potion from her cloak. "Here, this will dull the pain." Klin drank the potion with her help, and let out a sigh as the pain faded just a bit. "Thanks. But how—why?" Dreas shook her head, "Oh my dear boy, I have known about this 'deal' with the Guardians for a long time. Please accept my apology though. I wanted to intervene, but Joseph needed to see the full extent of what you have been going through on his behalf." Joseph froze and looked over at Klin. "What does she mean." Klin sighed. No point in hiding it any longer. "About seven years ago, back when you first started to fight others, Marth came to me. He said that what you were doing was far beyond pleasing, and he was going to kill you for it. So, I pleaded with him. Told him, I'll take any and all beatings that you incurred for breaking some stupid law or for standing up to them, as long as they did not harm you or mom." Joseph started at Klin, tears forming at his eyes. "You idiot! You selfless idiot! We could have taken those beatings together!" Celeste clenched her fists. "I don't care how much power these assholes have, people really let them do this kind of stuff?" Dreas nodded, "I'm afraid so. But enough chatter, let's get Klin back. His wounds need tending to." Joseph and Celeste nodded. Each of them put an arm around Klin and helped him to his feet. "By the way Dreas? What was it that you did earlier? With the golden fabric stuff?" Joseph frowned. "Klin, what are you talking about? I mean, I'm curious how she glowed, but there were not fabrics." Klin frowned, shaking his head, but stopped. That hurt too much. "Hmm. Intriguing. I'll explain later." Dreas said with a smile as she led them out of the city. That was fine with Klin. He had had enough of this place for the day.

Chapter 4

Fabric of Fate

They made it back home just as twilight was setting in. "Were back!" Klin cried hoarsely. "Oh good!" Lorelei called from behind the stairs, "I was just starting to get worr—Klin! What happened?!" Klin smiled darkly, "I uhhh, hi mom." Lorelei rushed over and examined him. "Get him on the kitchen table!" She ordered, and then spared a glance at Celeste. "Oh, hello." She said with a smile, "I'm their mother. Who you are can wait though." Celeste nodded hesitantly, obviously taken aback. Joseph and Celeste helped Klin into the kitchen, where Joseph lifted him onto the table. Klin rolled onto his stomach, already aware of what his mom would probably have to do. "What in the world happened?" Lorelei asked as she began to move around the table. Klin let out a small gasp as his back prickled and icy rolled over his back as his skin was healed. "Monastrath." Joseph spat. "That asshole whipped him!" Klin could sense his mother's anger and felt some fear when she asked coolly. "Oh? Really. So, where is he now?"

They made it back home just as twilight was setting in. "Were back!" Klin cried hoarsely. "Oh good!" Lorelei called from behind the stairs, "I was just starting to get worr—Klin! What happened?!" Klin smiled darkly, "I uhhh, hi mom." Lorelei rushed over and examined him. "Get him on the kitchen table!" She ordered, and then spared a glance at Celeste. "Oh, hello." She said with a smile, "I'm their mother. Who you are can wait though." Celeste nodded hesitantly, obviously taken aback. Joseph and Celeste helped Klin into the kitchen, where Joseph lifted him onto the table. Klin rolled onto his stomach, already aware of what his mom would probably have to do. "What in the world happened?" Lorelei asked as she began to move around the table. Klin let out a small gasp as his back prickled and icy rolled over his back as his skin was healed. "Monastrath." Joseph spat. "That asshole whipped him!" Klin could sense his mother's anger and felt some fear when she asked coolly. "Oh? Really. So, where is he now?"

"No need for that Lorelei." Dreas interjected, "I took care of him."

"How? And why were *you* there Dreas? And why did that pig of a person do this to my son?!" Klin heard Dreas pat his mother. "Your son has been protecting both you and Joseph by voluntarily taking punishments for acting out against the Guardians. I was there because tonight we need to tell them the truth." Klin craned his neck, barely able to see his mom and Dreas. His mother had a very concerned look on her face, but it was tempered by acceptance. "Very well." She said with a sigh, "I suppose it is time. Do you really think they are ready though?" Dreas gestured to Klin. "Do you think someone unprepared would be able to take this, and willingly too?" Klin shuddered violently as his mother finished her healing. He sat up and rolled the muscles on his back. "Thanks mom." His mom though was starting at him silently, looking between him and Joseph. "I suppose you are right as always." Lorelei admitted with a sigh. Dreas smiled and patted her. "I know. Now, come you two! And you also Celeste. We must know why a woman came all the way out here to find me."

"Uh, can I get a new shirt on first?" Klin asked, "This one's covered in blood now." Dreas shooed him, so Klin went and did that real quick. Once he came back down, he found everyone by the door. "Uh, why can't we talk here?" Klin asked. Dreas pointed her cane at him, "Well, we don't want any unwanted eavesdroppers now do we? Besides, your mother keeps the most horrendous of teas."

"Hey!" Lorelei protested indignantly, "I do not!" Dreas let out a cackle as she opened the door, "Oh right. You just can't make any properly." The old woman cackled to herself as she walked out. Klin just shook his head as he followed her. What made her think someone could hear them out here? He froze though as he neared the doorframe. Above it were some of those weird fabric threads, but they were gray instead of gold. "Hey mom, have those threads always been there?" His mom frowned and looked to where he was pointing. "No, they hav— wait, you can see them?!" Joseph frowned, looking between them. "Uh,

I can't see anything guys. Do you Celeste?" Celeste narrowed her eyes, "Well, not what they see. Look, there is a slight distortion in the air around the doorframe. That's a sign of air magic." Klin felt his heart skip a beat. "Air magic? Wait, then what I'm seeing then…"

"Is the actual spell that Weaver's see." Lorelei confirmed. "Yes, very intriguing." Dreas cut in suddenly, poking her head through the door. "All the more reason we get to my place! Come! Come! I'm hold and am bound to habits, so don't blame me when I get cranky that I don't have my tea!" Klin and Joseph gave one another a shrug and followed Dreas after their mom destroyed the spell above the door. They did not have to walk too far though. At the edge of the woods, about a mile from the Markus's house was Dreas's cottage. It was a simple wooden home, not very large with a small flower garden in bloom in front. Dreas pulled out a key and unlocked the door, shuffling inside. "Welcome to my simple abode Celeste." Dreas called as she walked off to the kitchen, most likely to prepare her tea. "Find a seat. I will be just a moment." Finding a seat proved to be a bit difficult though. There was hardly any furniture as most of the cottage's space was taken up with bookcases. If there was a wall, there were books against it. Different piles of books lay scattered on the ground also. There was a couch, rocking chair, a love seat and a small table that had most of the surface covered in books.

"Wow." Celeste whistled softly, "This is uh, well…"

"Amazing?" Klin offered. She shook her head, "Nah. Obsessive."

"Hmph, not my fault you are stupid." Dreas scoffed as she came back in, a steaming pot of tea with cups on a tray. Celeste jumped in surprise, turning bright red. "Sorry. Reading has never been my strong suit. No offense." Dreas set the tray down, pouring herself a cup. "There is nothing but offense in an idiotic comment like that, and so you shall earn what you waged." Celeste blushed even harder and hid her face. "Sorry ma'am." Dreas gave her an approving nod as she took a seat in her rocking chair. "Accepted. Now, where shall we begin. With our stranger, Klin's recent ability, or the family heritage?" Klin sat next to his mom on the couch wile Joseph took a seat next to Celeste. He and his brother looked and exchanged a silent conversation before Joseph said, "How about we start with Celeste? She came all this way to talk to you, so let's let her go first." Celeste looked at Joseph slightly bewildered.

"Are you sure? I mean, I know I just kind of walked into some sort of family drama, but I can wait." Joseph shook his head, "Nah, feel like it's only fair. Besides, I have a feeling that we'll end up helping one another."

Celeste snorted softly, "Are you two always this trusting?" Lorelei gave her a smile, "They get that from their father." Celeste shrugged, "Alright. Fair enough I suppose. Let's see, where should I start? Oh, I know. So, you two obviously saw that little Eastern girl, right?" Klin blinked a few times, "How—"

Celeste gave him a sly smile. "Because I'm talking to her right now. This sounds crazy, but there is a little girl trapped inside the blade. I…I want to help get her out and I heard of this woman who lives in Ala'Kathar with boundless knowledge." A twinkle appeared in Dreas's eyes. "Oh, and where did you hear such a thing?" Celeste shrugged quickly. "Oh, rumors. But I also heard rumors of some legendary blacksmiths not able to practice their craft to the skill they have. Turns out though they are kind of shitty smiths."

"Hey!" Joseph cried indignantly, "I'll have you know that if we had the same metal as your sword, we could make a blade even better!" Celeste rolled her eyes, "Sure. The other stuff in the store did not seem too terribly impressive. Are the other smiths around here that bad?" Joseph crossed his arms, pouting. "Ah, shut up. We're *excellent.*" Celeste let out a small giggle, her eyes glowing with mischief. "I was only messing with you." She apologized with a giggle, "Sorry about that. The work was good. Anyway, Dreas, do you think you could help me?" Dreas set down her cup and examined the blade. "What is the girl's name?" She asked. "Yatta." Celeste replied. Dreas nodded and reverently examined the blade. Klin watched her trace her finger along the blade, a small golden thread trailing behind. "Well, I know this." Dreas finally said. "Whatever placed her in this was not done with Elemental Magic. It was something that has no roots in goodness. Does she remember who she was?"

Celeste shook her head. "No. All she knows is this. She was from the East, and has been inside the sword for hundreds of years." Dreas gave a start at that. "Damn. I might have an idea then. Are you familiar with Cursed?" Celeste hesitated then shook her head. "Well," Dreas explained, "They are as the name implies. Cursed beings as the result of magical experimentation, usually with Natharian magic. Officially outlawed in most of the world, but at the same time, unofficially sanctioned. She is Cursed. I can say this though. You must go to Dremaria, for that was where she was turned into her present condition. From there, find her past and the facility she was created. Do this, and you might be ablet to undo what has been done." Dreas handed the sword back to Celeste. "Thank you very much Miss Dreas." Dreas smiled and nodded, "Of course dear. Now, what next?" Klin raised his hand, "Well, before we talk about dad, can we discuss my new apparent ability to see magic?"

Dreas looked at Lorelei, the two exchanging a silent joke it seemed. "Well, they might be connected." Lorelei admitted. "Well then why did we separate the two?" Joseph asked bewildered. "For politeness's sake." Dreas chuckled. "So, let's see. Your father is Jethro Markus the Immortal Hero." Klin and Joseph burst out laughing but stopped when they saw their mother's stoic face. "Oh…Oh crap." Joseph said reverently, "You are not joking." Lorelei let out a wistful sigh, "I somewhat wish we were. It would make your lives easier. He warned me that a man who lived as long as he had would not be able to provide a normal family life." Klin frowned, feeling like he had just got hit with a truck. Wh—what was one supposed to feel at information like this? "Okay. So, dad is *the* Jethro. But, if he's immortal wouldn't that mean—"

"That he would outlive you all?" Dreas finished. Klin nodded. Dreas gave him and Joseph a knowing smile, "Oh, do not worry about that. He can actually give up his immortality." Klin and Joseph blinked, "Wait what?" They asked in unison. Dreas shrugged, "He's not the only one who live through the Final Battle. You boys are very familiar with that time period. I'm the same Dreas from then." Klin crossed his arms and laughed, "You know, since we've actually known you for so long, I'm not nearly as surprised by that. It actually makes way too much sense."

"Uh, can I ask a few things?" Celeste inquired tentatively. They all nodded. "Okay, thanks. Sorry, cause I know there is some really deep revelations going on right now, and wow. I'm in the presence of a legend and a legend's sons. Anyway, I'm actually from Coronus."

"Oh, my goodness!" Lorelei exclaimed, "That's quite a long journey for someone to make by themselves!" Celeste shrugged, "I mean yeah, it kind of was. But anyway, if your Jethro's boys, then…where is Jethro?

The emperor has been searching for him the past five years." Dreas frowned, "Really? Why in the world did Gabriel not contact me? Unless—"

"Unless the Guardians have been interfering your contacts." Lorelei finished solemnly. "I've been worried about that for the past ten years. I barely get to communicate with my brother, and it's been a year since he's been here." Joseph crossed his arms, frowning, "Is that why Uncle Joshua hasn't visited us? Cause of the Guardians?" Klin stroked his chin. "Okay, can we slow down here? There is way too much information being dropped right now. First being that the Guardians knew who dad really was." Dreas nodded, "I'm ninety percent certain they do. Which explains all the precautions they have taken regarding you boys. For example, a legendary swordsman having two sons? What would their skills be like? Almost certainly great. And if they have the same sort of courage, they would assuredly lead a rebellion and overthrow those who misuse their power." Joseph began to grin widely, "Herk yeah we would! But, if they knew who dad was, does that mean they actually killed him?" Lorelei and Dreas looked at one another. "We…we don't know." Lorelei explained. "I've been carefully keeping track of their movements and supply chains. All evidence points to the fact that they have a permanent prisoner in their base, but whether or not it is your father is still uncertain."

"Well, what are we waiting for then!" Joseph cried, "If there is a possibility of getting our dad back, we should take it! I still have memories of him, and I miss him!!!" Klin felt a small spike of jealously. He really had nothing to remember his dad by, except vague affirmations that he was a really good person. He stuffed those emotions down and made sure to keep them locked. Dreas raised an eyebrow, "Oh, and how do you plan to do that? Run into the most heavily armed building in the city, with no training or plan? Hmm yes, please tell me more." Joseph flushed, hanging his head down. "Uh, right. But we still gotta do something, right?" Lorelei shook her head. "We need evidence that your father is in there. Otherwise, if we go in and take out the Guardians, the citizens will be out next enemy. They don't like them, but they fear the monsters more."

Klin crossed his arms and let out a growl, "Fine, then I think our next step is obvious. We infiltrate them." Everyone looked over at him in shock. "What?" He asked, "If we can't just break in, infiltrating would be the next step, right?" Lorelei and Dreas gave each other a look. "Well, that could work." Dreas admitted, "However, do you know what that would mean Klin? You and Joseph would have to submit yourselves to being the Guardian's servants." Klin nodded, "I know, and while that for sure leaves a really nasty taste in the mouth, I think it is not just necessary, but the only option." Lorelei nodded, "I agree. I would have done this years ago, but they would never have let me in. So far, they still have no idea you two know your father's true identity."

Joseph raised his hand, "Yeah, about that. What about the spell at our place you got rid of? What was that?" Lorelei let out a sigh, "It was a complex spell. It seemed like it would set off an alarm if the word 'Immortal' was said. Thankfully we're good. While complex, they were not able to make it so destroying it would set off an alarm."

"Alright, new question." Klin said, "How the herk can I see magic? I can't even use it!" Celeste looked over at him in surprise, "Wait, are you sure?" Klin nodded, "I mean, it literally developed today. So, yeah, I'm pretty sure." Celeste tilted her head. "Uh, that's not right." Dreas nodded, "I agree. There are two possibilities. One, you are a late bloomer in regards to magic. However, that still does not explain how you can see the Threads. Two, it is a weird side effect of being a child of Jethro." Joseph leaned back; his brow furrowed. "Uh, I don't understand either one." Dreas sighed, "Why did I even bother teaching you if you won't try to remember?" Joseph just gave her a wild grin. "I can't help that!" Dreas just shook her head. "Anyway, to answer your question Joseph, when you first start with magic, you can only see the spells *you* cast. You cannot see other's Threads. However, Klin can. It took Lorelei, how many years dear?"

"Twenty-three." Lorelei answered nonchalantly, "And that is considered fast for Weaver's. The average is thirty." Klin and Joseph's eyes widened, "Twenty-three years?!" Joseph exclaimed, "Damn Klin! That's kind of awesome you skipped all that!" Klin squirmed a bit in his seat. "Yeah, well, this only thing is just weird, okay? Anyway, the second theory?" Dreas nodded, a twinkle of a smile tugging at her lips.

"Yes, of course. The second theory is that because of Jethro's...unique way of coming into his power, there are bound to be weird side effects in his line." Celeste titled her head. "Uh, what do you mean by that? Cause, none of the stories mention anything like that." Dreas blinked a few times, "Oh! That's right! I'm terribly sorry. Sometimes being one to have witnessed these events makes me forget you young ones did not. So, you are all familiar with Jethro's legendary mastery of Light and Dark magic?" Celeste nodded excitedly. "Of course! They say he single-handedly beat back Malanus three separate times with that! And during the War of the Sculptors, he took dueled *three* Archeshtisi by *himself*!" Dreas chuckled, "I had actually nearly forgotten about that one. Actually, it was four, and Threa was there."

"Whoa, wait what?" Joseph exclaimed, "You mean Threa *herself* fought with dad?" Klin and Celeste just looked at him in bewilderment. "Uh, Joseph." Klin began, "If our dad was *the* Jethro, that means he was Threa's best friend." Joseph flushed, "Oh, right. Sorry, guess my brain's just lagging behind right now. This is just so much to take in. It doesn't really feel real yet."

"Yeah, I'll agree with that." Klin grunted. "Anyway Dreas. What about his powers?" Dreas took a long sip of her tea, gesturing to the others to take some. Klin, Joseph, and Celeste looked at one another and then poured themselves some tea. As soon as they did, Dreas spoke, saying, "As time went on, the stories changed and a key bit of history was lost. Jethro was not always a Weaver." Joseph spit out his tea right on Celeste. "WHAT?! How is that even—oof!" His cry of shock was cut short was Celeste decked him right in the face. "Dude!" She cried, "Not cool! I'm already covered in dirt, and now tea?!" Klin snickered as his brother rubbed his face, "Sorry, I kind of deserved that." Celeste nodded and sighed. "Apology accepted. I'll make that punch up to you, sorry." Joseph gave her a grin. "No problem. Dreas?"

Dreas shook her head and muttered, "I swear, I'm never going to be able to finish with how distracting you three are. Anyway, you know how Threa received her magic directly from Genus and Elenora?" They all nodded. "Well, on her deathbed, Threa passed her magic onto Jethro. Before then, he was just a simple blacksmith with incredible swordskills." A smile and look appeared in Dreas's eyes that Klin could only describe as wistful. "Ahh, you should have seen those days. Women would line up at his forge to watch him work shirtless and then spar with Geofrey." Lorelei let out a small sniff but kept silent. "Anyway, his power was directly from the Sculptors, and since that has never really happened, at least in written history, we do not know will happen as it passes down the line. Jethro never had children till you two." Klin and Joseph looked at one another and then shrugged. "Oh, okay. Quick question, how come neither one of us got magic?" Joseph asked. "What, do you think I know everything?" Dreas snapped, "Who gets magic and who doesn't is nothing quantifiable. That's a stupid question."

"So, what now then?" Klin asked. "That is up to you." Dreas stated, "But, I have a feeling our new friend here will want to help with whatever you do." Klin looked over at Celeste. "Honestly, I'm feeling pretty invested in this whole thing now. Besides, if they have *the* Jethro, like Heshtanus I'm going to leave this alone!" Lorelei gave her a smile, "Well, its nice to know that there are still some people who respect his legend." Celeste turned slightly red, "He may be one of my top hero figures."

Klin laughed. "Fair. So, what's the plan from here on out Celeste?" Celeste crossed her arms. "Why are you asking me?"

"You obviously having some combat training, so maybe you should lead?" Klin proposed. Celeste just shook her head, "You guys are way too trusting. You know that, right? For all you know I'm not even close to telling you the truth." Klin shrugged, "I mean, to be completely honest you're obviously hiding stuff, but you can't really trust us either. So, we won't ask." Celeste blinked in surprise, "Uh, okay. Guess that's fine with me. Based on everything you guys have told me, you need training. So, we'll train."

"Herk yeah!" Joseph crowed. "We can finally give it to them! Klin will no longer have to take those stupid abuses any longer!" Klin felt his gut twist as he opened his mouth. "Well, not quite." Joseph stopped, giving him a look that was somewhere between confusion and anger. "Why not?" Klin stood up and began to pace, "Well, if I suddenly learned how to fight properly, what do you think will happen?" A still silence fell upon them before Dreas said, "They will know you have been trained, and bring a small squad of Guardians after you boys, and possibly imprison the one who trained you." Klin nodded, "Which means I'm going to have to continue to submit myself to their abuse."

"Herking—that's not fair!" Joseph growled. "But unfortunately seems like the best option." Celeste countered. "Can't say I'm too happy about these assholes obviously abusing their power, but what can you do right now?" Klin titled his head as he inquired, "So, quick question. Why do you have such strong feelings about this?" Celeste crossed her arms and glared at him. "Personal. Anything else." He shook his head. "Don't want to talk about it, got it." Lorelei stood up with a yawn. "We've been talking for quite a while now. Don't you think it might be time to head to bed?"

"I guess we should." Joseph admitted, "We've still got work in the morning." Celeste got to her feet, "Well, guess I should start finding a place to stay then." Lorelei smiled, "Oh that won't do. You are staying with us."

"Are you sure?" Celeste asked warily. Lorelei gave her a warm smile, "Of course! We have plenty of room. It would be a shame to not host you, especially since you have agreed to help them." Celeste hesitated, then nodded, "Alright. Sure. But, you guys know as soon as we rescue your dad I'm out, right?" Klin frowned, "Yeah. I don't know why you would stay. To be honest, I'm still shocked you're helping us at all!" Celeste grinned as she walked past him. "Me too." Klin and Joseph laughed as they turned to leave. "Thank you, Dreas! Have a good night!" Klin called as he left. Dreas just gave him a smile as she watched them leave.

Dreas sipped her tea, relaxing in her chair as the Markus boys left. Klin was sharp, catching on that Celeste was not nearly as open as she appeared. Dreas had a very good idea of she really was, but as she was no threat, no reason in forcing her to reveal her identity. She still felt disturbed about last night. She had revealed a lot to the boys, but not everything. Dreas had not completely told the truth about why she had made the executive decision to reveal the truth about Klin and Joseph's heritage. Last night, she had received a vision, and one of gigantic proportions. She was still trying to make sense it all, but one thing had been clear. The events that were going to happen soon had Klin and Joseph at the center. Dreas was the last of the Seers, at least to her knowledge, and it had been three hundred years since she had last received a vision. Celeste's coincidental arrival was going to be the cog that made the wheel start. Suddenly, she heard a soft noise, like the flapping of wings made of crystal. Her heart froze. She knew that sound all too well. The boys were in for one Heshtanus of a fight up ahead.

Chapter 5

Plans in Motion

Darkness covered the land like a thick blanket as Klin ran through the woods, barely guided by the fain moonlight that pierced the veil. He crashed through the foliage, twigs snapping and dead leaves crunching underneath his feet. Low hanging branches scrapped his face as ran, yet he barely noticed because of the single emotion running through him. Fear. He ran from the terror chasing him. A being whose very knowledge of left him with a sense of immeasurable evil and malice; yet so powerful that he could *feel* the raw power of it swirling in the very air he breathed. He spared a quick glance behind him and saw its eyes. Eyes that held such hatred and malice that it felt like the heat of the anger was drilling holes into his body.

Then a giant shadow fell upon him. He looked up, and saw a giant bird flying overhead. The bird screeched out a warning, that almost sounded like words, yet Klin could not make anything out. He turned back and noticed the evil was gone. Klin turned and ran after the bird, a deep feeling that he could not abandon it, and there were others he needed to find. He ran, his coat tassels flapping behind him. He frowned as he noticed the brown coat he wore for the first time.

Suddenly, he came out of the woods and onto a small plain, and gasped in horror at what he saw. In the silver light of the moon, his brother knelt on the ground. Wearing a black coat and grasping a strange sword stuck into the ground, Joseph clutched his side, a pool of blood seeping through his fingers. Next to him was Celeste, who stood in front of him. Her sword was out yet she looked terrified. Three more voices cried out as two men and a woman ran over to them. A they reached them, five screams of terror rang out as black flames rose around

56

them. They were so high that Klin could not see them. "No!" Klin cried as he ran forward, but stopped as he saw him. A tall man stood in front of him. His body was well toned and muscular and even though the features of his face were blocked out, Klin could tell he had a chiseled and handsome face. As the flames rose higher though, Klin could see him clearly. The man's handsome face was marred by a twisted smile. Everything about the man was perfect looking. Except the smile. And his eyes, they were the eyes of what had been chasing him.

Klin took a step back, terror running through him. "What? Have you nothing to say?" The man asked, "I did all this, and you turn out to be a silent coward. Tsk, tsk. For shame Klin. I really thought better of you. You better prove you are worth keeping, or I shall dispose of you like your friends."

"Leave them alone!" Klin shouted weakly. The man smiled, and held out his palm. A ball of crackling black energy formed in the air above it. It was small, fitting in his palm, but Klin watched as it continued to grow in size till it was so big that it blocked out the moon. "Say good-bye to them Klin." The man said. *You know what you have to do.* A voice inside Klin whispered. The man threw the black ball. "NO!" Klin shouted.

Klin jolted up. His entire body shook from a cold sweat. Rosy light drifted through his window as dawn arrived. He took a deep breath and steadied his rattled nerves. It had just been a nightmare. Klin smiled, a nightmare was all it had been, and nightmares had never hurt anyone. He took some deep breaths. It was okay. The dream was already fading from his mind. He looked at the clock. Today was a Saturday, and that meant no work. As his heart rate settled back down, he nestled into his bed covers and went back to sleep. He need rest after the past two weeks.

"WAKE UP!"

"GAH!" Klin cried as he leapt up, punching Joseph in the face. "Owwww." Jospeh stumbled back, a hand to his face. "Damn dude, that smarts." Klin rubbed his still ringing ear, "Then don't herking do something like that! Ugh, what time is it?" Joseph pointed to the clock. It was eleven. Klin turned bright red, "Oh. Sorry." Joseph shook his head, chuckling softly. "Eh, it's alright. I would have done the same." Klin nodded as he got out of bed, rolling his shoulders. His muscles were sore from all the intense training Celeste had put them through. Lorelei had explained that she could heal the soreness, but it would not actually improve the muscles, just set them back to where they had been. That also meant though that he had extra bruises on his chest from Monastrath. Monastrath had gotten exceptionally aggressive with his beatings ever since that day two weeks ago. Still, he had not done anything as bad as the whip. Klin shivered involuntarily as his body remembered the pain. "You, okay?" Joseph asked.

Klin gave him a small smile. "Yeah. Just some bad memories is all." Joseph tilted his head, "The whip?" Klin just nodded as he took off his bed shirt and began to dress. "I swear, once we get dad out, I'm going to beat Mona to a pulp." Joseph growled. Klin winced from the pain of one of Monastrath's beatings as he put on his shirt. Klin chuckled at that. "That would be a pretty funny sight, but don't. Anyway, guessing Celeste is waiting for us?" Joseph nodded. "Yeah, she's getting impatient. Said you don't deserve any food before the match." Klin rolled his eyes as he followed his brother downstairs. "Well, she can be the one responsible for carrying me back when I faint." Joseph snickered at that. Once they got down, they found Celeste standing at the door tapping her foot rapidly. "Finally!" She exclaimed, "I was wondering if you were ever going to get up! Where you up late or something?" Klin rubbed the back of his head embarrassed. "Well, uh yeah. I sort of was doing alchemy till almost two.

"Seriously?" Celeste asked with a sigh, "At least tell me you made some that we can use today."

"Of course, I did." Klin replied, a touch offended, "I made both stamina and health potions." Celeste gave him an evil grin, "What, you think I'm going to stab you or something?" She cackled to herself as Klin and Joseph exchanged some wary looks. "Wasn't before, but now I am." Joseph said. That made Celeste give him a look that was sarcastically flirtatious and mischievous. "Oh, you should be. Anyway, chop chop! Let's get moving you two! This is going to be our last day, remember?"

"Oh, there is sandwich in the for you Klin." Lorelei piped from the living room suddenly. "If you are going to train, you'll need some food."

"C'mon Mrs. Markus," Celeste complained, "you know I said you can't have any food! He overslept! Teacher's orders." Lorelei gave her an even stare, "Yes, but mother's orders override teacher's. I say he eats." Celeste turned bright red and shuffled her feet. "Yes ma'am." Joseph's boomed across the room, and even Klin could not help but crack a smile. He quickly went and grabbed his food, which turned out to be an egg sandwich made with at least four eggs. "Fine. Eat on the way." Celeste ordered. "Yes ma'am!" Klin replied with a salute. "Have a good session boys!" Lorelei called as they left. "We will!" Joseph called back with a wave. They left the house and made straight for the woods. As they walked, Joseph asked. "So, Celeste. You must have had a pretty strict teacher. Who was it?" Celeste jumped slightly, "What makes you think that?"

"Just your own strictness I guess." Joseph shrugged, "You've been pretty warm otherwise I would say." Celeste stayed quiet for a bit before finally saying, "I mean, you're not quite wrong. My teacher was definitely strict, but I'm giving you guys the toned-down version."

"Yikes." Klin muttered in between bites of his sandwich, "Don't think I want to know who this guy is anymore." Celeste gave him a smile over her shoulder, "Oh trust me, you do not. Anyway, we're here. Grab your weapons. We're doing things a bit differently today." Klin and Joseph frowned but grabbed their wooden swords. In the woods, but not too far in was a small clearing. No bigger than ten feet in diameter, they had cut a swath of an arena. They left their training swords in a hollowed-out tree nearby when they were done. Celeste apparently knew a number of different fighting styles, and so despite the brothers not using one like hers, she was able to teach them regardless. Joseph had opted for using a great sword, while Klin had chosen dual short swords. Klin grimaced as he grabbed them. He was determined to beat Monastrath at his own game. "So, what are we doing today?" Joseph asked. Celeste grinned as she grabbed her own wooden sword. "You're sparring me."

Klin tilted his head. "Okay. What's different about this?" Celeste let out and exasperated sigh, "We've only been doing forms and kumites so far. You haven't actually truly sparred me. Just mock sparring. Today, you spar me for real." Klin and Joseph exchanged a worried look. "Oh, this is going to hurt, ain't it?" Joseph asked. Klin nodded, "Almost certainly."

"Alright," Celeste asked with a mischievous grin, "which one of you wants to go first?"

"I don't like how excited she is for this." Klin whispered to Joseph. Joseph just shrugged, "Eh, I'll do it." Celeste smiled, "Well then, step into the ring!" Joseph smiled as he readied his wooden great sword. The wooden weapon was twice as heavy as a normal great sword, but they had done this so that when they used real ones, they would have the advantage of being faster than their opponents. Even if both of them managed to defeat Celeste, they would still be inexperienced in a fight, no matter how fast they had progressed.

Klin moved off to the side to watch as Celeste and Joseph squared off. Joseph lowered his great sword as he fell into a fighting stance. Celeste though brought her katana to her side and held the weapon in her hand like a sheath. Klin frowned. Why wasn't she in the proper fighting stance? Celeste smiled as she rushed forward, her sword still sheathed. She jumped into the air and drew her sword far faster the Klin had expected. He watched as Joseph barely reacted fast enough to block the attack to his head. Celeste landed right behind him and immediately tried to slice his stomach. Joseph knocked her sword from him as he blocked and countered with a strike to her head. Celeste whipped he sword back with grace as she blocked Joseph's attack. "Now we're talking!" Celeste laughed. Joseph grinned, "Better try harder then!" The two continued to fight on, but after a few minutes, it became clear that despite Joseph's raw skill, he was at a disadvantage in this fight. Celeste was now completely on the offensive, with Joseph hardly getting time to block her onslaught. Then as Celeste went in for a stab, Klin noticed her stance was sloppy and unbalanced. Joseph must have noticed it also, for instead of blocking like he had been, he stepped to the side. Celeste stumbled forward, off balance by her own sloppy footing. Joseph quickly swept her feet out from under her. Celeste fell to the ground. Joseph then stepped on her sword hand and placed his sword on the nape of her neck. "So," he asked, "does this mean I win?"

"Yeah." Celeste groaned, "Can you get off my hand now?" Joseph leapt back, "Oh right, sorry." Celeste stood up, looking a little dazed before shaking herself. She proceeded then to brush the dirt off her skirt, saying, "Good job. You noticed my weak stance and took advantage of it. However, I still was not trying as hard as I could. This probably means though that you can take on some Guardians." Joseph grinned, "Nice." Klin crossed his arms, "Does that really say much?" Celeste shrugged, "You tell me. I've never seen them in combat." Klin blinked, "Then how can you say that he can take them in a fight?"

"You are way too easy to mess with." Celeste giggled, "I've been hanging around their training times. They kind of suck. How in the world do they keep this place defended?" Klin shrugged, "I mean, we don't have much a of scale to compare them with. To us, they are pretty impressive." Celeste nodded, "Yeah, should've known. The only one I've found truly skilled was Monastrath. If we are still planning to go ahead with this plan, we'll need to watch out for him. My advice, leave him to me." Klin nodded while Joseph rolled his shoulders, "Damn it. I was really hoping we could take him." Joseph muttered. "I get it." Celeste sighed, "But there is way too high a chance you'll get really hurt or killed if you fight him. He's an insufferable ass, but he's got skills to back it up."

Klin offered the waterskins they had brought as the two came over to him. "Nice job." Klin said as Joseph and Celeste gulped down the water. "That fight took only about five minutes maybe?" Joseph smiled, "So we know if I end up in fight that takes that long, then it's time for a strategic retreat." Celeste nodded, "Yep. That is if retreat is an option." They feel silent at what Celeste was suggesting. "Well, anyway," Celeste said cheerfully, "it's your turn Klin!" Klin sighed as he stomach churned from the nerves. Joseph was obviously the better swordsman, so he didn't think he had much of a chance at winning. Yet as he grabbed his two shortswords, his face became grimly determined. Even though he was going to lose, he wasn't going down without a hard fight.

As Celeste and Klin squared off, Celeste grinned at him. "What's with the grim look? I'm not going to kill you." Klin said nothing, instead he ran at Celeste. He sliced at her stomach, which she barely blocked in time. A flash of surprise flew across her face, before it was replaced by a determined smile. "All right then!" Celeste exclaimed, "We're going all out huh?" She swung at his collarbone, as if to decapitate him. Klin leaned back as the sword went over him, before coming back up like a spring, swinging both swords diagonally. Celeste jumped back, and then came rushing at him with a whirlwind of strikes. She feinted a blow to the head that turned into an attack at his ribs. Klin barely blocked before she was attacking his stomach and then his legs.

Soon enough, Klin was on the defensive. He focused all of his energy on defending against Celeste's relentless onslaught. After at least a minute of this though, he finally spotted an opening, and thrusted at her heart. Celeste leapt back and took a few steps away. She was watching him with a curious look on her face. Klin was breathing harder than he normally would from something like this. Was he not in as great a shape as he thought? He readied to attack, despite his exhaustion, and at the same time, he felt an electric current run up his back. Celeste began to rush towards him, yet time seemed to slow down around him. Each step she took seemed to be four times slower than normal. Klin was able to take in everything about her incoming attack. One foot was in the air as she ran, and only one hand on her sword as she lifted it up above her head, turning it for a diagonal cut. Klin realized that this was his chance. He quickly ran in, swept her foot out from under her, and smacked her stomach with his swords, knocking her to the ground. Celeste fell to the ground in a heap as she lost her grip on her sword. The sword rolled away with a clatter. Klin then placed his sword right over her heart. Celeste looked up at Klin with wide eyes. "How was that?" Klin gasped. His breathing had become very heavy and his body felt exhausted all of a sudden. Celeste nodded as Klin collapsed to the ground, no longer able to stand.

"What the hell just happened?" Klin muttered as he lay on the ground. He stayed lying even after he heard Joseph running towards him. It wasn't that he didn't have the energy to sit back up; he just did not feel like it. "That was incredible!" Joseph said as his face came into Klin's field of vision. "I've never seen you move that fast before!" Klin just grunted in response. "Uh, you want some help up?"

Klin sighed as he pushed himself back to his feet and brushed himself off. Joseph then handed him an energy potion. Klin took it gratefully and drank it. Immediately he felt renewed vigor flow through his body. "How in the world did you move that fast?" Celeste asked. Klin looked at her confused. "What do you mean?"

"Buh- what do you mean what do you mean?!" Joseph exclaimed, "You moved fast than I think either of us could follow there at the end!"

"I did?" Klin asked. "Yeah," Celeste said, "I didn't even know you were moving till I was down. Which that herking hurt by the way."

Klin rubbed the back of his head, "Oh, sorry. Must have hit you harder than I meant to." Celeste rubbed her stomach, "It's okay. But damn Klin! That was some intense speed. I had no idea you could move that fast." Klin just shook his head. "Neither did I. Are you guys sure it was mean and not either of you losing focus." Joseph turned red, "Well…that *is* a possibility for me." Celeste also blushed slightly, "I mean, I'm not nearly as good as you two think I am, so maybe." Klin just shrugged. "Well then, the truth is probably I got a burst of speed that made me move faster than I normally do while you guys just lost focus." The others nodded in agreement. That seemed fair, but still, something did bother him. What had been that weird feeling of energy right before he felt like time was slowing down?

"So, what now?" Joseph asked. Celeste shrugged. "Well, we got one more week of training before we go. I say, we spend the rest of the day having you two spar. You're on each other's skill level, so you'll improve that wa—" Suddenly, there was a loud rustle in the bushes. The three dove into a pre-prepared hiding spot under a tree. They not just chosen this spot on a whim, but in case they were found they could easily hide somewhere. They waited in silence next to each other, breathing shallowly. There was heavy footsteps and loud sniffing. "Are you sure they are here?" A voice asked. It was sweet, dripping with charisma and sounded like a man's voice. "Yes, my lord." Joseph's eyes widened as he stared at Klin. That was Marth. "My info says they come here everyday with that outsider." There was a low, bestial growl. "The pagom smells traces of them, so be grateful that it does." The man said. Klin peaked his head up, along with Celeste and Joseph and saw Marth with two creatures. One of them was a small, yellow leathery skinned creature with bulging eyes and long claws on all fours. The second was a crystal winged creature, with ice blue skin and beady red eyes. Marth gave a shaky bow to the winged one. "I-I am always grateful to you my lord." He replied, licking his lips. The winged creature crossed its arms, and that silky voice they had heard earlier passed from it's lips. "No need for such obvious suck-ups Marth. "They don't seem to be here right now. I want you to go by their house. If they are not there, make some sort of vague threats to the woman to get where they are. I don't like what's been going on."

"I understand my lord," Marth said, "But, they are still merely children. Why such—" The creature rounded on him, ice appearing in the air around him. "THOSE ARE JETHRO'S CHILDREN!!!" He screamed, "Need I remind you how difficult it was to capture him in the first place??! And you think his *SPWAN* are nothing to worry about? Do you want to lose the power I gave you?" Marth quickly shook his head, "N-n-n-no my lord."

"Then do as I say!" The creature snarled. "You have three days! If you have failed me by then, I'll kill you!" Marth prostrated himself on the ground, "Forgive me my lord! I will do as you say!" The winged creature nodded, "You better. I'm going to go and interrogate Jethro some more." The thing smiled, "It is time for our daily appointment after all." At that moment, the creature flew off. Marth got to his feet shakily and dusted himself off and walked off but the small creature stayed. Three ducked back down. Klin turned to Joseph and nodded. They were going to have to kill the thing. "Hey Celeste, can you—Celeste?" Klin asked. She was sitting there, shaking and breathing rapidly. "Hey, Celeste, are you okay?" Joseph asked quietly. "What's wrong?" She shook her head, and tried to speak, but seemed unable to. Suddenly, there was a loud growl. Klin looked up to see the monster above them, ready to pounce on them. "Herk!" Klin snarled as he swung his wooden swords at it. The beast let out a yelp as it was batted aside, rolling across the glen. Klin dropped the wooden swords and grabbed Yatta. "Sorry, need this." He explained quickly. He drew the sword, tossing aside the sheathe. The monster slowly got to its feet, shaking its circular head before snarling at him.

Klin shifted his feet into the fighting stance Celeste had taught him and held his ground as the monster charged at him. *Wait.* He thought. "Klin!" Joseph warned. Klin did not move though as the beast leapt through the air at him. Instead, he cut it in half. The creature's body disintegrated to ash before it hit the ground. Klin dropped Yatta, his nerves finally kicking in. "Wha—what was that thing?" Klin asked shakily. Joseph shoot him a look. "Later." Klin turned to see him crouching protectively over Celeste. Right. She was taking deep breaths and seemed to be calming down. "Hey, everything alright?" Klin asked. "What happened?" Celeste inhaled sharply, "I-I've seen that thing before." Joseph frowned, "Wh—"

"Doesn't matter!" Celeste snapped. "I've just dealt with those things before. I'm fine now though." Joseph and Klin exchanged a skeptical look, but they let it go. "Wait, I know where we've seen those things!" Klin exclaimed suddenly. "They're the monsters that attack the city!!"

"Herk, you're right!" Joseph growled, "But why in Threa are they working with the Guardians? I thought they killed them?" Klin walked over and picked up Yatta. *Sorry.* He thought. He got a mental image of a young girl giving him a small smile right before he handed her back to Celeste. "That big, winged guy said he put Marth in power." Klin said, "And he seemed to be in control of...whatever that thing was." Joseph frowned. "Okay. What are you getting at Klin?" Klin began to pace back and forth. "The Guardians don't protect us from the monsters. They're the ones who brought them upon the city."

"They're using them as some sort of messed up protection fee." Celeste said, "Damn." Klin nodded. This was not good. "Wait" Joseph asked suddenly, "Didn't that guy tell Marth to go threaten mom and look for us?" They fell deadly silent as a chill settled upon them like a heavy weight. "Oh herk." Klin cursed. "We gotta go! Now!" Celeste nodded, "I'll get prepared. You go ahead of me. They don't need to see us together. That will only get them more suspicious." Klin and Joseph nodded and ran off.

It did not take them long before they ended up back at the house. A mile off though, they stopped running. If Marth saw them bolting full speed he would probably figure out they overheard him. Klin stopped as they neared the front door, taking a deep breath. It was flung wide open. He and Joseph nodded and went in, letting Joseph go first. The living room was a mess. The furniture was overturned and the table was broken in half, but most concerning was the blood splattering the floor. "MOM?" Klin yelled and began to frantically search the house. "MOM? ARE YOU HERE?" Joseph called. "I'm fine boys." Lorelei replied wearily. Klin and Joseph spun around to see Lorelei walking out from her bedroom. Her face was set in a weary smile, and her hair

KEEGEN HORST

was a bit wet. "Mom, what happened?" Joseph inquired. Lorelei put her hands up to her hair, Air Threads spreading out as she dried it. "Well, Marth showed up. I think they are catching onto you two. He was quite insistent that I tell him where you were. When he threatened me, pulling his sword, I responded by showing him what it means to be afraid."

Joseph let out a low whistle, "*You* did all this?" Lorelei nodded, "I needed a shower after that. I felt dirty after dealing with him." Klin grinned, but he had some apprehension. "Mom, I appreciate what you did, but was it the right move?" Lorelei started at him quietly. "I know why you seem afraid. You are worried that they will come back with a vengeance. I will tell you this Klin. The only reason I waited this long was because you two could not protect yourselves. Now that you can, I have no fear taking them on now." Klin smiled, his heart warmed, but that warmth was quickly chased away when he remembered the event in the woods. "Mom, we got something to tell you though." Lorelei frowned as he and Joseph quickly explained.

"That's not good. Not good at all." Lorelei muttered. "Why?" Klin asked. "That flying creature was the same being that your dad left to face eleven years ago." Klin and Joseph's eyes widened. "What? Are you sure?" Lorelei nodded. "Based on what you told me. Boys...these monsters are Heshtisi."

"What?" Klin exclaimed, "You've got to be kidding! Come on, we know they're just bedtime stories!" Lorelei crossed her arms and raised an eyebrow. "You will accept that your father is *the* Jethro, but won't accept that the Heshtisi are real?" Klin turned red, "Well, when you put it like that." Joseph snickered but then stopped. "Wait, if one of them could talk, what kind was he?" Lorelei shivered. "Viscious. The Archtisi made to become the next Sculptor of Wind." Klin felt a chill run down his spine. "Wait, the Guardians are working with *him*? How do you know all this?" Lorelei gave him a small smile. "Being the wife of Jethro lets you see things that were only regulated to stories. But yes, I have met Viscious once before. This is bad. Very bad. If he wants you boys..."

"Well then, way I see it, we just have to free dad before he finds us!" Joseph crowed. Klin blinked at him. "Are you insane?! This isn't some low-grade bully! This is a creature straight from legend! A being

66

whose power is spoken of in battles that wiped out civilizations! And you want us to go up against *that*?" Joseph just snorted. "Who said anything about fighting him? Dad's beat him before, right?" Lorelei nodded, "I think exactly eighty-five times." Joseph grinned as he threw out his hands, "Then what's to worry about! We just have to sneak in, grab dad, and then let him take care of Viscious." Klin frowned. "Joseph, dad won't be in any state to do that. If he's the great hero from the legends, they would have to have kept him in a near death state to keep him imprisoned." Joseph just waved a hand dismissively. "Then just brew enough potions for him."

Klin opened his mouth to argue but stopped. That…was actually a pretty good idea. "Fine. But we should move up our plan. If Marth is out for us, we'll need to move quickly."

"Agreed." Lorelei replied, "Why don't you go start on some potions. I'm going to go talk with Dreas."

"What about me?" Joseph asked. Lorelei looked about, "Why don't you go find Celeste and inform her of the new plan?" Joseph shrugged, "Alright. She should be back soon though." Klin smiled though as he ran off to the alchemy tower. Things were getting really exciting now.

Chapter 6

The Path of Heroism

Klin stretched out with a big yawn as he pulled the covers off of him. He was really glad Sunday was still a day off because he had stayed up late again making potions. It had been close to three in the morning before he had climbed into bed. Yet the fruits of his efforts sat on his desk. Seven health potions, glowing a faint red, and six stamina potions a warm blue. He really needed to thank Dreas for continually getting him the ingredients he needed. He had made three of them last week after the encounter with Heshtisi, and then had to wait for Dreas to get him more ingredients. Speaking of which, what had his mom talked to Dreas about? They still did not know. He looked over at the time. It was ten in the morning. He quickly got dressed and went downstairs. He looked around but no one was in the living room or kitchen. "Mom? Joseph? Celeste?" Klin called. When only silence met him, Klin shrugged. They were probably moving forward with the next step of the plan, so he went ahead and make himself some breakfast and coffee.

As he was finished, he smiled to himself. A Sunday morning breakfast was not complete without a book to read while eating. He went back to his room and grabbed *The Complete History of the Magical Creations and Creatures of Threa*. He sat back down with his food and began reading. "*The Triamal,*" he read, "*is a gift from the Life Sculptor, Valoria. Valoria bestowed this power upon her chosen champion at the start of the War of the Nine. This is the oldest of the magical powers known to men. Whoever wields the Trimal has power of incredible scale. However, like all magic, the Triamal's power has rules and some limits. The Wielder has the ability to change into three different animal forms, an air, land, and aquatic animal. Yet the total amount of forms is six, as there are day and night forms. Each animal though has strength and agility far surpassing a natural animal or human. Yet it seems that one can only sustain this form for a certain period of time. Another note is that the amount of power the wielder depends on one's own physical abilities, and is tied directly to their natural power.*

Klin stopped and sat back. *What I wouldn't give for that kind of power.* Suddenly, the door was flung open. He looked up and saw Joseph running in. "Morning." Klin greeted with a smirk, "What's got you in such a hurry?" Joseph grabbed his wrist and pulled him up. "Come with me. Now!"

"Hey wait! What—!"

"Celeste is in trouble!" Joseph cried. "Monastrath's goons got her tied down. He demanded that you come!" Klin let out a curse and nodded as he went out the door with Joseph, expecting to have to go into town but instead found Monastrath and his two goons outside. Sure enough, they had Celeste pinned, arms behind her back. "What the herk do you think you're doing?" Klin snarled. Moanstrath's smirk changed to a frown. "Watch your tone Klin, or I'll have this pretty thing's arms snapped." Klin took a deep breath, steadying his shaking hands. "Alright, what do you want *sir*?" Monastrath smiled, "There we go! Was that so hard? Now, what I want is for you to admit that she's been teaching you how to defend yourselves, something that is *extremely* illegal, might I add."

"She's been doing nothing of the sort." Joseph spat. "So, let her go." Monastrath raised an eyebrow and nodded to Cenn, and there was a loud snap as Celeste screamed. "I said she hasn't been teaching us!" Joseph snarled, "Let her go!!" Monastrath sighed. "Do I need to break the other one?" Klin stepped forward, trembling with rage. "Oh, you're properly scared are you now?" Monastrath chuckled. "Good."

"If you're going to punish anyone, hit me." Klin said coolly, "You're an expert at that, aren't you?" Monastrath narrowed his eyes. "What are you up too?"

"Why are you upset?" Klin asked. "You love beating me up. Leave. Her. Alone." Monastrath starched his chin, thinking for a bit. "No thanks. I've been thinking I need to change up the routine so—" Klin didn't wait any longer as he decked Monastrath in the mouth.

Monastrath stumbled back, blood trickling from his mouth. He just started at Klin in surprise, while Cenn and Draco released Celeste in surprise. "HERK YOU!" Celeste screamed as she headbutted the two and stood up. "Don't just stand there! Get them!" Monastrath roared. Joseph though leapt forward and punched Draco in the head, knocking him out instantly. He turned to Cenn who just threw up his hands in surrender. "Not a chance asshole." Joseph spat as he kicked Cenn in between the legs. Cenn let out a squeak as he feel over, curling up into a ball. "Hah! You have been learning how to fight!" Monastrath crowed. Klin punched him in the face again. "Focus on me jerk!" Klin exclaimed. Monastrath wiped the blood from his mouth as he stared at Klin. "Fine then. Let's go." Monastrath leapt froward, unleashing at flurry of punches, almost all of which landed. Klin stumbled back, blood dripping from his nose. He had taken enough beatings by now to stay balanced though as he countered with a kick.

Monastrath leapt just out of range before leaping back in with a backhand. Klin's head snapped back as the sky became the ground for a moment. "Piece of shit!" Monastrath snarled as he kicked his ribs. "You think you can take me on?!" There was a loud crack as Celeste kicked Monastrath in the ribs. Monastrath fell over with a cry. "Broken bone for broken bone!" Celeste said as she spat on his face as Joseph helped Klin to his feet. "You okay?" Klin nodded, "Yeah, I'm alright." Klin walked over to Monastrath and stood over him with the others. "Stand down Mona." He said coolly. "Just leave." Monastrath climbed to his feet. "You think you can take me?!" He sneered, "I'm the most talented warrior this city has seen!" Celest let out a snort. "Damn, this city has some pretty bad warriors then." Kin froze as he saw Monastrath's hand slide towards his waist. The others had not noticed. What was he—shit! Klin felt that same weird energy spike as he had when sparring with Celeste. Time slowed down around him as he moved, grabbing the knife from Monastrath's hand and flinging it away. He stood breathing heavily over a stunned Monastrath. "Dude. How the herk did you see that?" Joseph asked in awe.

"What did you just do?" Monastrath asked. Klin stepped back. "I...I don't know."

"Don't lie to me!" Monastrath snarled, "You must have cheated somehow! There is now way you could have beaten me!"

"Oh? And what about me?" Dreas asked. Monastrath went pale as Dreas hobbled to them, Lorelei behind her with a stormy look on her face. "Just what do you think you are doing to my sons?" Lorelei asked softly. "Punishing criminals!" Monastrath growled. Dreas raised an eyebrow at him. "Do you have proof?"

"Well, I—" Dreas hit her cane against the ground, silencing him. "If you have no proof child, I suggest you leave. Unless you want a repeat of our last encounter." Monastrath stood up, glaring at her, then turned to Cenn. "Carry Draco!" He snapped, "We're leaving!" They watched the three leave and Klin felt a sense of satisfaction as they left. "Good herking riddance." Celeste spat. "I hate them."

"Anyone hurt?" Lorelei asked as she rushed towards their side. "Celeste had her arm broken, and I'm just a bit bruised." Klin explained. Lorelei let out a sigh as she set about healing their injuries. "The Guardians are worried." Dreas muttered. "This is not good." Joseph shook his head. "This is really not good. Things are moving way fast than I expected. I knew things were grim, but can we really do this?" Lorelei let out a sniff as she finished healing Celeste and moved onto Klin. "I warned you boys. But don't doubt yourselves. That will lead to certain failure." Klin nodded, "Yeah. We got this. Why don't we go into town and grab what we need?" Joseph frowned. "You saying we should strike tonight?"

"Yes." Klin replied, "The longer we wait, the greater the chance of the Guardians arresting us. We *have* to act now." Dreas gave him a smile. "My, my, I was not expecting such resolve so soon. Very well then. You three head into town. I'll help your mother with some spell instruction." Celeste frowned at Lorelei. "I thought you were an expert?" Lorelei gave her a small smile, "Well, it has been at least a decade since I have done any combat magic. This is a precaution." Klin crossed his arms. "Alright, let's go do this."

The three made it to the entrance to town and were met with the gates being closed. "Wait, what's going on?" Joseph asked. *Dong. Dong. Dong.* Klin's hands felt clammy and sweaty. "That's the bell for an attack!" Klin cried. "We need to get away from here now!" The three began to run towards the gates, the pressure on them now. As they reached the closed gate, they heard a loud shriek from behind. They turned around to see five more of those creatures that they had encountered in the woods. "What the herk?" Celeste cried. "They *are* working with them!" Joseph began to bang on the gate. "Hey assholes! Do your job and protect us!!" Klin spun, wishing he had a weapon right now. Suddenly the gate opened, and some guards ran out, charging at the monsters. "Get in you idiots!" They sneered. Klin bit back a retort, instead giving him a grateful nod as the three ran inside. The gate slammed shut behind them, and they all let out a sigh of relief. "Herk. That was intense." Joseph sighed. "And unusual." Klin muttered, "They don't usually attack this early in the day." Celeste frowned. "They have a set schedule?" Klin and Joseph nodded. Celeste crossed her arms and let out a sigh, "And no one thought that was unusual?" Klin turned bright red and shifted his feet, "Well, I mean I've thought about it but without proof—"

Celeste just shook her head. "Ah, whatever. Let's just get you boys your stuff." Klin and Joseph grinned as the made their way to their shop. Right as they made it to the store, they found Monastrath waiting outside. "Herking—can't you just lay off for once?!" Joseph exclaimed. Monastrath just gave them a glare. "I'm not here for you, I'm here for her." Celeste laid a hand on her sheath. "Oh, and why's that?" Monastrath flared out the cloak he was wearing, and Klin felt a chill run down his spine. "Because I want to invite you to a private dinner with me." Celeste just laughed, "You have got to be kidding! Not even an hour ago you had your idiots break my arm! Why the *herk* would I spend any time with you?" Klin opened his mouth to warn Celeste but was cut off by Monastrath. "Because, you have intrigued me. Your headstrong and unyielding will! Not to mention your combat skill. You make a perfect match for me." Celeste took a step back, revulsion on her face. "I can think of nothing more disgusting right now. Herk off jackass." An ugly sneer marred the man's handsome face. "I will excuse that insult for now as I doubt you comprehend the gift I am offering. Women in this town literally fling themselves in front of me vying for my affection. Yet I have accepted none. Now for you I extend an offer."

"Oh, my Genus you are conceited!" Celeste groaned. "I bet that number is way lower than you think. Herk off."

"Celeste, be careful." Klin hissed. "His cloak—" But he was cut off again as Monastrath took a deep breath, shaking with anger. "I will not ask again. Dine with me tonight."

"And I won't tell you again. Herk. Off!" Celeste yelled, spitting in his face. Monastrath snarled as he wiped the spit off. "That was not a request! IT was a command!!" He roared, leaping forward to grab her wrist. "How *dare* you refuse me!" Celeste moved with catlike reflexes, leaping backwards and drawing Yatta, gashing his stomach. Monastrath howled as he cradled his stomach with one hand. "GUARDS!" He screamed. At his call ten guards came running over, weapons drawn. "ARREST HER!"

"WHAT?!" Celeste squeaked. They grabbed her wrist and disarmed her before she even had a chance to retaliate. "You can't do this!" Joseph protested, "She was acting in self-defense!" All but one of the guards ignored him, and they began to cart her away. One of them at least hung his head in shame. "Let go of me!" Celeste yelled. "You assholes are going to regret this if you don't!"

Joseph spun towards Monastrath, his body trembling in rage. "Why you---" He pulled back his fist, but Klin stopped him. "Let go!" Joseph roared. "I'm going to break every bone in his body!"

"STOP IT!" Klin screamed, "He's a Guardian now!" Joseph froze, finally noticing the cloak around Monastrath. "Oh, so you *did* notice." Monastrath said evilly. "I was thinking of having you two arrested after that little humiliation. But I thought of something better. Guards! Destroy this worthless shop."

"NO!" Joseph and Klin cried in unison. Yet, they watched helplessly as the guards ran away, brining back barrels full of oil and some torches. They stood in a stupor, watching as their life's work went up in flames. As the store burned bright, Monastrath walked away cackling. "So long Markuses!"

Joseph and Klin trudged their way back home in silence. Nothing Klin could think of to say seemed to be appropriate, yet nothing needed to be said. What could be said was understood and was painfully obvious to them. So, it was in this sense of hopelessness that they arrived back home. As they approached the door, Klin thoughts dwelt upon Celeste's plight in a greater degree than they had until that moment. There was no excuse for what how he had dealt with that. He had had his chance to help, to warn, to prevent! Yet he had let others talk over him. Celeste's situation was hie fault.

Yet, before they opened the door, anger began to bubble up inside Klin overtaking the fear and misery. "What are we going to do about this?' Klin asked angrily. Joseph just looked at him sadly, "What *can* we do? Our one chance of arming ourselves is gone!" Klin looked over at Joseph in surprise. His brother's eyes which were normally so full of life, now stared at him dull and lifeless. Klin had never seen him look so…defeated. No matter how hard things got, Joseph always kept his optimism, even when he had been beaten down and spat upon. "I had my chance to do something," Joseph spat, "and I just stood there like an idiot as she was carted off like an animal to the slaughter! What do you think we can do to help her now? Well?!"

"We both did." Klin whispered as he placed a hand on his shoulder. "We both messed up. But we can't give up yet. Maybe mom will know something.

Lorelei was sitting on the couch waiting for them. Dreas must have gotten her some cloth for she was knitting. Multiple needles hovered in the air next to her, knitting what looked like gloves as Lorelei knitted some with her own hands. Klin saw what looked a knot of gray, shimmering threads encircling the cloth and needles. "Ah, you're back!" Lorelei exclaimed happily, "Wait, where's Celeste?" Joseph could not meet his mother in the eye, but Klin did his best. "She—she got taken by the Guardians. Specifically, Mona." The needles clattered to the ground as Lorelei covered her mouth. "Oh no…what happened?" Joseph explained quickly, anger creeping into his voice as he did. "Bastard!" Lorelei exclaimed. "Fine. We just have to change our plans slightly now. This is a double rescue mission."

Klin frowned, "But mom, we don't have any weapons." Lorelei gave him a small smile, "True. However, I was planning on us doing this once you three returned. We're going to open your father's closet.

Klin and Joseph looked at each other, a hidden excitement that both felt. For years they had speculated at what was in their father's closet, for there was something odd about it. For one the lock could not be picked, no matter how hard they tried, (in fact Joseph was *really* good at picking locks now,) and the wood could not be destroyed. One time they had taken a forge hammer and tried to break it open, but instead the hammer at burst into a thousand tiny iron shards. "You're going to open dad's closet?" Joseph asked skeptically. Klin looked at Lorelei, also slightly skeptical. Lorelei nodded and flashed a smile at them, "Yes, I think it's time the darn thing was opened."

They all headed into Jethro's former room, and as they surrounded the closet, Klin noticed something he never had before. The entire closet's surface glowed with faint light. Gold and purple light flowed off of it, moving in ways that reminded him of water. He was transfixed by the movements. The way the magic itself looked was glowing and sparkling like water, yet as he looked closer, he could almost discern a pattern to the movement, as if it was alive. "Well, that explains why we could never get it open." Klin grunted. Joseph started at him expectantly. "Oh, right sorry." He apologized with a small blush. "There's some really, really complex looking spell." Joseph titled his head. "Aright, I'll take your word for it. Explain though real quick why this is complex."

"The Threads are not really Threads." Lorelei cut in. "At least, not how we see them. Your father never explained to me how he did this, but instead of fabric looking, the spell has a liquid look to it."

"Oh. Uh yeah that sounds complicated." Joseph responded. Klin nodded, fascinated by the sight. He was already trying to figure out how one could transform the state of matter of *magic itself!*

"So if the door is locked by a spell," Joseph asked, "and only masters can see it, how are you going to unlock it?" Lorelei gave him a scolding look, "And why do you assume that I can't see it? Have I not told you boys that I *am* a master, Weaver?" Joseph flushed, "Sorry." Lorelei nodded and turned to the closet. Klin then watched as Lorelei sent a small Wind Thread into the center of the gold and purple water. The water began to coalesce around the Thread, seeming to try and absorb it. Lorelei let it, and then all of a sudden, the single thread burst, growing in size as three more Threads encircled it. The three on the outside than began to push back at the watery spell. Klin watched in awe as the Wind Threads separated the gold water from the purple. As soon as they were separated, a keyhole appeared in the center of the closet. Half of the keyhole was formed from glowing gold light, and the other by purple light. Lorelei formed a string of Threads and Wove them together into the shape of the key that was needed. There was an audible click as the Thread key went in. Suddenly all of the purple and gold magic disappeared.

"Whoa, what did you just do?" Klin asked in awe. Lorelei smiled at him, "Simply Wove in a way that would counter the spell in place. Now granted I only knew what to do because your father showed me how." Joseph frowned, "Hold on, if you knew how to unlock it, why only now do it?"

"Because I don't know how your father made that spell." Lorelei sighed, "What is in here is dangerous if they fell into the wrong hands, and so when I opened it, I knew I could never put the safeguards back in place. Your father knows how to do a lot of things with the Weave that most of us can only dream of doing. He's a genius when it comes to magic." Klin barely listened though as he stepped up to open the closet. Whatever was in here was so important that their mother didn't want it left without the spell on it. Klin thrust open the mysterious doors, excited at what treasures lay behind it. He found some old trousers and shirts and a burst of stuffy air.

"What?!" Joseph exclaimed, "Are you kidding me? All this hype for a few clothes?!" Lorelei though just giggled, "Watch." She moved past them and pushed on a panel in the back. The panel did not look any different at all compared to the rest, yet it sank back a bit as Lorelei pushed on it. Klin and Joseph watched in surprise as a click was heard and the entire back wall slid back and to the left to reveal a stone staircase winding down into to the earth. "Ah, now everything makes sense again." Joseph said wryly, "I honestly should have guessed a secret staircase. We've gotten immortal old ladies, a talking sword, and a brother who can't use magic but can see it. Why in the world didn't I see something so blatantly normal coming!"

Klin looked over at Joseph with a raised eyebrow. "You call secret staircases normal?"

"Compared to everything else that I just listed, yeah." Joseph replied as he descend down the stairs. "Fair enough. They are a tad cliché." Klin shrugged and followed. Unlit torches lined the walls, torches that leapt to life as they neared them. "Torches?" Joseph asked as they descended, "No one has used torches as a lighting source for at least five hundred years!"

"Well," Lorelei explained fondly, "your father always had a bit of the flair for the dramatic." After walking for about five minutes, they finally came to the end. The room they had entered into was massive, and slightly chilly. The back of the room had to lay at least a hundred feet away, and the side walls were at least fifty feet from the entrance. Hundreds of shelves and chests filled the room with various objects upon them, and from the ceiling hung a glowing ball of golden light that illuminated the entire room. "Welcome to Jethro Markus's Collection Room." Lorelei proclaimed majestically.

"Wow," Klin whispered, "this place is impressive." Joseph nodded in agreement, at a loss for words. "Look around for anything that might help us." Lorelei said, "But uh, please don't touch anything till you've read the label. There are a lot of cursed objects in here." Klin and Joseph looked at each other, their faces breaking into grins before running off to explore.

Klin went over to a bookshelf labeled, "Ancient Magic Texts." The books on it were leather-bound, and when he opened one up, in surprisingly good condition. Although he received a slight surprise. It was written in Aldonean, one of the three ancient languages of Threa. Klin frowned, when the label said ancient, it meant *ancient*. Aldonean had been dead before the time of the Disciples! Luckily though, people still devoted themselves to studying the language, and Klin was one such person. His proficiency in Aldonean was nothing more than the basics, and so it took him a few minutes to figure out the text. Klin almost laughed out loud though when he read the title. *How to Accelerate the Growth of Corn*. With a smiled, he closed the book and put it back on the shelf.

Klin proceeded to look around some more, and came upon two stone masks, carved into the likeness of an elephant and a crow. He began to reach for one but stopped remembering what his mother had said. He bent down to read the label. *The Masks of the Seveljarnian Balgarths*, he read, *These, are spirits that inhabit masks and take control of the wearer. (These two were an s-class type and a real pain in the ass.)* Klin decidedly did not touch the masks and quickly left, thankful he read the label. Klin passed a few more curious baubles that seemed like they had a magical purpose but set down a small marble orb as a stone pedestal caught his eye at the back of the room.

Upon the pedestals rested three swords, two sheathed and one laying upon a rack. The unsheathed sword was massive, coming in at probably six feet in total length. The handle was a dark ebony with a black leather wrapping. The guard was curved like a crescent moon, and a red handle guard sported from the side. On the pommel was a red thorn looking spike. The weapon had two blades, one smaller and thinner than the other, joining at the bottom into one and the tips of the blades curved outward. The blades though looked like steel yet shone with a glimmer that steel did not have. "Hey Joseph," Klin called, "come here! I think I found something!" Joseph emerged from behind a shelf, wearing a long black leather coat with a red trim that he wore open. In his arms he had what looked like a similar coat, only brown. "What in the world are you wearing?" Klin asked.

"A densar leather coat!" Joseph replied excitedly, "These things can give us better protection than any armor out there! Here, I grabbed one for you also." Klin stumbled as Joseph tossed him the coat, barely catching it with a slight grunt. "It's heavier than I expected." He commented. Joseph shrugged, "Yeah, but go ahead and put it on." Klin sighed as he put on the coat. He was surprised when the coat's weight disappeared as soon as he put it on, plus he immediately felt the air around it him become a comfortable temperature. "Whoa." Klin said. Joseph grinned at him, "Yeah, these things have some weird properties. Anyway, what did you want to show me?" Klin pointed to the swords behind him. Joseph walked over towards them with a spring in his step. Klin just shook his head in amusement as Joseph's eyes widened like a little kid receiving gifts on his birthday. While Joseph examined it, Klin spotted the label for the weapons.

These are the last of the weapons that Zechariah Marrobreath made Klin read, *Took me seven hundred years to finally track them down. They have never been used in combat. In fact, no one knows why Zechariah made these. He only made weapons for people he deemed worthy. These three swords are the only instance of him breaking that rule.* Klin looked up at the weapons with wide eyes. These swords had been made by *the Zechariah Marrobreath*?! The most legendary blacksmith to have ever lived?! Klin nudged Joseph and pointed at the label. Joseph looked over at him and surprise "These are-what the-holy Sculptors!" Joseph exclaimed, "Do you think we should take them?"

"Did you see any other weapons? "Klin asked. Joseph shook his head. "Alright, then yeah, we better." An excited gleam shone in his brother's eyes as he reached for the greatsword. Joseph picked up the weapon and swung it around a bit. Klin leaped back with a cry, "Hey, watch it!"

"Whoops, sorry." Joseph replied sheepishly, "But man, this sword feels great! It's far lighter than it should be! It weighs about the same as a shortsword. Gah, what's going on?!" Klin's eyes widened as he watched as the sword began to change. The boys watched as color seeped into the blades. The thicker one becoming a dark black, while the other became a crimson red. "Wh-what just happened?" Klin asked perturbed.

"I don't know." Joseph answered, "Something weird happened though. All of a sudden, I felt a current of... something flow from me and into the sword." Klin eyed the weapon warily, "That can't be normal."

"Oh, you think?" Joseph replied sarcastically, "But, it seems like it was harmless. Welp, your turn now!" Klin turned to Joseph startled, "W-what?! What do you mean my turn!" Joseph pointed at the two swords that still lay sheathed. "I mean you still need weapons, right? This works out great considering you prefer a dual wielding style." Klin sighed as he cautiously reached out for the swords. He only picked up one and unsheathed it. The sword had a triangular handle with a gemstone set into it. Yet the gemstone was dull and colorless. Klin frowned, wondering what kind of gem it could be. He examined the rest of the sword. The blade itself was also a bit curious. The bottom half was curved like a lightning bolt, yet straightened out to a normal blade on the upper half. Stepped away from Joseph and took a few practice swings. He smiled. The speed at which he swung was incredibly hard to make controlled swings, yet with practice he could get it the hang of it.

Klin set down the sword and unsheathed the other one. The second sword was identical. "So, these were made to be a pair it seems." Klin picked up both swords and went through the basic forms with them. He nodded in approval to himself and was about to sheath them when he let out a surprised gasp. A tingling feeling, that over his heart and moved to his fingertips, flowed through him. He watched, as with Joseph, as his blades began to become colored. One became a bright fiery red, while the other a striking lighting blue. The gems also become filled with color, the one on the red blade becoming a ruby, and the other a sapphire. "I was wondering if it would happen to you also." Joseph said, "I wonder what it is that makes them do that? Did you see any magic?"

"No," Klin replied, "I didn't see any Threads at all." Joseph frowned, "Huh, if it's not magic, then what the heck could it be?" Klin just shrugged as he shakily sheathed the weapons. He felt drained all of a sudden. Joseph was not showing any signs of it, but as Klin looked into his eyes, he knew that he felt the same. *Why did the swords drain us of energy?* Klin thought, *Well, at least I've got a few spare energy potions. We'll need those before we put our plan into action.*

"Oh, I'm going to need something to attach the swords to." Klin realized, "Let's look around and see if we can't find something." Joseph nodded and placed his sword on his back, where it just stuck. Klin froze as he started at the sword. "Uhh, Joseph? Do you realize that your sword is just *sticking* to your back?" Joseph looked over his shoulder in surprise, "Oh, would you look at that! That's pretty neat! Come on, let's find you something." Klin just shook his head as Joseph ran off unperturbed. A few minutes later and they had found a black leather sword harness. Klin attached the sheathes and put it on. Joseph surveyed him, "Looks nice! Now come one, let's head back to mom."

The two made their way back to the entrance where Lorelei stood waiting for them. She gave them a small smile as she saw them. "Well, you boys look ready then." Klin and Joseph looked at each other, "Yeah, I think we're ready." Joseph said. They went back up the stairs and closed the secret door. Moonlight now filtered in from the window. They had spent more time down underneath than Klin had realized. He looked over at Lorelei and Joseph. They had lost precious time. Time in which who knows what had been done to Celeste. "Alright," Klin stated, "I think it's time to go rescue Celeste."

Chapter 7

A Night of Blood and Ash

As the moon become covered by the dark clouds, plunging the night into an inky black of darkness, Klin, Joseph and Lorelei lay in cover behind some bushes. They lay about sixty feet from the Guardians' Fortress. Four soldiers stood guard by the gate. Two in front of it and two patrolling the wall. As the guards on the wall turned to continue their patrol, Klin whispered, "Alright, let's go."

Lorelei wove together a small draft and sent in near the guards, covering the noise she was about to make. She grabbed Klin and Joseph by the wrists and created a small, but incredibly strong draft around her, sending them propelling up into the air. Wind whipped about them as they flew up, Klin and Joseph's coats flapping about in the air. Klin swallowed hard though as his stomach plummeted. He felt sick as he looked down at the hundred foot drop. Klin then watched as Lorelei made adjustments to the Threads. All of a sudden, the wind died down, but they stayed in the air. Lorelei then leaned forward, and they shot towards the Fortress, flying silently above everyone.

Klin held his breath as they neared a guard and did not release it until they had set back down. The courtyard was dark, with torches only placed sporadically on the walls. They had landed in a dark spot, using the night to conceal them. The guard above them halted and peered down at them. Everyone became absolutely still. The guard had a torch in hand, and thankfully his eyes were not adjusted to the dark, so he just shook his head and continued on. Klin let out a small sight of relief and whispered, "Alright, now we just need to make it to the weapon storage without being seen. Follow me." They moved in a zig-zag pattern, moving through patches of darkness and avoiding all torch-lit areas.

Finally, they neared the single wooded door that led into the room where they stored weapons, which would lead then lead them into the main Fortress. Klin was glad Joseph had managed to snag a map of the layout earlier in the week. Yet right before they could open the door, they heard an awful screech from the wall to their right. Klin turned to see what had made the horrendous noise and felt his heart skip a beat at what he saw. A creature on all fours stood next to a guard. It had a round, yet squished looking head, and bulbous eyes that stared hideously at them. He stood up on it's hind legs, showing human like hands on all four limbs with wicked looking claws. It's skin though was a sickly yellow. The creature screeched again, and pointed a singular claw at them. The guard frowned, like he could not see them, but took the horn at his side and blew it. All of a sudden bells began to ring and shouting was heard from guards.

"What the herk?!" Joseph snarled, "They have them in *here?!* "A pagom," Lorelei cursed, "a minor heshtisi. Their might be higher ranking Heshtisi inside, so be careful." Klin looked around, noticing all the guards that were running around searching for them. "That doesn't matter right now! Come on, we need to get insid—look out!" Lorelei turned as the pagom, which had crawled down the wall, leapt at her with a loud scream. Lorelei gave the creature a cool stare as she whipped out a dagger, slashing the creature's stomach open as she stepped to the side. The creature screamed in agony as black blood and entrails began to spill from it. Klin and Joseph stared in a disgusted trance at the gore. Lorelei walked over to the creature and stabbed it in the head, stilling its cries. They watched as the monster turned to ash, including the blood and entrails.

More pagom screeches we're heard in the courtyard, and they could see the torches of guards heading their way. "Damn it!" Klin cursed, "We didn't plan for this. Come on, let's head inside and hope they lose us!" Klin opened the door, and as he did the guard with the dead pagom cried out, "Halt! You're under arrest for tress-" He was cut off as Joseph rushed him with a scream. The guard was so taken aback that he just stood their dumbly as Joseph hit him over the head with his sword, knocking him out. Klin sighed as he yelled angrily "Come on guys!" Joseph looked over startled before running inside. Lorelei though just stood there, staring at the guards rushing towards them. "Mom, what are you doing?" Joseph asked, "Come on let's go!"

Lorelei turned and smiled at them, "Go ahead boys, I'm going to buy you some time. They don't know how many they're looking for, and if they don't find us out here, they'll look inside, making it just that much harder to rescue Celeste. Now go!" Before either could protest, Lorelei ran off, and sent a blast of air at them, shoving them back and closing the door at the same time. "Damn it all!" Klin cried, "What is she doing?! She said that she can't fight them all by herself!" Joseph placed a hand on his shoulder, "Don't worry, mom's smarter than both of us. If she gets in danger, she'll get out of there. She won't throw her life away." Klin clenched his fists, fighting back the urge to head out and help. He began to move towards the door, but Joseph tightened his grip on his shoulder. "Don't." He ordered, "Remember, we're talented but still new. What do you think you'll add?" Klin took a deep breath and nodded. "Yeah, yeah. I know. Fine, let's move."

Joseph gave him a satisfied grin as they made their way deeper in. Klin though could not shake off a sense of guilt as they left. They passed hundreds of weapons before they came to the door that lead into the main Fortress. They opened the door and found themselves in the main hallway. Klin stifled his disapproval and he heard Joseph snort in derision as he looked at the ostentatious interior. Plush velvet carpets lined the floor and gaudy golden goblets and candelabras decorated highly polished and gem studded tables. There was so much gaudiness in just the main hallway that it hurt to look at. "Doesn't seem like much of a place for warriors." Joseph muttered.

"The carpet muffles our footsteps nicely though." Klin said with a grin. Joseph grinned back as they ran through the hall, the carpet indeed muffling their footsteps. They passed numerous doors, but they never saw any one to stop them. "Guess mom is keeping them busy." Joseph said. Klin nodded, silent in his worry for their mother. Finally, the hallway, exiting into a massive rectangular room. A massive crystal chandelier hung from the ceiling, filling the room with bright light. Numerous circular tables were pushed against the walls, and straight ahead of them were a two flight of stairs, curved around a raised platform that looked like it might be a stage. At the top of stairs was a terrace that overlooked the room. "Is-is this a ballroom?" Joseph asked incredulously, "The herk is a ballroom doing inside of a fortress?"

"Well, this *is* our home also you know," Klin and Joseph snapped their gaze back up to the terrace. Lounging lazily against the railing was Monastrath. "And it looks like a few rats have sneaked into it." He scowled, "I really don't like rodents you know. "Monastrath then thew himself over the railing, a new black cape with a blue trim billowing behind him as he fell. He rolled as he hit the ground before popping up and striding towards them in one graceful motion. Each step he took had the grace of a panther. "As soon as I heard the alarm go off, I figured it had to be you two worms." Monastrath purred in a silken voice, "I mean who else would be stupid enough to try and break in here. I'm glad I did as I was ordered. He was right. You two *would* come here tonight after all." Klin frowned, stiffing, but not drawing his weapons yet. "Who was right?" He growled. Monastrath just gave him a smirk, "Oh, you'll meet him soon enough. But not before I have my fun with you." He finished, caressing his sword's handle.

Klin and Joseph quickly drew their swords, assuming fighting stances as they stared at him. Monastrath looked at them surprised before he began to laugh, "What in the Eight? You two found some toys and think you can take me on with them?" Monastrath continued to laugh, and almost doubled over from mirth. "Shut up," Joseph growled, "you're going to tell us where Celeste is, and then we're going to beat your ass." Monastrath's face broke into a grin, "Ah so predictable. Too bad you two didn't come earlier. You could have preserved her 'dignity' I think you would say? Or is it chastity? I lose track of what prudes call it." Klin felt blood rush to his head, "What did you do to her you piece of filth?" Monastrath gave them an evil grin, "Oh, I just had a bit of fun with her. She probably will deny it out of shame. I did have to chain her up though to start…"

"You bastard!" Joseph roared, "I'm going to cut up that pretty face of yours and scar it so horribly that no woman will ever look twice at you again!!!" Monastrath just laughed as he drew his sword, "Come and try it!" Before Joseph could charge him, Klin grabbed his wrist, holding him back. "Let go of me!" Joseph protested. Klin simply started at his brother while Monastrath watched in amusement. "Awww, look at this!

Your brother is a coward! He doesn't want anyone to fight! Still the same idiot who takes beatings like a dog. Knowing what's good for him." Klin ignored Monastrath and kept a firm grip until he felt Joseph's arm relax. "Let me handle him." Klin whispered, "I'll distract him while you go and find Celeste." Joseph hesitated. Klin could see the conflict in his eyes. "Let me do this." Klin whispered firmly, "I *need* to be the one to fight him." Joseph's eyes softened in understanding. "Alright," Joseph relented, "Kick his ass for me, and make sure you're in one piece when I see you again."

Klin flashed a grin at him, "Don't worry. Upholding both promises will be a cinch." Joseph smiled at began to run towards the stairs. "Oh, so both brothers are cowards after-" Klin cut Mona start off as he swung at him, provoking a curse from the burly man. Monastrath quickly blocked the strike. As the two stood with locked swords Klin said, "You talk too much." Monastrath let out a decidedly unattractive snarl as he pushed Klin off of him. Klin stumbled, forgetting the proper stance as he moved back. Monastrath then whistled and as Joseph crested the stairs, the screeches of pagoms were heard.

"Let's see him survive those things." Monastrath said menacingly. He then leapt at Klin with incredible speed, trying to stab him. Klin stumbled in his haste to block the attack, and as he did not have the proper footing, almost fell over from the force of the blow. As he went back, he tried to fall into the proper stance, but his mind came up blank. Monastrath wasted no time in pressing his attack. Klin blocked two attacks to his waist but was staggered by both. "Come now! Where was that bravado? Falling away with your skill?" Monastrath grinned and brought his sword down in a diagonal strike to the head. Klin brought both swords up quickly, his feet finally assuming the proper stances. Monastrath's sword got hooked in one of the crevices in Klin's swords. Monastrath's eyes widened in surprise as his sword stayed stuck in between the blades. Klin grinned at him and shifted his weight, tossing the man to the side. Then before he could recover, Klin kicked him in the ribs, sending him rolling across the floor.

Klin ran over to him, intending to disarm him before he could stand back up, yet he wasn't fast enough. Monastrath stood up, spinning in a circle as he sliced outward. Klin barely leapt back in time to avoid the blade. "You got lucky there." Monastrath growled, "It won't happened again." He then launched an all-out attack upon Klin. Klin was barely able to block the numerous blows that were coming at him. Monastrath moved with such speed and grace that he almost could not see the attacks coming. Klin began to panic as he fell back under the relentless assault, arms barley responding in time. Then he noticed a mischievous smile upon Monastarth's face, and the almost lazy way in which he swung he sword. *Shit,* Klin thought, *he's only playing with me!* He had known that Monastrath was exceptional with a blade, but this was a whole other level of skill! *I need a plan*, Klin thought as he sidestepped a thrust, gaining a brief moment of respite. *I won't be able to last any longer than a minute at this rate! My arms are already getting weak. I need to end this now!*

Klin took a deep breath. What he was about to do was extremely risky, but it was the only thing he could think of. As Monastrath began to rush him again, Klin ran at him and threw one of his swords. Monastrath blocked the sword with a look of surprise. Then, while his vision was covered Klin jumped, hoping to leap over him and hold his sword at the neck. Yet just as his first foot began to leave the ground, Monastrath kicked Klin in the stomach. He let out a gasp as all of the air was knocked form him, and almost fell over, but Monastrath hand shot out and grabbed him by the throat. "Really?" Monastrath mocked, "That was your big plan to defeat me? That was pathetic! Did you really think you could jump over me? You train for a bit and think you're an expert?!" Monastrath's grip tightened around his throat, blocking off all air. "You see, this is what pisses me off. You can't do anything, yet you carry yourself like you're better than all of us! Well, you're not!" Klin desperately gagged as he tried to take in air, his vision starting to fade. Monastrath punched him, saying intbetween hits. "Why. Can't! You! Get! THAT!" Monastrath slammed him into the floor with a snarl. He removed his hand from his throat. Klin gasped as he drank in the air. Monastrath though placed his boot upon his chest and began to press down. Klin screamed as he felt he bones on the verge of breaking. Monastrath laughed, "Just surrender and I'll make the pain as minimal as possible." Klin looked up at him and spat in his face. Monastrath growled as he pressed down harder. Klin cried out in pain. Yet despite his whole body aching and the pounding in his head, he desperately tried to think of something. His sword that he had thrown was just next to him and in reach. As he began to reach out, Monastrath stomped down on his hand. "Ahahah, can't let you do that."

Klin turned and looked up at Monastarth, his eyes fuming with an unbridled rage. This man, no this *animal*, had tortured him and beat him down all of his life, and here he was once more winning because Klin was too weak to fight back. Rage continued to build up inside of him, slowly consuming his entire being. "Why won't you just give up already?" Monastrath asked angrily as he kicked Klin in the ribs. Klin heard a crack with that kick. "Why won't you just submit to your betters!"

"My betters?" Klin snarled, "You pieces of filth don't even deserve to breath the same air we do you contaminate it so badly!" A small part of him was surprised at what he just said, but the majority of him didn't care. It felt good to say that. Monastrath stepped back, startled by the sheer force of anger emanating from Klin. That had been all he needed. He grabbed his swords and leapt to his feet, fighting against his own body which screamed in protest. As he did, the world began to slow, and he felt a rush of energy flow through him, just like his duel with Celeste. As he moved towards Monastrath, he took in every inch of the man's startled and surprised face. Klin relished the look with glee, for in his eyes was also the beginning of fear. *Now's my chance to end this.* Klin thought. As he wondered where to strike, he smiled sadistically. He swung both swords at Monastrath's face as he blinked, striking with extreme precision.

The world returned to normal as Monastrath fell to the ground, screaming in pain. He was clutching his face. "Damn you!" Monastrath screamed as he tried to stand up but fell back down. He removed his hands and began to grope around for his sword. Blood poured from two wounds on his face. Klin had cut his face, starting from the jaw, and working up towards the temple and over his eyes. He had cut deeply, but only scratched the eyelids. Klin smiled, relishing the pain upon his foe's face and committed it to memory. "I'll kill you for this!" Monastrath screamed. Klin just smiled twistedly, "Not if I do first." He whispered and began to walk towards him. As Klin hovered over Monastrath, he froze, realizing what he was about to do. He was about to kill the man. And he was enjoying it. Klin stepped back as Monastrath now lay on the ground, moaning pathetically. *What am I doing?* Klin thought. His stomach churned as he realized the darkness of what he was doing. He started down at Monastrath, half of him wanting to gleefully kill the man, while the other half felt sick at the prospect. While he stood in conflict, he heard shouts and the clanging of armor coming from the hallway.

He didn't have time to stick around. Klin shook himself, and the darkness retreated. He moved up to Monastrath and tossed him a healing potion. It would do nothing about scaring, but he would at least live. "What the herk is this?!" Monastrath hissed. "Something to keep your pathetic life alive." Klin replied cooly. "Drink." Monastrath hesitated, but then gulped it down. As soon as he had drained the bottle, Klin whacked him over the head hard with the sword pommel, and then ran up the stairs, chasing after Joseph. As Klin ran, he took out one of the remaining three healing potions he had stored in his pocket. He drank it and felt his wounds begin to heal. However, the potion did nothing for the revulsion he felt for the heinous act he had just committed.

Joseph gave a half glance behind him as he saw Klin leap at Monastrath. *Kick his ass,* Joseph thought as he turned forward and climbed up the stairs. He did not look back once more, too afraid of what he might see if he did. He was proud of his little brother for all the initiative that he had been taking, but this one was riskier than he liked. As Joseph topped the staircase, he saw another spiraling stone staircase leading up. He figured that had to be the way up to the prison. As he moved towards it, he heard a faint whistle from the ballroom. At the same time, multiple pagom emerged from the ceiling, screeching at him. *The herk did they come from?* Joseph thought, *No matter, just kill them for now.* Joseph brought his sword down into a fighting stance as three pagom encircled him. Four more stayed at the staircase, guarding it.

Joseph smiled even though the ugly bastards were snarling at him. The pagom in front of him leapt at his face. Joseph sliced it in half in midair, before spinning in a circle, killing the other two as they also jumped to attack him. Only ash hit the ground. Joseph turned to the remaining four, which screeched angrily at him. He just chuckled internally. These things were just crazed beasts. Joseph rushed the four with a yell. They stumbled back, confused at his screaming. With two strikes, four more piles of ash decorated the stairs.

The Guardians seriously thought these things were a threat? Right as he began to climb the stairs though, he heard a scream from above him. Joseph turned to see a pagom falling at him. Joseph tried to jump out of the way, but the heshtisi's claws ripped his thigh. Joseph grunted and quickly dispatched the thing. Joseph knelt down inspecting the wound. It wasn't very deep thankfully, but it hurt a lot. *Guess they're smarter than I thought*, Joseph thought ruefully, *If I find anymore in a larger number than this, I'll be lucky if a scratch is all I get.* Joseph ascended the stairs, determined not to underestimate the pagom again.

As Joseph ascended the stairs, he heard footsteps ahead of him. Joseph rushed forward with a scream as he came around the corner. Two very surprised looking guards stood there. "What's up?" Joseph asked as he stabbed one in the stomach and cut off the sword hand of the other. Blood splattered the stones as the two men fell to the ground, screaming in pain. "Try not to move too much." Joseph instructed, "And use the cloth of your capes to bandage the wounds. I'd rather not be responsible for killing you guys." The two men looked up at him with confused wide eyes but nodded. Joseph continued on. He had more important things to do. He had only been climbing for another minute when he heard more footsteps. *How many damn people are on this staircase?* Joseph thought in annoyance. He froze though at the sight of the man who came around the corner. "Why is it always you?" Joseph asked exasperated.

Marth Cra'son stood staring down at him, his gold armor sparkling in the torchlight. "I could ask you the same thing." Marth sneered, "Why is it always *your* family that gives me trouble?" Joseph shrugged, "Have you tried to stop being such an asshole? I hear that drops your number of enemies drastically." Marth looked down haughtily at him, "I should have just left your family to starve. It would have saved me a lot of trouble." Joseph assumed a fighting stance, "Pity that. I really don't like the way life is going anyway." Marth struck first, slashing at his midriff as he drew his weapon. Joseph blocked the attack and used the momentum of the block for a head strike. Monastrath stumbled back, barely getting the block up in time. "Whoooa!' Joseph whistled, "What's this? A leader of the Companions is barely more than a novice swordsman?" Marth growled as he struck again. Joseph casually blocked the attack. "Look at that poor foot work folks! Does this man even know how to properly hold his weapon?" Joseph mocked. Marth snarled and went for a thrust. Joseph sidestepped, quickly switching his sword to his left while grabbing Marth's wrist with his right. He twisted his hand, forcing Marth to drop the sword. Marth cried out in pain as Joseph used his wrist to control him and force him to the ground. Joseph clucked his tongue as Marth began to pound the stones, "Well you're really pathetic. Do you even practice? Dude, I've only had three weeks of training and I took you down like it was nothing! And you call yourself a warrior."

"Yes, yes I'm a fraud, now let go!" Marth cried, "This hurts a lot, so please let go!" Joseph frowned, "You think I should give you mercy? After *everything* you've done to me and my family. After all the suffering you put us through?!" Marth shrank back the best he could as Joseph loomed over him menacingly. "Thing is, you're right." Joseph whispered, "I am going to show you mercy. But here's the thing. I'm not doing it out of the goodness of my heart. I want nothing more than to kill you, but I know that isn't good enough. No, for true justice, I'm going to expose you and let the people judge you. Maybe they'll exile you. No one really likes you, you know. Whatever fate they decide though, I'll make sure that it's worse than death. Then, and only then will you realize the suffering you've inflicted upon everyone in this city."

Marth just looked up at him with wide eyes, "No please, just kill me then." Joseph quickly twisted the man's wrist, snapping it. Marth screamed in pain. Joseph let go of him and quickly grabbed Marth's sword. "Get out of here while you can." Joseph spat, "I know you're a coward and won't stick around to die." Marth began to run. As he did Joseph paused, "Actually, you're such a coward that you'll probably skip town before the night is over. Soo.." Joseph rushed over and jumped in front of Marth. The cowardly man's eyes widened in terror as Joseph smacked his legs with the front of his blade. There was a loud snap as Marth crumbled to the ground screaming. "Know this," Joseph said as he began to walk up, "I don't actually enjoy this. You just were unlucky." Joseph didn't look back at the man, who was now blubbering on the ground. He felt guilty at what he had just done, but what he had said was true. He had not enjoyed a single moment of that violence.

Joseph continued climbing, not seeing anyone else. After a minute or two, he found himself at the top. "About time." He muttered and opened the door. A dank and somewhat rotting smell filled the air. Joseph nearly gagged at the foul stench. *They actually keep people in this?* He thought horrified. The prison was dark and not very well lit, but there was just enough light to make out those in the cells. Joseph began walking inwards, examining the cells. Almost every cell was filled. Each person in them shrank back in fear as they saw Joseph approach.

Joseph shook his head. He knew a few of these people had been legitimate criminals, and not just scapegoats of the Companion's tyranny, but still no one deserved to live in this state of fear. Joseph scoured the entire prison, looking for Celeste. After about ten minutes, he had narrowed his search to the back of the prison. As he was about to search the nearby cells, Klin's voice called out. "Joseph, are you in here?" Joseph turned around, and yelled back, "Klin, that you?"

"Yeah, where are you?"

"In the back! I've narrowed my search down back here!"

"Joseph?" Celeste's weak voice called near him, "Is that you?" Joseph spun around. Her voice had come from the cell next to him. "Yeah," Joseph said assuredly, "Hey Klin! I found her!" Klin arrived shortly. Joseph spared a quick glance at him. He looked unharmed thankfully. Joseph then returned his attention to Celeste. She lay in the back of the cell, slumped against the ground with her wrists shackled above her. Joseph motioned for Klin to move back as he swung his sword at the cell door. It cut through the iron bars like butter. He kicked the door in and rushed over to Celeste. He wasted no time in cutting her free of the shackles.

"Thanks." Celeste said weakly as she tried to stand up. Her legs buckled though and she fell. Joseph caught her, and she let out a small gasp of pain. He frowned and looked her over. Her jacket was torn and her arms and legs were covered large, dark bruises. "What did they do to you?" Klin asked. Celeste gave them a weak smile, "Oh, just the usual beatings. That creep Monastrath though tried to rape me." Joseph's eyes flashed with fury, "He wasn't successful was he? Cause if so, he's got a lot to answer for."

Celeste shook her head and gave them a smile, "No, thank goodness. I kept kicking him in the crotch, which bought me about ten minutes after each attack. After I did that about six times, he put me in the shackles and tried to force himself on me. I bit his nose a couple of times, thankfully you guys tripped the alarm when you did, because I wasn't sure I could keep him off for much longer."

"Don't worry about him." Klin said, "I don't think he'll be causing trouble for a while." Joseph frowned as he looked at his brother. A dark and scary look was upon his face. "Anyway," Klin said, "let's get going. Here, take this first." Klin pulled out a healing potion, which Celeste drank gratefully. Joseph sighed in relief as he watched her bruises fade away, and life began to come back into her eyes. "Alright, can you walk?" Joseph asked. Celeste nodded. "Right, let's get going then." As they exited the cell, Celeste cried out, "Wait, where's Yatta?" Klin sighed, "We don't know, and we don't really have the time to search. We need to get out of here."

"No." Celeste replied stubbornly, "I'm not leaving without Yatta!"

"Oh for the love of- we don't have time for this!" Klin growled.

"I'm going to search for Yatta with our without your help Klin Markus!" Celeste yelled, "Maybe Joseph will help me?" Joseph looked between the two warily, "Uhhhh."

"Klin? Joseph?" A weak voice called out, "Is it really you?" All three turned around to see who was speaking. A thin, gaunt man clothed the bars of his cell, starring at them with wide brown eyes. He had gray hair with black tips that flowed all over, and a wild beard. "It must be you." The man said, "I know those coats."

"Um, who are you?" Klin asked. Joseph stared at the man with narrowed eyes. Something about him seemed familiar. Then memories began to flash back. Trim the hair and beard, turn the gray into brown and this man was, "Jethro Markus," Jethro said, "your father."

Chapter 8

The Rematch

The three stared at Jethro in shocked silence. No one moved and not even the sound of breathing was heard. Klin and Joseph's father, who had been taken eleven year's ago, was right in front of them, smiling. Finally Joseph spoke up, "Well, you don't look quite how I remember you." Jethro let out a hearty laugh. The laugh betrayed nothing of his weakened condition, sounding warm and full of love. "Well now," Jethro said, "isn't that true? I would think that you two are just an illusion, conjured by my captors if it wasn't for those swords you hold." Klin glanced down at his swords, "Yeah, these are one of a kind. But how do we know you are who you say you are?"

"Klin!" Joseph scolded, "What the heck?" Jethro just shook his head, "No, it's a legitimate question. Anyone could claim to be me." Klin nodded, "Yeah, so tell us something that our father would know. Maybe name something in the Collection Room?" Jethro raised his eyebrows at them, "Setting the bar a little low aren't we? Unless you've memorized everything in there, I could say anything and it could be real."

"Yeah, well," Klin flushed, "just humor me." Jethro shook his head, "Well let me think. Hmm, well the coats that you're wearing are densar leather, the swords are the last weapons made by Zechariah Marrobreath, and there are some Balgarth masks in there. And oh, some Aldonean texts down there." Klin looked at the Jethro in awe, before saying, "Alright step back from the door." Klin cut the door down. Jethro tentatively crept out of the cell.

Father and sons stared at each other for a moment. Then Klin and Joseph tacked their father with hugs. "How did-why di you-" Klin babbled before sobbing into his father's shoulder, gripping him tightly.

"We've missed you dad." Joseph whispered as a few tears trickled down his face. Jethro smiled warmly as he embraced the two. "It's good to see you two once more." After an appropriate amount of time for the tearful reunion, the boys withdrew. "How long have you been here?" Klin asked.

"Ever since they built this place." Jethro replied, "They never took me out of the village. Thought there was too great of a chance of me escaping if they did. They were right of course." Joseph laughed, "Guess even in a really weakened state you would've figured out a way to escape." Jethro flashed a grin at the two boys before almost falling over as the boys stepped back from him. Klin and Joseph grabbed their father's arms. "Heh, guess I'm still pretty tired." Jethro said weakly. You two wouldn't happened to have learned some alchemy would you?" Klin smiled as he produced the last swirling blue concoction and handed it to him. Jethro took it gratefully and chugged the whole thing.

"Ahhh, that hits the spot!" Jethro exclaimed. He then thrust out his hand, and Klin watched as golden Threads appeared around his hand, along with purple Threads. In the brief time of two seconds, Klin guessed there were about fifty Threads of both kinds circling the hand. The Threads then disappeared as a sword appeared in the air and fell into Jethro's hand. Then a glow of pure white encased Jethro. The light was so powerful that it blinded the rest of them. Once it had faded, the thin, gaunt, unkempt man was gone. In his place was a strapping man with defined muscles and a trim goatee and gray hair that just barely touched his shoulders. "Whoa." Celeste exclaimed softly, "You know for being old, he looks *good*. Especially considering what he's been through."

"Celeste!" Joseph yelled, "You can't just say my dad's hot! That's just weird!"

"Why? I'm just stating a fact." Celeste replied a roll of her eyes. Jethro just smiled, "Well thanks. I like to consider myself quite the looker. Anyway, we need to get going I believe." Klin rubbed the back of his head, "Oh right, the Guardians know we're here so we need to get the heck out of here."

"Not without Yatta!" Celeste yelled.

"Seriously, not this again." Klin sighed, "We've been over this, we don't have the time! Now come on!" Klin began to run towards the exit, not pausing to see if anyone followed. He heard the clatter of three pairs of feet against the stones though as he ran. "So, who's Yatta?" Jethro asked.

"Little girl trapped in Celeste's sword." Joseph replied. Klin looked behind to see Jethro nodding sagaciously. "Ah, I see. Most likely a case of Shadewelding a Cursed. I've seen a case very similar to this one, so I might be able to help." Celeste stopped running, "Wait, are you serious?" Jethro nodded, "Yep. I've seen a lot of stuff kid. We can grab her on our way out."

"Hold on," Klin interrupted, "we don't even know where she is." They had reached the stairs and had begun to descend them. "Oh, on the contrary we do." Jethro grinned widely, "You see, my sword has a few special things about it. You saw the one restoring me to full health. Another is I can sense where it is at all times, so I know where they were keeping it. I bet they are also keeping Yatta in there as well." Klin paused for a moment before saying, "Alright lead the way then. But this is our last stop." Jethro nodded and took the lead. He led them through a maze of corridors, never faltering at which path to take as they navigated through the fortress.

As they ran Joseph suddenly asked, "Hey guys, shouldn't we be seeing at least some Guardians? I mean, this is their home." Klin frowned. It was strange that they hadn't seen anyone yet. Marth had not been on the staircase like when he came up also. Right as he was about to say something, they entered into a giant room, almost as big as the ballroom had been. Various items of increasing value were on display at the sides of the room. Inlaid vases, golden platters upon carved oak tables and fancy weapons that looked more showing that practical. "Yatta should be in here." Jethro said. "If not, there should be a smaller room in the back behind those thrones." Jethro pointed towards three thrones made of marble. "I would check in that room first. We can stay out here and search." Celeste nodded and ran towards the back room, with Joseph following close behind. Klin and Jethro then began to search around. As Klin rifled through a pile of swords stacked haphazardly, he asked, "Why are none of the Guardians after us? You think mom's been keeping them distracted?"

Jethro spun around from his pile of loot, a look of surprise on his face. "Wait, your mom's here?" Klin nodded, "Yeah, she's been fighting them outside while we rescued Celeste. She wanted to keep them distracted." Jethro ran his fingers through his hair as he sighed, "That woman. Your mom is incredible, you know that." Klin stared at his father, watching him ruffle his hair. "Huh, oh yeah." Klin looked away and continued to search. Joseph just shook his head. The awkward energy was getting to be a little much.

"Hey! We found Yatta!" Klin and Jethro turned around to see Joseph and Celeste running towards them. Celeste had Yatta's blade at her waist once more. Klin smiled, "Good. Let's get out of here then." At that moment, a dark and sinister laugh resounded throughout the room. The laugh filled the room, the voice's presence pressing down on them. Joseph and Celeste stopped moving, their weapons drawn. Klin had also drawn his swords, warily searching for the owner of the laugh. "Leaving so soon?" The voice asked, "But you haven't even met your host yet!" Klin froze. That voice sounded eerily familiar. Jethro cursed and summoned a white ball of fire in his palm as his eyes scanned the room like a hawk.

Then, out of the corner of his eye, Klin noticed a black cloud of fog descend from the ceiling. It was so dark that it was nearly invisible. "What is that thing?" Klin asked pointing at the fog. Jethro's eyes narrowed in a fierce anger as the fog darted towards Celeste and Joseph. "Stay away from them Viscious!" Jethro roared as he shot the fireball at the cloud. The fog cloud dodged the fire. Joseph and Celeste began to move out of the way of the fireball, but it disappeared before it got close. "Hold on!" Joseph shouted, "Did you call that fog Viscious?!" The cloud laughed and began to take a humanoid form. The creature before them still seemed indistinct and immaterial. His skin was black, with wisps of smoke swirling off of him. Wings of pure smoke spread out behind him with terrifying majesty. Ice blue eyes shone out from the form, staring at them.

Viscious the Eighth Archeshtisi, gave a bow as he finished taking form. "Ah, it is such a pleasure to finally meet the Markus sons in person. I've just been *dying* to meet the two of you. After all, you've caused my lord quite a bit of trouble." Klin stepped back, his heart beating so fast that all he could hear was the *thump, thump, thump*. His legs became rooted in stone, his arms trembling and feeling like liquid. Viscious gave him a twisted smile, "No words from the brave Klin? I expected at least a witty response from you since this whole operation was your idea."

Klin's eyes widened. *H-how did he know that?!* "Shut the herk up you creepy bastard." Joseph exclaimed. "I don't know what the heck you're doing here, but you can crawl back to Heshtanus!" Viscious walked clucked his tongue, "So rude and crass. We barely know one another and that is how you greet me? Jethro, you raised such bad children." Klin tightened his grip on his swords. "Shut up! I bet you are the one responsible for keeping him here! We missed so much time with him because of you!!" Viscious shrugged, "That is true. Now, before we do anything rash, may I propose a contract?" At that moment, Joseph had snuck up behind the monster. "Propose this bitch!" Joseph growled as he sliced his back. Viscious snarled as he spun around and tried to backhand him. Viscious moved faster than Joseph could respond, but Viscious's claws meet steel with a loud *clang*! "Huh, dad?" Joseph asked in surprise. Jethro grunted in affirmation as he pushed Viscious back with a kick. *When did he even move?* Klin thought. He had just been right next to him. "This is your only waring Viscious." Jethro said, "Give up now." Viscious laughed hysterically, "GIVE UP?! ARE YOU GOING SENILE OLD MAN! DON"T YOU REMEMBER WHO WON LAS-ARRGH!"

Suddenly, a dome of dark magic, who's purpose Klin couldn't figure out had appeared around Viscious and within a millisecond of it appearing, white flames bearing the Threads of light shot out and engulfed Viscious. "You talk too much." Jethro said. Viscious burst out of the flames and rushed at Klin. "You're going to pay for that Jethro!" Viscious cried, his wounds healing at an exponential rate. As he neared Klin, all the smoke from his body turned into translucent crystals. Without thinking, Klin raised his swords, and blocked Viscious's claw attack. Viscious took two more swipes, which Klin blocked as well, but they were close and not at all graceful. As Klin blocked two more, Jethro was suddenly at his side, stabbing Viscious in the ribs. Viscious snarled as Klin and Jethro teamed up and pressed their attack upon him. As they pressed in upon Viscious, the Archeshtisi let out a clattering noise. Suddenly pagom screeches filled the room.

Klin spared a glance and saw numerous pagom advancing towards Joseph and Celeste. Jethro let out a smirk as he unleashed a flurry of quick blows. "Come on Viscious, pagom are the best you can do?" As if to back up his words, the death cries of pagoms sounded out. Viscious snarled and as Klin swung at his head, his body become smoke and the blade went right through. Klin stumbled from the unexpected lack of resistance. Viscious then stabbed Klin, his claw re-materializing at the last second. Klin let out a gasp as his stomach was punctured. Viscious then went for his throat, but Jethro blocked while simultaneously spinning, grabbing Klin, and leaping out of the way while leaving a white wall of flames behind him.

"Klin!" Jethro yelled as he set him on the ground, "How bad is it?" Klin tried to speak but coughed up blood. "Stay here." Jethro spoke quietly, "I'll take care of him." Klin's vision began to become hazy as Jethro loomed over him. Yet through the immense pain, he could make out his father's expression. It was like looking at the dark clouds right before a storm. A fury of nature so powerful that the very air darkened to compensate for the power and anger of the clouds. Klin began to close his eyes, consciousness beginning to fade. In the back of his mind, he realized he could feel his life slipping away. *I'm dying*, Klin thought, *and I don't even seem to care.* "Klin. Klin. KLIN!" He could hear his brother's voice, but why was it so faint?

He felt a trickle of some sort of sweet-tasting liquid between his lips. Klin swallowed it, and felt some energy return, and the pain dull. All of a sudden, his vision cleared. Joseph and Celeste were standing over him with concerned looks. "Don't scare us like that." Joseph said.

"Wait, what just-" Klin noticed that in Joseph's hand was the red liquid of a healing potion. Klin smiled half-heartedly, "You should really save those you know." Joseph handed him the rest of it. "Shut up you moron." He replied. Klin laughed softly as he grasped Joseph outstretched hand and stood up. The three turned around then to face Jethro and Viscious.

Jethro was relentlessly assaulting the Archtisi To simply call Jethro a master swordsman would have been an understatement, and an insult to his skills. No, as Klin watched his father duck and weave while swinging his sword with deadly precision and grace, he knew Jethro was no master. He was an artist, and his sword the brush. The fluidness and grace with which he moved seemed like it was not of this world. All three had stopped trying to advance and stood watching the fight in a fixed stupor of awe.

"Hold on," Celeste said, "guys I think your dad is getting tired." Klin frowned and studied the fight a little more closely. As soon as she said it, he noticed that Jethro was slowing down, and his movements were not as graceful. "Shit," Joseph muttered, "Of course, he's going to be slowing down. He's been in here for way too damn long." Klin nodded and cried, "Then let's stop standing around!"

Klin rushed forward with Joseph and Celeste at his side. All three broke off and encircled Viscious, hoping that he had to focus too much on Jethro. As they moved in to attack, daggers of ice appeared in the air above them. "Ah, ah," Viscious tittered, "this fight is personal!" The daggers came flying at them. Klin hit the ground and heard a loud, *thunk*, as the dagger impaled itself in the stone behind him. As he got back up, Viscious let out a hideous scream. Yatta's blade was jutting out of the demon's ribs while Celeste stood grinning. She kicked Viscious to remove the blade, knocking him close to Joseph. Joseph jumped up, slicing the Viscious's back open. Another scream, and another kick, and it was Klin's turn. Klin cross cut Viscious stomach and then leapt back as Viscious tried to swipe at him.

Viscious snarled as inky black liquid dripped from his wounds puddling the ground. Klin spared a glance at Jethro. He was breathing really hard. *Damn, he's nearing his limit.* But so was he himself. His body was on the verge of trembling, his muscles taught with exhaustion. Viscious then leapt forward at Joseph with far more speed than he had shown to have before. Joseph never even had a chance to block. He was flung across the room, a stream of blood flying through the air after him.

"Joseph!" Klin screamed. Suddenly Viscious was right in front of him. Five ice daggers appeared and as Klin just barely moved his wrists, the daggers impaled him. He screamed as his body became pierced by ice cold needles. Two through his forearms, two through his calves, and the last one hovered right above his head. Klin lay pinned to the ground as Viscious stood over him laughing. *I'm sorry dad*. Klin thought as he realized he was about to die.

Jethro stood behind Viscious, his sword only a mere five inches from splitting the bastard's skull open. Yet he had been forced to stop as Klin was held hostage. "Better not move at all Jethro," Viscious crooned, "or the kid dies." Jethro cursed his own ineptitude. *I'm so weak! My body feels so sluggish! I can't even save my own son!* Anger coursed through him like a river, the rage of a father. *What the hell can we do?* Jethro thought. Out of the corner of his eye he saw Joseph get back up from where he had been flung. Even in this grim situation, Jethro felt a spark of pride as he saw him stand tall, despite the harsh gash across his stomach. *Wait, where's the girl?*

Out of nowhere, Celeste appeared and with a well-placed roundhouse, kicked Viscious in the head. *Who the hesh is this girl?* There was an audible *crack*, as Viscious was sent flying, but Celeste let out a shriek and fell. Joseph rushed over to her while Jethro advanced towards Klin. Jethro stood over his son, the dagger at his head on the ground now. Jethro was about to remove the daggers when he sensed a presence behind him. Jethro spun just in time to block an attack to his head. Viscious was already back, his neck healed. "It seems I found your weakness Jethro." Viscious gloated. Jethro pushed off Viscious's claws and began a vicious assault. "I won't even give you a chance to get to them." Jethro snarled. He inflicted three wounds before Viscious responded, "Too late for that. I've got that pathetic one on the ground already. He's a sitting target right now."

"Joseph!" Jethro yelled, "Go help your brother!" Jethro spared a glance at Klin, and saw multiple ice daggers appear around him. Jethro quickly weaved a fire wall around him, and melted the ice. "I would but now you put fire around him!" Joseph yelled back, "And Celeste can't walk!" Jethro cursed as he cut of Viscious's arm. Viscious howled and leapt back. "Enough of this foolishness." Jethro charged him, but as he swung at the Arctisi's head, Viscious's body became transparent and foggy. Jethro went clean through his body, stumbling from the lack of resistance. Jethro spun around, looking for the black fog cloud, the telltale sign of Viscious's assassin form. Yet he couldn't see anything. *Damn it, where did he go?!*

Jethro scanned the room hurriedly, desperately trying to find the bastard. As his eyes rested near Joseph and Celeste, Viscious all of sudden appeared right behind them. "Look out!" Jethro's warning was too late though. Viscious grabbed both of them by the neck, his claws digging into their exposed flesh. "I would stay still Jethro." Viscious tittered, "Unless you want these two dead. Drop the flames around the boy. Now!" Jethro growled as he complied. "Now, I'm going to give you a choice." Viscious said slowly, "Either you can surrender now, and let them all live, or you can keep fighting me and watch all three die. Oh, and if you're wondering why you couldn't see me, well you're not the only one who learned some new tricks."

Jethro stood absolutely still, trying to figure out what he could do. Hundreds of daggers had appeared around Klin, and if he even put Threads near Klin, Viscious would send them into him before he could finish. As Jethro stared at Klin and Joseph, he wondered why the two did not use their magic. He could see the glow of the fabric on them. They had the power prepared in them since before the fight began, yet they had never even woven a single Thread. "I'm growing impatient Jethro!" Viscious exclaimed, "So you have ten seconds!" Jethro's mind began to move a light speed. "Ten!" If only he had his full power. "Nine!" Then he could move at light speed and catch Viscious by surprise. "Eight." Stop thinking of what you can't do. "Seven." Think of what you can do. "Six." Maybe he could signal his sons now is the time to use a spell? "Five." Why won't they do it though? "Four." Wait, the shimmer around them, it pulsed almost as if it was contained. "Three." Wait, contained? That was it! "TWO!" Jethro wove faster than he ever had before. "ONE!" Jethro sent the discreet Threads at Klin, hoping he still remembered the counter spell. "ZERO!" There!

Klin gasped as he felt a massive burst of energy flow through him. There was so much, that he felt as if his body could barely contain it. The daggers flew at him, and almost instinctively, he grabbed the energy and willed to save himself and his brother. There was a loud *whoosh* all around him, and at the same time he heard Viscious scream in pain. Klin stood up and looked around him. A dome of flames and lighting was circling around him, creating a protective shield. All of the daggers had been destroyed. He then turned to where Viscious was, and saw that

Joseph and Celeste lay on the ground coughing. Viscious though was clutching a burned claw, the one that had been holding Joseph. Viscious turned to Klin, and for the first time, he saw genuine surprise in the monster's eyes. "How!" Viscious cried, "I sealed their power years ago!"

"Yeah, and I destroyed that seal." Jethro said with a smile. "I got rid of Klin's and just did Joseph's." As if on cue, a purple aura appeared around Joseph as a rush of energy flowed through him. Both brother's wounds were also healed by the absurd amount of power coursing through them. "Gah, this isn't over!" Viscious yelled and just disappeared. "Oh herk yeah!" Joseph yelled as his aura disappeared. "The coward ran away." Klin smiled and let go of the magic also and rejoined the others. "Wait, don't-!" Jethro yelled as he ran towards them. Klin turned and saw Viscious appear once more in front of them and shot two daggers straight at him and Joseph's hearts. "NOO!" Jethro cried. He jumped right in front of them. The daggers made a sickening sound as they pierced his body. Jethro slumped to the ground in front of them. "DAD!!" Joseph and Klin screamed in unison.

Visciosus laughed, "The fool. I knew he would do that!" Klin reached out mentally and grasped at the absurd amount of energy once more. "I'LL KILL YOU!" Klin screamed. Viscious laughed as he summoned more daggers, this time all around them. "You don't even know how to use that power!" Viscious cackled, "So how in the world are you going to kill me."

Klin looked at Joseph, who had also resummoned his magic. "Like this." Klin said. He felt three different sources of energy, and grabbed the one that felt the strongest. Then, something happened between the two brothers. Something rare. They knew exactly what the other was thinking. As Viscious lowered his hand to send the missiles at them, a circle appeared around the three. Rippling purple energy on Joseph's side, and glowing golden energy on Klin's. The energy's rose up and formed a dome around them, disintegrating the daggers upon contact. "WHAT!" Viscious screamed in a tantrum like way, "THAT"S IMPOSSIBLE!" Klin and Joseph then together lowered the dome and formed a sphere in front of them. Viscious's face then changed from one of rage to one of fear. "No, wait this is impossible!" Viscious cried out. Klin and Joseph lowered their hands, the purple and golden energy twining together in the sphere. "See you in Heshtanus buddy." Joseph said.

A massive blast of golden and purple energy was sent straight a Viscious. He let out a brief scream, but it was cut off from the roar of the blast. When the beam disappeared, all that remained was a scorch mark on the ground where Viscious had been. Klin and Joseph looked at each other, nodding grimly before collapsing to the ground. "Damn," Celeste said softly, "I think you guys killed him. What did you two just do." Klin shook his head as he sat on the ground. He had no idea what it was they had just done. At least it was finally over. "Klin, Joseph." Jethro said weakly. Klin leapt to his feet and ran over to Jethro, almost falling over as he ran. "Dad!"

Klin and Joseph knelt down next to their father. Jethro looked up at them smiling. His skin was pale and he lay in a pool of his own blood. The daggers had missed his heart, but narrowly. "You can heal yourself, right?" Joseph asked shakily. Jethro shook his head, "No, I don't have the energy needed to even patch up a scratch." Tears formed at the corner of Klin's eyes. "Then, you're not going to die, are you?"

Jethro coughed up blood, "I'm afraid I am. I'm sorry you two, but I couldn't let you die. Not after I failed as a father and left you alone for eleven years."

"You were about to make up for it though." Joseph sobbed, "You were going to come back with us! We were going to be a family again!" Jethro smiled weakly, his eyes beginning to gloss over. "I'm sorry boys. I tried to help, but it looks like I failed once more. Tell your mother I'm sorry. But I'm so proud of you both. I love you Joseph. I love you Klin. Good-bye…" With that, Jethro the Immortal Hero, was immortal no more. Klin and Joseph began sobbing uncontrollably. How long they sat there, he had no idea. Finally, Klin wiped the tears from his face and stood up. "Come on," he stammered, "we should leave." The two stood up and walked over to Celeste. Joseph picked her up and carried her. Together they left the fortress in the new light of the rising dawn.

Chapter 9

The Path of Honor

Deep in the forest of Edearan, to the south of Ala'Kathar lay the remote city of Edeaven. The city of Edeaven is peaceful place full of honorable warriors. A place so far removed from the rule of the king that it almost rules itself with no royal taxes or oaths of allegiance to the king. Yet in this bustling city, with more people than the capital itself, a dark interior lurks underneath the face of virtue. And so in this city, three threads of the weave of fate are laid. Threads that shall weave a tapestry with the others that come before them.

The summer heat of the noon sun beat down upon the cobblestone road of Edeaven's streets. People bustling about throughout the streets like fish through a stream. Sticky humidity filled the air. It pressed down heavy, almost chocking those whom it found. Another typical summer day in Edeaven. Walking down the twisting maze of streets and buildings that made up the city was a young man and a little girl accompanying him. The man looked to be seventeen to sixteen years old and the girl about ten to twelve. "Ander," the little girl said gaily as she moved about with a skip, "Can't we stop at Brom's for some pastries?"

Ander back at her and smiled, "We can do that later. Right now, father told us to get you a new dress, remember Kyoko?" Kyoko crossed her arms stuck her lips out in a pout. "But I don't like wearing dresses! Why do I need another one? Daddy should know I'll just throw this one out as well." Ander rubbed his temple, sighing, "I really wish you wouldn't antagonize him. You may be his favorite but even he has his limits with you." Kyoko cocked her head to the side, a look of befuddlement upon her face. "What do you mean I'm his favorite? He loves both of us. Same with mom." Ander ruffled her hair, which Kyoko laughed at and flailed her arms in an attempt to make him stop. "You're right," Ander replied, "He does love us both."

At least that is what Ander said. His sister was sometimes too pure for this world. Ander Dyon was a boy of seventeen, past his year of reaching manhood. Yet unlike everyone else he knew that was his age, he did not quite look the part. He was just about average height, and had brown hair of medium length. His bangs went farther than the rest of his hair and was parted down the middle. He had striking purple eyes and pale, but not unhealthily so skin. Yet Ander was extremely skinny. He barely had any muscle mass and if one felt him, all they would really feel would be bones. He wore a white, short-sleeved tunic with a blue trim on the collar, waist, and cuffs. His gray, slightly baggy pants were held up with a corded belt.

His sister Kyoko bouncing about next to him was twelve and starting to mature. She had long brown hair that was put into ponytails and bright blue eyes. She was barely above Ander's waist in height. She wore a light blue shirt with a dark blue skirt. Even though she hated dresses, Kyoko really liked skirts for some reason. She wore some shorts underneath them also, for Kyoko was a very active girl. As the two were walking and nearing the tailor's shop, they passed a woman in a dress with a swooping neckline coming out of the shop. Ander pointedly looked away, his face beginning to turn red. Kyoko however sniffed and said, "Women should have more respect for themselves! Grownups should not look like whores." Ander suppressed a laugh which came out as a snort. Kyoko picked up on stuff that she really did not understand sometimes. "Kyo, what did I tell you about using that word?" Ander scolded. His sister looked up at him with innocent eyes. "Grownups?"

Ander looked around before whispering, "No, whores." Kyoko gave him an impish grin, "Oh, that. You told me I'm too young to know that word! But Sasha uses it all the time."

"Yeah, but Sasha needs to not say stuff like that maybe." Ander countered, rubbing his wrist. It was still a little sore form yesterday. Ander shook his head, ignoring the pain from bruise along the nape of his neck and said, "Come on, let's see Brom."

The two went inside the shop, and as they entered the owner, one lovely Madame Jade Ringsore, came up to them. "Ah, if it isn't my favorite pair of customers!" Jade said. Ander gave her a small smile, "You say that to every customer." Madame Jade gave him a mischievous grin, "Well that's because anyone who gives me money is my favorite."

"But if everyone's your favorite, then no one actually is." Kyoko replied confused. Jade let out a hearty laugh, "Exactly my dear! Now, how can I help the two of you?" Kyoko rolled her eyes, "Father wants me to have a new dress."

"Again?!" Jade exclaimed, "But what happened to your last one?" Kyoko paused, her face turning slightly red, "It may or may not have been brutely destroyed in a fight three weeks ago." Jade tossed her black hair back and scolded the girl. "Why in the world were you fighting in a dress?! Honestly, I know you love the things, but there is better attire to wear to a fight in."

"I can't help it." Kyoko said cunningly, "I want to look beautiful while I destroy my enemies!" Ander just shook his head as Madame Jade lead Kyoko back to her work room. He knew better. Kyoko had purposely worn her last dress to her latest fight to she could find an excuse to throw it out. That fight though had been her fault for instigating it, so Father had punished her for that, but Ander was proud of her nonetheless. Not only did Kyoko always stand up for herself, but she was a talented warrior, unlike him. Kyoko was skilled in both wind magic, and with the lance. It was always a funny sight to see this small girl wielding such an large weapon, and not only that, but sweep most opponents away.

While waiting for Kyoko, Ander took out a small book from his pocket and sat down in a chair to wait. The book was *The Adventures of Jethro Markus, Vol. 3*. It was Ander's favorite book. He had read it countless times and never got bored of it. He opened it up to a random chapter and read. He smiled at the one he had selected. It was the account of Jethro's battle against the Seveljarnian Belgroths. He loved how Jethro had just stumbled into the town, and rather than leaving them, he had gone out of his way to not only destroy the monsters, but had also spent a whole month helping the people recover. Jethro was the type of warrior that everyone in Edeaven should try to be. Many claimed to be like him, but almost none actually were.

Ander put the book down. Just thinking about the hypocrisy of most of the citizens left a sour taste in his mouth. Unfortunately, he had been getting that taste a lot lately. Luckily Kyoko and Jade exited just at that moment. Kyoko was wearing a knee-length pink dress with a blue floral design all around it. She spun around and asked, "How do I look?" Ander smiled and said, "Like a warrior princess." Kyoko grinned. That phrase had become their code for, "You look great but I know you're ready to destroy that dress."

Madame Jade sighed, "Just please don't destroy the dress before the tournament. Your father won't be happy about that." Ander laughed uncomfortably, "Yeah, he wouldn't. I'll make sure she shows up in that dress."

"Don't worry Ander," Kyoko said, "I'll be extra careful today. I want to commemorate your victory with my adorable presence."

"Of course." Ander stammered. Jade remained silent but looked at him with an unreadable face. "Come on Kyoko, we'll be late if we don't get going." Kyoko nodded and went out the door. Ander pulled out the money that his father had given him and gave it to Jade. "Here's the money. This is the same as the last four I'm guessing." Madame Jade took the money, but looked Ander over as she pocketed the money. "I don't know what it is you do for your sister to adore such a pathetic brother. It's beyond all of us as to why she admires you. You better win today. The last thing any of us want to see is her disappointed." Jade eyed him for moment then said venomously, "But I suppose she's used to it from you by now. It'll take a miracle for you to win today." Jade smiled at him maliciously, obviously hoping for a reaction. Instead Ander just smiled and said, "Miracles happen to those who need them the most you know. Have a nice day Madame." Madame Jade's face curdled as she turned with a *huramph* and walked away. Ander sighed and went outside to meet his sister.

When Ander got outside, he found Kyoko couched down, petting a cat. "Look" She exclaimed, "This guy loves me!" Ander smiled as the black cat began to rub against her dress, purring loudly. "Come on Kyoko, we need to get to the arena." Kyoko nodded and began to walk in front of him. She ran about, skipping and running in circles, and walking upon the various walls alongside their path, giggling and laughing all the while. To many, Kyoko was strange, seeming to find jokes in the strangest ways. Yet to Ander, she was someone who took pleasure in life itself. "Hey Ander," Kyoko asked as they neared the arena, "do you know if Sasha will be watching today?" Ander shrugged, "Don't know. She has class today."

"Aww, that's too bad." Kyoko said, "I was hoping she would get to see you destroy your foes with me!"

"Haha, y-yeah." Ander rubbed the back of his head as he looked away. Why did she have to have such faith in him? "Ohh, we're here!" Kyoko yelled excitedly. As the giant structure of black stone loomed over them, Ander felt his spirits drop to the same cool temperature as the shade that they came upon. The Edeaven Area. Young people who wanted to prove themselves as capable warriors or gain prestige and honor would gather here to compete against one another. Today though was special. It was not just any old tournament, but The Battle of Disciples. Only the bravest and most skilled warriors fought in this tournament for the once-in-a-lifetime chance. Permission to go to the capital and enter the school of The Magnum Commander. The leader of the entire army of Ardaven. Everyone in this tournament had been training all of their lives for this tournament. Excited spectators were gathering at the gate. Ecstatic chattering from the crowd spilled over them as they anticipated the exciting fights that they were about to see.

"Look at all the people here big brother." Kyoko said. Ander simply nodded mutely and started rubbing his left wrist. Kyoko looked over and beamed at him, "Don't worry so much Ander! You got this!" Ander plastered a smile on his face, and forced himself to stop rubbing his wrist. "Well, I suppose I better head in." Ander said. Right as he was about to leave, he felt a tapping on his shoulder. He jumped and spun around. "Hahaha! What are you that nervous?" Ander's face broke out into a genuine grin as he saw who it was. "Hey Sasha. What are you doing here? I thought you had classes." Sasha grinned, "We got out early today for the tournament. So I figured I'd come and watch you."

Sasha Inezena was the daughter of one of the wealthiest families in the city and was well known for her beauty. She had long flowing blonde hair and stormy gray eyes that could pierce a man's soul with both their softness, and their intensity. She had warm, flawless skin and was wearing a pink shirt and simple white skirt and knee-high boots. Despite her immense beauty, she always wore simple clothing, and only ever adorned herself with her signature jade colored choker. Yet, to the citizens of Edeaven, she was a strange one. Not only did she not have a boyfriend, despite her numerous suitors, she had also been best friends with Ander since they were kids. "So, you think you got this one?" Sasha asked. Ander paused and looked over at Kyoko. "Yeah, I think I got this."

"Excellent!" Sasha replied happily, "Well then, I suppose Kyoko and I will go find a seat. Good luck Ander!" Sasha took Kyoko's hand and the two girls began to walk towards the gate. "Good luck big brother!" Kyoko yelled, "You can do this!" Ander gave her a thumbs up, but noticed Sasha turning back to look at him. She had a concerned look on her face. Ander's face fell as he turned away and headed towards the competitor's entrance. He should have known that he couldn't fool her. His earlier bravado began to fade as he showed the guard his ticket and his mark. The guard looked over his mark and ticket and then snorted. "You better not ruin this tournament Violeter." Ander winced at the name, and replied politely, "Believe me, I don't want to." As Ander went in, all confidence he had returned to the abyss in which in usually resided in.

Thirty minutes later, Ander sat on the bench in the waiting room. His match was coming up. Luckily he had been third on the rooster. The crowd outside roared like a lion, and he could hear the faint clanging of metal and the scraping of sword against armor. He had been given his choice of weapon and armor, yet what he had chosen seemed to have shocked the armorer. Ander clutched his weapon tightly, feeling the polished wood grip sink into his hands. He was going up against Tam Buckley, a strong warrior who had already proven himself in battle against monsters and had almost won the tournament last year. *Why do I have to fight him first?* Ander thought, *Because of this, there's no way I'll be able to satisfy father now.* It looked like tonight would be another dinnerless night. Ander sighed at the thought. He had already been denied breakfast, and he had had only enough money to buy a snack beforehand. Many wondered why Ander was never able to gain any weight, despite all the rigorous training he was put through. It was simply because he was malnourished at home. Despite living in a luxurious house and being rich, Ander usually went to bed hungry, and went till noon without food. After a certain point his appetite had begun to adjust and so he stayed alive despite his lack of food.

Ander lifted his head up as the crowd burst into a rancorous roar. "And that's that folks! We have a winner!" The announcer shouted, "Give us five minutes to clean up the blood and clear the arena, and then we'll move on to our third match of the tournament!" *Wait, bl–blood?* Ander thought. His stomach plummeted and he felt sick all of a sudden. There was a knock on the door all of a sudden. "Hey Violeter, you ready?" Ander stood up and gripped his weapon in determination, doing his best to steady his nerves. "Yeah, I'm ready."

Ander stood in the entrance tunnel to the arena, waiting for the call of the announcer. The guard in front of him was beginning to brief him on the rules. "We want to see clean, honorable fighting. Got that? Thee judges will decide what constitutes dirty after the match ends, so don't stop until you or your opponent concedes." The guard eyed him distastefully before saying, "But in your case you'll concede first. We do have a healer on standby, so anything short of killing is allowed. That's about it then. Got it?" Ander nodded, his face as grim and determined as he could be. The guard looked at him, and sighed. "Kid, why are you doing this? Everyone knows you won't make it past this round. Why not give up?" Ander looked the man in the eyes, and gave him a small smile. "I made a promise to do this, even though I know I don't stand a chance. I'd rather disappoint everyone for failing rather than running away."

"You got guts kid." The guard replied smiling, "I wasn't rooting for you before, but now I am. Don't make this fight easy for that bastard. Good luck Ander." Ander's eyes widened. He had not been expecting that. "ALRIGHT LADIES AND GENTELMEN!" The announcer shouted, "IT'S TIME FOR OUR THIRD MATCH! Our contenders are well known for this one. Please welcome, a returning fighter, one who made a splash with his insane skills and brute strength last year. TAM IROAS!" The crowd went absolutely wild as, Ander assumed, Tam walked out onto the arena. "His opponent is no well less known, although for different reasons. Please welcome the son of the former Captain of the Guard, ANDER DYON!" Ander took a deep breath as he walked into the bright light, covering his eyes. The crowd let out some polite cheering, but over them all he heard one bright voice. "YOU

GOT THIS BIG BROTHER!" Ander turned to see Kyoko leaning so far forward that she was almost falling out of her seat, while Sasha desperately tried to keep her in.

As Ander walked into the middle of the arena to meet Tam, a tall man with bulging muscles and short blonde hair, he heard the crowd begin to mutter. He figured it was probably because of his choice of armament. Unlike Tam, who wore plate armor and bore a shortsword. Ander on the other hand had no armor and held a quarterstaff in his hand. As soon as the two met, Tam examined Ander and his equipment, before bursting out in a derisive laugh. "What in the world? No armor and just a quarterstaff? Are you really that confident that you can beat me?" Ander said nothing, shifting his feet into a fighting stance, pointing the end of the staff at him. He felt his hands begin to shake form lack of nutrition. "What's this? It looks like Ander is raring for a fight!" The announcer exclaimed bewildered. "Well folks, shall we grant him his wish?!" The crowd roared in approval. "Very well, the crowd has spoken! Let the fight, begin!" Tam let out a giddy cry as he leaped at Ander. Ander stepped back and brought the end of the staff around and smacked Tam in the side of the head. Tam let out a yelp as he was sent sprawling to the ground.

The crowd fell silent as Tam got back on his feet. "Lucky hit." He growled. "You won't get another." Ander remained silent and thrust the staff at his clavicle. Tam backed up in surprise, and brought his sword down upon the staff. Ander brought it to the side, moving around the sword and smacked him in the nose. Tam cursed as his head was flung back and a loud crunch was heard. "What was that about not getting another hit?" Ander asked.

"Why you cocky little bastard." Tam growled, "I was going to go easy on you but it seems you need a lesson in humility." Tam rushed forward, swinging wildly, Ander started to duck and weave, nimbly avoiding the attacks. Then as Ander went to dodge a blow to the legs, Tam's sword swerved upwards. *Oh crap.* Ander tried to move back, but was far too slow. Ander cried out as his ribcage was sliced open. Ander clutched his wound, his hand sticky with his own warm blood. The crowd screamed, ravenous for more blood. Tam stood over him sneering. He pointed to his nose, which was bleeding and said, "Blow for blow, and blood for blood." Ander looked up at him, and placed both hands back on his staff. Tam snorted and tried to backhand him. Ander though ducked and thrust his staff straight at his neck. Tam let out a chocking cry as he moved backwards, gasping for air. *Now's my chance!* Ander thought, *My plan actually worked!* Ander ran forward and smacked Tam's sword out of his hand. But as he did, Tam leapt at him with a snarl.

Ander shouted in surprise as Tam was suddenly on him, wrestling for his staff. Ander tried to fight back, but he just could not beat the man's brute strength. Tam ripped his staff from him and tossed it away, but kept a firm grip on Ander's wrist. "You actually did pretty good." Tam rasped, "Which is why I'm going to only beat you up a little." Tam's face broke out into a big grin as he picked Ander up by the throat. Ander started to claw and kick, but there was just not power behind any of his blows. He felt weak and shaky. He had used up all of his strength already. Tam slammed him into the ground and punched him in the stomach. Ander let out a soundless gasp as all the air was sucked from his lungs. Tam then picked him back up slammed him face first into the wall. The crowd which had been cheering wildly before had now fallen silent. Tam dragged him against the wall for a bit. Ander screamed as his parts of his skin were ripped from his face by the rough stone.

The crowd began to mutter in discontent as they watched the brutality that Ander was enduring. "What's this?" The announcer exclaimed, "It seems that Tam is no longer the crowd favorite, and to be honest I can see why! "The crowd now began to boo and heckle Tam. Tam just snorted as he picked Ander up and said, "Alright, I've had my fun. Do you concede?" Ander felt his body start to go limp as conscience begin to fade. His face was a bloody mess and one eye was swollen shut. His arms were scraped and bruised, and he had felt one if his ribs crack. Ander opened his mouth to concede but all that came out was a croak. "Well, if you can't say anything, I suppose that means you still want some more!" Tam leered. Tam brought his fist up and flung it at Ander's face. Ander closed his eyes, and heard a yelp as he was dropped to the ground. He groggily opened his eyes to see blood dripping from Tam's curled fist. The crowd had gone silent, for standing above Ander was Kyoko. "Leave my brother alone!" Kyoko screamed.

"Out of the way kid." Tam growled, "This is interference with a match. Get out of my way or I'll hurt you too." Ander smiled though as he saw Tam eye Kyoko warily. "I wouldn't do that if I were you." Ander rasped as his voice finally returned. "My sister is far more talented than I am." Tam snarled but otherwise did nothing else.

Ander heard rushed footsteps behind him and someone shout, "Stop! Ander is obviously unable to continue! Anymore fighting for any reason will result in disqualification." Ander felt himself be picked up and placed on a stretcher. "The winner of this match is Tam." The announcer shouted half-heartedly. "I think we can all say that we now have a greater appreciation for Ander." The last thing Ander heard as he was taken off the arena field was the muted sounds of Kyoko and Sasha's voices.

Ander walked through the streets of Edeaven by himself. He rubbed his side. Even though the healers had fixed him up, he still had bruises on where he had been hit. The healers had told his sister and Sasha that he would be fine, but both of them had refused to leave. As soon as he had woken up, he told them he was okay and to watch the rest of the matches and that he would join them soon. He felt a little bad for lying, but not terribly. He sighed as he rubbed his wrist, heading east. Why did he think he had ever stood a chance in that fight? He should have known his plan would fail, just like everything else that he did in his life. Ander had never shown skill in anything. His intelligence was average, his athletic skills were below average, and any project he attempted end in failure. Well, all except one.

Dong, dong, dong, dong, dong, dong, dong, dong, dong, dong, dong, dong, dong. Ander looked up at the giant clock tower in the center square. He was not expected to be home till at least nightfall. After everything he had just endured, he wanted to leave the crowded streets and loud noises of Edeaven. As he walked down the street, passing by all the vendors and shops, he noticed that every once in a while people would point at him, whispering. People of all ages did it, and as soon as they looked at his eyes, the crowd would part around him. Ander quickly put his head down, making sure to avoid eye contact. It was well known that anyone with purple eyes was a warning of things to come.

Anyone who had ever borne the violet color had brought disaster and death with them.

Why can't people just accept me? Ander thought bitterly, *But then again, why should I care? They're all assholes anyway.* After about half and hour of walking, Ander found himself at his destination. The Wall. At sixty feet high and twenty feet thick, no one had ever breached it. The city wall had stood impregnable and invincible since the Era of the Sculptors. Or so the city's historians said. Ander wasn't so sure since they called Ala'Kathar the Last Bastion of Humanity. That had to imply that the city had been taken at some point, right? But the reason he was here, was because the wall had a weak spot. If one went to the eastern gate, or the Earth Door as it was named, and walked two hundred yards to the east; you would find a hole. This hole was hidden behind a large rose bush, which is why it had not been patched yet, and it was right behind a bakery. The thing was barely wide enough for a single person, yet Ander had no trouble fitting in it. Ander ambled over to the hole, checked his surroundings, and then went in. Only warriors were allowed to leave the city and the penalty for transgressing this was four years in prison. When he saw that no one was around, he pushed the small opening in the bush aside and crawled in.

Ander wriggled and squirmed through the hole, barely able to see against the cold ground and dark stone till he was able to see the light from the other side. Ander slowly pulled himself out into a brush covering. Cautiously he moved the branches aside and peered up above him. Not a single guard in sight. Ander burst out of his hiding spot and ran into the forest hunched close to the ground. He ran deep into the woods, climbing over fallen trees, cleaning himself off of spiderwebs that he didn't see, (and checking himself for the rest of the trip for spiders) until he finally ascended a hill, arriving at his destination, a grove. This grove was Ander's secret hideaway. Strong oaks formed a protective barrier around the place, hiding him form any possible prying eyes. A small stream flowed down the center of the grove from a pond about fifty feet in diameter. That pond in turn had a beautiful waterfall splashing into it, creating a crystalline mist in the air by it. Pond lilies decorated the surface of the water, and the large golden and red Fiare fish could be seen swimming in the brilliantly clear water. Yet the main spectacle of the grove were the scores of flowers the decorated the ground. Flowers of all colors and breeds grew in beautifully coordinated rows and filled the air with their sweet aroma.

Ander let out a content sigh as he laid down on the ground, brushing aside the flowers he had worked hard to grow. He had discovered this place about ten years ago now, after being punished by his father and being yelled at by both his parents once again. Back then, there had been only a few wild flowers. He still did not know why he had done it, but after that day, he had come out every day he could to take care of the field, buying new seeds and getting the tools he had needed. This was the only project he had ever done that had not ended in disaster. He had made sure to not let even Sasha or Erok come here till a year later, when he got to see all of his hard work pay off.

He closed his eyes as he basked in the warm summer breeze. Up here by the water, the weather was actually kind of nice. Maybe he would go for a swim. Ander let the beauty and quiet of nature clear his mind, forgetting about the horrible events of the day, and the worse things that awaited him when he got home. "I thought I would find you here." Ander sat up quickly, startled and turned to see Sasha. A sad smile was on her face as she stared at him. "It's not nice to lie you know." She scolded, "You really upset Kyoko you know."

"Sorry, but I needed to be alone." Ander replied. He turned his head away, staring at the flowers, "Besides, I don't need Kyoko coming out here." Sasha just shook her head with a sigh, "You should've just told us then. You know we would haven't followed you." Ander raised his eyebrow, "Oh really, then why are you here?" Sasha blushed and sat down next to him, clutching her skirt, and said sheepishly, "Well, not immediately."

"So, you here to try and cheer me up after that pathetic performance?" Ander asked.

"Yes, I am," Sasha answered fiercely, "and it wasn't pathetic. You did a great job!" Ander just snorted derisively, "Yeah, and owlbears can fly. I was barely able to do anything. I can't believe I was so stupid as to think that I actually stood a chance." Ander put his head in his palm, and then yelped as he was poked in the ribs. "Ow, what was that for?"

"You need to stop being so pessimistic." Sasha scolded with a pout, "You should really have more confidence in your abilities. So, what if you didn't win the fight? You got close to it and did a really good job."

"Yeah, and you think that'll be okay to tell my dad?" It was quiet for a moment before Sasha replied meekly, "Maybe." Ander sighed as he looked at Sasha and smiled, "I appreciate the pep talk, but I come here to forget about that type of stuff, remember? Can we change to subject please?" Sasha eyed him critically. "I promise I'm feeling better." Ander assured her.

"You swear?"

"I swear." Ander said solemnly. Sasha narrowed her eyes, "Your serious voice says otherwise. Come on, you need to be passionate!" Ander could not help it. He burst out laughing. Sasha started to laugh too. "Good, now you're cleared to change the subject." Ander gave her a small smile as his fit of laughter subsided. "Thanks Sasha, I mean it."

"You're welcome. Anyway, I have two things I want to do. First, I learned a really cool move today. Want to see it?"

"Sure." Ander nodded with slight surprise. Sasha went over to the pond. The sun had begun to set, casting a golden glow upon the grove. Sasha held out her arms and raised them upwards. As she did, hundreds of tiny droplets rose up from the pond. She held them in place, letting the golden light filter through and create tiny rainbows. From each droplet, the rainbows connected to another. Each droplet was an island, connected by a bridge of rainbow. "Wow," Ander breathed breathlessly, "it's beautiful." Sasha turned back to him and smiled, "I'm not done yet though." Her hands formed fists, as if she was grasping a line, and acted as if she was giving the invisible line a shake. The droplets flew high into the air before shattering, creating a colorful crystal mist. Ander gave her a boyish grin as he laughed, spinning around in the mist. "That was incredible!" Sasha flushed suddenly, "You think so?"

"For sure." Ander nodded, "You really are an incredible weaver." Sasha waved her hand dismissively, "Not really. Besides, that move doesn't really have any practicality. It's just to help with precision and minute control."

"Well, it gave us beauty," Ander replied, "isn't that enough?" Sasha frowned, creating a small dimple in her cheek as she thought, "I suppose you're right." Ander grinned as he crossed his arms and rocked back and forth, "I'm a real dispenser of wisdom you know. Kyoko tells me so all the time."

"She's twelve," Sasha snorted, "anything you say she'll take as gospel." Ander just laughed, "You're just jealous of me. But anyway, what was the second thing?"

"Oh, that's right!" Sasha exclaimed, "You'll never guess who I saw before your match!"

"Who?" Ander asked curiously. "It was Erok!" Sasha answered excitedly. Ander froze, "Wait, really?!" Sasha nodded vehemently, "Yep, and he said that he wanted to meet us in the Brandyshire later today. Actually, it's probably almost time for us to meet him."

"Well then," Ander exclaimed, "what are we still doing here? Let's get going!" The two turned to leave. Erok was back! It had been years since they had seen him. Ander began to walk away, a skip in his step as he moved. As they neared the edge of the grove though, the skin on his back began to crawl. Ander stopped and turned around. He let out a gasp. In the dark brush, a pair of glowing eyes stared back at him. He started at them transfixed and stepped back as the owner let out a low, deep growl. "Ander?" Sasha asked, "What's wrong?" Ander's legs began to shake as the creature continued to growl at him. Those eyes. Those glowing, fierce eyes pierced him with a hungry look. "Ander? Ander!" He spun around, his breath ragged. "Hey, are you okay?" Sasha asked worriedly, "You look frightened."

"There's some sort of creature. In the underbrush there." Ander pointed at the spot, but much to his surprise, the creature had disappeared. "Ander, there's nothing there." Sasha said softly, "Are you feeling okay?"

"Y-yeah." Ander replied shakily, "It's just probably a visualization of my inner demons." He gave a warbly laugh, "Come one let's go."

"O-oh, okay." The two left the grove, but Ander no longer walked with that skip. Whatever that thing had been, its eyes had been purple. And not just any, but the exact same shade as his.

Chapter 10

The Second Trio

It was almost seven by the time Ander and Sasha were back inside the safety of the city. Neither of them had seen any sign of the creature on their way back. As they headed down the darkened streets, lit sparsely by the fire or light stones mounted on iron poles, Ander pondered on what that mysterious beast could have been. The Eastern Woods were home to all sorts of beasts, or at least they supposedly were. After all, this was his first time seeing any confirmation of any monster that was supposed to dwell within the forest. Yet there was one type of monster that everyone knew existed somewhere deep in the trees. The Saromanthian Spiders. No one knew where they had come from, first being documented thirty years ago. The Saromanthian Spiders were giant spiders with abdomens that were as big as a man and eyes a wide as gems. They spit a harsh venom that not only ate away at the flesh but froze the wound over. Not only would you feel acid searing into your flesh, but the ice would continue to secrete acid as it froze over. It was an extremely slow and painful way to die. Yet the reason Ander thought of them was because of their eyes. They were said to have violet eyes.

The problem was though, they had not been seen in almost twenty years now, but he could not think of anything else it could have been. Ander kept these thoughts to himself though and so it was that the two of them walked in an unnerving silence until they arrived at the Brandyshire. The Brandyshire Bar and Mill stood at the southern end of the city, where the small Lorkathan river ran through. The bar was also one of the most paradoxical places in all of Edeaven, simultaneously being a business and feeling like a welcoming home. The building itself was enormous, being able to hold over two thousand people and three floors. Brick siding lined the outside and a large wooden sign proclaimed the name of the place.

The two entered and found the comfort the bar's paradoxical nature. The floor was made of polished oak, and numerous fireplaces dotted the walls, although none were lit as it was near the end of summer. Instead of fire, a small ball of frost hovered in each hole, colling down the place to a comfortable temperature. Stairs led upwards to the next two levels, with the center of the second and third floors open so that one could observer the stage and watch the night's performance. While the place was big, loud, and incredibly noisy, it also gave the feeling of being quaint and homelike. A feeling which one would normally feel at a local café. Most places traded that feeling for spacious room, but here at the Brandyshire, they had achieved both.

"Good evening, Master Dyon, Mistress Inenza." Ander and Sasha turned towards the counter to see the owner of the bar, Johnathan Brandyshire. "Good evening Mr. Brandyshire." Sasha replied with a smile, "How are you doing tonight?" Johnathan grinned back at the two, "Oh it do be a good night it tonight. We're quite booming right now with the tournament being close to over for the day. Anyhow, I got quite the shock when who do be coming in and reserving a spot, but old Master Erok! He's changed quite a bit since he left five years ago. Your stuff is already paid for so you can head on up to your usual place. I hope you three enjoy yourself-oi! You there, stop bothering my waitress!" The muscular man rushed away to a man trying to grope one of the female servers bustling about. Ander and Sasha gave each other a mischievous grin. "I almost feel bad for the poor guy." Ander said, "Almost, but not quite." As if on cue, there was a loud crack and a storm of cursing. The two burst out laughing as they left Johnathon to deal with the drunken pervert and went up the stairs.

Up to the third floor the climbed and headed on over to a both in the corner. As they neared their usual spot, Ander spotted a waitress walking away, giggling. Sitting at the booth, with his feet propped up on the table and a mug of beer in his hand was Erok the Orphan. Erok had left five years ago, disappearing one day. He had always talked about leaving, but Ander and Sasha had never been sure if he would. Yet now he was back.

Ander stopped, and stepped back a little, taken aback by the person he saw before him. The Erok sitting in front of him and the Erok he knew were very different. The boy he remembered was an emancipated kid with oily reddish-brown hair that had fallen to his back, and pale, freckled, sickly looking skin. The Erok in front of him was bulging with muscles and tanned. His hair was cut short, with his bangs parted to the side. Yet both had the same glistening eyes. A fierceness that challenged the world that had wronged him, daring it to try and push him down even more. Erok leapt to his feet with a grin when he saw the two, throwing back his finely made black cloak with a flourish. "Ander, Sasha! It's great to see you guys again!" Erok crowed as he pulled them into a hug.

"It's great to see you again too." Ander exclaimed happily. He looked his old friend over. He no longer had to wear poor and worn clothing. Besides his cloak, he wore a nice gray shirt and gray pants and some black leather boots that did not look cheap. "Come on and sit down." Erok said, "I just ordered our usual. I didn't know what to order for drinks though, so I took a bit of a guess. Probably some purple wine for Ander, and earl gray tea for you Sasha." Sasha sat down and smiled, "Well, you guessed right. Ander can't really handle the bitter stuff yet. Although I would have been fine with something alcoholic." As Ander sat down next to Erok, he noticed him move a strange looking crossbow. Erok shrugged, "I figured you were still the responsible one. Am I wrong?"

Sasha raised her eyebrow, "How is wanting some wine being irresponsible? I only want some. And to answer, yes, I'm still the responsible one. Do you have any idea how hard it is to keep him and his sister out of trouble? I need some wine for that." Ander turned his head and muttered, "What the heck, you make it sound like I'm a problem child. What are you, my mom?" Erok burst out laughing, "Well, I'm glad somethings have changed. How are things here? I only just got back this morning and haven't heard anything."

Ander just shrugged his shoulders, "Eh, there's not much to tell honestly. The lord is the same, the laws are the same, and the relations between everyone are still the same, and people are still assholes here." Erok let out a sigh, "And here I was hoping for something different.

Suppose I can't expect a miracle. Even with the possibility of war on the horizon, the people of Edeaven still stay the same." Ander and Sasha glanced at each other before Sasha asked with trepidation, "What do you mean war?" Erok looked at them with shock, "What, you mean you haven't heard?" Both of them shook their head.

"Damn" Erok muttered, "this place gets more and more secluded every year. Anyway, Turmaky had been gathering troops and their food supply requests have gone up. Some think that they're finally putting down the rebellion in Xaldinor, but this army seems far too big to be for them." Sasha pursed her lips into a frown and asked, "But the Turmakians aren't exactly known for their kindness, so why wouldn't this just be them trying to crush them once and for all?" Erok leaned forward and lowered his voice, "Well, that's because they're gathering soldiers from every part of the empire. They never conscript soldiers from the area that they fight. It has something to do with their religious tenants or something. No, this seems like an army to fight an empire." Anders eyes grew wide, "You don't mean..."

"Yep," Erok replied as he leaned back, "all signs point to Turmaky going to war with Coronus."

"But that's insane!" Sasha yelped softly, "They've always been scared of Coronus, and for good reason. What's changed?" Erok crossed his arms and slouched down in the booth a bit, "Well, Coronus hasn't been very unified recently. People are becoming divided in the various provinces. It's actually kind of scary how close it is to becoming like Aradaven."

"But why are they divided?" Ander asked, "They've always felt a strong bond as Coronians." Erok shrugged, "Not sure, but I have heard rumors that it has something to do with the princess. I can't say much more on it, mainly cause that's all I know. But basically, Turmaky thinks that Coronus is weak right now and sees an opportunity to get rid of their biggest threat." Ander shook his head. This was crazy, but why had this not made their way to them? Especially since if Coronus did go to war, that meant that they would probably ask for help from them. "Well, that's enough doom and gloom news for now." Erok said, "Do you guys have any pleasant news for me?"

"Well," Sasha answered shyly, "I recently graduated to Rivarin."

"Hey!" Erok yelled, "That is good news! Our Sasha's now a full-blown water weaver now! And hey, the food's here too. Let's celebrate that!" The same waitress who had walked away giggling came over with their trays. She was a small and plump blonde girl. Peppered and grilled pork rose over the smell of roasted vegetables. She gave Sasha her steaming hot tea and Ander some local Brustleberry Wine. As Ander took reached for his cup, he felt something strange. His stomach let out a low rumble as a ravenous hunger filled him at the smell of the pork. "Thanks love," Erok said with a wink, "this food looks almost as good as you." The waitress gave him a wide smile and somehow managed to bend over and place his food down in a sensual way. Ander almost spit out his sweet wine, and turned away, his face bright red. Sasha though gave Erok a dirty look. As soon as the waitress left Sasha asked disgustedly, "Uh, what in the world was that? I didn't take you for a sleaze Erok Noson."

Erok's face darkened ominously. "I'm only having a bit of fun." He spat venomously, "It's not like I forced her to give me that view." Sasha didn't reply, btu the air around the table became uneasy. "W-well why don't we drop it for now?" Ander put in diplomatically, "Erok, please don't hit on anyone else, and Sasha, please don't talk about it. Agreed?" Erok nodded and picked up his mug of ale, while Sasha looked away irritably and muttered, "Fine, as long as he doesn't do it again." Ander let out a small sigh as the mutual truce fell into place and they turned friendly once more.

"So Erok," Ander asked, "What have you done these past five years? All we know is that you and Deboo left one day to, 'find yourself?'" Erok smiled as he leaned back, "Well I hope you two have time for some stories, because I've got the quite the wealth of them now. I suppose I should start with, how I got a job."

"Yes please!" Ander exclaimed, "I really want to know how you went from orphan to…well this." Erok grinned tossed his bangs up with his fingers, "Well, I'm a mercenary now first off."

"No way!" Ander shouted; his eyes full of awe. "Oh yes." Erok replied with a silly grin, "Now granted it wasn't the first job I got after I left. That honor belongs to being a stable boy in the Capitol."

"You've been to the Capitol?" Sasha asked intrigued, now full of some of that same awe. Erok nodded, "Yep. You know how I did odd jobs here and there to make money? Blew all of it on getting there. But the nice thing is that since no one knows that you're from the slums there, getting a job was much easier. So, there I am, working and sleeping in these stables, earing two topazas a day. The only reason I was better off than I had been here was because my master's wife feed me homecooked meals. Anyway, one day I'm in there working, when all of a sudden, a bunch of bandits show up to try and steal the horses. Now, I really liked my master and his family, so I grabbed the pitchfork and told them to get lost."

"Problem was I had forgotten that these guys also had weapons. They drew their swords, and one guy rushed me, thinking it would be easy. I had gained a lot of muscle now by this point, at least a healthy amount, so I stabbed the guy straight in his heart. Unfortunately, I wasn't able to remove it from him fast enough. The other bandits rushed me, so I dropped my only weapon and ran up into the loft, pulling the ladder up behind me. Now luckily for me these guys were not that smart and also blinded by rage. (They pretty much just wanted to kill me rather than steal the horses at this point.) Yet luck was on my side this day. Up in the loft was a crossbow with a full quiver. I knew it was the owners, but I still have no idea why it was up there, and when I asked later, he didn't know either. Anyway, I loaded a bolt in, and shot one of them right between the eyes. Faster than they could react, I loaded more and killed them all, one right after the other. I think they were just in too much shock."

"After I killed them, I was shaking kinda badly form the adrenaline. Then this guy just waltzes in, looks at the bodies, looks up at me and whistles. He calls up to me and says 'I saw that entire thing kid. That was impressive, especially for a stable boy. I was about to come take care of them for you myself. Talent like that would be wasted here. Why don't you come with me? I can show you how to utilize it properly, and I can give you a better offer.' So accepted the guys offer, found out his name was Kyrl, a mercenary. He trained me for five months, got me my first job, and then after that I just started raking in the money."

"Wow," Ander whispered in awe, "that's amazing. You've kept your promise and risen up in the world." Erok nodded with a grin, "Yep, we're equals now, all of us." Sasha just shook her head, "We've always been equals."

"Maybe in your eyes, but not mine." Erok replied solemnly, "But get this, not only I am talented with a crossbow, but it turns out I'm something of a genius." Erok reached over and grabbed the strange crossbow, placing it on the table. There was no string connecting the bent bows. The bows though had indentures on one side, and juts on the other as if they were meant to be connected. "I call this the Shearcraft crossbow, mark one." Erok proclaimed proudly, "You won't find anything else like it in all of Threa. Mainly because I built this myself. You see, you place a cartridge full of bolts at the bottom here. Then it gets loaded into a chamber when you pull this." He pointed to a small handle that looked like it would come straight back at the base. "Then the bolt is placed on this slab here, which flings it forward. The Shearcraft can hold up to eight bolts and shoot up to two hundred yards. The only downside is that I have to make these bolts since nothing else will work."

Ander whistled, thoroughly impressed. Then the three continued to talk and eat. All of a sudden though, Sasha exclaimed, "Ander, you ate all of it?!" Ander paused, looking down at his plate in surprise. He had eaten all of it. When was the last time he had been able to stomach a plate that big? Normally he could only eat a third of a normally sized meal, but the meals here were twice as big. "I guess so." Ander replied. His stomach growled at him, "And I think I'll order seconds." Erok's jaw dropped, but he quickly closed it and beamed, "Well look at that! You're finally becoming healthy!" Ander just smiled but didn't say anything. Honestly, he was a little worried. One did not just all of sudden become ravished like this in one day, right? Erok pulled aside another waitress, ordered more food for Ander, and when that plate arrived, he gobbled down that one also. The three friends though talked and talked, sharing anecdotes from the past five years. After about an hour, the clock in the bar chimed loudly nine times.

"Oh no!" Sasha yelped as she stood up, "It's late! I better get him or dad's going to be mad!"

"Ah," Erok winked, "your old man still worries about you having a naughty night life huh?" Sasha puffed out her cheeks indignantly her face turning a pale shade of red, "You know full well that's not the case!" Erok just sipped some ale and said, "Alright, whatever you say." Sasha just shook her head as she walked away, her face still red, "Well, I'll see you guys later." After she left, Erok got up and stretched. "Well, I better get going too. I was a long journey here, plus Deboo is probably getting anxious without me."

"O-oh okay." Ander said. He got up and looked away rubbing his wrist, "So, um, will you be here tomorrow?" Erok paused and looked over at him in surprise, "Of course. You didn't think I would just show up here and take off after only one day, did you? I need to spend some time with my best friend!" Ander smiled weakly and looked away embarrassed, "Well, you've changed, so I was a little worried I guess."

"I haven't changed that much." Erok replied gently, "So don't think about it too much. Well, I'll see you tomorrow!" Ander gave him a wave as he left, and said to himself, "Yeah, see you tomorrow." Ander sighed as he made his way downstairs. Now that everyone had left, there was no excuse not to return home by now. Hopefully his father wound not hear about his defeat until tomorrow. Ander ran his hand over the master-full railing as he walked down the stairs and made his way the door. As he was passing the counter, all of a sudden someone leapt from their stool and moved in front of him. Ander stepped back surprised, and at the same time a sinking horror fell upon him as he realized the person was Tam Iroas. "Well, well, who do we have here?" Tam asked gleefully, "The Violeter toddler at the bar drinking away his shame? What did you try and get some milk from your mommy? Oh wait, she wouldn't even give you the milk from her own breasts!"

Tam burst out into a vulgar roar of laughter, a few of his friends chuckling a little uncomfortably. "Can you please move Tam?" Ander asked politely, "I just want to leave." Tam just crossed his arms with a raised eyebrow, "Why, too afraid to stand up for yourself? You just going to accept my insult and leave!" Ander backed up a bit and replied, "W-well, I just don't want any trouble." Ander started to try and walk around him, but Tam snatched his hand and pulled him close. "You should've thought of that before you made a fool of me back at the tournament." Tam growled, "Because of you, the judges allowed my opponent to cheat! I lost to someone weaker than me, and it's all your fault!" Ander looked more closely at Tam and saw that his cheeks were flushed, and his eyes were red and puffy. "I'm sorry," Ander apologized meekly, "but I don't know if that was in my control." Tam twisted his arm. Ander let out a yelp and whimpered, "Ow, please stop, that hurts."

"You know what pisses me off the most about you Ander Dyon?" Tam snarled, "Your cowardice and readiness to just roll over and accept anything! And somehow you actually got people to pity you more than you do today!" Tam lifted Ander off the ground by his arm. Ander quickly looked around, looking for any possible help. Yet Johnathan was nowhere to be seen and all the customers near him were either jeering at him also or pointedly looking away. Ander's hope was extinguished and as Tam raised his fist back, he resigned himself to another painful fate. He was used to these types of beatings by this point. He closed his eyes. He found that if he didn't see the hit coming, it usually hurt less. Darkness surrounded him, but no pain punctured it.

Ander frowned as he opened his eyes, which quickly shot wide open. Everyone nearby was silent, for a man was holding Tam's wrist. "The herk old man!" Tam yelled, "What's your deal! Let go of me!" The man in front of them was tall, well over six feet. He was well toned and obviously had a very strong grip, for Tam was struggling to shake him off of him. He also looked to be at least fifty. He wore a sliver shirt and vest with tan pants and a brown duster. He wore a strange brown leather hat that looked sun worn. He had a sun-weathered face and long tangly brown hair and a close-trimmed beard with gray in it. The man's dark brown eyes glared menacingly at Tam as he said, "For a city so obsessed with honor and glory, not many of ya actually live up to it. Now, I'm gonna count ta three, and if ya haven't dropped the kid, your wrist is going out commission. One, two…"

Ander fell to the ground and sat staring up at the man in shock. The old man grunted in surprise, and turned around, sitting down at a stool and grabbing his lone mug of beer. Tam's face though curled into a snarl as he glared at this strange old man. Tam's nearby friends stood up, a few of them cracking their knuckles. Ander began to rub his wrist vigorously. Tam's friends might not approve of what he did, but they were loyal to a fault. The old man though didn't even turn around to face them, seeming to be completely oblivious to them. As Tam approached the old man, Ander noticed a lot of customers became uneasy and looked worried. But something was strange about their attitude. To Ander, it seemed as if they were worried for Tam and his friends. "What's your name old man." Tam asked with mock politeness. "Joshua." The old man grunted. The bystanders let out a mutter and someone said, "Don't do it Tam!" But Tam ignored them and roared, "Thanks old man!" Tam swung his fist at Joshua's face and there was a loud slap as the man's face snapped to the side. Joshua held his head in the same position and rubbed his cheek, "Welp, guess that's three." Joshua said. Then as quick as a viper, he snatched Tam's wrist and broke it. Tam howled as he fell to his knees.

"Get him!' One of Tam's friends cried. Joshua sighed as he stood up, with his mug of beer still in his hand, "Herking kids." Ander watched in awe as Joshua kicked up his stool with one foot and sent it flying into three of the goons. Two of the others rushed at him, one swinging at his head and another at his kidney. Joshua casually caught the one by going for his head by the wrist and swung him in the path of his friend. The man let out a gasp as he received the horribly painful punch. Joshua then shoved them to the ground and knocked out his friend with a kick to the head. "Look out!" Ander cried as the three from earlier stood up cursing. Joshua took a swig of his beer, before he threw it straight up into the air. Ander looked up, guessing it was almost touching the ceiling of the third floor.

The first goon stepped up, only to have his ears clapped and his groin kicked. The man fell with a howl. The mug was now falling. The other two stepped up, one aiming a kick at Joshua's stomach. He caught the man by the leg, and before the man could try and escape, lifted him off the ground. He then proceeded to swing the man around and throw him into the last guy, before sticking his hand out and catching his mug. Joshua chugged the rest of the beer and gasped, "Ah, not a single drop gone." Ander looked at the old man with admiration. Who the heck was this guy? Joshua simply turned around and sat back down. There was some laughter from the crowd as they shook their heads at all the men groaning in pain on the floor.

Ander smiled and stood up, brushing the dirt from his clothes. As he was about to leave, he noticed Tam was staring daggers at Joshua, and snarling soundlessly. Ander watched in horror as Tam pulled out a knife and rushed at Joshua. At that moment, he felt something strange enter him, something primal feeling. Anger welled up inside of him as he rushed at Tam without thinking. Ander let out a howl as he threw a punch at the man's chest. Tam looked over in surprise just in time to see Ander punch him square in the chest. Joshua turned around, reaching for his belt but looked surprised to see Tam fly through the air past him. Ander felt bones crunch underneath the skin as his punch made contact. Tam went soaring and crashed into the wall behind the counter. He slumped to the ground soundlessly.

Ander was breathing ragged and erratically. He looked around, his heart beating fast and his whole body in a numb shock. Everyone was staring at him silently in shock, but Joshua looked at him curiously. Ander tucked his head down and ran out. Something weird had happened there. He had felt his arm grow *bigger and hairier*. He ran outside, confused as he entered the moonlit streets.

Chapter 11

A Feral Awakening

The lamplights glowed with an unnatural light, casting a warm glow upon a silver street. The fire elemental stone inside the post flickered as the energy inside it was slowly consumed. Ander passed a lamper climbing up to one and replacing a stone. The woman saw him and gave him a friendly wave. Ander just held up his hand in return and plastered a smiled on his face. As soon as he was out of sight, he slumped down, dragging his feet as he made his way home. He had been putting off this moment ever since the tournament had ended.

Ander Dyon's relation to his parents was far from what one would call ideal. Hardly any love was shown to him, from both his mother and father. Russ and Maria Dyon were accomplished soldiers, accumulating great wealth and glory during their time. Russ had become Captain of the Guard at the remarkable age of nineteen, and his then sweetheart had been his second in command. Both of them had been well respected for not only their skills, but also for their defense of the city during the siege of Edeaven. A battle which his parents had led the city to victory, being outnumbered thirty to one. The Guard had never seen their like before, and probably never would again. But for Ander, he was glad that there had not been anyone like them since.

So it was with a heavy heart that Ander came to the center of the Emerald District and stopped in front of Dyon Manor. The manor was spectacular looking with three floors and almost as large a large lawn. It loomed above most of the other expensive houses in the area too. Ander quietly walked up to the ten-foot-tall rosewood doors and tried to open them quietly. Unfortunately, they sounded like thunder as he opened them. Ander winced as he walked in. At least everyone on the first two floors would know that he had come in. Ander's heart dropped as he finally looked around him. The main foyer wasn't even empty. Servants bustled about the place, finishing up their jobs for the day. A few of them had paused to look at him, but quickly resumed their tasks. The head servant though, one Doyce Patterson, stood at the top of the grand staircase surveying everything. He spotted Ander and beckoned him to come up.

Ander dragged his feet up the stairs with his head held low. "Young master," Doyce said once he reached him, "Welcome home. Your father though is awaiting you in his study." Ander sighed and nodded, turning to head up to the third floor. Before he had even taken two steps though, the middle-aged man called out to him. "You know, you could wait to see him? He...he doesn't seem to be in the best of moods right now." Ander turned around and smiled at Doyce, "Thanks, but it'll only be worse if I put him off." Ander turned and climbed up the stairs and muttered, "Besides, when is he ever happy?"

The wheel of fate spun, and Ander's fate became set as he entered the hallway and stopped in front of his father's study. Ander gave a light rapping of his knuckles against the door. "Come." Russ's muffled voice called form within. Ander opened the door and walked in. Large bookcases lined the walls, with hundreds of untouched books filling them. Behind the stately desk that his father sat behind, (his chair currently not facing him) was the armor of the city guard. Black plate armor with golden gauntlets, boots, and a gold stripe over the waist. A golden eight-point star marked the brow of the helm, indicating it as the armor of the Captain of the Guard. The normal armor of the guards was black with a golden stripe at the waist, but this armor had been specially made for his father. Ander's eyebrow twitched like it did every time he saw it. It was so ostentatious, yet he could not deny that it looked incredible. Russ did not deserve it. "Sit down son." Russ said quietly. Ander obeyed and took a seat as Russ spun his chair around. Russ had short dark brown, and close-cut beard that was mostly gray. He still had the body of a solider and his brown eyes still had the hardness of a soldier to them. "So," Russ began coolly, "I assume the reason your home so late is because you were out celebrating?" Ander stiffened slightly. *He doesn't know then!* Ander looked up at his father and nodded, "Yeah, we went to the Brandyshire and celebrated. I may not have won the tournament but I did win a few-"

"HOW DARE YOU LIE TO ME!" Russ roared, "Do you take me for a fool?! I was there to watch you! Not only did you lose but you had to have Kyoko rescue you! You two rely upon each other too much!" Ander shrank back under his father's fury and whimpered, "I'm sorry father. I did my best! I almost won though." Russ's face darkened and his face stilled into a dark, calm anger. "Almost is not good enough. Now, are you going to tell me the truth about why you were at the Brandyshire, or are you going to lie to me again?" Ander shrank into his chair, wishing it could absorb him and he could just disappear. "Sasha and I went there because Erok came back, and we wanted to see him again." Russ narrowed his eyes and leapt to his feet. "Erok! I thought I told you to end your useless friendship with that lowlife!" Russ yelled.

"But he's a mercenary now dad!" Ander protested, "He had a job and is now well respected!" Russ slapped Ander across the face. Ander winced and held his stinging cheek with one hand. "I don't care what he is now." Russ growled, "Once a lowlife, always a lowlife. Especially with who his mother was. But do you have any idea how humiliating your performance was for me? The son of the most talented Captain, losing to Tam of all people! People already think you're a useless person, and now you're proving it!!! Do you have any idea how that makes me look?!"

"I'm sorry father." Ander quietly whimpered, "I don't want to make you look bad."

"Then try harder." Russ growled. Ander kept his cheek cupped and looked at his father out of the corner of his eyes. Russ was staring at him, his brow furrowed in contemplation. "Maybe I should give you some motivation to try harder." Russ muttered, "No matter what I do, you never seem to try your hardest. Maybe I should separate you and your sister." Ander felt his heart stop. "What?" He whispered incredulously, "No, you wouldn't." Russ started down at him, his eyes cold and devoid of any warmth. "You never try. Maybe if your sister wasn't here to distract you, we could get some results. Say, you finally win a tournament and then you can see each other again. Maybe at least once a year."

"NO! DON'T TAKE ME AWAY FROM ANDER!" Russ and Ander spun around in surprise to see Kyoko burst into the room. "Kyoko!" Russ shouted, "Were you listening in on us?!" Kyoko ran up to Ander and grabbed his arm, burying her face into his side. "Don't let him take me!" Kyoko sobbed. Ander stood up and hugged Kyoko. "Please father," Ander pleaded, "don't do this. I'll work thrice as hard, just don't separate us." Russ stopped, staring at them. His eyes softened, and a deep pain shone in his eyes. Ander's heart skipped a beat. Was it true? Was his father finally going to show some compassion? Russ walked up to him and knelt down. "Oh you kids." Russ whispered, before backhanding Ander across the face. The room spun, stars flashing across his vision as he hit the ground hard. "WHY CAN'T YOU JUST EVER DO AS I SAY!" Russ screamed, "Why do you always question and disobey me! I'm your father, and what I say goes!" Ander started to stand up, but Russ kicked him in the stomach, sending him flying into the wall. Ander let out a gasp as his body bounced off and he slid to the ground. "All that training, and you just sit there and let me do this to you." Russ growled as he calmly walked over to him. Ander lifted his head and with half closed eyes, saw Kyoko watching in horror. Russ then began to kick him in the ribs. Ander fell on the floor and curled into a fetal position.

Russ stood over him and began to repeatedly kick him. "Come on. Get up!" Russ yelled hysterically, "Get up and show me that spirit to try that you boldly just said you would have. Show me how hard you're going to try!" Come one you worthless boy! STAND UP!" Ander just stayed curled up, his whole-body aching. The pain seemed to immobilize his will to move. "Stop!" Kyoko pleaded, "Dad, what are you doing? Please stop! That's Ander you're hurting please s-aaaah!" There was a loud smack and the kicking stopped all of a sudden. Ander opened his eyes and saw Kyoko lying on the floor. "Shut up." Russ said quietly, "You're annoying me. Stay on the ground." Kyoko looked weakly up at Russ in shock and slowly tried to push herself up, "Dad?" Russ spun around and slammed Kyoko's face into the floor. "I thought I ordered you not to get up!" Russ yelled. Kyoko made not a sound as Russ lifted her up. She hung in the air limply. "Kyoko?" Ander whispered meekly. Then he noticed. Blood dripped down from her head. "You kids are so damn selfish." Russ muttered as he set Kyoko gently down on the ground. He turned to Ander, "Look what you made me do. Now I must go and get her looked at."

Ander pushed himself to his feet, blood roaring in his ears. Russ turned and looked at him in surprise. "What, you're finally getting up?" Red hot anger coursed through his veins. "Shut. Up." Ander growled. Russ raised an eyebrow at him, "Excuse me? What did you say?" Something inside of him had awoken as he saw his sister bleed. "I said. Shut. The herk. Up." For seventeen years Ander had endured this, but as he looked at his father standing over Kyoko's unconscious and bleeding body, he had found his limit. "You brat, how dare you-"

"NO!" Ander roared, "How dare you! How dare you stand there and hurt your own daughter! How dare you call us selfish and worthless, when the most damn selfish and worthless bastard is standing right here in front of me!" Russ glowered as his whole body shook with rage. He moved forward and threw a punch at Ander. Ander dodged and punched his father in the gut. Russ barely grunted as his picked him up and threw him against a bookcase. Glass shattered, sprinkling around him as he hit. Russ walked over to him. Ander tried to stand but slipped on the broken glass and cut his palm. Slick blood covered his hand and Ander let out a small yell at the pain. Russ snorted, "Pathetic, one ounce of pain and you give up." Russ punched him in the face, knocking his head back. *I am pathetic.* Ander thought, *I can't even land a single blow on him. What was I thinking? I can't do anything.*

Maybe so, a small voice said in the back of his mind, *but that did not stop Erok did it? A boy with less and harder circumstances. He rose up and fought back against this world! And you? Are you going to let some old man beat you and get away with hurting your sister? You're a weak hunter if you let the prey win.* Ander stared at his father who was looking down at him disappointedly. "Here I thought you had finally found your fighting spirit." Russ said with a shake of his head, "Guess I was wrong." Ander swabbed his tongue around his mouth, tasting blood. He spit out some blood and said, "Don't count me out yet *father.*" Russ frowned as Ander leapt to his feet, a newfound strength surging through him. A raw power coursed through his muscles, his blood, his very soul! It felt the same way it did back at the bar. Time slowed down almost to a standstill as in his mind's eye, he saw a wolf with purple eyes. It looked him straight in the eyes and grinned before disappearing. Time resumed as Ander leapt at his father, acting without thinking as a sort of primal instinct took hold of him.

Ander wrapped his hand around Russ's throat. As his fingers closed around the exposed neck, his body began to morph. His arms grew larger and dark grey hair began to sprout and cover his body. His hands became padded and clawed. His mouth grew longer, and his teeth became sharper and longer. His ears went to the top of his head and became triangular. His legs become bowed, and his eyesight became sharper. Russ's eyes became wide with horror as he watched his son transform into a giant, humanoid wolf. "I thought I told you," Ander said, his voice deeper and more guttural, "to shut up." Ander spun and threw Russ into the bookcases. Glass went everywhere as Russ was flung against them with such force that the bookcase broke and caved in. There was a loud tumbling of books and a quick shout from Russ. Ander waited, but Russ did not get back up. He lay there, unmoving. Ander's heart leapt in panic as he ran over and checked Russ's pulse.

He let out a sigh of relief as he found out that he was still alive. That was when Ander saw himself in the broken glass. He stumbled back in shock, looking down at his claws and arms. "W-what the herk is going on!" Ander exclaimed in fear. "Wait, Ander?" Ander spun around and saw Kyoko staring at him, her eyes wide. "Ander, what happened? What did you do to dad?" Then the door was flung open, and there were a bunch of servants clustered around the door. "Master? Is everything alright?" One of them asked, "We heard a loud crashing and—MONSTER!" The servants screamed as they turned and ran at the sight of Ander. "Wait, it's just Ander!" Kyoko shouted. "Brother, just tell them it's you!" Ander started at Kyoko, before turning to the door and running. His hear pumping wildly. His mind raced, wild and full of fear. "Wait, big brother!" Kyoko shouted, but Ander ignored her as he ran out the door. Crazed and scared, Ander ran down the stairs, passing by screaming servants. He burst out the doors and ran into the night, his body full of tense power and lean strength. He used this new body to propel himself across the city, running on all fours, heading to the only spot he could think of. As he reached the Eastern Wall, he leapt straight up, and flew over the wall. He heard some cries of surprise from the guards as he soared over their heads. Ander hit the ground with barely a jolt and took off running into the woods.

Erok jolted upright, throwing his bedsheets off of him. The loud bonging of the warning bells could be heard faintly in the distance. It grew louder and louder as each district set their bells off. *Aw herking herk.* Erok thought as he leapt out of bed and grabbed his Shearcraft and cloak. He was glad he had slept in his clothes. Erok ran down the stairs, almost falling as he stumbled upon the last step. Damn beer, why did it have to have such adverse effects? Erok walked into the common room, which was in absolute chaos. People were running about talking and yelling. Erok groaned put a hand to his head at the noise.

Erok finally spotted the innkeeper, and grabbed the man's arm, "Hey, what's going on?"

"We're not really sure." The man replied, "Apparently some sort of monster attacked the Dyon Manor! Mr. Russ is in critical condition and the children are missing. People are saying he fell in defense of his kids." Erok grabbed the man by the collar, pulling him close, "What? The kids are missing?!" The man nodded, obviously confused, "Yes. We think the monster kidnapped them. It ran off into the woods-hey where are you going?!" Erok ignored the man and threw open the door, rushing out towards the stable. No way that asshole would protect his kids to where he would almost die. But…still, something was wrong. Erok's heart beat in time with the music of fear that played in him. Erok threw open the stable doors and ran up to the giant owlbear sitting by the other horses. "We need to go Debboo." Erok said. "Can you pick up Ander's scent?" Debboo let out an affirmative screech and walked out of the stable. Erok hopped on top his companion's back, the navy feathered and grey furred animal sticking its beak into the air, sniffing. Then Debboo let out a triumphant screech right before he took off running at a breakneck speed.

"Come on buddy!" Erok encouraged. The two traveled across the city, the green light of the moon in its life stage shining down upon them. As they neared the wall, two people ran out in front of them. "WHOA!" Erok shouted and pulled up on Debboo's reigns. "What the herk is wrong with you peo-oh shit. Hi Sasha." Sasha looked up at him, her arms crossed, and an eyebrow raised, Kyoko standing next to her. "Want to try that again?" Erok cleared his throat, his cheeks turning slightly red, "Not really." He muttered, before saying louder, "What the heck are you guys doing out here? I heard Kyoko was kidnapped by some sort of monster, along with Ander!"

"I wasn't!" Kyoko yelled, "And neither was my brother! He, well, something's wrong with him and he ran off into the woods!" Erok raised his eyebrow and looked over at Sasha. "She came to me right before the alarms went off." Sasha explained, "I'm not sure what's going on, but all I know is that Kyoko is telling us what she saw. So, whatever is going on, we should find him." Erok sighed, shaking his head. He pointed back and said, "Well then, come on. Let's go get him then. Debboo's already got his scent." Sasha nodded as she picked up Kyoko, placing her behind Erok before climbing on top herself. "Wait, does this mean that monster, Ander, attacked your dad?" Erok asked suddenly. Kyoko nodded. "Dad...I, well—I mean..." Erok shook his head, "Don't worry about it Kyo. Just glad that bastard got what he deserved finally. Now, hold on tight!" Erok commanded and kicked Debboo's side. Debboo let out a small cry as they took off. Once they got to the wall, the owlbear leapt from house to house, using their roofs to get continually higher. Debboo finally leapt onto the wall, and they ran across it, passing by some very startled and surprised guards. A few of them let out some halting cries, but they ignored them. Finally, they reached the east wall, but as they did, Debboo halted all of a sudden, and began to paw the ground, like he was warning an enemy. "What is it buddy?" Erok asked concerned.

"Wait, where are the guards?" Sasha asked. Erok stopped and realized that Sasha was right. The usual lamplight of the guards was missing. Then to his right he heard a soft hissing. Erok turned just in time to see a Sarmanthian spider leap at him from over the wall. Quick as a viper, Erok pulled his knife from his sheath and leapt off of Debboo. He flew over the spider and stabbed it right in the head. The creature landed right on Debboo's side. Kyoko let out a scream as she finally noticed it. Debboo looked at the dead spider lazily before smacking it off the wall. "Everyone okay?" Erok asked. Kyoko shakily nodded, and while Sasha seemed slightly flustered, she nodded also. Erok nodded and moved towards Debboo, but his foot kicked something metal with a loud clang. Erok looked down and muttered, "Damn, I guess I found where the guards are." Dead bodies covered the ground. The faces were half melted and covered in frost the glistened and rose like a mist into the night air. Now that Erok had noticed, he could smell the metallic scent of blood, and saw that many of the bodies were missing limbs. "Come on." Erok said, "We need to find Ander quick."

"Wait," Kyoko protested, "What about everyone in the city? They don't know about this!" Erok sighed as he climbed onto Debboo, "It looks like this was a contained attack, so everyone else shouldn't have anything to worry about. Besides, we need to find your brother now that we know these spiders are back."

"But-"

"Well tell them on our way back!" Erok groaned, "You happy?" Kyoko nodded, looking pleased with herself. "Stupid Dyons." Erok muttered as they leapt off the wall and took off into the woods, "You always are trying to make me act noble."

Ander sat with his arms hugged around his legs, his face buried in them. He sat next to the pond within his little hideaway. He lifted his head, trying to take comfort in the scenery. The water sparkled in the moonlight, but the green light gave it an almost eerie look. A cool summer's night breeze blew across him, giving him the calming scent of all the flowers. His breathing was finally returning to normal, and his panic slowly fading. His body was back to normal. He had transformed back almost as soon as he had sat down. *What in the sweet name of Threa is happening to me?* Ander thought, *I've never heard of anything like this before. What the herk is this?* Ander looked down at his hand, turning it over. Not a trace of a wolf's paw remained, yet in the back of his mind, Ander could *feel* something lurking, waiting to be free. *What kind of monster is in me?* Ander pondered, *And can I even go back home?* Ander remembered the anger, the animalistic rage that had been in him. A storm that he could not control. What if it happened again, but this time to someone he actually cared about? Erok, Sasha, or worse, Kyoko?

Ander clenched his fist, no, he could not go back. Too many people could get hurt if he did. Then, he heard rustling from the brush. He turned and looked towards it but froze. His arms turned to jelly, and his legs would not move as he saw three Saromanthian spiders slowly approaching him. As big as a grown man and green leathery skin as hard as iron, these spiders could strike fear into most anyone with a single violet glare. As Ander stayed in place, frozen by fear, deep in the back of his mind he almost hysterically thought, *Well, I don't know what you expected, coming out into the woods this late.*

Ander finally found his voice and shouted, "S-stay back! Don't come any closer!" The spiders stopped, and then Ander noticed something that made his heart stop. Atop two of the spiders were children. A boy and girl, looking to be about eight or nine, wrapped in blue webbing, their mouths covered by it. Yet their eyes were uncovered, and he could see the soul-piercing terror that was in them. The spiders began to click and snap at each other, before turning around. Ander breathed a sigh of relief as they ignored him, but his heart felt heavy as they left. The children began to scream, through their muffled mouths, and one of them sounded on the verge of tears. "I'm sorry," Ander whispered tears forming in his own eyes, "but I can't help you. I'm useless."

Hmph, a deep throated voice snorted, *this is the newest Vessel we must serve?* Ander looked around startled, but he could not figure out where the voice was coming from. "Who's there!" Ander shouted. Yes, it is a little disappointing, isn't it? A prim sounding voice replied, *I was really hoping this boy would prove more courageous!*

What the heck is going on?! Ander thought as he spun in circles, trying to discover the source of the voices. Then he finally noticed something strange. The spiders were frozen in mid motion. *Hmph, I think the kid can be.* A deep, gruff voice said, but not as deep as the one before. *He just needs to learn and grow.* "Who are you people!" Ander shouted hysterically, "Stop talking like I can't hear you!" There was laughing from all three voices before the first one he had heard said, *Sorry kid, but we had to freak you out. Especially since you were going to leave those kids. We are the Triamal, the Life of Valoria, and warriors against Death.*

Ander's head began to spin, and he fell to the ground. "The Triamal? You mean, *the Triamal?*" Ander got the strangest sensation of a creature, not a human, nodding at him. *That's right,* the second voice said, *and we have the unfortunate privilege of serving you as the next Vessel.* Ander shook his head in befuddlement. It all felt too dreamlike. "But how am I the

Vessel?" All of a sudden, the voices became more sustainable than they had been. *That is a story for another time kid.* The first voice said, *For now, you need to make a choice. Will you grasp the power before you, and save these children, or will you run away like the coward you are? Make your choice now!*

Ander felt a jarring sensation and heard the spiders scuttling away, and the children's muffled cries for help. Ander got to his feet, and found his body was no longer shaking. Plenty of fear still resided within his heart, but something else was there, overpowering the fear. "I will save them!" Ander shouted. Three faces appeared around him and nodded. It was so quick and brief, that he did not get a good look at them, but he knew they were animal faces. *Then let the world hear our unified cry!* The voices said in unison. A phantasmal coin appeared in Ander's hand. On one side it had a wolf, and on the other, some type of fish. Ander flipped it on instinct and caught it. The wolf side was facing up. Ander ran at the spiders and as he did, he felt his body begin to change once more. All of a sudden, he was leaping on a spider with four times the strength of a wolf.

His claws ripped through the skin like butter, and it let out an unnatural screech as it's face was ripped apart. Ander picked it up and threw it against a tree, where it seized to move. The other two began to click menacingly at him, their violet eyes full of calculated malice. Ander howled at them, and the howl sounded like five wolves howling in unison. The spiders shrank under the howl, which allowed Ander to blind them with two quick swipes. The screeched and began to spit out green blobs of venom randomly. With the precision and grace of a predator, Ander leapt over them, cutting the webbing binding the kids to the spiders with one hand, and grabbing them with the other. Then with his hind claws, Ander kicked down, cutting into the brains. The spiders stilled and Ander set the children down, his body reverting to normal. He paused, surprised at his own skill. It seemed all those training days had not been in vain after all. *A body must have the energy to carry out such skills.* One of the voices remarked, a hint of praise in his voice.

"Ander!" Erok yelled. Ander spun around in surprise, seeing Erok, Kyoko, and Sasha all riding Debboo towards him. All three dismounted and ran over to him. Kyoko tackled him with a hug, nearly knocking him over. "Don't ever leave me like that again!" Kyoko yelled, tears in her eyes. Ander bent over and hugged her back and whispered, "Don't worry, I won't." He looked over at Sasha who was smiling at him, but there was an inquisitive look in her eyes. *Oh no, how do I even begin...* Luckily, before either of the girls could ask, Erok yelled, "Holy shit Ander! What in the herking herk happened here?"

"I'll explain later." Ander said, "For now, can you help me free these kids?" Erok nodded and pulled out a knife and began to cut the children free. As soon as they were freed, the kids began to sob. Sasha ran up to them and hugged them, caressing and comforting them. "Shush now." Sasha whispered, "It's okay now, you guys are safe."

"Alright, you've got some explaining to do." Erok said, "Like why you left, what happened at your house, and how the herk you killed *three Sarmanthian Spiders by yourself and unarmed*!?"

"Well, that's uh, a bit of a story." Ander replied evasively.

"Well, start talking then." Erok replied with a raised eyebrow. Ander sighed and took a deep breath. Right as he opened his mouth though, Kyoko shouted, "Spiders!"

"Shit." Erok cursed under his breath, "Fine then! Make my night better why don't you! Ander, help Sasha keep the kids safe. Kyoko, create a wind barrier to stop venom from hitting them!" Ander looked over to see five spiders emerge from the darkness. "Hold one shouldn't we talk about this?" Ander asked meekly. Erok pointed his right arm up at a tree, a grappling hook on it. "We already have!" Erok shot into the air, landing on top of a branch. Erok shot two and cursed as a clicking sound could be heard. He reloaded before nailing the other three in the head. Ander shook himself out of his stupor and turned and ran to Sasha and Kyoko. Seven more spiders emerged. "They keep coming!" Ander shouted. "Yeah, I herking know!" Erok shouted back as he killed five of them.

Ander rushed at them, willing for the coin to appear again, but nothing happened. Ander let out a small curse as the remaining two leapt at his sister. Kyoko shrieked but watched as wind slices cut off the spiders' legs. They fell to the ground, looking a little confused right before Debboo grabbed them. With a roar he ripped them in half, tossing the corpses away. "Thanks, Debboo." Kyoko said weakly. Yet the nightmare wasn't over yet. More and more spiders began to emerge, clicking and hissing at them. "Oh, *come* on!" Erok moaned, "How many of these things are trying to kill us?" Ander shrugged and then turned to Debboo and said, "Debboo! Can you get these children back to the city?" Debboo let out an affirmative screech and gently scooped up the children, who were staring around with fear. The owlbear then took off running towards the city. "Well, this is a fine mess we're in. I suppose we could try and run?" Sasha said. Ander nodded mutely. "We need to kill as many as we can." Kyoko protested, "Remember the guards who died? I bet these ones are headed for the city."

"Herk, you're probably right." Erok muttered as he landed next to them. The spiders were now slowly trying to enclose them. "Fine, I guess we can play exterminators tonight." Erok spent the rest of his clip, killing eight that had gotten to close. Some other spiders spat their venom at them, but Kyoko's wind wall blocked it. They watched the green spit just fall to the ground. "Ander, since you're light on your feet, try and distract them so we can get some good openings." Ander gave an unsteady smile, "Glady." Sasha stretched out her hands and a watery whip appeared in both.

Ander charged at the spiders, and as he did, he heard Erok mutter, "Heh, and you said you hadn't changed." Erok unleashed a volley of bolts at the spiders, killing eight while Ander heard the cracking of a whip the whooshing of wind. Ander ran in between all the spiders, whopping and shouting, generally trying to make noise and get their attention. It worked, and a little too well. All of a sudden, he had at least twenty spiders with their attention on him. Ander ducked as they spit at him and heading the sizzling sound of melting flesh as the spiders hit each other. For what felt like hours, the four fought like this. Ander had never been in such prime form before, nimbly moving about and avoiding attacks with a reaction speed he had never shown before. His entire body felt heightened.

The sickly scent of blood soon filled the air, weighing down heavily on them with noxious smell. Yet no matter how many they killed, more kept coming. "Guys, try get up here with me!" Erok finally called out. Ander turned and ran towards the tree Erok was in. "Duck!" Kyoko yelled. Ander hit the ground without even thinking and as he stood back up, there was a cracking noise and a thunderous crash as the tree Erok had been in fell to the ground. Sizzling green goo glowed at the cracks, the split tree now freezing over. "Erok!" Sasha screamed. Kyoko landed from above and held out her hands in front of her. Suddenly the air around them stiffened and became stale. "I just formed a barrier around us!" Kyoko said, "I won't be able to keep it up for long. Go check on Erok."

Ander nodded, "Thanks sis." Sasha and Ander ran over and began to search the fallen tree, and finally found Erok. He was lying underneath a thick branch. "Erok!" Ander yelled, "Are you okay?"

"No," Erok groaned, "I think my legs are broken, maybe a few ribs, and my legs are stuck. So, herking heshatnus get me the herk out!"

"Hold on," Ander said, "I'll try and get you out." Ander began to try and lift the branch up, but it was just too heavy. "Damn it." Ander exclaimed, "I can't lift it."

"Look out!" Erok screamed. Ander spun around to see a spider leap on him. He heard Sasha shout, but then fall down. She must not have been able to summon any magic. Ander fell to the ground, the spider on top of him. He grabbed it by its pincers, desperately trying to keep it off of him. The spider bore down on him though, slowly growing nearer to him. "I won't let you hurt them." Ander snarled and *pushed*. As he did, he saw the coin appear next to him. A sudden strength filled his body and rolled, tossing the spider to the side. Ander grabbed the phantom coin and flipped it. This time, there was a bird face him when he caught it. *Oh my, now the hunt begins.* The prim voice said with satisfaction. Ander felt his body transform once more.

His arms elongated and grew feathers, turning into black wings. His mouth became a beak and his feet talons. His eyes turned red, and his vision grew clear, and he could make out the tiniest of hairs upon the spiders. Ander flapped his wings and darted at his foe and clawed the spider in half with his razor-sharp talons. "Ander?" Sasha asked in wonder. "Yeah, it's me." Ander replied, his voice sounding similar to the second voice he had heard. He then flew over and lifted the branch off of Erok. "Kyoko! Take down the barrier. I got this." Ander yelled. Kyoko was looking back at him, and jolted out her shock as she nodded before running over to Erok. Ander soared high into the air, before dive bombing some of the spiders. His claws sank deep into one's head, and he clutched and flew high up into the air, before performing a loop, and throwing the body down at the last minute.

It hit the ground with such force that it created a small shockwave. A dust cloud covered the ground, but this proved no problem to Ander. He could see easily through the cloud. Ander flew down and grazed across tens of spiders, purple blood flying through the air behind him. Ander flew through four times, killing about maybe forty of them total. He then flew up high out of range of the venom and hovered, looking around the forest. "This is the last of them!" Ander cried out, "I don't see any more coming!"

"Stay at that height then!" He heard Sasha shout, "Kyoko and I are going to do something!" Ander watched as a huge gust of wind gathered all the spiders into one spot, and then he saw Sasha perform the move she had shown him earlier that day. Only the droplets were far bigger this time. Then, the water froze and formed into daggers of ice. Ander watched as a hailstorm of ice ran down upon the spiders. Anytime they tried to run away, they were blown backwards right into the deadly rainfall. In a matter of mere seconds, all of the Sarmanthian spiders finally lay upon the ground, silent and unmoving.

Ander landed, transforming back to normal. "Sasha, Kyoko that was incredibl-"Ander stopped as he caught Sasha. "Sasha! How much did you use?" Kyoko asked. Sasha grinned at them, "It was worth it though. Think of all the people we saved." Ander nodded, and asked, "Can you stand?"

"I think so." Sasha replied as Ander helped her to her feet. Sasha wobbled for a moment before stabilizing. Ander let go of her and then turned to Erok. "Don't even think about trying to help me up." Erok said. "My legs are for sure broken. Just wait for Debboo." As if right on cue, the great owlbear emerged from the woods, but there was a man on his back. "Whoa there, big boy." The man said, "Look like we're here." As Ander took in the man's wild appearance, he realized he knew who this was. "Hold on, you're that guy who helped me at the Brandyshire!" Joshua nodded as he dismounted, grunting, "Heh, good memory kid. Didn't think you would remember." As Debboo walked over and picked Erok up, Erok asked, "Alright, so you know this old geezer?"

"Watch it kid." Joshua growled, "The name's Joshua Rickstone, and you may only address me that way."

"I'll address someone who rides Debboo without permission however the herk I want!" Erok spat back. Joshua raised his eyebrow, "Spunky one, aren't ya? Well, the owlbear let me ride him so I'm not sure who you should be angry at." Debboo squawked in agreement which made Erok mutter, "Fine, I guess it's okay." Ander cracked a smile, and then started to giggle. Suddenly, everyone was full blown laughing. They laughed and laughed unit they could not anymore, their sides hurting. As they finished, Joshua muttered, "Damn kids are crazy. Now why did I come here again? To confirm something, remember? Ah yes, mighty kind of ya." Ander and Sasha looked at each other unnerved. "Um, are you okay?" Sasha asked cautiously.

"Why wouldn't I be?" Joshua asked confused. Sasha and Ander slowly moved in front of Kyoko as Sasha replied, "Oh, no reason." Joshua shook his head and turned to Ander and barked, "Hey kid! You're the Triamal, aren't ya?" Ander stepped back and stammered, "Wh-what? What makes you think that?" Joshua just grinned and walked over to him, "You're a terrible liar kid. I knew it! Back at the bar I thought I saw it."

"Wait, what's the Triamal?" Kyoko asked, "And what does it have to do with my brother?" Joshua looked over, seeming genuinely surprised, "Wait, you mean to tell you kids don't know what the Triamal is?" Everyone shook their heads, Ander doing it to feign ignorance. Joshua let out an annoyed sigh, "What the herk are they teaching kids these days? This is basic history! Very well then, the Triamal is a power passed down through the generations, tracing back all the way to the Age of Sculptors. It's a gift from the Life Sculptor Valeria to us humans as a means of defense against Romevan. It allows one to transform into different beasts. I'm not sure how it works exactly, but I do know somethin' about it. The wielder always carries a coin and bears a tattoo."

"Oh!" Kyoko exclaimed excitedly, "Ander can transform into a wolf and bird! He must have the Triamal." Joshua looked over at Ander and grinned, "Still want to play dumb?" Ander sighed as he shook his head, "No, I guess not. But, how did you know? I only just found out a few hours ago."

"Look on your left tricep." Joshua said, "I saw it at the bar." Ander frowned and rolled up his sleeve and felt a small jolt of surprise as he saw a tattoo there. It was a red t, with the end point spiked down. "So, where's the coin?" Erok asked. Ander shook his head numbly, "Don't know. I don't have one." Joshua frowned and said, "Really? I saw you transform thought back there." Everyone turned and stared at Joshua. "What?" He asked, "I figured it would be better to try and get you to confess. People are more comfortable when they confess rather than being confronted."

Ander crossed his arms and asked, "Well, alright. So, what do you want with me then?" Joshua let out a short, barking laugh, "About time you asked that. Quick tip kid, next time someone' tryin' to figure out your identity, ask them what they want first before givin' 'em anything. But here's the thing. I'm a bit of an adventurer, unlike yur merc friend there."

"Wait, how did you-" Erok began before Joshua cut him off, "I've been around long enough that I can recognize your kind. Ya'll have the same lustful look in yur eyes. Anyway, we adventurers just travel around doing our best to help people, and if ya hadn't noticed, the world be changing right now, and not for the better. I need the help of the Triamal, and you need training. I can help with that. You light my cigar and I'll light yours. What do you say?"

"Hold on!" Sasha yelled, "You're a complete stranger and you expect him to just pack up and leave with you?! You must be insane" Joshua's left eye twitched then grunted, "Would he be losing much if he did? I've been here for a few days. No one respects the kid. I saw the tournament and I had to stop some pathetic louche from beating the shit out of him. Herk, I'm pretty sure the only one who actually loves the kid is his sister there."

"Hey!" Erok exclaimed, "I may be injured, but if you question our friendship again, I will break every bone in your body!" Joshua gave him a grin as he replied mockingly, "Oh, I'm soooo scared. Whatever you say kid. And miss, before ya get your panties all wound up, why don't we listen to what he has to say first?"

Everyone turned and looked at Ander. He gulped before he said, "I-I suppose I should start from the beginning." So, Ander told them everything that had happened to him since they left. From the bar to his house, and finally when he got here. He even told them about the voices. "So, you see," Ander said, "there really is nothing here for me." Erok and Sasha stayed silent as they looked at him, their faces unreadable. *Damn, so they do think I'm a monster.* Ander thought. "Oh Ander," Sasha cried, tears forming at her eyes, "you've dealt with so much today." She flung herself at him in a hug. "Don't you dare leave without me big brother!" Kyoko cried as she grabbed also. Ander just stood there dumbfounded. "Wait, you guys don't think I'm a monster?" Erok laughed, "Ander, you're way to kind to be one. Yeah, you might look scary, but your just a big old teddy owlbear."

Ander grinned at them, relieved as his heart felt warm. "So, kid?" Joshua asked, "What's yer answer?"

"I'll go with you." Ander replied with a solemn nod. He then looked over at his sister and asked, "I hope you don't mind if she comes though?" Kyoko looked up at him, her eyes shimmering with gladness. "Herk, I'd be a horrible person to separate you two." Joshua replied with a soft look in his eyes.

"Hmph, well I'm coming also." Erok said, "I'm not letting him go off with someone he doesn't know. Plus, I don't have any cause to trust you yet." Joshua let out a raucous laugh, "Yer a smart one all right! You'll be great for fighting wikenshires!" Erok and Ander looked at each other in confusion. "Well, I'm coming also." Sasha said, "Someone needs to keep the two of you in cheek, otherwise who knows what kind of trouble you guys will get into."

Erok and Ander gave each other a grin. "That's not something we can actually argue against." Ander said. Erok shrugged, "Especially with our track record, but wait, what about your parents?"

"Don't worry," Sasha said, "I have a plan for that."

"That was fast." Ander muttered. Joshua coughed and said, "Well I won't oppose any of ya coming. So, if yer coming, grab whatever you want to take with ya and then meet in front of the western gate at sunrise." Everyone nodded in affirmation before turning and heading back towards the city. As Ander neared the wall, he felt a surge of excitement flow through him. A new life awaited him with the rising of the sun. One in which he could not only be a person who was respected, but also someone he genuinely liked. Yet, this all was happening so fast. First the spiders, now leaving! He felt like they should wait a day still. "Uh, Mr. Rickstone?" He asked. Joshua stopped, "Yeah?"

"Why? Why do you really want me along?" Joshua paused, a pipe in his mouth about to be lit. "Kid, I appreciate you willing to come along, but why do *you* want to join?" Ander waited, Kyoko staring up at him curiously. "I-I mean, well you said you are an adventurer…and well I just thought…that maybe…" Joshua held up a hand, smirking at him, "That you can learn to be a hero?" Ander nodded, turning red. "But you are one!" Kyoko cried. "Look at what we just did!" Joshua let out a smoke ring and shook his head. "He did one good act. It might have been heroic, but that don't make you a hero yet. Listen Ander, I'll level with ya. I just got a message, and a place I got to head to. I think you'll be invaluable. Plus…yer not infected." Ander paused. "Infected?"

Joshua nodded solemnly, "You heard me. No damn infection of maggots. They get in yer blood and suck out all of the—well maybe yer not ready to hear that part. Young ears and all. Anyway, head on in with the others." Ander nodded, feeling elated. This man was…strange for sure, but a fatherly warmth he had never experienced radiated from him. Ander was a good judge of character, at least he thought so, and this man…he just instinctively trusted him. Whatever awaited him from here on out would be amazing, and this was the first step to the change he wanted.

End of part one

Beginnings and Endings

INTERLUDE ONE

Viscious walked down the underground corridor, his icy wings shimmering and casting rainbows behind him as he walked. He looked behind him at the spectacular sight and gave a satisfied nod. It was only fitting that his presence created more beauty than there had been before. Yet the satisfaction quickly faded as his eyes beheld his left wing. It was shattered and broken at the upper half. A horrible scar that marred his perfect appearance.

Viscious began to unconsciously growl lowly as he remembered what those two brothers had done to him. He knew he should not have played with them for as long as he had, but he had not expected their magic to be so powerful! But the younger one, the younger one terrified him. And anything that scared him must be eliminated. Viscious clenched his fist remembering that his escape had been pure luck only. How in the world though had those two managed to pull off the United Hearts spell? Not even Lavina and Malanus had been able to perform that one, and they were the strongest Archeshtisi!

Viscious walked towards his destination, his mind deep in the brooding thoughts of revenge, but he set them aside as he reached the door. He opened it and stepped into the dark room. It was a small stone room with nothing in it except for a stone table with a black gem on top of it. Dark runes were inscribed upon that gem, runes that cowardly humans would never dream of engraving. Viscious walked up to the gem and immediately knelt down.

A black projection of his master, the only one more glorious and perfect than he, Romevan, was cast upon the floor. With his head bowed, Viscious meekly said, "My lord, I bring news of my visit to Ala'Kathar." Viscious recounted everything that had happened to him and waited with bated breath for Romevan's response. There was silence and a bead of sweat dripped down Viscious. "So, he has played his hand." Romevan said, "Most intriguing. Do not worry over Jethro's death my servant. It seems he was too great a man for us to break. We never would have gotten anything from him. If only he would have ended up in my realm, instead of His after he did. His children however, may be of use to us."

"My lord?" Viscious asked, "Is it not concerning though that this one child can use *three* elements?"

"You act like this is unusual for us Viscious." Romevan replied, a hint of amusement in his voice, "Are you worried about them?"

"Well, it is possible for higher beings like us" Viscious answered incredulously, "but not for humans! We know how do to do it but have not quite achieved it! How is this possible?"

"Ah Viscious, you are the most intelligent of all my servants, but you still fail to see the larger picture. Here me and listen well, for this is what we shall do about them." His master explained his plan, and Vicious smiled as he realized what it meant. "A brilliant plan as always my lord."

"Now go and carry out my will. But before you leave, tell Damian to report to me. I wish to know how his pets did against Edeaven."

"Of course, my lord. Praise be to you forever!" The gem turned off and Viscious stood up. He left the room with a smile on his face. Those children may have been Jethro's kids, but they were not him. This was going to be quite a bit of fun.

Chapter 12

Leave-takings

Clouds darkened the sky as a cool front flew in. A faint smell of iron tainted the air, hinting at the storm that was fast approaching. Klin stood in front of his father's grave, alone and silent. Jethro's tomb was placed in the center of the graveyard. No special ornamentation, no statue, only the name and death date were inscribed upon the gray stone slate. The world's greatest hero, a man who had served the people to the end, lay in a common place unrecognized and unappreciated. Klin balled his hands as he stared the tombstone. The injustice of it was absurd and yet the town seemed to have gone through changes so they could ignore their hero.

It had only been a week since the deadly battle with Viscious, but Ala'Kathar had gone through major changes. The Guardians had been disbanded and all original members had been imprisoned with the rest on trial. The city which had praised them had viciously turned on them as soon as they had gotten the chance. Klin had hoped that Monastrath would be put on trial but the slimeball had claimed that he had been forced to act like that under duress by his father and the others. Everyone was so ready to add more sins to the Guardians that they had believed him. A new leader had been elected and new laws were being drafted. Yet Klin ignored it all and came to the grave every day for things were in some ways still the same.

Half the town hated them for exposing something that had benefited them while the other half practically worshipped them in an awed god complex. Yet that awe was fear at the same time, and despite giving them what the asked for, the fear that those who had freed them would turn on them was all too present. All in all, no one still wanted anything to do with the outcasts, whether heroes or villains. *What would you think of all of this dad? Are you okay with all of this? Did we do the right thing? Everyone either hates or loves us. We saved a city, and the people are resentful for it.* It was the same questions that he thought every day, every time he came across the grave. The thoughts would just not leave his mind. The deafening crack of lightning filled the sky. He sighed as he turned and began to make his way home, his questions still left unanswered. What was next for them now that they had won? Klin made it home not a moment too soon, for the clouds released a downpour of rain.

Klin made it to the doorstep with only mildly damp clothing, yet his coat, while it had drops of water on it, was left remarkably dry and still quite warm. He opened the door and paused as he saw his mother, brother, Celeste, and Dreas all sitting in the living room staring at him. "Uh hi," Klin said awkwardly, "did I do something wrong?"

"No, but we do need to talk so sit down." Dreas snapped. Klin obeyed but shot Joseph and inquiring look. His brother just shrugged. "So, what's going on?" Klin asked. Dreas stared quietly at each one of them individually before she said, "We need to discuss our next move concerning the Heshtisi."

"Hold on, what?!" Klin exclaimed.

"The Heshtisi," Dreas replied dryly, "the demonic creatures bent on taking over the world at any cost."

"I know what they are." Klin snapped back, "But what I don't understand is what you mean by *our* next move."

"You took on this task to destroy them, did you not?" Dreas asked.

"Whoa, whoa, whoa, slow down granny, I uh mean ma'am." Joseph corrected as Dreas shot him a glare, "We never made any such promises. All we said was that we wanted to help our home and find our dad. Both are done."

"Yeah," Klin nodded, "We accomplished our goal. What else is there to do?" Dreas sighed and looked them angrily, "I had expected better from you two! Yes, you drove out those weaklings, but they were only a fraction of the power that Romevan holds with the Heshtisi! They *will* be back. There is no doubt about that."

"What? Why would they come back?" Joseph scoffed.

"Maybe you should shut up and find out." Dreas replied. Joseph sunk into the couch meekly as Dreas continued, "Yes, it's true that you drove out the Heshtisi. But the thing is they will be back. Romevan I'm sure has not changed his principles, just his methods. He despises anyone or anything who dares fight back against him. Do you have any idea what this means for you three?!" A heavy silence fell upon them as a dread realization sunk in. "He's going to be after us now, isn't he?" Klin whispered.

"But how?" Joseph asked, "How in the world would he know about us? Didn't we kill all of the Heshtisi?"

"We don't know that for sure." Celeste replied with a shake of her head, "We only killed what we saw. According to Lorelei, there were some that definitely turned tail and ran after you two killed Viscious."

"Shit." Joseph muttered, "I thought for sure we were clear. What are we supposed to do now then?"

"Finally, you understand the gravity of the situation." Dreas snorted, "There are only two options. Do you know what those are?"

"It's either we fight back, or run, isn't it?" Klin answered softly. Dreas nodded, "Yes, those are your only two options. Either way, you will have to leave Ala'Kathar."

"Wait, we can't just leave!" Joseph yelled, "This is our home! If they want to come for us, we'll just stay and fight them!"

"Yeah, because us four and a bunch of amateur soldiers are totally going to be enough to hold off the Heshtisi." Celeste replied sarcastically. Joseph flushed and opened his mouth then closed it. "Face it," Celeste said, "you guys are going to have to leave. As painful as it is, you can't stay."

"Well-uh gah! Damn it all! There has to be something else we can do besides running away like cowards!" Joseph yelled; his brow turned down in frustration. "There's nothing cowardly about running away from a battle that you can't win boy!" Dreas scolded, "It is wisdom to know what you can and cannot do! Only idiots and fools with delusions of grandeur stay to fight a hopeless battle. The Heshtisi will only come back here for *you two*. No one else. It would be selfish to drag this town into more of this family's problems."

"Now you're saying that this is our fault?!" Joseph cried, "For the love of the Eight!"

"I agree," Klin said, "you can't blame us for this!"

"Be quiet you two!" Lorelei snapped, "I thought I had raised you two better than this! You two did the right thing, but it comes with consequences that you have to own up too! Are you going to shirk from them just because they ask you to sacrifice something?! Your father never ran from responsibility, so what would he think of the both of you doing it?"

"Well, we'll never know, will we?" Klin answered bitingly, "It's not like he was ever here as a father for us." Klin's head snapped to the side as his vision was filled with stars. "What the-?"

"Shut up!" Celeste screamed, "How the herk can you sit there and say that?! I didn't know your father but even for the brief moments I got to spend with him, I could see the deep love he held for the both of you! How can you resent him for something that was out of his control! At least you have your mother!" Klin sat silently starting a Celeste. She moved to slap him again, but Klin caught her hand. She then tried to slap him with her other, but Klin caught that one also. "Let go so I can smack you!" Celeste screamed. Klin stood up and gently put her hands down by her side but did not let go. "Thank you." Klin whispered and sat back down, releasing his grip. "Yeah, well, you need it." Celeste muttered. She sat back down but with far less passion. "Alright, so we need to leave," Klin said, his voice cracking a bit, "but where do we go?"

"South." Lorelei answered, "You uncle knows a safe haven down by the sea that he can take us too."

"Us?" Joseph asked. Lorelei smiled, "What, you didn't think I would let my babies go off on their own, did you? I already sent a letter to my brother explaining everything. We'll meet up with him and then he will guide us there." Klin paused as he looked at Dreas, Lorelei, and Celeste. "You three have been planning this already, haven't you?" Celeste smiled softly, "You got it. Things needed to get done, and you two weren't doing anything about it so I figured I'd help out. I might as well go with you also. I made myself a target also by helping you out. Plus, I can probably get passage to the East. I understand you uncle has a lot of connections."

"Alright then, so when do we leave?" Klin asked.

"Tomorrow," Lorelei replied, "Try to pack somewhat lightly but take anything that you think will come in handy."

"But-" Joseph began. "Oh, come on!" Klin snarled, "I've accepted it so why cannot you? We *have to leave! There is no other choice!* Do you *want* to sacrifice all these innocent lives. Is that what you want?!"

"KLIN!" Lorelei scolded. Klin stood up, glaring at his brother who just sat there dumbfounded. "I'm going to go pack." Klin muttered and stormed upstairs. He slammed the door as he entered his room. Why was Joseph still protesting? Didn't he understand that at this point, they had to leave! Feeling furious he began to pace. After a few minutes he began to calm down. With a sigh, Klin grabbed his traveling bag, something he had never used for the purpose it was made for. Mindlessly, he began to stuff miscellaneous mishaps and belongings into it.

He really shouldn't blame Joseph. He was originally on his side after all, but then why did he feel so *angry?* This anger had been festering underneath him like and infected wound, pussing and oozing, sometimes barely hurting and at other times coming full force. Why? Why? *Why?* WhywhywhywhywhyWHYWHYWHY?!!!!! With a sudden roar, Klin slammed his fist into the wall beside him. He turned to his pillow and started to punch it. Hit after hit, he just kept slamming his balled fists into it. Finally, he stopped. Breathing heavily, he looked about his room. Clothes and books lay strewn across the floor. His sheets were all jumbled and bundled. He looked at himself in the mirror. His hair was slick with sweat and even more of a mess than normal, if that was possible. His eyes though. They were wild and crazed, like an animal. A dark light shone through them.

A chill blew down his spine. That look, what was he doing? Disturbed, Klin sat down on his bed, his face in his hands. *Tap, raprap, tap.* Klin looked up. "Come on in Joseph." Joseph opened the door softly. "Hey," he said, "you alright?" Klin remained silent, not sure what to say. "Damn dude. Is this what you call packing?"

"No." Klin replied sheepishly, "Hey, listen I'm sorr-"

"Don't." Joseph said softly but forcefully, "Just don't. I deserved it. Granted that was a bit over the top, but you know me. I need over the top stuff when I'm being an ass." Klin laughed, but there was hardly any mirth in it. "Yeah, I know."

Joseph let out a sigh as he leaned against the door frame, "I guess I'm just not ready to leave is all. At least, not permanently." Klin frowned, "They never said anything about leaving permanently."

"Then why was there an air of finality in their tones?" Joseph asked. Klin looked down at the ground, groping for an answer and found none. "Face it," Joseph said, "when we leave, it will be for good. Are you really okay with that?"

"Yes." Klin answered without hesitation, "The only thing here for us is mom and this house. What else has this Light forsaken town given us? Nothing!" Joseph stared at him for a moment, "Yeah, I suppose you're right."

"Besides," Klin said, "We can finally be heroes like we've always talked about. Traveling the world, helping people from country to country." Joseph simply nodded and lounged in the doorway. "Hey, so I kinda have another reason for visiting ya." Klin looked up at him inquiringly. "I think I know what's been bothering you lately?"

"Oh?" Klin laughed hollowly. Joseph ignored that nodded, "It's because of what I did to those Companions, isn't?" Klin paused, "The ones you brutalized?" Joseph nodded. Klin hesitated, as much as that would make sense, it did not seem like that was it. "Yeah, I think you're right." Klin lied. Joseph nodded, "Listen, I'm going to do my best not to kill people if I don't have to. But I'm going to make them wish they were dead." Klin examined Joseph's face. A dark look had crept into it, yet there was a noble look also, like moonlight in the dead of night that was teetering on the edge of a cloud. "Boys! Come on down and eat!" Lorelei's voice echoed form below. "Be right there!" Joseph called back, "Come on. Let's go eat. It'll be our final meal here after all."

"I'll be down soon." Klin said with a half-hearted smile. Joseph gave him one last look before turning and heading out. Klin sat thinking and reflecting. No, it wasn't Joseph's questionable actions that had him upset. It was a deeper and more personable problem. It was his actions against Monastrath. The ecstasy he had felt as his blades had torn through his flesh and bloodied the steel which wanted to lap up the crimson water. No, what disturbed Klin more than anything was the knowledge that if he ever killed, he would delight in it. And that made him angry. "Klin, are you coming down?" Lorelei called. "Coming!" Klin replied. Joseph was right. He should enjoy this while it lasted.

Chapter 13

Lessons for a New Life

Klin rubbed the sleep from his eyes, wishing for a nice cup of coffee. Unfortunately, that simple pleasure was denied to him on this chilly late summer morning. A navy darkness covered the land. In maybe an hour or so the rose of dawn would bloom upon them, but for now they had to stumble about with little light to guide them. "Whoa Strider." Klin soothed his gray coated horse, "Easy buddy." Celeste gave him an approving look as she sat upon her horse, "Nice," Celeste called, "I knew your mom had said you guys had skills with horses, but I didn't think they would be average."

"Thank you?" Klin answered skeptically. All of them had horses of their own. Dreas had gone out and purchased them a few days ago. The last time Klin had ridden a horse had been when Dreas's old horse Tommy had still been alive. She had taught them to ride on that old thing. All four horses were laden down with supplies. Celeste sat upon a chestnut male that she had dubbed Darby, while Lorelei sat upon her own mare, a black with gray spots all over it. Joseph sat upon a proud white horse, it's coat as pure as snow, yet he had named her Cider. "Honey, I still want to know why you named your horse Cider." Lorelei asked.

"Well, it's simple." Joseph replied grinning, "it's fitting." Celeste just shook her head in amazement. "But why do we have to leave this early?" Joseph complained. Lorelei sighed as she double checked her straps before climbing on, "I told you; we need to leave unnoticed. We really don't know if Romevan has any spies here still and we do not want to be followed."

"Yeah, but does it have to be so damned early? I'm barely awake!" Joseph whined. With the clopping of hooves, Celeste rode over and lightly smacked Joseph across the face. "Ow! What was that for?" Celeste grinned, "You awake now?"

"Yeah." Joseph muttered. Klin grinned, suddenly not tired anymore. "Shall we get going then?" Klin asked. Everyone nodded. "Alright then, let's ride!" Lorelei shouted and kicked her horse into a sprint. "Aren't we supposed to be quiet?" Joseph asked before he took off after her. They rode down the main road at a brisk speed. They did not encounter anyone upon the road and as they neared the end of the city's domain, Klin turned back for one last look. Despite all the horrible things that happened to him there, Klin still felt a nostalgic attachment to the city. It was still his home. Slight light broke upon the sky and as Klin looked to the sky, he saw smoke rise above where their house was. "Hey, mom!" Klin yelled and pointed at the sky. Lorelei looked back and her face grew dark at the sight.

No one said anything as they rode. Klin shivered as a chill went up his spine. He buttoned his coat to his waist, the rest of the coat flapping in the wind. He looked up to the sky. A storm was coming so at least it would put out the fire.

They rode through the rest of the day, eating their lunch while riding. It lightly rained upon road, but the storm withheld itself until they were clear of it. Eating drinking though while riding was a new experience, and one he definitely had not acquired the skillset for. He was pretty sure he had spit half of his waterskin all over himself while trying to take a drink. They had only stopped twice since leaving, and that was when Klin had reserved to take drinks. No one had spoken that much while they rode.

Joseph and Celeste had been the only ones to hold any real conversations and they only talked when they had slowed to a trot to let the horses try and catch their breath. Otherwise, the only sound that could be heard was the steady clopping of the horses. Finally, as the sun was in the last two hours of setting and everyone's rears cried out in pain, the call came. "Alright I think that's enough for today." Lorelei said haltingly, "Let's make camp here for tonight." They all dismounted, there legs popping as they forced them into a different position to walk.

Lorelei led them a reasonable distance into the woods, far enough to be away from everyone but close enough that they could still find the road if they needed to. They tied their horses to some trees and set about getting camp ready. Klin and Joseph walked about looking for some wood to be used for the fire while Celeste stayed and helped Lorelei get dinner ready.

As Klin and Joseph wandered through the woods, Joseph let out a dry laugh, "They always leave out the boring, not so fun parts of traveling don't they?" Klin smiled as he found a good-sized branch, "No kidding. My butt feels like fire after that." Joseph laughed and filled his arms up with fallen branches. "But you know, I'm actually kind of enjoying this. It's weird and different, and a little painful and uncomfortable, but I like it in the end." Klin nodded. It was new, but it was not an unwelcome experience. "Think we've got enough firewood?" Klin asked. Joseph raised his eyebrow as he offered the pile of sticks that rose to his chin. Klin placed a few more from his pile into Joseph's before turning away and heading back to camp. He heard Joseph muttering under his breath as he followed close behind.

"We're back." Klin announced as they returned, "This should be enough for the night." Lorelei nodded and pointed to the circle of rocks placed in the center. Klin and Joseph dropped the sticks and Celeste moved forward with some matches. "Are those puny things going to be enough?" Joseph asked. Celeste looked up with some annoyance, "If your competent they are." Five dead matches later, there was a roaring fire with deer roasting atop it with some carrots and onions. "So, how many matches you have to burn through to be competent?" Joseph asked slyly, "Twenty? Ten? Six?" Celeste just gave him a glare and a rude gesture. The deer smelled tangy and aromatic, making Klin's mouth water. "So, I do have a question." Joseph asked, "Not that I'm complaining but why did you have us stop so early. It's like maybe five thirty at this point. Seems a little early to stop." It was indeed a bit early as the sun was just now beginning to set and the sky shedding its noon blue for a fleck of gold.

Lorelei turned the spit over, examining it before she replied, "Well, we're nearing bandit infested roadways and I'd like to try and cross those sections quickly during the day. They've been known to rob and kill while travelers sleep. Plus, the last of the woods ahead are Spprigan infested." Joseph rubbed the back of his neck, "Oh, that makes sense." Klin shot up alarmed, "Wait, we're near Spprigan country?!" Klin asked. "Only in a confined area." Lorelei answered, "We should be able to make it through with no trouble at all tomorrow." Klin nodded; they were nocturnal after all. "Wait a minute," Celeste shrieked," you're telling me that I crossed through Spprigan territory on my way here?! I didn't have any fire when I came through here last!" Klin and Joseph burst out laughing, while Lorelei tried to hide her laughter. "This isn't funny guys!" Celeste pouted, "I could have died!" Her pouting though made everyone laugh even harder. "Ah, looks like the food's done." Lorelei announced smirking.

Lorelei handed out the food, disarming Celeste's agitation. Celeste gobbled down the food voraciously. Soon enough Celeste was in good mood once more and everyone began to talk and joke as they ate. Everyone except Klin. "Mom, can you show us how to use magic?" Klin asked suddenly. Silence pressed down upon them. Lorelei finished eating and set down her plate. "Klin, magic is both wonderous and extremely dangerous." Lorelei replied quietly, "Why do you want to learn?" Klin lifted his head and locked eyes with his mother, a flamer burning within. "I want to get stronger." He said morosely. He clenched his fists, "We lost dad because we couldn't help. Because we didn't have the strength! Joseph and I had this power within us, but now herking clue how to use it! If we had, then just maybe…!" Lorelei looked at him sadly. "Alright, you don't have to say anymore. We'll begin right now. At least as much as is universal."

"Wait, right now?" Joseph asked shocked, "And what do you mean as much as you can? Can't you teach us fully?" Lorelei shook her head. "From what you two described, neither of you have the same elements as I do. There are basic rules of mastering the conjuration of magic and controlling it, but the applications of each element are different and vary." Klin nodded, "Yeah, I kinda knew about that. I tried to grab the 'source' as the books called it but got nothing."

"What?!" Lorelei barked sharply, "You tried to summon magic on your own?!" Klin hesitated. His mother looked furious, something he had not been expecting. "Y-yeah." Lorelei balled her fists and leapt to her feet. "Do you have any idea how dangerous that was! You could have easily killed yourself! Magic is not some spectacle to be looked at and examined! It's volatile and dangerous. One misplaced thread, one spec of ignored animana, and you're dead!" Klin crumpled under his mother's wrath. "I'm sorry." Klin said lamely, "I just thought I should know how. Isn't that why we train kids at such a young age? So, they don't kill themselves?"

Lorelei deflated and rubbed her eyes, "Yes, that's true. But still, you should have come to me from the very beginning then." Celeste clapped slowly from her seat on the ground. "And here I thought you two couldn't get any dumber."

"Hey!" Joseph cried indignantly, "I wasn't a part of that!" Celeste raised an eyebrow, "But you would of if you'd known." Joseph promptly shut up remained silently standing. "Come on, let's begin then." Lorelei sighed. Klin and Joseph grinned at each other. "Now then, before we do an applying, let's start with the theoretics." Lorelei said. "First the Threads of Weaving. Threads are what hold the world together. Shaped by the Sculptors, Threads form the foundations of everything in the world. Anyone who is able to access and control those Threads we call Weavers. Now there is a Source of the Threads, which we call the Weave. Each Thread has a Source, but each of those Sources are connected to a larger Source, The Weave. Make sense so far?" Klin and Joseph nodded.

"Good. Now here is where things get a little more complicated." Lorelei said solemnly. "The more powerful a Weaver is, the closer they are to their Source. We measure the increments in what's called animana. Animana is also what powers your magic. It is directly tied to your energy, and some think you are using your soul itself to power the Threads. The closer you are to the Source, the more animana you have, and the more powerful your Weaving will become. Yet here's the thing. Those who have multiple elements, or Duowoven, have different animana for each of their elements."

"How do you increase your animana?" Klin asked.

"It depends on the element." Lorelei replied, "For example. For me, I had to learn empathy to grow closer to my Life Source, and detachment for my Wind Source. But animana also acts like a muscle. The more you use it, the stronger it becomes. You can get very close to the Source by just training and using magic, but you will always be behind someone who has trained both morally and physically."

"Wait, so the strength of our magic is tied to our morality?" Joseph asked, "Then why in Heshtanus was Viscious so damn powerful? Shouldn't that bastard's magic be really weak?"

"Like I said you can train in two different ways." Lorelei answered darkly, "While training your character is better, the physical aspect can get one infinitely close to their Source. Not to mention Viscious would have been using Natharian magic." Klin shivered as a chill ran down his spine. He'd heard of the terrible and gruesome things Weavers had done with Natharian magic. Most villains in the fairy tales he had read had been Natharian Weavers. "Anything else we should know?" Klin asked. Lorelei thought for a bit before saying, "Oh, yes. Spells, or as some Weavers like to call them, Cloths. Spells are just Threads arranged in a way that makes a new or desired reality by the Weaver. There is an infinite combination of Threads, but there are rules. Threads are not arranged randomly. Somehow the numbers and thickness of the Threads matter for what is made. We're not sure exactly why some things require a certain thickness or number, or even length! Yes, even the length of the Thread matters."

"What do each signify?" Klin asked curiously.

"Length shows the size of the object you are creating. The thickness shows how much power is stored within the spell, or how much was used. Finally, the number of Threads determines the complexity of the object." Lorelei explained. "The more complex and the more components required for the spell to work like desired, the more Threads are needed. For example, if I wanted to give the instruction to heal, I would actually spend more animana than if I added an extra thread to say, 'heal this wound.'"

"So, the number of threads lessens the amount of animana?" Joseph asked. Lorelei shook her head, "Not always. It really depends on the spell. Some require more threads, and therefore more animana for the spell to work properly, while other more basic spells use more Threads, but less animana than if they used less Threads. A lot of spell devising requires experimentation. But experimentation is dangerous. Some

Threads placed in a certain way can create a spell that you cannot cut off, and once you start it, it will not stop till it achieves its desired effect. Most of the time, it means draining you completely of life. Knowing one's own limits and the rules of Weaving are needed for experiments."

Klin nodded, "Alright, so then how much energy is one animana?" Lorelei shrugged, "It costs no more effort than flexing you little finger for some, while others it almost knocks them out. It all depends on how close you are to your Source. Besides making spells more effective it makes something strenuous less so. It's like lifting weights. For some ten pounds is a lot, while those who have trained their muscles, ten is hardly anything at all."

"You said one anima then is different for how trained a person is," Joseph said, "and that thickness determines how much animana is used. How much animana is used for the thickness then?" Lorelei smiled, "Well that's a good question. Someone actually looked into this. A Weaver by the name of Arthur Porter I believe. He observed that one millimeter is one anima. One centimeter is five, one inch ten, and then one foot is seventy-five aniamani." Joseph frowned, "So is there a pattern? Cause I partially see one."

"Not really." Lorelei replied, "You would think that for every millimeter one animana would be used, but it does not seem that way. He did observe though that you add one animana in between each size. So right before you hit a centimeter, you have a four-millimeter Thread that uses four animana. But enough of the theoretical stuff. It's time for you two to practice this."

"Sweet!" Joseph exclaimed, "We're done with the boring stuff." Klin rolled his eyes. "Yeah, but it's important. Besides, it's not *that* boring." Lorelei crossed her arms, "Alright you two, settle down. Now close your eyes." Klin and Joseph eyed each other and shrugged before obeying. The darkness of the mind enveloped Klin, as he squeezed his eyes shut. "Now focus. Envision a path. Search for it in your mind. Klin obeyed, and all of a sudden, even though he was sure his eyes were closed, found himself in a dark space. He seemed to float in the air yet felt solid ground underfoot. He looked around and noticed than some areas were less dark than others. The lighter dark seemed to form a path, so he followed it, and was soon brought to a divergence. "Have you found the Thread or Threads?" Lorelei asked.

"Yeah," Joseph replied, "I see a dark purple thread. It's really big. It looks like the type of rope you use to secure boats." Klin frowned, "I see three Threads. One light blue, one red, and one golden one."

"*Three* threads?" Lorelei exclaimed in shock. "Are you sure?" Klin hesitated, confused. "Yeah? Why is that bad?!" There was a pause, "No, it's just I've never heard of someone having *three elements* before. By all rights, it shouldn't be possible."

"Maybe dad did something that gave him the third?" Joseph postulated hesitantly. There was a pause. "Yeah, that's probably it." Lorelei said dismissively, "Anyway, grab one of the threads that you see before you." Klin stretched out his hand and grabbed the gold Thread in front of him. He gasped in surprise. The Thread was cool, yet warm at the same time. He could feel an energy running through the Thread beneath his hands. "Gah!" Klin cried as the darkness suddenly shifted around him. He knew he was moving, but his body never moved nor did the Thread seem to pull him along. When everything stopped moving, he found himself staring at a giant, golden liquid sphere. It pulsated and glowed, almost seeming to ooze at times. The Thread lead straight into the center but the light was so bright that he could barely make that out.

"Now grasp the thing you see in front of you," Lorelei said, "And try and absorb it." Klin recoiled back. "What?" He cried, "How in the world are we supposed to do that?"

"Just relax." Joseph called back, "Go for it without thinking. I did it and it's not that hard." Klin turned back to the sphere and let out and exasperated sigh. "Why can't they just tell me instead of 'follow your instincts' crap?" Klin muttered. Angrily he reached out and touched the sphere. That same energy he had felt under the Thread now flowed into him. Klin cried out as his entire body was racked with shaking and spasms. He ground his teeth as he tried to focus and regain control, but the more he fought, the worse the spasms got. Little by little, he tried to force his way into the sphere. He pressed his palm against it, yet some sort of force pressed back and flung his hand back. His hand began to shake so hard that he could not control it. Klin turned back to the sphere with a ferocious growl and yelled, "Damn it! I won't be denied!" and plunged both hands in.

He struggled and fought until he had his entire body in. Klin grinned and then the power hit him. He let out a soundless scream as thousands of little needles pierced him. Not only did he feel them on his skin all over, but even in his stomach, heart, throat, eyes. They were everywhere. The pain was like nothing he had ever felt before. He fell to the ground shaking as fire engulfed him. "Klin! Klin! Klin! KLIN!" With a groan Klin opened his eyes and found himself lying on the ground staring at the sky. A phantom like pain lingered throughout his body. Celeste and Joseph were staring down at him. Celeste's face was pained and full of concern. Joseph was frowning and looked panicked. "Wha-what happened?" Klin croaked.

"You collapsed all of sudden, screaming in pain." Celeste choked. "You scared the shit out of us." Klin groaned and looked over and realized Lorelei was clutching his arm. A soft green light emitted from her palm. He then realized something. "I can't feel your hand." He breathed. Lorelei looked up alarmed. "What did you do?" Klin shook his head, "I don't know. I just tried to grab and absorb, like you said." Lorelei turned pale, "This should not have happened. I-I've never even heard of this happening." Klin clenched his fist and winced. Moving anything but his head flared up immense pain. Even talking hurt. "Here, is this doing anything?" Lorelei asked. Klin flexed his hand. Considerably less pain than before. "Yeah." Klin nodded. Lorelei let out a held breath as she began to slowly heal Klin.

Once she was done, Klin stood up. "Thanks mom." Lorelei looked him up and down. "You are sure you're okay now." Klin nodded and moved a little stiffly. "What the heck was it you were yelling though?" Joseph asked. Klin frowned, "What do you mean?"

"You kept yelling out some weird words." Joseph replied, "At first I thought it was gibberish, but then I realized it was forming a sentence. You kept shouting the same thing." Klin frowned. He had no memory of saying anything. "It was Ancient Threan." Celeste explained. Everyone turned to look at her in surprise. "What?" she demanded, "I had a proper education. Unlike you two. Anyway, he kept crying, 'Lavosna est dumacosa Genus me.' Which means-"

"The Light of Genus shall purge me." Klin translated. When Celeste looked at him in surprise he smiled mirthlessly, "I did my best to educate myself properly. But I don't have any idea what that means nor why I would say that. It's a weird thing."

"Maybe you were just spitting out random thins since you were in pain?" Joseph offered. "I mean, people say nonsense when they are incoherent, right?" They all looked at Lorelei who just shook her head, "I have no idea." She said, "All we can do is guess." Klin nodded and then rolled his shoulders, "Alright, guess we better get back to it then."

"Hold on, what?" Lorelei exclaimed shocked. Klin frowned and looked at his mother. "I didn't achieve what this session was for, so shouldn't we resume?" Lorelei's eyes flashed. "NO!" She yelled, "You just collapsed and are exhausted! *Any* more practice could kill you! I forbid you from trying to access anymore magic for the night!"

"But-"

"I said no!" Lorelei barked. Klin shrank in on himself as he sat back down. "Okay." He said meekly. Lorelei nodded and sat down. "Don't worry about it too much." Celeste said gently. She reached out her hand awkwardly before pulling it back. "So what if you can't practice right now? You'll still be able to tomorrow." Klin nodded absently and then smiled at her. "Yeah, you're right." Celeste grinned back. The tension in the slowly went down as they sat in silence. "Alright, things are way too quiet!" Joseph proclaimed. "Everyone is also way to down in spirits!" He got up and went over to his bags and began to rifle through it. Celeste frowned, "What are you-what the heck?! Why did you pack that!" Joseph pulled out a guitar and sat down. "Because, I figured we could use the music on bad days." Joseph replied casually. Klin smiled and shook his head, "Of all the important stuff you brought, you grabbed that?" Joseph eyes him, "Well not all of us are bookworms you know." Klin flushed and looked away as Joseph started up a song. Soon enough he had the entire group singing along, there spirits rising as high as the smoke from the fire.

For the next few hours, they sang and talked, growing closer. "Alright, we've had our fun." Lorelei laughed, "But I think we should all go to bed." The three agreed and turned in. Klin snuggled under his blankets and closed his eyes. He listened carefully. As the campfire began to burn out, the shallow breathing of the rest of the group could be heard. Carefully Klin threw off his blankets and got up, and went deep into the woods where he would not be disturbed. *I need to get stronger.* Klin thought, *Even if I have to risk death to do so.* Klin closed his eyes and found the Threads and for the third time grabbed the golden one. The darkened landscaped moved and changed as he was brought to his source. As Klin began to walk towards the sphere, he stopped as he noticed something. The air and the very energy in the Thread felt different. He looked at the sphere. It was no longer of a liquid-like substance, instead solid. It also did not glow nearly as brightly. Klin moved forward and placed his hand on the sphere. He did not even feel the energy this time. He clenched his fists and growled, slamming his palms on the sphere. A dull thud resounded from the thing. "Come on!" He screamed, "Why won't you let me win?!" Klin fell to his knees in despair. *Why?* He thought, *Why am I so pathetic that I can't even do something so basic!*

Yeah, a voice whispered back. *You are pathetic, but not for the reasons you think. Do you really want to act like* him, *with this win/lose view?* Klin paused, "No" he whispered, "I don't want to be like that. I will take what comes my way, even if it hurts." Defiantly Klin got to his knees and meekly placed his hands on the sphere and felt a crack. He frowned and pressed against it and watched as the sphere shattered like glass, and a massive burst of energy flowed into him. Klin gasped as his eyes were flung open. He stood still and struggled as he felt the magic trying to escape, trying to find an outlet. Finally, it stopped and stabilized. Klin smiled, the magic was his, and it was time to use it.

Celeste rolled over, her regular nightmares beginning to fade. She held in a groan with some struggle. Tonight's dark dream had been one of the worst in weeks. *Snap!* Celeste froze, and lay absolutely still, pretending that she was still asleep. The nocturnal noises from the animals had stopped. Celeste listened intently, even the fire had gone out. Then she heard it. A low snappish hummin crept up from the woods. Rhythmic and musical, but yet the tune carried and air of peril, making her heart beat faster, feeling like it would burst from her chest. She listened even more and then shot her eyes open. The humming was coming right towards her. Celeste quietly wrapped her hands around

Yatta. The footsteps grew closer. Celeste rolled over and finally saw what it was that was coming to her. *Oh no.* Celeste thought, *They aren't supposed to be here!* Celeste threw her blanket at the Spriggan as she leapt to her feet, ready for a fight.

Chapter 14

New Rules=New Game

The willow figure of decaying bark that formed the creature screeched as it tore Celeste's blanket to pieces. It's petulant green eyes stared malevolently at Celeste. "Hey guys!" Celeste yelled, "Might want to wake up now!" She heard Lorelei wake with a shout. Celeste spared a glance to see Lorelei staring at her in bewilderment. "What is-Celeste look out!"

Celeste whipped back and saw the Spriggan leaping at her. Celeste blocked with a grunt. "Gah, you smell bad." Celeste growled as she shoved it off of her. The monster stumbled back with a hum. Celeste gave it a hum herself as she chopped of its arm. The Spriggan screamed as it stumbled back, throwing back its horned head into the air, revealing teeth whiter than bone. Celeste didn't want to get bitten by those. "You shouldn't have done that." Lorelei said as she stood next to her, "They regrow, and they come back angrier."

"Of course, they do." Celeste complained, "I mean, it's not like things can be easy or anything, right?" As if on cue, the Spriggan's arm came back. The wood elongated and intertwined as it reformed the arm in one smooth motion. "Also, Joseph get the herk up!" Celeste yelled. Joseph just snorted and rolled over in response. "I am so killing him after this." Celeste muttered. "Agreed." Lorelei scowled, "Look out, here it comes!" Celeste parried the arm as the Spriggan lunged forward and cut off the same arm again. Almost immediately though the creature swiped with its other arm, no longer seeming to feel pain. Celeste let out an involuntary cry and as she stumbled back and tripped over her leg. The Spriggan not expecting clumsy prey stumbled above her before being flung through the air. It slammed into a tree and lay in a heap.

"Hurry, finish it off!" Lorelei said. She stood with her arms outstretched, "I'm keeping it down, but I can sense more coming now!" Celeste nodded and scrambled to her feet and rushed forward. She kept her body low and had Yatta in her sheath as she approached the Spriggan. The monster tried to spear her with a claw but Celeste slid under it before leaping up, and as she did she spun in the air, unsheathing Yatta and decapitating the thing. Sickly green blood oozed from the wound as the body slumped to the ground. "Was that flourish really necessary?" Lorelei asked. Celeste turned back with a grin, shaking the blood off the blade. "Probably not." Lorelei shook her head as her daggers floated to her. "That must have been a young one though to die so easily." Celeste's heart plummeted, "What do you mean by that?"

"Full grown Spriggan's regrow *any* body part." Lorelei explained, "Which means we need some sort of destructive magic or fire to kill them." Celeste wet her mouth that was surprisingly dry all of a sudden. "So that means its just a matter of how long I can last then." Lorelei nodded gravely. "Great, just great." Celeste said, struggling to keep her voice steady. "Why don't we get the boys who specialize in that magic up then?" Celeste stomped over to Joseph and Klin's blankets, "Alright fire boy I hope-shit! Klin's gone!" Celeste shouted. "What?!" Lorelei shrieked. "Where is he then?"

"I don't know." Celeste replied. But she had a pretty good idea of why he was not there. He was going to get his ass beaten. Celeste then turned her attention to Joseph. "Ugggh!" Joseph whined, "What's with all this noise! I'm trying to sle---owowowowow! What's that for?!" Celeste stepped back and leveled her blade at his face. "That's for being a heavy sleeper and not helping us!" Celeste scowled. She smacked him on the head once more for good measure. "Help you with what?!" Joseph exclaimed confused, "Shit! Behind you!" Celeste spun around to see a Spriggan right behind her. This one was twice her size and it's limbs were longer and broader than the previous one. Before she could react, Joseph had leapt to his feet and tacked it.

She watched as Joseph and the Spriggan grappled on the ground. The monster swiped its claws across his face, but Joseph just grunted as he got behind it. Grabbing by the arm and with a hearty cry, Joseph threw the Spriggan into the tree with a crunch. "I think I broke its back." Joseph exclaimed. Celeste ran forward and stabbed it in the heart. The Spriggan gave a cry, but the wound closed almost instantly. "Well shit," Joseph cursed, "they heal?!" The Spriggan grabbed the sword and threw it to the side. *Damn it Yatta.* Celeste thought, *I thought only I could grab you now!* Four more screeches were heard. Celeste turned to see four more Spriggans approaching. "Celeste!" Joseph yelled.

The world reoriented itself as the Spriggan grabbed her and they tumbled to the ground. Celeste let out a scream as the Spriggan sank its claws into her side. "Damn you!" She shouted as she grappled with it. She grabbed the monster's wrists and struggled to keep the powerful limbs from reaching her. Then she turned her hips and wrapped her legs around it's neck. All of sudden, tons of wooden spikes sprang out from its head. Celeste gritted her teeth as she kept in her scream and snapped the Spriggan's neck. The creature went limp. Celeste scrambled out from under it but winced as she tried to stand. Her legs were too weak from all the wounds, and she was losing a lot of blood. There was a loud *snap!* as the Spriggan's neck was placed back to normal. It eyed her evily. Then with a roar, Joseph grabbed it from behind and slammed its face into the ground. A purple aura then surrounded him and with a vengeful cry, purple energy streamed down his arm in a mist.

"HERK! YOU!" Joseph screamed. The Spriggan's head imploded, leaving a steaming black mark on the stump of its neck. Breathing heavily he turned to face the others, murderous glint in his eyes. Lorelei was slicing them to pieces with her air weaving, but they kept healing. "Mom! Celeste needs some healing! I got this!" Joseph rushed forward as his mother glanced back at him and nodded. Joseph grabbed his sword from next to his blankets and rushed them. Lorelei glided over quickly and knelt down next to her. "You need to be more careful." Lorelei scolded. As she healed her with one hand, she summoned Yatta with the other. Celeste sighed with relief as the pain went away and took Yatta gratefully. "Be very careful though." Lorelei said while staring Celeste in the eyes, "Any more wounds like that and you'll pass out. I wasn't able to replace the blood yet."

"Yeah, yeah." Celeste replied as she quickly got to her feet, "I got it." She ran into battle to help Joseph. He was backed into a corner by three of the Spriggans. One of them lay dead with a smoking neck.

Joseph's stance though was shaky, and he was breathing heavily. Celeste ran up as Joseph blocked all the Spriggan's with his massive sword and then she activated Yatta's power. Celeste felt an immediate drain on her strength and nearly stumbled. Celeste thrusted her sword into its heart from behind, but it made no wound. Celeste then willed Yatta to un-phase and ripped the sword out. The Spriggan fell to the ground screaming and twitching. The other two spun around, allowing Joseph to kill them. She watched though as the wound did not heal and the life left the monster's eyes.

"What the heck did you do?" Joseph asked, gasping for air. Celeste shook the blood with a sweep of her arm before sheathing Yatta. "I wounded it from the inside." Celeste explained tiredly, "Yatta has the ability to phase through objects like a ghost. I noticed that your method seemed to kill them from the *inside*, so I tried that." She then looked away as she realized Jospeh's state of attire. "Also put on a shirt!" Lorelei walked up to them. "Interesting" she mused, "They only heal from wound dealt externally. That's useful to know. But we have twelve more coming. How are you guys doing?"

Celeste struggled to her feet and gave a weak grin, "I can keep going." Joseph shook his head, "I can swing my sword but don't expect any more magic out of me." Lorelei nodded and then cursed, "Damn they're here." Celeste looked around but could not see anything. "Where?" She asked. Then she heard something whistle through the air. *Thunk, thunk, thunk, thunk.* Celeste gasped as she fell to the ground. At least four sharp objects were embedded in her back. "Celeste!" Joseph cried. Celeste gasped for air. *Those damn things shot me in the back! What the herk can these things* not *do?!* She heard the clashing of steel and some shouts from Lorelei. She looked over, her vision was growing blurry. She saw Joseph struggling to protect his mother. Seven of the Spriggans had surrounded them. She watched as green blood oozed from four of their mouths, and Lorelei began to sweat. *Get them!* Celeste though. Humhohummmm. Celeste's heart stopped. She forced herself to roll over and found a Spriggan looming over her. Celeste tried to swing her sword, but she found herself frozen in fear. *No!* Celeste thought, *I won't die this way! I won't!* But despite her defiant thoughts, past nightmares resurfaced and she no longer saw the monster in front of her. Instead she saw one worse. "NO!" Celeste screamed, "GO AWAY!" The Spriggan let out a glorified hum and brought its claw up in a spear like way and went up in flame.

Celeste stared with an open mouth as the Spriggan screeched in pain as its body cracked and went up in flame like kindle. "LEaVe! Them! ALONE!" Klin roared. Celeste watched as he emerged from the darkness and held up his hand. A stream of fire leapt to life and fell upon the Spriggans like a tidal wave. They screamed and flailed as they tried uselessly to put themselves out. Lorelei ran over to Celeste, and said something to her, but Celeste was not paying attention. Klin stood with his fist clenched. A breeze blew, ruffling his hair and coat, and placing cinders and embers in the air around him. Yet she was morbidly enraptured by his face. His eyes glowed with a deep, dark light and his face was contorted with an ugly sneer. The last thing Celeste thought was that this was someone whom both their enemies and allies would fear. Then darkness wrapped her in its embrace.

Chapter 15

New Rules for Another Family

Ander walked alongside Kyoko; their belongings strapped to leather packs across their backs. Rosy light was just beginning to filter down through the leafy cover above them. Dark bags rested under everyone's eyes except for Joshua and Erok. "How much farther do we have to walk?" Kyoko whined. Joshua spared a glance at her, "We've only been walking a couple of hours kid. We go till late afternoon." Kyoko held her head low, groaning as she began to trudge along. Ander could not exactly blame her. He was feeling the same way. Joshua's idea of dawn had been two o'clock in the morning and they had been heading west since. "You kids need to learn to look for the difference in light!" Joshua had told them, "At exactly midnight the sun begins to come back, and at two we get light!" Ander shook his head. He was beginning to think he had agreed to follow a crazy man.

All of a sudden there was a crash behind them. Ander spun around and saw Kyoko lying face down on the ground. "Kyoko!" Ander cried, "Are you okay?" Kyoko twitched as she gave a muffled, "No! I want to sleep." Ander sighed and gave a pleading look at Sasha who just shook her head. "Come on Kyoko," Ander cooed, "I know you can get up. We need to keep going."

"No!" Kyoko cried, "I'm tired and sore! I want to sleep!" Ander thew his hands in the air and grabbed Kyoko's arm and pulled her up. Kyoko just went limp and leaned backwards moaning. "Uhhhhghghghg!" She cried. Sasha moved up to them. "Come one Kyoko" she pleaded, "we need to get out of the forest. If we don't we might have to fight more monsters. You don't want that do you?"

"If I sleep now I can kill them later." Kyoko replied stubbornly. Sasha's eye twitched as she held out her hand. "Fine. I'll be harsh. Don't say I didn't warn you." Ander jumped back, knowing what was about to happen. A ball of water appeared above Kyoko's closed eyes, then it fell down on her. Kyoko squealed and leapt to her feet. "Sasha!" she complained, "I'm all wet now!" Sasha crossed her arms, "But you're awake now also, correct?" Kyoko gave her a stink eye, "Yeeeahh. I guess so." Sasha nodded in satisfaction, then grinned. "Next time don't be so stubborn sweetie, then I won't have to be mean."

Kyoko nodded solemnly, "I won't." There was a sudden updraft that blew. Kyoko mattered her hair down after she was done. "Quite messing around kids!" Joshua yelled without even turning around. "We need to get out of here before nightfall!" Ander winced. "Sorry! We're coming!" Sasha called back. The three caught up to Joshua and Erok. Erok had gone and found a healer before they had left and so was walking alongside Debbo. Erok looked over at Kyoko, who was slumping down exaggeratedly. He leaned down and picked her up. Kyoko let out a surprised squeak as she was placed on Debbo's back. "You can ride on Debbo and nap." Erok said.

"Really?" Kyoko asked, "That alright with you Debbo?" Debbo cawed affectionately in response. Kyoko wrapped her arms around the owlbear's neck, burying her face in his soft gray feathers. In almost no time they could hear her soft breathing. Erok smiled and patted Debbo's side whispered, "Thanks buddy." Debbo nudged him with his beak playfully. "You know," Erok said as he turned to the others, "I'm surprised at how quickly Kyoko accepted all of this and adapted."

"Well she stayed happy for twelve years living with that bastard." Ander snorted, "She's obviously made of stranger stuff than anyone of us." Erok nodded quietly and crossed his arms. "So what happened when you went back?" he asked softly, "You didn't have to confront your parents did you?" Ander shook his head, "No, thankfully not. Everyone was still in a panic from before. My parents were at the infirmary and all the servants but Doyce had left. I told him Kyoko and I were leaving. The poor guy began to tear up at that but he actually helped us pack. I think he's the only one from that house who will miss me. He was too good of a man to work there. I did leave a note for my parents though, letting them know I'd left. Didn't want them to think I was dead, but I doubt they would care."

"Probably not." Erok snorted shaking his head. "Never did like your parents, and that was before I learned the full story." Ander smiled at him. "That man's a coward." Joshua said abruptly. Ander looked over at the old man, "Who my dad?"

"No, the butler." Joshua grunted, "He's a coward. Don't know how long he worked there, but my guess is longer than two years, correct?"

"He's been there longer than I've been alive." Ander said smartly. Joshua eyed him and continued, "And he never tried to stop you the entire time he was there, correct?" Ander hesitated, "Well no but-"

"There you have it!" Joshua interrupted, "A true coward! Probably was only nice to you to alleviate his guilt. Man is probably to scared to eat a hornet's nest!"

"Um, any sane person is scared to do that." Erok replied confused and looked at Ander. Ander though said nothing. He wanted to argue back, but Joshua made some powerful points. "So how did your parents take your leaving?" Ander asked instead. Sasha shrugged, "Well it wasn't—by the Eight! Are you *drinking* right now?" Joshua was taking a long swig out of his metal flask. The faint scent of alcohol could be smelled coming from it. "A spirit an hour keeps the spirits from power." Joshua replied with a refreshed gasp. Sasha just stared at him incredulously. "That is the most ridiculous answer I've ever heard!" Sasha exclaimed, "You justify drinking this early with *that* explanation?"

"Oh, just you wait," Joshua grinned, "One day when not enough people are getting drunk, the ghosts will come and rule over us. Now I'd appreciate it if ya didn't critique my habits or I won't be paying for your traveling expenses. Stuff like rooms and food and the like." Sasha turned bright red and shrank down, "Please don't do that." She muttered. Ander's jaw fell into a ridiculous grin. He turned and looked at Erok who also wore a lopsided smile. "How the heck did he know she's a cheapskate?" Erok whispered not so quietly. "Her hair." Joshua grunted, "Cheapskates always have left parted hair." Sasha's face became a dark red as she grabbed the top of her head. "A-anyway." Sasha stuttered, "We were talking about my parents."

"Ah yes," Erok said with a wink at Ander, "The far more entertaining subject for sure." Sasha turned and glared at him. Erok just looked away innocently while Ander stifled a laugh poorly. "Go on!" Erok mocked, "We're listening. Captivated, enraptured, and on the edge of our seats waiting with the suspense of the story!" Sasha eyed him and muttered something under her breath. "Well there's actually not much to tell." Sasha shrugged, "Things went smoothly and without much problem. I came back, found my parents pacing about anxiously and they grabbed me in a hug. They'd heard about the attack and were worried. After they had calmed down I told them that you guys were leaving and I was going along to help you. It didn't take much to convince them. My parents are really sensible you know. I just hope my siblings can forgive me. All in all, though it wasn't that difficult."

"Oh yeah," Erok asked, "how old are your brothers and sisters now?" Sasha smiled softly as a warm light entered her eyes. "Well, Jovena is fifteen now. Markus and Vena are twelve and then Damian is ten. Karoline is nine and Jack eight. Finally, little Sevena is six." Erok whistled, "Dang, they're all so old now. I remember when half of them were born!" Ander smiled and then stopped. Sasha turned her head and tired to hide her face. "Sasha," Ander said comfortingly, "please don't lie to us. I noticed you were barely keeping it together on you way back. Just because leaving wasn't hard for the rest of us doesn't mean you have to put on a face."

Sasha spun around and looked at Ander, taken aback. Her eyes began to mist and soon hot tears were rolling down her cheeks. Ander moved closer to her awkwardly, not sure what to do. "I-I am going to mi-miss them!" Sasha cried, "I feel so terrible! I left them and they aren't even fully grown yet!"

"Don't worry," Ander whispered, "You'll get to see them again someday." Sasha continued to cry as they walked. When she finally calmed down, she said with a bit of a croak, "There is one thing I'm confused on. Why were they concerned about me?" Erok frowned and stared at her narrowed eyes. "You're kidding, right?" Erok asked, "What kind of question is that? They were worried about you of course!" Sasha hid her face and flushed, "Well, yeah I guess but what had them so worried?"

"How should I know?" Erok snorted. Ander frowned and moved closer to Erok. He studied his best friend's face, looking into his eyes. Erok darted his eyes away. "Thought so." Ander said, then pointed dramatically at him, "You're lying. Why?" Erok turned around astonished, "How did you—"

"Your voice gets slightly deeper when you try and lie." Ander replied with a wave of his hand. "Now, you going to explain to me why you lied?" Erok sighed and re-adjusted his wrist grappling hook. "I thought I would do you guys a favor and not tell you about it."

"Enough beating around the bush!" Joshua barked, "Just tell them!" Everyone jumped at the sudden shout. "Fine!" Erok shouted back then sighed, "Remember those kids we saved from the spiders? Well they weren't the only ones. The entire city was attacked, not just one area. They were still tallying up the numbers when I asked a guard, but at that moment they had a reporting of over four hundred children missing last night." Ander stumbled and almost fell to the ground. Sasha stopped and slumped to the dirt. "Over. Four. Hundred?" Ander cried out hoarsely. Erok nodded. Sasha glared at him and yelled through the tears, "Why didn't you tell us?!" Erok balled his fist and shouted back, "What would've been the point?! What point does it serve for you guys to know?! You're just upset now and going to be blaming both of yourselves for this now! I know you already are, even though there was nothing you could have done!" Ander took a step back and sat down, his heart beating wildly. This was just too much. It-was-too-the kids-four-too-hundred-so many-the spiders.

"Ander!" Sasha yelled. Ander's sight came back into focus and he saw Sasha and Erok kneeling in front of him. Sasha was gripping his wrist. "Calm down buddy." Erok comforted, "Listen to me. This is why I didn't want to say anything. But know that I have, yeah a lot of people went missing. But think of it this way, we did what we could. We saved who knows how many more kids from being added to that list? We killed so many of those spiders last night. We helped people buddy, so focus on that and not what we failed in." Ander nodded and began inhaled through the nose and exhale out the mouth. Soon his breathing and heartrate was back to normal. "You kids did a good thing." Joshua said, "But evil is enormous. It takes a lot more than three kids doing good to stop it. But don't fret too much. Three good people shine a lot brighter than a hundred evil men." Ander nodded drearily, walked with a lot less vigor. The heavy weight of the seriousness of what happened that night fell down upon them. No one spoke for the rest of the trip.

"Alright, ya slowpokes, you can stop!" Joshua halted. "Oh, thank the eight!" Erok cried and flopped down upon the ground. Kyoko dismounted Debbo and lightly danced about as she moved next to Ander. He gave her a weary smile as he placed his pack on the ground and sat down. It had been a very long day. He looked up at the setting sun. It had to be close to five or six. "What you lazy kids doing?" Joshua scolded, "We still gotta set up camp!"

"Uh, with what?" Sasha asked, "None of us have own anything that we could have packed for this." Joshua ignored her and began to whistle a tune. It sounded like a lullaby. Joshua instead reached into his coat and pulled out a metallic cube as big as his hand. It had some strange carvings on it and the metal was faintly tinted blue. He began to fiddle with it, moving his hand over the cravings in a pattern. Once he was done, the cube began to glow a neon blue. A beam of the same color shot out from it and stopped in midair. Where the beam ended, a portal big enough for a person to step through appeared. Through it was a blue nothingness, an seemingly infinite void. Joshua stuck his hand into it and began to move about. When he pulled out, he was holding a rolled-up tent. He did it again and pulled out three more. "What the herk is that thing?" Erok asked.

"What, you never seen a tent before?" Joshua asked confused. "No, the cube!"

"Well, it's a cube like ya just said."

"Argh!" Erok stomped away, angrily slouched over. "I think he meant what is it's function." Sasha put in politely. "It stores stuff in an interdimensional pocket. I call it my ass." Joshua said plainly, giving them a look like they were stupid, "Don't they teach you kids how to think these days?" Ander leaned over to Sasha, and whispered, "I don't think we'll get a straight answer from him." Sasha sighed and picked up a tent, "Yeah, you're right. Let's get stuff set up." Ander nodded and picked up a tent, almost falling over from the weight. It was heavier than it looked. Then, after much struggling, (and some help from Joshua and Erok,) they had the tents up, a nice fire, and some soup on its way.

"Man, I could eat three bowls I'm so hungry!" Kyoko exclaimed, spinning about. "Well then stop running about!" Ander gently scolded with a tiny smile. "No!" Kyoko cried as she leapt into the air, flying about. "Hey, pay attention kid." Joshua reprimanded. "You need to have some attention when cooking."

"Sorry." Ander apologized with a blush. Joshua just looked at the brown liquid and said, "Go ahead throw the onions in now." The grizzled handed him some diced onions, which Ander threw in and began to stir the concoction. The others were barely conscious it seemd. Sasha lay on a blanket, barely awake while Erok lay against Debbo. Ander though began to feel the uncomfortable silence fall upon him and this strange man. "So, uh you never actually told us where we are going." Ander said.

"We are going downriver." Joshua muttered as he chopped some carrots. "There's a guy I know who can take us down the river for free." Ander frowned, throwing in the carrots. "Why are we going down the river?" Joshua snorted as he placed some oregano in front of him. "You sure ask a lot of questions. Good. There are some people I have agreed to take care of also. My nephews. I'm supposed to meet them. Was actually on my way when I ran into you four. I'll train you on the way, and maybe you'll get some real help from my friend."

"Okay." Ander replied, "What are your nephews like?" Joshua paused, "They are kind, with generous souls like their father. They care about people, some might say too much, to the point where they won't stand up for themselves. I say those people are stupid. Both of them have fire within them. Fire that will get them into trouble." Ander nodded and then asked, "Do you have a family? Or ever wanted one?" The slicing sound of the knife stopped. Ander looked over at Joshua, who was frozen. His face had gone slightly pale. "Joshua?"

"Spirits begone." Joshua muttered, "Spirits fear me." Ander stopped and tentatively reached out his hand towards Joshua. "Joshua? Are you okay?" Joshua turned to him, a wild look in his eyes and tossed him the knife. "Finish the soup." He said brusquely and walked away. Ander barely caught the knife, nicking his finger as he did. He saw Joshua go and sit down away from everyone else and produce his flask. Ander shook his head and continued working on the soup like he had been asked. "He's like dad." Kyoko whispered from above him. Ander did not look up as he replied, "How's that? He hasn't tried to beat me yet." Kyoko gently floated down next to him, staring at Joshua. "He barely remembers how to love." Erok grumbled, walking up to them. Ander stopped and looked over at Kyoko. Her eyes were full of sadness and pain as she said, "No, that's not it. He loved *too much*, and then had it taken away." Ander and Erok shared a look with each other. Erok raised his eyebrow. *You going to tell her how off that is about your dad?* Ander shook his head. Sometimes it was children who had the best insights into the minds of adults.

"Damn Ander, that was a good meal!" Erok proclaimed with a burp. They all sat around the fire, bellies warm and full of food. "I just followed Joshua's instructions." Ander shrugged, "I didn't do anything special."

"Well, it was delicious nevertheless." Sasha smiled. Ander returned the smile, embarrassed. "Ugh, I'm tired now." Kyoko yawned. She flew over to Debbo, who lay curled up. "You were the only one who got any rest here." Erok pointed out with a bemused smirk. "Yeah, and I need sleep." Kyoko pouted, "Using magic is *exhausting*." Kyoko picked up Debbo's paw, or at least tried to. Debbo opened one eye lazily and stared at the child. He let out a soft coo and picked up the paw, letting Kyoko snuggle into his feathers. "So, I'm guessing everyone's had their fill?" Joshua asked. All of them nodded, surprised. He had not spoken a word since he had sat down to drink. "Good. It's time for some training then."

"...What?" Ander asked as Joshua walked up to him. Joshua crouched down and grinned, "What? Did you think this would be a nice and easy camping trip? You agreed to train under me or have you already forgotten?" Ander turned red and leapt up, "I haven't! But we've been walking all day! I'm exhausted and the last thing I want to do is exert myself more!"

"And we'll be walking all day tomorrow. And the day after. And the day after that one." Joshua replied coolly, "That really only leaves time for training when we stop."

"But if we all train, then we won't make much progress." Sasha pointed out. Joshua looked at her lazily. "I don't remember saying I'd train you others. I believe you forced your way into this trip, not me inviting ya. Besides, I only want to train scrawny-ass over here."

"Why only me?" Ander whined. Joshua stood up and towered over him. "Because yer the weakest. The others here are at least competent in a fight and have skill. But most importantly, they have confidence. Something you sorely lack." Ander crossed his arms and stared at Joshua defiantly. "And how do you know that I'm the weakest? You've never actually seen me in a fight!" Joshua cocked and eyebrow, "Oh and I wouldn't be so sure of that. I saw yer fight in that tourney. Wasn't too bad, if you and your opponent had been twelve-year olds." Ander turned bright red as the shame of the fight was brought back to the front of his mind. "Come on, he didn't do that bad!" Sasha exclaimed, coming to his defense. "No, I did." Ander muttered sorrowfully. "Fine! I get it! I'm bad! So where do we start!"

Joshua laughed heartily, "Now that's more like it! So, first thing's first. You're the weakest of the group, but you have the most power within due to the Triamal, so we need to focus on getting you to be able to control it." Ander tilted his head, "You know how to help me control it?"

"Not at all." Joshua grinned, "But I taught a fish to swim once, so how hard can this be?" Ander stared at Joshua in disbelief. "What?! But that doesn't-there is not connection-I mean—"

"Ahh, just shut up and listen!" Joshua slurred. Ander squinted at the man. His face was cherry red. *Oh no, he's drunk.* Ander realized. "Now, close your eyes and focus!" Ander quickly obeyed. "Now, ask the Spirits for their power."

"Wait, what Spirits?" Ander asked, as he opened his eyes in confusion. "The Triamal Spirits! And close yer eyes!" *Oh, right duh.* Ander thought. He had almost forgotten about them after they had spoken to him. *Hey, Triamal Spirits?* Ander spoke into his mind. *Yes?* A deep voice replied. It sounded like the first one that had spoken to him. *Can I uh, have some power?*

No.

Oh, okay. "They said no." Ander said aloud and opened his eyes. "Oh did they now?" Joshua growled, "So ya pompous bastards are going to be stubborn, eh? Come on out and fight me you stuck up, glorified

song birds! Or better yet, have your pathetic excuse of a vessel try and do it!" Joshua taunted. *Oh, I like this one!* The deep voice chuckled. *He's loud and vulgar.* A prim voice said, I say we fight him and put him in his place. He's obviously drunk, a third voice put in, so I say we do it but not beat him too hard. *AGREED!* The other two voices said. The coin that had appeared last time he had transformed materialized in his palm. Without thinking Ander flipped it. This time, it was a side he had never seen before. Was that some kind of fish engraved on it? Immediately his body began to transform. His skin turned gray and leathery, while gills began to sprout from his neck. His eyes gained more lids and his nose grew into a snout and became just slits. The teeth became feral and pointy, and fins appeared on his arms and back. "Holy herk!" Erok exclaimed, jumping slightly, "You can turn into a herking shark?!" Ander examined his webbed hands and feet. "I guess?"

"Yep!" Joshua cried, "And I'm gonna wrestle with it!" Joshua bounced on his feet and then fell into a casual stance. Ander charged at him, and as he was about to throw a punch, he faltered. Joshua just stood there not making any movements. Why would he—suddenly Ander was flat on his back, his arm twisted up behind him. "Again." Joshua said gruffly, "But this time don't hesitate. If you are attacking, you have to fully commit or pull out." Ander nodded as he got to his feet, then threw another punch. Joshua caught it with hardly any effort, twisting the wrist. "Owowowowo!" Ander squeaked.

"Sloppy." Joshua muttered, "Not only that, but a snail could move faster. Come on kid actually try!" Ander growled as he threw another, only to be caught once more. "Not nearly fast enough." Ander then kicked him in the stomach, sending Joshua flying back a couple of feet. Somehow, he managed to not fall, his recovery looing graceful. "There we go!" Joshua laughed, "Now the real question is, can ya hit me again?" Ander charged him, crouched low and aiming for his legs. Right before Ander could grab him, Joshua crouched down also, knocking his hands away, grabbed his waist, and suplexed him. Ander lay on the ground in a stupor, his head spinning and his vision blurry. Dimly, he felt himself change back to normal. "Nice try." Joshua said, pulling Ander to his feet, "It was a good idea. Main problem was your stance. It was as bad as cleaning a litterbox and feeding the feline a tune sandwich."

All Ander could think to say was, "Have you done that before then?" Joshua nodded solemnly, "Far too many times. I attribute my tolerance to horrible smells to that. But, that's not important yet. What is it that I know yer skills now." Ander stared at Joshua incredulously, "Wait! I thought you said you already knew them?!"

"I'd watched ya." Joshua replied with a tip of his head, "That's not the same as experiencing them. Now that I have, I can begin to teach. Now, time for bed!"

"Wait, we're done already?"

"YeP! See ya kids in the morning!" With that Joshua stumbled into his tent. They heard a loud thump. Ander rushed over and saw that Joshua was lying face down on the ground, completely out. "How much did the old coger have to drink?" Erok exclaimed. "That flask can't hold more than an ounce of alcohol!" Sasha shook her head, "So not only is he a regular drunk, but a lightweight one at that." Ander stared at Joshua silently, then ran into his tent, grabbed his blanket and threw it over Joshua. Erok gave him an inquisitive look, "Why not just leave the drunkard like that? He deserves if for getting wasted." Ander shrugged, "I'm not sure why. It just seemed wrong to leave him like that." Erok looked at him, then got up, "Whatever. I'm going to bed."

"Well, anyway I think you did pretty well!" Sasha said. Ander gave her a skeptical look. "I mean, you got a solid hit in." Sasha continued hurriedly, "That's more than what you usually get."

"I guess."

"I bet you'll be seeing massive improvements soon enough!" Sasha proclaimed. Ander slouched down, "As long as he doesn't kill me first." Sasha placed a hand on his shoulder. "Well, Joshua's training is already less brutal than your first training session." Ander smiled grimly, "Yeah, that's true." His hands ached at just the mere memory of those first few days of training. The skin peeled back from relentless hits. He had been seven. "Well, I should probably get some sleep." Ander said. "Yeah," Sasha replied. He turned to his tent and crawled in, but he could feel Sasha's eyes on him the entire time. *That was quite an underwhelming performance.* The first spirit said. "Quiet you." Ander growled, "It's not like you helped me out at all." Ha! We're not going to be quiet for a while. The third voice laughed, Our time with one another has only just begun! "Greeeat." Ander groaned. Besides, we have somethings that need to be discussed. The second voice proclaimed. "Can't it wait? I'm freaking exhausted." *No, it cannot. But fear not, for we can accomplish both of these things. Sleep, and you shall see.* With that ominous note, Ander flopped down onto his traveling blankets. Even though his body was weary, his mind was far too active to let him sleep. After much tossing and turning, he finally fell asleep.

Ander opened his eyes, awoken by the heavy scent of pine needles. He was standing in a meadow, surrounded by flowers as far as he could see in one direction, and in the other a tall, dark forest of evergreens. Yet in the distance, far off at the end of the flower field stood a mountain, tall and proud. "Where am I?" he wondered aloud. At that moment and strong, yet refreshing breeze blew over him, almost like it was caressing him. "Nowhere, yet somewhere in between what is real and fake." Ander spun around to see three men standing behind him. All three had dark black hair and dark tan skin. The first man was tall and barrel chested. He wore leather pants and a wolf's pelt wrapped across his chest. His hair was shaved on the sides, yet the top was longer and pulled back into a very short ponytail, which seemed to accentuate his feral eyes that gleamed yellow. The second man was shorter than the other two, standing even shorter than Ander. He wore simple leather pants, and no shirt. In his hand was a fishing spear. He had long wavy hair, and a slit like nose and slightly bulbous eyes. The third man was taller than the others, but was much skinner with a lean frame. He was dressed in white pants and shirt, yet his outfit was distinguished with a cape made of hawk feathers. He held a book, and inquiring eyes peered at Ander from behind a pair of spectacles. He had a hooked nose, not unlike that of a bird's beak. He had curly, short hair. Ander looked them all over and asked to the man with the wolf pelt. "Voice one?" The man smiled, "The name's Lupis," he said in a low growl, "And this is Adamer, the half-naked one. The wimpy looking one is Sean"

"I am *not wimpy*, Lupis!" Sean cried indignantly. His muscles flexed out as his body tensed, revealing a very fit and strong body. However, compared to the hulking form of Lupis, he seemed childish in comparison. Sean readjusted his glasses, "Anyhow, we are the Spirits. We called you to the Dream Realm so we could meet."

"Dream Realm?" Ander asked, looking about in awe at the landscape once more. "Yes," Sean answered with a small smile, an excited look in his eyes, "This is the area where souls can meet and commune even if physicality separates us from one another. Since this is an area where in which the spiritual and physical combine in a unique way, a new blend is formed in which the cognitive can meet!" Ander cocked his head, "Uhhhhhh, what?" Adamer sighed. "Dream world allows us to physically interact with each other when the real world won't let us." He cast a glare at Sean, "Keep the scholarly stuff to a minimum, would you?" Sean blushed, slightly abashed, "Sorry. I will be keeping that in the forefront from now on."

"Let's get back to business." Lupis snapped. He turned his attention back on Ander, his yellow eyes boring deep into his mind. "Yes, you are very confused. Confused, excited, but most of all, angry at being so overwhelmed." Ander took a step back, "How-!" "Silence for now boy!" Adamer said coolly. "All will be explained in time. Just be patient." Adamer nodded back to Lupis, who continued. "It is only natural for you to be this way. Your circumstances for acquiring this inheritance are...unique to say the least."

"What do you mean?" Ander asked, "What's the normal way for the Triamal to, uhhh, inherit you said?" Sean flipped open his book and began to skim through it. "Well, first off," Sean said, "There are normally signs at birth that whole cities will look for. The Hero Jethro also tends to help in figuring out who it is. He gives directions, explains signs, etcetera. You had none of that. We're still not sure why Jethro never gave any guidance to his generation. Herk, we're still not sure why none of the signs were even *looked for*! Especially not by the Edeavens!" Ander frowned, "Hold on, what does my home have to do with this?" Adamer crossed his arms. "Do you know the history of the Triamal boy?"

"Of course!" Ander replied, slightly hurt, "It's taught in our basic history books!" Sean began flipping through the book once more. He looked up and shook his head at Lupis. "As we thought, you only know what has been preserved." Lupis said solemnly. "So, tell me, what is it that you know? Hmm?" Ander hesitated, feeling for some reason that he was being lead to a trap. "W-well," He began tentatively, "The Triamal is a construct, created by Valoria to help humans against Romevan during The Great War of The World."

"Huh, so that's what they call it now." Sean muttered. Ander frowned, "Why, what do you know it as." Sean shrugged, "This must be a recent thing, in the past hundred years. It used to be known as the War of the Sculptors, or even the Celestial War." Ander furrowed his brow, remembering something about the old names and the reason for the change. "Oh, I remember now!" He exclaimed, "The name was changed because it added too much mysticism to the time. The Heshtisi and Sculptors are really just by products of a time full of myth and superstition."

"WHAT!" Adamer roared, "What blasphemy and arrogant thinking is this?!" Ander shrank under the fury that was in the man's eyes. "B-but the Sculptors were just humans of science who were given spiritual status due to-"

"Foolishness!" Adamer roared, "Is mankind really so ready to forget their past?! THEIR HERITAGE! THEIR HISTORY!"

"Calm yourself Adamer!" Lupis barked. "You are frightening the child!"

"But—"

"Peace!" Lupis turned his face upon Ander. Ander let out a small sigh of relief as Adamer began to calm down and compose himself. "Thank you." Ander said, but immediately wished he had kept quiet when he saw the look in Lupis's eyes. He was barely containing his rage himself. "Wh-what did I say?" Lupis let out a sigh. "You will understand soon enough. Please continue child." A small irk of anger spread through Ander. He was seventeen now! A man for two years! "Well, that's all I really know. The coin was made by Valoria, teacher of Life Magic, and somehow it can be passed down through the ages. The Wielder always ends up doing great and heroic deeds, because the world is always in need of it."

"Well, at least they didn't distort that." Sean muttered. "As for the Coin, do you know how it was created?" Ander paused, tossing out a guess, "She created you guys?"

"Hmph, with the downfall of spiritual goes basic tenets I suppose." Adamer growled. Sean gave him a sidelong glance before responding to Ander. "No. Not even the Sculptors could create ex nihilo. There is only one who can do that. We are humans just like you."

"Wait what?!" Ander cried. "I-I have *three people in me*?!" Sean nodded, "To be even more precise, we are Lucari." Ander's head started to spin as he muttered, "Great, I have three shapeshifters in me." Lupis shook his head, "Calm down boy. We are not *in* you. We merely exist alongside you." Ander vaguely took that in, a small comfort. He was still thinking about the fact that the Triamal was made up of humans! "So, um,--"

"How did this come to be?" Adamer asked? "Well, we were devout servants of Valoria herself, back when that actually mean something. Little known fact about us Lucari, our whole people are actually Valoria's dedicated servants. We were among the finest in each of our tribes, in both body and heart. Valoria was looking for people like us to make her gift to men. However, a grave price was to be paid for our help. We would lose our bodies, existing only in spirit for as long as this Coin exists. We were told all this, then given a choice. We prayed, and decided this was our fate. So, we gave our power."

"So, I'm merely borrowing your guys' power then?" Ander asked. "Did I say lend?" Adamer asked, "I believe I said 'gave' boy. No, the power you hold is now completely yours." More and more questions began to swirl through Ander's head at all this information. "So, I know the Lucari are shapeshifters, but they are not very open to strangers, so we know very little about them. What makes the Triamal different from one of the Lucari? Also, why a coin?" Lupis closed his eyes, and muttered something, and then began to explain. "We Lucari are blessed with the ability to transform into beasts, and beasts of abnormal size. Usually, we have human traits in the beast's form, not always though. However, we have one form. One only, and it can only be used once a day. You, however, are blessed with not just one Beast Form, but six! Three for the day, a land, an air, and an aquatic, and then three for the night." *Huh, so that's why!* Ander thought, thinking back to the different animals he had already transformed into. "Okay, so what else is different?"

"You can transform a theoretically infinite amount." Sean answered, "What limits you is your strength. You now have access to your animana.

Are you familiar with what that is?" Ander nodded, "Yeah, my friend Sasha is a weaver." Sean smiled, "Ah yes, the girl. Well, that saves some time. Your transformations draw upon your animana. Because you haven't been able to use it prior, it is somewhat small. Let's see if—aha!" A glowing green bar appeared in the air in front of Ander. It looked like the measuring gauge some farmers would use to see how much rainfall they got. He walked up and began to inspect it. It was barely longer than his hand, going down to his elbow. There were numbers etched upon the surface, and a small green liquid within it. "Be thankful." Adamer said, "Not many have the privilege of ever actually being able to see a physical manifestation of their animana. We can barely do this because of being in the Dream Realm right now." Sean nodded and pointed to the gauge. "As you can see, the max right now for you is twenty. Each transformation takes ten at the moment. So right now, you can only transform twice before draining it all."

"What happens if I try to transform while it's empty?" Ander asked. Sean paused and looked to Lupis. "You risk death." Lupis said firmly. Ander swallowed hard. "Got it. How do I increase it then?" Adamer shrugged, "How else? Constant training. You are still unused and new to this. So you must train. Train until each form is just an extension of your body, each transformation as easy as breathing." Ander's heart sank as he thought of that. "That sounds, difficult."

"Hmph" Lupis snorted, "So is anything worth doing in life. But I forgot, we are overseeing one who despairs easily. A coward." Lupis's words sank into Ander like a knife through the heart. "I-you- I don't—" Andamer lifted an eyebrow, "I believe he is trying to argue. But it seems he sees truth in your words Lupis." Lupis nodded, "Yet he shows fire. A weak ember that is not even hot enough to light a candle, but it is there. That is more than used to be." Ander paused, anger starting to build up in him now. "Why do you talk as if you guys know me? Have known me forever!" Sean peaked at him with that hawk-like face, "Ah, that's right. The exact way we come to you isn't really known. But come now, did you not make the connection earlier. We have been present since your birth. We have been in a coma though, only able to observe and not speak until now." Ander curled his hands into fists, "If you could see," he growled, "then why the herk did you wait so long to actually help me!"

"We could not." Adamer growled, "Believe me, we wanted to, but only once the Wielder has reached a certain growth of soul can we bestow upon you the power of your birthright. You took longer however than most." Ander sensed the sneering undertone to Adamer's voice, which only served to enrage him even more. "I've seen others look at me the way you do now!" Ander screamed, "I also know what they think about me when they get *that* look in their eyes! If I disgust you that much, why did you chose me? Huh? Why!?" Lupis gave a glare at Adamer, before giving Ander a steely look. The cold fire in those yellow eyes froze him, extinguishing the anger within him like water upon flame. "I shall answer multiple questions. One, we do not choose who we serve child. Second, you do not disgust us like those whom you have dealt with before. You are not our favorite or first choice to be honest, but we still bear a love for you for working your way towards the virtue you should be. Finally, the reason the Triamal is centered in a coin, why we do not choose? That is because that coin is the Life Seed."

Ander froze, all hints of anger gone at Lupis's words. "Wh-what?" Sean nodded, "It's true. The reason this power is yours by birth? Life Seed." Ander's head began to swim, and he fell to the ground. "Boy!" Adamer cried, "Are you alright?" "The Life Seed." Ander muttered. The Life Seed. The physical manifestation of the source of Life Magic. And he was wielding it! "I-I thought the Seeds were just legends!" Ander exclaimed. "I understand that one." Sean said, "To be completely honest, we did to till we were placed within it. Now, to be a little more precise, the coin is simply a fragment of the whole Seed. The rest of it remains hidden somewhere in the world." Ander nodded, "So, then the Seed choses the next wielder? But I thought it had not conscious?" The three Spirits looked at each other, before Adamer began to slowly try and explain. "We-we are not fully sure about how the Wielder is chosen. Let us leave it at that, shall we?" Ander nodded. This was starting to hurt his head! So much to know!

"So, what now?" Ander asked. Lupis extended a hand, smiling. Ander took it and was pulled to his feet. "Now, we begin to show you how to control your power." Lupis said. "Are you ready?" Ander paused. He had a feeling that this would be the hardest thing he had ever done, even harder than the training and education he had received from his father. As if the Dream World could sense his hesitation, the landscape changed. Ander was by himself, watching two different paths. One was if he refused. He left Joshua, and went back home with Sasha and Kyoko. He saw himself going home, begging his dad for forgiveness. His dad gave it, and his life continued. He lived a peaceful live, continuing on as he was. He was not happy, but he was peaceful. The other one, he saw himself with the group he was with, plus three shadowed figures. They all waked down a narrow path, one small slip and they fell off. At the end was a blackness colder than death, yet hotter than the sun. It emitted light, yet he could sense that the darkness hated all things that gave off life, itself most of all. It wanted nothing more than the complete annihilation of all creation, for only then would the light be gone. That darkness terrified him, yet he walked towards it, for the darkness was not the end goal. It was what lay behind it. A light so powerful that it was blinding to anything that looked at it. The light was blazing with fire, yet that fire was brilliant with the warmth of a spring day. A light of life. A light of love so powerful, that all selfish acts seemed incomprehensible under the weight of its gaze. This was the goal for which Ander and his companions strived. That light promised peace, warmth, and joy.

Suddenly Ander found himself back in front of the Spirits. From their looks, he could tell not a single moment of time had passed for any of them. *What was that? A vision of some kind?* Whatever it was, it had helped him see clearly. "I accept." Ander proclaimed proudly. All three of the Spirits grew big smiles so wide he thought their faces might split. "Then we-wait!" Lupis cried, "You must wake! You are in danger!" Ander jolted upright. There were screams outside. He looked to his side, and saw Erok was not there. He threw off the blankets and was about to run outside when a hand grabbed him, covering his mouth with something. "Sleep beckons you." A voice whispered in his ear. He smelled a sickly-sweet scent drift up to his nose. It was not coming from the rag. *A dark weaver!* Ander thought and passed out.

Chapter 16

The Evils of Men

Klin rubbed his eyes, not wanting to open them. His whole body ached and felt lethargic, plus his head was pounding. But his body forced them open as he felt his balance start to slip. He jolted upright in the saddle, regaining a proper grip on the reins. "Getting a little sleepy there?" Celeste called from behind. Klin back to her. Celeste wore a big grin. Klin just scowled, "Yeah. You try going through this kind of training and little rest." Celeste just smiled sweetly, as she squeezed gently, riding up right beside him. Celeste lowered her voice, "Well maybe you should stop sneaking off for extra magic training." Klin stiffened; she had figured that out! "If you did, maybe you would also start showing better results. There comes a point you know where you start to *lose* more progress than you make when you push yourself like this." Klin started to scowl but stopped when he saw the look of genuine concern on her face. "I-I'll stop doing that then." He replied softly, so as his mother would not hear. Celeste nodded satisfied and rode up on ahead next to Joseph. The two began to chat cheerfully, leaving Klin at the back.

Klin sighed remorsefully. Celeste was right. He needed to have more balance. It had been a few weeks now since the Spriggan attack, and he and Joseph had undergone non-stop training since. They would ride all day, receiving lessons on the more scholarly side of magic that did not require practice from their mom. Then, at night, while dinner was being made, Celeste would teach them more swordplay. Turned out Celeste had been holding back on them quite a bit. "I was putting my skill level at what I thought you would encounter before." Celeste had explained, "Now you'll see what a true master looks like!" Celeste fought with more grace and ferocity than either of them had expected. Klin had lost his matches in seconds. Now it was usually half a minute before he lost. Joseph though could now hold his own. He always lost in the end of course, but at least he could get a few strikes in. Klin could never get off the offensive. After about two weeks of this and no improvement, Celeste had taken him aside and said, "Either you're holding back, or you're not as talented as I originally thought. Either way you need to start trying harder!"

That had made Klin mad, but of course he now realized the reason he had not been improving was because he had worked himself beyond what any reasonable person should. But the only reason he had kept sneaking out to practice magic was because Lorelei refused to show them more than that basic control. "Master that, then we'll move on." Klin had asked if that was how she had been trained, but the brief hesitation in her answer had revealed that her answer was a lie. She was scared. For some reason, his mother did not want them to learn magic. So, Klin had undertaken it as his job to teach himself. The results had paid off. He could now do more than just summon each element. He could suspend a ball of light next to him and have it follow. He could create a continuous stream of fire, and his proudest achievement so far, he could now have a bolt of lightning split off into three more bolts.

"Hey Klin," Joseph cried out, breaking his line of thought, "why don't you get up here with us?" Klin smiled, "Maybe because you're too loud and annoying."

"What the heck I am being too loud over?" Joseph asked and gestured to the fields of grass that stretched to the horizon. "What? Can't here the grass growing now?" Klin just laughed and rode up beside them. The plains filled his nostrils with the scent of dry grass and fading pollen as the season slowly began the change to fall. The scenery along the road was a golden orange ocean, with pockets of wild flowers here and there. "So how much longer before we see the next town?" Joseph asked. "Not exactly sure," Celeste replied, "but we should begin to see it at the end of today, right Mrs. Markus?" Lorelei just nodded, not turning back to even look at them. Klin frowned. This was the second day that his mother had barely been responsive. What was bothering her? "Well, you boys will soon see something unique." Celeste went on, "Plain cities are a little different than your own little town."

"I don't know if were little." Klin replied, "And what could be so different?" Celeste just shook her head, "Oh believe me, where I come from, your city is what we call a village." Joseph raised an eyebrow, "And where exactly do you come from? All you've said is that you lived somewhere in Coronus. Must have been an important city for you to say that."

"Yeah," Klin said, taking the same playful tone as his brother, "Plus those parents of hers must be really successful merchants to be able to get such a unique sword. Maybe they're minor lords!"

"That really doesn't matter!" Celeste said quickly, "My hometown is of little importance. It's really not that big or important." Joseph laughed, "Well then how can you say we are from a small town?" Celeste rolled her eyes, "Because idiot, my parents are *merchants*? That means I got to travel a bunch. I've been to the capitol city before, and lots of other cities bigger than your home."

"Oh." Joseph replied lamely, which just made Klin burst out in a laughing fit. "I swear," Celeste mumbled, "if you were half as smart as you were handsome, you'd be fine." Klin paused and looked at Joseph. He had not heard that. A sly smile crept across his face. Celeste kept looking ahead, no longer looking at either of them. Oh, he was going to remember this for sure. "So Celeste, random questions but what is your favorite color?" Klin asked. Celeste looked at him in surprise, "Uh, why?" Klin shrugged, "We've been traveling together and known each other for a while now, but we really only know each other for training and bits of personal stuff here and there. I want to get to know my friend better." Celeste turned and hid her face, most likely blushing. "So, you consider us friends then?" She muttered. Joseph got a stupid grin on his face, "Well yeah! Do we mean so little that you don't consider us friends yet?" Celeste shrank in on herself even more, "Well, uh no-I just-well…" Klin and Joseph just burst out in uproarious laughter. "So what is your favorite color then friend" Joseph asked. Celeste shot him a glare in a failed attempt to cover up her flustered face.

"Well, if you must know," she pouted, "It's sky blue." Joseph looked genuinely surprised by that. "But you were so much black and red!" Celeste crossed her arms, before quickly grabbing the reins again as she realized her mistake. "You have no idea how hard it is to find traveling clothes in that color. How about you two, what are your favorite colors?"

"Black." Joseph proclaimed proudly. Celeste rolled her eyes. "How predictable."

"Hey!" Joseph protested, "I'll have you know I have good reasons for that color! I'm not so stereotypical and wanting a dark and brooding color choice. It's black because of this. It's the color of good soil, a color that one believes can nurture. Plus, the dark sky gives rise to the star lights and moon." Celeste stared in awe at Joseph while Klin hid a smile. He had reacted the same way when Joseph had first explained. "I-I'm sorry." Celeste replied, "I just wasn't expecting such a noble answer. I expected that from Klin." Joseph started laughing. "What?" Celeste asked. Klin cleared his throat and said, "My favorite color is blue." Celeste stared at him, waiting for him to explain further. "Wait that's it?" Celeste asked? Klin nodded shyly, "I just like blue okay." Joseph just continued to laugh, "This is the one time he doesn't have some bullshit analyzed meaning behind enjoying something." A small flash of anger sparked across Klin's face, cutting off Joseph's laughing. "Bullshit analyzing?" He asked coldly. Small beads of sweat appeared on Joseph's forehead. "Uh, sorry. Was just a joke. No meaning behind it." Klin began to say something scathing in return when Lorelei barked from ahead, "Stop it you two." Celeste hid a snicker as the two brothers slouched shamefully.

"A mother's voice puts even the most angry siblings in line, huh?" Celeste asked with an evil grin. Joseph just scowled at her. Celeste gave him a sweet smile in return. "Everyone, stop!" Lorelei exclaimed. Klin obeyed more out of surprise than worry, before asking, "Wait what's wrong?" He began to scan the landscape, looking for whatever had made his mother bark out that order. "Look, over there!" Celeste shouted, pointing ahead of them, "There are some people ahead and they look injured! Come on!" Celeste kicked her horse into a sprint as she charged ahead. "Celeste wait!" Lorelei called, but her plea was lost to the wind. "Ahhh, damn it!" Joseph growled as he kicked off after her. "Another day of chaos." Klin muttered as he and his mother followed suite.

When they got there, they found two women and a man in what looked like at one time nice clothing. Dirt and grime covered their bodies, and there were pale stripes of just healed wounds on their faces and dark bruises all over. Klin also noticed splotches of dried blood on their clothes. Celeste had already dismounted and was moving towards them. "What happened here?" She asked. "Please," the man rasped, with a dry throat, "help us!" Joseph though leapt in front of her before she could get too close to the man. "Hold on!" He barked, "We don't know if we can trust them! They might be acting!" The two women began to cower and shrank back even further, somehow seeming to be corned even in an open field. Celeste glared at him, but did not move any closer. "Do they look like they could be acting!" Klin snapped. "They're covered in just healed cuts and bruises!" Joseph looked startled and gave the strangers a more discerning look. He did not say anything though as he stepped aside. "Sorry for him." Celeste apologized, much scorn in her voice. "How can we help you?"

The man looked up at them, incredible melancholy in his eyes, "You friend here is wise to be so careful. We are victims of an eagerness to help ourselves. No apology is needed during these violent times." His voice, despite being dry and raspy, rang with an air of command and nobility. This was a man used to the upper crust of society, Klin thought, and one who desperately tried to act it. "Victims of eagerness?" Lorelei asked with a frown, "Explain." The man nodded and opened his mouth but one of the women cut in, her voice on the edge of hysterics. "We were traveling from Marsh to Cleana. Then along the way, we ran into another group. They said that they were the victims of bandits. They had had everything stolen. We thought nothing of it, despite the fact that they were not roughed up or wearing decent clothing. We pulled out money to help them, and then were pounced on by some scum vagabonds!" The woman cut off as she began to tremble. The other one picked up the story, "They tied us up and took us to their hideout, some abandoned fortress." She shivered and closed her eyes, "There we were thrown in cages and treated like pigs! And oh, the things they did to us!" Celeste gave them a pitying look as she asked gently, "How did you escape?"

"A man, some noble by his dress." The man answered, "He came in with a small group, maybe twenty or thirty men, and fought with these villains. We had lost all hope of anything, especially once we found out they were slavers." Klin frowned, "Hold on, slavery's been outlawed though for the past two-three hundred years in Ardaven." The man looked at him with wide eyes, "What backwater village are you from? The king reinstated it twenty years ago." A chill ran down Klin's spine. Lorelei and Joseph looked just as troubled. He and his brother locked eyes, communicating wordlessly. *We should have heard this from the merchants. Why would they not tell us?*

No idea, but there's something weird for them not to say news this big. Once the man realized they were not going to give their town of origin, he went on. "Well, he fought like he was in the pits of Heshtanus itself. But it wasn't enough. Their leader was obviously extremely skilled, probably killing about a third of the slavers himself. However, his men were just simple farmhands. They were quickly overwhelmed. He freed about half of us, btu once we saw that he was going to lose, we fled. We saw them tying him up as we ran." The man suddenly threw himself at Klin, grabbing his arm as he sobbed and pleaded. "Please! Save him! We fled like cowards instead of trying to stay and help our savior! We left him to rot!" Klin hesitated, unsure what to do with this man clinging to his arm. Celest though exchanged some sort of look with his mother, before moving closer and taking the man by the hand. "Shh," she soothed, "We'll go and rescue him. Don't worry. Your job is done. We'll save him."

"We will?" Joseph exclaimed. "Yeah," Klin growled, his grip tightening on the reins, "we will. How far is their hideout from here?' One of the women stood up, pointing behind them, "Not too far. About half a day's ride from here." Klin nodded. That was not bad at all. Joseph narrowed his eyes. "Wait, how long ago were you freed?" The man had gotten control of himself once more and said "Earlier this day. Why?" Joseph and Klin froze. He saw the air thread flying almost too late. "MOM!" Klin screamed. Lorelei calmly held up her hand, and the razor blast of wind that was about to him them was deflected upwards.

The strangers screamed and five men, rough looking and surprised, were lifted out of the grass into the air. Klin stared at his mother. All the air threads holding these bandits in a bind had come from her. "Looks like you were followed." Joseph growled. "Guessing they were hoping to use you as bait." The bandits began to struggle uselessly in the air, so Lorelei tightening the air around them, solidifying it into bands constricting their movement. One of them began to weave a thread but Klin shot a small bolt of lighting right next to the man's head. "Next one hits the source if you try that again." Klin said coolly. The man froze, intense fear spreading across his face. "So, now what?" Celeste asked. The nobles were still curled up in fear as she stood next to her horse. Joseph drew his sword. "I think the answer's obvious."

"Hold on!" Klin cried, "What are you doing?!" Joseph glared at his brother. "What does it look like? I'm going to slit some pigs throats!" Klin's face contorted in anger, "They're bound and defenseless! We can't do that!" Joseph just gave him an even stare. "Killing defenseless animals don't have the same rules as humans." Klin was about to argue further when they heard one of the men begin to gurgle. They turned around to see a slaver; blood pouring from his mouth as the life faded from his eyes. One of the men gave a soundless scream as an air thread wove down his throat. Soon enough the other four lay dead in the grass, blood staining the golden sea.

All three turned to look at Lorelei, her face pale but hard as stone. "Mom?" Klin asked weakly. It, must have been a suicide from the slavers, right? But the weaver among them died first. Lorelei swallowed hard before dismounting. She walked over and healed the travelers, before remounting. "Come on, let's move." She said. Klin though made no move as everyone else began to leave. The bloodied corpses pierced into his soul. Their dead eyes pleading for mercy. "Klin!" Celeste shouted, "Come on. We need to get out of here." Klin spurred his horse into motion, his eyes tracing the bodies until he was behind everyone else. He sneezed as they rode. The metallic smell was still rank in his nostrils. They rode on, complete silence among them. Evening fell, and they could finally see the stone fortifications of the fortress off in the distance.

"Why?" Klin finally asked. It came out as barely more than a whisper, but his mother heard it. She never even looked at him as she replied, "I'll do anything to protect my family, and not everyone can be spared. You'll understand one day soon enough, unlike your father." Klin sat silently in the saddle. It was not a lack of understanding the feeling, but the impulse to give in that he was confused on. "Hey!" Celeste cried, "There are three, wait no! Four people up ahead of us!"

Klin narrowed his eyes, straining them to the extent to try and see. Sure enough though, there was a group of four people ahead of them. "Hold on," Lorelei muttered, "It can't be!" This time, it was her who took off without any explanation. Joseph sighed, "This again?" They took off in pursuit, and as they got closer Klin realized what it was that had made his mother run like that. "Brother!" She cried. The tall man dressed in strange fashion turned around. One of his campions pulled a crossbow pointing it at them. The man smacked it away and gave them a smile. Klin pulled to a stop, slightly slack-jawed. What the herk was Uncle Joshua doing here?!

Ander sat hunched over in a ball, his arms wrapped around his legs as he barely rocked himself back and forth. The cold metal of the cage bit into his skin, his usual clothes replaced by sackcloth that hung loosely over his body. His stomach growled, making him flinch from the sharp hunger pains. It had been four or five days since he had eaten, and he had lost a surprisingly amount of wait, and by that next to none. Then again, he did not have much to lose in the first place. He let out a heavy sigh. Only one day with Joshua and he had for the first time in his life, had had enough to eat. This was nothing new at least. "Hey kid." Ander jumped slightly, banging his back against the cage. "Sorry." The voice said. "Didn't mean to startle you."

Ander turned himself to look towards the cage beside him. The small, barred window in the room let in barely enough moonlight to let him see his fellow captive, although all the colors he saw were tinged turquoise from the moon. The man had black disheveled hair that had once been combed back. He wore a faded coat that seemed to have been silk or something or expensive material but was now torn up. Ander still could not figure out why these greedy men had let him keep it. He seemed to be fairly young too, not much older than Ander. "You don't need to be afraid to speak to me you know?" The man, Nathaniel was him name, replied with a raised eyebrow. Ander had heard the name spoken by their captors. "Oh, uh sorry." Ander rasped, his voiced barely working, "I was just surprised since you hadn't spoken since you got here." Nathaniel nodded. "Understandable. I guess someone who barely speaks, and only to his enemies would be slightly intimidating."

Ander nodded in agreement. It was better than just admitting most people intimidated him. Nathaniel had shown up yesterday morning. He really did not know much more than that. He had been brought in with thirteen other men. Nathaniel was the only one left now. "So, uh who are you?" Ander asked, "And why are you here?" Nathaniel gave a small chuckle. "I appreciate it when people are straightforward. I grow quite weary of people always beating around the bush. My name is Nathaniel Aradoth, a minor lord of Derid. It's a small town to the south of here, not much to see. However, we have constantly been raided by these brutes and slavers. Those clever bastards use portals to escape with their goods. So, I came to put a stop to it. Almost did, however my band was not well trained. We ended up captured as you can see. And I believe I'm the only one left alive. Either they'll ransom me or kill me. It all depends on what is stronger for them; their greed or wrath. How about you?"

Ander's stomach gave a growl so loud that anyone in a five mile radius could probably here it. Nathaniel frowned and tossed Ander a loaf of bread. Ander stared at it in awe. "W-where did you get this?" Nathainel shrugged, "Swiped it from a guard. I was going to eat it, but you seem to need it more." Ander clutched it like it was sacred and bowed his head. "Thank you!" He began to devour the loaf like a wolf, and in between bites, he told his story. "I was drugged about two weeks ago. *Much much* I don't really know how far I am from where I was taken. I woke up one night to one of them knocking me out. Been here since. They feed me every once in a while, and beat me if I beg for food. That's about it."

Nathaniel was quiet. "Why were you on the road though?" Ander froze, debating on what to say. He decided to just be honest. "Well, I'd rather not say. Apparently, I'm in danger that I'm not fully aware of I think?" Nathaniel let out a small laugh, "Now that's intriguing. Someone on the run but they don't know why." Ander blushed, but really did not know why he felt shame. Then all of sudden, he realized Nathaniel had said something very important. "Hold on, did you say they use portals?"

"Yes. Why?" Ander slouched down, a feeling of hopelessness taking over him. "There's no way my companions will find me then, huh?"

Nathaniel was very quiet for a while before he answered, "Well, I found this place, so I'm sure your friends will too." Ander nodded glumly. There was almost no way they would find him, and why would they even make the effort? If they did it would only be because of Ander's power, not because they wanted to rescue the person wielding it. Feeling full and re-energized, Ander lay his head down to go to sleep, feeling for the first time in months somewhat satisfied his life. A life of slavery would not be too bad, right? They would probably treat him better than his father.

Clink, clack, swish, slash! Ander popped up, banging his head on the cage. The noise of his collision masked the sound of the window's metal bars falling to ground. Ander watched silently as a man dropped from the window. Two odd looking swords were in his hands, and his dark coat flared out around him as he hit the ground in a crouch. The man stood up, sheathing one of his swords, and began to look around. His eyes stopped on Ander. He began to walk aggressively towards him. Ander scrambled to the back of his cage, and shrieked as the man swung his sword, breaking open the cage. It began to fall to the floor, but the man caught it with lightning fast reflexes.

"Quiet!" The man whispered harshly, "Do you want to alert the guards. Ander snapped his jaw closed, terrified, but nodded in assent. "My name's Klin." The man whispered, "And I'm here to get you out. I know some friends of yours. Erok and Sasha?" Ander felt his heart jump for joy and he nearly shouted with glee. He restrained himself though as Klin continued, "How many are here?"

"Just me and that guy over there." Ander said quietly. Klin nodded and walked over, freeing Nathaniel. Nathaniel got out of the cage, holding himself proudly as he brushed himself off. "Thank you, sir, now how may I help my rescuer?" Klin seemed about to answer when they heard the jangling of keys. Klin rushed over to the door, sheathing his last sword. He was right in front of it as it was opened. The man gave a cry that was quickly turned into a wet gag. Before the man could grab his sword, Klin had curled his fingers by his palm, struck the man in the nose, and then quickly gotten behind him and was choking him. The man gasped and struggled to make Klin let go, however Klin seemed to have an iron grip, and the poor man could not get his hands close enough to force him to let him go. After what seemed like forever, the man dropped to the ground unconscious. Ander finally stepped out of his cage, his pack screaming in the pain of sweet relief.

Klin started to rifle through the man's belongings, grabbing the keys. Nathaniel walked up to him, and Ander heard him hiss, "Why didn't you kill the man?" Klin stiffened, and gave Nathaniel a cool, level look. Ander gulped. It remained him of the same look his dad always gave him. "It would have been murder." Klin snapped, "And I don't want to be one." Nathaniel snorted, "It really would not have been. You see the world far too black and white." Klin looked like he was about to say some sort of scathing reply, but Nathaniel threw up his hands defensively. "I'm sorry. That was quite rude of me, and this is not the place to be discussing this sort of thing. How about we talk about this later, over some good food and drink perhaps." Klin's face softened immediately, and Ander could have sworn he grinned as he replied, "Apology accepted."

"So, uh what's the plan from here?" Ander piped. Klin turned to him, a mischievous grin spreading across his face. "Just wait." They all stood around in awkward silence. Klin had his head slightly tilted like he waws trying to listen for something. The silence lasted for so long, Ander could hear his own terrified and anxious heartbeat. Finally, the signal was heard. A massive boom was heard. "Alright! Let's move!" Klin yelled with a slight whoop. They ran out the door, into a dimly lit stone hallway. It looked like no one was around. Klin took the lead and never paused as they ran. The corridors were a twisting maze of paths, yet he never hesitated in choosing. "How do you know which way to go?" Ander asked in between panting breaths. "I don't!" Klin replied.

"Herking daredevil." Nathaniel muttered. "Oh shit, by Nath's own luck!" Klin cursed. They had run into what looked like a dining room. Three men who looked absolutely wasted sat slumped on over the table. They lifted their heads and looked at the escapees uncomprehendingly. Both sides just stared at each other till one of the slaver's eyes went wide. "Rwnauays!" The man slurred. Ander acted without thinking and tackled the nearest bandit. The two hit the ground with a thud, tumbling over one another. The man let out a yell and threw Ander off of him. That spurred everyone else into action as the dining hall became a fighting ring. Ander scrambled to his feet, squaring up his foe. The bandit pulled out a knife, and a hunting knife at that. The man chuckled evilly as he saw Ander's face pale. The man began to slash about wildly, doing his best to wound him. Ander danced about, but hardly gracefully, almost tripping over his legs no less than seven times as he avoided the bandit's blood-thirsty iron.

"Stop running you runt!" The man roared. Ander backed up and tripped on the table bench, falling back on top of the table with a cry. He felt one of his ribs crack and his side flared in pain. He stifled a groan and saw the man standing above him, grinning. "It's slaughter time piggy!" He cackled and brought the knife down. Ander threw up his hands without thinking and screamed in pain as the knife plunged into the palm of his hand. The man paused, looking confused as to why Ander was not dead. He gritted his teach and knew he needed to take advantage, He grabbed the man's wrist with his other hand and twisted, hard. The bines shattered as the man screamed in agony, letting go of the knife. Ander yanked the weapon out, wincing all the while as blood gushed from the open wound. The bandit though had recovered, and had bloody murder in his eyes. The man gave a great snarl as he leapt at Ander. Yet luckily, at that moment, Nathaniel leapt in front of him. Blood splattered the stones as man hung by the neck from his thin blade. Nathaniel had found a rapier somehow.

With great elegance and smoothness, Nathaniel removed his blade, the body dropping to the ground. He shook the blood off. "Bastard," he snarled, spitting on the body. "Thanks." Ander gasped, gritting his teeth. Nathaniel frowned, and knelt down next to him, a look of admiration in his eyes. "Here, lets take care of that." Nathaniel quickly ripped a part of his coat off and tied it around Ander's wounded hand. "You are a brave man Ander." Ander turned red, and mumbled some sort of thanks back to him. "Not really though, I was terrified." Nathaniel nodded, "Well, we all were I believe." Ander paused after a sudden realization. But that thought was quickly pushed away by Klin's scolding voice. "You two done or can we get out of here now?"

"Right, sorry!" Ander cried and ran over to Klin. He noticed the other two bodies though. One had a stab wound through the eye, and the other lay on the ground with no discernable wounds. Nathaniel though took a bit of his time getting over. He first went over to the dead body and removed a rapier sheath from it. "Isn't that supposedly a sin?" Ander asked, "Stealing from the dead I mean?" Nathaniel smiled, "Not when it was mine in the first place. Never use a precision weapon while drunk my friend." Klin's face took on a stormy expression that made Ander shiver. When Klin saw Ander's hand though, his face did a complete one-eighty. What was with this guy? "Once we get out, my mom can heal you hand." Klin said.

"Um, okay." Ander replied warily however Klin did not seem to notice. "I need you to stay behind the two us." Klin ordered, "You're weaponless and not dying on me. Now let's move." They opened the door and apparently this one lead outside, because what they found was absolute chaos. The night ran red. A man near them immediately turned around and moved towards them, but feel to the ground with a crossbow bolt protruding from his heart. Ander looked to the wall and saw the brief flash of a dark cloak. "Looks like the plan's working." Klin muttered. He ran forward, and the two followed. Halfway across the grounds, they halted as Klin leapt to protect a man in black. The man flashed Klin a grin as he helped take down the foe Klin had halted. Klin then began to try and make his way back to them, but was stopped as more of the slavers converged around him and the other man.

Crack! Crack! Crack! Three sounds like a whip cracking against thunder broke the air around them. Ander jumped, clutching his ears. The men that had been approaching him and Klin lay dead on the ground. Joshua stood a few paces away, a smoking revolver in his hand and a giant sword as tall as him slung over his shoulder. Ander had only ever seen guns with the elite guards, but never had he actually heard one fired. The courtyard fell eerily silent. Ander cautiously looked around. There was hardly any movement except for a few dark silhouettes "Is that all of them?" Sasha called out. "Yep!" Erok called from the wall's top. "All clear!" Ander released a pent-up breath that he had not even realized he had been holding. "Shall we get out of this hell hole?" Nathaniel asked. Ander smiled wearily, shaking his head vehemently, "Yes, please!"

Chapter 17

Fate's Intertwined at Last

Celeste crouched down, wiping the blood off of Yatta on the grass. She would need to grab a cloth later and properly do it, but for now she would do her best. *How's that?* Celeste asked. *Much better. That feeling of blood, it's so icky.* Yatta heaved in relief. *I know* Celeste thought, *but it was necessary.* There was some silence from Yatta, and she could tell the child was thinking hard. Celeste could sense Sasha though beginning to give her an odd look. Celeste felt a slight rush as she realized she had been whispering to herself. Instead of giving her an explanation, Celeste decided conversation was the best route. "That was some impressive water weaving there!" Celeste praised, spinning around, sword behind her back. Sasha looked startled, "O-oh, thank you." Celeste skipped around to the other side, grinning, "Are you an Oceanus?" Now Sasha really looked flustered. Poor girl did not get many compliments, did she? "No, I'm just a Rivarin!" Sasha replied quickly, "And a recent one at that! You must not have seen many of us then to think that."

"Ha! As if! My father employs many Oceani, and most of them have raw strength, not technical skill like you." Sasha's former shyness quickly faded, and for the briefest moment, Celeste thought she saw a flash of contempt in her eyes. But it must have been her imagination because Sasha asked very politely, "What does your father do?" Now it was Celeste's turn to feel some sort of panic. "Oh, he's a farmer." She replied. "Must be one rich farmer then." Celeste simply nodded, "I mean he's not *that* wealthy. Oceani just come and go is all! I see maybe one or two a year and they don't usually stay on." Sasha gave her a skeptical look. *She doesn't believe you.* Yatta whispered. *Yeah, I can see that!* Celeste exclaimed annoyed, *Just, watch though. I'm a master of deflections.*

Celeste noticed the one scrawny boy standing by the gate. She assumed that was Ander based on the descriptions given to her. "So, I'm guessing the scrawny one is your boyfriend then?" Celeste asked with a playful nudge. Sasha's face turned bright red, and her eyes took on a panicked look. *Bingo.* "No! What? I mean—hold on, what in the, why would you think that?!" Sasha babbled. "But yes! That's him! We're just childhood friends!" Celeste kept her stupid grin, which just made Sasha blush even harder. She turned away and started to walk towards Ander at a rapid pace. Halfway there she broke into a run and tackled her friend in a hug.

Celeste just shook her head, standing in place as she noticed Joseph, Klin, and Joshua walking towards. "Well, that plan worked flawlessly!" Joseph crowed, windmilling his arms. "We should have Uncle plan more often!" Celeste sheathed Yatta, placing her hands on her hips. "Oh yes," she drawled sarcastically, "who would have guessed taking out the guards silently first would work soooo well?" Joseph flushed, and muttered, "Yeah, well I did most of the work taking them down you know." Celeste twirled in a circle, "Oh I know. Good job by the way." Joseph smiled, and an uncertain look appeared in his eyes, but it quickly disappeared as he said, "Well thank you." Suddenly, they heard a slight whirring. They looked around to see Erok falling gently down the wall. He disengaged his grappling hook, falling next to them. "What, can't take the normal way down?" Celeste asked. Erok just shrugged, "This way's faster."

Klin let out a heavy sigh, a flame appearing in his hand, giving them proper light to see by. "Can we all just head back to camp?" He said, "I'm exhausted."

"Alright old man," Celeste teased, "we'll get you back for your bedtime."

"Hmmm, whosaidmyname?" Joshua blurted out with a jump. Everyone just ignored the crazy old man though as they headed to the entrance, standing next to the two freed prisoners. Now that she was closer, she was able to get a better look at the two of them. Ander was smaller, but not much taller than herself. He was scrawny, obviously insecure and anxious, yet she could tell a quiet strength lay within him, just waiting to flourish. Celeste smiled at him. He was not her type, but she could already see that his potential was what Sasha liked in him. However, the other man bespoke the opposite in everything. Confidence to the point it was probably folly, aptitude in many things, a learned man, and a glint of wisdom shone in his eyes. He was also incredibly handsome.

"You must be the noble, Nathaniel Aradoth, right?" Joseph asked to the older man. "That is correct." Nathaniel replied warmly, "I assume I have you all to thank for my freedom? Tell me, how can I thank you?"

"We can discuss all that in a more comfortable place." Klin cut in, "For now why don't we all head back to camp?"

"That sounds wonderful!" Nathaniel exclaimed, "But uh, I don't suppose you have any food prepared, do you?" Klin nodded. "Wonderful!"

"Wait!" Ander yelled, "Where's my sister?!"

"Don't worry," Celeste soothed, "She's back at our camp with these two's mother and the owlbear." Ander smiled, relaxing and nodded. Suddenly Klin stiffened, "Damn it! That's right!" He grabbed Ander by the arm and ran off with him towards camp. Everyone paused surprised, then turned to look at Joseph. "Why's everyone looking at me?" He cried indignantly, crossing his arms, "I don't know what he's thinking half the time myself."

"Y'all need to pay more attention." Joshua spoke quietly, "Ander's hand was covered in bloody bandages. And it was still a'bleeding. Now, why don't we join them?" Joshua strode forward, seeming not to notice the air of shame that feel upon everyone. They all followed after him soon enough, but it was much quitter and more subdued.

Their camp was actually not too far from the fortress. Nestled in the grass about thirty feet from the fort, was a unique sight. Joshua had revealed to have some very interesting items on him. At first, all one could see was tall grass. But upon closer inspection, the top of a tent could be seen poking out from the ground. Joshua's hand hovered over the top, and five symbols appeared in the air. He pressed them in a certain order, and then the top opened. They followed him down and inside. At the bottom was a very big open space. Big enough for about five more tents, which were pitched, and an owlbear to stand up at full height comfortably. A fire blazed in the middle, an air spell placed above that dispersed the smoke, filtering it from the air around it. Klin,

Kyoko, and Ander sat around chatting, bowls of soup in their hands. Celeste noticed that Ander was not wearing the bandages Joshua said he had had on.

However, a pile of bloody bandages lay next to Lorelei, who was tending the fire. A big pot, most likely from Joshua, sat above the fire, a delicious smell emanating from it. Celeste's stomach began to growl at the smell. Lorelei smiled at them all encouragingly, "Please, come get some food! I made more than plenty." Celeste was already running to grab a bowl. "You don't have to tell me twice!" With much gratitude, they all grabbed food. Lorelei had not been kidding when she said she had made plenty. They had enough for everyone to not only have seconds, but thirds too. Celeste and Joshua eyed each other though as they stood over the pot, just enough left for one final serving. "So kid, you think you can actually eat a fourth?" Joshua growled, his hand twitching. Celeste stretched her hand, flexing each finger. "Oh yeah. I'm still growing old man." Joshua raised an eyebrow, "Alright, so neither of us will back down. So why don't we make this interesting?" Celeste cracked her neck. "Oh, and how's that?"

"Only one way to settle these things. Standoffs. Grab that there spoon first, and ya get the final serve."

"Deal!" Celeste cried. The two lowered their hands, the tension rising as they stiffened their muscles, preparing to draw first. "On your mark," Lorelei exclaimed, "GO!" Celeste darted her hand out like a snake, but if she was a snake, Joshua was a lightning bolt. He snatched the spoon so fast, it looked like it had teleported into his hand. "Nice try." Joshua smiled wryly, "You're the first person to almost out eat me. And closest I've ever seen to being beaten in reflexes." Celeste crossed her arms and sat down by Joseph, sulking. Joseph though looked at her in awe, "You know, he's not lying. I've never seen someone get that close to beating him." Celeste glared at him. Close? How had she been close? She had never stood a chance! *You know, taking defeat like this is not very nice.* Yatta chimed in. *Oh, be quiet you.* Celeste growled back. There was brief silence. *Sorry* Yatta whimpered. Celeste immediately felt bad and guilt. *No, I'm sorry. Here, you need to eat.* She took the feeling of love and want she had for Yatta and transmitted it to her. *Thank you,*

Celeste. I'm going to sleep now. Celeste smiled as she felt Yatta's presence leave her mind.

"So, uh how did you guys find me?" Ander asked, now that everyone had had their fill of food. "I thought there would be no trail?" Celeste looked up, intrigued. This group of weirdos actually had not told them how they had found Ander. "Astronomy." Sasha replied. "Erok paid attention to the stars' placement in the sky when they opened their portal. Between him and Joshua, we were able to figure out exactly where you were thanks to them."

"You people are quite the skilled group then!" Nathaniel praised. "What could a lowly noble such as I have to give so skilled a party in thanks?"

"I mean, money's always nice." Joseph said shrewdly. Klin elbowed him in the ribs a little roughly. "Hey!" He protested, "We need money. It's not like any of us are rolling in cash."

"Still." Klin muttered. "We shouldn't ask for rewards." Celeste jumped in surprise as Nathaniel let out a hearty, warm laugh. It had the same warmness and love as her father. She frowned though. Something felt slightly off. That frown though was quickly dispersed by what Nathaniel chuckled out. "Ahh, the innocence of youth! If only we could all think in such black and white terms. Maybe then we would not create gray."

"Wise words." Lorelei said solemnly. "Although I'm not very surprised to her such things from you. We heard about the reason you were imprisoned from some of the slaves you helped escape." Nathaniel shrugged, "I like to think I'm a decent fellow, but nothing more than that. I'm just an average man who was born into power and doing my best not to abuse it."

"Ah, so you are the governing lord of Cleana then." Sasha proclaimed. Nathaniel nodded, "Yes, and not a very good one if I'm being honest. I'd much rather spend my time in scholarly pursuits than running a town. I don't understand my people that well, so I constantly fear ruing their lives with one callous decision." Joshua snorted, hanging out at the edge of the group. "Ya at least care for them. That's more than I can say for most of them black hearted lecherous nobles."

"That's far too true, isn't it?" Nathaniel sighed. Klin though, who had been sitting patiently and seemed about to burst like a waterskin filled to the brim, blurted out, "So, you said you're a scholar? What of?" An excited sparkle was in both of the men's eyes. "Philosophy and magic." Nathaniel replied. Celeste groaned inwardly as Klin sat up like a stick had been stuck up his back. She had heard enough philosophy from him this past week. Her heart took on an even more horrified feeling, when Joshua took an interest, drawing closer. "What fields ya study?" He asked, "Many can pass themselves off as smart but they're really quacks." Ander and Erok exchanged a very sarcastic look, but Celeste ignored them when Nathaniel answered. "Well, I study ethics and the various uses of elemental stones." Now the noble had everyone's attention.

"So, yer a Stoner then!" Joshua cried. Nathaniel glanced over awkwardly, "I mean if you want to call me that fine. But I prefer the official name of Haereomist." Celeste suppressed a snort. Intellectuals could be so damn haughty. "So, are you a Weaver then also?" Sasha asked. Celeste rolled her eyes not too inconspicuously. That was such a dumb question, especially coming from someone who could use magic. Nathaniel though was for more charitable in the question than she herself would have been. "Yes. I use fire and light specifically."

"Hey that's the same as Klin!" Joseph yelled excitedly. "Of, course he can use lightning also though." Klin glared at Joseph, a murderous look in his eyes. Celeste was barely close enough to hear him hiss, "You idiot! That's not something I want broadcasted around!" Nathaniel burst out laughing rancorously, "Oh! That's a good one!" Celeste sniffed indignantly. It was one thing for Joseph to blurt that out like an idiot, but it was another for this puffed up noble to make fun of her friend! "Hey Klin, show this blue-blooded, sliver-spooned arrogant man how wrong he is!"

"Excuse me?!" Nathaniel cried, leaping to his feet. "What did you just call me!?" Celeste smiled wryly, "You heard me, you egotistical puss head." Nathaniel's face contorted in rage, turning as red as a beet. "You upsih peasant! Don't insult your superiors!" Celeste's smile grew into a massive, shit-eating grin. *Oh, if you only knew.* She thought. Klin though leapt up in between the two. "Hey!" He yelled, "Knock it off!

We just got done fighting. We don't need any more!! Now apologize!" Celeste began to smirk when Klin barked at her, "You're the one who needs to apologize."

"What?" Celeste huffed, "But he started it!" Klin turned a glare on her that was so bone-chilling, that any thought of arguing died on her lips like flowers with almost no soil in the pot. "From where I'm standing, a normal person's reaction is to take it as a joke." Klin growled lowly, "And it's not your place to decide what I reveal. It's *my* secret, not yours." Celest nodded, a deep feeling of shame and a slight pang of hurt. "I'm sorry." Celeste apologized with a bow, "He's right. I should not have said such awful things." Nathaniel sighed and gave a bow also, but it was not as low. "I'm sorry too. I should not have reacted so violently. My sincerest apologies." Celeste nodded in a half-hearted recognition and sat back down. Her chest felt like it had syrup in it from the shame. *Remember your true worth now?* A small voice in her head whispered. *You forgot for a bit during your travels, didn't you?* "Now, if everyone's calmed down!" Klin said tersely, "I'll show you why Miss Hissy Fit got so angry." Celeste shrunk in, wishing she could cover her face with her jacket. That would only make her shame more obvious though. Klin took a deep breath, and then held out his palm upward. A dancing flame flashed above it, before a crackling bolt of lightning, barely contained. Finally, a white ball of light lit up the cavern before flashing out. "By the Nine." Nathaniel whispered, "You were not joking. By all the laws we know this should be impossible!" Klin sat down, his recent anger replaced by shyness. Celeste looked over at those who had just joined them. Ander, Erok, Sasha, and even his uncle were looking at Klin stupefied.

"Yeah, it should be impossible," Klin said, staring at his palm. "But somehow, it's not for me." He looked up tentatively. "Well I'll be damned," Erok chuckled, "no wonder you guys were so confident he could take care of himself." Kyoko leapt into the air and began to circle over Klin, poking and prodding him. "Hey!" Klin complained, "What the heck are you doing?"

"Huh, well nothing seems different about him." Kyoko declared, "Maybe we should have him take off his clothes and see then?"

211

"Kyoko!" Lorelei gently reprimanded, "That is not appropriate!" Kyoko hunched her shoulders and blushed. "Sorry." She then flew back over next to Ander. Celeste frowned though as she caught Ander giving Lorelei a glare. She sniffed softly. If he disliked her for putting a child in her place, maybe he should have done it first! "Anyway, enough about my brother." Joseph stated, "Poor guy looks like he's about to cry from all the attention you guys are giving him."

"Am not!" Klin sulkily protested, crossing his arms. "Uh huh, sure you are big guy." Joseph replied, not even trying to hide his grin. "So how about you guys tell us why you're travelling together? You never did tell us."

"Well, we did have more important matters to attend to." Erok replied dryly.

"Wait, you were not all traveling as one?" Nathaniel asked. Joshua shook his head, "No. Why would we do that? Fusion is a messy and complicated matter." Everyone gave him an exasperated look but ignored him. "We only meet near the fortress today." Joseph explained. "So, let's all be quiet and let them explain." Everyone followed his advice as they listened rapturously to Ander, Eork, and Sasha with Joshua adding in a few comments here and there. (Not all of them making sense however.) From the tournament to the battle in the forest, to Ander's kidnapping, it was quite the story to behold. There was a brief silence hanging over them as they finished the story. A silence that Celeste decided to break. "Under the Eight's Holy names!!!" Celeste exclaimed, "You're the herking Triamal?!"

Ander seemed to be trying his best to withdraw like a turtle as they all looked at him in awe, giving them a slight nod. "Yep." He squeaked out. "I'm the Triamal." Joseph just began to laugh warmly. "Well, no wonder our uncle wanted to snatch you up! I knew there had to be something special about you."

"Why didn't you use your power to escape though?" Celeste asked confused. Ander turned even more red, if that was even possible. "Well, uh I don't have full control yet." He mumbled. "Plus, I didn't have enough energy to transform from the way they treated me." Celeste eyed him skeptically. Something about his voice felt like he was not fully telling the truth. "Anyway," Klin said, "since we were supposed to travel with our uncle, why don't we all travel together from here on out?" Erok looked at him suspiciously, examining him with a critical eye. "Why? What do you get out of it?" Klin sat with a stupefied look, as if someone had just slapped him across the face for offering a sweet to them. Sasha though glared at Erok and said condescendingly, "Because it's the logical thing to do. They already explained that they were looking for Joshua, and he confirmed these two are his nephews."

"Yeah, I know that." Erok snapped, an icy undertone freezing them. "I was here, remember? What *you* failed to remember however is that Joshua admitted he hasn't seen them for what, five or seven years? They never told us *why* they are looking for him." Erok turned his gaze upon the others, his furrowed brow like a searchlight that revealed all. "You just show up when we happen to need help the most, claim to be his nephews, and help us out. So what, now we're supposed to be all buddy buddy? Only an idiot would trust you guys at face value."

"Now hang on just one minute!" Joseph protested, "We helped you guys out! Why would we—"

"Oh, shut it." Celeste snapped, "Even I can see that he has a point. They told us their story. Now we tell ours." The atmosphere become silent, as everyone waited expectantly for the story. Klin let out a weary sigh, "Well, the truth is we need Joshua to lead us to sanctuary. We've been on the run." Ander frowned, "Sanctuary? What do you guys need to get away from?" Klin looked them dead in the eye and said softly, "Romevan." Erok snorted derisively, "Oh come on! If you're going to lie, at least make it a believable one!"

"Shut up kid." Joshua growled, "I have a letter saying exactly that. You wanna know what I was *really* doing in Edeaven that night?"

"Replenishing your alcohol supply?" Joseph asked.

"Uh, well yes." The grizzled man replied sheepishly, "But that was just a bonus! I have many contacts, and I was checking on them. I had just read that letter when those punks showed up." Erok fell quiet, nodding. Celeste noticed however, that he showed no signs of shame or wanting to apologize. "So, who is this big bad guy?" Kyoko asked. "Is he using the Romevan from fairy tales name?" Klin shook his head. "No. It's the real one. It began what, two months ago now?" So, the two brothers wove their tale. Celeste and Lorelei spoke when needed, but for the most part, the two told the story, especially the ending. A melancholy and solemn silence fell upon them, only the crackling of the fire being heard.

"Damn." Erok whispered. "You guys actually *did* all that?" Klin and Joseph nodded. Erok sighed, "That story is just too weird and cohesive for it to be made up. I'll trust you for now." Sasha put her hand under her chin, eyes contorted in deep thought. Celeste felt a slight stab of jealously. How did that girl look pretty even while thinking like that? She would never be able to look that way. "There's something I still don't understand though." Sasha pondered, "Why exactly was your father to warrant such interest from Romevan himself?" Erok's previous trust vanished from his face in an instant. "Hold on. Yeah, who was he?" Celeste had learned her lesson from before, so she stayed quiet. Klin and Joseph exchanged a subtle look. She had been with them long enough by now to know they were very nervous and trying to figure out how to tell them no, and still have them trust them. Luckily, Joshua was there. "Don't worry about that." He said quietly, "they'll tell you when the time is right. Just know that their father was a great and saintly man."

"The herk!" Joshua cried, "You not been listening! He married my sister! Of course, I knew him you idiot! I'll be damned if I had not known the little shit who got married to my baby sister! He was a great man and one of my best friends!!" Celeste was startled as tears began to trickle down Joshua's face. He had not known, had he? Uncle Joshua turned his back on them, and sat down away from them in the all encompassing darkness. "Why don't we call it a night?" Lorelei suggested quietly. "One of us is already asleep anyway it seems." Everyone smiled gently as they saw Kyoko lying on Lorelei's lap. "Yeah," Erok agreed, "Let's go ahead and turn in. Goodnight, everyone." He went ahead and climbed up atop Deboo and snuggled into his feathers. Lorelei carefully picked up Kyoko and carried her to one of the tents. Everyone was assigned their tents. Celeste let Sasha go in first, giving one last look at Joshua, not sure if she should talk to him. However, Lorelei was walking over to him. So, she went inside and threw her sheets over her. As she fell asleep, the usual nightmares came, only this time a new one joined their ranks. The fires were joined by blood.

Chapter 18

The Price of Life

Spring had come after a long and harsh winter. Diane was out her sickness and recovering fine. "Come on!" Andrew yelled, "Let's go out and play." The little boy grabbed his arm and dragged him outside. The eight-year-old wasn't that strong, but he could not bring himself to fight against the child's smile and pleading eyes. The two went outside, a river breeze wafting across their island home. Dominic stood near the woods, practicing his swordplay. The boy would be a master soon enough. Josephine sat crouched under a tree by the flower field reading. He smiled warmly, glad to see her outside. Josephine was a delicate creature, and at eighteen, she was a flower just now in full bloom. "Come on dad!" Andrew yelled, "Let's play tag." He grinned as he brought his attention back to him. "Alright, but yer going to hafta run fast to be able to escape the Snickerdach!" Andrew squealed with delight as his father began to chase after him. Then he heard the loud gasp of someone being startled awake.

Joshua shook his head as he returned to the present. That had been the strongest one in year. "Damn brain." Joshua muttered, "Ye can't do want I want. Must be the Snickerdach again." He took out his flask and took a swing of beer. The comforting tingle of alcohol filled his whole body as the faces faded from his sight. He knew he shouldn't have stopped drinking this week. But he'd just felt so damn responsible! "Joshua? Why are you still up?"

He turned around and saw the girl, Celeste was it, walking up behind him. "Keeping watch." He lied, "Someone has to." Celeste gave him a flat look as she said, "But isn't the whole point of this whole underground thing so you don't have too?" Damn. Sleep was not an inhibitor for her brain it seemed. "Well why are you up?" Joshua deflected, "Can't sleep or you just enjoying the cavern air?" Celeste sat down next to him, "No, it was just a dream. Startled awake and all that."

"Mmmm, must a been a pretty intense dream then."

"Oh, it wasn't *that* bad." Joshua looked over at the girl. Her eyes had the same look as when they had been walking back to camp. She had hidden it with a smile and had probably even fooled herself. Eyes sunken and listless, as the reflections of blood upon the ground and the entrails of a man you'd just gutted danced in front of them. She could fool herself, but she couldn't fool him. "So, yer seeing their faces, huh?" Joshua asked quietly. Celeste jumped. "What?"

"The men you killed." Joshua explained, "Tonight was yer first time, wasn't it?" Celeste looked away, wrapping her arms around herself. "Yes." She whispered, "I know we were justified killing them. They probably deserved more than death. But, all I see is their faces before me. Staring at me accusingly, angry, and scared." The poor girl shivered as she hugged her legs tightly. Joshua was silent for moment, before he said, "I'd tell you it gets easier from here, but I won't. Cause that would be a lie and give you false hope. If killing gets easy, if it becomes like breathing for you, then you've become no better than them. You should always hate it."

"What about the faces?" Celeste asked, "Do they always stay?" Joshua looked her dead in the eyes and said, "If you forget, then you've joined them. One who says they remembers has forgot, and the one who forgets remembers. So yeah, I remember those faces." Celeste looked at him confused, before shock and finally pity flashed across her face. "Isn't it okay though to forget them?" She asked, "There's always hope."

"Hope left this world twenty years ago kid." Celeste stared at him for a while. She obviously wanted to say something to try and comfort him. In the end she chose the right option and went back to her tent. Soon enough, her slowed breathing joined the chorus of everyone else. There was one more person now who would not turn out like him. "Cheers!" Joshua muttered with a dry smile, and drank deeply to his victory.

Klin woke up at the crack of dawn. The top of the tent somehow let light into their cavern. No one else was up yet though. The soft, yet heavy breathing of his brother fogged up the air near him. He shivered as he threw off his warm blanket. Fall was approaching now. He softly trode over to the horses. They barely noticed him. He pat Strider's snout, getting an affectionate bump from him. Klin grinned and grabbed the food from the packs. He brought the food over to the fire, placing it down. Smoldering ashes and warm coals were all that were left of last night's flames. He grimaced, and went back to the horses, grabbing logs from Cider's saddlebags, thankful for his mother's foresight. He threw them onto the coals. Unfortunately, the coals were now so few, and so weak at his point for any spark. With some effort, Klin summoned a small flame and got a roaring blaze going again.

Ten minutes later, the tangy smell of bacon and toast wafted across the air. One by one, he could hear everyone begin to stir. However, Ander was the only one who emerged from his tent. "Good morning." Klin said, somewhat cheerfully, sipping some coffee. Ander stared at him groggily, stumbling over to him. Dark bags hung under his violet eyes, yet even with that much obvious lack of sleep, there should have been a slight sparkle to them. Klin grabbed a plate of bacon and toast, and then handed it to Ander, sitting down next to him. The two began to eat in silence, but Ander barely eat. Only nibbling here and there at his toast. Klin studied him for a while. The hunched shoulders, downcast gaze, and lack of energy. "Couldn't sleep because of guilt, huh?" Klin asked.

Ander whipped his head around, eyes wide. "How—" Klin just laughed, "Dude, your whole body language just screams, 'I'm guilty." Ander turned away, eyes down. "O-oh. Gotcha." Ander set the toast down. Klin's laughter died, and he nudged Ander, "Go ahead and keep eating. Starving yourself won't solve any depression." Ander gave him a look in between a glare, and thankfulness. But he picked up the toast and took a huge bite. Soon enough, his plate was cleared with the voracious energy of a wolf. Klin smiled at him. "Nice work! You do have an appetite! Now, what's wrong?"

Ander sighed, "I normally would not want to tell anyone this. But, you seem a little different about this kind of thing. It's just, when I think back, I should have fought back more. I thought I had finally changed! You know? Grown stronger, more courageous! Yet, when the time came,

I failed spectacularly. Back into my old cowardice." Klin just snorted, "What, you think one victory is enough to change a person?" Ander flinched back, like he was expecting something else to follow. "No one truly changes first try you know. We rise and fall in an endless cycle of trying to overcome our faults. So, you fell, and it was a pretty hard fall. But, it seems like you're not at the bottom. At least not yet." Ander grinned wryly at him. "You know, that is some really blunt advice. But somehow, very comforting." Klin laughed softly, and patted Ander on the back. "Well, you need pain before any healing."

Ander's countenance though fell, his face darkening all of a sudden. "What now?" Klin sighed, a ting of annoyance. Ander turned bright red and tried to hide his face. "Oh, um, well, my friends. I'm, well I'm afraid they hate me now." Klin raised his eyebrow. "Seriously? That's what you're worried about now? Normally I would say you should, cause I probably would myself. However, would people who hate you go to this length to rescue you?"

"Well no, but—"

"Shut it. No buts." Klin reprimanded, "It seems to me you have some great friends. If they hated you, based on last night, I'm ninety-percent certain Erok would make it vocal." Ander laughed, a genuinely warm laugh. "Yeah, that's very true! Thanks, Klin. I just need to have your confidence." Klin smiled, "You're welcome." It was easy to put on a show when someone else needed that reassurance. "What are you guys talking about?" Kyoko yawned as she emerged from her tent. She was rubbing her eyes as she floated towards them. Ander shook his head as he grinned at her. "Oh, just friendly stuff. And Kyoko, we've talked about this! It's dangerous to use magic half awake!"

"Not when I've done this one so often." His sister grumbled. However, she did land back on the ground, and eyed the food greedily. Klin handed her some, and soon enough everyone else was out and eating. (Except Joseph. Celeste had to go in and kick him awake.) Once they all had had their fill, they were packed and ready to go. "So how far is your village?" Klin asked as he led Strider over. "About a full three days ride from here." Nathaniel replied. "I know we did not really talk about it last night, but I would like to ride with all till then."

"Uh, we kinda figured that." Joseph ridiculed lightly, "What we going to do? Make you walk after rescuing you?" Nathaniel just shrugged, "Well, you should never assume another's kindness. Thank you very much!" Erok cleared his throat not so subtly. "Don't mean to break this up, but we need to figure out the logistics of traveling together. As you can see, we don't really have many mounts. We'll need to have people ride with one another. I can take three on Debbo, myself included. That's the only one we have."

"Unless you include Ander." Joshua snickered. Lorelei smacked him on the back on the head. It was actually pretty amusing to see her fly up to reach his head. "I can ride with Ms. Lorelei!" Kyoko pipped. Lorelei gave her a motherly smile. "I would be happy to let you ride with me."

"Alrighty then, Ander, Sasha, why don't you ride with Erok?" Joshua suggested, "You three get along well." Ander and Sasha nodded, and Klin was pretty sure Sasha blushed slightly. "Okay, then I can take Nathaniel." Klin offered. "Then you can ride with Joseph, uncle."

"Sounds good. Any objections!" Joshua exclaimed. "Nope." Everyone replied. Joshua nodded, and with a grin hopped up on Cider next to Joseph. "Hope this thing don't have fleas." Joshua grumbled, "They suck all the melatonin from you, ya know."

"Uh, what?" Joseph asked, a bewildered look plastered on his face. "Just don't let 'em bite me! Now let's go!" Joshua cried, kicking Cider into action. "What the—UNCLE!" Joseph screamed, fighting to gain control of Cider as they bolted off like lightning. "Well, I suppose we should follow them." Nathaniel said with a shrug.

Three days came and went little to no excitement. Klin discovered that Erok was a voracious reader, and so the two of them had some very engaging conversations about they different works they had read. Erok had a very keen mind, and often gave deep insights, however they were overshadowed at times by his crude comments. It turned out that Ander had a few surprises up his sleeve too. Despite a lack of skill and his meek personality, he really loved wrestling. He knew all the technical terms and techniques, talking about them a bright fervor with Celeste and Joseph. Sasha would talk with Lorelei and Kyoko, and occasionally personal conversations with Klin and Joseph.

"You have six younger siblings?!" Joseph cried, "How do you stand it? I can barely keep this one in line!" Klin raised an eyebrow at him, "I think you have it backwards brother dear." Sasha laughed, giving them a warm smile. "Well, it's definitely hard. However, I love them all quite a bit. They all have so much life to them! It's never boring. Heartache at times sure, but love so bright it warms your soul." Lorelei had a wistful look as she stared at Sasha. "Their father and I always wanted more. I hope that big family has not dissuaded you if you ever marry." Sasha shook her head, "Oh no. I've seen the beauty and would love to have it myself." Celeste though shook her head, "Man, I can't imagine all the pain though! That's a lot of labors!" Sasha smiled at her, "Well, that many is not everyone's calling." Klin though could have sworn he caught a disdainful sneer covered by the smile. She was incredibly sweet and kind though. Must have been his imagination. Celeste looked down and muttered, "Yeah, I suppose you need to be strong enough for that many."

They also discovered that Nathaniel seemed to have a dabbled interest in almost everything they could talk of. "Why yes, I am a fan of sparring and wrestling matches. However it is more of a side hobby than a true passion." Or, "Ah yes, Derick Malvory, on of my favorite writers. I just adore his blend of prose and poetry in a story. Of course Zachequette Marque is another favorite. What, you've never heard of him? A hidden gem my friends, a hidden gem indeed." Klin remembered this comment, mainly because he then proceeded to ask, "Well, maybe you could recount a few of his stories for us?" Nathaniel laughed, "Oh course! I would be delighted to retell one of his stories. Hmmm, now which one?"

"Ah! I know! The Man with Nothing. You'll have to excuse my lack of poeticness, as I will be retelling this from memory. Our tale begins in the First Age, during the time of the Sculptors' War. It was one of those rare decades where neither side was actually doing any fighting, just plotting. For immortal beings, what is a decade to them but a year of working out the details? One man, by the name of Joshua Malan, however decided to take advantage of the peace. Born into a poor family he had little, growing up with barely the needed amount of anything. Yet he grew into manhood like a flourishing flower, being a big man with quite an amount of strength. About halfway through his life, he earned a job as an ox tender to one of the local lords, which allowed him to tend for his family and earn more than enough food for them."

"Yet eventually he was framed for theft by one of the servants, and was dismissed. However, his master was suspicious of mal intent and so gave Malan his own little pot of land and a small home. Now, magic was in these days much more rare than it is today, and far more mysterious to our ancestors. One day, as Joshua was tending to his squash, he noticed that one of them was far larger than the rest. Joshua was very warry, for the soil was poor and hard. There had also been stories of a new breed of Heshtisi had appeared, one which lured you in through gifts and guile. He grabbed his pitchfork and destroyed it."

"Immediately he retreated in fear, expecting some friend to pop up and eat him. When nothing happened, he grew sorrowful, realizing that he had destroyed one of the few gifts given to him in life. The next day he went back out, and much to his surprise, over half of his crop had grown to enormous size! This time he wasted no time in harvesting all of them. Yet he still kept a warry eye out for any Heshtisi. None came. And for months, Joshua's crops only produced exceptional food in size and tase. Soon enough, he amassed enough money to buy more land and a nicer home. Joshua though pondered what could be causing all of this. The soil was far from good, and the seeds were nothing special."

"He realized one day, after cutting himself and then watching two threads heal himself, that he had Life Magic. He had been unconsciously pouring in magic to the plant's growth. Joshua hired some workers, as his fields got too big for him alone. He would walk along, infusing them with his magic. Soon Joshua was the richest man in the land, with a wife and children. He was finally living a life of peace and comfort. Every day he was thankful for the gifts he had been given."

"Then, one day, he met a stranger at his doorstep. The man was poor, dressed in rags and emaciated. The man meekly asked Joshua for some food. Malan, being a man who understood what it was like to be in that position, took the man in. He dressed him in silk and nursed the man back to health. 'My goodness!' The stranger exclaimed, 'How blessed are you! All this wealth and rich ornaments! If only I were this fortunate!' Malan inquired to whether the man had any family. 'I confess I have no living relatives.' The poor stranger replied, 'It is just me, poor old Tom these days.' Joshua, his heart moved by pity and love asked, 'Well how would you like to work here for me?'"

"Tom was ecstatic and accepted with flowing tears. Tom proved to be a hard and valuable worker, and more than that, a great friend. Soon Joshua and Tom learned to love each other like brothers, but even brothers have their sins. Despite Joshua's unending love and charity, Tom grew jealous, coveting all that his friend had. So, Tom connived to bring Joshua to ruin. At first, he just wanted the things that Joshua had, but soon his jealousy twisted him to want nothing more than his complete destruction. The plan started with a small finding; discovering Joshua's power. Sly Tom, slowly and carefully persuaded Joshua to stop making his rounds 'Why should you work? Let me do it for you! I myself have life magic you know. Spend time with your family.' Through such seducing words, and with some clever illusions, he demonstrated his 'magic'. Slowly the quality of the Malan's crops faded and the wealth began to fade. Joshua paid no attention to his waning coffers, donating just as much as he always did to the poor."

"Tom had also convinced his wife to keep her wealthy life style, despite the lack of funds. Joshua would often berate his wife for her ostentatious living, but would not budge on giving to the poor as much as he did. His wife, enraged by Joshua, left him, taking their kids. But she still had claim to his money. Bit by bit, Joshua fell into debt and ruin, till he lived in nothing more than a hut. It was now only him and Tom. As the two sat in the muck and grime, Tom was enraged. Joshua, covered in rags and dirt, smiled at him. 'You are my truest friend Tom. A brother who never abounded me, nor betrayed me, even at my lowest points. Thank you.' Tom looked into those pure and innocent eyes, full of love and felt something deep within him. A burning hatred so powerful that if felt as if his entire body was aflame. With a cry, he seized Joshua by the throat in a manic frenzy. Joshua was well three times Tom's size and weight. However, he did not resist. He looked at Tom with deep hurt, but more than that, a deep forgiveness. Tom married the wife, and took control of all the wealth that he had hidden. Yet those eyes haunted him for the rest of his days."

Nathaniel finished his story with a solemn flair. "That's it?" Klin asked, "Tom got away with it, never punished?" Nathaniel shrugged, "That is how the story went."

"But the villain got away unpunished!" Joseph protested, "It's not fair!"

"What an altruistic way to view it!" Nathaniel scoffed, "There is no one true villain here. If Joshua had not been slothful and imprudent, you could say that. However, it is rarely that men work in ways of such black and white at you seem to think." Joseph cast his head away, fuming in silence. "That's not fully my problem." Klin muttered, "Only one of them was punished." Erok nodded in agreement, and so did Sasha. "If you think the guilt and torment ain't enough," Joshua barked, "then you ain't ready for this world! Mercy and justice mush go hand in hand!" Celeste shook her head, "Was it really imprudence, or supernatural charity?" Ander nodded in agreement, "I see Malan as a hero, one who loved enough never to harm." Erok just snorted, and Sasha seemed to be struggling to stay silent. "Personally, I agree with Klin." Nathaniel sniffed, "Except for one key fact. This story just shows us, despite our proclamations of good conquering evil, all light fades to dark eventually." Klin shifted in his saddle, a slight confrontational tension building in him. "That may be true for temporal things," Lorelei said softly, "but what about the Eternal?" Nathaniel scoffed, "The eternal? That is just a concept! No intelligent person believes in that. The dark is the only thing that is everlasting, for all candles burn out eventually. All fires fade." For the rest of the ride, that was the only time Klin ever saw disdain and hatred on Nathaniel's face.

They arrived at Cleana late in the evening on the third night. The crescent moon's pale gray light shone down on them, giving the fields of wheat an enigmatic feel. The star however illumined most of their path. "Wow." Sasha wondered, a breathless look of awe upon her face. "I've not seen so many stars before." Ander nodded silently, his head tilted so far back, Klin was mildly concerned about him breaking it. Celeste also had a look of wonder on her face, but she was better at concealing it. "Can tell who's from major cites." Nathaniel chuckled softly. He also turned and looked at Klin and Joseph. "So, why are the two of you not amazed? You said you were from Ala'Kathar. That city is immense also."

Klin and Joseph gave one another a smile and shrugged. "Eh," Klin replied, "We lived far enough on the outskirts that the lights really did not affect our view. The one that should be called out is Celeste. She's travelled enough that she should be over it."

Celeste turned bright red and scowled at Klin. "Maybe I don't take beauty for granted!"

"Neither do I." Ander put in, "I've seen the stars like this from a few trips outside the city. But I never grow tired of looking at them." Celeste gave Ander an approving smile, which just made Klin give them a playful scowl. The village though came into view. It was not large at all, especially compared to the places everyone seemed to come from. There were maybe a hundred buildings in total. Torches lit the way through town, not Light-Posts. There was also really only one main road for traveling, with small dirt, foot-ridden paths on the sides instead of tile. "Bit of a rustic town." Joshua grunted, yet he had a small grin. "Yes, it is." Nathaniel sighed longingly, "I've done my best to get modern inventions to us, but I just do not have the funds. So, you'll have to excuse some modern conveniences. Things like Light-Lamps and Shock-Chandeliers, and Fire-Baths are not in this town."

Erok shrugged, "Can't speak for everyone else, but it wasn't until recently that I got to experience those things. I won't complain if I don't have them. They're a luxury, not a necessary for me." Nathaniel smiled warmly at the mercenary. "I'm glad you are so frugal. Well, now that we are here there is something I must do, and I hope you will join me. First, I should visit Old Barne at his tavern before heading back to my own home. They should know who all died, and that I am alive." Klin looked over at Nathaniel in surprise, "Wait, you actually speak to them, and as friends?"

"Of course, why wouldn't I?"

"Well, you're a better noble than most." Joseph snorted. "Anyway, what's the name of this tavern?" Nathaniel pointed to a three-story building near them. "There. That's the Green Isle." They all joined him as they made there way over. In faded gold lettering hung a sing nailed to the door proclaiming the name of the place. A dark green island was painted on it roughly. The building itself looked old, with faded wood. Loud music though echoed out and the shouts and carousels of drinkers could be heard within. When they opened the door, a strikingly luscious interior greeted them. Silk carpet lined the stairs and polished wood floors reflected the firelight. Fancy works of art hung upon the walls, and exquisitely designed chairs sat before each table and the bar. The place also seemed very busy tonight, almost at max capacity.

"Nate, is that you?" A grizzly voice called out. The party turned to see a gnarled old man with a squished nose and an eyepatch over his right eye, hobbling towards them with a cane. Nathaniel spread his arms out, "It is! I made it back safe and sound." The old man laughed, "Glad ta see my old eye ain't deceiving me yet! We'd thought ya died out there!" Nathaniel took on a grim smile, "Oh I would have too. Luckily these kind folks saved me, and solved the source of our problem."

Old Barne gave them a critical look. "Hmm, you don't look like much, except your old geezer there. But if ya did it, ya did it. So, where are the lads you took with you?" Nathaniel shook his head quietly. Klin cast his head down ashamed. If only they had gotten there sooner! "Damn." Barne whispered, "They'll be missed." He then closed his eyes, tucking his thumbs in and touching the other eight fingers to his forehead, and then his thumbs. "May their souls rest in the Nine," Barene prayed, "and may their souls be sculpted into a better life." Nathaniel proceeded to do the same, then looking expectantly at the others. Klin, Joseph, Ander, and Sasha quickly followed their example. Erok did not move. Joshua however said the same line, except "By the Eight," and did not have his thumbs touch his forehead. Lorelei also did the same. "Thank ye." Barne said, "Not many strangers oblige us anymore."

"It's rare for anyone to follow the Way of the Sculpted outside of Edeaven." Ander said. Nathaniel nodded, "True. Much of this world has forgotten it's history. That will soon change though I think." Joshua muttered something under his breath. "Anyway Old Barne, may I get up and let everyone know that I am here?"

"Of course." Barne replied dryly, "You own half this place." Nathaniel let out an exasperated sigh, "Those were gifts Barne, gifts!" Barne just laughed heartily, (if somewhat hoarsely.) "Yeah yeah. Just let 'em know drinks are on the house tonight. For the lost, and the returned." Nathaniel gave him a grateful hug and then walked over to the stage. The music stopped, and so gradually so did the cacophony of talking. Once there was complete silence, Nathaniel began to speak loudly. "My friends! I have returned, but not in as much joy as we had hoped. The slavers are all dead, but at a hard price. I could find none of our children and I was the lone survivor. They had greater numbers than we anticipated and were led to believe. We were taken prisoners and once by one, executed. Thankfully a group of heroes dared to attack the scourge of the plains! Those strangers in the back are our heroes!"

Everyone turned around and stared at them. Klin cast his gaze down, and began to fidget, not really sure what to do with himself. "I hope to continue the search for our dear little ones!" Nathaniel continued, "But tonight we drink in bitter happiness. Grief for our lost, but triumph over our enemies! Take joy that they are now dead!" There was a resounding cry, but at the same time it was subdued. Everyone was handed a drink, and they all drank for the dead and the living. Nathaniel walked back over to them, and said, "Come, drink with us my new friends." Joshua grinned ruefully. "Don't have to tell me twice." He exclaimed. Klin shifted, unsure, but Joseph grabbed him by the arm. "Come on, let's now waste their good will!" Klin just laughed as he was dragged into the revelry.

Chapter 19

The World In Gray

"And it's no-nay-never!" *Clapclapclap,* "No nay never, no more! Will I plaaaaaay the wild rover! No never, no more!" The crowd erupted into cheers as the song finished. Drinks clacked together in celebration before being downed. Klin smiled, taking a small sip of the ale he had been given. He had never heard that song before, but the energy had been so infectious that he could not have helped but try and sing along. "Another song!" Joseph cried, sitting at another table. "And someone get me another beer please!" That marked his seventh beer. His brother's face was beginning to get a tinge of red to it, and a lopsided grin was plastered on his face. "Hah!" Celeste mocked, "You can't handle another!" She herself was on her sixth drink, Klin was pretty sure. Joseph flashed her a smile, "Oh yeah? I'm not even getting started! I'm not even tipsy yet!" Celeste laughed raucously, "Well neither am I! Shall we have a competition?"

Klin just shook his head as those two incited another eruption of babbling cheers. "Well, they're having fun." Ander commented. He simply nodded as another song began. Klin had enjoyed himself at the beginning, but once he had sat down and had time to think, something about this did not quite feel right to him. It felt as if no one was really mourning those men they lost. It just felt as if this was another party. Shouldn't there be some melancholy amongst everyone? He sighed though, tapping his foot in time to the new song. Klin and Ander sat alone for the most part. They had joined in the revelry for a bit, and then once they had sat down, the villagers had come over to interrogate them for their side of the story. Once they had gotten it though, they had pretty much been left alone for the most part.

Lorelei and Kyoko had retired early, taking one of the rooms upstairs. Nathaniel had been kind enough to pay for their lodgings for the night. Klin was glad too. He was looking forward to a nice bath. It had been a while. Nathaniel though himself ran about talking to every person in the inn. Sasha was surrounded by a men at one of the tables while Erok and Joshua sat at the bar talking quietly. As the newest song ended, Klin was able to hear one of the men say to Sasha, "Come on sweetheart, it's getting pretty late. Why don't you let me walk you to you room?"

"No thank you." Sasha squeaked. Klin sighed, and got to his feet. "Where are you going?" Ander asked. "Be back." Klin grunted. He walked on over to Sasha. She was giving all the men a half hearted smile, but there was a mix of panic, pity, and disgust in her eyes. Klin stopped behind her, hands in his pockets. "Hey Sasha," Klin said, tapping her on the shoulder, "Ander wants to talk to you." Sasha leapt to her feet, almost knocking over her chair, "Oh, okay! Thank you!" The other men began to get up. "Privately." Klin said coolly. Sasha rushed off, casting him a grateful look. The rest of the men sat down, and Klin turned to leave.

"Oi, just who do you think you are kid?" Klin sighed, turning around. It was the guy who had been close to being very aggressive. He was still on his feet and had looked like he had no intention of sitting back down. *Oh boy*, Klin thought exasperated, wiping the man's spittle off his face. The man was shorter than him by a good five inches, but fairly muscular. "You looking for a fight pal?" The man spat. "No." Klin shrugged, "But I guess you are." Before the man had anytime to react, Klin punched the man in the face. He stumbled back, rubbing his jaw. A small amount of blood trickled down his mouth. "I was gonna let you off easy!" The man roared, and charged him.

Klin just moved lightly to the side, and stuck his foot out. The man stumbled over it like a wild boar, tumbling to the floor in a heap of limbs. "Anyone else?" Klin asked. The rest of the men vehemently shook their heads. "Good." He nodded to them all, and then turned to walk away. As he did though, was smacked on the back of his head. Klin fell to the ground, his skull pounding. He rolled over with a groan, and found the drunkard looming over him with a sneer. "Havn't they 'ver told ya never to turn yer back on an enemy!" The man slurred. *Crap.*

The drunk man leapt at him, legs pinning his waist. Klin went to grab his waist for leverage, but as he did, he was punched in the face. Klin stayed silent as he was repeatedly punched in the face. He struggled back, looking for a chance to retaliate, however he was having trouble focusing and seeing straight from the onslaught of punches. Suddenly, the man was ripped off of him. "That's enough!" Nathaniel cried. Someone grabbed Klin's arm and lifted him to his feet. He used their arm as a support as he got his bearings. Nathaniel was holding the man by the scruff of his neck, and he looked pissed. Klin looked over to see his uncle staring daggers at the drunk. "He started it!" The man whined. Joshua made a movement for something at his waist, probably his gun. Klin wasn't too sure. His right eye was completely swollen over as blood trickled from his mouth and over his face. "Yes, and you gave him more than triple what he gave you!" Nathaniel roared.

The drunkard tried to shrink away, but it was a hard thing to do with the man you're trying to run from holding you. "I saw the whole thing! You are well outside the realms of what is required by justice! Now get out before I decided to lock you up in my dungeon!" Nathaniel threw the man forward. He barely caught himself, and then scampered away like a cat, terrified of a promise he knew would be carried out all too well. Nathaniel glared at the rest of the men, and then walked over to Klin. "I'm sorry about that. I would have helped sooner. I wanted to give you your chance to take care of it yourself first thought." Joshua nodded at him approvingly. "You've got yer issues," the old man said, "but I'm growing to respect you. Now kid, why don't you go see yer mother? She'll fix you up. She won't be asleep yet." Klin nodded, "Thanks Uncle, I will."

"Uh huh." Joshua replied non-committally and walked back to his seat. Before Klin could leave though, Nathaniel tapped him on the shoulder and leaned in. "Why don't you come talk to me after you get done?" He whispered, "I have something that may be of interest for you."

"Uh, okay. What is it?" Nathaniel just smiled. "I'll tell you once you are done. Let's just say it's important." Klin nodded, "Alright then. I'll be back in a bit." As he walked up the stairs, he could not help but wonder what it was Nathaniel wanted to talk about that required secrecy. He did not wonder about that for too long though once he stopped in front of his mom's roon. *Shit. This is not going to be fun.* He knocked lightly on the door, half-hoping she was actually asleep. Unfortunately, Joshua revealed just how much he knew for being so strange. The door opened to reveal a slightly tired Lorelei. Her eyes though quickly became wide awake as she saw her son's face.

"What in Heshtanrus did you get into now!?" She exclaimed. Klin sank down, "Uh, high mom." She leaned out the door and looked around. "What, no Joseph?" Klin shook his head, going a shade of red that was not because of the blood on his face. "No, not this time. This was all me." Lorelei sighed, "Well, what are you waiting for? Get in here young man." Klin shuffled in, making to sit down on the bed. "What are you doing?" She scolded, "You'll get blood o the sheets. Sit on the chair over there." Klin obeyed silently and sat in the chair. "Alright, so what happened?" Lorelei asked, placing her hands on his face. Klin winced at the touch, and explained the whole thing.

He finished his story just as his mom finished healing his face. She sighed, "So you started it?" A flare of anger popped up, "I'm mean kinda." He replied indignantly, "He threatened me." Lorelei gave him a very cool, even look. "Klin Gabriel Markus, did you or did you not throw the first punch?"

"Yes." He grumbled. "But he deserved it! You heard what he was trying to do!"

"Whether or not he deserved it is not the issue." Lorelei explained gently, "He might of, or he might not have. However, this is something I thought you learned from our time as the oppressed. No matter how much they insult you, no matter how much they threaten, you let them attack first. Always."

"Why's that?" Klin growled, "In this case I caught him by surprise. If I had been paying attention, that would have been the end of it. Why should I not attack first?" Lorelei pursed her lips, a slightly worried look on her face. "Do you know who you sound like right now?" Klin shook his head angrily. "Monastrath." Klin's whole body went cold. "What? How? Wait, no I am not!!!" Lorelei crossed her arms. "You have become arrogant, thinking you can do what you want, carry out things like you want. Yet you do not have that authority, even if you want to do it for far more noble and good reasons." Klin placed his face in his hands. Was he really acting like Monastarth? That guy had deserved it right? Or, maybe his mother was right. He felt something tug at him, a deep desire. In that moment, it was all consuming. A want for power to *have* that authority. Of course he would use it better! Why wouldn't he? He was a good person, right?

"Klin?" Klin snapped his head up as Lorelei stared at him, concern and love shining on her face. "Klin, honey, are you okay?" That desire disappeared, and he smiled. "Yeah, I'm good now. Thank you. I was wrong." The concern did not disappear from her eyes, but she did smile at him. "Alright. Well, you're all fixed up and good to go."

"Thank you!" Klin exclaimed as he leapt to his feet. Once he had one foot out the door, he heard Lorelei call, "Now beave yourself now!" He turned back and gave her a smile, "Don't worry. I will." Klin rushed back down the stairs and looked around for Nathaniel. He saw him sitting in a corner at a booth by himself. He waved at him, and sat down next to him. "So what is it that you wanted to tell me?" Klin asked.

"Did you catch what the reason I said we left after the bandits was?" Nathaniel spoke softly. Klin frowned, "Yeah, you mentioned they were kidnapping the children here. You never told us that we rescued you, did you?" Nathaniel shook his head, "No, we were so caught up in the moment I never got a chance too. But don't you think something was off? We never found a single trace of the children, even with the portals they use." Klin furrowed his brow and crossed his arms. "Well, we did not really look around the place that hard. We sort of went and went out immediately. But, granted I suppose I should have seen something. So then that means, either they are still there, or they were never there at all."

"Precisely." Nathaniel praised, "There was quite a bit of extra room, so they may have hid them well. However, I was asking around and discovered something that might help us. Two days ago, another child was kidnapped." Klin froze, "Hold on, we had gotten rid of them all! They should not have been able to get here! You guys killed everyone! I only left two alive! There's no way they would try something like that now."

"I agree." Nathaniel replied, "So I think that we were wrong about who was enacting these kidnappings." Klin leaned back, shaking his head, "Okay, but then who would be doing it?" Nathaniel leaned forward, folded hands on the table. "I have an idea based on this. We assumed it was the bandits for multiple reasons. First, we had been getting word of all the smaller villages suffering under those louts for a while. Kidnappings and robberies and the like. Second, it always happens at night, and there is no sign of struggle. And we knew they used portals, so we assumed that was the reason why. Here is what is suspicious though. No one ever saw them happen. We were just going on speculations. However, we finally got a sighting from our local doctor, Horst Mavory. He claimed he saw them take three of the children from off the street."

Klin shrugged, "Okay. I'm not sure I'm seeing where this is going."

"Patience." Nathaniel soothed, "There are many pieces to this puzzle. The next piece is this. Horst does not often leave his house. He conducts lots of research there. Most of the time, the sick are brought to him. Next, it was night. He is not a night owl, and he hates being out after dark. So that is strange in it of itself. Now here is the real strange part for him. Horst just made a request for a new scalpel to be made, according to our blacksmith. He said he broke his recently in a surgery. What is odd here is that he has not had to perform surgery for at least a month. I asked around some more, and no one has any idea who needed it. News of the ill spreads fast in a village this small."

Klin felt a chill as cold as ice run through his blood. "You don't think he's…" A very grave look feel on the minor lord's face. "It's possible. He's a known Life and Dark Weaver. He can make himself invisible, so that would make a lot of oddities fit together." Klin balled his hands into fists, hiding them under the table, "Alright, so what can we do about it?" A big smile spread across Nathaniel's face. "I was hoping you would ask that. We will head over to his house and investigate."

"Hold on, what about the others?"

"Well they are not in prime state of mind right now are they?" Nathaniel replied with a raised eyebrow and gesturing to the very drunk Joseph and Celeste. Ander and Sasha were talking, but it was obvious they were exhausted. Erok and Joshua were on their sixth drink by now too. Klin nodded. He had had all the alcohol flushed from him when he was healed, but that only worked if you were not tipsy, let alone drunk. "Alright, let's do this then." Nathaniel clapped him on the back, "Glad you see such reason! More people might have scared him anyway, this is for the best. Besides, you seem the most skilled warrior here." Klin stood up, red in the face, "I don't know about that. Anyway, let's get going."

The two got up and went on outside. Klin blinked a few times, trying to get used to the dim lighting. Nathaniel pointed down the south side of the village. "Horst lives that way, at the edge of town." Klin nodded and followed Nathaniel. The buildings they passed were made of a patchwork of clay, shoddy wood, and thatch roofs. Almost none of the homes had glass windows, and if they did they were gray and smudged. There was hardly any light from the homes, which gave there walk an ominous air, seeming like the homes could fall atop them at any moment. "When I said we were not that well off," Nathaniel whispered, making Klin jump, "I meant it. We really do not have that much going for us anymore." Klin shook his head, confused, "I was looking at the map as we were traveling. According to it, this place should be a major stopping place for merchants and anyone wishing to do any sort of trade or travel. Shouldn't the kind help you out?"

"That child?" Nathaniel sneered, "He's the reason we have so little trade. Not only does he impose such ridiculous taxes on us that we lose half of what we make, but he does not even care to see why the merchants have stopped coming through. Bandits rule the roads these days, and he does nothing. You may not realize this, coming from the sheltered city of Ala'Kathar, but this country is dying. It has been for a while. We need real change, and soon." Klin feel silent, not really sure what to say. He really was in no place to say anything here. Ala'Kathar was such on the edge of the kingdom, that they really were not taxed. And for all the Companion's many faults, they did take care of the poor. Well, all the poor except his family. They had probably only done it to keep up appearances for something that made them seem redeemable, but still.

Cough, cough cough. Klin whipped around, drawing his swords. He relaxed though when he saw a man slumped over in an alleyway. He frowned though as he looked at him. Something seemed…off about the poor man. He could not place it though. He had barely put one foot forward before Nathaniel grabbed his arm tightly and hissed, "What are you doing?! Are you crazy?!" Klin looked over in confusion, "What are you on about?" Nathaniel pointed a finger, two Light Threads began to form. Each one was a centimeter wide and a millimeter long. They entwined around each other, and formed into a sphere. A small ball of light shot froward and hovered in the air above the man. Klin let out an involuntary cry of horror at what he saw. The man, or creature, had skin that was a deep yellow, like a faded page and just as leathery. It clung to his skull, outlining every bone. The nose was gone, revealing the boney slits. One arm was swollen and inflated, while the other looked like it was about to fall off. The stomach was bloated while the chest looked caved in.

"W-what is that?" Klin asked, feeling nauseous. "That," Nathaniel whispered pitifully, "Is lephthrima. More commonly known as Valoria's Breath. They very air they breath can be contaminated. That would be the other reason we are not doing well at the moment. It has taken have the village, and right now, not even magic can heal it. No one has figured out what works. The rates are slowing down finally, but come, we need to go." Klin let himself be torn away, but the look in the man's eyes lingered in his own mind. The indescribable pain that was there, the poor man could not even see them as his whole existence had been reduced to suffering.

"We're here." Nathaniel said. Klin jolted his head up, aroused from his ponderings. They have stopped in front of a big, two-story house. Unlike the rest of the houses, this one was made of brick and wood. Solid, good oak too by the look of it. "Alright, so I've got a plan to distract him. Once I do, I want you to start looking around, okay?" Klin nodded, "Sure, but what's the plan?" Nathaniel smiled assuredly, "Just trust me." He moved up to the door and knocked. They waited awhile, but there was no response. Nathaniel and Klin frowned at each other, before he tried again. Again, no response. He tried three more times with equal results. "Oh come on." Nathaniel muttered, then with a raised voice, "It's only nine! Come on out Horst! I know you're not asleep you insomniac!"

"But I already am out." A gentle voice said behind them. Both of the men jumped and spun around, Klin reaching for his weapons, but stopped himself as he saw a short old man. The old man had a sad, teasing smile upon his face as he peered at them from behind a thick set of glasses that contained sparkling blue eyes. White wispy hair touched his scalp in a mess, but a very neat, short trimmed beard graced his face. "Ah, Horst!" Nathaniel cried, "I didn't realize you were out! You're never out at this hour! How are you?"

"I'm still alive, aren't I?" Horst replied, laughing as Nathaniel hugged him. Despite the man's white hair and gently wrinkled face, he looked to have a strong and muscled body. "I'm glad you're alive." Horst continued, "I was afraid you had died. Thought we would be having another funeral without a body."

"You almost did." Nathaniel answered, "But thanks to this brave man here I lived." Horst turned his attention to Klin, giving him a look over. "Well," Horst muttered, "Did you know? Thank you very much. You must be an individual of exceptional talent and bravery." Klin shook his head, as he realized what Horst was thinking, "Oh no! I did nothing out of the ordinary. Anyone would do the same! Besides, I had help! It wasn't just me!"

"Well, my thanks still stands." Horst said with a bow, "I wish all thought such as you. That such acts of incredible kindness were ordinary. Anyway, to what do I owe the pleasure of our lord visiting?"

"Well," Nathaniel began, "We were hoping you might help us. Klin's mother here is a Life Weaver like yourself. An Animare by her skill. However, you are clearly better so we were hoping you might be able to teach us some of your tricks. Her healing is lacking compared to yours. Wait, are you okay? You've been crying!" Horst's eyes were dried and bleary, tinged with red. He sighed, taking off his glasses. "Yes, unfortunately I have been. My reason for being out late was... not pleasant. I just returned from the Olesson's. I found little Lily in the street with a cut stomach. I did my best but I found her too late." A grim hush pressed down on them. Klin felt slightly ill. "How did she receive the cut?" He asked quietly. Horst looked up in surprise, before shaking his head. "Not sure. I examined it and it seemed likely it was an accident. Falling upon some large rock's edge or the like. She did not have enough strength to talk though." Klin balled his fist. He hoped it was just an accident. If not, well that person better pray he did not find them. "I'm very sorry." Nathaniel comforted, placing his hand on the doctor's shoulder. "I'll go visit them tomorrow." Horst gave him a weary smile, "They would appreciate that. But come now! Come on in. You must be getting chilly standing out here. I would be glad to help."

Klin was surprised. Cold? He realized he could see everyone's breath. *Huh. These coats* do *regulate temperature. Nice.* Horst unlocked the door and waved them in. There was a creaking of gears as a light stone suddenly flared to life, revealing a comfortable looking sitting room. The floor was partially covered by a purple carpet, and peaking out under it was a nice oak panel floor. Soft pillows were atop two green couches, and three more chairs sat near the fireplace. Atop the mantle were placed many pictures of a younger Horst and a young woman. "That's my wife." Horst said melancholic, when he noticed Klin staring. "She's long since passed though, so don't expect anyone else but us."

"Any children?" Klin asked. Horst shook his head. "No, we never had any of our own. Maybe divine punishment for sins of our youth. Would you like some tea?"

"Yes please!" Nathaniel exclaimed joyfully, "Mint if you have it." Horst gave a small bow, shuffling into the kitchen. Once he was out of earshot, Klin turned to Nathaniel and whispered, "Are you sure it's him? He seems like such a kindly old man with a pure heart." Nathaniel shrugged, "So can I if I want to. I have a nasty side I'll have you know. We all hide various demons. And remember, I don't know for sure. We're only here *because* of that fact." Klin nodded, and did not dare broach the subject any further. Luck too, for at that moment Horst came back in. "You guys were very quiet." He inquired, holding a tray with clay mugs of tea, "Is everything alright?" Nathaniel gave Horst a reassuring smile as the old man set down the tray, "Nothing's wrong. We have just had an exhausting past few days. Silence is very rejuvenating you know."

Horst nodded sagaciously, "Hmm, that it is." He took a seat in one of the armchairs, as the other took a seat on a couch. "Now, what can I help you with my friends?" Nathaniel took a sip of the tea, before saying, "Regrowth of limbs. His mother can heal minor wounds but nothing serious like that." Horst's eyes leapt to life. "Really?! For shame! I get that regen is no easy task, but that used to be a requirement to become an Animare! Very well though, listen closely." Horst then began to ramble on about such things as cell wall and nuclei. Most of it went over Klin's head with all the technical jargon, but he made an effort memorize what Horst was saying nonetheless. "What about head wounds?" Nathaniel asked, "And nerves, the brain, and bones?"

"So many questions!" Horst exclaimed haughtily, "Can this woman even call herself a weaver?" Klin bit back a retort. His mother had been the local doctor for the most part back home. Never got money for it either, and that was before she was forbidden to be paid by the Companions. "Well, not everyone has received the erudite education you have." Nathaniel cooed. Horst sighed, "Yes, you're right. I must remember how much more learned I am than most."

Suddenly, Nathaniel sat up straight and said, "Oh my goodness! Why in the world didn't we bring her? We all must be so exhausted as to have overlooked such a simple thing! The one we want to hear this is not even here! What do you say we move this and go find the lovely mother?"

"Excellent idea!" Horst proclaimed, jumping out of his chair with surprising vigor. "My legs could use some stretching so why don't we go to her?" Nathaniel nodded. "That sounds like a very fine plan. But, may I suggest one of us staying behind?" Horst frowned, "Why's that?" Nathaniel gestured to the time. It was almost ten. "Well, I may not have been back long, however I remember that the crime rate was just going up when I left. I assume that has not changed?"

"No, it has not." Horst replied, "Ahhhh, I see what you mean now. This house is a prime target for thieves. Very well, I think that would be good then. "Klin raised his hand up to his cheek, "I can stay." Horst smiled, but there was a small wariness to it. "Really, thank you. Make yourself at home. Just don't go downstairs." Nathaniel frowned, "Wait, isn't that where you keep your patients."

"Used to be." Horst replied, "Now the basement is a mess. Must have been a leak, but there is a lot of water damage and mold. I've been waiting to get it fixed, but I'm at the lowest on Lithman's list of work. I do all my work upstairs now. Why?" Nathaniel shrugged, "Eh, I just had not heard was all." Horst gave Nathaniel a quick glance, before smiling at Klin as they walked over to the door. "Well, this should not take more than an hour or two. See you then!" Klin waved back with a smile, "See you." Horst and Nathaniel went out into the night, Horst practically running from excitement. Klin shut the door, and quietly looked out the window. They were already out of sight. So, Klin got to work, He ran up the stairs, despite the suspicion Horst had shown talking about the basement, he wanted to check upstairs first. Besides, he had time. He doubted Nathaniel was stupid enough to put his mother in a situation the reveled they were lying.

Klin silently climbed the stairs, almost not making a single sound. At the top, he came into a long hallway with four gilded doors. He opened the first one on his right. In the room was a desk and shelves with various jarred liquids. Some of the jars had more than liquids in them though. He decided to check the desk first. It was immaculate, not a single speck of dust on it. A stored quill and ink were the only things on the desk, placed neatly on the center right. He opened up the drawers and found stacks of papers. He placed them on the desk and started to leaf through them but frowned. *What kind of doctor needs to code their papers?* Klin thought. He put the papers back, and then went over, opening the door in front of this one. Inside this was a stainless steel table in the middle of the room. Various medical tools were on small metal tables, with bookshelves pushed as far against each other as possible. *Well, he wasn't lying about working upstairs now.*

He had to cover his nose though at the strange smell wafting in the room. It was just nasty. That was all he could think of to describe the smell. He quickly left the room when he noticed the books ranged from medical to leisure. The next room though was strange. Not because of what was in it, but because of the lack thereof. Absolutely nothing was in this one. The only noticeable thing was that the walls had chipped, pale blue paint on them. Klin closed the door and went over to the final door. A large, ornate bed was pushed into the corner, drapes handing off of it. What immediately caught his attention however were the four tables in the center, placed apart at four points in a cross shape. Each table held at least seven candles, all of them lit, and picture frames?

There was also a small bookshelf and writing desk, but Klin ignored them and went to the bottom table.

Ten candles surrounded a picture frame. Klin gently picked it up. It was the doctor, at least thirty years ago, with a smiling face pressed against a little girl's. The girl was smiling as if she could not imagine a happier place to be. He narrowed his eyes, examining the picture more closely. He could see the bare traces of colorless Threads. This must be an example of Light Impress. He set the picture down, slightly annoyed that he had found nothing besides those coded papers yet. He went over to the right table. Twenty candles surrounded this one. The doctor looked older in this one, and a young woman stood next to him, proudly bearing a paper. Klin thought it might be a medical license based on the look. He moved on to the left table. Seven candles near this one. The doctor and his wife and a young boy together. The married couple looked ecstatic, but the young boy looked very uncomfortable. Finally, he examined the top table. Seventeen candles and a picture of a young man with a sly smile as he held out his hands, surrounded by water. *The hesh are these? They seem like some kinds of shrines.*

Suddenly, it clicked. They must be his child—wait he said he did not have any so who—oh, duh, adoption is a thing. Feeling slightly stupid, he decided to check the desk and bookshelf finally. He leafed through them, most of the books being fairy tales and fantasy novels, most of them being meant for children. Then, he found in the drawer of the desk four leather bound notebooks with dates on the cover. He grabbed the earliest one, 2973 A.R.-2984 A.R. and began to read, skimming and jumping around.

Atsla 26, 2973. I have decided to start a diary. With all the intensive training that has become normal for my life, I am hoping that writing my thoughts down will help relieve some of the stress that keeps popping up in me. Nothing to write down today except my own personal thoughts on this diary and my resolution.

Markian 19, 2975. I have just met the most wonderful woman ever! I was working on my research at the bar, when this woman came over and sat down next to me! Me! She asked what I was working on, so I told her. Instead of running away like everyone other woman has, she asked questions! Finally, I have found a worthy companion to hold an intellectual conversation with. Her name was Mira. Mira Contema. Ahhh, what a wonderful name! I hope our time together tomorrow goes well.

Darshen 3, 2978. Mira and I have been married for two years now, and we still have yet to conceive any children. I know the lack of fertility is weighing heavily upon her. I wish I could do something for her, but even Life Weaving can do nothing for that. I just pray that N can bless us.

Genua 6, 2978. Glorious day! Oh happy world! I could sing the praises of N and all of creation! Mira is pregnant, and not only that but I used my magic to check on the children. We have quadruplets! Quads!

Atsla 1, 2978. Mira's health is bad. Very bad. She can barely walk or eat. I fear for both her and the children. Please N, bring them to safety and health.

Celeriam 5, 2978. Oh, thank N! Mira has recovered from that nail-biting month of illness. I will have to make an offering in thanks.

Elenortic 19, 2978. Mira is in bed. She finally passed out from her weary weeping. The quads...they were stillborn. I had to perform surgery to save Mira, but it cost us. We will never be able to conceive again. Unless I figure out a new spell. I will work until I discover it.

Elenortic 18, 2983. It seems the pain of our loss is finally dulling. A unique individual came through town today. A man with a long blue coat and black and brown hair. He saw us and somehow, with just a glance, figured out our deep pain and sorrow. I'll never forget his words. "The pain only becomes more tolerable with time. Bear it, and never stop loving. Turn the pain into the stronger force of love. But be there for the children who need a loving hand that only you may give."

Elenortic 20, 2983. Our neighbors died today, leaving behind their seven-year old. It was the strangest thing. They got sick out of the blue yesterday morning, and it got exponentially worse. Nothing I did helped, and I could not figure out what was wrong. It looked like parablue leaf poisoning, but that's ridiculous. It's a plant native to Sudarn and the only supply of it is in this house, under lock and key. It is a cure for muscle spasms when applied to the skin, but a poison when made into a tea. Anyway, we adopted poor Emily. I do not expect us to replace what she has lost, only help her through it. It is a good thing Mira and her are so close though. That will help immensely.

Threaten 15, 2984. The parents of Gabriel died today. We adapted him just like we did with Emily. Poor boy was only five when he lost his parents. I'm worried though. The parents seemed to have died from the same, unexpected sickness that resembled parablue…just like Emily's. I checked and the supply is diminished. I have not had to use parablue for two years, and I keep meticulous track of my medical supplies. Someone killed them. I hate to think it, but Mira was close to Gabriel as well… no that's ridiculous! She would never do something like this.

Klin closed the diary, disturbed. He opened the next one on the shelf, but hesitantly, scared to think of what he might find within the pages of this new diary.

Valorian 1, 2987. A third family almost died from parablue poisoning. Luckily, I have discovered a spell to cure it. I will write it down here, and in my records. Seven, five inch threads woven together in the shape of a rose. Place the spell on any flower, roses work best, then place the flower atop the afflicted's heart, and the poison retreats, being drawn into the flower. The flower wilts and gains a soft blue light. Burn it within an hour or the poison will become gaseous. But, I'm going to start investigating who our killer is.

The next five pages of the diary were torn out. Klin flipped through, scanning rapidly, but there was no mention of his investigation. So, he continued to read.

Darshen 3, 2989. We've had to adopt yet again. Third family died. We took in the two children, Jal and Sienna. They are three and two respectively. The other two I fear are close to discovering what they should not though.

Klin slammed the book shut, his stomach feeling like a ship tossed about at sea. Woozily, he set the diary down. He shut his eyes and swallowed, trying to keep his most recent meal from splattering on the floor. Tentatively, Klin reached out and grabbed the fourth and final diary, terrified of what he might find within.

Elenortic 15, 3015. It had been years since that horrible disease stole my entire family from me! I cure and spit the fact that I was the only one never to contract it! Now, that same damned disease is slowly spreading throughout this home. I thought when we came here, Mira and I could escape it. Instead, I might have brought it to these people. That fool of a lord Nathaniel though does nothing but study his herking Stones! We need a cure! And I will get it.

Darshon 21, 3016. I have almost done it!

Atsla 21, 3016. I have reached the stage in my research where I require live subjects. Luckily the children, when I ask them, say they would love to help. I will take them away tonight.

Atsla 24, 3016. The village has been in an uproar over the missing children. I hate to do this to them, but they wouldn't understand. They've never understood my genius, those imbeciles! Things have to be sacrificed for moving forward! I know this better than anyone! Everyone always talks about how you must sacrifice for love and to grow as person you must sacrifice. But when you are asked to sacrifice for what truly matters, people rebel and spit on you. They'll see though soon enough. I'll have to do something to throw the scent off of me though. Nathaniel is too clever for his own good. Maybe those bandits could help? I have lots of money I no longer need.

Klin dropped the diary, not caring for any propriety at the moment. He had all the evidence he needed. It was time to check out the basement, and rescue some children.

Chapter 20

And Justice for All

Klin practically fell over himself as he ran out of the room. He slid down the stairs, riding along the railing. He jumped off, gliding across the room, keeping his speed and stopping at the window to peak outside. No sign of the doctor or Nathaniel. Good. That gave him plenty of time. Hopefully. He dashed over to the door and tried it. It was locked. Even if the basement was moldy, why lock it? He took a few steps back, and then charged the door, hitting it with his shoulder in a jarring jolt. "Ow!" Klin exclaimed with a wince. He clutched his shoulder, massaging it. That had hurt way more than he had expected. He rolled his shoulder around as he thought of what to do next. Maybe a few more charges would break it, but also his shoulder. He did not have the build to do that. As Klin rolled his shoulders, the sheathes upon his back smacked against his spine. He stopped mid-stretch, then smacked himself in the face. *I'm such an idiot!*

Klin drew his red sword, casually thinking that he should really name them at some point, and began to slice at the lock. The metal lock fell to the ground with a metallic tinkle, much like a bell. The door swung open easily. Klin grinned, and looked down the stairs, the smile quickly fading. It was pitch black. He closed his eyes, concentrating as he tried to remember how Nathaniel had made that light orb. *Come on!* Klin thought, as sweat began to trickle down his face. *Just let me cast this simple spell!* All of a sudden, something clicked within him. A wave of energy poured into him, warming his center of being. Klin's eyes flashed open as he formed two Threads in his palm, forming them into a sphere. He cut them off and a small orb of golden light floated in his hand. He grinned, then leaned on the wall as his legs began to buckle under his weight. *Damn it!* He thought, *That took way more animana than I thought.* Lorelei had been right to warn him about the dangers of even small spells for him at the moment. He had not built up the proper stamina for Weaving yet.

He steadied his breathing, in the nose, out the mouth. In the nose, out the mouth. Once he could support his own weight once more, he straightened up and held his palm out. The light orb flew and hovered around his hand, going five feet in front of it as he descended the stairs. As he went down, he noticed that the light barely illuminated anything, despite being extraordinarily bright. The darkness seemed to be enclosing him like a ravenous beast, eager to feast upon anything that lived. Hesitantly, he began to increase the orb's output by feeding a small, one centimeter thread into its center. He barely noticed a drain of his strength, but while the glow became stronger, it lit up fare less. He stopped and placed it back at its original strength, becoming very concerned. This darkness could not be normal. All of a sudden though, the stairs ended, and because he had not been paying any attention, Klin stumbled as he hit level ground. He fell to the ground, and winced as he hit cold, hard, smooth steel flooring. *Ow.*

His hands and knees smarting from the sudden impact. He got to his feet, but in complete darkness. His spell had been dispersed. He was not sure if it was because he fell, or if something else had put it out. He swallowed with a slight choke; the darkness all encompassing and pressing on him from every side. The only sound he could hear at the moment was the rapid beating of his own heart. *Okay, okay. Just stay calm Klin. You can do this. Just summon another orb! And not die from the exertion.* He focused, concentrating hard as small trickles of sweat slipped down his forehead. He could do this! Twice he got nothing more than a sputtering of light like a candle blown about in the wind. Finally, on the third try he got one, but he had let instinct take over. The orb was massive, having a circumference of teen feet. *Shit.* Klin thought as he collapsed to the ground. The light though spread out, rays of golden light reaching every corner of the room as the darkness fled. Klin suddenly realized he could see intricate Weavings of purple Threads disappearing under the light. His suspicions had been right.

That darkness had been the work of Horst. *Maybe I produced a spell stronger than it?* Klin thought, positing an answer.

Klin pushed himself to his feet though, despite his muscles feeling like liquid and his knees shaking like leaves on a tree. He got a good look around and realized that the room had another light source. He extinguished his spell, examining the numerous five feet by five feet light stones lodged into the ceiling. Their light revealed a room of decent size, allowing probably around ten people to fit in comfortably. The stainless-steel floor that he had fallen on, (twice now and it hurt) reflected the light off it. Shelves with jars lined some of the walls and a wooden counter stood by. It was made of a dark mahogany and seemed a little out of place compared to the sleek metals everywhere else. Yet in front of him were six steel walls. They were placed haphazardly it felt like and formed boxes yet did not reach the ceiling. Curious, Klin walked over to the nearest one and found an opening just wide enough to fit a door. Inside was a raised bed and a table filled with surgery tools next to it. On the bed though lay a young boy. His hands and legs were strapped down and his eyes were close.

Klin ran over to his side. "Hey, are you okay?" Klin asked worriedly. The boy did not even act like he had heard him. Klin grabbed the child's wrist, checking for a pulse. He sighed in relief as he felt one, then froze. Something was wrong, he could feel it. At that moment, the boy's eyes flew open, staring at Klin in a soundless horror. He smiled, patting the boy's wrist. "Don't worry," He said gently, "I'm going to get you out of here." The boy just gave him a confused look, like he did not understand him. Klin frowned. *Does he speak a different language?* The boy did not look like he was from a different country though. He had the brown eyes and white skin of Ardaven. No, it was not that. Suddenly, he felt a chill run up his spine as realization settled upon him like a revelation from above. He had never heard his own words when he spoke them. He could not even hear his own breathing! The boy let out a soundless yell, and Klin felt something bounce off his shoulder blade. Klin spun around, hands on the handles of his swords. The good doctor Horst was standing a bit away. He was holding a bent scalpel and looked very surprised. *Herk.* Klin cursed as he drew his swords. He did not waste any time as he leapt into action, swinging for both Horst's face, and the left hand that held the scalpel. Horst was able to dodge the first strike, but let out a soundless scream as his hand was cut off.

Klin sheathed his swords and leapt back, glaring at the man. Horst glanced at him, and then gave him a nasty smile. Klin froze as ice gripped his heart, as the bloody stump of a hand regrew. The hand on the ground broke down into ash. *Shit*! He had forgotten how skilled this man claimed to be! Looks like it was backed up! Hundreds of purple threads filled the air, leaving a blackness as thick as ink and darkener than the moonless night and the stars covered by thick clouds. *Shitshitshitshit!* Klin felt himself panicking as his sight was now useless. Horst could be anywhere, and he bet the man could see in this. Suddenly, he was kicked in the stomach. He fell to the ground, his head bouncing against the floor. Groaning without even the ability to hear it, he pushed through the pounding pain of his head and pushed to his feet. He summoned a small orb, worried what anything stronger might do to him at his point. He could only see his hand. Klin chucked the light to where he thought the table was, trying to recenter his surroundings. He was rewarded by seeing an old, wrinkled hand lying on the bed. *Gotcha!* Klin thought triumphantly as he charged. Just as he was about to cut it off, he noticed something strange. The hand was too small to be Horst's.

Klin's heart skipped a beat as he increased the output of the orb. It was the boy. His hair, once brown, was now silver and the skin was wrinkled like worn parchment. The eyes were glazed over. Klin felt for a pulse. There was none. *Vicisous's small...the Hestanus happened?!* Out of the corner of his eyes though, he spied a green thread forming behind him. Klin leapt to the side as a spear of green energy fly where he had been, impaling the young corpse. Letting out a roar, Klin let a blast of fire out, shooting towards where the spell had started. He saw the silhouette of Horst dodge out of the way as the fire splattered against the wall. He felt a spike of adrenaline fill his body. Fueled by anger and a want to survive, Klin summoned the orb that had broken the darkness the first time. The orb was enough to break this darkness spell, and as all the light flooded back into the room, Klin froze as the horror he saw.

Horst stood by the entrance, his arms held behind his back in a very composed way. Yet the man before him was not the old man. All the wrinkles and saggy skin were gone. Instead, what looked like a twenty-year old version of the doctor stood before him. He gave Klin an approving look before holding up his hand casually. A beam of purple energy shot out, racing towards him. Without thinking, Klin sliced at it, and actually cut the beam. As the beam dissipated, Horst looked just as shocked as Klin felt. *Mental note. I can someone how cut through magic with these blades.* Klin took advantage of the shock, shaking his own off and charging Horst. He stabbed the doctor in the chest, watching as he let out a soundless gasp of pain before kicking him in the stomach, pushing him off his blade while removing it at the same time. Blood splattering the pristine floor, ghastly in the light. Yet the wound began to close immediately.

Horst held out his hand, green Threads forming around it, but Klin gave the doctor no chance to focus. He was faster and began to relentlessly attack the man. At least, he thought he was faster. Horst nimbly dodged all his strikes with uncanny grace, but the spell was not able to be finished thankfully. Horst was using all of his concentration just to avoid Klin's onslaught. Klin let out a grin though as he saw what might be an opening. He sliced at the man's neck, Horst going up to defend, but he stopped mid swing and transitioned into a spinning kick. He himself had to stop though as a green beam came at him. Planting himself down just barley in time, he crosses his swords, blocking the attack. However, the beam did not disappear, and instead continued to press against him. The light emanating from it was so bright that he could hardly see his surroundings. With great effort and strain, Klin was able to hold it off with one sword, and then use the other to destroy it. As he did though, he noticed Horst was no longer in front of him.

Suddenly, a roaring pain erupted as something pierced his back and through his stomach. Klin screamed as he was kicked to the ground. *Damn it.* Klin thought shakily, *He snuck up behind me!* He dropped his swords and fell into a puddle of own blood. *Not good, not good. That's a lot of blood already.* There was a massive popping of his ears, as if a great pressure had been released from them. "Hmph, you really though you could outsmart me?" Horst sneered, "I'm the most brilliant doctor this world has ever seen!" Klin's eyes went wide as he realized what had just happened. "I'll give credit where credit is due though." The doctor continued, "You lasted a remarkably long time against me. That fool of a lord couldn't even figure out what I was about to do to him. I'm impressed." Klin groaned as he was kicked and rolled over by Horst. "Screw you, you crazy bastard!" Klin coughed, spitting blood.

"Is that anyway to treat your savior?" Horst spat. Klin watched as the green Threads he had seen healing Horst formed in the air around his gut. Klin squirmed as they began to heal him, however he felt an intense pain as hot as fire racing along his stomach and back. He screamed, the pain like a hot coal in his stomach. "I need you alive." Horst whispered, a mad gleam in his eyes, "I need to replace the child you killed." Fire raged inside as Klin softly, yet angrily replied, "You're the one who killed him you sick psycho!" Klin screamend though as thousands of knives ran along his back and arms. "I did not!" Horst snarled, "You forced my hand by meddling where you should not! And you'll pay for your crime by replacing him! By saving others!" The pain subsided. Klin shakily raised his head and looked at his arms. No blood. What..had..that been? "I can activate your pain receptors." Horst said, almost gleefully, "So if you don't want to feel like your being skinned alive, I suggest you be a good boy."

"TO HERK WITH THAT!" Klin roared. With a burst of energy, he grabbed his swords and scissor kicked Horst, knocking him flat on the ground. He rolled backwards, bouncing up to his feet. "I honestly can't believe you have the energy to keep going!" Horst laughed. Klin just snarled in response. That burst might have been all he had left. Horst leapt back up as Klin began his final push. His muscles roared with the leftover pain of those torments and his whole body felt sluggish which let Horst dodge all of his sloppy attacks with ease. The doctor grabbed Klin's wrist as he stumbled, and then gave it a sharp twist. Klin yelped, dropping his left sword, but made Horst pay by cutting off that hand that had grabbed his. Horst just shook his head amused as he healed the wound. "Enough of this foolishness." Horst commanded.

A green glow hung in the air before Horst as hundreds of green threads began to form. The amount of energy required for the spell was enormous! It had to take a *minimum* of five hundred animana, *I have to do something, quick!* Klin thought in a panic. Then, a plan leapt to his mind. Something he probably should have done from the start. He ran over to the wooden counter and leapt on top of it. Klin looked over at Horst who had momentarily paused his spell, examining Klin with curiosity. "What are you doing? It's fruitless you know." Klin gave the man a defiant grin as he held up his hand, summoning a crackling ball of lighting. "Wining." Klin answered as he threw the bolt onto the floor. Horst's eyes widened in horror as he realized what Klin was doing far too late. Klin kept a steady flow of magic into the spell as lightning arced across the floor. Horst screamed as the floor became a light show of blue sparks, crackling energy dancing upon the ground and flashing into the air. Klin eventually closed his eyes as the flashes became too bright for him. When the screams finally stopped, Klin ended the spell, opening his eyes.

Horst lay on the ground, slightly smoking but still alive. The air smelled acidic and coppery with the faint smell of charred flesh. Klin hopped down, walking over to the doctor and picked up his fallen sword. His wrist hurt, but luckily was not broken. "I-I-I don't un-understand" Horst wheezed, "I thought you were a light and fire weaver!" Klin sheathed his swords, standing over the man, arms crossed. "Yeah, well I got a third."

"But that's impossible! That breaks all the known rules!" Horst exclaimed. Klin's eyes flashed with fire as a boiling feeling began to brew. "Yeah, I exist outside those rules. But I exist so as to stop those who break the more sacred rules. Those who transgress what it means to be good. Those who violate the sacredness that is beauty and truth! And *you. You have broken a lot of them.*"

"What are you going on about?" Horst coughed. "I read your diaries." Klin replied coolly, "I know enough." Horst's skin became deathly pale, even more so than he already was, as his eyes went wide with fear. "No. Nonononono! Please you don't understand! I had to protect them! I had to protect them all!" Klin kicked him in the face. "I don't want to hear any of your bullshit!" Klin screamed, "All I care now is that you face justice from the families you destroyed!"

"Klin, is that you?" Klin spun towards the stairs and saw Nathaniel walking in. His clothes were torn and bloodstained. A great big piece of his shirt was missing, leaving his stomach uncovered. "What?" Horst wheezed, "I thought I killed you?" Nathaniel replied with an even, cool stare as he said, "Maybe next time, check the pockets of the man you know who experiments with alchemy and elemental stones." The lord pulled out a half-drunk potion of healing and swirled the contents around a bit. He then looked Klin up and down. "Wow, you look terrible. Hear, drink this. You exhaust your magic power?" Nathaniel asked. Klin gratefully took the potion, and felt his muscles being restored, although he still felt exhausted. "Maybe? I used more than I should have been able to. All of a sudden, I could cast spells with animana that wasn't there previously." Nathaniel nodded sagaciously. "You probably experienced Overhaul. It's a phenomenon where weavers who have completely exhausted their magic push through and try to keep casting. Normally, this ends with them using their own life source and dying. However, sometimes a weaver gets lucky and has all of their magic restored, gaining the ability to cast higher spells than normal. It also exponentially increases your magical energy."

Klin frowned, "Wait, but how come it only happens sometimes?" Nathaniel shrugged, "Not sure. But what we can tell, you cannot be trying to achieve Overhaul, otherwise you will not be able to. Don't try it again though." Klin nodded, "I won't. Now, what do we do with this one? Imprison him? Also, how did he find out?"

"It seems that he had some sort of magical alarm. As soon as you entered here, he stopped and stabbed me in the stomach with this blade of darkness. As for what to do with him, we kill him."

"What?!" Klin cried, "No we can't do that!" Nathaniel looked over at him, a cool gleam in his eyes. "Yes, we can. I am judge in jury, remember?"

"Yeah, but the families!" Klin protested, "They should be apart of this! Plus, would not a prison sentence be better? We can't just slaughter him here! How would that be just?"

Nathaniel straightened his back, and asked, "What is justice? Very few men know and even fewer can met it out. Do you know what image we use for justice Klin?" Klin nodded, "Yeah, a hammer."

"Do you know why we use a hammer?" Klin shook his head. "Because we won't acknowledge what justice is," Nathaniel explained. "The wicked losing their rights. So why *do* we call the tool of justice a hammer? It does not seem the proper tool for justice. A spear would be far more accurate and fitting. So why a hammer? Because men are weak and fail when we are needed most! We are not willing to do what must be done. Justice should have scars left upon the sinner and a blunt weapon just won't do that. But a spear shall damage them for more than a hammer. Justice must be piercing and precise, not crushing and crude. So I ask you Klin, are you skilled enough and strong enough to pierce where you should?"

"I-I don't know." Klin stammered. Something about what Nathaniel was saying felt right, but a small part of him was wanting to rebel against it. "Come on Klin." Nathaniel cooed. "I heard the anger in your voice beforehand. I know you can do this. I know you want to do this."

"P-please! Have mercy!" Horst whimpered. Klin looked at him and his whisper turning into a roar. "Mercy? MERCY?! You *dare* ask for mercy now?! Where was your mercy when you killed that boy? Where was your mercy when you took these children from their families!"

"It was mercy that drove me to do those!" Horst replied in a mixture of a snarl and whimper. A deep, burning desire filled Klin. It was a hot, flaming liquid that flared to life within his chest. A sudden new energy flared through him. Klin started into the doctor's terrified eyes. He saw the man begging and scared of death. Klin smiled. Just then, one of the children began to cry. The darkness fled and Klin suddenly felt very tired and sluggish. "I'll do it." Klin said quietly, "Just get the children out of here first." Nathaniel studied Klin, seeming to see straight into his soul. Klin felt like squirming and was very uncomfortable. "Alright." Nathaniel finally said and walked away to help the children. Klin shook his head. For a brief flash of a second, he thought that Nathaniel's eyes had been yellow, and full of disappointment. Klin turned to Horst, "I hope you are truly sorry for all you've done." Horst just started past him into empty space with glazed over eyes.

"Got them." Nathaniel called. The nobleman returned with five children. He had two of them in his arms, with the other three clutching his legs as he escorted them out. As he passed by Klin he said, "We'll come back later for the bodies." Klin nodded as they went up the stairs. He waited till their footsteps could no longer be heard before drawing his blades. "I'll try and make this as quick as possible." Klin whispered. He closed his eyes and slit Horst's throat. Horst began to gasp and trash about on the ground. Soon, the good doctor lay dead in a pool of blood and ash flaked off during his spasm. The dead body began to rapidly transform back into its true age. Klin took one look, then turned around and puked. The eyes still stared at him accusing and asking *why*? But Klin had no answer for them.

End of Act II

Chapter 21

Heshtisi and Men

Sasha sat backwards atop Debbo, staring off into the distance. She was still surprised that the carriage could hold a sleeping owlbear and not show any signs of strain or breaking. Then again, there were a few things that were special about the carriage. The covered wagon moved at a celeritous pace, the landscape moving past them as a blur of colors. Nathaniel had been quite generous in giving them these experimental wagons. Four windstones had been placed on each of the wheels, each one releasing a small but powerful gust of wind to rocket them forward. Attached to the front were two horses. They had both wind and earthstones on them. The wind to help pull and keep speed, and the earth magic within allowed the horses to withstand the speeds that they were not built for.

"I still can't believe the speed and effciancy of these." Klin said. He was also laying against Debbo's side, an open book laying on his leg. Erok. Sasha rolled over to look at him. "No kidding," she replied, "It's only been a day since we left and we're already at the Edeaven Forest!" What would normally be a three day journey, accomplished in one! "Who knew that prick actually had the smarts to back him up?" Erok commented as he lounged against the sides. Klin just shook his head, "He's not a prick. I thought you would have figured that out by now." Erok waved a hand around dismissively, "Eh, you would thinks so. Birds of a feather flock together or whatever." Klin simply gave Erok a glare as he picked up his book and continued to read.

"Why must you be like this?" Sasha asked with a sigh. Erok crossed his feet, placing his hands behind his head. "I have no idea what you mean your majesty." Sash let out an even more exasperated sigh, "I'm sorry about him Klin." Klin peaked out from behind his book, "It's alright. So, does being this near to home make you homesick at all?" Erok chortled, "Why in the world would I miss that hellhole?" Klin set down the book again, a surprised look on his face. "It's still your home, isn't it?" Erok snorted, "That shithole stopped being my home as soon as I left. I don't have any found memories of that place."

"I understand that Ander had a hard time there, but what happened to you?" Sasha took a sharp breath. *Oh no. Klin, you blissful fool.* A stormy look overtook Erok as crossed his arms, he hands balled into tight fists. "I'll forgive your rude and dumb question this once just because it seems you are unaware, yet seeming at how buddy-buddy you've gotten with Ander, I really doubt you didn't know. I'm an orphan. No family in the that city. I grew up on the streets since 'no strangeres' are allowed in the orphanages. Gangs and thugs are always looking to steal from kids like me. Take away even our nothingness. I learned how to survive, but *nothing* about it was easy. So tell me Klin, why the herk should I have a found memory of that place?" With a loud clap, Klin shut his book and stood up. "Because you at least had friends to help you through it." He snapped, "I'm headed to the front." As Klin walked away, Erok snappily cried out, "Have fun with the old man!" With a swish of his coat, Klin turned and went to the front to sit by his uncle who had the reigns. Once he was out of ear shot, Sasha turned to Erok, about to scold him, but stopped.

Erok had his eyes trained on Klin's back like a hawk. She followed his gaze and noticed the small hole in the back of the coat. "You're not going to get him to explain you know." Sasha said with annoyance. Erok snorted, "I will if I annoy him enough."

"Is that why you're being such an ass to him?" Erok placed his hand over his mouth, "Gasp! Did Sasha just *curse*?" Sasha flicked her pointer and index fingers at him, making Erok sputter as ice cold water was splashed directly on his face. "Why the herk am I the only one you do this to?" Erok grumbled as he wiped his face off. "Because you're the only one who needs it." Sasha explained sweetly. Erok gave her a distrustful glare, which quickly turned into apprehension. "So know that you've come back to your senses," Sasha asked, "are you going to explain what about Klin is bothering you so much?"

Erok raised an eyebrow," I really can't believe I'm the only one bothered by this. You remember when he came back to the inn?" Sasha nodded. He had shown up with Nathaniel, his shirt tattered and covered in blood. Lorelei had nearly fainted from the shock. "Okay, so what about it?" Erok crossed his arms, "After it was clear he was fine, I went and talked to Joseph. Their coats are made from Densar hide."

"What?!" Sasha exclaimed, drawing a look from Joshua. She blushed before continuing, "But Densar are extinct!" Erok rolled his eyes, "Yeah, I know. How they herk they got ahold of those things, Joseph wouldn't say. But doesn't that make the tale they gave us a little more weird?" Sasha hesitated. "I don't know. It seems to add up. Nathaniel asked for Klin to help him investigate a citizen and it turned out to be more hostile than he expected." Erok snorted derisively, "Yeah, and I want to know what kind of 'citizen' is a Weaver that is powerful enough to pierce a Densar hide! Those things are damn protective you know." Sasha nodded, thinking she understood where this was going now. "So you're worried that the citizen Nathaniel locked up will be able to break free and want revenge?" Erok froze, indecisiveness on his face. "Well, not quite." He explained, "I'm worried about Klin really. His eyes. When he came back…they were the eyes of someone who had just killed."

Sasha began to laugh, "Oh come on Erok!" She giggled, "I think you're reading too much into things that aren't there! Klin, killing? Come on, that seems impossible." Erok let out a chuckle, "Yeah, you're probably right. I'm just being silly. Probably all this stress. The dude is way too naïve to want to kill." Sasha smiled back. Erok did have cause to be concerned about Klin though. He had become quiet and bit reclusive since they had left Nathaniel's Domain. Sasha turned back around and looked at Kyoko, who was sleeping at her feet. She ran her hands through her beautiful brown hair. At least this one was still the same. Ever since they had left Edeaven, it felt like everyone was changing or on the verge, and Sasha was still not sure if that was a good thing or not.

"Ugh, now I'm getting bored." Erok complained as he stretched out and began to ruffle through his pack. "Want to play a game Sasha?" She looked over, interested. "What kind?" Erok pulled out a small drawstring bag, a mischievous grin plastered on his face. "Oh, just some dice games. We can even bet!" Sasha sighed, "No. We barely have enough money as it is, so I'm not losing any of it on betting."

"Oh come on," Erok replied, rolling his eyes, "It's not like the amount of it is going to change." Sasha gave him one of her disapproving glares, "I said no."

"Buzzkill." Erok grumbled, "Ander would have played with me. Too bad he's too busy chasing after that Coronian girl." Sasha's heart fluttered rebelliously, "You don't really believe he is, do you?" She scoffed. Erok's eyes resumed their mischievous light, "Why? You still wouldn't happen to have a crus-"

"I do not!" Sasha shrieked, her face flushed a bright red. "I'm his friend so I need to be concerned about who he's trying to woo." She explained with a strained voice. "Uh huh," Erok answered with a cocked eyebrow, "Suuure."

"Ooooh stop thinking that!" Sasha yelled! "Oi!" Joshua snapped, "Keep it down back there! Your loud noises of argumentation will attract faires!" Erok and Sasha looked at him confused, but obeyed. "Sooo," Erok drawled, "Going to play? If you don't I might just have to warn Ander." Sasha crossed her arms and huffed, "Fine, you win." As she climbed down off Debbo, Kyoko yawned and sat up. "What are you guys doing?" She asked as she rubbed her eyes. "Dice. Want to play?" Erok offered. "Sure!" Kyoko exclaimed with glee and leapt down next to them. Sasha was about to protest, but she stopped as she noticed Erok subtly pushing his coin pouch away. Debbo also awoke, and gave a soft squawk as he nuzzled Kyoko, who laughed and began to pet him. "So, what are we playing for?" Sasha asked. Erok tapped his chin, "Hmmm, how about this? Double tens, and the winner gets to tell a story. They get to go for a bit, till I tell them to stop. Then, we play again and the next person who wins gets to continue the story."

"Oooh, that sounds fun!" Kyoko said, "Let's do it!" Erok nodded, and took out the dice and cup. He went first and rolled two ones. "Blast! Romevan's Eyes already?" Sasha and Kyoko laughed. Thankfully, the only time he tried to censor himself was when Kyoko was around. "Okay, my turn now!" Kyoko exclaimed. She snatched the die and cup, and rolled two tens. Even Debbo showed interest, his head leaned over and looking at the roll. "Yay, I win already!" The young girl giggled, " Now let's see, what sort of tale should I tell?"

"Whatever you want." Sasha replied. Kyoko looked at her with a fake pout, "Well you're no help bimbo." Erok burst out laughing as Sasha went bright red. "EXCUSE ME? Wh-where did you hear that word?!" Kyoko looked at her innocently, "From Celeste. She called you that. I'm guessing its not a nice word then?" Sasha kept back a growl, as Erok was sent into an even harder bout of laughter. "It is not!" Sasha exclaimed, "And for the record, I am definitely not one!" Kyoko looked down, "Sorry Sasha. I won't call you that again." Sasha gave her a nod, before turning an ice cold look upon Erok. He wiped a few tears from his eyes. "What you giving me that look for?" He asked defensively, still smiling, "It was hilarious! Butonlybecasueitwasn'ttrue!" He continued quickly, holding his hands up to protect his head. Sasha just mumbled, "Let's just hear her story." She was going to have a few words with Celeste later. Kyoko sat by them thoughtfully for a bit before suddenly exclaiming, "Oh, I have one now!"

"Alright, let's hear it then." Erok prompted as he leaned back. Kyoko nodded and cleared her throat. "There once was a beautiful lady. She had dark black hair and was a very powerful Weaver of both air and life. Every man that knew her wanted to marry her, but they were all horrible and mean! Then-" "Hold up." Erok cut in, holding his hand up, "Going to have to win once more if you want to keep going." Sasha scooped up the dice and rolled. A five and nine. She handed them off to Erok. "Her- I mean- are you kidding me?" Erok exclaimed. He had gotten Romevan's Eyes again. "Too bad." Kyoko said, imitating his voice as she rolled. "Yay, I win again!" Erok rolled his eyes, "Now this just isn't fair." Kyoko stuff her tongue out at him. "Anyway," she began, "This woman was very skilled at magic but hated fighting. One day though, the lady met a young girl who had no parents. She was lonely and scared at not being in a familiar place. The pretty lady, moved by kindness, asked her if she had a home. The girl told her no, so the lady asked if she would want to live with her. The girl practically yelled with happiness as she said, 'I would love to!' The girl then went to the lady's house."

Kyoko stopped, and handed the dice to Sasha. As she was shaking them about, the wagon came to a violent stop. As she hit the floor, the dice spilled out. Two ones. "What's goi—" Kyoko was hushed was Klin turned around, leaping down from his seat, a finger pressed to his lips. Klin crawled carefully to them and whispered, "Armed men. Uncle said to keep down and be quiet. Likely bandits." Sasha had a sinking feeling her stomach. Joshua was not a negotiator. "Keep Kyoko safe," Sasha muttered to Erok, "I'm going up."

"Sasha wait!" Erok hissed, but she ignored him as she crawled to the front of the wagon, hugging the side as she crawled up to the front. "Is she always like this?" Klin whispered. She could not see his face, but she could already see the scowl on Erok's face as he responded, "No. Just when she thinks she's 'doing the right thing." Sasha smiled to herself, and carefully peaked over the edge of the cart. Seven men stood in the road in full armor and armed to the teeth. No helmets though strangely enough. The man at the front held up a hand in greeting as he came closer. He was fair of face and genial looking; the only one of the seven actually. The other six men looked like hardened, cold-blooded killers with no idea what the word hygiene meant. "So, mind explaining what all this is about?" Joshua asked gruffly.

"Oh, we just need you to pay a toll." The man replied jollily, a charming smile flashing across his face. "Toll? On the road to Markthath?" Joshua snorted, "First I've heard of this." The man shrugged. "Word travels slowly across Ardaven. Bandits roam and communication is slowed because of the lack of unity. The lord of Markthath instituted this. Helps him pay for hired hands to stave off the bandits." Joshua nodded, "Makes sense. So, how much is this toll? I need to keep track of my savings. Money for whiskey and beer, and oh! Hats and clothes. Gota stay up to date with fashion am I right? Oh and food I guess."

"Right, of course." The man replied, his eyes showing some trepidation now. "Seven emeraldas." Joshua rubbed the back of his neck, rolling it around. "Well hot damn. That's a step price for Hershing toll. So, what you bandits saving up for?" The man's eyes widened in surprise before laughing, "What are you talking about?" Subtley, Joshua's hand went to his side, and Sasha stiffened, her muscles taught. Joshua had his revolver at the ready. "Don't play dumb." Joshua growled, "Even a lord has his hired hands have an insignia of his house out in the open." The thugs exchanged looks with one another before their leader chuckled. "Well, you're a sharp one aren't you? Very well then. Hand over everything you own, including any women that may be on board. This job is stressful you know? We need to let some of that out."

Joshua leaned back, "Sure you don't want to just take the seven emeraldas and call it good? Greed's a bad look on ya you know." The leader just smiled, the other men drawing their weapons, evil grins upon their faces. "No, I like this better." Joshua just shook his head, "Have it yer way." *Bang.* "Wait!" Sasha screamed, leaping up. The bullet that Joshua had shot was now suspended in a small ball of water, floating an inch from the leader's face. The bandit had gone deathly pale as he stared at it. "Wh-what the herk?" He stammered. "Please, nobody needs to die." Sasha pleaded. "Kid, what are you doing?" Joshua hissed.

"Negotiating." She snapped. She turned her attention back to the leader, and dropped the bullet. It clattered against the ground as the ball broke in a splash. "What, are you offering to go with us?" The man asked, trying to flash a smirk, but the best he got was a slack-jawed open mouth. His bravado was completely shattered. Sasha just stared at him coolly. "I think a discussion would serve everyone better."

"And what if we don't wanna?" One of the thugs cried out. Sasha gave them all a level look. "There are seven other people across the two wagons. That gentle looking woman driving behind us? She is an air and life weaver. A Halny at that. The others are all skilled warriors as well." All the thugs paled, as the leader nearly squeaked, "Very well, a discussion seems like a fine idea! What is it that you had in mind?" Sasha sat down beside Joshua. "Well," She inquired, " I want to know first off why you feel the need to be so menacing and rob people for a living." The bandits all burst out laughing, a few of them so hard that tears formed in their eyes. "Is it really that funny a question?" She asked crossly. The leader wiped tears from his eyes, and replied, "No, sorry lass. It more from surprise that anyone cares about us. A genuine inquire about us requires a genuine response. First, what's your name?"

"Sasha, and yours?"

"Well Sasha, the name's Edathon. As for why we became bandits, well its simple enough. One bad thing and society stopped caring about us, so we stopped caring about them." Edathon explained. Sasha nodded. *Perfect, just what I expected.* Speaking out loud, she said, "But aren't you doing exactly what they wanted?" Edathon narrowed his eyes. "What do you mean by that?" She spread out her arms and gestured around them. "This. Becoming bandits, robbing, killing. Isn't this exactly what they expected of you? In my eyes, it seems like instead of paying no head to what they thought, you molded yourself to become exactly what they expected of you. How is that not caring?" The men all looked at each other, while Edathon stroked his beard. "Your logic makes sense lass, however, you can't change the heart with just logic."

"Why not? Doesn't is make sense to follow what makes the most sense?" Sasha shot back, "Don't we follow what makes sense to us?" Edathon chuckled, "Aye, that it is. I suppose I've grown comfortable with my lot in life. I would like to change, but at this point I just don't see it as actually possible."

"It's never too late to change for the better." Joshua put in suddenly, his voice full of morose and melancholy. "Trust me on this one." Edathon stared in shock at the man who not even five minutes ago had been ready to put a bullet in his head. "You really believe we can change don't you?" Sasha nodded. Edathon gave her a true, genuine smile. "Well then, I actually think we might try and start over. First time someone good has ever shown us kindness, and that gives me hope. What do you say boys?" The men cheered, rattling their armor. "There's something special about you miss." Edathon said, "I hope you can continue to show that something special to others like me. Farewell."

"Wait!" Sasha cried, and began to reach for her money pouch, "At least let me give you something to help get you started!" Edathon turned around, a small smile on his face, and opened his mouth to say something right as his head exploded. Sasha watched as the stumped corpse fell to the ground, gore covering her. She touched her face, fingers slick with blood covering them. "Wha--! SASHA GET DOWN!" Joshua screamed, yet all she could do was stand in place, stuck in a daze. She felt light headed and nothing seemed real. The bandits began to scream as they looked around, searching for their foe. Two more died like Edathon, heads gone. "SASHA, DAMN YOU!" Erok bellowed, leaping up next to Joshua. The two had their weapons in hand, and fired. Sasha simply watched as a grotesque creature that had appeared, fall to the ground, claws falling limp on inches from her. Two heads it had, one smaller atop the other, and that was all she took in before the body turned to ash. "Someone get this girl out of here!" Joshua roared, killing another creature as more began to appear. Sasha felt she could not comprehend anything. How had they not noticed them. How had she not-what was happening-two more dead-Eork- Ander!

Suddenly, she was scooped up by someone, and found herself carried back into the wagon. "Hey, can you hear me?" Klin shouted, yet his voice sounded buzzing and distant. Sasha finally focused in her vision and saw Klin standing over her. She realized she was on her back, feet propped up. "Y-yeah." She replied. Klin nodded, "Okay good. You're hyperventilating. Need you to down, okay? Everything is alright." *Oh, so I am.* She thought to herself, and began to go through the breathing exercises her master had taught her. Klin gave her a soft, reassuring smile. "Good, now I need to head out. Stay here." He wiped his brow, and that's when Sasha finally noticed the blood on his face. Without thinking, she reached up and cupped his face with one hand. Klin stiffened, "Uh Sasha what are you *gasp*" Klin stopped as the cold energy he would be feeling raced through him as Sasha healed his wound, and then passed out.

Klin caught Sasha before she hit the ground, checking her pulse. She was fine. He shook his head as he threw a blanket over her. Damn Edeavens. They were dramatic about everything. He drew his swords and raced back outside. These monsters were going to Heshtanus for this. He entered into chaos. There were about twenty of those monsters, and they had split into two different groups. The remaining bandits had formed a circle, and were fending one group off, but it was not going well for them. Erok and Joshua were advancing towards the bandits, but were facing some of those monsters, trying to break through. Celeste and Joseph were guarding their wagon from the other half of the monsters. He deliberated for a brief moment before charging towards his brother. His uncle was more skilled than first glance.

Celeste was atop the wagon, fending off any that got to close, but she would be overwhelmed soon enough. Joseph kicked one away and decapitated it while it was stunned, but took a nasty slash to his cheek from another. Joseph snarled, turning to it but Celeste quickly killed it. Both creatures they had killed feel to ash. They needed an opening though to kill anymore. "Raging flame!" Klin yelled, his arm outstretched. It did what he intended. The monsters spun around in surprise while Celeste and Joseph leapt out of the way as a blast of fire emitted from his palm, hitting the centermost monster. It screamed and thrashed as it went up in flames, catching another on fire in its wild movements. Joseph and Celeste took advantage of the confusion. Celeste leapt down, killing two in diagonal cut, while Joseph performed a spinning attack, taking down three more. The last one rushed at Klin, but he sidestepped it, cutting it down the middle. "You guys okay?" Klin asked. The two nodded. Klin moved up and checked inside the wagon. Lorelei held Kyokko in her arms. The poor girl was curled up in a ball, eyes shut tight. Ander stood by, trembling but a grim look upon his face. His eyes were so dark they almost appeared black. "Stay here." Klin ordered, "You guys can protect each other." Ander nodded, while Lorelei cast him a worried glance. Klin simply gave her a reassuring smile before running towards Erok and his uncle, Celeste and Joseph following suite.

He slowed down though as he realized the two had broken through and were going at the last five. Three piles of ash and two bodies told the tale of their batt—wait, two bodies? Klin's eyes widened as he the bodies leapt up. Black blood splattered the ground from their wounds, and they seemed to be gripping something. "DUCK!" Klin screamed. Erok and Joshua hit the ground without hesitation, but the last two bandits spared a glance. Whatever the monster had thrown, it hit the bandit and his head exploded. Klin suppressed his stomach's intense urge to puke, stopping to steady his vertigo from the revulsion. Celeste and Joseph dashed past him and killed the two monsters that had been pretending to be dead. The final bandit though threw his spear at one of the four monsters still by him. The creature was impaled in the chest, and turned to ash before he could even remove it. The bandit stumbled from using more force than necessary, and Klin watched in horror as the last bandit was leapt upon by the remaining three monsters. Everyone was too fart to help him, but it would not have mattered. They tore him to pieces so fast that he never had any time to scream.

Klin felt all the blood rush to his head, crossed his swords, fire and lightning racing across them, and roared,""DIIIEEEE!" The monsters turned as a massive blast of fire and lighting, intertwining speed at them. There was a large explosion as the attack landed. Rock and dust flew through the air. When it all settled, a small crater was all that remained. Klin coughed, a splatter of blood pouring out of his mouth, and feel to the ground. *Damn it.* Klin thought, *That was a mistake.* "KLIN!" Joshua yelled, "Are you okay?" Klin tried to push himself up, but he could not muster enough strength, and fell back down. He cocked his head to see his uncle standing over him worriedly. Uncle Joshua began to check over him for wounds when he saw the blood, and stopped. "DAMN IT ALL KLIN!" He roared, "I thought we had into that thick skull of yours not to cast above your level!!!!!" Klin shrank down under the raw fury of his uncle.

"The dynamics of investiture and opposing elementals are downright deadly!!" Joshua continued, "Have you learned nothing?!" Klin just tilted his head in confusion, "Uh, I don't understand what you just said?" He croaked, the taste of blood still strong. Joshua stopped, and muttered, "Damn your mother! She's too busy worried about protecting you that she hasn't even shown you *why* she needs to! Cockatricing woman!!!" Klin just shook his head. He never would understand his uncle's train of thought.

"Despite all that, you did good kid." Joshua sighed softly. "What do you mean? They all died." Klin replied gravely. Joshua sat down next to him, and sighed, "Aye, but you can't save everybody kid. Just be grateful none of the ones you love died." Klin wanted to argue more, but nodded instead. He was too tired for that. "Klin, are you okay?!" Joseph cried suddenly. He and Celeste had reached them. "I got him," Joshua waved airy, "Go check on the others." Joseph and Celeste looked to him. Klin smiled and waved them away. As they left, Joshua sighed, "C'mon Klin, let's get you to yer mom." Joshua grabbed his arm and wrapped it around his shoulder.

Klin's legs felt like jelly as he was helped up, but he managed to stay up. "Okay, so what the herk were those things?" Klin asked. Joshua shook his head, "I-I actually don't remember. I feel like I've met them before while helping your old man. But, I can't remember now. They're heshtisi though for sure." Klin nodded. He had suspected as much, but he was glad for confirmation. As they passed Edathon's body he looked away and asked, "What did they do to the bandits?"

"Air stones." Joshua grunted, "Have to examined the ground for them to be sure, but that's what it seems like."

"Hey, uncle?"

"Yeah?"

"We should bury them right?"

"Yeah kid, that sounds like a good idea."

Chapter 22

Ghosts of the Past

Celeste wiped the sweat from her brow as she placed the shovel down. The sun had painted the sky a brilliant golden orange as it slowly fled as twilight began to settle in. Pink mingled with the yellows and blues. A truly breathtaking evening for a graveyard. Celeste flexed her hands, sore from gripping the shovel handle for so long. Her hands had not truly felt so worn since the early days of training. Swinging a sword around with Selene till they were both on the ground, battered, bruised, and exhausted; yet happy. She shook her head. Now was not the time to be dwelling on her. Yet, it was inevitable while she was in a graveyard.

"You finally done over there?" Joseph called. Celeste turned around and gave him a sour look. "Yeah, no thanks to you I might add." Joseph walked over with that infuriating grin, and held out his hands with a shrug. "Hey no," He retorted, "I dug, what, four of the graves? I think I deserved a break. You only had to dig two." Celeste gave him a sweet smile, the sides of her mouth tugging slightly, "Oh but I'm such a weak girl who needs help." Joseph just snorted, "Uh huh. Sure. Tell that to my bruised shoulders."

"And your bruised ego?" Celeste asked innocently. Joseph's face flushed red as he opened his mouth and closed it again. She crossed her arms and pouted, sighing, "You could have a least pretended to care about me you know." Joseph cocked his head in confusion, "Uh, what? You always beat me!" Celeste sighed, brushing her hair back as she turned away. "That's not what I'm talking about."

"Oookaay??" Celeste just shook her head as they returned to the main group. Men could be idiots sometimes. They saw Klin hunched over a freshly dug mound, his face hidden behind his drooped hair, damp with sweat with Sasha standing by him. Even though he had been nearly dead from exhaustion, he had insisted on helping. He had dug with Joshua's help of course, being forced to take breaks as needed. "He's not taking this like I expected." Celeste whispered softly. Joseph followed her gaze. "Yeah, I think he blames himself for this. He kept muttering about 'if only I'd been stronger.' I'm going to talk with him later. See if I can get his head out of his ass." Celeste let out a snort of laughter, trying hard to stifle it. She patted her face, calming herself down, and then looked over to their wagon. Lorelei, Kyoko, and Ander and Erok were helping to set up camp. Joshua sat with his back against a tree, a small plume of smoke emitting from his pipe. Lorelei still had dried blood on her clothes. Black as ash from some gruntlets that had made it in the wagon. Celeste did her best to not glare at Ander. She was still mad about his ineptitude.

The weakest always made large, boastful promises that they could never uphold. She had come across enough men in her father's service like him. Erok sat hunched over a small candle of flaming wood, and straightened up as he saw them approaching. "Ah good, you guys are done. We're going to need some more wood for the fire. Can you grab some Celeste?" Celeste's shoulders slumped down, and was about to tell Joseph to go do it when she caught Ander staring at her. "Yeah, sure." She said, and began to walk towards the woods. "Here, I can help too!" Ander said, rushing over to her. Celeste whipped around, gritting her teeth, "No thanks." She squeezed out, "I can handle this on my own thank you."

"Don't worry." Joseph cut in, wrapping an arm around Ander, "You can help me out with cooking! I'll need the help bud." As Joseph led the annoying boot-licker away, he turned around and gave her worried look. Celeste stood still in shock for a moment, then quickly walked away. That oaf could not usually tell when she was bothered, much less who was bothering her! And the fact that he *clearly* understood she needed some space! The nerve of him! But, she was glad he had picked up on it. Ander had been not-so-subtly hitting on her the whole day, and she was growing tired of him and his unwanted attention. Then his failure to leap into action when it counted had only increased her dislike of him this day. How could he say he loved Kyoko, would protect her, when at the first sign of danger he froze like a deer in a hunter's line of sight?!

The boiling rage in her felt like it was about to burst and hot enough to brew tea, when she snapped a twig beneath her feet. Oh...wait. She was supposed to be collecting those. Celeste sighed wearily as she bent down and began to pick up pieces of wood. After collecting a few pieces, she stopped and looked around. "Wait, where am I?" She thought. Celeste had the horrible realization she had no clue which way their camp was. She shoved down the spike of panic that was trying to drive itself into her. She took a deep breath, calming her nerves. *Okay, I know I always just walk in a straight line when I don't care. So, just turn around. Easy, right?* Suddenly, there was a loud rustling in the brush near her. Celeste froze, her body poised to strike like a viper. There was no more noise. Complete silence. Celeste relaxed. Probably just a rabbit. That was when she realized two things at the same time.

First, she did not actually have Yatta on her. She had left her back at the camp. Second, the entire forest was as silent as death. No crickets, birds, or any other animal made a single noise. "Who's there?" Celeste challenged to the forest and shivered. The air had gone cold. Maybe that was because she had just issued a threat without a weapon. "Who are you? Why are you following me?!" Celeste continued on stubbornly. Her breath was now visible in small little clouds. "Oh there is no such need to use that tone my dear."

Celeste's heart stopped, and despite herself, her legs began to shake. She stilled them, but she knew that voice. She could never forget that silky smooth voice. "N-no. It can't be you!" Celeste blurted out, "Klin and Joseph killed you! We watched you die!" Viscious let out a small sigh as he emerged from the trees, hands behind his back as he gracefully floated forward, his icy wings casting a rainbow, marred only by a giant black scar on the top of the wings. "Humans really have not gotten any better with their silly assumptions on things, have they?"

"GUYS! COME QUICK!" Celeste screamed. But her cry for help faded unnaturally quick, like a bird shot down midflight. "Please don't do that." Viscious pleaded with a wince. "You're lucky I already set up the barrier around us." Celeste froze as dread began to creep up into her. She cast a look behind her to see a rapid movement of air forming behind her, completing its entrapment as it came full circle around them. "What do you want?" Celeste snarled. Viscious gave her a charming smile. "Well well, straight to business. I like that. I just want to talk. I believe you to be the most reasonable one. However, my appearance seems to have shaken you a bit. Maybe my true form will help things?" Celeste let out a gasp as Viscious closed his eyes, and his form shifted and changed. In place of the demon was a man of equal height and slender, yet lean build. He had dazzling icy blue eyes and short golden blonde hair. His sculpted jaw moved as soft lips revealed dazzling white teeth in an embarrassed smile. He wore a soft blue silk shirt that exposed a bit of his chest, while a dark blue cape fluttered behind him. All in all, he was a gorgeous man.

"*This* is your true form?" Celeste asked breathlessly. Viscious nodded, "Yes. Although a great use of anima is needed now to transform lately, so I can't use it as often." Celeste felt a great calmness wash over her like cool spring water. He was human. Maybe she had overreacted? "Alright, but you still haven't explained what you want."

"Ah, yes! My apologies." The man replied, "See, I would like to make a deal with you." Celeste felt a spark of anger, "And what happens if I refuse to even listen?" Viscious looked at her sadly, "Well, then we go our separate ways. Although it would be quite foolish to reject an offer before you even hear it out, don't you think?" Celeste nodded. That made perfect sense. "Very well. Continue." Viscious smiled, "I knew you were smart. First, I should ask a question. Do you know where all magic finds its source?"

"In each of the elemental fabrics."

"Right, but where do those find their source?"

Celeste frowned. "I'm not sure." Viscious let out a sigh, "I suppose he was right. Humanity *has* forgotten most of its inheritance. Each element was born from the Sculptor in charge of it. They do still teach who the Sculptors are, right?" Celeste nodded, "Yeah. They are beings with divine-like power who created this world." Viscious held up a hand, "Yes, but also no. They did not create this world, only formed it from the material available. For they themselves were created. But anyway, do you know what each was given as a domain?" Celeste cocked her head. "I believe so. Let's see, its been a bit. Genus for Light, Eleanora for Dark, Valoria was Life, and Bonaventure was Earth. Then there was Darshon for Fire, Sasara over Water, Atlas with Lightning, and then Celerious with Air." Viscious gave a small clap, "Excellent! I'd begun to believe normal people no longer paid attention to them! Wonderful to find someone who knows history! But, I suppose I should have expected as such from your family." A chill went down Celeste's spine. "How do you know my family?" She demanded. Viscisous gave her an impartial stare, "Forgive me, but I know many things Celeste Elizabeth Farvor'Coal. For example, your great desire to see Selene again." Celeste could barely breathe, her heart frozen still. "I see I have your full attention now. Better explain since I let the cat out of the bag so to speak." Viscious smiled as he began to explain. "See, I am looking for something. Something that someone in your band of misfits can get me. See, I cannot get it myself though, so I need your help. In exchange for your help, I will bring your sister back."

"Wha-what do you mean bring her back?!" Celeste sputtered. Viscious extended a hand, summoning a small black ball of light that glowed ominously, but with a pale beauty. "Many forget that there was a ninth Sculptor. Nath. He was cast out and spurned for something he never even did. Punished for an act that he could have committed, but never did. He has a magic all of his own you know. Natharian magic. Humans speak of it in hushed tones, for the Eight made sure to hunt any who practiced it. Fearing the great power and potential it has, for Natharian magic is not limited by the elements. It transcends all, the limits being the users power and imagination. And the resurrection of the dead are not beyond that power."

"HA!" Celeste barked, "Nothing can bring back the dead. Otherwise, I would have heard of this." Viscious stared at her before sighing. "Very well, I suppose I must prove it." Suddenly, a doe was thrown into their midst. Its eyes were wide as it thrashed about, constrained by the very air. Viscious snapped his fingers, a slice of air slitting the does throat. Celeste watched as the doe's eyes were drained of light. Viscious gently placed the deer on the ground, and waited a bit, then held out his hand, and recited in a booming voice. "By the power granted to me by the Lord of all, I command you to rise!" Celeste gasped as she watched as the blood flowed back into the wound, the slit throat closing. Suddenly, the doe leapt up, shook its head, and pranced off into the woods. "Believe me now?" Viscious asked.

Celeste nodded. "I can do the same for Selene," The man crooned, "All you need to do is get me what I want." Celeste's heart began to pound against her chest. This man had enslaved an entire village, and in the process had ruined Klin and Joseph's childhood. But, then again, the Companions had been the main force in that. A man offering to raise someone; they must have had a good reason for it all, right? "Very well, I'll do it." Celeste said. She could finally make amends for her sin. Viscious let out a triumphant smile. "I knew you would see reason. Now, there is this crystal orb at the pirate haven you are headed towards. You must get ahold of it someone how. Return it to me, and you shall have Selene back. Then, use this to let me know you have it." Viscious handed her a black stone. Engraved in it was an eye surrounded by a heptagon with two pair of horns at the top and bottom. "The Eye of Romevan." Celeste whispered. As she did, a breeze rattled the trees. "Yes. Just whisper my name and I shall come."

"How will I know who among us gets it?" Celeste asked. Vsicous just let out a knowing smile, "When the time comes, you will know by the Water's cry. With that, I must be off. Any longer and your friends will get suspicious. Oh, and do me a favor. Tell the Markus boys that their father was not nearly the hero they think him to be." With that Viscisou snapped his fingers and disappeared in a whirlwind. When the wind died down, he was gone, nothing left expect a large pile of wood perfect for a fire. Celeste gave a quick look around before gathering the wood into her arms and setting off back to camp. Her head swam with the amount of information she had been given, but most importantly, a deep sense of shame and guilt lurked underneath her heart. She buried the guilt and shame, focusing on what she would get out of this. Besides, its not like she had been asked to hurt anyone. A deal with him was not the same as betraying everyone. So then why did she feel so uncomfortable?

"Celeste?!" She jumped, startled by the sudden appearance of Ander. "Celeste, there you are!" He cried gleefully. She glared at him, picking up the wood she had dropped. "What are you doing out here?" She sneered, "I thought I told you I was fine alone." Ander took a step back, avoiding her eyes. "W-well, I mean, night...it's night and you hadn't returned so I got worried. Especially when I couldn't pick up your scent all of a sudden." Celeste finally noticed how dark it was, the stars their only waying of seeing at the moment. She was about to thank him, when suddenly what he had said made her red with rage. "*EXCUSE ME?* You were following me this whole time???! And smelling after me like some dog?!!" Ander covered his face, "No that's not—"

"Save it." She snarled, "I don't want to hear it. You stalked me. I have nothing to say to you!" Ander crouched down, squeezing his eyes shut. "Just get it over with!" He mumbled. Celeste froze. "What are you doing?" She asked. Ander peaked one eye, "You-you're not going to hit me?" He asked. Celeste frowned, shaking her head. "No, why would I do that." Ander eyed her warily as he stood up. "Oh, okay." Celeste's guilt came back even harder, but this time she knew it was over something else. She let out a deep sigh of regret. "I'm sorry Ander. That wasn't very nice of me. I understand that you were just looking out for me."

Ander smiled, "I understand. And I wasn't stalking you or following you. I just have enhanced sense of smell when transformed, and well Joshua had us training. Well, just me actually. But, I promises I would never try to disrespect you!" Celeste gave him a reassuring grin, tinged by her exhaustion. "I know Ander. I just let emotions get ahead of sense. C'mon, lets get back to camp." Ander nodded, and grabbed some of the wood. Together they entered camp, and found an angry Lorelei glaring at them. "Just where exactly where you two?! You should have been back an hour ago young lady! Because of you, I haven't been able to finish cooking yet!" Celeste shrunk down, "Sorry ma'am. I uh, got lost. Ander found me on my way back." Lorelei crossed her arms, "Well, what are you waiting for? Throw the wood in. Then, you get to eat last *and* clean the dishes." Celeste and Ander quickly threw the wood in the pit.

Klin gave them a mischievous smile, "Well, looks like someone's on her bad side." Celeste gave him a cool, even stare. "Shut it spiky." Klin lit the fire, and then began patting his hair as Celeste took a seat while they waited for dinner. She simply sat quietly as everyone talked about various things. An hour later, dinner was done. Celeste devoured three dishes and then got to work cleaning. Once she was done, she went to her sleeping bag and lay down. As soon as she did, a young girl of about eight appeared by her. She had jet black hair tied back in a ponytail and wore an Eastern dress without sleeves. The top of the dress was white crossing over a blue underneath. If Celeste had to guess, it was from Sundarn, but Yatta herself could not remember. Yatta crouched down by Celeste, hugging her legs and stared at her with those piercing blue eyes. "Why did you leave me?" Yatta asked. "Got caught up in all the chores." Celeste mumbled, "Didn't mean too."

Yatta blinked, "You're hiding something from me. What is it?" A sharp spike of panic went through her. That others would be easy to deceive but Yatta? She would be hard. "I have no idea what you're talking about." Yatta just stayed there, staring at her. It took all of Celeste's will power to not start squirming under that piercing look. Finally, Yatta got up and walked over to her prison, where it lay next to Celeste's sleeping bag. "Alright, I believe you. Now I need food or the power won't work long." Celeste nodded and thought about what she needed to give Yatta. For whatever reason, Yatta needed emotions mixed with purpose to have energy. If she went too long without anything, she basically became drowsy and weak. Celeste in the end shrugged and just decided to give her this whole day's worth. That would keep her feed for a month at least. Celeste closed her eyes and concentrated, giving all of it.

As they neared the end of the day, Yatta suddenly began to vomit and retch. "Yatta! Are you okay? What's wrong?" Yatta stared at her, eyes brimming with tears and a deep look of betrayal. "You-you promised!'" Yatta accused, sobs beginning to form, "Yo-you promised me! But you are just like to the rest." She disappeared, a sick feeling in the air was all that remained as Celeste jolted awake. The embers of their campfire crackled pitifully as everyone lay sleeping. Celeste was shaking, but she barely noticed. She was cold, very cold now. "Celeste?" Klin asked. He stood up from his crouched position by the campfire. She had not noticed him at all. "Hey, are you okay?" He asked.

"Y-yeah," Celeste replied shakily, "Why wouldn't I be?" Klin frowned as he sat down next to her. "No, you're not. You're crying." Celeste wiped her face, her face wet from the hidden tears. She stiffened as Klin suddenly placed his coat around her. "Wha-" Klin shushed her, "You looked cold."

"Won't you get cold though?" She asked. Klin just grinned as he held out his hand, a flame flickering in and out. "I doubt it." Even though the flame was gone, she could still feel some of the leftover heat. "Besides," He continued, "My shift is over. Good night Celeste. Everything will be alright." With that he walked over to Joseph and gave him a small kick in the ribs. There was a muffled yelp as Joseph jerked up on his elbows. She could tell from his position that he was glaring at Klin. Klin just ignored him and bent down, whispering something to his brother before trotting off to his own mat. Joseph gave a big old stretch as he got up, throwing on his own coat. He paused though as he noticed Celeste.

"Why the Heshtan are you up?" Joseph asked as he sat down near her. "You need to sleep." Celeste hugged her legs tight after she removed Klin's coat. "Maybe I don't wanna." She muttered. She stared at Joseph, his eyes glowing in the dark as he examined her. She turned away, feeling like he was seeing too much. "Hmph, it's those nightmares again, huh?" Celeste whipped her head back around, "How-"

Joseph snorted derisively. "I'm not as much of an idiot as you seem to think I am Celeste. I see the way you tentatively lay down, as if something will for sure bother you when you sleep. Most nights you wake up in the middle of my shift, and always you try to take first watch as if to postpone sleep. Then, when you do sleep, I often hear you mumble either Yatta's name, or some girl named Selene." Celeste glanced away and hugged herself even tighter. It was a very cold night after all. "I don't want to talk about it." She growled. Joseph sighed and threw his coat over her face. "Hey!" She sputtered indignantly, "What was that for?" Joseph gave her a roguish smile. "You were obviously cold so just wear the damn thing already."

"You could have been a little more gentlemanly about it." She snapped. Joseph crossed his arms, eyebrow cocked, "And have you bite my head off for it? No thank you. You needed a rude awakening." Celeste stared at him before giggling softly, "I suppose you're right. Thank you."

"No problem, Celeste." He replied softly. He then took Klin's coat and lay it back over his brother before sitting down next to her. The two sat together in the soft dark night. The fire crackled gently as Celeste wrapped herself up in the massive coat. All that could be heard was their breathing. She cast a glance at Joseph, his golden eyes acting like searchlights in the night as he kept watch. He had not pressed her, nor tried to bring it back up. He had only tried to make her feel better, and he was content with just that. She let out a sigh as she resolved herself. "I guess I'll talk, especially after everything we've been through. You deserve to know at this point." Joseph turned to her, but not looking overtly expectant. Celeste took a deep breath and began to explain. "I haven't been completely honest with you guys. You see well-um, I'm actually the daughter of Antoine Farvor'Coal, one of the Six Great Noble families of Coronus. Pleasedon'tbemad!" She squeaked at the end. Joseph shook his head, "Don't worry, I'm not. Surprised, like really surprised, but not mad. So, why not tell us the truth?"

Celeste gently tugged at her bangs, "Well, I wanted some help from someone who wouldn't be doing it for a reward first off. Those kind of people are going to be more reliable. Second, tensions with other countries have been rising and so I could easily be branded an enemy. Plus, I wanted people to help me for me, not for my father." Joseph nodded, "Okay, that makes sense. But why not come clean earlier?" Celeste shook her head, "I guess I just started to enjoy being treated as just another person, and not some flower people ogle at. I'm ninety percent sure that most compliments I get are just from my station."

"So how does this tie into the nightmares?" He asked. She hunched down, "It's-kinda of a long story. Are you sure you want to hear it?"

"Not like I got anything better to do." He shot back. Celeste took a deep breath, "Alright then. It all began two years ago. The day I first met the Heshtisi..."

Chapter 23

Lady Celeste Elizabeth Favor'Coal

"Lady Celeste! Please wake up! It's nearly nine!" Celeste groaned as she cracked an eye open. Sunlight streamed in small beams, finding their way in-between her closed shades. Fiora stood over her, glaring at her fiercely. "Five more minutes." Celeste muttered from her pillow. Fiora gave an exasperated sigh and marched over, throwing open the curtains. Celeste let out a hiss as light flooded the room and hit her in the face. "Really Celeste? What are you a Scal'gatha?" Fiora said crossly. Celeste hid her head under her pillow and hissed playfully. "Maybe. I am a creature of the night my dear Fiora. Call me Celeste Nightwalker."

"Well Miss Nightwalker, would you like to get out or shall I help you?" Fiora shot back.

"I'm up!" Celeste yelped, leaping out of bed and nearly falling on her face in the process. Despite the woman's petite frame, Fiora was quite strong, and used that strength quite well in getting sleepyheads out from under their comfortable beds. Fiora gave her a satisfied smirk before she walked into Celeste's massive closet. "So, what would you like to wear today ma'am?" Her muffled voice came from deep inside the space. Celeste was now sitting at her vanity, a brush in hand. "Eh, I don't really care." She replied. Her bed-head was particularly bad today. The left side of her hair was sticking out completely horizontally, and the right side was matted down and slightly damp. Looks like she had drooled again. Celeste began to methodically attack her hair. "Also, drop the formalities Fiora. It's just us you know." Fiora let out a deep sigh from the closet. She seemed to do a lot of that these days. Fiora poked her head, her strawberry colored hair falling down in small strands from

275

under the blue headband. "You know I'm not supposed to though." She protested. Celeste stopped brushing, hands on her hips, "And how long have we been friends?"

"Ever since we were four." Fiora replied with a roll of her eyes, but she was smiling, "I can't ever forget when you *constantly* remind me." Celeste grinned back, "Which is why our friendship trumps formalities." The two giggled as they went back to their tasks. The girls were the same age of sixteen. Celeste had secured Fiora's position as a maid and her personal handmaid four years ago. Even if Fiora had not been pretty, Selene would have made sure she kept the job. Selene called Fiora, "The perfect good influence upon our mischievous Celeste."

"But are you sure you don't want to choose?" Fiora asked slyly, "Or have you forgotten what day it is already?" Celeste paused mid brush. "Uhhh...our best friends forever anniversary?" Fiora rolled her eyes, "Sculptor's you're still half-asleep. It's your sister's birthday today." The brush clatter to the floor as Celeste began to frantically pull at her hair. "SHIT! Argggh, how could I forget!" She leaned back on the stool, and pinched the bridge of her nose. "Damnit! I haven't even gotten her present!" Fiora threw up her hands. "Are you serious?" Celeste turned to her with pleading eyes. "Shit, you are serious." Fiora moaned. "Fine, we'll run into to town after breakfast. I'll see if I can figure out something to get your father's permission. Everyone is waiting for you at the moment. You'll owe me though."

"This and every other day." Celeste replied with a small laugh. "But thank you." Fiora nodded, smiling before she turned around. "Alright, so which dress you want?" Celeste did not even hesitate as she called back, "The black and purple one!" Celeste began to resume brushing her hair, with even more ferocity than before. "It's Selene's favorite one on me." Fiora came out holding an off the shoulder black summer dress with purple frills. She set the dress down on Celeste's bed and then walked over to her. "Here, let me do this." Fiora ordered, "You'll tear out your hair doing it this way." Celeste let her have the brush as Fiora began to work through the hair. "You know, I still marvel how you can keep it this long." Her friend marveled. Celeste's hair ran all the way down to her ankles. Celeste shrugged, "I hardly ever feel the weight anymore. Plus I love it this way." *More importantly,* She thought, *I actually look decent like this.* But it was a lot, especially compared to Fiora's short wavy hair that did not even touch her shoulders most of the time. "Do we want to do anything with it today?" Fiora asked. Celeste shook her head, "Nah, that would take too much time at this point. I better change and get down there."

"Finally, you're speaking some sense." Fiora said approvingly. Celeste stood up and changed into the dress. Once she was done, she spun around, letting the bottom twirl up. "So, how do I look?"

"Like a proper lady." Fiora said in a deep, mocking voice. "Why thank you." Celeste replied in a trim, high voice. "I make it my duty to strive towards the noble ideal everyday of my life. Berating, obnoxious, and bitchy of course!" The two girls burst out into laughter as they left the bedroom. Celeste suddenly took off sprinting down the hallway. "Hey, wait for me!" Fiora called with a laugh. Celeste skidded to a stop, her bare feet turning slightly red against the wood floor. "You just need to get faster slowpoke!" With that, she spun back around and launched herself on the banister. She slid down, her hair flying behind her like some sort of fay creature. As she neared the end of the stairs, her father came into view, and right in trajectory. "Look out Papa!" Celeste yelped. Antoine turned around, his eyes widening just before his daughter slammed into him, sending the both of them into a heap on the ground.

Celeste quickly scrambled off of her father. "Are you okay Papa!" Antoine pushed himself up in an acrobatic leap that was impressive for a man of his age. He rolled his neck and arms a bit as he laughed. "Yes, I'm fine. I told you this would happen one day, didn't I? Are you okay dear?" Celeste turned her face down sheepishly, "Yes, I'm fine. Sorry about that." Her father was a short, stocky man, barely taller than his daughter by an inch. He had short blonde hair that had a single spot of gray on the top, that was combed back a bit, and a trimmed beard to a triangular point. He shook his head, "When are you going to stop doing that though?" Celeste crossed her arms, "When I'm old and decrepit like you." Antoine raised an eyebrow, "Well this old and decrepit man can still sire a new daughter to replace his ungrateful one."

"Um, ew!" Celeste gagged. Antoine just let out a roar of laughter. "You make it too easy somedays. Come, let's eat. Your sister and mother already ate." Celeste began following her father as they headed towards the dining hall. "What, not making them wait like you did?" She asked. Antoine cast a glance back at her, "No," He replied a hint of reprimand on the edge of his tongue, "I would think others should not go hungry because one member of the family is 'a party animal, and creature of the night.' I think that is what Selene related what you said last night?" Celeste blushed furiously, but met her father's gaze. "I..uh may have had too much to drink last night I suppose." Antoine snorted, "By too much you mean two ales?" Now Celeste was very red. Just then, Fiora came running up behind them, her breathing sharp. "Ah, there is my daughter's handmaiden." Antoine barked. Fiora stopped, a timid look coming over her. "I'm wondering, are you not supposed to keep her in check." Fiora nodded tenativly, "Yes my lord. However, she would have slid down in her undergarments if I had not made sure she was dressed." Antoine looked at Celeste who shrugged. "Eh, that does sound like something I would do." Antoine sighed, "Unfortunately it does."

He then turned to Fiora and smiled, clasping her on the shoulder. "Ohh, stop looking so scared my girl. I thought by now you would be able to tell when I'm just messing with you. I hope you know I cannot think of any friend better for her. You do as best a job as you can. Now, some breakfast?" Fiora gave a bow, "On it my lord." She scampered off ahead, while the nobles took to their seats. The dinning hall was the second most decorated area of the mansion. The table itself was made to seat at least fifty people, and was crafted from dark oak. The legs of both the table and chairs had dragon scales carved upon them. The backs of the chairs themselves had a dragon's head at the top, fangs bared in a fearsome snarl. Various paintings of landscapes from around the Favor'Coal domain hung on the walls, and a large crystal chandelier hung above the center of the table. Fiora brought out their food, eggs, sausage, and biscuits covered in a savory gravy. Antoine smiled gratefully as his food was set before him. "Thank you Fiora. And give my thanks to Mr. Bartote." Fiora bowed as she scurried off, most likely starting whatever chores were scheduled for the day. As they dug in, (the food delicious as always,) Antoine asked, "So Celeste, what present have you gotten for Selene?"

"Oh, umm-you see…" Antoine just burst out laughing. "Oh Celeste, you're such an airhead. I'm not surprised you forgot. So, taking Fiora out after breakfast?" Celeste relaxed her shoulders. "Precisely. Figured I'd take someone with good taste." Antoine raised an eyebrow, "You ask me for advice you know." Celeste gave her father a critical eye as she looked over his outfit for the day, which was a bright, baby blue suit with a golden shirt. "No offense papa, but you have none."

"No taste!" Her father sputtered indignantly, "I bought you that dress you are wearing! And that outfit for your date that you had! I picked those out didn't I?"

"Even a broken stool is able to stand twice a day." Celeste recited. "Clock." Antoine corrected, "It's clock Celeste. Even a broken clock is right twice a day."

"Eh, my point still stands." Celeste waved a hand dismissively, "Besides, didn't you chase that boy out? Wouldn't exactly be proud to bring that date back up." Her father crossed his arms, his face clouding just at the memory as he growled, "That bastard deserved what he got for such pig-like audacity He kept making allusions to having sex with you on your first date!! I still don't get why you're still upset over that." Celeste finished her food and stood up, "Because *I* wanted to be the one to chase him out papa. Inspire *true* fear in the pig. I had a whole line prepared and everything!" Antoine cracked a smile. "Oh, and what was it?" Celeste leaped on the table and grabbed a fork, wielding it like a sword. "If I ever see your face again, making moves on anyone I know, I shall take this sword and gut you! Roasting you over a fire upon a spit like the pig that you are!" Antoine clapped as Celeste gave a bow. "Wonderful! I'm sorry I deprived you of that opportunity! Might have actually made him change his ways." Celeste laughed and bent down, kissing her father on the check. She hopped off of the table, and walked backwards, waving as Fiora followed her. "Bye Papa! Be back soon then!"

Antoine smiled, shaking his head, "I'll give Selene some excuse. She's in the chapel with your mother at the moment." Celeste nodded, and quickly turned away, hiding her face from her father. "That woman is *not* my mother." She hissed under her breath. Fiora glanced at her, and gave her hand a squeeze. The sudden burst of anger disappeared though as they exited the through the large stately doors and out onto the rough paved road. Foreign cherry trees were in the midst of blooming, their soft petals blowing about in a graceful dance as the warm wind glided over them. Celeste smiled at the sight. Those trees were her favorite. She was quite happy that their family had close ties with Sudarn. "You gotta love spring." Celeste remarked. Fiora let out a wistful sigh. "Yeah. The perfect temperatures, beautiful plants blooming; all the perfect ingredients a season of romance."

Celeste rolled her eyes. "Don't tell me that you're still mooning after that boy?" Fiora's face flushed bright red. "Just because I mention romance doesn't mean I'm in love! I can appreciate it without having it!" Celeste gave her a flat stare as exited the Farvor'Coal estate. "Ohh, okay." Fiora assented, "I am. But don't tell anyone! Especially Selene. You know how aggressively…supportive she can be about these type of things." Celeste cocked an eyebrow, "Um, and I'm somehow better?"

"At least when the guy is standing right next to me."

"That's fair. Selene just doesn't care about images."

"That's something I do admire about her." Fiora praised, "But I don't have that strength, so I don't like being embarrassed." *Yeah*, Celeste thought to herself, *its easy not to care about images when you are perfect.* Out loud she said instead, "You know what this means now though?"

"Oh no!" Fiora wailed, burying her face in her hands, "Don't you dare!" Celeste grinned, and grabbed Fiora's hands. "Ohhh yes. It's apart of our pact."

"Do we *really* have to though?" Celeste crossed her arms, "Yes! A promise is a promise." Fiora looked at her, shoulders slumped in defeat, "Well, I suppose I have no choice. Besides, if he gets scared of you, he can't be the one." Celeste broke into a wide smile, "Now that's more like it!" As they began to near closer to town, Fiora asked, "So, do you even know what you are going to get her?"

"Of course." Celeste snorted, "Just because I forgot it was today doesn't mean I forgot what I should get her!" She spun around, walking backwards with her arms behind her head, "There's this jacket at Millie's that Selene has had her eye on for a while. It's actually far more expensive than most clothing because there is magic sewn into the clothing." Fiora crossed her arms, "Heh, I'm impressed. I totally thought we were going into this without a plan. So, two questions. One, why am I here? Two, why did you wait till now to get it then? You were in town yesterday also."

Celeste turned around, blush appearing at the edges of her cheeks. "Oh, I see now." Fiora remarked, "You were with *him*. Well that answers both my questions." Suddenly, Celeste grabbed Fiora and dragged her into a nearby bush. "Wha—"

"Sshush!" Celeste hissed. Fiora peeked out above the bush, and Celeste tried to push her head back down, but was unsuccessful. Fiora ducked back down and rolled her eyes. "Really, why are we hiding from Claude?" Celeste opened her mouth, prepared to give a very logical explanation, but closed it as she felt very foolish all of a sudden. "Yeah, why are you two hiding from me?" The girls screamed as they leapt to their feet. Celeste, not thinking, spun around and backhanded Claude across the face. He fell on the ground with a slight yelp, but was soon laughing. "Ow, that hurt." Claude moaned in between chuckles. Claude was a tall, and muscular man with short, curly blonde hair and the beginnings of a beard. "Serves you right for sneaking up on us!" Fiora sniffed. "Hey, I didn't do anything wrong." Claude muttered. Celeste crossed her arms and pouted, "Keep telling yourself that. Why the herk you do that?" Claude raised an eyebrow. "I mean, when I saw you dive behind a bush and then Fiora staring at me, I was naturally curious. Anyway, why are *you* here? Isn't the party soon?"

Celeste waved her hand, "Whether the urge to hid in the bushes hits me is none of your business first off. Second, I uh, need to get Selene's gift." Fiora pointed her thumb at Celeste. "Yep, airhead here forgot to grab it." Claude laughed, "Well, that sounds just like her." Celeste glared at him, "Well *maybe* I wouldn't have forgotten if someone hadn't taken up all of my day yesterday."

"What, is it a crime to be friends now?"

"Yes! Wai-wait Imeanno!" Claude just started to laugh even harder, even Fiora giggled. Celeste just flushed red. "Oh forget I said anything." She moaned. "Oh, don't worry," Claude teased, "I'm sure you'll forget before I do." Celeste threw a punch that Claude barely dodged. He let out a yelp and whistled, "Damn, if I hadn't known that was coming that would've hurt." She then proceeded to give a light kick to his shins, which made him let out a small curse. Fiora crossed her arms, "Oh come on. No way that actually hurt." Celeste flushed, "Oops. Sorry."

"Apology accepted." Claude replied, "But damn, that actually hurt. You've gotten stronger this year." Celeste smiled, "Comes from taking down idiots."

"*Clauuuude. Claude* where are *youuu?*" Celeste's face dropped at the sound of that voice. "Ah herk. Speaking of idiots..." Fiora turned to Claude with an accusatory look, "You're hanging out with *her?*" He shrugged, "Well, I mean we are friends. In the most generous sense of the word." A young girl their age came speed walking towards them. She was taller than either of the girls and had dark, silky black hair and green eyes. She had alabaster skin and was quite curvy. As she neared them, she hiked up the edges of her pink silk dress, making a face of disgust as she moved through the trampled dirt and grass. "Why-oh." Marie's emerald eyes narrowed to snake-like slits as she saw who Claude was with. "Hello Celeste. Fiora." Celeste gave her a very wide smile. "Hello Marie, it is so ever nice to see you." Claude shifted uncomfortably as the unseen daggers flew from the girl's eyes. Marie hated Celeste purely for the fact that she was more popular than her, (and she considered herself better than everyone else of course.) While Celeste hated her for the much more just and sensible reason that Marie was a piece of shit. Marie was so arrogant and girly that she really felt like a young girl's novel antagonist, and comically so.

"What brings you into town?" Marie asked in a sickly-sweet voice. "Oh, just on my way to pick up Selene's present."

"Oooh, how sweet. Such a loving sister to get her a present as soon as possible. I hope it's not something plain like one of those jackets?" Celeste clenched her fists, but kept her face smooth and emotionless. "Oh, and why's that?" Marie smiled, almost a sneer, "Well they are made out of leather aren't they? Wouldn't want it to be one of your relatives." Claude looked horrified, and was about to say something, but Celeste just began to laugh, nearly doubling over from it. "Oh, don't worry Marie, I was going to get the snakeskin one. You know how Selene likes to wear her victims."Fiora stifled a snort. Marie's face went deathly white, before her face curled into a snarl, "Why you--!" Celeste just shrugged innocently, "What? We're talking about Selene

282

aren't we?" Marie pointed a finger like she was about to say something, but Celeste took up a loose fighting stance. Her shoulders were relaxed, but her feet poised to leap like a cat. Marie noticed that a least, and crossed her arms. "Yes, so I suppose you'll need to get two of those. I know how much Selene loves for you two to match. Too bad only one of you will look nice in it."

"Marie!" Claude barked, "Enough!" Marie took a startled step back. "Right, of course." She replied trimly, "We should get back to our date." Celeste's eyes widened, her mouth going slack, "Date?!" Marie smiled devilishly as she wrapped an arm around Claude's. Claude shrugged her off and glared at her. "Just head back. I'll meet you at the café." Marie's eyes widened, but she did as he asked, slinking off. Celeste did her best to keep calm, but her lip was beginning to tremble. Claude turned to them, his face full of embarrassment. "Sorry, her parents and mine pressured this. Really, why couldn't they let me choose you? I'll see you later tonight, Celeste." With that Claude took off running, while Celeste stood there stupefied. "Di-did he just???" Firoa stook rooted like a tree, just as stupefied, "I believe he did. I suppose that's one way to confess. Lucky you." Celeste began to grin from ear to ear as an uncontrollable amount of energy flooded through her. Once the girls finally entered town, Celeste had a sudden thought. "Hey Fiora, you know what this means now?" Fiora looked at her skeptically, "What?" Celeste just grinned, "You get to uphold your half of the deal too now." Fiora laughed, "Oooh, good. I like this part of it more." It was going to be a fun night.

An hour later Fiora and Celeste stood in the back courtyard at the manor. Four large cherry trees stood at cardinal points of a lard sand arena. The area was ringed with large, rectangular red stones. The Farvor'Coal's family training ground. Only members of the family were allowed to enter the ring and spar or do any kind of practice. Only very close friends or those who received a special invite were allowed within the circle. Even then, that was a rare occasion. (Unless you were Fiora.) There was a sacredness to this spot, a sacredness born from tradition and familial history. This was also Selene's favorite spot to just sit and listen. It had also been their mom's. "Go on," Fiora said, "I got stuff I still need to do. I'll catch you later."

"Thanks for the help." Celeste said softly and waved her friend good-bye. She turned then, gripping the box which held the present, and began to walk towards her sister. Selene was two years her senior, and breathtakingly gorgeous. She had blonde hair like Celeste, but it bordered on silver. She wore it cut to her neck, and layered bangs. She had beautiful purple eyes that would seek you out, glowing like gems. Her skin was flawlessly smooth, her body slim but muscular, and more curvaceous than Celeste. Selene also stood a good five inches taller than Celeste. In both appearance and skills, her older sister was better than her. As she got near, her feet crunched some dead leaves. Selene turned around, and smiled. "Ahh, there you are. Don't tell me you just got up sleepyhead?" Celeste grinned, "As if Papa would let that happen. Nah, I had to go into town for your present."

"Oh come on lazy!" Selene teased, "Even on my birthday you're last minute!" Celeste sniffed, and turned her head. "Well, maybe you don't deserve it!"

"Ah no! I'm sorry! You are the most thoughtful and loving sister I could ever ask for!" Selene flattered as she kneeled. Celeste smiled, "Weeeelll, *maybe* I could give it to yooo—eek!" Celeste let out a shriek as her world reoriented itself as her feet were swept out from under her. She threw the present out and fell into a roll. She turned around behind her, leaping back up to see Selene on her feet, holding the present with one hand. "Wow, nice recovery." Selene praised, "But deduction for falling in the first place." The two sisters stared at each other before bursting out laughing. Celeste tackled her sister in a hug. "Happy birthday you jerk!" Selene wrapped her in a warm embrace. "Thanks you dirty scoundrel!"

"So how does it feel to be an old lady now?" Celeste asked. "Eh, not that different from you." Celeste rolled her eyes, "You're just jealous of my **maturaty**." She proclaimed dramatically. Selene crossed her arms. "You know, pretty sure that response just undermines the answer?" Celeste waved her hand dismissively, "Blah, blah, blah. I'm mature, you're not. So, you going to open the present you so rudely stole or not!" Selene smiled and grabbed the present. She gasped as she opened it and removed a black jacket with a purple trim and buckles along the sleeves. "Oh Celeste, this is great! Thank you!" Celeste nodded, "I know you've wanted this for a while, so I may have had Millie put it on reserve for you since. Even better, the jacket has multiple defensive enchantments in the thread itself. Most weapons will only leave a scratch with their first hit." Selene turned to her, smiling slyly, "Ah, so you didn't get one for yourself then."

Celeste shook her head, "No, that would be wrong of me I feel. Besides, I wouldn't look good in one of those anyway."

"Nonsense!" Selene reprimanded, "You look good in most anything! So go put yours on and meet me back here for a spar." Celeste stared at her as her sister's words began to register. "Oh no, you didn't." Selene grinned, "Oh but I did."

"But it's *your* birthday." Selene shook her head, "Yes, and yours is not for a good while. It's mine, and so I choose how it is celebrated. It means as much to me for you to match with me as it does the present received."

"Okay, but what about your dress? Shouldn't we be ready for the party?" Celeste asked. Selene put a finger to her chin, "Hmm, maybe. Unless this is my party, and so I decide the dress code. Not Marianne. Now go get changed so we can sweat!" Celeste beamed, nodded, and took of running to her room. She blew by a flustered Fiora who was cleaning the stairs. She opened her door and found a nearly identical jacket to the one she had just given Selene. The only difference was that it had a red trim and was smaller. She quickly changed out of the dress, and into a classic outfit for her. White shirt, short skirt with shorts underneath. Celeste completed the look by strapping her katana, Scarlet, to her hip, and ran back out.

As she ran down the hallway, she collided full force with her stepmother. "Watch were you're going!" Marianne snapped. Celeste eyed her tersely, and bowed. "I'm sorry about that. I wasn't paying attention and was too caught up in my own energy." Marianne was a stout woman, with large arms and body, and just the slight beginnings of fat. She had dark, brown hair done up in a tall bun, and a makeup plastered face that made her normally light skin seem as white as a dead woman. Celeste then tried to move past her, but was stopped as Marianne commented snidely, "And just where do *you* think your going dressed like *that*?" Marianne's blue eyes narrowed as she examined her. Celeste took a deep breath as she turned around, forcing herself to unclench her fists. A mixed sense of dread and annoyance filled her, but she answered anyway. "To the Four Trees. I'm going to spar and a dress would get ruined."

"Hmph! On today of all days!" Marianne's mouth curdled, "Have you forgotten that it is your sister's birthday?! You should be spending time with her, and not swinging around some blade like a brute of a man!" Celeste took a deep breath. She cannot let her antagonize her today. As much as she wanted to rub a sarcastic comment in this bitch's face, she shouldn't. "Oh, but I am actually." Celeste said, with what she hoped was convincingly genuine humility, "Selene is the one I'm to spar with. She asked me to go get changed for this." Marianne crossed her arms, glaring like a snake, "I suppose though that *you* were the one who suggested sparring in the first place. Selene needs to be focused on her lady-like duties for tonight. She'll have a lot of suitors for tonight, and she will need to look more than presentable! Not like some sweaty mutt like you." Celeste physically had to restrain herself from drawing Scarlet. "I'll be sure to pass the message on." Celeste replied with a barely restrained voice, "Now may I leave please?" Marianne waved her hand. "Fine. I don't know how your father expects you to find a husband with that personality of yours."

"At least I'm not a fake." Celeste muttered. "What was that?!" Marianne snapped. Celeste just smiled sweetly, "Oh, just about how kind and beautiful you are." Marianne narrowed her eyes. "Just get out of her." She spat. *With pleasure.* Celest thought. She calmly turned and walked away, but not before making sure her middle finger was conspicuously extended while gripping the hilt of Scarlet. As her heartbeat began to slow, Celeste let out a sigh of relief. She was lucky she had not received any punishment this time. She had gotten worse for less before.

She noticed though that Fiora was still cleaning the stairs at the bottom, and had not noticed her yet. Celeste quietly got near her, before leaping over her. Fiora did not even bat an eye as she smacked Celeste's leg. Celeste let out a yelp. "I believe I warned you about doing that again." Fiora chided from the floor. Celeste grumbled to herself, rubbing the red spot. Damn, that had hurt. The pain though was gone by the time she made it to the arena. Selene had also changed it seemed, into a long red skirt, and a black shirt under her new jacket. "What's with you?" Her sister asked, "You looked like a cat licking it's wounds."

"Met 'mother' in the hallway." Celeste puffed, "She said to make sure you don't look like a mangy mutt later tonight. To be *presentable* too allll the men." Selene let out a sigh. "Ah, I see. She punish you?" Celeste shook her head, "Nah, I controlled myself." Selene nodded, "Good. That woman is such a bitch. So. Ready to fight?" Celeste rolled her shoulders and drew Scarlet. "Oh boy am I ever." Selene smiled, drawing her sword, Yata. Still seemed like a weird name to Celeste but to each their own. "Oh, wait." Selene held out her hand, and a flurry of wind flew around Celeste. She could feel as the wind quickly braided her hair into a tight bun. "Wow." Celeste whistled, "You're getting pretty good at that. How's it look?"

"Like Fiora did it." Selene replied, "Oh, and I put up the barriers at the same time, so we can go all out today." Celeste grinned, "Alright, but you asked for this!" Celeste rushed her, falling into Sasara stance, her legs just barely bent, but the feet loose and fluid. She unleashed a flurry of vertical strikes. Selene parried them all gracefully, retaliating with Bona stance. She stabbed at Celeste's kidney, but she quickly placed her sword vertically, pressed against her arm as she let the strike pass through. She then swung at Selene's wrist, but her sister was no amateur, and her stance was solid. Rapidly and fluidly, Selene reversed her grip and knocked Celeste's blade up before slicing diagonally. Celeste leaped back as Selene continued her momentum, spinning and switching grips midspan. Celeste decided then to take a risk. As Selene's back was turned, Celeste stepped in with a vertical overhead slash, locking blades with her sister. Celeste smiled as her sister gave her a surprised but admiring look. The two leapt back, both more wary as they eyed one another. Celeste focused in, her attention to detail enhanced by the rush of adrenaline flowing through her.

She noticed that Selene's strands of hair were beginning to float up. "Shit!" Celeste yelped as five distortions appeared in the air only a few feet from her. She could just barely make out the blades as they shot towards her. Celeste parried the first, cut through the other two as they went for her calf, then spun around as the final two shot at her ribs on both sides. As she knelt close to the ground, Selene leaped at her with a horizontal slash to the head. Celeste fell down to the ground, ducking into a push-up position. Selene let out a cry of surprise as for a brief second, she lost her footing. *There!* Celeste swung her legs around, tripping Selene. Her sister fell forward through the air while Celeste rolled forward, coming up with a slash. But as she did, Selene rocketed forward through the air, parrying Celete's attack while simultaneously sending a blast of wind into her. Celeste let out a stifled cry as she was hit by a solid blast of wind in the stomach. It sent her tumbling backwards. Dazed, she laying staring up at the sky trying to regain her breath. Just as she was about to, the edge of a sword fell gently on her forehead. "I win." Selene giggled, then extended a hand out.

Celeste sighed as she took hold and got to her feet. "I have to say," Selene commended, "You actually almost had me there. You get better every time we do this. I'd wager you'll be better than me one day." Celeste shook her head, "I doubt it. You're such a skilled weaver and swordsman, that it'll be impossible for a non-weaver like myself to surpass you. Besides, you say that every time." Selene sheathed Yatta, and looked thoughtful, "Well, first off I say it because it is true. You just need more practice is all. You already have a skill most do not have. Being able to see the first signs of a spell without even weaving. That's an incredible skill you know. Only reason you deflected my House Move was because of that." Celeste just snorted, "That's also because you didn't do the full move. If you had done the entirety of Air Immobilizer, definitely would have lost." Selene just smiled, "Well, I don't want to kill you, you know.

"Could have fooled me." Celeste huffed. "Again?" Selene nodded and took up her stance. Celeste eyed her footwork. That was a new one, that or her footwork was sloppy. Her feet were close together, one of them raised on her toes. Celeste grinned as she leaped forward, drawing Scarlet out straight into a strike. Selene nimbly dodged to the side, jamming Yata's handle into Celeste's stomach. Celeste let out a gasp as the air was stolen from her. Then, before she could recover, she received a solid smack to the back of the neck, knocking her flat on the ground. "Normally you would be left without a head." Selene said smugly, "So I think I win."

"What—even was—that?" Celeste asked in between ragged breathes. Selene got down and helped Celeste up. "Keep up straight and deep breathes. Helps get your breathing back." Celeste glared at Selene, "I already know that." But she did it anyway. "So, you going to answer my question?" Selene crossed her arms, "It's a foreign technique, like all of our sword skills. It's called cat stance. It's not normally used with a sword, but the purpose of it's meant for quick, rapid movements. Hence, cat." Celeste shook her head. The stance had looked so unstable. She had thought it would be a piece of cake to destroy it. Man, she still had so much to learn. She was never going to catch up. Silently, Celeste fell into a fighting stance. "Again?" Selene asked, "Alright. Guess you wanted to be humiliated!" The two girls smirked at one another, and were about to start when their father called. "There you girls are!" Selene looked over, so Celeste took that moment to attack. Selene deflected the blow without even looking at her, and knocked Celeste to the ground. "Nice try." Selene said casually, and then turned to greet Antoine. "Hello father. Did you need us?" Celeste got to her feet, muttering under her breath before focusing on Antoine, and paused. Their father had traded his suit for his armor.

He wore red greaves and gauntlets, with gold speckled across them, but the father up the greaves and gauntlets went, black encroached until it merged into the black chest plate. Their house colors, the colors of a coal in fire. Antoine also wore a black shoulder cape with a purple dragon emblazoned on the back. A mix of their colors with the Royal Family's crest. "What's going on Papa?" Celeste asked concerned. Antoine sighed. "King Gabriel called an emergency meeting just now. All his generals are needed and so is the Talon." Selene frowned, "W-what's going on?"

"He didn't say." Antoine said grimly, "I came to let you girls know that I'm leaving right now." A lump formed in Celeste's throat. "But it's Selene's birthday! You promised you'd be here!"

"Celeste!" Selene barked. Celeste flinched abashed. "Father knows all that, but something must be truly wrong for His Majesty to call a meeting so suddenly. Father is just doing his duty." Celeste looked away, feeling very childish, "I know." She muttered, "Sorry." Antoine smiled, and gave them both a hug, which kind of hurt. "It's alright. I'll do my best to be back before the party ends." Selene nodded, "Thanks father. Say hello to the princess if you see her. Tell her I'm up for a rematch any time." Antoine laughed, "Looks like someone hasn't gotten over that loss." Selene went red, "I-I just want to see how much I've improved is all!" Celeste snorted. Princess Veronica was the only person she had ever seen beat Selene in a duel. "Still embarrassed about losing to a twelve year old?" Celeste taunted."

"That was two years ago!" Selene shot back, "She's no longer twelve!" She began to puff her check out angrily, but that only sent their father into an even harder bout of laughing. His laugh fell short as he quickly became somber though. "I better get going. You two behave and listen to your stepmother."

"Yes, we will." The girls said in unison. Antoine gave them one last loving look before turning to leave. After their father let, Selene looked Celeste over. "Well, you are absolutely covered in dirt." Celeste looked at her hands. Dust and grime coated them, and she had a thin layer over her face also. She felt gross, but it had been worth it. "So, should we go and wash up?" Selene proposed, "We still have about two hours till the party." Celeste shrugged, "I guess we should." The sisters turned back to the mansion. As they trudged across the arena, chatting about who would be at the party, Celeste felt a great leap of excitement within her. Little did she know that night would be the most horrific of her life.

Joseph watched as Celeste's breathing slowed, her face peaceful. She had fallen deep asleep. He smiled, even though the story was cut short; telling him what she had seemed like it had been therapeutic for her. After a good twenty minutes, he gently picked her up and placed her back in her sleeping bag. Celeste did not even stir. Joseph then went and resumed his post by the fire. He went through the night without his coat, even when his shift ended, he left it on Celeste.

Chapter 24

The Pursued

Joseph awoke with a loud, large yawn, stretching his whole body out before sitting up. "Well good morning lazy bones." Klin said coolly, "Get ready. You're going into town." Joseph was still blinking blearily as Klin tossed Joseph's coat on him. Joseph clawed it off his face, grunting. "Wait, what's going on." Klin walked over to him. "You and Erok are heading into town. We had a raid on our provisions last night. Uncle forgot to store them, and *someone* didn't notice the raccoons and bears grabbing our food till it was too late." Erok rubbed his head, and shrugged, "What? Not my fault those things are slippery." Klin just glared at him before stalking off. Joseph started too quickly changed but stopped. "Wait, where is everyone else?"

Erok raised an eyebrow, "What, you want them to see you naked?" Joseph pulled his shirt over, "Uh, not really. Really just want to know why we're the only ones here." Erok rolled his eyes, which irritated Jospeh a bit. "They all went to go train. Your mom wants to do some things with Kyoko, and while Sasha and Celeste give Klin more training in magic and swordplay. Joshua I think is training Ander some more." Joseph's shoulder's slumped, "Maaan, I want to join!"

"Maybe don't sleep in so much next time idiot." Erok snorted. Joseph began to do some stretches, keeping his face emotionless. It was fine when Klin did it, (usually) but there was some venom in that statement. "Oh, just toss me Black Rose and let's go then." Joseph replied. Erok looked around confused, "Uh, toss you what now?" Joseph pointed to his sword, "Black Rose. Finally named it. What do you think? Perfect name right?" Erok shook his head and tossed the weapon at him. Joseph caught it, spun it windmill fashion, and with a flourish placed it on his back. "Was that needed?" Erok asked. Joseph shrugged, "I mean it fully woke me up. Sooo, maybe?" Erok glared at him as he stalked past him. "Let's just get this over with." He growled. Joseph followed after him, hands in his pockets, "Well aren't you just a ball of sunshine." He muttered under his breath.

As they went down the forest trail, Joseph began to take in the natural beauty. Fall was in full force now. The trees were a canvas of reds, yellows, and oranges. A few birds flew about here and there, chittering probably about leaving soon. Some squirrels scampered by, gathered nuts in their cheeks and paws, and a few deer ran across the path. Joseph took in a deep breath, allowing his lungs to be filled with that nice autumn air. Too bad the tension from Erok was tainting the experience. "So, Erok," Joseph inquired, "You know the name of this town?" Erok didn't look back. "Yeah, Hunter's Rest. I've been here a few times over the course of my work." Okay, at least he wasn't trying to bite his head off at the moment. Progress. "What did you need to come here for? What's the town like?" Erok looked back at him with a grim smile, "Oh, just needed to hunt down this one guy named Mark. Dude gave me quite the chase, but I finally found him here. Shot him in the heart and then sent his head back to my employer." Joseph kept his face neutral and started walking besides him. "Alright, so what about the town itself?"

Erok shrugged, "Well, as the name implies, tones of hunters and trappers. There's a small mountain range to the west of here. It's so small that not many maps actually have it on them. But, during the winter, most of them come down to the town and live there for the winter. It's a bit rowdy, lots of bars for its size. Oh, and there's like three really good brothels there. Other than that though, not much goes on. Farmers surround it, so we should find plenty of food." Joseph nodded, but thought to himself. *This guy is Ander's closest friend? He seems way too... not innocent?* Eh, he would think of a better word another time. "Okay, seems fair. So, another question for you. Did you fall asleep during your watch?" Erok snapped his head at him, eyes narrowed, "No! Even if I had what's it too you?" Joseph just laughed, which made Erok look at him *very* confused. "It's okay." Joseph chuckled as his laughter died down, "Almost everyone has done it before. You don't need to lie about it. Honestly, I bet Klin would have been *waaaay* less angry at you if you hadn't lied." Erok shook his hand at Joseph, his face turning slightly red, "How do you know I'm lying?! I just said that I'm not!! I'm a logical, smart guy who knows the pointlessness in lying!!"

"Yeah, sure. It's *completely* logical to get worked up like this and explain in a totally not calm way that you are innocent." Joseph remarked snidely. Erok's face got even more red, and Joseph thought he was going to try and hit him. Erok unclenched his fist though and took a deep breath. "Yeah, okay you're right. Sorry for over reacting or whatever." Joseph raised his eyebrow, "Pretty shitty apology, but one I'll accept, nonetheless. It's okay dude, you can chill. I'm not judging you for falling asleep. Pretty sure the only thing you are being judged on is lying. And honestly, it's probably only Klin." Erok shook his head, "Easy for you to say. You were asleep and so didn't see their faces."

Joseph shrugged, "True. But I'm a people person. I get a pretty good feel for what people are thinking or that they are hiding something." Erok looked at him skeptically. "Uh huh." Joseph decided to ignore that. "Eh, you don't have to trust me on that. Just throwing it out there." Erok said nothing as they continued on. Joseph was fine with that. He at least got the guy to stop being an ass to him for the moment. The rest of the walk was done in silence. When Hunter's Rest came into sight, the sun was at about the ten o'clock position. "Alright, so what do we need?" Joseph asked. Erok pulled out a two lists, and two coin purses. He tossed one to Joseph. "Take this list, and then split up. We should be able to find everything in about twenty minutes." Joseph pocketed the money and nodded, "Alright, sounds good. Meet back here then when we're done?"

"Sure. Just don't get lost and make me come find you." Joseph just rolled his eyes, "Yeah, yeah. Just focus on your own job." Erok gave him a smirk as they headed into town. This town had no wall, which was still kind of weird for Joseph to comprehend. But it was decent size. Maybe about a thousand people lived here. This was not your normal countryside village at least. There were at least four smoke plumes that he could see. So more than one blacksmith or baker was here. He waved to Erok as they split up, and then checked his list. *Alright. Simple enough. We need twenty pounds of meat. Seven dozen eggs. And oof, that's a lot of horse feed. That's going to be expensive.* With grim determination, Joseph set out to burn a hole in their finances. First stop was the butcher. It took him a bit, but he found one. He walked in, raw meats hanging around and the smell of blood and freshly quartered flesh in the air. "Hello?" Joseph called out.

A man came out from a door behind the stone counter. Yep, he was a butcher alright. Big beefy arms, scraggly beard, and dark eyes that seemed to enjoy handling a knife a little too much. The man stopped, and gave Joseph a strange look. "Yer not from around here, are ya?" Joseph examined himself, "Uh, no. What, I am I dressed that strangely?" The man gave a terse snort, "Not exactly dressed like a farmer, are ya? What can I do for you traveler?" Joseph walked up to the butcher and pulled out his coin purse. "I need twenty pounds of meat." The man grunted, "That's quite a lot. Got some sort of lord's party going on or something?" Joseph shrugged, "No, just have a lot people I'm travelling with. Eight others to be exact."

"Is that so?" The butcher asked, genuine curiosity in his voice. "You merchants?" Joseph smiled, "That would be more profitable. No, just some travelers on our way to a new home." The butcher leaned nodded, "Ay, can respect that. So, how what kind of meat?" Joseph gave him the specifications and then waited as the butcher went and got them. After Joseph paid him, (a slightly painful emeralda,) the butcher asked, "What's yer name?"

"Joseph. And yours?" The man smiled, "Garth. I hope you have a nice trip Joseph." Joseph returned the smile, "Thank you. I hope you have a nice day yourself Garth!" Joseph walked out carrying the three bags of meat, and had the sudden thought. *Shit, how am I supposed to carry the rest of this shit? Eh, guess I'll figure that out when I get to it.* Joseph hoisted the bags into a better position to carry, and then headed on to look for a farmer's stall. He found one, and bought the eggs. Again, he was asked his named and commented on being from out of town. Joseph precariously balanced the eggs and meat, thinking. *Man, I thought this wasn't that small a town for strangers to be such an oddity. Do I really stand out that much? More importantly, there's got to be a better way to transport these. Wait! I got it!* He had been working on new spells lately. One of the thoughts that he had was that often shadows hid things, so maybe...

Joseph placed down his groceries and tapped into his Source. Taking hold of four Dark Threads, he began to weave them into a sphere. The sphere was about the size of a large ball. He tied them off and a purple sphere appeared in the air, but in the center was empty space. He went ahead and placed a bag in it. Then, reached his hand back in after waiting a minute, and pulled it back off. "Sweeeet." Joseph triumphed with a smirk. He went ahead and put the groceries in and set out to find the last thing on the list. As he was walking, he kept tossing the coin purse about. It was getting kind of light. *Huh, guess we don't really have unlimited funds. Ooh! The wanted board! Maybe if we run into some bandits we can turn them in for a reward!* Joseph stopped as he came to one of the town's notice boards. On it were the usual wanted posters and legal declarationssss...wait.

Joseph froze as his eyes fell upon a wanted poster of Klin. "The herk?" He muttered. Quickly he scanned the rest. He was on there also. He looked around. No one was around. "Wanted for treason and conspiration against the crown?! What in the Eight?! Any who help hide or transport them without notifying the Seekers are hereby convicted of conspiracy also. Reward: 8,000,000 emearladas." Joseph frowned, "Hmm, not a bad price for us. Nice. Wait, no! This is bad! Real bad!" He turned and saw another wanted poster. It was Nathaniel. He was wanted for fleeing from Seekers. Finally, something clicked in his head though that should have fallen into place as soon as he saw the poster of himself. Garth had recognized him, and that mean he and maybe Erok were in danger. Joseph turned and sprinted at full force. His heart pounding.

As he ran, he noticed that the streets were oddly empty. Not a single soul in sight. It was noon, high time for business. "Herk." Joseph cursed. They were already here. Suddenly, he found himself in a circular street, a fountain bubbling in the center. He came to a halt, and began to spin around. Which way now? "Halt. Joseph Markus, you are under arrest." Joseph spun around to see a man standing in one of the streets. About ten men were with him. Joseph let out a brief sigh of relief. They were just normal town officers. Not Inquisitor's. Dark blue armor and the local lord's insignia on their chestplate. "I don't suppose we can talk this out at all, can we?" The officers began to move towards him, drawing their blades. "Oh, come on!" Joseph whined, "Can't a guy know why

295

the herk he's even wanted? I mean I just found out about this crime I committed!" This actually gave the officers some pause, looking slightly confused. That's all Joseph needed. He wove ten threads around them in a thirty foot diameter. As he completed the spell, a dark cloud submerged all of them.

The officers began to cry out in surprise. Joseph took advantage of it and charged them. *Oh shit. I don't know how to make it so that I can see!* He followed the sounds of the panicked voices, keeping his own sword on his back for now. He nearly bulldozed into the first guy. Right before he did, he jumped, and kicked him in the face. The man fell down with a clatter. Joseph hopped on him and beat his face until he was unconscious. He shook off the blood from his knuckles and grunted as a sword bruised his back. He spun to barely see a second officer looking very confused as he beheld an unmarked Joseph. Joseph shrugged before roundhouseing him in the side of the side. The man went flying with a cry, and there was a large clatter as he heard multiple crashes. "Striiiike!" Joseph crowed, "Oh fuck!" Jospeh ducked as a fireball went flying over his head. *Okay, they got Weavers. Really should have anticipated that.* Suddenly the dark cloud dispersed as in the center, a flare of fire went outwards like a hurricane cloud.

Four men stood where the fire had been, glaring at Joseph. Four other soldiers were just not extracting themselves from each other. Joseph's shoulder's sagged. All that and he had only taken down one guy. "Surrender! NOW!" One shouted. Joseph sighed and drew Black Rose. "Herking Heshborn idiots" He muttered, "Sure we can't talk this out?" The four men in the center charge him. "Fine then." Joseph growled, "I'll lay you fools out." They attacked in a line, side by side, all trying to stab. Joseph swept their blades into each other, knocking them into one another. Then, he brought the sword back up to his right shoulder, and gave a diagonal slash across two them. Black Rose cut through their armor as blood spurted out. "Bastard!" One of them cried. Joseph formed a fist, holding the Black Rose with one hand. Purple energy coalesced around it. "Don't worry! It's a shallow cut!" He said cheerily as he punched in the guy's chestplate. The armor crumpled, and the man let out a gasp for air. Joseph then punched the other one in the face, and stomped on the third officers head, knocking them both out.

The fourth man began to scuttle backwards on his hands. "Please! Don't hurt me!" He cowered. Joseph turned, seeing the five soldiers he had knocked down finally up on their feet. "Sorry, gave you that choice at the beginning of this." The man's face curdled into a fierce sneer as he tried to get up. Joseph grazed his forehead threw his sword down. While the man was stunned he grabbed the man by the collar and heatbutted him, and then gave two solid hooks to his head. The man's eyes rolled back as he was knocked out.

Joseph threw him to the ground and turned as the final five cautiously approached him. One, them was holding a flame in their hand. Joseph popped his neck, and picked his sword up. Suddenly, a crossbow bolt protruded from one of the officer's forehead. Two more flew into the two beside him. The three fell to the ground. There was a zipping sound, and Joseph looked up to see Erok flying through the air on a grapple. He stopped above the two, and fell. His crossbow came together, and he stabbed one in the throat, spun around cutting off the final officer's sword hand before unlocking the crossbow, and shooting him in the head.

As the final officer fell to the ground, Erok shook the blood off his crossbow. "What in Heshtanus do you think you are doing!!!" Joseph roared. Erok glared at him, "You know a thank you for saving you would be nice." Joseph knocked the crossbow out of his hands. "No the herk it's not! Not with a rescue like that! You herking killed them!" Erok crossed his arms. "So? They would have killed you." Joseph grabbed Erok by the collar, lifting him in the air. Erok's eyes widened, as he grabbed Joseph's hands, trying flutily to force him to let go. "We. Don't. Kill. Humans." Joseph growled, "Got that? Or shall I beat your face in for a reminder?" Erok's eyes narrowed, "Is this what this is? You think you're better than me? Huh? More moral cause you don't kill? Hate to tell you, but this kind of trip doesn't allow for that kind of morality." Joseph roared and threw him against the ground. "I got them down without killing. So can you." Erok just laughed, "That what you think you did? Pretty sure some of those wounds were lethal. Face it, you have the arrogance to think you can control a life" Joseph picked him back up and threw him off. "And you have the arrogance to think you can control death." Erok rubbed the back of his head, his palm becoming bloody. "Just stop it, okay? You and your brother are too naïve. Not all life is worth preserving. Got it?" Joseph clenched his fists but paused. "Maybe, but in this case, they were. Let's get out of here." Joseph turned and began to make his way out of town, doing his best to not focus on the blood that covered his fists.

They came back to their camp and found everyone huddled in a circle. "Yo, what's up?" Joseph called. Joshua spun about, pointing his revolver at them. "Whoa, wait!" Joseph yelped. Joshua relaxed, holstering the weapon. "Get yer asses over here." Joseph and Erok looked at each other confused but obeyed. Erok set down his bags. (He had gone back for them before they left.) Joseph went straight for the center of the circle, wanting to know what had caused such intrigue. He let out as gasp as he saw a man, his clothes stained in blood. "Is… that Nathaniel?!" Klin was kneeling next to him along with Lorelei. "Yeah," he replied with a low voice, "He stumbled in, half-crazy from blood loss and passed out."

"He said a few things." Kyoko piped, "Most of it did not make sense. But he did say one thing. 'They are coming for you.' He seemed to be really upset. Miss Lorelei has been healing him since then though." Joseph nodded and crossed his arms. "I might have an idea about what to make of that." Celeste looked over, and then did a double take. "Wait, why are your hands covered in blood?!" Joseph examined them and sighed. "That…has to do with his statement, I think. See, here's the thing. Klin and I have wanted posters."

"WHAT?!" Klin exclaimed, leaping to his feet. "For what?!" Joshua crossed his arms and leaned back against the wagon while Joseph and Erok explained what happened and what he had seen. Klin shook his head, "What in Heshtanus do the Seekers want with us?"

"No idea." Joshua growled, "But I have a feeling our friend here will be able to tell us when he wakes up. He's wanted also. And considering the shape he's in, they found him." A chill went down Joseph's spine as a sudden realization hit him. "And if they found him, they'll be able to find us." Ander held up his hand, "So, what do we do now then?" Joshua strode forward and threw out his cube. "We get the herk out of here! Well? MOVE!" Everyone scrambled into action to help pack. Kyoko and Lorelei used their wind magic to compile most stuff in a pile as everyone else threw them in the cube. In a mere three minutes, they were packed and in the wagon. Joseph pulled out the groceries and quickly handed them to his mother, dissipating his own spell. Lorelei gave him a grateful smile, then the horses were whipped into action. They took off, speeding across the ground as the wind whipped across them. He looked back. Even in the daylight of noon, a weird feeling of darkness washed across him. The sun was high, yet a clump of clouds were forming in front of it. Despite everyone safe and sound in the wagon, he could not shake that sudden, inescapable feeling that they were being watched. It was malevolent, intelligent, and most of all, weirdly familiar.

Viscious grinned as he watched the fools run off. The old man was spooked right now. That was good. So many in this group were unexpected, contingent factors. But one's that his master had foreseen. Romevan really was the most perfect creature to be able to expect something like this. Things were looking up for his master once more.

Chapter 25

Looming Twilight

The chill wind settled upon Klin as he helped everyone unpack. They had been traveling nonstop for almost four days. Joshua had wanted to make sure that they left no room for their pursuers to find them. The horses were ragged though, after covering hundreds of miles and almost no rest. Kyoko was feeding them at the moment, her normally cheerful face worn with exhaustion and care. They were now in the hills of Mar, with Lake Markus in sight from the top of the hill they were on. Not many trees in this area, which left Klin feeling open and naked.

The sky though was mixed with pinks and gold, the waters of the great lake reflecting them into a gleam of ominous bronze. Klin shivered as he set down a container of food, casting a look at Nathaniel. He had only just awoken a few hours ago. When Klin had asked him what had happened to him, Nathaniel had replied quietly, "Wait till everyone is together." And then had said nothing else for the rest of the trip. A haunted look though remained in the man's eyes. Klin was very worried about that, for the look he saw in his eyes was one who had seen death. "There, now we can get some food prepared!" Lorelei proclaimed with forced cheerfulness. "Klin, why don't you get Nathaniel a snack? He'll need something in him at this point." Klin nodded and grabbed an apple. "Here," Klin offered. "You've got to be starving at this point." Nathaniel glanced at it and muttered, "Not hungry." Klin frowned, and shoved the green orb into his hand. "Don't care. Eat." Nathaniel looked at him, slightly confused, but began to eat. Soon enough, the apple had disappeared. Klin grinned, "See, told you." Nathaniel smiled softly at him, "Thank you. I suppose now I should tell what happened. Let us gather everyone."

Klin nodded and helped Nathaniel up, keeping an eye on him as they went over to the campfire. Or, at least the pile of wood that was supposed to be consumed by the flames. "C'mon Erok, how are you not able to light a fire?" Celeste asked irritably. Erok, Celeste, and Ander were all gathered around the wood pile as Erok tired to get a park going. "Hey, I'm a well-travelled merc." Erok shot back, "I've endured many a harsh night with intense weather and damp ground."

"Because you can't get a fire by yourself?" Celeste inquired. Erok glared at her, "Ah shut up. What do you know? Stupid woman. Watch and learn Ander. I'll give you a lesson in some manly skills." Ander shifted uncomfortably but gave him an encouraging smile. "Uh, okay. Cool." Celeste stood with arms crossed, giving Erok a patronizing smile as Erok began to rub two sticks together, struggling to get a spark. "Shouldn't you help them?" Nathaniel asked. Klin shook his head, "Nah, this is way more entertaining. Just wait till Celeste gets annoyed and takes over."

"I give her twenty seconds till she snaps." Joseph whispered into his ear. "Gah!" Klin yelped, spinning around. Joseph just laughed uproariously. "Hey there." He replied innocently. "Sneaky bastard." Klin muttered, "I'll take you on though. Two topazas says she takes longer." Joseph smiled, "You're on." Twenty seconds later, Klin reluctantly handed over the money as Celeste got the fire going. She gave a sulking Erok a triumphant smile as she warmed herself by the newly roaring fire. "Thank you." Joseph gloated.

"Hmph, wouldn't think we were running for our lives from ya'lls behavior." Joshua stated. Klin and Joseph jumped, and then looked away as they began in unison, "Well, uhh—" Joshua gave them a confused look, "What? Did you hear mean complaining about it? This is good. Means you'll be able to survive when things get worse." Joshua walked over and sat down, as Klin mouthed to Joseph; *worse?!* Joseph just shrugged. Klin rolled his eyes, understanding the statement of; *well, we are good.* "So, we going to hear what happened to ya, you blue-blooded prick? Or you going to wait till my hair turns yellow?" Nathaniel nodded, slight annoyance in his eyes, "Yes, I was just waiting till everyone was ready." Joshua took out his pipe, and called, "Alright everyone! Gather around! It's story time!" As everyone moved towards the fire, finding a spot to settle down, (except Lorelei who worked on dinner with Sasha,) Nathaniel leaned over and whispered to Klin. "Your uncle. He seems a little, well…"

"Crazy?" Klin finished, "Yeah, we know. Took you long enough to realize that." Nathaniel shook his head, "Well, as long as you know you are following a madman." The group fell deathly silent as they waited in anticipation. "Well, you going to tell us why we found you half dead, hundreds of miles away from yer domain?" Joshua asked impatiently. Nathaniel gave a gracious nod, "Yes. But before I do, how much do you know about our governing system?"

"Not much." Klin admitted, "We lived so far from the capitol that we've never even seen a royal soldier before. All we know is that our current king is Charles Ardaven XII. We never really heard much more than that." Joshua shook his head. "The hesh you been teaching these kids little sis?" He asked incredulously. Lorelei did not even look up from her cutting. "Things that they would need if we ever ended up on the run. Like now." Joshua nodded, "Ah, excellent foresight. Just what I would expect from my baby sister." Klin heard his mom mutter something that did not exactly sound like a compliment. Joshua puffed out a smoke ring, and said, "Very well, I can tell you kids. So, some history lesson for ya. Five hundred years ago, Ardaven was a unified powerhouse, rivaling Coronus itself. Then, some nobles got all uppity and decided to stage a rebellion. They lost, all of them killed. However, the king lost three-fourths of his army during the civil war. Not exactly a force you can just replace. So, without the man-power to enforce his rule, lots of nobles ended up becoming pocket kingdoms. So, somewhere along the line, nobles ended up sending him a monthly sum of taxes, or bribe money as I call it, in exchange for being left alone. So officially the high blooded, stuck ups answer to the king. Unofficially, he prays ya keep him funded while do what ya want, right?"

Nathaniel nodded, "Correct. Only thing I would correct is that the nobles have to answer to highlords, which are similar to the Coronus Great Families. They decide which family gets to be in charge of what domain. However, unlike the Coronus Great Families, they actually live in the castle. Though, they typically do not bother with us too much."

"Okay," Joseph interrupted, "This is cool and all, but what does this have to do with anything?" Nathaniel's face darkened, "Well, I wanted to make sure you understand our history, for the day after you left, I had a battalion lead by a Seeker show up."

"Wait, what?!" Celeste exclaimed. Even Joshua looked unnerved by that. Joseph put a hand to his forehead. "Herking Heshtanus! We knew they were after us, but holy shit!" Ander and Sasha exchanged a confused look, before Ander raised his hand. "Uh, what are Seekers?" Klin looked at Ander incredulously "How the herk do you not know what a Seeker is?"

"Well, our city is very removed from the rest of the kingdom." She replied awkwardly, "We kinda only learn about local political things, and not the rest of the kingdom." Erok nodded in agreement, "They're right. About ninety percent of Edeaven knows almost nothing about the outside world. I found out about Seekers only after I left. But to answer, Seekers are the king's personal force of elite warriors and generals. They were founded in response to the civil war. Their job is to find and eliminate possible rebels. In reality, they are higher than any noble, answering only to the king and so act almost like thugs."

"So, what the actual herk was a Seeker doing in Mar?" Joseph asked. Nathaniel looked downcast as he explained. "That's what I wanted to know. Now, I'm no fan our current king due to his hedonistic...hobbies, but I would never dream of overthrowing him. So, I sent a servant to the Seeker to ask why they were here and if they would like to stay in my manor. My servant returned with their head on a silver platter. They had a note attached to the head, a spike driven through the skull." Klin felt his stomach retch and rebel, while Ander actually turned and puked. "Wh-what did it say?" Sasha asked tentatively. Nathaniel took a deep breath and closed his eyes. "For the crime of consorting with foes of His Majesty Charles XII, you and your domain of Mar have been condemned to death." A shocked silence settled upon everyone. Nathaniel opened his eyes, pain and rage shining in them. "Outraged and confused, I used some of my elemental stones to set up a meeting with the Seeker. We communicated via air com, so I never saw her face to face. But when she gave her name."

Nathaniel shuddered. "What, what was her name?" Ander asked. "Misha." Joshua whispered, fear in his voice, "Misha Varden. Head of the Seekers. A woman known for exceptional skill and ruthlessness. Am I right." Nathaniel nodded, "Yes, unfortunately. As soon as I learned who she was, I was terrified beyond belief. I asked why she was here. She said that she was pursuing an elite group of criminals. They had overthrown their hometown and slaughtered the king's men. Apparently they are so fierce and ruthless who harbor them have declared themselves rebels. I asked for their names. She said they are probably using false ones, and so described them. Two brothers. One, older with long black hair, and yellow eyes that send a chill down the spine. The other, younger with messy brown hair and eyes. Both are tall and wear coats of an unknown material, one that seems to have magical properties. They have strange swords, one a great sword of black and red. The other with two shortswords of red and blue."

The camp fell silent as all eyes turned to Klin and Joseph. They looked at one another, eyes wide. "Naturally, I assumed your innocence," Nathaniel went on, "especially after how you all helped me. But Misha took my shocked silence as all the proof needed to condemn me. She gave me a twenty-four-hour warning. At the evening of next day, she would attack us, and there would be no prisoners. So, I let the people know. We gathered all who could fight together. Then, we gathered the women, children, and some elderly. We sent them away. Misha may be the head Seeker, but she has no experience with sieges. At least that is what I thought. She had a force hidden and waiting for them. We...we could hear their screams all the way from the manor."

"Why didn't you try and save them!" Ander yelled, leaping to his feet. Nathaniel's eyes flashed as he spat, "SILECNE! We did try to save them! Do not speak to me of heroics till you yourself are outnumbered and outclassed yourself! Only Joseph and Klin have a right to speak of morality to me you coward!" With each word that was said, Ander flinched and cowered, as if he was pierced by arrows. "No! How dare you!" Sasha exclaimed, leaping to Ander's side. "You have no idea how much he has been through! How much courage it has taken for him to even be here!" Nathaniel raised an eyebrow, "Oh really?" He drawled, "Then maybe he should use some of that courage to take initiative for himself." Sasha opened her mouth to, but Klin leapt up. "QUIET! ALL OF YOU!" He bellowed. At the same time, the fire flared up, forcing everyone to shield their eyes. Klin took a deep breath. "Stop this. Both of you apologize. Now."

"What?!" Sasha cried indignantly, "But did you hear what he said?!" Klin glowered at her, "Yeah, but you took it farther." Sasha crossed her arms but took a deep breath. "Fine. No, you are right. I'm sorry." Nathaniel gave a gracious nod, "And I am sorry myself. Especially to you Ander. Those were horrible things to say to you." Ander gave a weak smile, but that was all. Klin heard Sasha mutter something under her breath, something like, "I apologized first at least." He decided to ignore her and sit back down. As he did, he saw Lorelei smiling at him approvingly. "So, you did try and save them?" Erok asked curiously. Nathaniel's face became grim once more as he continued. "Yes. I gathered what men I had and rushed to their aid. As we got closer, we found ourselves wading through dead bodies. As we fought to save them, I was astounded at these savages' brutality. They had men attacking them, yet they would turn their backs to them in favor of spilling an innocent civilian's blood. They would rather die than allow these people to escape. No regard for their own personal safety, just an insatiable bloodlust."

"That's horrible." Lorelei whispered. Kyoko's eyes were wide, tears beginning to form at the edges of her eyes, hands clutching Lorelei's shirt. "It got worse." Nathaniel trembled, "As we fought futilely to save them, we suddenly realized that there was a bright light. We turned to se our home up in flames. Shocked and with barely any men left, I had no idea what to do. Then, suddenly I found myself in the air. My men had created a spell and told me that I must let someone know what had happened here. I wanted to stay, but they refused. They flung me across the plains, with such speed that I could just barely see the fact that they were about to be surrounded. I knew they had died when the spell ended, and I was cast to the ground. I got up and ran, but they pursued me. I was wounded by some blades, but I was able to get away somehow."

"Hold on," Erok inquired, "You would have had to run for days to have caught up with us. How the herk did you manage that?" Nathaniel pulled out two stones. A green one and a grey one. They were both dull and bleak, but Klin could make out some words inscribed in Ancient Threan on it. "Hold on, is that a wind stone?" Klin exclaimed. Nathaniel nodded. "Yes. This thing gave me the boost I needed to run for as long as I did. Other one constantly replaced my blood and stamina, making sure I did not die. Both of them are depleted so much so that I doubt they will ever work again. I poured some of my own energy into them to make them work as long as I did." Klin and Joseph exchanged a worried look. "Wait, that looks like the stones the Gruntlets used!" Ander yelled. "Nathaniel furrowed his brow. "Gruntlets. What's this about now?"

"Oh, just some Heshtisti we ran into." Celeste replied causally. Nathaniel's eyes widened. "I had assumed that the King was after them due to Klin's unique magic repertoire. But if the Heshtisi have found you also...was this a chance run in do you think?" Joseph nodded, "Most likely. I mean, there a few weird similarities going on right now, but we pretty much decided it was a chance run in." Joshua let out a low, guttural, growl. "I'll be damned if anything with those things are chance." Klin just rolled his eyes, "Yeah but you see conspiracies in every tree branch."

"That's cause the wood mites are after us." Joshua snapped. Nathaniel gave a derisive snort, but ignored their uncle otherwise. "I have a question for the both of you at his point." Nathaniel said, his face stern, "After all that has, I happened, I feel like I deserve to know the truth. You told me most of it when we meet. However, there is one key piece missing. Who was your father to warrant such attention to the both of you?" Joseph and Klin looked to one another, and nodded. "No, you do." Joseph replied, "And honestly, kinda getting tired of hiding the fact." Klin took a deep breath. "Our father was Jethro. Jethro Markus, the great hero of the Threan Warriors. Hero of a Million Acts of Kindness. That is who our father is." Erok burst out laughing but stopped when he realized no one else was laughing. "Oh, come one," Erok scolded, "You can't be serious?" He took a look at Celeste, Klin, Joseph, Lorelei, and Joshua's faces. "Oh herk, you are. Herking Hesh. Wait, that means this old coot was his brother-in-law?!" Joshua grinned, puffing out a cloud of smoke from his pipe. "Yep. And fun fact, he was damn proud to be related to me after he married my sis." Celeste frowned, "Please tell me he's lying?" Lorelei shrugged with a faint smile, "What can I say? Jethro had an uncanny ability to see a person's true nature." Ander just shook his head. "Wow. Just, wow." He said sort of lamely.

"Things make much more sense now." Nathaniel muttered, "Thank you for sharing this information with me. It also makes me know what I shall do next. Allow me to accompany you to the safe haven you are headed too." Klin jumped in surprise, "Huh, wait why?" Nathaniel smiled, "Is it not obvious? Whatever is going on, you all are apart of something much larger than it first appears. I must help you and do my part." Sasha smiled, "That is so noble of you! We would be happy to have you!" Celeste leaned back, and muttered under her breath, "Says the one ready to strangle him ten minutes ago." Sasha looked over at her and asked sweetly, "What was that?" Celeste scratched her nose and did not look at Sasha. "Oh, nothing." Joseph stifled a laugh. "Well, any objections to this?" Klin asked. The others shrugged, and Ander said, "I really can't think of why we wouldn't. I mean, aren't we all already kind of a group hobbled together by chance?"

"Well said kid." Joshua praised. "You're now with us blue-blood. Congrats on being the second one." Klin frowned. "What the herk are you babbling on about now uncle?" Celeste had become weirdly still, and Joseph was giving their uncle a shocked look. Klin was really confused but offered his hand out. "Welcome aboard Nathaniel."

"Thank you-get down!!" Klin suddenly found himself tackled to the ground as something whizzed over Nathaniel and his heads. "Are you herking kidding me?!" Joshua cried, "They found us already?" Klin rolled up, and found three men emerging from the woods, their bows drawn. "No sudden moves, or the girls die!" The center man shouted. "Oh, you wish it were that easy." Celeste growled, drawing Yata as she charged. The soldiers were obviously not actually expecting a female attacker, and so were taken off guard as Celeste stabbed one in the throat. The other two pivoted, about to shot, when *bang, bang*. Then fell down, revealing Joshua looming behind them, the barrel of his revolver smoking. "Sis!" Joshua barked. "Already on it." Lorelei replied, as she knelt down by the soldiers.

Klin watched as his mother healed the throat of the one Celeste had attacked, before stabilizing the other two. "He kid," Joshua said gently, "disarm them please." Kyoko looked up at Joshua tentatively, but did as he asked, creating an airstream to take their weapons. Erok then walked up to them, a bundle of rope in his hands. "Her Mrs. Markus, some help?" Lorelei nodded as she restricted the soldier's movements. "Why did you not kill us?" One yelled. Erok began to tie them up, ignoring them. "Hey, answer me!" Erok finished up, and then drew his knife, pointing it at him. "Huh, you didn't even flinch." Erok said causally, before twirling it around, reversing his grip and holding it at the man's throat. "I'm impressed. You have steel. Especially for some lowlifes." The man just glared silently at Erok. "Now as fer yer question," Joshua said, "Well, I can't be going and get these kids hands dirty yet, now can I?"

"You think you can scare us?" The same man spat. "My, my you love to talk, don't you?" Celeste complained, "Face it. You're just embarrassed at how fast we took you down." Klin turned away at that moment and began to pace. Something felt off to him. Why only three men? And why just seemingly regular soldiers? "Hah! Owl got your tongue!" Celeste sneered, "Looks like I was right!" Klin walked over to where the scouts had shown themselves. He found their footprints just barely outlined in the soft earth. "Alright you three, start talking." Eork said, "How did you find us? And more importantly, how did you catch up to us?"

"We're not talking!" One of them squeaked. He sounded younger than the rest of them. Klin pushed them out of his mind though. He needed to focus. He reached out to his Fire Source and summoned a small flickering flame tongue. He crouched down, bringing the flame closer to the footprints and examining them. They had been single file right up to when they revealed themselves it seemed. They were well trained then. So why had they been easily caught off guard? Klin was becoming more and more unnerved by the whole situation. He decided to follow the trail and was soon out of earshot of the others. It did not take him too long to find the end of the trail. As he did, a chill went down his spine. The trail did not bring him to a camp like he had expected, but the middle of the woods. The trail's start had deep imprints, like they had fallen out of the sky! Yet even stranger was the gouged dirt behind the footprints. It was formed into a curvature, almost like a wheel had gone through it, yet there was only one and no hoofprints. *What kind of Romevanin handiwork is this?* Klin thought bewildered.

Suddenly an ear-piercing scream filled the air. An icy cold gripped his heart as he turned an ran towards the source; it had been from camp. As he feet pounded against the ground, he heard rustling from behind. He cast a glance back, and saw the gleam of steel in the firelight. There were more soldiers! Damn it all! Luckily, they seemed very intent on staying hidden, so Klin continued on. However, a small voice in him began to whisper. *You could stop them now. You have the element of surprise. Light their hiding spot on fire. Finish them!* He shook his head violently. NO! He would not kill! A small weight was lifted from his shoulders as he ran, hearing no more movement. However, that was insignificant compared to the iron chain in his heart, keeping his earlier thought in place. Was he really so ready to kill someone so casually? They were not even for sure they wanted to kill them, so why should he be so ready to kill these soldiers?

Klin was so preoccupied with his thoughts, that he did not even notice he was back in camp and ran headlong into Sasha. "Oooow!" She yelped as they fell to the ground. Klin immediately leapt back up, "I'm so sorry!" He apologized profusely, "Here, let me help you up." Sasha rubbed her forehead as he helped. "It's fine." She replied sweetly, "But where were you? We were just about to head out to find you." Klin scratched the back of his head. "Oh, right sorry about that. I kinda followed their footprints to see where they came from. But that's not the issue! I heard a loud scream and found more soldiers!" Sasha nodded grimly, "Yeah, we know about them. As for that scream..." Her face turned pale as a nauseated look came over her. "You can ask Erok about that." Klin turned around, "What happened?" Kyoko was crouched down on the ground, visibly shaking. Deebo was near her, nuzzling her affectionately while Ander hugged her. Yet he was also trembling. Joseph and Nathaniel looked grim, but stoic otherwise. Erok and Celeste though were arguing with one another, while Joshua and Lorelei looked on with disappointed faces. Klin looked over at the soldiers, and saw blood splattered all over the ground. The young one was blubbering like a new born child. "WHAT DID YOU DO?!" Klin bellowed as he stomped forward.

Rage began to boil up inside him, raging like a volcano about to erupt. He grabbed Erok by the neck and lifted him up. "What the herk?" Erok cried, grabbing Klin's wrists. "You damn brothers! Again?!" "What. Did. You do?" Klin spat. "Klin, stop it!" Celeste cried. Klin turned, glaring at her so intensely that even Celeste stopped, a worried and scared look on her face. "Not until he explains!" Klin growled. Erok's face contorted into a snarl, "I got them to talk you moron!"

"Through torture?!" Klin yelled angrily. Erok gripped his wrists, trying to break his grip. "Oh, what would you have had me do? Ask nicely and then bribe them with sweets for being good little boys?" Klin crossed his arms and began to choke Erok. "Wrong answer."

"KLIN!" Celeste screamed, "STOP IT!" Klin stared Erok in the eyes, and something broke in him, his anger abating. He let go. Erok feel to the ground, coughing harshly. "The herk is wrong with you?" He rasped. "I—" Klin paused and swallowed his apology. "I don't want you to ever needlessly hurt someone ever again, got it? Or I'll show you exactly why I'm given this power."

"Hey bro?" Klin turned his head, Joseph had his hand on his shoulder. "Was it actually needless though?" Klin looked at his brother incredulously. "So, you agree with him?" Joseph shook his head, "Yes and no. Erok went too far, but a few threats and some scratches was needed." Klin took a deep breath, "It was still wrong." He muttered. "Yeah, but we got bigger problems you herking adolescents!" Joshua snapped, "I shouldn't be the responsible one here yet here I am! We got soldiers coming, and based on the info Erok got us, we got less than ten minutes! So, let's move it!" Joseph nodded. "Alright, good point. We are nearly packed. So, we'll see you three later then."

Klin frowned, "Wait, what's happening?" Joshua pointed to their stuff. "I'll explain while we pack." Klin nodded and began to help out. "Alrighty," Joshua began, "Apparently the Seekers are tracking our location the massive amounts of magic we're giving off. You and Ander each give off such massive amounts of anima that even a low level weaver can find us. So I'm going to take to two of you and throw them off our trail." Klin shook his head in wonder, "But how? We'll still meet up and they'll find us."

"Yeah, and when they do they'll find an open field. With traces of magic." Klin paused, confused and then it clicked. "Wait, you're basically going to have Ander and I release every ounce of magical energy we have, creating a cloud that we can then hide our trail in." Joshua grinned, "Yep! He gets his smarts from me you know sis." Lorelei shook her head in annoyance. "Sure Joshy." Joshua actually flinched, "Uh, please don't call me that." Ander raised a hand. "How are they tracking us though? That still hasn't been explained."

"We have no idea." Lorelei replied, 'By all means, this thing very idea goes against all we know about the elements. Yet, these soldiers are convinced that is how they found us, and they gave a very detailed path of where we have been, so they do know something. And that is what worries me." Celeste furrowed her brow, "Well, if this thing goes against all we know about magic, how do we know this plan will work?" Joshua and Lorelei exchanged a grim look. "We don't." Joshua replied plainly, "We'll be taking a risk here."

"Um, this is a pretty big gamble though." Ander squeaked. Klin folded his arms, "Yes, but it might be a reasonable one. Skilled weavers can sense magic from one another and spells when they are close together. In theory that is. From what I understand, only a handful of weavers ever achieve this. So, theoretically, the same logic will apply here but on a bigger scale."

"And yet, what if it doesn't work?" Sasha asked quietly, "It will be just you three against a whole battalion of Seekers." Joshua walked over to Sasha, his usual intensity gone as he crouched down, meeting her eyes. He gingerly placed a hand on her shoulder and gave her a warm, reassuring smile. "Hey, worst ain't gonna happen. But if it does, you can be sure I'll die before I let anything happen to them." A stunned silence fell upon everyone. Uncle Joshau was not only being tender, but sane? Klin spared a look at his mother. Deep understanding was in her eyes, something also of a mix between pride and sadness. Suddenly, a horn sounded from the woods.

"Shit, we've wasted too much time!" Erok snapped, "We need to go. Now!" They quickly finished throwing stuff into their wagons. Before they left, Lorelei ran over and gave Klin a quick hug. "Come back, alright?" Klin squeezed his mom's shoulder, "Don't worry. I'm kind of special, remember?" Lorelei grimaced, "It's that fact that worries me." Joseph just gave him a wry smile as he hoped up and grabbed the reigns. "Just don't die." Celeste remarked, "I've begun to grow found of you idiots." Klin grinned, "Same to you. Keep Joseph safe." Celeste grinned back, "What else you think I'm going to do?" As Klin climbed into the wagon, Erok stopped him and grabbed his wrist. "Keep Ander safe, you here?" Klin nodded, "Don't worry, I will. Erok paused, and looked like he was about to walk away but sighed, shoving something into Klin's hand. "Wha-"

"It's an air stone." Erok explained, "In case you guys need a quick escape. It has three charges and I expect it back. That and, an apology. What I did was wrong, and I'm sorry. I did take it too far. But so did you, don't forget that." With that, Erok jumped into his wagon. Klin watched Ander disengage from a hug from Sasaha, and hopped into the wagon beside him. As soon as he did, Joshua whipped the horses into action and they took off at a breakneck speed. Klin watched until the others were out of sight and turned around with a sigh. "You might as well try and get some sleep." Joshua yelled back over the wind. "From here on out, things are going to get pretty rough." Klin looked over to see that Ander was already conked out. "Yeah, good point." He said quietly. He shifted into a better sleeping position, and with a heavy heart, drifted off into dreams.

Chapter 26

Misha Varden

Dark woods, a distant black bird with red eyes above. An evil, murderous presence behind. A clearing with all of his friends in the center. Black flames erupting, stealing light instead of producing it. Then a human face and figure outlined in shadow, slowly walking towards him. **"Join me."** The man said, his voice richer and smoother than honey. **"Join me and it all will end."**

"NOOOOOOOOO!" Klin awoke screaming. Sweat beaded on his forehead, and he was shivering. Sunlight hit his eyes, forcing him to squint. As his eyes adjusted, he was able to make out the outline of his uncle snoring loudly in the corner. His hat was tipped over his head and his body scrunched against the wall. He looked oddly comfortable. "Uh, you okay?" Ander asked. Klin jumped, and noticed Ander had the reigns. "Oh, yeah sorry about that. Just a nightmare." Ander nodded, and yelped as the wagon tossed around a bit. "Bad horses!" He scolded and turned his attention fully to the front. Klin smiled and leaped up front with Ander. "Got this?" Ander gave him a wobbly smile, "Yeah, just uhh, experiencing a mild bump is all." Klin laughed. "Alright. How did you sleep?" Ander shrugged, "Eh, not bad. Woke up at the crack of dawn, so decent enough." Klin frowned, and looked up at the sun, immediately regretting that as he nearly blinded himself. It was almost eleven. "So, when did you learn to handle horses?" Ander gave him a sidelong glance.

Klin blushed embarrassed as he rubbed the back of his head. "Sorry, guess that came out kind of rude huh?" Ander smiled, "It's okay. I am bad at a lot of things, so surprise is only natural." Klin frowned, "What do mean?" Ander shrugged again, "I meant what I said. I'm really bad

313

at doing almost anything. Yet taking care of horses is like the one thing I excel at and enjoy. I'm useless at everything else."

"No you're not." Klin replied matter of factly, "You got the Triamal power. And you've done a lot of great things with it." Ander looked at him, eyes profoundly sad. "Have I? I feel like the only time I have actually used them well was my first transformation. Since then, I really haven't done much. I—I can't actually transform right now." Klin stayed silent, somewhat shocked. "You mean…you can't use your power right now?" Ander nodded, tears forming at the edge of his eyes. "Yes! And I have no idea why! Why chose me? Why chose me if I'm so damn useless that I can't even utilize this power?!"

"Hey Ander?" Ander looked over and Klin hit him lightly on the head. "Uh, that didn't really hurt." Ander said confused. Klin rolled his eyes, "Wasn't supposed to dummy. Let me tell you something. Only one right now expecting you to be perfect with your powers is you. There is not really any instance of a Triamal Host being in any sort of situation like yours. You've been doing a really damn good job with the cards you have been given. Have more faith in yourself. Stuff like this takes time." Ander wiped some tears away. "You're probably right. But, I hope I can be of use soon." Klin grinned, "I think you've been more helpful than you realize. It will take time for you to see it though." Ander nodded slowly, "Maybe. We'll see I guess."

"I'm curious though." Klin began, "How did you get into horse care?"

"It was a part of my training." Ander explained. " 'All warriors should know how to ride!' Sure, but horses don't scream at you for clumsy strikes." Klin frowned, confused and concerned. Ander's hands were beginning to shake a little. "I'm not that familiar with Edeaven's customs. What exactly were you being trained for?" Ander looked at Klin like he was crazy. "Uh, to fight?"

"With a weapon?"

"No, just, fighting in general." Ander replied confused, "Is-isn't everyone expected to know how to fight?" Klin shook his head. "No. I spent almost my whole life just having instinctual fighting techniques. The kind that get you laid out on the ground by someone larger than you. Even now I really only know the little swordplay and whatever

Joshua has taught us." Ander sat up straight, "Wait, you're telling me I have more experience than you?" Klin smiled, nodding excitedly. This was a perfect chance to build him up! "Yep! And I've only learned the proper way to use a sword for what, two months now?"

"Absph—only two months!" Ander sputtered. Klin smiled reminiscently, "Yeah, feels longer though now." Ander slouched down, becoming silent. "Okay, what's wrong?" Klin asked annoyed. Ander looked over surprised, "Huh? What?" Klin crossed his arms. "I asked what's wrong. You've been going up and down between happy and sad this whole time. What's wrong?" Ander leaned forward; eyes focused on the horses. "Well, um…I-I'm not exactly sure how to explain." Klin shrugged, "Just go ahead and try." He encouraged, "I find that once we start we end up figuring it out as we go." Ander stayed silent, and for a while all that could be heard was the horses heavy hooves clopping into the dirt. "Well," Ander began, "have you ever felt that no matter what you do, you're never getting better at it?"

"All the time." Klin sighed morosely. "Well, that's how it is for me." Ander explained, "Except that its with literally anything I do. Nothing helps. I'm always stuck and never get better at anything that I try to do. Then there's you." A hint of venom crept into his voice. "Mr. Perfect at everything you try." Klin frowned, slight anger creeping in, but he pushed it down. "You know that's not true. I struggle deeply with magic. Every spell I cast I barely keep it under control. I can't cast many spells above the level of a five-year-old. You and I struggle similarly; me with magic, and you with the Triamal." Ander's face turned bright red, but not in anger. He covered his face and bent over, "Oh, right. Sorry Klin." Klin clapped him on the back, "It's okay. You sound like you've had a rough life, so don't worry too much about it, okay?" Ander flinched and sat back up. "You're such a good person, you know that, Klin?" Klin smiled half-heartedly. "Not really, but thanks.

"No, you are!" Ander exclaimed, "You have so much power! Power that most I know would kill for, yet you've remained noble and just!" Klin raised an eyebrow, "And you?" He retorted, "You're so quick to lift up others while putting yourself down. You are in the same boat as me, yet I've never met someone so gentle and kind. Take some pride in yourself Ander. As soon as you can recognize one virtue in yourself, I bet you'll find that you will start to excel at a lot of different things. I'm sure your parents are proud of you." Ander stiffened suddenly. "Yeah, sure." Klin frowned. Everything had been going so well up till now. What-...oh. "Ander, do your parents hate you?" Ander spun, his eyes wide. That was all the confirmation he needed. "Ah, so they do." Klin whispered, his heart aching for Ander. "No! They don't!" Ander denied frantically, "They love me! I just disappoint and make them ashamed with my failures! I-I-I"

Suddenly, Joshua popped up, embracing Ander in a warm, tight hug. "Kid, you don't have to lie anymore." Both Klin and Ander stayed in a shocked silence. Klin shook himself, and grabbed the reins from Ander, allowing him to fully enjoy the hug. Yet Klin was somewhat confused. In all of his memories of the brief visits from his uncle, he had never seen him act so much like a father. "Um, can you let go of me?" Ander rasped, "You're starting to choke me." Joshua grinned, "Hehe, not till you say you're father is a sick bastard."

"Gah, fine!" Ander snarled, "My father's a herking messed up, son of a whore with a cow for a mother!" Klin stared at Ander in shock as Joshua let go of him with a whistle. "Damn kid! That wasn't what I told ya to say! That was better than a bee's sex dance!"

"Uh, excuse me?" Ander replied confused. "Yer excused." Joshua dismissed, "Now Klin, pull us over. This should be a good spot." Klin nodded and stopped the carriage. "Alright, now what uncle?" Joshua tipped his hat back and stared up at the sun. "Uncle?"

"Something ain't right." Joshua growled. "Everyone out, now." Ander and Klin obeyed, scrambling out of the wagon. They had learned by now not to question Joshua. He was crazy, but sometimes that craziness was justified. They had made it out of the woods and were now in the plains. Dead grass swayed gently in the wind, but other than that, nothing else could be seen. Kin drew his swords though as the three of them stood back to back, Joshua pulling out his massive greatsword in addition. "Stay human Ander," Joshua whispered as he slipped him a knife, "We want to get the drop on them."

"I don't even know if I could transform even if I wanted to." Ander moaned softly. Klin felt a chill crawl up his spine. "Uh, what?"

316

"Not the time for this, but he's been having trouble shifting." Joshua growled. Klin sighed, "Herk." And began to focus in on the area. He took in each detail, as focused as a hawk, trying to figure out what had spooked his uncle. Then, he heard it. It was faint and far off behind him, but it was the sound of dozens of metal pieces scrapping against one another. It stopped almost as suddenly as it started. "Shit." Joshua muttered, "I should'a seen that come'n."

"What, what is that?" Klin asked bewildered, turning his head every which way. "Portals." Ander replied. At that moment, space in the air in front of him ripped apart. About two hundred yards away, a black line appeared. Then the ends formed a circle. After that the center line formed into a catlike pupil. The figure blazed purple before disappearing, fading away to reveal another area on the other side of the portal. Out of it came four heavily armed soldiers. They had red vests over their armor, but the armor itself was black as raven wings. "I hate noon." Joshua muttered, "Everything bad happens at noon."

"What do we do now?" Ander squeaked in a poor attempt to mask his fear. "I counted seven portals, each with four soldiers." Joshua quickly explained, while Klin began to confirm what his uncle said was true. "One from each had a spear, while the others had swords. No bows." Klin shifted, taking a better fighting stance. "Yeah, I can confirm that. Ooooooh shit." Joshua spared a glance at the both of them. "When I say go, you two go."

"What about you?!" Klin hissed. Joshua chuckled, "I've survived four weeks in a horse's ass. I can survive this. Now get!" Klin sheathed his swords and was about to follow Ander into the wagon, but a rolling wall of flames suddenly flared to life around them. Ander was in the wagon, but the flames separated both him and Joshua. "Ander!" Klin screamed. The flames were strong enough that he could barely see his friend's face. "Just jump through it!" Joshua yelled, "Yer coat will protect ya!"

"Are you so sure about that?" A voice purred. Klin spun around to see a woman in a red coat striding towards them. She had short blonde hair and short bangs brushed to the side of her head. A single pink strand of hair though could be seen. She had a light tan skin, and starling red eyes with a fierce, piercing gaze. She wore no armor, but that made Klin

317

more nervous than the soldiers rushing to them. The fire had come from her, and based on the threads, she was very, very powerful. "I read about his coat." The woman said, "And it's not invincible. These flames will burn anything they touch to ash. So, do you want to take that chance?" Joshua stepped in front of Klin protectively. "Misha Varden." He spat, "So ya are leading this shit show." Misha smiled at him and gave him a little wave. "Joshua Rickstone! I did not think I would be seeing you? How are you?"

"Worse for wear now that I've seen ya." Joshua growled. Misha placed a hand on her heart, "Is that anyway to talk to a former lover?" Klin's jaw dropped. "What?!" Joshua shook his head vehemently, "Don't know what in the herk you think we were lovers! I never loved ya! It was one sided ya crazy bitch." Misha shrugged, "Not my fault you missed out."

"Ain't my fault yer a cow, yet here we are!" Joshua exclaimed and drew his gun, firing off a shot. Misha did not even flinch as a small blast of fire in front of her, destroying the bullet. She had done that so fast Klin had not even see the threads. "Oh shit." Klin muttered. Misha just simply shook her head. "I see you haven't changed Joshua. Pity. Now, hand over the boy before I have to hurt someone."

"Like hell I am!" Joshua snarled. "These kids haven't done anything to warrant this!" Misha tilted her head, "Actually, I have the testimony of one Monastrath Cra'Son that says otherwise." Klin stiffened as his heart stopped. Misha noticed and gave him a sly smile, "Ah, I see. So you *do* know him." I a bit of anger began to creep into her voice as she continued. "So, you can verify his account of the numerous cases of rape and murder that you and you're brother are responsible for then?"

"What?!" Klin yelled, "That's ridiculous! This is all because of that bastard lying?!" Joshua began to point his gun at numerous soldiers. "This is downright stupid. My nephews would never do something like that!" Misha frowned, giving them a cool, steely stare at them. "Ahh, so they are family are they? That makes sense. However, was he lying about the scars on his face then Klin?" Klin stayed silent. He could not move a muscle as the memories of that night flooded over him. The tearing of flesh as he swords bestowed their mark upon Monastrath's face. "What in the blue grass are you talking about?" Joshua exclaimed,

"Klin beat that ass in a fight, but he didn't turn his face into a picture. Right kid? Kid?" Klin's hands began to tremble, the face and scream replaying in his head over and over again, but most of all, the gleeful feeling of triumph and pleasure. "So, you did do." Misha said coolly. "He also mentioned the pleasure you took in it. I have no stomach for scum like that."

"No! I never wanted, I didn't'- I-" Klin just kept stammering, not sure what to say. "AAAAHHHH, shut the HERK UP!" Joshua screamed, "Don't keep torturing him with yer hypocritical accusations! You take glee in it yerself! So, get to the true reason some Seeker is after us." Klin shook his head and snarled, "He's right. I'm guessing these are just excuses. So cut the crap and get to the point." Misha's eyes lit up, a smile creeping onto her face. "They said you were smart, so I'm glad to see it's somewhat true. Yes we need you Klin Markus, but not for the reasons you may expect. However that information is classified."

"Oh my herking...all this yapping and still now answers!" Joshua moaned, "You suck at this you know? Ander now!" Klin spun around to see that Ander had climbed up atop the wagon without anyone noticing. "See you later!" He cried, and jumped off with arms outstretched only to face plant into the ground. Klin winced as the soldiers began to laugh and grabbed Ander, who simply hung limp and unconscious. *C'mon bud! You can do this! Get up!* Klin internally pleaded. "What was that?" Misha laughed in bewilderment, "The great Rickstone's plan hinged on a novice Weaver?!" Klin stopped, and realized something. *She does not know about Ander.* "Now where is the other one?" Misha demanded. Joshua gave her a grin. "No where near the herk here loser." Misha narrowed her eyes, "Don't lie to me! I can sense his presence! He's here!"

Klin and Joshua exchanged a quick look. *Ander's anima was stronger than Joseph's then!* "Nice call uncle." Klin whispered. Joshua just grinned. Misha became furious, clenching her fists as she shouted. "Tell me where he is, and I'll let you and that boy go!" Joshua just laughed, "No thanks." Misha crossed her arms, "Fine!" She sniffed, "I should have known that would not work. Tell me now, or that boy dies!" The soldiers crossed their blades, holding them right at Ander's throat. Joshua slowly began to shift himself, placing the soldiers in his line of sight. "Shoot them, and I'll kill him myself!" Misha warned coyly.

Joshua froze, and then shrugged. "Alright. What am I, crazy?" Then, faster than a blink, Joshua whipped his revolver out and nailed the two guards in the head. "Oh yeah, I am!" He cackled.

"RICKSTONE!" Misha screamed, tossing a fireball at Ander. Klin leapt in front, slicing through the fireball and destroying it. "What?!" Misha shrieked, "That should have melted the blades!" Klin said nothing as he charged towards the wall of flames, which Misha was now behind. "Are you crazy?!" Misha yelled, "You'll die!" Klin stayed silent as he leapt forward. All of a sudden, the flames disappeared. Klin smiled as he hit the ground and rolled forward. He was wanted alive. He came up, swinging his swords in an x-strike. Misha backed up with a curse, drawing her shortsword. Klin spun, slicing at the stomach. Misha blocked it and then created a burst of fire with her left hand. Klin tried to dodge, but was too slow. The burst was small, but powerful, sending him tumbling backwards. "So, you can see my Threads." Misha mused. "Men! Focus on the old man!"

Klin scrambled to his feet, wincing as he did. That blast had made it through his coat. His stomach was red and crisp from the burn, and hurt like hell. Klin counted half the soldiers converging on his uncle, who was dueling three soldiers at once. Klin watched in awe as his uncle cut a spear in half, kicked the man away before ducking under the strikes from the other two. As he ducked, he spun around coming up into a diagonal slice, decapitating both of them. Joshua then drew his six-shot, and the other soldiers who were advancing froze, becoming extremely wary. Klin was almost to his uncle when he saw a flurry of Fire Threads at his feet. He leapt back just in time to avoid the flames suddenly erupt from the ground. "And just where do you think you are going?" Misha asked. The rest of the soldiers were right next to her. "Tsk, tsk. I wanted to see your skill first." Misha clucked.

Klin shifted into a defensive stance. This was bad. Keep her talking. "And if I disappoint?" Klin asked warily. "You die." Misha said coolly. "You there! Fight him!" A young man was shoved forward and he stepped towards Klin. Klin frowned; this man seemed familiar. As the soldier advanced, Klin could see the anger and terror in his eyes. It was the soldier Erok had tortured. Klin nearly did not get his swords up in time to block from how distracted he was trying to figure out how he had got here. He thrust the blade away, creating an opening, deciding that really didn't matter right now. As the soldier stumbled, he reached out to his Lightning Source, and tried imbuing his sword with a small electrical field. A light blue of crackling electricity swarmed around his blade as the metal made contact with the soldier's breastplate. The soldier's eyes went wide before he convulsed, collapsing onto the ground unconscious. "Impressive." Misha commended, "Skilled in swordplay, magic, and ingenuity. With more training you'll be just what we need."

"And what the herk is that?!" Klin cried out, exasperated. "Classified." Klin sighed, crossing his blades over his chest, reaching for his Fire Source. "Getting real tired of that answer." He grumbled. Misha frowned as she noticed the threads he was weaving. "What are you-?" She was cut off however as Ander yelled, "Just what was I thinking?" Soldiers began to yell in panic. Klin turned, grinning as Ander transformed into his giant hawk. "Damn kids." Misha muttered, her attention fully on Ander for the moment. He was diving straight for Joshua. Misha began to form some sort of spell, but Klin did not wait to find out what it was. He instead fired of his own. Fire and lighting leapt to life around his blades, and with great force, he scraped the blades against each other as he opened his arms. A giant blast of fire and lighting intertwining was let lose at Misha and her soldiers. The soldiers screamed in fear, but Klin could see multiple Threads from multiple Weavers forming. There was a massive explosion as multiple spells came into contact with his. Dust flew up and wind threw back his coat. He covered his face, barely able to see. Once the dust died back down, he could see Misha staring at him with a mixture of awe and appraisal. "I almost am impressed!" She said, "That much power from so simple a spell? I wonder though, how many more do you have left in you though?" Klin was breathing heavily by this point but doing his best not to let it show.

Misha shook her head in disappointment. "Still resisting? Fine then, I'm done playing around. Men!" Misha snapped her fingers, and a bolt of flame snaked its way towards Klin. He danced around it, but as he did, three soldiers charged him in unison. He avoided the magic, then leapt back as the men with swords attacked. He was able to dodge them, but the third man had a spear. He barley brought his sword around to knock the blade of the spear away quite awkwardly. As he was about to counterattack, he was hit in the back. He fell to the ground, his back was strangely warm, and his head a bit dizzy. Before he could recover, a metal boot smashed his right hand. He screamed as the bones were crushed. "Don't move." A soldier above him growled. He was then grabbed by the neck and lifted up harshly. "Ready to surrender?" Misha asked.

Klin snarled soundlessly. She just shrugged, "Well, their blood on your hands I suppose then." Klin froze and looked over where Ander and his uncle where supposed to be. They were pinned to the ground. Ander's arms were cut in multiple places, blood dripping in clumps over them. Joshua had a large bruise over his eye, but other than that did not seem to beat up. "So, what will it be?" Misha whispered, "Surrender and they can go. Resist and we kill them and then take you." Klin's mind raced, pushing through the pain. He was pretty sure he was bleeding from a wound on his back and his right hand was unusable. Suddenly, he remembered two things. "I have one question for you beforehand." Klin proclaimed, "Are you familiar with my father?"

Misha gave him a humoring smile. "No. Enlighten me." Klin shrugged, "Well, you see he was a great warrior. Brave and clever. But most of all, stubborn. Something my brother and I inherited from him. Now mix that with the Rickstone side and you get a mountain." Misha frowned, then paled as she saw the blue threads of lightning nearly finished. "And you're supposed to be the smart one." Klin chuckled, and then cast the spell. The area around him exploded in an electric burst. Misha was knocked to the ground, while the soldiers were knocked out by the sudden electrical shocks sent through them. At the same time, Klin began to run, weaving an outline of himself using the Light Source. *Please work!* He pleaded and stepped into the outline. The world slowed down as he moved, seeing each and every detail of those around him. He could feel his strength being sapped at the same pace as which he moved, as fast as light. It was enough though to get him to his uncle and Ander. He grabbed them in a tackle, and with his good hand, pulled out the stone Erok had given him. He ended the spell. "Later!" He yelled, and activated the stone. There was a bright golden flash, and when it faded, Klin found they were in a new area.

They were sitting on a cobblestone road. In front of them was a city wall, about a mile off. They had made it out. "Excellent job kid." Joshua coughed, a dribble of blood coming out of his mouth. "You saved us, so how bout we save him now?" Klin nodded as his uncle bent down to tend to Ander's wounds. "What happened?" Joshua shook his head. "Simple. He's not used to his power. He did a great job at first, but as soon as they recovered he lost control. They snuck up and got his wings. He must have tried to change and failed. I ran out of bullets and they had him hostage." Klin nodded, wrapping Ander's arms up with some bandages Joshua had given him. "He's bleeding fairly badly." Klin remarked, "and he has a deep cut on his back. We need a healer." Joshua stared at him, "Yeah, for him and you." He grunted. "Frist Ander." Klin said though gritted teeth as tired to lift Ander up. "Then we can worry about other things." Joshua nodded, "Sure. But you ain't carrying him boy!" Joshua slapped Klin's good hand and picked up Ander with the ease of picking up a cat. He shook his head, muttering something as the two went to the city.

Chapter 27

Wounds That Never Close

Celeste watched the wagon fade from sight as they went their separate ways. "They'll be okay, right?" Sasha asked, her face full of worry. "Don't worry." Lorelei assured her with a soothing hand, "My brother may be insane, but he is more than capable of keeping them safe."

"One man can only do so much though." Erok put in dryly. "I'm sure they'll be fine though." Sasha snapped, "Unless you don't trust Ander?" Erok crossed his arms, looking sullen, "It's not Ander I don't trust. It's Klin I'm worried about." Kyoko tilted her head, "Why are you worried about Klin? He's a better fighter than my brother." Erok shook his head, "Sure, that's true enough, but it's his self-sacrifice tendencies I'm worried about. I'm betting he'll do something stupid because of some noble ideal or some bullshit."

"That may be true." Nathaniel said, "However, I believe you are underestimating the value of that willingness to sacrifice." Erok rolled his eyes, "Oh great. This week has just been one self-righteous bastard after another lecturing me on morality." Nathaniel kept his face stoic, but just stared at Erok silently. Erok shifted uncomfortably before scoffing. "Whatever." Suddenly Joseph piped up, "Well Erok, you are right to a certain degree. However, Klin's smart enough to only resort to self-sacrificing as a last resort. So if he does, we'll probably have bigger problems on our hands."

"How is that supposed to make me feel better?" Sasha blurted out annoyed. Joseph looked over his shoulder, reigns sturdily held. "It wasn't supposed to." Joseph said matter of factly, "I'm just giving the facts. It's up to you whether to keep hoping in the face of them. As for me, I'll continue to trust in them." A silence fell over as every one looked at each other, hope and love in their eyes. "He's right." Celeste remarked, "So, maybe instead of worrying, we should all just keep some sleep for now." Lorelei gave her an approving smile, "Agreed." Celeste watched as everyone settled down. Kyoko, Sasha, and Erok all snuggled up to Debbo. She was still surprised the owlbear could fit in the wagon. Lorelei gave her a smile, but her eyes showed the worry for Celeste. "Are you not going to sleep?" She asked. Celeste shrugged, "I think Joseph could use the company." Lorelei nodded. "Alright. Wake me though if you need someone to take over, okay?" Celeste gave her a grin and a thumbs up. Soon enough, everyone was fast asleep, even Nathaniel would had barely spoken a word. Celeste then turned and crawled onto the seat next to Joseph. "While I appreciate you staying up with me, I have a feeling there is a selfish motive in there." Joseph remarked with a small smile.

Celeste let out a deep sigh. "I suppose it is." Joseph tilted his head a little, "Worried about the nightmares?" There was a brief silence as Celeste debated on telling him the rest of the story. "Yeah," She finally admitted, "And, well, I never did finish telling you what happened. Sorry."

"Eh, no worries." Joseph replied with a chuckle, "It allowed me to see how cute you are when you actually sleep peacefully." Celeste recoiled in surprise, her face going bright red. "Wha-shut up!" She cried as she punched him in the arm. Joseph just laughed, (although he was rubbing his arm.) Celeste was just glad the dark hid her face at the moment. "Sorry, couldn't resist." Joseph apologized. "Oh, you were just joking. Got it." Celeste replied breathlessly, but her heart sank. *Wait, why am I upset at that?* Celeste shook her head, a little confused. "Yep, that's me, the jokester." Joseph said a little weirdly, rubbing the back of his neck. Celeste frowned. Was he lying? He was avoiding eye contact. But why would he lie? She shook her head again. No! Now was not the time for this! Wait, what even was this??? Suddenly, Yatta materialized between them. "Well Celeste, are you going to tell him or not?" She asked exasperated. "GAH!" Joseph yelped ins surprise, then immediately struggled to recover control of the horses. Celest gripped the bottom of her seat, trying to hang on. After things had settled down again, Joseph turned to Yatta exclaiming, "Where the herk did you come from?"

"Well, that was rude." Yatta pouted. Joseph and Celeste stared at her and said in unison, "What?!" Celeste then turned to Joseph, "Wait? You can see her?!" Joseph threw up a hand, "Well apparently!" He then reached out tentatively and poked Yatta in the face. His finger went right through her, creating a ripple like effect across her face. "Please stop." Yatta sighed, "That feels weird." Celeste released a pent up breath that she did not know she was even holding. They weren't asleep then. "How are you able to appear before him?"

"He held me once, so that was enough to create a connection." Yatta explained. A mischievous grin overtook her face as she leaned in and whispered, "Plus, depending on the relationship you have with certain people, it makes this a lot easier." Celeste pulled back, startled. "What does that mean?" Yatta's eyes shone with mirth as she shrugged, then moved over and sat on Celeste's lap. It was the strangest feeling, one that she still had not gotten used to. Her brain told her she should feel something. The warmth of Yatta's skin, the weight of her body, the breathing. Yet nothing other than a vague impression of the air around her being slightly heavier. "So, story time?" Yatta asked gently. "It will do you good you know." Celeste sighed, "Yeah, yeah, I know. Alright Joseph, I'll finish the tale and tell you what happened on that Sculpted-forsaken night."

The golden pink sky danced lights off the manor's windows, almost camouflaging the lanterns strung about the place. Pavilion tents with tables of gourmet foods had been set up all around the grounds. Both the front yard and in the back. Some Light Weavers had been hired also, placing small multi-colored balls of light to hang in the air, giving the evening a magical feel to it. Celest though had done her best to hide by eating cake in a corner. Guests milled about eating and drinking, conversing and playing games. However, despite all there was to do, one of her father's subordinates had still found her. He was chatting about some political nonsense. Ugh, nobles. Celeste had tuned him out and was nodding along and properly acting indignant at the appropriate moments. This asshole was only talking to her to get in good graces with her dad, so he did not deserve a proper conversation on her end.

"Celeste!" Fiora cried. Celeste tuned back into reality to see Firoa come running over. Her strawberry hair was done up in a loose bun with curled strands falling to the sides. She wore a pink satin dress that Celeste had gifted her last year.

"Excuse me my lord." Fiora explained with a bow, "But her sister asked for her."

"Oh, very well then." The noble replied and walked off. Celeste crossed her arms. "Wow, corners me to talk my ear off and then walks off without a word." She complained. Fiora gave her a smirk. "Oh, he'll be even ruder if he finds out I lied. Come on." Celeste grinned as she let herself be lead away. "So, where are we going to go then?" Celeste asked. Fiora turned back around and gave her a sly smile. "Oh, just the dance." Celeste's heart dropped a bit. "Oh, great."

"Oh, come on, it'll be fun!" Fiora led her over to the dueling circle. The sand had been covered with a makeshift wooden floor. Lanterns were hanging from the trees, while multicolored lights were strung through the air between the trees. A stage had also been built and a band played upon it while guests danced to the music on the ring. Tables and chairs had also been brought out, with more food and drink on them. Fiora guided them over to a table though and promptly had them sit down. "Wait, I thought we were going to dance?" Celeste asked confused. Fiora rolled her eyes. "Honestly, it's almost as if you aren't a noble's daughter! Don't you know anything about proper courting etiquette? We wait to be asked!" Celeste crossed her arms and snorted. "Fiine. But I'm not waiting too long." Fiora smiled softly, chuckling a little. "I should have guessed that. Good thing I placed us in view of the guys." Celeste sat up straight and saw Samuel, Fiora's crush, and Claude go to each other as a slow song began. They were giving each other overly exaggerated moony-eyed looks while stupid grins were plastered on their faces. Celeste and Fiora looked at one another, and just shrugged. Boys would be boys.

"Looks like we might have a bit." Fiora whispered, "So I'm going to go grab a drink. Be back." Celeste nodded and sat patiently, but at the same time wondering where Selene was and if she should go look for her. At that moment a young girl's voice piped up suddenly. "Celeste Farvor'Coal?" Celeste spun around, looking for who had spoken. She was surprised to see a familiar face. The girl behind her was about thirteen or fourteen, just hitting puberty. She had a soft face and was not much shorter than Celeste. The two most striking things about her though were her emerald eyes which shone as brightly as any start in the night, and her long crimson hair. She wore a modest dress of pale purple, plain and not even silk, despite the fact that this young girl was Veronica Winters, daughter of Emperor Gabriel Winters of Coronus Empire. "Veronica!" Celeste exclaimed delightedly, leaping up to grab her in a hug. Veronica squirmed a little but giggled softly. "Hello there." She said behind giggles. Celeste released the princess, looking her up and down. "What are you doing here?" She asked. "I thought you would be stuck at the castle?" Veronica shrugged, "Father said this was an important enough event that I could go to, despite the emergency meeting that he called. It's not like I'm old enough to be a part of it anyway."

Celeste smiled, "Well, I'm glad you're here. Have you said hi to Selene yet?" Veronica nodded. "Yes. I told her she will not be able to escape a duel with me this time." Celeste laughed. This girl was one after her own heart. "Well, does that mean I am challenged to a duel also?" Veronica crossed her arms, "Pleeease! Unless you have gotten more proficient since our last duel, you are even worthy of fighting." Celeste narrowed her eyes, "Better watch that mouth young lady. It'll be eating dirt soon enough." A friendly fire was lit in those emerald eyes as Veronica smiled mischievously. "I have my sword with me. Shall I ask my guard to fetch it so we may duel?" Celeste cackled evilly. "Yes please little princess."

"What's this, you guys just meet and are already ready to fight?" Selene demanded. The two girls spun to see Selene with her hands on her hips, a mocking look of disapproval on her. "And you weren't going to let me watch!" Celeste and Veronica looked at one another and then the both of them bowed. "Very well, would you like to officiate this duel?" Veronica asked, "As a token of our sincerest apologies?" Selene grinned. "Very well, I accept that."

"Sheesh, you nobles!" Fiora exclaimed, "All you ever do is think of dueling!" Veronica raised an eyebrow at her. "Oh? And would you prefer

328

that you peasants do all the fighting?" Fiora leaned in and whispered to Celeste. "I also forgot how annoying she is."

"I can hear you, Miss Fiora. You may be older but I am still your princess." Firoa recoiled back, "How--?" Veronica rolled her eyes. "You are neither as quiet nor as subtle as you would like to believe you are." Celeste burst out laughing, "Oh that is so true." Fiora glared at both of them. "Yeah, well look who's talking Celeste." Celeste just kept laughing, ignoring the death glares from Fiora. "So, when shall we duel?" Veronica asked. This time, it was Fiora's turn to look triumphant. "After one dance. Celeste agreed to do at least one." Celeste looked over, slightly startled, "Wait, when did I agree to that?"

"I think that is an *excellent* idea!" Selene replied emphatically. "While those two get some guys to dance with them, how about you and I talk?" Veronica nodded, "Very well, that seems fair. I look forward to kicking your butt Celeste." With that the two walked away. "Such an interesting girl." Fiora muttered. Celeste just smiled. "Oh, I don't know. I find her charming." Fiora let out a snort, "Charmingly arrogant maybe. She's on the brink right now. In a few years she'll be insufferable if she doesn't change." Celeste rolled her eyes, "Oh please, you're over exaggerating. In a few years that'll arrogance will be justified." Fiora shook her head, "Arrogance is never justified Celeste. Maybe you should stay away from philosophy." Celeste crossed her arms, glaring at her friend. At that moment though, the girls turned to the dance floor, recognizing that the music had stopped. They stared at Claude and Samuel, the two giving mock bows to one another. Then the two boys turned and immediately began to head their way. Samuel was a man of average height, and had a skinner stature than Claude, but he was by no means without defined musculature. He had long dark hair that tumbled a bit around his face and a bright smile that was welcome among any group.

He wore a pink dress shirt with a black overcoat. He looked Fiora up and down and smiled. "Wow, guess we unintentionally matched! Guess that means we should dance huh?" Fiora rolled her eyes, "Seriously, that is by far the dumbest way to ask someone to dance I have ever heard." Samuel cocked his head, looking very confused. "So, is that a no then?"

"No! Of course, I want to dance with you!" Fiora laughed and grabbed him by the hand, dragging him out to the dance floor. Celeste grinned, knowing that Fiora had probably found out somehow what Samuel was going to wear. "Well, those two seem to be having fun." Claude chuckled. "Yep." Celeste replied, now a little distracted. Claude wore a golden dress shirt that was barely able to conceal his bulging muscles. "So, uh want to dance?" He asked. "Yep!" Celeste squeaked, barely able to keep her voice under control. As Claude took her by the hand and lead her out, Celeste saw her sister out of the corner of her eye with Veronica. Selene sprouted a mischievous smile as she walked over to the conductor and whispered something to them. They nodded and began to play Quartet No. 2, Celeste's favorite song. Huh, it seemed like Selene really *had* learned how to be properly supportive.

As they danced to the song, Celeste found it hard to lock eyes with Claude. "I noticed that you and your sister aren't dressed that fancy." Claude remarked. "Selene has to show off her new move tonight." Celeste explained, "Sort of difficult to do that in a fancy dress." Claude nodded, "Ah yes. The famous Farvor'Coal rite of initiation. How's her signature move look?"

"Deadly and beautiful. Just like her." Celeste replied. Claude smiled. "And you? What's your excuse for not wearing a dress?"

"My sister directly asked me to wear this." Celeste replied a little testily. "Ah, well it suits you."

"What, think I can't pull off a dress?"

"No! Not that at all! You just look graceful in anything you wear is all." Celeste felt like a match had been lit on her face as the entire surface went red and warm. That was when she heard the screams. A dead, torn body hit the ground behind Claude. Claude spun around in horror. "What the herk?" The head was gone and the body was so mutilated she could not even tell what gender it had been. Everyone around them froze in a silent horror. A strange snarl was heard and Celeste turned around to see a small, yellow skinned creature leap at her. "Get back!" Claude yelled. He pushed her behind him, backhanding the creature away. As he did though, it's talons ripped through his sleeves and flecks of his own blood splattered the ground. Celeste spun around to see six more leap down from the tent, some landing on the guests and tearing into them. That was when the pain and mayhem finally set in. The six creatures began to advance towards her and Claude. Two guests lay dead nearby, their throats torn to shreds. "Shit." Claude muttered. As the closest beast lunged at them, Selene spun through the air above them, slicing it apart. The monster crumbled to dust as Selene landed, pivoting on one foot and killing the other five in one fell, magic backed attack. "Are you two okay?" She asked. Celeste nodded, "Yeah, thank you. What are these things?" Selene shook her head. "I'm not fully sure. I have a few ideas though. Right now I'm going to see why our guards are not helping us. Stay together and keep each other safe!"

"Wait!" Celeste cried out, but Selene had already run off. "Damn this all to Heshtanus!" Celeste screamed. Claude looked over at her concerned. *Shit, where is Fiora though?!* Celeste thought, her mind a buzz. Suddenly she noticed two things. Princess Veronica was running towards them, her rapier drawn. Secondly, she saw Fiora running towards the manor, being chased by a small hoard of those horrendous monsters. "Fiora!" Celeste yelled. Her friend cast a terrified look back at her. "Damn this all!" She snarled and charged after them. "Celeste! Wait!" Claude shouted. Celeste spared a glance back only to yell, "Veronica protect him!" And kept running. "I can protect myself!" Claude yelled back. *Whatever, but Fiora isn't a fighter!* First Celeste ran towards the cherry tree nearest the house, scooping up her sword as she passed. She drew the sword out of the sheathe, tossing the sheathe to the ground, and ran the hardest she had ever run. Her footsteps become like steps of wind from her speed. As she drew near, she leapt forward, flying through the air. She cut one of the beasts right down the middle so fast it did not even have time to cry out as it dissolved into ash. The other two beasts were so focused on Fiora that the did not even notice her. So she dispatched the other two, reliving them of their heads.

"C-Celeste?" Fiora stammered, shaking and tears in her eyes. "Are you okay?" Celeste asked hurriedly. Fiora nodded. "Yes, b-b-but Sam-he-they.." She could not finish as she broke down crying. Celeste turned and noticed the body that lay near them. It was Samuel's. He was a bloody mess with his chest torn open, and his normally twinkling eyes now dull; the mouth frozen open in a soundless cry. Celeste closed her eyes and struggled not to puke. Celeste took a deep breath and moved in Fiora's line of sight, taking her by the shoulders and squeezing them gently. "Alright I need you to listen to me carefully. Run to the banner that has our crest on in the dinning hall. Behind it is a steel door. Put my ring in it, and you'll be able to get in. You can call my dad from there. Now whatever you do, don't come out unless me, my sister, or dad get you." Fiora nodded, her eyes wide as she clutched Celeste's ring. "What about you though?" Celeste turned back around, surveying the mayhem, her heart thumping. "I'm going to carry out my duty. Now go!"

Fiora turned and ran inside. Celeste charged, prepared to send these demonic creatures to Heshtanus. Veronica and Claude were fighting together. They had managed to fend off a lot of the creatures and seemed to be doing quite well all things considered. Claude had found a knife and was dealing out fatal wounds while Veronica spun and danced around with her rapier, gutting the creatures with frightful grace for a young girl. There were quite of few of the monsters advancing towards them though. So, Celeste snaked around to them, killing six imps in one fluid motion. Down, step, upper vertical, step, down vertical, and finishing off with a spin, killing three more. She ended with her back to Claude and Veronica. "Wow, very nice." Veronica commented as she killed an imp. "I had them." Claude growled. The last two imps leapt at them before Celeste could spit back a reply. "Watch it!" She cried. One leapt at her, and she sidestepped it, cutting it's head off. The other continued on to Claude, who threw his knife with a snarl. He nailed it right between the eyes. The creature feel to the ground in a pile of ash. "The herk Celeste!" Claude yelled angrily, "That think could have killed me!"

Celeste's eye twitched as she gestured to the chaos raging. "You mean like those on the ground?! Don't know if you noticed, but I've been saving your sorry ass! Now go help those who are still alive! Get them into the house and in a safe place!" Claude clenched his teeth and looked like he was a bout to argue, but instead he took a deep breath and asked, "Alright. What are you going to do though?" Veronica lightly hit Claude on the arm. "Do not ask a noble what she will do. If she so deigns not to share, follow her orders!" Celeste allowed herself a small smile as she wiped the blood and ash from her blade. "It's okay Veronica. No need to scold him. I'm going to clear the way. Veronica, stay with them princess." Veronica nodded, "Of course. It is my duty." Celeste smiled, "Good. Now, if you guys can get this crowed clamed and to follow you." Celeste killed some more imps as they approached, and then ran off, killing some here and there with a few swift strikes.

"Everyone! Get your asses over here!" Claude bellowed from behind. Celest allowed a small smile as the people began to make their way over. Celeste was able to rescue a few more, but the bodies of guests were piling up now. She made her way to the mansion, deciding that going straight through would be faster than going around. She flung open the door open, ran through the kitchen, slid across the dining table, and threw open the front door. The scene she entered was filled with the same chaos of war. The lush green grass, just recently reborn, was now covered in blood and gore. Her family's guards were engaged with distorted and disfigured humanesque monsters. Gray warty skin and two heads, one atop the other. Celeste watched as a guard slew one. It turned to ash like the imps. She stared though, stuck in horrific fascination as one of the monsters cut off the head of a guard and then began to gleefully mutilate the body. It dropped its sword, ripping and tearing in a blood-crazed glee with its claws. Celeste's stomach churned at the vileness. She swallowed the incoming vomit, and broke out of her stupor. Screaming, she bolted and gutted the monster.

The monster did not even look at her as she gutted in. As it turned to ash, she spun around, hearing heavy footfalls. Another one of the warty-skinned creatures was there. She blocked a strike from its crude blade, kicked it in the stomach, and decapitated it. The heads hit the ground before crumbling. "Celeste!" She spun to see her sister flying towards her. "What are you doing here?" Selene scolded. Celeste pushed her sister aside, killing a human-esque monster that had been about to puncture Selene's neck. "Helping you!" Celeste retorted. "Now focus!" Selene nodded, "Fine, but stay close!" She sent a swathe of air slices out in front of them, cutting through four imps. Celeste placed herself in a defensive position next to her sister. "Like I would have herking run off by myself!" The two fell into place, defending against the onslaught of Warties, (as Celeste was now calling them,) and Imps. They watched each other's backs, not letting any beast get close. "Did you contact father?" Selene asked as she stabbed a Warty. Celeste cut down four imps in succession as she replied, "Got Fiora on that. Also got Veronica and most of the guests to safety."

Excellent job sis." Selene grunted, ducking a imp as it leaped over her, right into Celeste's blade. Suddenly, they heard some panicked screams. "Over there!" Selene pointed. A guard lay on the ground defenseless. "I see him!" Celeste yelled back. She began to run over, but as she did, she felt a gust of wind push against her back. She was launched into the air, suddenly unbalanced. She curled up into a ball, flipping through the air. Celeste saw the Warty looming over the guard. She uncurled herself, landing on the creatures shoulders, her sword going through it's head. Celeste plummeted to the ground as the Warty fell to ash, sending a jolt up her legs. "Thank you!" The guard said through barely contained tears. Celeste picked up his sword and helped him to his feet. "Your fight's not over yet." She said gently. The guard nodded, the fire of resolve appearing in his eyes. "Of course, my lady!"

"Celeste!" Selene warned. A chill rattled up her spine as Celeste spun, noticing about ten Warties converging around them Selene had even more and was isolated. "Shit!" She cursed as she placed herself to the guard's back. "Behind me my lady!" The guard cried, leaping in front of her. "What do we do?" Celeste growled. The guard spared a glance at her, "I'll distract them and hold them off. Once I do, run to your sister."

"What?! No! You'll did that way!" Celest protested fiercely. The guard gave her a warming smile. "You extended my life for a few minutes so I may extend yours for hopefully years to come. I had a daughter too once. I do not wish for his lordship to suffer the same. Now go!" The guard leapt forward, cutting down two Warties with a surprise attack. "GO!" He commanded. Celeste ran through the opening and heard his last cry of opposition. "FOR FAVOR'COAL!" She could not help but turn to see the man's last stand. The eight Warties all attacked him at once, impaling him. He sputtered as his sternum was pierced eight times but spat his blood on their faces and with a dying gasp, was able to cut off the heads of four of the monsters. Celeste screamed and fell to her knees. The-there was so much blood. So many dead. The monsters turned towards her with a growl and hiss that sounded like some sort of language, and they began to converge on her. "Kill, kill, killkillkillkill!" One the monster's screamed. It broke off from the others, tossing aside its sword and leaping at her. Celeste tried to swing at it, but her lethargy was too much. The beast batted her hand aside, knocking the sword away. It then sank its fangs into her arm. Celeste screamed and punched it in the face.

It let go, stunned briefly, so she scrambled back but it grabbed her leg. There was a loud snap as the Warty twisted her leg. Celeste howled in agony, blinking away the spots of black. She reached out her hand, trying to grab her sword, roundhousing the monster in the side of the head. She felt bones crack like glass against her foot as the monster howled, falling over. Celeste finally was able to crawl to her sword and just in time. She stabbed the beast in the heart as it pounced at her. The body went limp as it fell to ash, covering her in it. She coughed and blinked furiously as it got in her eyes and throat. She felt a deep sense of horror though. There were still three Warties, and she could not see really.

Suddenly there was a loud gust of wind, some howls, and another gust of wind, but much gentler and warmer. Celeste opened her eyes and found Selene standing in front of her, blood dripping down her face. "Selene, you're hurt!" Celeste cried. She tried to get up, but let out a whimper as her leg released a lighting bolt of pain. "And you are hurt far worse!" Selene replied angrily, "So sit the herk down!" Celeste shrunk in on herself and nodded as her sister tore off a piece of her jacket and wrapped the bite wound on her arm. "What about the others?" Celeste asked, "They're still in danger!" Selene shook her head. "No, they're not. That was the last of them. We're done." Celeste looked into her sister's eyes. They were filled with anger, regret, and exhaustion. Her face was pale and she kept missing the spots she needed to wrap the bandage, and kept having to go back. "You've used up too much magic. You're starting to get vertigo. So sit down."

"I will once you're fine." Selene sniffed. Suddenly there was a loud crash as the whole earth trembled. Selene froze, "What was that?"

"Wow, I was not expecting us to have to bring in the syndican." Celeste and Selene turned to stare at a noble. It was the man who had been trying to talk to her earlier! He was simply strolling across the blood-soaked ground like it was an afternoon walk by the pond. "I guess the Farvor'Coal family's reputation is no exaggeration." He said with a smirk. The remaining guards drew their swords and advanced on him, circling him. Only ten of their original thirty men remained. "You."

Selene hissed, "Are you responsible for this?!" The lord shrugged, "In a way, yes." He looked at the guards disdainfully, and sighed, "I suggest you do not try to detain me you foolish men. You'll die before you can." Sweat began to drip down the men's faces, but they held their ground. "Now, which one of you is Celeste?" He asked. Selene pointed Yatta at him, and snarled, "I am! Now what do you want?"

"What are you doing?!" Celeste whispered angrily but Selene just ignored her. "Well, you going to answer me?!" Selene shouted. The lord rubbed his chin, "Just as fiery and impatient as the reports said. Kill her." He snapped his fingers and a giant boulder was flung from the tree line at them. Selene leaped into the air, flying at it. Celeste watched in awe as her sister sent the rock straight back to sender. "Damn it!" The lord cried, "She *has* been chosen! Quickly, we must kill her!" Suddenly, a roar so loud broke the air that it sent violent vibrations down Celeste's whole body. The source was close, but all Celeste could see was darkness. Something that big should not be this hidden! Celeste watched though as Selene flew higher, almost to the roof of their manor, before slicing directly in front of her at the darkness. The roar was head again, and a crash as something stumbled backwards. Celeste then realized the great wall of darkness *was* the creature. It was of immense size, standing around twenty feet tall. Its skin was made of obsidian, which was why should could not see it at first. It had barely any discernible features, other than that its skin was shaped like armor, but it moved like it was its flesh. Finally, two large red eyes gleamed out from a dark helmet. Bright red ooze, glowing like lava, dripped from its arm where Selene had wounded it. The men scrambled away, letting the lord get through. Luckily though, the creatures blood only looked like lava, and had none of the dangerous properties of it.

As the lord broke away though, he shouted to the syndican. "What in the Great Lord's name are you doing?! KILL HER!" Celeste though watched with glee as her sister did what she does best, be awesome. Selene flew around the syndican like a hawk, and with the predatory efficiency of one also. Selene darted around, slicing and raking her sword along the creatures side. The beast could be seen clearly in the night now, thanks to the glowing red wounds across its body. But then, the unthinkable happened. Selene swopped up, and then stumbled in the air, running right into the swing of the syndican's fist. It swatted her down directly into the ground. There was a loud crash as the ground broke under her, creating a small crater. "SELENE!" Celeste screamed, her throat raw from the ferocity of it. "Damn it." The noble cursed, "You stupid sisters! We've been tricked. Kill her now!" The guards began to rush to Celeste, but were blocked by the syndican's hand. They scrambled back, trying to stay alive. "I'LL KILL YOU!" Celeste screamed, pushing to her feet, ignoring the pain that was coursing through her. Yet, she was only able to take one step before collapsing. *No! I need to get up! I need to fight back!* Selene was counting on her! But, Selene had lost-no she never loses, but she had-yet-but. Tears streamed down her face as the noble walked towards her. She was going to die, and there was nothing she could do about it. Tears began to stream down her face as she bowed her head.

"What are you doing to my daughters?" A deathly calm voice rang out. The noble froze, his face turning pale as he turned around to see her father walking towards them. "You use Natharian magic. So, I sentence you to death." Antoine snapped his fingers and the noble erupted in blue flames. He screamed, but not for long as he was quickly reduced to ash. "Secure my daughter!" Antoine barked, "I have the beast." The guards rushed over, surrounding and protecting Celeste as her father strode up to the syndican. The beast roared at him, but Antoine did not flinch. Instead, he drew his rapier, blue dragon wings of fire erupting from his back. "Cease your existence." He declared. Suddenly, he was gone, a smoldering patch of flames where he had been. All of a sudden, the syndican screamed as her father appeared behind it. Giant wings that had been behind Antoine were now on the monster's back, but they were not harmless. Talon marks were also raked across the chest, and wherever the wounds were, fire began to pour out from them. Celeste watched as one by one, the flames exploded in the wounds, then more flames appeared, consuming the enlarged wounds. The beast moaned, falling to its knees as its body slowly crumbled to dust.

Antoine turned, sheathing his weapon before bolting to Selene's side. "Let go of me!" Celeste screamed as she smacked away some guards trying to hold her back. "My lady, please let us help you over at least!" One of the guards pleaded, "You are in no condition to walk."

Celeste just snarled and cried out, her tears obscuring her vision. She barley even noticed when a guard scooped her up and carried her over next to Selene. Now that she was by her side, Selene would be alright, right? Selene lay in the small crater, her body splayed out at odd angles. The brilliant white of her bones could be seen peaking out. "No. No, nonononono!" Celeste mumbled hysterically, "You'll be alright. Right? You have to be!" Selene turned her gaze to her. "Hey," She croaked, her voice mangled, "Don't worry. Everything will be okay." Antoine brushed her cheek, and grabbed her hand. "Shush now darling." He choked, "save your strength."

"No, I must apologize." Selene protested, "I failed you Celeste. I'm sorry. Take care of Yatta for me."

"NO! You haven't!" Celeste yelled, her face red and throat raw from tears. She grabbed her sister's hand. "Stay with me. Don't die. Do-don't leave me!" Antoine gently pried her hand away, whispering, "Celeste, she-she-she's gone..."

"NO!" Celeste screamed, "NO! She just needs a healer! Somebody get a healer!" Yet the vacant, one violet but now grey eyes could not lie. No healer in the world could fix the malady that which Selene was now afflicted with. "She's gone Celeste. I'm sorry."

Joseph was silent as Celeste finished her story her face lightly wet. Just as she was wondering if he would say anything at all, (and becoming very self-conscious about it,) Joseph pulled her into a hug with one arm. Celeste stiffened, caught off guard, but relaxed quickly as she found himself buried in his side. It was a strong and tight hug, but warm and full of empathy. "I'm sorry you had to go through all that." Joseph whispered, "And I'm sorry that there are people who would want to do such a thing. I know how it is to lose your hero." Celeste looked up as something splashed her. Joseph was crying! Celeste was so taken aback, she was not sure how to react at first. She decided not to think about it though and hugged him. The two stayed that way as they comforted each other in their sadness.

Chapter 28

Purpose

A stream of light broke through the darkness behind his closed eyes. Ander blinked furiously, trying to clear the sleep from his head as he shielded his face. *Where am I?* He though groggily. Soft, plush blankets lay over him, fighting his will to get out of bed. His head felt like it was on a cloud, and not pillows. "Ah, yer finally up." Ander turned his head and saw Joshua sitting in a chair nearby, smoking a pipe. He had removed his coat and vest, and had a small book and pen in his hands. "Bout damn time too!" Joshua exclaimed, a grin poking out from the pipe, "Was beginning to wonder if you would ever get up!" Ander sat up, his head spinning. "Ugh, wow. How long was I out? What happened? I remember Misha, and you guys were hurt! Then…something hit me."

"Calm down kid." Joshua soothed, "We got away thanks to Klin and the little trinket Erok gave him. We're good. As for how long you were out, I think three days now." Ander threw the sheets off of him and leapt to his feet. "Three days!" Ander shouted, but then stumbled as he hit the ground. Joshua leapt up, catching him. "Whoa there kiddo. You're still weak so take it easy. Give yer body time to get used to standing up again." Ander shook his head, "But, I don't understand, why was I out that long?" Joshua looked him over and nodded. "Give yerself a look in the mirror, then you might know. Also, might want to speak to them crazy spirits. The voices in yer head probably got something to say now."

"Wait, how—" Joshua just shrugged and opened the door. "I got too many voices myself. Everyone's got them, right? Come down for food when yer ready." With that, the crazy old man closed the door and left. Ander shook his head, totally bepuzzled, but his heart rate was slowing down again. He thought Joshua somehow knew about the Spirits! But it was just him being insane. His curiosity at the old man's last comment though intrigued him. There was a full body mirror in the corner of the room, so Ander went over and let out a gasp at what he found. His body had changed! His once sickly frame was now very healthy looking. He was still slim, not growing much wider, but the bones once able to be counted were now hidden by a healthy layer of muscle. His arms and legs looked the part of one who had been trained from birth to be a warrior. His chest was slightly wider and more muscular too. But what was most striking was the fact that his tattoo had changed. It was now black, with green blades of grass nestled at the bottom of it. "What happened to me?" Ander muttered. *Your body is changing as a result of growing more acclimated to the power of the Trimal.* Lupis explained.

Ander jumped, "Gah! Well, well, haven't heard from you guys in a while." He shot back spitefully, "Almost forgot you guys existed." *Hmph, it's not like we wished to stop conversing with you.* Sean grumbled, You *cut us out.* Ander crossed his arms, "And how did I do that pray tell?"

The magic of the Trimal is more unique than you realize. Adamar explained. It is bound to one's soul more closely than the magic of a Weaver. Or, maybe more accurately, the spell itself *is* the source of the magic. Because of this, if you act shamefully in times when you are most needed, we are separated from you. "O-oh. I see." Ander stammered lamely. "That would explain why I've been having trouble transforming, huh?" Ander received a mental image of the three nodding. "So, what brought you back?" *Your bravery.* Lupis answered, a hint of pride in his voice. *You knew there was no guarantee you could transform, and you knew that that battle was one you could not really win. Yet, your selfless love for the others is what brought your power back.* Ander felt a warmness spread throughout his body. "So I did good?" As one, the spirits replied, "Yes, you did good." Ander smiled, and turned to his bed, putting on the clothes that lay there.

They were not his clothes, but new ones. He had a dark blue, long-sleeved shirt. As he put it on, he felt something weird by the cuffs. He started to examine it and found a deep pocket. *What in the world?* It is for daggers. Adamar said, I believe your mercenary friend and the drunkard did this for you. "Wait, so you guys hear things even when I'm asleep?" *Yes.* Sean replied, And before you as, yes we will relay any information of importance to you. Ander grinned, "Well, that's helpful." He continued to look around the room, in case he missed something. Good thing he did, for he found two daggers, just the right size to put in his sleeves, but not without some difficulty. He ended up cutting his palms, but got them in there. However, the wounds he had created were closed within the minute! "Uh, guys? Is this normal??" Lupis chuckled, *Do not fret young one. This is simply one of the powers of the Triamal. You will gain more as time goes on. The healing takes longer depending on the wound, but with training, your healing can be increased also.* Ander grinned, "That's awesome! I guess we should go down now though, huh?" Yes, there is a man of great interest you will want to meet.

Intrigued, Ander left the room and found himself on a loft overlooking an inn's dinning room and bar, with a theater stage taking up a good hundred feet. *Where the heck are we?!* Ander thought, *The cost for a night must be insane!* He spotted Joshua though. He had his hat on, but still no coat or vest. And everyone else was with him! Ander rushed downstairs, sprinting towards the others, bumping into tables and chairs prompting curses from customers and breathless apologies from himself. When he finally reached them, Erok was doubled over from laughing. "Damn Ander? Can you turn into a bull now? I think you hit every bit of furniture possible on your way over!" Ander turned bright ride, casting aside his gaze, so he didn't see Sasha charging at him, embracing him in a hug. "Thank the Eight you're okay!" Sasha exclaimed. "Sorry." Ander replied, returning the hug awkwardly, "You know how me and sleep are." Sasha smiled at him, and then pulled away frowning. "Hold on, something's different about you."

"No shit Sasha." Erok exclaimed, rolling his eyes. "He's got muscle now! Ander's finally becoming a man!" Klin shot Erok a dirty look, like he wanted to say something, but kept quiet. Ander frowned as he studied Klin. There were dark circles under his eyes and he had a cup of coffee in his hands. He was slightly slouched and deflated. "Hey, are you okay Klin?' Ander asked, concerned. Klin turned and gave him a low energy smile. "Yeah, I'm alright. I've been having to expel a continuous amount of magic since we got here, so I'm just tired." Ander nodded. That made sense, but his eyes. They did not have the dullness from physical tiredness. His heart skipped a beat though as he say Celeste.

Her hair was especially lush today. Joseph was sitting next to her and scarfing down some food. Lorelei and Kyoko were at the end, just chatting with the others. Lorelei looked over and smiled at him. She nudged Kyoko, who stopped speaking.

"Ander!" She squealed, leaping up and flying over to Ander, wrapping her arms around his neck. Ander stumbled back as she stopped floating. "Gah! Kyoko, that hurts!" Kyoko giggled as she let go of him. "Sorry. I'm just happy that you're alright." Ander patted her head. "Thanks, Kyo. Means a lot." She floated back over to her spot and handed him a plate of food. "Eat. You've got to be hungry!" Ander gratefully took a plate of seven eggs, four pieces of toast, and eight strips of bacon. He could feel his mouth salivating at the smell. He dug in, listening to the conversations of everyone. "So, what are we doing about training?" Joseph asked to Celeste. She shrugged, "Don't know. We can't continue till we're safe. I know you're just *dying* to get back to fighting me."

"You can only wish we weren't." Klin mumbled from the bottom of his mug. Celeste raised an eyebrow, "Oh, you think you're better than me?"

"Let me use my damn magic, and we'll see how the match goes."

"Ugh, we've been over this Klin. Can't rely on your fancy bolts of light for all fights."

"Best fighters use all they can."

"Best fighters also take the time to master what they can." Celest shot back triumphantly. Klin grumbled something in his cup once more but spoke no more on the subject. "Hey, Erok?" Kyoko asked. "Yeah Kyo?"

"Can you teach me how to shoot that crossbow?"

"Herk yeah I can!"

"Absolutely not!' Sasha scolded. "She's too young for that thing!" Erok rolled his eyes, "What are you, her mom? It's not like she's been trained to kill since birth or anything like that." Sasha's eyes bugled a bit as she put her hands on her hips. "Excuse me?! I know I'm not her mom but *someone* has to look out for her and act like an adult!" Erok gestured towards Lorelei, "And she's not?" Sasha went bright red in the face. "Ah-well-um-I mean…" Lorelei held up a hand. "It's okay Sasha. I appreciate the concern you show towards her. One that might be better

342

emulated by the men she has been looking up to." Both Ander and Erok turned bright red. "Now wait just a damn minute!" Erok protested, "You can't speak to us that way!" Lorelei crossed her arms. "How would you like me to talk to you then? Like your mother? If you were my boys, I would never let you speak to Sasha like this first. You sir, are in need of some manners. However, I also think you are bright and that Kyoko should learn to handle your weapon."

"Hah! Take that!" Erok crowed. There was a small whip of air, and a yelp as Erok leapt from his chair. "Speak with some manners young man." Lorelei said darkly. Erok rubbed his rear, but sat down with a healthy dose of fear on his face. "Yes ma'am." Ander turned to look at Joshua. Was he…*snickering*? "By the way," Joseph asked, "When's this guy we're supposed to meet gonna show Uncle?" Joshua took a long drink of his beer, and then looked in the mug. "According ta this, in three seconds." All of a sudden, the doors were flung open and a small group of men walked in. The inn went dead silent at the sight of them. They were all big and brawny with sun-weathered faces and a soft scent of salty air brought with them. The man at their head though stood out from the rest. He had dark, smooth skin that seemed very well taken care of. He was just as muscular as the others but stood above the rest. He was shorter than Joshua, but not by much. He wore a light tan flaxen shirt and pants that had the cuffs torn. Over his shirt was an orange, sleeveless vest that he straightened with a charming smile. His black hair stood up straight with an orange, cloth headband tied around his head. He had a hammer and crescent sickle thought hanging from his waist, and a ukulele slung over his back. "Yep, right on time!" Joshua cried out, waving at the newcomers.

The man smiled and looked at everyone in the inn. "Long time no see tredos!" The rest of the customers let out a friendly cheer of greeting as the other men with the leader sat down with the customers. The leader looked over at their group though and began to approach with a scowl. Ander tensed up, and he wasn't the only one. Erok had his hand casually by his crossbow. He stopped in front of Joshua, who had his chair leaned back, feet propped up on the table and eyeing the dark-skinned man. "After all this time, after all that you have done, you have the nerve to show up here?" The man growled. Joshua took a long drink from his mug. As he finished, he pulled out a second pipe. "So, a smoke to catch up then?" The man laughed boisterously, "Of course you old scoundrel! Come here!" Joshua got to his feet with a smile as they hugged. After they pulled apart, Joshua introduced him. "Well guys, this is Beppo Calist. He's the head of the Coronus Liberation Sailors and our ticket ta safety."

Klin frowned at them. "Wait, I think I've heard of them. Aren't they just pirates with a fancy title?" Beppo placed his arms on his hips indignantly "How dare you! We are a faction officially sanctioned by the royal crown! But, in a way, you are correct." He ended with a laugh. Celeste crossed her arms. "Well, I'm not quite sure how you guys can help us. I'm quite familiar with your work, but a life at sea doesn't sound great to me to be honest." Ander raised his hand, "Um, I'm not familiar with these guys at all, so can someone please explain?"

"The C.L.S. or the Coronus Liberation Sailors are a group of sailors who roam the seas on the lookout for suspicious or illegal ships." Beppo explained, "Most of the time we stop slavers from getting to Coronus and raiding our lands. We also tend to stop them from getting back to Turmaky or Ardaven. Every once in a while we are a part of the official navy, but that is only in times of war or when it seems like we might be heading to war."

"Cool, but that still doesn't explain how that helps us." Joseph mumbled in between bites of food. "Ahh, would you pipe down." Joshua complained, "You kids are so impatient!"

"It is fine tredo." Beppo calmed with a wave of his hand. "It is only natural to want answers, especially at their age. But, to sate your curiosity, it is not our organization itself really that will help you, but the place we conduct our doings." Celeste narrowed her eyes, "Hold up there bud. I'm pretty high in the know about army stuff, but I have never heard where you guys have your headquarters at." Beppo let out a small chuckle, "Well, who are you to expect to have such knowledge?" Celeste turned bright red, and began to mumble, "Well, uh, I uhh... might just be the daughter of Antoine Farvor'Coal. I um, haven't told everyone here that yet..." Beppo's eyebrows went up in surprise. "Well now, this is a welcome treat! I will be very happy to hear your thoughts on how we do things then Miss Farvor'Coal! It has been a while since any from your family have visited."

"Hold on!" Erok cried, "Are we just going to blow over the fact that she's a herking noble?!" Klin looked over in surprise; even Joshua seemed taken aback. Lorelei just smiled at her, and leaned in and whispered, "I see Joseph is the only one not surprised. You chose a good man." Celeste went bright red and began to ramble at Lorelei. Ander thought sat confused at how he had heard that. *The Triamal powers gave you enhanced hearing.* Sean whispered, *Just try to act like you heard nothing.* Ander gave him a mental nod, but sudden confused feelings rose up in him. Why did she feel like she could not tell any of them this? Why did she feel like she could not tell *him*? "So, anything to say for yourself about this Celeste?" Sasha asked, a bit huffily. Ander turned towards her with a bit of a glare, "Sasha! She probably has good reasons!" Sasha gave him a surprised look, and a brief flash of hurt brushed across her face. Celeste placed her hands between her legs, hanging her head. "Thanks Ander. But, well as for my reasons. I have two. First, if my true station was found out as I traveled, that could cause problems. Daughter of the head general of the Coronus army in another country? They would think I was there for espionage or something. Second...well I just wanted to be treated liked a normal person, you know?"

Klin nodded. "I understand. Joseph and I were never really afforded that either." Joseph nudged her, "Like hesh we do. You should count yourself lucky you had the chance. Still waiting for mine." Ander smiled as he quickly put in, "Y-yeah! I mean, being treated like a noble must suck!" Celeste just stared at him. "You saying my life sucked?"

"Wait, no! That's not--!" Celeste just smiled and laughed, "Oh lighten up Ander! I'm just teasing." Ander smiled weakly, his heart still thumping from that brief scare. "Yeah, of course. Heh." Sasha gave Celeste a dirty look, one that was not unnoticed by Ander. "So mister, what is so special about your base?" Kyoko asked. Beppo smiled at her, "Glad you asked young miss. The thing about it, if one speaks the name without someone wanting to bring them there, they forget."

"What?! How is that even possible?" Klin asked. Beppo leaned forward with a smile. "Magic tredos."

"Hah!" Erok snorted, "There's no such spell! If so, we would have records."

"Ahh, shut the hesh up!" Joshua snapped, "Goes for the rest of you too. Let the man explain you yapping crikets. Ya need to open yer minds more! Just because you haven't heard about it in some tight-necked academic report don't mean it don't exist. Reason we call most scientific laws discoveries and not inventions." Beppo gave him a respectful nod. "This is true. He speaks wisdom on occasion."

"Ahh, shut it Calist. I never speak wisdom. Those damn fireflies make it too noisy to think." Joshua retorted. Beppo just shook his head, "As I said, on occasion. Now, let me tell you more tredos. We know not how this spell came to be, so do not ask for I hold not the answers. We do know however that about five hundred years ago, Jethro Markus gathered a small group of Coronus's best Weavers and worked with them to cast it. This was when Coronus was about to go to war with Turmaky for the, hmmmm...I think third? No! Fifth time it was." Joseph and Klin exchanged a knowing look with one another. "Ah, that is right!" Beppo exclaimed, "You two are his sons! That is why you are even here!" Klin and Joseph then shot their uncle a nasty look.

"What?" Joshua asked. "I just said yer my nephews. He already knew who married my sis."

"That's true." Lorelei put in, "And might I add this? I have kept your lineage a secret because of the danger at home. I think at this point you boys can proclaim it openly now. The enemy already knows. There is no longer reason to keep it hidden." Kyoko suddenly leapt in her seat. "Yeah! I think it's a good idea! I know I would if I had him for a dad!" Ander felt a sharp pain in his chest. Everyone but Lorelei and himself had missed the hidden malice in her voice. "Wait just a damn minute." Joshua began, "Something's wrong." Ander just shook his head but stopped. Something was wrong. "Where's that blue herder Nathaniel?"

"Calm down uncle." Joseph answered casually, "He's just out getting supplies for us."

"Why?" Beppo asked confused, "You will all be my guests! You will not want for comfort while with me." Lorelei crossed her arms and glared at Joshua, "Well, that might have been nice to know." Joshua turned bright red, "Well, uh you know how I like my surprises." Lorelei stood up and began to walk away. "Yes, I know."

"Shit, hold on sis!" Joshua cried as he went after her. Ander cocked his head in confusion, but Klin just shook his head. "Later."

"Anyway," Beppo said, "I heard we need to leave as soon as possible. So, how does this afternoon at three sound?"

"Do we really get much of a say?" Joseph asked.

"No," Beppo smirked, "I just like to be polite." Ander shrugged, "Well, that still gives us about three hours. Should be more than enough time-wait. You guys hear that?"

"Hear what?" Celeste asked. Ander blushed. Right. Enhanced hearing. He continued speaking though. "It sounds like a group of men arguing. There's now a scuffle of feet and some shouting. My hearing's been improved." Erok raised an eyebrow. "You're kidding right? No one's hearing is this good." Klin tapped Erok on the should and then held his palm out, summoning light, fire, and lightening in quick succession. Erok went bright red while Joseph snickered. "Wait, they're coming in!" Ander declared. At that moment, the door to the inn was flung open once again. "Oi! Be careful with my herking door!" The owner shouted as twelve brawny men decked out in weaponry walked in. "Alright," the lead man shouted. He had a bald head and a long nose. "Which one of you milk drinker's is this criminal's traveling group?!" The men behind him parted to reveal a very badly beat Nathaniel carried with them. "Aw herk." Erok cursed, "These guys are mercs."

"You sure?" Ander whispered. Erok nodded, "Yeah. They each got a silver medal across their waist. Sure sign there."

"Speak up and we won't hurt ya!" The mercenary continued, "Don't fight back and he lives!"

"Are you herking kidding me?" Celeste grumbled, "He got caught that fast?" Joseph looked over at her with a level stare, "I'm more concerned at how fast they got accurate wanted posters." He said as he pointed to the piece of paper they held. On it was no longer Klin, Joseph, and Nathaniel, but the others as well. "I'll take care of them." Klin whispered sharply but was pushed back down by Beppo. Gentle, but firmly. "Do not worry tredos, I will take care of this one."

"We ain't gonna wait forever!" The leader cried angrily. "Calm down you louts!" Beppo shouted jovially as he walked over to them, "You are disturbing the nice peace here." The mercenaries all burst out laughing. "You want yer ass beat?" One of them shouted. Beppo put a hand to his chest. "Now that's just rude tredos! Did I even threaten you?"

"What do you want smartass?" Their leader growled. Beppo gave them a charming smile "I wish to make you an offer. How much is the reward for bringing him in?"

"10,000 emeraldas." The leader grunted, "And 40,000 if we bring in the rest of them. You'll have to fight all twelve of us for him." The other men began to jeer and leer menacingly. Beppo sighed, "My, do you always think with your biceps? I said I want to make an offer! What if I gave you eighty thousand for him? That's twice what you would get for all them." The mercenaries began to mumble excitedly, and a greedy glint came in their leader's eyes. But his eyes narrowed in suspicion. "What would you get out of this?"

"Well," Beppo explained, "He and his companions are under my protection, and I assure you, I can pay that amount." Beppo snapped his fingers and one of his men ran over. "Do you know what this is?"

"A bank voucher." The merc snapped, "I'm not an idiot." Beppo nodded, "Of course not. Just had to make sure. Now, take this to the city's bank and ask them to pay you. Tell them Beppo Calist sent you." The mercenary suddenly turned deathly pale. "Yo-you're Beppo Calist?" Beppo bowed, "In the flesh tredo." The merc snapped his fingers and his men dropped Nathaniel, looking far less confident than they had a few seconds ago. "He's all yours sir!" The leader said in a panic, "I'm so sorry! We didn't realize they were under your protection! Come on men, there's better ones out there!" They all piled out as if the inn were on fire. Ander started, frozen in awe at what he had just seen. Klin thought leapt over to Nathaniel's side. "Can someone go get my mom?" Kyoko flew away, "I got it!" Soon enough, both Lorelei and Joshua were back. Lorelei rushed over to Nathaniel's side and began to heal him. "Huh, guess you must have quite the name, huh?" Erok asked. "Yes," Beppo replied, "Especially among mercenaries. They tend to know me quite well. I am surprised you have not though. You must have not been a very good one."

"Hey asshole!" Erok snapped, "I made quite a name for myself!"

"Erok…" Joshua warned. Beppo stood still for a moment. "My apologies," He said, "I meant not ill will, merely a joke. I have heard of you Erok Noson, even if you have not heard of me." Beppo gave him a low bow, "How about we share a drink on my ship as recompense?" Erok crossed his arms, "Fine."

"I'm glad we can have all these moments of solidarity." Klin snapped, "But how about we get back to why everyone's here?" Ander flinched involuntarily, his body shuddering at what that tone of voice implied. Sasha reached out and squeezed his hand, giving him a worried look. He smiled at her reassuringly and let out a deep sigh. It was okay. His father was not here. But, why was everyone just so damn pissed today? "What happened Nathaniel?" Klin asked.

"Damn mercenaries followed me back from the market." Nathaniel explained, "They jumped me right before I came in. Sorry, I'm not used to having to deal with this sort of stuff."

"Well, ya better." Joshua growled, "This is yer life now."

"Hey!" Klin cried angrily, "He's helped us a lot! Show some understanding!"

"Klin," his mother soothed, "calm down please."

"Yeah Klin," Erok said snidely, "Show some more of that garbage you like."

"Excuse me, what's that supposed to me?" Klin growled. Erok crossed his arms, "Come on, we gotta do this again? That stupid naivete shit you pull." Joseph leapt to his feet and grabbed Erok by the collar. "Don't attack my brother just because you don't like being an asshole." Joseph snapped. Erok just hung there casually, "Again? This always you're first response? To attack and threaten like an animal? Maybe you should be dealt like one!"

"Everyone! Please calm down!" Lorelei begged. "Yes, please stop this." Sasha implored. "Or what?" Erok asked, "You guys will compliment me into stopping? Appeal to my conscious? Newsflash, but that ain't how the world works! What are you going to do when you can't sweet talk someone down? When you meet someone who *likes* being what you condemn as evil you self-righteous pricks? Huh? What then moron?!" Joseph just growled and punched him in the face. Erok flew back a bit, rolling as he hit the ground. He wiped some blood from his mouth as he got up. "Finally! Been waiting for an excuse!" Erok leapt forward and punched Joseph in the gut. Soon enough the two were in a full on brawl. "Guys! Stop!" Sasha yelled. "Why?" Celeste asked, "That asshole needs this." Sasha whipped on Celeste. "What do you know about him you selfish bitch!" Celeste raised an eyebrow, "Oh, I'm the selfish one?!" Ander watched in shock as the group devolved into chaos. Celeste was dodging splashes of water from Sasha, slapping her face when she got close, while Klin and Joshua shouted at one another. Erok and Joseph continued to fight while Lorelei pleaded uselessly. Ander turned and saw Kyoko hiding under the table, trembling. "Guys, stop." He whispered. "I said stop!" He shouted, but no one listened. "I SAID STOP" Suddenly, everyone froze, looking at him. "WHAT ARE YOU ALL DOING?" Ander continued, "After all that we have been through together, now you want to turn on one another? You guys should be ashamed! We've literally fought back-to-back to keep each other alive! We finally have our end goal in sight, and now you want to argue and fight?" Everyone looked at one another, heads hung in shame. "The kid is right." Beppo said, "I am disappointed. I expect there to be better behavior, or you will face the same disciple my men do. Come, let us clean up this mess." The group nodded and set to work.

"Sorry about that." Joseph said. Erok waived a hand, "Don't worry, I deserved it." Sasha gave an awkward hug to a Celeste who looked like a drowned rat before drying her off. Klin and his uncle continued to glare at one another, before smiling. "Good work tredo." Beppo whispered to Ander, placing a hand on his shoulder. "A true man stops conflict. He does not create one." Ander smiled, his body feeling warm. That…felt really nice. Once they were finished, Beppo looked around and said, "Come! We must prepare." Joseph frowned. "For what?" Beppo shook his head. "Do you have the memory of an old man? To set sail of course!"

Chapter 29

The Sasara Archipelago

Klin leaned over the side of the *Water Maiden's* deck. The silvery light of the moon reflected one the clam surface of the ocean. The water was a vast as the plains and gave off ripples like the grass did. He let out a smile. That trip over the plains felt like years away now. Klin looked up at the moon, the color a testament to how long it had been since they left. It had been purple then. Beppo's ship cut across the waves smoothly though, like a ghost floating across the land. As he continued to stare into the heavens, the wind rustled his hair, and he wondered what was wrong with him. He had been feeling increasingly angry ever since their battel with Misha. But, he had a feeling that fight was what brought these feelings to surface. "Klin?"

"Oh, hey Nathaniel." Klin greeted softly, "What's up?" Nathaniel shrugged, "Not much. Figured I should check up on you. They have dinner done now." Klin hugged himself as he resumed leaning against the ship's railing. "I'm not hungry."

"Alright, what's wrong?"

"What? Nothing's wrong."

"Yes. It is. It's okay, you can trust me." Nathaniel said, placing a gentle hand on his shoulder. Klin sighed, "Okay. Well, you know how I basically started that fight back at the inn?"

"Yes. That was…unfortunate." Nathaniel replied awkwardly. "Hmph, yeah unfortunate." Klin grumbled, "But, well, I just—I don't know! I feel so angry at everyone and I don't know why!" Nathaniel nodded understandingly. "I see. Do you know when these feelings started." Klin looked at Nathaniel and began to ponder, "Huh, I think actually ever since we left your home."

"Why then?"

"Because maybe that's when everyone started to act stupid!" Klin exclaimed, "It feels like we are rushing to safety, but no real plan! There feels like so much that is still being kept from us too! Somethings still are not adding up!" Nathaniel nodded, "Sounds like you are just in being upset right now Klin. Have you asked them about it?" Klin frowned, "I think once."

"Then they are wrong to hide this from you." Nathaniel declared before leaning over and whispering. "I'd be skeptical. If they will not tell you, then they have a goal, one they are trying to manipulate you towards. They will make it seem like it was your idea, when it was theirs." Klin laughed, "Oh come on. That's just stupid."

"Is it? You told me that your mother and the old woman you studied under hid a great many things from you and your brother. And now that you know all these things, is it not clear that your path was decided for you a long time ago?" Nathaniel whispered in his ear, "You were talked to, but this plan was made without your knowledge." Klin paused. He was right. "Why do you trust them so much?" Nathaniel continued. Klin jumped a little, "Because they love me."

"Do they though?" Nathaniel asked. "Can you really be so certain of that fact? Would not they tell you everything if they loved you? Would not they have given you a *choice* if they truly love as they claim?" Klin waved his hand back in anger. "Shut up! What do you know?" Nathaniel though was unfazed by Klin's angry glare. Instead, pity and empathy shined in his face. "I can see that you are hurting. I see it clearly in your eyes. I know I really am the only one who has tried to help so far. I will go for now but think on this. Who are the ones truly hurting you? The ones pursuing you, or the ones you are with?" Nathaniel turned and walked away, leaving Klin grappling with statements that seemed too close too reality for his taste.

Ander smiled as Nathaniel sat down next to him. "How did it go?" Ander inquired. "Pretty well." Nathaniel replied with a smile, "He just needs a bit of time to himself, then he will be back to himself in no time." Ander let out a relieved sigh as he laid back, staring at the stars. "That's good, I was really starting to get worried." Ander yawned. Klin had had nothing to eat today, and Lorelei was too busy looking after Joseph's seasickness. "Well, I think I shall turn in for the night." Nathaniel said. Ander sat back up and waved him goodbye. As soon as he was out of earshot, Joshua, who sat across from their little fire, said in between his pipe, "I don't like him."

"Yes, we know." Celeste complained. Ander's heart skipped a beat as he remembered how close he was to her. A whole five feet away! "You never did say why you dislike him so much groga." Beppo asked through a pipe of his own. Joshua's eyes narrowed, "His hands are too red." Erok rolled his eyes, "Ugh, there he goes again! Old man's crazy."

"That may be, but I am not the one who followed his lead across the country." Beppo chuckled, "So who is crazier?" Erok crossed his arms, "We really didn't have much of a choice."

"Jabberwocky!" Joshua protested, "I gave you kids a choice!" Beppo elbowed him smiling, "But not much of a choice when one wants to do the right thing, eh?" Celeste began to giggle and smiled at Ander, "Guess you're the good one then huh?" Ander was glad for the firelight as his face went red. "Oh, yeah I guess then." There was a brief silence that settled about them, then Ander suddenly blurted out, "Beppo do you have a wife?"

"Bit of an intrusive question for someone you just met!" Beppo laughed. Ander hid his face. "Sorry." Beppo sat up a bit waving his hand, "Oh no tredo! No need to apologize! Kids your age are always thinking about love, are they not?"

"Are not!" Celeste protested. "We got more important things to worry about." Beppo raised an eyebrow, "Oh, like what?" Celeste crossed her arms, "Like maybe staying alive?" Beppo threw out his arms like an eagle, "But what is the use of being alive without love meardo?"

"Oh no, here he goes." Joshua groaned. Beppo ignored him and continued, riled up now. "Love is the most powerful force in the world! It has overcome armies, mountains, and even time itself! It is the greatest and most precious thing a human can hold within their heart! Love can create, and love can protect. It is what we humans were made for! To love and be loved!"

"Yeah, well not everyone has romance." Erok said dryly. Beppo raised an eyebrow. "And when did I speak or romance tredos? You young people always think when love is mentioned, that romantic love is the only kind. For shame! A pursuit of only romantic love will destroy you."

"And how can that be?" Ander asked confused, "Isn't romance a good thing?" Beppo puffed out a few smoke rings and nodded sagely. "It is. However, if you shut out all other kinds of love in your pursuit of it, you will find yourself devoid of any love." Ander, Celeste, and Erok exchanged skeptical looks with one another. "I mean, I don't know if you are wrong," Celeste said, "But this sounds overly poetic to be true."

"Hmm. I believe the true poets are the ones who see reality the most clearly." Beppo mused, "So I will take that as a compliment meardo. Maybe a song will help with my point." Joshua let out a groan, "Damn it kids. Just as I thought we'd get through the night without one." Celeste crossed her arms and gave Joshua a flat look. "You can leave you know."

"And miss Beppo's singing!" Joshua sputtered, "Like hesh I will!" Beppo smiled as he took out his ukulele. "See, I knew you always enjoyed my songs groga. This is a song though of man, and the lengths he went to pursue love." With that Beppo began to sing. His voice was just as rich and smooth as when he spoke, only now there was a deep hypnotic rhythm to his voice. Ander was held captive by the sound of his voice as he sang.

"My name shifts, swirling its own course.
Once bred I was serve blindly
Bred I was to envy dryly
Bred to fight and love all sin.
Soul of confliction
No love received.
Raised by one whom shuns
I called him father and he called me son,
But no love existed in that voice
Love I craved, Love I sought
Love nonexistent from the parent that begot.
Dark, stained, and bought was his soul
I abandoned the endeavor
Rebellion is my only joy.
A lover I sought to fill the gap,

One I found, or so I thought
The servant of the father, and his best.
Our love and joy, it could not last
For what is laid on lust can never be built.
Father, I rejected, my fate I carved into the face of death.
Flung was happiness into the past
Loyalty prevailed over carnal pleasure and hate conquered my
own loyalty
Son I was no more!
My name shifts over sands of time
Its course changed by a flimsy wind
Made by a choice born of hate!
Once I betrayed the creature who made me, I am foe
Hunted I flee, stronger I grow
Death I will bring to thee.
Love will be won back
Love that I crave!
Is it just, is it black?
The soul conflicts
But it matters to me not,
His demise is my only quest, no room for love in this blackened
heart
And if I am evil, he its essence.
The son should surpass the father, and fate take its course.
I see many paths, a test
Any I choose, I am led back
To you, a fate worse than death.
As I give breaths, love abreast of me
Love devoid in me
Arrogance and hate my only truth.

Beppo finished, posing dramatically with one hand on his ukulele, the other in the air. "Wow, that was beautiful." Ander whispered breathlessly. "Who's it about though?" Erok asked. Beppo shrugged. "I do not know. It is an ancient song, one composed during the War of the Sculptors. Some say it is a man who joined Romevan, others a leader during a civil war. Either way, the author remained anonymous when he wrote it, so we many never know. Yet all agree his fall is tragic."

I guess you were right then." Celeste said softly, "Love is powerful in both directions. Whether you are overflowing with it, or because you don't have an ounce of it within you." Beppo grinned, "I'm pleased my lesson was not lost. Now, it is late and sweet dreams beckon me. I suggest you head their siren call as well. Good night tredos!"

"Good night captain!" Ander waved. Joshua leaned back, stretching out. "You kids should get to bed. We'll be at the haven early tomorrow." Erok frowned, "Wait, we're headed somewhere in the Sasara Archipelago right?" Joshua nodded. "Okay, so then we should still have two more days left. Joshua gave them a sly smile, and got up, walking away. "You kids need to pay better attention. Look closely tomorrow then." As he went into the cabin, he left the three puzzled. "Magic?" Ander asked. "Probably." Erok admitted. It was a wonderful world they lived in.

Chapter 30

The Island of Paradox

Klin awoke to the ringing of a bell, blurrily opening his eyes. He rolled over in his hammock, looking out the window. It was barely morning. The rose tint that dawn brings was not even showing. It was still mostly dark out. It was that strange time between light and dark, but the bell kept going off. *Okay, what is going on?* Klin thought annoyed. He threw himself out of bed and stumbled out the room. As he climbed from the first lower level and onto the deck, the bell stopped. He looked around in annoyance. As soon as he gets here, the stupid thing stops. He looked around and found Beppo at the helm with a grim look on his face. "Hey, what's going on?" Klin asked as he climbed up next to him.

"Turmakian ship." Beppo replied, "And a warship at that. Things my get ugly tredo." Klin shrugged, suddenly very awake. "Eh, I'll be fine." Beppo gave him a sly smile. "Really? You do not look very intimidating at the moment." Klin looked down, realizing he was still in his pajamas, shoeless and weaponless at the moment. "I still got magic." He mumbled; his face warm. Beppo chuckled, "Might want to use it to fix that bedhead then." Klin felt his face get warmer as he uselessly tried to get his hair to lay down. "Martin!" Beppo shouted, "Go below and make sure our guests stay there please!"

"What about Rickstone sir?" A short stocky man shouted back. "I'm already here." Joshua growled as he emerged from below. "But I'd say the others will be trying to come up, so ya better lock the door, Marty." Martin looked over at Beppo who nodded before running off to do that. "What about me?" Klin asked. Joshua came over next to them. "Kid, yer the only one I trust to *not* screw things up. Even if yer hair does look like a rat's nest." Klin crossed his arms. Why was everyone picking on his appearance today? "Captain, we we're next to 'em now!" A sailor shouted. Beppo nodded and handed the helm to Joshua, who began to grin like a little kid. "Uhhh, should you be handing that to him?" Klin asked. Beppo nodded, "He can't do much damage. Do not worry so much." With that, Beppo walked down to the deck, while Klin scanned around. There was a thick fog that lay about the sea. Suddenly, he saw the ship. On their starboard side was a ship half the size of the *Water's Maiden*. It had two sails instead of the four on theirs, and only had one lower level, while Beppo's ship had six, making it so they towered over the ship. The wood of the ship was painted red, expect for the deck which had blues, oranges, and yellows all bleeding into another, making it seems as if the crew walked atop fire. A golden flag with a blue, eight-pointed star in the midst of a red flame hung from the top of the ship. It was Turmaky alright.

"Hello there!" Beppo called. "Is there anyone aboard I may speak to?" A man with dark pink hair and a heavy beard walked to the edge. "That'd be me." The man called back in rough common. "I'm the captain. I trust so you are also?" Beppo nodded. "Yes my friend, and unfortunately I must ask you a few questions before letting you go." The captain stiffened but began to laugh. "Stop us? Ye have done nothing of such." Klin tensed up himself, touching his fire source. Beppo leaned against the railing, looking down at the ship with a steely calm look. "Maybe it seems that way. However, I have seven Oceani down below, messing with the current to keep you in place. Then there are three Halnie who have taken the wind out of your sails." The captain became visibly pale and began to shake. Klin grinned, until the man screamed, and he realized he was not trembling out of fear.

"How dare ye do this?" The man yelled, shaking his fist at them. "What right have ye?!"

"Now, now." Beppo clucked, "That's a very uncalled for reaction, especially for a man in foreign waters with a warship. I'm merely doing my job in the C.L.S." The man fell silent as Beppo continued. "Well, I see you understand the situation now. So, tell me your name and why there is a warship in Coronian waters." The captain kept silent, only staring at Beppo. "Come now tredo, I'll have to take your ship if you do not answer!"

"My name is Dratnit." The captain spat, "As for our business, that is for us alone." Beppo frowned, straightening up, one hand on his scythe. "Listen Dratnit, tensions between our countries are not good right now. We simply need to know why you are here, and then you can be on your way! Do not do anything that would worse the tensions 'friend.'"

"You dare threaten me?" Dratnit scowled. "We are mighty Turmaky! You do not scare us!" Beppo patted his hammer. "I should. Now, explain." Dratnit turned to a man beside him and began to whisper something in his ear. The man nodded, and red threads appeared in the air beside him. "Fire ball!" Klin warned. Klin leapt in front of Beppo, firing one of his own. The two meet and burst into sparks. "Now that was the exact *opposite* of what you should've done." Joshua shouted. Beppo nodded at the captain and said, "I will mourn your souls tonight. May they find peace." At that moment, seven large pillars of water shot up around the Turmakian ship and crashed down upon them. Klin heard faint screams amidst the loud cracking and splitting of wood. Once the water resumed its normal level, there was no sign of the ship. Klin went to stand by his uncle, a feeling of horror within. "Why…"

"Because war is brutal." Joshua answered softly, "We try to help, but people make their choices in the end. Ain't nothing we can do about that." Klin shook his head, "This fells wrong though." Joshua nodded, "Death does that to ya. It was self-defense though." Klin glared at his uncle, "But they still died!" Joshua handed the helm back to Beppo, "And what would you have done? Sacrifice some of yer men to take them alive? Those Turmakians would have had no reservations about killing our men." Klin bowed his head. It felt wrong, but his uncle had a point. "Yeah, well I still don't have to like it." Beppo chuckled softly, "At philosopher this one is. Just like his father and uncle. Let me allay your troubled mind my friend. Killing others is an evil, but there is not always personal moral guilt for it. We must simply do our best to navigate the evil present." Joshua laid a hand on Klin's shoulder. "World's imperfect nephew, so sometimes the best choice ain't really the best." Joshua patted his head, ruffling his hair before walking way. "Now can someone get me some booze?"

"Land in sight!" Klin jolted awake as the lookout shouted it again. He was back in his cabin, having decided to take a nap after all that had happened in the morning. He stretched out and rolled out of the hammock. He changed into his day clothes, and then washed his hair and face. Suddenly, the bell began to ring in a rhythmic interval. One, two, three, gong! One, two, three, gong! He headed topside and found most of the others already up there. "Morning Klin!" Kyoko greeted. He smiled, waving back at her while shielding his eyes from the sunlight. "Morning Kyoko." He took a deep breath as the salty sea air brushed across his face. "Morning sleepyhead." He turned and saw his mother walking towards him. "Hey, I was up early!" He protested, "I was just up *too* early is all." Lorelei smiled and squeezed him in a hug. "Oh, alright. I'll let it pass. This time. It is almost eleven." Klin let out a small whistle, and then stopped as Joshua walked by. "Wait, Uncle you said we would be there really early today!" Joshua looked over his shoulder at him and shrugged. "Not accounting for enemy warships. We'll be there soon now."

Klin shook his head as Joshua went and sat with Erok and Ander. "Where's Celeste and Sasha at?" He asked. "Well, Celeste is with Joseph." Lorelei explained. "Poor thing is still seasick. I could only help so much. As for Sasha, she's down below tending to Debo." Klin nodded. The owlbear had been neglected as of late. "Ah, good! You are up!" Beppo called from above. Klin looked up to see Beppo sliding down a rope from the Crow's Nest. "I'll need you to tie secure yourselves with this." Beppo said, handing them some very thick rope. Klin frowned, "Uh, why?"

"Things are about to get rough tredo." Beppo explained as he began to help Klin tie himself. Lorelei had already gotten herself secured and he could see her using magic to get the others. "You see that island?" Beppo asked, pointing to the horizon. Klin squinted and could just make out a large island out in the distance. "Yeah?"

"You will not for long."

"What do you—" Crack! The sky became intensely dark after a bolt of lightning flashed across it. The dark was as thick as soup and it began to pour down rain with thunder and lighting danced about. "What the herk happened?" Klin yelled. "Later!" Beppo yelled back with a wacky smile. Was he enjoying this?! "Alright men! You know the drill!" Beppo shouted and began giving out orders. "Oceanani! Shields up!" Pillars of water rose up around the ship, barely above the railings. "Overhead winds now!" Klin looked up and saw a barrier of wind over them. A bolt of lightning struck at them but was veered away as it hit the barrier. Klin still felt his ears ringing though. "Derik!" Beppo shouted at the helmsman, "Guide us home!"

Yes captain!" The ship suddenly turned hard starboard. Klin grunted as he was dueenly in danger of falling into the sea. Despite all the protection they had, the ship was still being battered and tossed about. As a wave hit, Klin slipped and lost his grip. "Shit!" He yelled as he fell over the railing. Just as he was about to hit the water, the ship turned hard port. His jerked, leaving him slightly breathless as he was pulled back over. Klin went flying back and was suddenly lying on the deck. "Ow." He wheezed, "That was not fun." His stomach and back hurt now. Someone grabbed him and propped him up. "See why I had you tie down?" Beppo asked over the noise. Klin nodded. "Yeah, thanks." Beppo slapped him on the shoulder, "No problem kiddo. Now, we should be safe." As if on command, the rain suddenly stopped and the storm vanished without a trace. Even their wet clothes were dry once more. "What the—" Beppo just grinned and gestured towards the island in front of them. They were closing in on a giant port. At least ten ships were docked there, with room for another twenty ships at the least. "Welcome to the C.L.S.'s home!" Beppo declared proudly, "The island of Solanthis, or as it is also known, the Island of Paradox. The Island you must have been to, to be able to get to."

Chapter 31

Sanctuary

"Thank the Eight!" Joseph cried, "Solid land!" Celeste shook her head and elbowed him lightly. "Could you really not handle the ship that well?"

"You try having a sensitive stomach." Joseph grumbled. Celeste just grinned as the followed the crew off the dock. The sea air had begun to mix with the island's vegetation, giving off a smell Celeste could only describe as tropic. She had never seen such a place though before. Despite being in the middle of fall, the temperature was nice and warm. The air still had some humidity, but it was not overwhelming. In fact, it was quite pleasant. Many of the trees had big, wide leaves with fruit hanging from many of their branches. "Follow me tredos!" Beppo shouted, waving his hands. "It is easy to lose oneself here!" They left the dock and found themselves passing under a stone gate. Through it was an expansive city. The streets bustled with activity. People walked about through the seemingly random maze of streets, each alley and street connecting in a weird crisscross of confusing layout. As they let Beppo navigate them through the confusion, she heard Klin call out. "Hold on, not everyone here is a soldier."

Sure enough, mothers and fathers walked the streets with their children by their sides. "Ah, yes I suppose that would seem strange to you." Beppo explained, "You see, being a part of the C.L.S. means intense commitment. We built this city here long ago. Half our life is on the sea, and you almost never can return to mainland. So, we bring our families here. The sea is no place for raising children. But, being one of us should not require that sort of sacrifice, no?" Erok nodded, "That makes sense. It's actually kind of beautiful that you guys do this."

"Yeah," Klin agreed, smiling, "It really is." Celeste smiled as she watched all the people simply *living*. "Mommy, mommy! Look at the pretty lady!" Celeste spun around to see a little girl jumping up and down, pointing at her. "Hi pretty lady!" Celeste smiled, waving back. The mother let out a tired sigh but waved back at Celeste. "She's got good eyes." Joseph whispered. "What?" Celeste asked startled. Joseph jumped himself. "Huh? I didn't say nothing."

"Really? I could have sworn—"

"Nope. Nothing."

"So where are we headed?" Ander asked. "I can't make sense of this path you are taking us through." Beppo cast a smile back at him. "Ahh, you are sharp my friend! If the layout of the city seems confusing, well it was intentional. In case of attack, we have the advantage, no?"

"I'll say." Sasha cried, "This place is the most confusing layout I've ever seen! I've been in caves that make more sense!" Erok frowned, "When have you been in caves? I thought the bugs in there made you squeamish?" Sasha turned bright red, "Well, I went exploring with Kyo one day. She insisted and Ander was...tied up with his father."

"Yeah!" Kyoko piped, "Sasha and I had so much fun though! You should have been there Erok! The cave was huge! And we found this nest of massive spiders!" Sasha shuddered and placed a hand on Kyoko, "Yeeeah. Can we not talk about that please?" Erok started to laugh. "Wait, didn't you drown them all immediately?" Ander asked, "And then Kyo had to stop some sort of monster spider cause you nearly passed out from the sight?" Erok just began to laugh even harder as Sasha hung her head, face bright red now. "What kind of spiders?" Klin asked curiously. "Oh, they were morthan spiders!" Kyoko replied perkily. Celeste winced at that one. Those things could grow to reach waist level. Not sure she could blame Sasha for her reaction. Although, they were actually quite friendly towards humans. They did not kill humans, and if they did, they never ate them. So, they would have been fine if she had not killed the babies. "Anyway," Erok said to Beppo after his laughter had subsided, "How often have you guys had to defend this place?"

"No once." Beppo replied. "In the entire history, or just under your leadership?" Joseph asked. "Never. In our entire history." Beppo said solemnly. "This is why it is such a safe place for you. The unique nature of the place is to thank."

"You alluded to that earlier." Lorelei said, "You called it a paradox. Why?" Beppo grinned, "Ah, so many questions! Well, to begin you must have been to this island to get here in the first place! Those who have never been can never reach here! That storm that appeared, it was strange, no? That is because it protects the island. Only those who have been here can navigate through it. No amount of luck can get you through it. The winds blow and the currents change, all to redirect you. The storm does not appear to those who have been here, so it has been a while since we have experienced it." Beppo chuckled. Joseph scratched his head, "So, you said our dad is responsible for it?"

"Forgive me, but I had to lie." Beppo apologized, "You see, we have another island that is a small base. That one was built by your father, with many a useful protective spell, and well known. Any who could overhear us cannot know about Solanthis. No, he did not cast the spell over this island. We think it is a remnant from the War of the Sculptors. For over two thousand years this island remained unmapped. Now only Coronus has accurate maps, and even then, it is only select few."

"Hold on." Joseph asked, "If this place was undiscovered, and the spell has been on it for who knows how long, how in Heshtanus did you guys get here?" Beppo shrugged, "Unknown. We have no real idea."

"An-and you're not bothered by that?" Klin asked bewildered. "Nope." Beppo answered cheerfully, "Who cares how? We have it now, no? Sometimes you should just accept the oddities of life." Klin was shaking his head and mumbling to himself. Celeste sighed. Looked like someone was going to lose sleep tonight. As they got closer to what Celeste assumed was the center of town though, the ground began to slope steeply. At the top of the hill, looming over all the other buildings in the city was a temple. It was built with marble that was a cool blue. Four pillars and a roof with stained glass windows were all she could make of it from her current position. "What's that temple up there?" She asked.

"That tredos," Beppo said quietly but firmly, "is something we are not allowed to talk about. I will say this though. That temple was here before we built this city."

"What's so special about it?" Erok asked, "It's just a building." Beppo nodded, "Ay, that it is. But there is something in there, guarded so well any who have gone in to get it have never returned." Celeste felt a chill run down her spine, despite the warmth outside. "Not true!" Joshua snorted, "At least one person has to have come out for ya to know! I know ya know what it is Calist!" Beppo laughed, "That is true my inebriated friend! And if the Crown found out I told you, well I would have my head lopped off like that!" Joshua just laughed, "Ahhh come on! We know that fancy fop wouldn't have it in him! Besides, I'm sure he would've told me at some point." Celeste punched Joshua in the arm. "Excuse me!" She cried indignantly, "Did you just call the most noble man in Coronus a *fop*?!"

Joshua rubbed his arm. "Damn kid, you hit like a paradox." Beppo stepped over to them with a disarming smile. "Do not be too offended meardo. Your loyalty to his majesty is admirable, but this groga has good authority to poke fun at our loveable emperor." Everyone looked at him in bewilderment. "You have got to be kidding." Ander said. Lorelei let out a sigh, "He does. Sculptors know how he ended up having it, but he does." Kyoko's hand suddenly shot up. "Oh, oh! I know! It's because he's crazy!"

"Shut it kid!" Joshua snapped, but his eyes held a twinkle and a barley hidden grin was on his face. "I ain't crazy! I'm unbalanced!" With that, he fell flat on his face. Everyone laughed as Klin helped him back up. Joshua pushed his hat back into place, said with dread, "Damnit. Guess I should've had less to drink." He then winced, which made everyone laugh even harder. "Oh great." Sasha moaned, "He's already drunk."

"And I fight better this way!" Joshua declared, spreading his arms out wide. "First thing we're doing we when get to this place issssss training!" Everyone groaned, except Beppo who let out a boisterous laugh. "You young'ins have no appreciation for hard work anymore." Joshua complained. "It's not that." Klin protested, "We were just hoping to have a moment to rest now that we have finally reached our destination."

"Eh, rest and you'll get soft and pudgy." Erok said with a shrug. Sasha raised an eyebrow at him. "Uh, don't act like you don't want this Erok. I saw you clench your fists."

"Well at least I'm not voicing my complaints." Erok shot back. Klin sighed, "C'mon Erok, really?" Erok and Klin began to shoot daggers at one another. "Alright, everyone calm down." Lorelei said soothingly, "I'll have a nice meal for everyone once you are done." Joseph rolled his shoulders. "Now that sounds like a deal! What are we waiting for?" Beppo looked over his shoulder and gave them a sly smile. "Oh no." Celeste moaned, "You and that crackpot planned something." Beppo placed a hand over his heart and cried dramatically, "What? How could you suspect such a thing from me?" Joshua muttered something under his breath, and swatted at the air in front of him. "Ahh, ya'll see soon enough."

Yep, soon enough they reached the top of the hill. At the crest was a wall made of white stone with an iron gate. Men walked around, but surprisingly there were no guards. The gate was up, so they just walked in. To their immediate left and right were large sands pits, with rocks outlining many different arenas in them. Some archers were practicing in the distance, past another gate to the left. A large building lay near back of the wall in front of them. That building was very large, spanning almost the entirety of the wall at three hundred feet and then another two hundred feet out towards them in width. Past the wall to their right though was the Temple. The cool blue stone did not really reflect the sunlight, instead almost seeming to absorb it, giving off a serene and water like feel in both color and texture. "Alright tredos!" Beppo proclaimed, "Let's get started!" Everyone let out a reluctant affirmation. Kyoko raised her hand and looked at Beppo. "Uh, before we do, can I ask you something?"

"Of course, mearda." Beppo replied sweetly. Kyoko put a hand to her chin. "I've just been wondering, what are the words you keep saying?" Beppo smiled. "Well, the one I just called you, mearda, means little girl. It is my native language. You see, I am from Zalcath" Kyoko titled her head, "Oh! Okay! What about tredos?"

"My friends, is what it roughly translates to. Meardo means young miss about." Beppo explained. Klin frowned, "What about the one you keep calling our uncle?" Beppo's face fell, a tinge of sadness on his face. "That one…I will tell you that one another time, yes? Along with where I come from, sound good?" Celeste began bouncing on the balls of her feet excitedly. "Sure. Let's train though." Beppo laughed, "Very well meardo!" He went over and grabbed some wooden weapons and handed them out. "Hold on," Klin said, staring at the wooden staff he had been given. "This isn't my expertise." Celeste suppressed a smile. She had figured out what was going on the moment Beppo had handed her a dagger. "Not yet it isn't." Beppo replied, "So far you have been training in the basics of one weapon. However, in the life you will lead, the weapon you want will not always be on hand. You must use what you can." Erok looked at his spear and lifted it. "Eh, this can't be too hard."

"Man, why do I have to use a rapier?" Joseph complained loudly. "Cause yer a brutish lout." Joshua growled. Everyone laughed, while Joseph just made shoeing motions at them. "So, each weapon is to compliment out normal fighting style?" Ander asked. Beppo nodded, "More or less. Makes you think in different ways in combat. Now, I'll split you up and have my men drill you in basics. Then, comes the fun part!" So, they followed the instructions. Klin and Sasha with staffs, Joseph by himself with his rapier, Kyoko and Erok with spears, Ander with a battle-axe, and finally Celeste with her daggers. They drilled, going over basics again and again. Celeste though was doing some mental games. Her father had been very through in his training, which meant she was above basics with daggers. Forcing herself to act like a novice was difficult. *Why don't you just show them your skill?* Yatta asked while her instructor showed her how to parry. *Because then they'll start asking more questions.* Celeste explained. *But Joseph already knows.* Yatta replied, *And you let them know before we got here. What worries you?* Celeste let out an inner sigh. *I'd rather they think I'm a bit of a loser Yatta. They know my lineage, but they don't need to know how much of a failure I really am. I'm never going to be able to step out of my sister's shadow. I'd rather they think I'm some sort of loser. It's what I am.* Yatta stayed silent, but Celeste could sense her disapproval, and her confusion. That was okay though, she was used to not measuring up to people's expectations by now.

After three hours, Beppo called them all back to him. "Excellent work tredos!" He praised, "Now for the real test! Who wishes to fight me first?"

"Awww, hesh yeah!" Joseph cried cracking his neck and stepped forward. He was about to grab a great sword from one of the nearby weapon racks, but Beppo stopped him. "Ah-ah-ah! Use your rapier." Joseph mumbled some creative curses before taking a fighting stance with the rapier. "He's going to get his ass whooped." Kyoko stated cheerfully. Joshua let out a chuckle while Klin and Celeste smiled at one another. Oh, he was so dead. Beppo picked up a wooden hammer and tied a pouch around his waist. Then he grabbed a wooden sickle, which he let hang from his belt. "Alright Joseph, come!"

Joseph leapt forward with a half-shout, half laugh. He slashed aggressively as Beppo dodged it. Joseph stumbled as he missed, so Beppo rapped his knuckles with his hammer. Joseph yelped and dropped the rapier. "Tsk, you wasted too much energy there." Beppo scolded, but he had a twinkle in his eye that said he was trying not to laugh at him. "Who's next?"

"Oi! I'm not done yet!" Joseph cried as he scooped his weapon back up. Joseph charged at Beppo, leaping upwards for a strike. Celeste watched in amazement as Beppo quickly pulled a wooden marble from his pouch, threw them in the air and hit one with his hammer. It darted through the air like an arrow and hit Joseph square in the forehead. He fell to the ground unconscious. "Boy's too damn arrogant." Joshua muttered, "Alright, who's next?"

"Shit." Klin muttered and raised his hand, trudging out to the field while Joshua lifted Joseph from it. Klin lasted longer than Joseph, but he was far more cautious. In the end though, the result was the same as the previous match; he was soundly beat by Beppo. Joseph had regained conscious quickly, and so was making jabs at Klin as he walked back, holding his forehead. Sasha went next and barely lasted twenty seconds. It was clear to Celeste that she had never had any sort of weaponry training. She shook her head. Weavers should never rely purely on their magic. Erok went after. His proficiency with the spear surprised her. He showed a lot of ingenuity by not being afraid to use what some considered underhanded techniques. He would throw sand up using the butt of his spear or make like he was going to throw the spear, but would not, causing Beppo to be caught off guard. He almost one too when he finally threw the spear, but Beppo regained his composure and caught the spear. Erok simply held his hands out in a shrug and walked off. Kyoko went next but was quickly disqualified for using magic. She walked off sulking. Then it was Ander's turn. Celeste crossed her arms. This was probably going to be the most pathetic match.

Ander turned and gave her a soft smile. Celeste simply made some sort of disgruntled sound. "Alright tredo" Beppo said gently, his voice warm and comforting. "Just give this your best shot."

"Alright." Ander replied. Celeste perked up, catching the confidence in his voice. Ander planted his feet and swung, almost falling over as Beppo dodged. He surprised Celeste though as he regained footing, but kept the momentum going, turning it into a spinning horizontal attack. Beppo just barely avoided that one before smacking Ander in the face with the hammer. Before he could recover and reorient himself, Beppo hit his stomach, making him double over and collapse. "A bold move young one." Beppo said gently, helping Ander back to his feet slowly. "But you were too slow with your reaction speed. You must improve with that! Do that, you will be a formidable foe indeed!"

"Okay." Ander nodded. For once the pathetic kid did not seem discouraged, but hopeful. Celeste cocked her head, a sudden thought popping into her head. Why did she hate Ander so much? By all means, he was an incredibly kind and sweet person. Why did she ignore that part? "Alright, last one." Beppo said jovially, "Then we can all go eat!" Joseph let out a whoop. "Yeeeah! Kick his ass though Celeste!" Celeste smiled, blushing somewhat. "I'll try, but no promises."

If you win, you can prove *you made it to her level.* A small voice in the back of her head whispered. Celeste ignored it though. That was an impossible task for her skill, and she knew it. She would not be able to win this fight. "Let's go!" Beppo yelled. Celeste nodded and leapt forward, not giving Beppo time to pull out those marbles. Soon as he did, this fight was over. Just because she knew she was going to lose did not mean she wasn't going to give it her all though. Beppo blocked her flurry of strikes, but surprise flashed across his face for a brief second. Beppo twisted his hammer, weaking her grip on one of her daggers.

Celeste pulled back before he could force her to drop it. Beppo quickly pulled out some marbles after she retreated. *Shit.* She thought as she ducked down, wooden marbles whizzing overhead. She rolled forward as three more marbles flew at her. As she came up from the roll, she deflected some marbles off the blades. "Whoa!" Joseph cheered, "That was herking awesome! Keep it up!"

Beppo gave her a smile and unleashed a hailstorm of those stupid marbles. Celeste was able to either dodge or deflect them, slowly closing the distance between them. Finally, she got close enough that he stopped, pulling out his sickle instead. He swung down at her with both. Celeste managed to lock her daggers, blocking him. Yet, Beppo was a lot stronger than her. It was all she could do to stop him from falling on her. If she disengaged, he would hit her. Celeste glanced down at his stance. It was uneven! Celeste quickly hooked her foot around his ankle and pulled it out from under him. Beppo fell with a surprised cry. She then quickly knocked his grip loose on the sickle with one hand, and with the other freed the hammer. He fell to the ground hard, so she pounced on him, daggers to the throat before he could get up. Beppo laughed at her. "Well, well! Looks like we had a fox hiding amongst the sheep!

"Wow!" Klin said excitedly, "That was an incredible display of skill you two!"

"Thanks." Celeste replied bashfully as she helped Beppo up. She had actually beat him! But that small voice began to whisper again. *Selene would have done it faster. This doesn't prove anything.* "I don't know if you could have done any better!" Sasha praised. Celeste felt her heart drop, all her excitement fading. Yeah, this was her limit, wasn't it? Celeste just nodded, plastering a smile on her face, not really feeling like talking. "Alright, let's go eat now!" Erok declared. They went over to the building, talking excitedly over what they had learned. Celeste hung back, trailing behind the others. Suddenly Joseph stopped and walked with her. "You okay?" He asked. Celeste plastered another smile on. "Yeah, of course." Joseph stayed silent, frowning. "You're lying." He finally said, "But, I won't push it for now. We can talk when you're ready." Celeste jumped in surprise at his insight. Joseph hurried back to the others before she could say anything though. She shook her head.

Sometimes that man was a mystery. "Don't be too proud to belittle yerself." Joshua said quietly. Celeste nearly screamed. Had he been behind her the whole time?! "What the herk is that supposed to mean?" Celeste demanded. "It means what I said." Joshua replied gruffly, "Clean those branches from yer ears. They usually have termites in them." With that he walked off. She crossed her arms. Crazy old man. Yet, his words did bother her. The bid about belittling herself. The branches talk was stupid. His words stayed in her head as she joined the others, pondering over them the whole time they ate.

Chapter 32

The Daily Routine

Ander stretched, letting out a loud yawn as he blearily blinked away his sleep. His arms were sore enough that they hurt to move, and his legs bore some bruises from those wooden marbles. They had spent another three hours training after they had eaten. By the time they were done, the sun had set. Ander was so weary by the end of it that he ate with the others, and went straight to bed once he had been shown his room. Ander rolled out of bed, ignoring the stiff muscles and sharp pains they released. He had endured worse from his father. Besides, these pains were proof of growth, so he was not bothered by them at all. His bare feet though alighted on the cool wooden floor.

A single window let light into the room, allowing him to judge that it was sometime around eight in the morning. The room itself though was very nice. Two beds, two desks, their own bathroom and bathtub, and a bookshelf filled to the brim. Ander looked over at second bed. It seemed like Erok had already left and left his bed a mess. Ander made both beds and then walked over to the window. It granted a view into a tropical forest that lay beyond the wall. Ander opened the glass pane and leaned over the ledge, closing his eyes as he listening to the chittering of insects, the twittering of birds, and movement of small animals beyond. He just simply let himself enjoy nature. It had been what, three months now? Three months since he had been able to relax and just listen to things without worry or anxiety. *Hmm, this is nice.* Lupis said, jolting Ander's eyes open. *Really boy*, Adamar laughed softly, *You must not be so surprised when we speak.* "Yeah, but for a whole month you guys said nothing." Ander retorted. *Yes, and who's fault is that?* Sean asked. Ander got the distinct image of the man casually examining his hand. Ander

372

turned bright red. "Yeah, okay. You're right. So, you guys have anything useful to tell me or what?" Lupis snorted, *Keep that attitude in check boy. In this case, yes we have something we wish to instruct. But, we are still people first and foremost, so we wish to be friends with you in the end. Not every time we speak will be as teachers. It will hopefully be as comrades.* "Oh, okay." Ander replied lamely. Now he just felt like a jerk.

Anyway, Adamar put in, *you already have a great love of nature and respect for life. So, you meet the requirements to learn one of the many skills you will gain.* "What is it?" Ander asked, intrigued. *Life force!* Sean explained excitedly, *It allows one to feel the presence of creatures, and "see" their life force. For your first time,* Lupis instructed, *close your eyes.* Ander obeyed. *Now, imagine your soul, pulsing and beating. Can you see it?*

Suddenly, a golden light leapt to life, burning itself in his mind's eye. Ander gasped, his eyes flying open. He was suddenly aware of just how *alive* this jungle and building was. He could feel the bird that was high above him. The ants outside in the dirt. The snake coiled around a tree. The people outside sparring, a cook in the kitchen. The person in the room next to him, fast asleep. He hunched over, curling up, overwhelmed at the number of things he could sense. *Simply will it to stop.* Adamar instructed. Ander did, and it all vanished. He sat on the ground, breathing heavily. The amount of sensory input…it had been more than he could handle. His mind still rung with the sensation of it. "How in the world do you guys think I'm ready for this?" Ander cried. *What? You think we want you to start at that level?* Lupis asked scornfully, *We're not your father. No, we want you to start at a more basic level. Sensing animals within five feet of you. The more accustomed you get to this power, the more you will be able to handle and expand.* "Okay, makes sense." Ander replied, "But how do I do that? And what kinds of animals?"

Ander could sense Sean thinking hard about that one. *Hmmmm, well how about this? It actually takes more effort to sense things as small as bugs, so we won't worry about them for now. Yet, rational souls are the hardest to sense. So, nothing larger than a cat, but nothing smaller than a bird. As for how, well, Adamar?* Adamar nodded, giving a smile. *I got it. You see Ander, most of this power is turning a conscious act into a subconscious act. Nothing more than a state of being. You are aware of your action to breath, yes? Once you activate the power, imagine some sort of seal on your soul. Bit enough to restrict, but not douse and extinguish the power. Place a number on it for the strength if you wish.* Ander nodded and envisioned a metal seal wrapped around the golden light, a big green "1" labeled on it. The same rush as before happened, but it was much less overwhelming. He could tell that the power only extended in a five foot radius; both by instinct and by a bird just about to land on the window. *Good!* Lupis praised, *Now young Ander, try to keep this up for at least an hour!* Ander smiled, his heart warm and fuzzy. He had never been praised over something so small before. Plus, he had successfully done something on his first try! That was a first also!

Suddenly there was a knock at his door. Klin walked in a saw Ander staring at him. "Oh good, you're up." He said blearily, "And dressed. Good." Ander frowned. "Why wouldn't I be dressed?" Klin let out a weary sigh, "Erok said you like to sleep in your underwear, and then gave me a look like he knew first-hand before he left."

"That dirty liar!" Ander cried indignantly, "I always have a shirt on!" Then he turned red, "And more so pants of course. He's the one that normally sleeps near naked…" Klin just nodded groggily, "That makes too much sense."

"Uh, so why are you here?" Ander finally asked, shifting his feet around awkwardly. Klin jolted up, the dark bags under his eyes more prominent. "Oh, right sorry. Beppo wants you. He asked if just you could join him for the day."

"Huh?" Ander cried, "W-w-why me?! And why are you telling me? Did I offend him?" Klin frowned, "What? No of course not. Everyone is spending the whole day with someone else. I have to go with your sister. Erok's hanging out with Joshua. The girls are together, and my mom and brother. As for why I'm telling you, well Beppo said he wants you to feel like you can refuse. Without feeling pressured. Looks like that didn't work. By the way, whole thing's optional for all of us. Uncle said if we're going to stop trying to tear each other throats out 'like a pack of wild terbulloos', we need to actually get too know everyone else."

"Oh, I see." Ander replied lamely. He just sort of stood there feeling embarrassed at his little panic attack there. Then, he felt something else. He felt flattered. "Uh, well knowing all that, I guess I can't refuse now, can I?" Klin gave him a big smile, "Knew I liked you. There's a reason we're friends." Ander practically leapt backwards, leaning back with such surprise he thought he would fall over for a moment. "We're friends?!" Klin winced, hanging his head sullenly. "Sorry, was that presumptuous? IF you find it that upsetting—"

"No!" Ander squeaked, his face bright red. "No! I've just—well—no one—that is." He stopped and took a deep breath. "It's just a rarity for someone to like me, let alone want to be my friend." Klin just stared at him silently. Ander shrunk down and felt like hiding. He probably did not want a sob story for a friend. Suddenly, he found himself being hugged! Klin stopped, placing his hands on Ander's shoulders, a big smile on his face and some tears glistening the edge of those brown eyes. "Me either." He said softly. Ander smiled and the two hugged. "To the start of a great friendship!" Ander declared, "Now let's get this day started! So, um, where is Beppo?"

Ten minutes later, Ander was jogging to the front gate. Beppo stood leaning next to it. His dark, muscled arms glistened in the sunlight. "Ander!" Beppo greeted happily, "Glad to see you accepted my offer!" Ander smiled and felt some pride at the fact he was not breathless from a small jog! "Well, it seemed like a once-in-a-lifetime opportunity." Ander replied. Beppo laughed, "Well, I hope it is not! I hope for us to stay acquainted, and then become friends!" Ander blushed. That was two people in a row today who liked him! He felt the sudden urge to sniff himself, but resisted, wondering if Celeste had dumped perfume on him in his sleep. She had threatened to do that one day. It was only a matter of time before she made good on that threat. "Now, shall we get going?" Beppo asked. Ander nodded, "Sure. So, what are we doing?"

"We are simply going to do one of my daily routines." Beppo said as they left the main area. "Oh, okay." Ander replied, feeling a little disappointed. He was not sure what he had been expecting, but it was not something so...normal. "Don't look so glum tredo!" Beppo chuckled, "You will still learn plenty since I am here! If you do not want to be, you could be with Joshua instead of Erok,"

"No thanks." Ander answered hastily, "Joshua scares me." Beppo let out a boisterous laugh at that. "I would never have thought one of you to be so honest about him! Hahaha! But, I understand, he is a fearsome warrior!" Ander nodded vehemently, "Yeah, and he constantly smells like whiskey or beer and not to mention he's insane!" Beppo nodded solemnly, "Yes, he has his flaws. He did not use to drink so much you know, nor was he quite so crazy."

"Wait, really?" Ander asked, "He didn't always spout off about jaberwockys and ghosts? And other weird things?" Beppo raised an eyebrow, "Now I did not say that. He has always been strange. It has just become more…exaggerated than it used to be." Ander frowned, "What happened to make him like this?" Beppo shook his head. "I do not know tredo. There are only two people who know. His sister, and our Emperor. I just know that it was so traumatic, that he is almost never sober." Ander felt a stab of regret and sadness pierce his heart. "I see. I wish I could have known him before that then. You have such respect for him, that he must have been an amazing man."

"Was?! No! He still is." Beppo chuckled, "Just wait. The amount of love and care he has for you and your friends will become apparent over time. He never could stop being a father."

"Yeah, well we don't need one." Ander grumbled. "Hmph, the fact you say that only proves your need for one young one." Beppo snorted. Then he resumed more gently, "You have had not a great father, no?" Ander snapped to attention, "How—" Beppo just laughed, "Your immediate distaste of a paternal figure says it all tredo. That and Joshua and Miss Lorelei told me all of your stories." Ander stayed silent as they walked. When they neared a busier section of the city, he finally decided to speak. "Yeah, to say I have a bad relation with my dad would mean I would have even *had* to have some sort of relationship with him in the first place. I've been coming to understand how bad he really was, at least logically. In my heart, I still see him as someone who messed up, and loved me. Not this hateful figure Erok always made him out to be." Beppo nodded, "That will take time tredo. In the meantime, try not to take out your anger on the good parents, yes? Like Miss Lorelei and Joshua."

Ander sighed, "Alright—wait! Joshua's *married*?" Beppo laughed, "Of course! Did you miss the part where he is a father? And a good one to twelve children."

"T-t-twelve?!" Ander asked incuriously, "How does he even support them all?" Beppo smiled at him, "His adventuring of course. He goes away for a few months, makes money, and then stays home the rest of the year. He has made quite a large sum this way. True adventurers are quite profitable. He owns his own island with a mansion."

"Huh." Ander mused, "He really doesn't act like most rich people. Except the way he throws around emeraldas. That's about it."

"To be fair, you do not act rich either."

"I was never allowed to use most of it." Ander shrugged. Beppo nodded, "That may be for the best. Ah, here we are! The market! Let us enjoy the life here now, yes?"

"Uh, sure." They walked among the stalls and various shops. Most people had their shops set up outside, a canvas overhang making it their "inside". Many people would wave at them, flashing Beppo great smiles. Every once in a while, Beppo would stop and speak with someone. They would tell the Commander about life. Their family, funny stories, or troubles they had. Any sort of trouble actually. Beppo would often give a quip, and then offer some wise advice. One person asked about love. "Ahh, love!" Beppo replied longingly, "You young ones always love to hear advice on that! But we all could, no?" He laughed before giving his advice. The young man walked away deep in thought. Every once in a while, Ander would introduce himself, making sure to neglect his unique power. And, every time Beppo would remedy that. Ander had never received so many approving looks in his life! Next, they went to the docks where Beppo checked in on crew members. He was meet with warm welcomes and a list of supplies.

"Your men really love and respect you." Ander commented as they left. Beppo simply shrugged. He seemed actually embarrassed. "People will give back what you give them. They are my men, but they are *people*, and not numbers. They are family." Ander smiled at that, and said wistfully, "I hope to belong to a family as caring as yours someday." Beppo frowned and coked his head in confusion. "Do not the friends you are with count?" Ander snapped up, his eyes wide. "Wait, you can do that? I mean, Erok is *like* a brother to me but I've never thought of him in that way. Does...that make sense?" Beppo just smiled, placing his hand on his shoulder. "Ander my boy, at some point in everyone's life family is what you make of it. Now, we are nearly finished with the day. It is what, three now?" Ander's stomach growled in response. Those fruits they had been given only lasted so long. "Yeah. So, what now?"

Beppo grinned, "Well, I had a more personal reason for inviting you." Ander leaned back a bit, "O-oh, what's that?" Beppo let out a raucous laugh, "Do you distrust me so Ander? Do not look so scared. You are not in trouble. In fact, quite the opposite. I have a gift for you. I hear you have interesting forms as the Triamal." Ander frowned, "What do you mean? I'm still not sure how they work by the way. The spirits haven't explained all of that yet." *Well, you have not asked.* Lupis hummed, a hint of humor in his voice. *Once this man is done, we shall explain all that you ask young one.* Beppo looked confused and turned to Ander. "Was that one of the Spirits tredo?"

"Wait, you can *hear them?*" Ander exclaimed, "No one's ever heard them before!" *That is because we deemed this man worthy of our presence.* Lupis explained, *We are impressed by this man's virtue.* Beppo tilted his head down, "It is a great honor that you have bestowed upon me Spirits. Why don't you explain to Ander then while we walk back?"

Ah, a splendid idea! Sean exclaimed with glee. *Now, who wants to go first?*

How about I do? Lupis offered. *I shall lay the outline, and Beppo Calist, we have deemed worthy to hear. Listen well, for you may offer insights young Ander may not have.* Beppo gave a solemn nod. "Very well, I shall do my best caperi." Lupis smiled and began to explain. *Now, you have noticed that the coin you bear can determine what form you have. You have three. Land, water, and air. I grant land, Adamer water, and Sean air. Each form offers two animals, one for day and night. You know all the night forms. Yet, you still have to successfully transform into a form beyond air in the day.*

"Right, thanks for the refresher!" Ander said, feeling something click into place. "So, do you guys know what my other day animals are?" *Tiger and seal.* Sean answered, *and before you ask, the animals are predetermined per person. That might have been obvious, but I don't think you have ever actually asked. You remember our first conversation, right?* Ander nodded, "Yeah. You guys explained about the forms back then. So much has happened, and after not being able to talk to you guys for so long, I kind of forgot about it. Almost chalked that all up to a dream."

"Interesting." Beppo mused, "So what makes Ander's forms different? Past Triamal's had to work to have "dire" forms. Yet he has them already, and not only that, he seems to be able to take on humanoid aspects for his wolf form." *The young one is tainted.* Adamer explained, *We were just as surprised at the humanoid aspect. Only a once did we see that. With the first bearer, Matthias.* Ander suddenly got the image of Sean swatting Adamer on the head. *Don't call it a taint you idiot!* Sean scolded. *That is quite possibly the worst way of phrasing it!* "Uh, so what is it?" Ander asked curiously, his dread disappearing before it could even manifest as an emotion. *Ahem, sorry.* Adamer apologized sheepishly, *that was careless of me. I will explain what it is rather than name it. It is easier. We think you past suffering is the cause. Your magic went into overtime to keep you alive. Much of what you went through, and the nutrition you received, should have killed you.* Lupis nodded. *Yes, you would be dead without the magic of the Triamal. But now, the floodgates are permanently opened, the stem of magic almost impossible to close. What should be a small river of magic is now a tidal wave.* "So, is my humanoid wolf a bad thing?" Ander asked. Sean shook his head. *No! Far from it young one! However, you are using so much magic that it is making it impossible for you to actually grow due to the immense strain as a result. We waited to tell you because we wanted you to grow accustomed to your powers and learn some control before we tackle this.* "Why wait?" Beppo asked. "Let him start now. Have him become a normal tiger."

Yes, an excellent idea! Sean proclaimed, *Why not give it a go Ander! You have been able to limit Life Force, so why not this as well?* Ander gulped as he pulled out the coin. A tiger and falcon on each side. "Uh, is there a way to decide for sure which of these two I get?" He asked. Lupis shook his head. *Not yet, I'm afraid.* Ander nodded his head a few times, "Right, okay. Sure why not." Adamer stood in his mind with his arms crossed. *You know what to do know. So, do it.* He said encouragingly. *Adamer, we must work your pep talks.* Sean sighed, *You've been around for what, two millennium now, and still can't do pep talks.*

What? Adamer asked confused, *He knows how to limit now. So how is that not encouraging?* Ander chuckled, feeling much more at ease as he closed his eyes and envisioned his soul. This time though, he brought to mind that gauge the Spirits had shown him what felt like so long ago. It flashed across his mind, the gauge bubbling over and a waterfall of green liquid pouring into it. Ander could feel an actual strain from keeping it in sight. He quickly imagined a damn with a flood gate closing over the waterfall. Suddenly, the liquid stopped, and the gauge stopped overflowing. Ander's eyes flashed open and he tossed the coin up in the air, grabbing it as he began to transform. His body shrank and he fell on all fours. White fur grew over his hands as they became paws, and red stripes appeared across his body. "Well, well," Beppo laughed, "aren't you a handsome tiger! Unique, no?" Ander rowled happily, feeling increasingly happy and joyous. "Follow me, my now furry friend!" Beppo said jovially.

Ander paced behind the commander happily, getting used to his new body. Using all four legs was different for sure, but not unpleasant. It was actually kind of fun. *Ander, you lost focus.* Adamer said suddenly. *You are no longer using Life Force.* Ander felt a pit form in his stomach. He had been doing so well all day too! "I'm sorry!" Ander cried, "I'll get back on that!" Lupi frowned, *Why are you apologizing young one? We asked for an hour. You gave us nearly six. That is far beyond what we asked. You did fine. No need to push yourself more for the day.* Ander blushed under the praise, and suddenly realized he was purring. He quickly stopped, embarrassed. Luckily, Beppo had not noticed, or at least was pretending like he had not. It was hard to tell if that smile was in response to his achievement or amusement. They made there way back to their quarters. Once there, Ander transformed back as instructed. Beppo led him inside. They passed a few of the others, who were outside training with Joshua. Ander winced as Sasha was soundly pummeled into the ground. Joseph and Nathaniel were off to the side, practicing magic it seemed. Due to him being a scholar, guess it made sense he would know spells outside his own elements. Ander saw everyone but Klin and Kyoko though. He would have to ask about them later.

Beppo led him inside the building though, and they went through a few turns before getting to their destination. "This is my office." Beppo explained as he opened the door into a very nice room. A polished birch desk sat at the far end of the room, with a giant sliding glass door leading to what seemed like a private garden. Three couches and numerous cabinets adorned edges of the room. Up on the walls were quite a few paintings of mostly men, and a few women. "Portraits of our leaders." Beppo answered when he saw Ander starting at them. Ander nodded, not failing to notice the portrait of Beppo himself. He looked younger in it. He did not have his hair in the headband, and it was much shorter than it was now. He was still incredibly handsome though. "So, you have your own private garden?" Ander asked. Beppo smiled, "Yes. It is more for my wife, Sierra."

"Ah-ha!" Ander cried, "So, you *are* married." Beppo laughed softly, "Yes, I am. Sierra means the world to me tredo. She is not here though. She went to the capital on my behalf. She took my son with her too, so he may see the wonders the city has to offer. So, unfortunately you will not meet them yet. They will be back before too long though. Only three more days." Ander smiled at the loving and tender look on Beppo's face. The amount of love in his eyes practically lit the room. "Now, let us do what we came for. Your gift is on my desk." Ander tentatively approached the desk and found a black velvet box that could fit in one's hand. Ander looked back Beppo, and he nodded. Ander opened the box and found a silver chain necklace with a green, oval shaped crystal hanging from the end. "What is it?" Ander asked. "That tredo, is a Life Stone." Beppo explained, "Spell already imbued. It contains a familiar." Ander shook his head, "Mr. Calist, I can't accept this! This must have cost a fortune!" Elemental stones this pure were pricey, let alone one infused with a spell of this caliber! "Oh, it is not trouble." Beppo replied with an amused smile, "I earn too much money sometimes. Besides, I have not much use for it. Take it Ander." Ander gave him a bow, "Thank you." Beppo waved his hand. "None of that! Bows have too much respect to be directed at me." So, Ander gave the man a hug instead, Beppo did not hesitate to hug him back.

Ander emerged from the embrace. "Thank you Beppo."

"Of course, tredo. Now, listen well. You can only summon you companion once a day, and for tow hours." Ander put the necklace on. "Got it. Thank you again." Beppo clapped him on the back and led him out, where they did some training with Joshua. After they were done, he went to with the others to the dining hall. Lorelei was in there, already pulling out plates for them. "So, has anyone seen my sister?" Ander asked. Joseph shook his head. "Nope. Neither she nor Klin have come back yet. Don't worry though. Knowing Klin, he'll be bringing her back right about…now!" Joseph spun around to look at the doors, pointing at them excitedly. They waited for five minutes before Joseph began to mutter something, stalking off as he sat down. As soon as he had sat down, the doors opened and the two walked in. "Oi!" Joseph shouted angrily, "You're late!" Klin frowned as he walked in and looked at Ander. "Uh, what?" Ander just laughed, "He's mad that his prediction was off." Klin grinned impishly, "Ah, so he was going to try that. Glad I purposefully had us walk slow then."

"You little—you did that on purpose?!" Joseph cried. Klin snickered as he sat down next to his brother, the two arguing playfully. Celeste and Sasha sat across from them, exasperated looks on both their faces. Erok just laughed as he sat down next to Ander and Kyoko, a plate of chicken with caramelized onions, peppers, and rice for their dinner. "So, what did you and Beppo talk about?" Erok asked. Ander shrugged, "This and that. I mainly just joined him on his daily routine. We got to figure out more about my powers though! Oh, and he gave me this!" Ander proudly presented his Summon stone. Erok let out a low whistle. "Daamn. That a Life Stone?" Ander nodded, "Yep. It can summon a familiar too." Kyoko tilted her head. "Huh, it's very pretty." Ander smiled as he put it back down his shirt. "Yep. Oh, this is delicious! Anyway Kyo, what did you and Klin do?" Kyoko's face lit up. "Ah, well we went into the forest. Saw a lot of cool animals I've never seen. They were so colorful! A few birds played with me, and then Klin went to the beach with me, and we talked. He played with me after." Erok frowned, "What did you guys play?" Kyoko gave them a sweet innocent smile, "I won't tell." Erok sighed and looked over at Klin. "Oi! Pretentious ass, what game did you play with Kyo?" Klin looked over and replied, "Tag, oh one who smells of ass." Erok laughed. "That was a good one! I'll have to remember that one!" Klin and Erok grinned before turning Klin went back to his conversation.

"Are you two on good terms now then?" Ander asked. Erok nodded. "Yeah. Dudes still got a stick up his ass, but…after talking with that crazy ass "cowboy", I understand why he does. I still think he's too naïve with his optimism, but well…I *want* him to scold me now and again." Ander blinked a few times. "Wow. That's…impressive." Erok shrugged before pointing his spoon at him. "Now don't go thinking my whole moral code will align with his, because it won't. I'll still sleep with whoever I damn feel like for one. But I do realize I might be letting some of my morals go off track. So, a reminder now and again won't hurt, but that doesn't mean I want one every day. I'm going to talk with him after dinner about it." Ander nodded, smiling. Kyoko piped up suddenly though. "I think he'll need some reminders too." Erok frowned. "What do you mean?" Kyoko shook her head. "I promised I wouldn't say more than that. Sorry Erok." Erok just shook his head and sighed. "Nah, you got nothing to apologize for Kyo. Keeping personal things a secret is usually good, so don't sweat it. Anyway, Ander can you go check on Debo for me? Don't know how long this chat with Klin will be."

Ander grinned, "Sure. I feel like we've been neglecting him anyway." Ander wolfed down the rest of his food and handed his plate to a washer. He then went back outside and went to the side courtyard where the archers practiced. That courtyard also doubled as a stable. They surprisingly kept a few horses, and the courtyard here was bigger than the main one and had plenty of lush grass. Ander found the owlbear up against the fence, laying down. Debo perked up when he saw Ander coming over with a bag of meat. Ander grinned as Debo nearly leapt on top of him, nuzzling his face. "Hey! Guess you missed me?" He laughed as he tossed him a slab of meat. Debo jumped up, devouring it in one bite. Ander continued to feed him and then spent some time petting him. After that, he bid Debo farewell and went back in. He joined the others by a fire and enjoyed the games and songs they played. They did this late into the night. It was well after midnight before they dispersed. Ander and Erok went back to their room, just flopping onto their beds. Erok passed out almost immediately. As Ander lay on his bed, slowly letting himself drift off, he smiled as he realized something. Today was the first truly good day he had ever had.

Chapter 33

Traitor

Two weeks had passed since they had arrived on Solanthis. Two weeks Celeste had spent trying to find that crystal orb for Viscious. Two weeks of frustration and nothing to show for it. She had scoured every inch of the island. The forest held three caves, and no secret passages. She had been in every important building and room. All but one. The mysterious Temple loomed ominously over her as she cautiously climbed the steps to the entrance. No guards today. Guess the holiday meant no guard duty either. It was the first day of winter, and as Coronus tradition had it, everyone was out celebrating the first snowfall. At least, they would be on the mainland. Here it was barely forty degrees, bordering on fifty. Celeste had left Yatta in her room. After the first time she had tried to enter the Temple, Yatta had begun to scold her. That, and the child was beginning to ask too many questions. Questions that the answers for might cause trouble. Yet, Celeste already knew she was a bad person. So, despite the heavy, awful, disgusting weight on her chest, she walked forward into the Temple. She did not need some stupid girl stuck in a sword to constantly reminding her of that. Besides, Yatta would not understand.

Celeste had not virtues or skills to save her. She had to do this. Selene was the only one who understood. Who could make sure she *was* a good person. So, what if she was working with Viscious, the one who had killed the Immortal Hero? What was one more sin on her path? If she was going to end up in Heshtanus, why not work with the ones who were there?

Celeste put her hands on the giant stone doors. They were cool to the touch, and very smooth. They were also a darker shade of blue than the columns. She pushed, and with some effort, opened the doors. She walked in, hands on the handles of her daggers. She had decided to borrow some from the armory. A normal sword would have looked too suspicious, but she was adept enough with these things that if trouble came, she could handle it. The inside though was surprisingly well lit. Chandeliers hung not too far above, their chains keeping them low enough that they were not at the absurd heights the Temple ceiling was at. The floor though was a patchwork of color as the stained-glass windows cast their light down. The air itself had a tinge of saltwater to it but had to coolness of sitting beside a river on a spring day. Rows of pew lined each side, with the center cleared all the way to an altar. Celeste frowned, noticing that something was floating above the altar. She wanted to rush over and inspect it, almost certain that the orb was the thing floating. It was very spherical at least.

Instead, she waited, inspecting the stained-glass windows and taking her time looking over each one. While the predominating theme of the temple was blue, all colors could still be found tastefully placed in the different widows. Surprisingly though, each countries symbol for water could be found at the base of each window. Both the East and West. Celeste felt a sense of awe at seeing that. She had never heard of any art uniting the East and West. It had been centuries since they had worked together. This place was definitely old. There were various people whom she had no idea who they were supposed to be on many of the windows, but the last two near the altar were of Water Elementals. Their watery wings blazing with ethereal beauty. Then, at the back of the temple in the sanctuary was the largest window. It depicted a woman whom Celeste recognized almost immediately. She was tall, with tan skin and a slim frame. She wore a pure white, long-sleeved dress and was barefoot. Her piercing blue eyes and hair though was what let her know who this was; Sasara, the Sculptor of Water. Her hair was dark blue at the head, but turned lighter and lighter, with hints of green and turquoise as it went down, till the ends were white. Celeste was familiar with all the different depictions of the Sculptors, as her father was deeply religious.

However, she was not familiar with this one. Often Sasara had a lighter skin tone and did not wear a dress so modest. It was usually flashy, with a range of different colors. White was a first. The hair color though was nearly constant though, but she had never seen it so detailed in the colors. A sudden realization washed over her though. There was one of two things. One, the symbolism in this depiction was older than they had record of, or two; the person who had made this had seen Sasara in person. Celeste felt awe as she realized what kind of history she was in the presence of. There was a inscription under the window, in Ancient Threan. She almost ran out then and there to find Klin to translate it for her, before remembering she was not supposed to be there. So, she turned her attention back to the altar. Floating above the turquoise marble was a dark blue crystal orb, floating in a ball of suspended water. That had to be the thing Viscious wanted! Celeste dashed forward, reaching out her hand. As she did, the water began to spin furiously as a strip of water was flung at her. Celeste's eyes widened in surprise as she just barley managed to dodge the water flying by her face. She felt a sting and touched her cheek. Blood stained her fingers. Celeste took a few steps back, watching as the water became still again.

"Celeste? Is that you?" Celeste spun around, hands on her daggers, but relaxed as she spotted Nathaniel. She frowned though as she asked, "What are you doing here?" Nathaniel walked towards her, raising an eyebrow. "I could ask the same of you. I have been coming here everyday since we arrived." Celeste squinted her eyes suspiciously, "I thought Beppo said this place was off limits."

"He did. To those without the proper permission, which I happen to have." Celeste's heart began to beat rapidly. Crap. "Oh, sorry. I have permission myself; I just did not realize it was that easy to obtain, especially to us outsiders." Nathaniel gave her a cool, piercing look. Celeste was beginning to think he had seen through her lie when he shrugged. "That is fair. Since you are here, join me in prayer?" Celeste blinked, "Oh, I did not realize you were religious." Nathaniel smiled, "What else would one do in a Temple? I am just quiet about it." Celeste looked over at the altar and pointed to the orb. "So uh, do you know what that thing is then?" Nathaniel shook his head. "No, unfortunately not. All I know is one would need a Water Weaver to get near it." Of course! Sasha! Celeste contained her excitement, merely nodding. "However," Nathaniel continued, "I could read that inscription under the window of Sasara if you would like." Celeste nodded excitedly. "Yes please!"

"It reads thus: To those who gather under roof or sky, may you look upon the majesty of Her visage, as shown by a servant blessed to give, and keep faith she will protect and aid." Celeste tilted her head. "Huh. So, whoever made it saw her face. That's incredible. Well, I should probably get going now though." Celeste began to walk away, and suddenly felt the hair on her neck stand up. She dropped to the floor, a loud whoosh flying overhead. She rolled to the side, more air magic hitting where she had been. She leapt to her feet, cutting through three more slices of air. "Alright Nathaniel, you skunk faced piece of shit!" Celeste yelled, "Who the herk are you?" Nathaniel placed a hand down and covered his heart as he bowed. "Forgive me Miss Farvor'Coal. I thought it prudent to test you." Before he could continue, Celeste was atop of him, daggers to his throat. "Test? You better talk fast before I slit your throat."

"I am sorry," Nathaniel explained quickly, "but these days imposters seem to be everywhere. When you claimed to be a Farvor'Coal, I grew suspicious. Especially since you had kept that from everyone. I think only Beppo and I truly grasp the severity of who it is you claimed to be. I thought checking that you were telling the truth was necessary. Only Celeste Elizabeth Farvor'Coal could be capable of avoiding a magic attack unaware of the spell, and without being a Weaver herself. I was merely worried you might seek to do Klin harm." Celeste lowered her daggers and looked at him in stunned silence. "What kind of idiotic, hair-brained worry is that?!" Celeste yelled angrily, "And why Klin in particular?!" Nathaniel winced, "I suppose I deserved that. As for Klin? Well.." He shrugged, "You seem to have a seductive effect on the men around you. Ander, Joseph, and you seem to pay Klin special attention." Celeste pointed her dagger at him, muttering, "I should cut out your tongue for that." But she was blushing furiously.

"It's not like I treat the guys any differently though." She grumbled, "Klin's like a brother, and a good friend now." Nathaniel nodded, "I see. My deepest apologies. My imagination ran wild. But, you do seem to have an effect on—"

"Shut it!" Celeste flushed, "Or I may not forgive you!" Nathaniel nodded, "Very well. I shall let you leave then."

"Oh, thank you soooo much my lord."

"You don't have to mock me."

"And you don't have to try and kill me, yet here we are!" Celeste cried as she marched out the Temple. As she left, something began to gnaw at her. Something at about that encounter bothered her, but she couldn't quite put her finger on it. She shook her head. Whatever, she had more important things to worry about at the moment. She had a plan forming, but she was going to need help for it. She went back to her room and pulled out the stone Viscious had given her. It was time to get her sister back. "Celeste? What is that?" Celeste turned to see Yatta sitting on her bed. Yet, she fuzzy and transparent. She was normally solid. "Why do you care what it is?" Celeste snapped. Yatta flinched but said, "You've been acting weird lately. Is everything alright? You haven't been taking me with you the past week."

"Maybe because you're annoying!" Celeste replied with a nasty bark, "Only reason we're together is because you were my sister's! I'm only doing what she wasn't able to do! That's as far as our relationship goes!" Yatta's eyes began to brim with tears, her face stuck in shock and horror. "Celeste…"

"Just go away!" Celeste screamed. Yatta vanished without a word. Celeste felt tears beginning to form in her own eyes as her stomach turned in revulsion over what she had just done. Did…did she actually feel that way? What was happening? Why did she keep acting like this?! She shook her head. Later. She..she could sort all this out later. She clenched the stone tightly and took a deep breath before wiping her eyes. "Viscious. Are you there?" She whispered. Silence for a bit, and then the stone glowed a faint gray. "Ah, Miss Farvor'Coal. It has been so long, I'd nearly thought you had forgotten about our deal!"

"No. It just took me this long to figure out how to fulfill it." Celeste explained. "Ahh." Viscious hummed, "So, do you have it?" Celeste hesitated. This was her last chance to turn back. "Not quite." She said, "There are intricate spells around it. I have an idea on how to get around it though, but I need help."

"Well then, please tell me what assistance I can offer!" Viscious purred. Celeste explained her plan. "Think this could work?" She asked after she had finished. "My dear," Visicious praised, "I myself could not come up with a better plan. Give me one week. Then we shall enact it, and you shall see your beloved sister once more." The stone's glow faded and Celeste was left alone in silence, suddenly wanting a fire despite the warmth outside.

Joseph pressed his blade hard against his uncle's, their swords locked in a battle of strength and will. "Give up old man." Joseph taunted, "I've got this one—ahh!" Suddenly, Joseph found himself flat on the ground. Damn it. Uncle Joshua stood over him, blade against his throat. "You let yourself get distracted." His uncle grunted, "Even if victory is in sight, always be aware of yer surroudings" Joseph climbed to his feet, waving a hand. "Yeah, yeah. Got it, but you have to admit, that was my best match yet!"

"Yeah? And? It was a 4/10." Joshua scoffed, "Yer still dead at the end. Yer talented, but don't let it go to your head. Don't want to turn out like that Mona kid, do ya?"

"Herk no!" Joseph exclaimed, "That might be the single-handedly most insulting thing you've ever said to me Uncle!" Joshua just chuckled softly. "At least you got a moral compass. Even if it does point at 0.4 latitude, 57 longitude." Joseph just grinned, "Uh thanks. Again?" Joshua shook his head, "Are ya crazy kid?! We've been at it fer three hours! I want a break!"

"Awww. Sounds like the old man needs a nap!" Joseph taunted. "Ahh, shut up before I whup yer ass for the hundredth-thirty first time!" Joseph stopped smiling and looked at him confused. "Have you actually been counting?"

"Of course! It's how I keep track of you boy's progress! So, shut it." At that moment, they heard someone shouting indistinctly. Joseph and Joshua frowned as they looked at the entrance to the courtyard. A young man burst in, his eyes wild and armor loosely hanging on to him, as if he had just put it on in a rush. "Army! Ships! Beppo! Ardaven!" The man rambled breathlessly. "Whoa! Calm down dude." Joseph soothed, "You're not making sense."

"Herk!" Joshua exclaimed. "The Seekers of Ardaven are herking here! Now you gotta find Beppo? Right?" The young man nodded, giving Joshua a look of awe. "Well, what you standing around here for!" Joshua roared, "Get!"

"Uncle.."

"I know." Joshua growled, "It don't make sense. Good thing it's our specialty, eh? Come on, we need to round up the others."

Chapter 34

The Downfall of Peace

Klin stood in Beppo's office with his brother. Beppo sat at his desk, a visual communication stone atop it. "In five minutes, you're supposed to talk with Misha." Beppo said, a hard undertone to his voice. "Stay calm and reveal nothing. Let me do the talking unless she addresses you directly. Understood?"

"Yes sir!" The brothers exclaimed in unison. Beppo nodded, "Excellent." His face softened for a brief moment, but then he shook his head, the hardness returning. "This bitora will pay." The stone began to flash a golden light. Beppo's face became hard as stone, and twice as unreadable as he growled. "She is early." He pressed the stone though, and a life-sized Misha of golden light was cast from the stone. "Are you the famed leader of the Coronus Liberation Sailors?" Misha asked. "I am." Beppo answered. "So, can you explain then why a whole fleet of Ardaven ship are in Coronian waters?"

"Are the boys with you?" Misha asked, completely ignoring Beppo. Klin felt a spike of anger run through him but said nothing. Beppo motioned them forward as he said coolly, "Turn around." The projection of Misha did and nodded as she saw them. "Ah, excellent. As for why we have a whole fleet, well that is simple. You are harboring Ardaven fugitives. We have come to take them into custody, as is our right."

"Under the Trinity Treaty, their fate is decided by the Emperor." Beppo replied in a monotone voice. "Attempting to recover them is in violation of that said treaty, and may I remind you, any country who violates the Treaty will have the other two countries against them." Beppo looked at her and said softly, "Do you *really* want both Coronus and *Seveljarn* against Ardaven?" Misha gave him a sly smile, "True. We

391

do not want either of you to be our enemies. However, the treaty states that the fugitives must make it to land. Crossing into foreign waters is not enough. According to both Seveljarn and Ardaven maps, this island does not exist. Therefore, they are not on land, and we are in our rights to take them. Therefore, if you continue to withhold them from us, *Coronus*, not Ardaven, will be in violation of the treaty and we shall consider it an act of war." Beppo's face became as stormy as the seas he sailed. "You wouldn't dare." Misha gave him a nasty smile, "Try me. I know war with us is not something you can afford, especially with the aggression that Turmaky is making right now."

"Yet what criminal warrants this many Seekers?" Beppo asked, "What crime have they committed? They have killed no one. The man who said such things is a lair, and a deep enemy of theirs."

"Oh, I know." Misha said casually. "WHAT?!" Joseph roared, "THEN WHY THE HERK HAVE YOU CHASED US SO FAR?!"

"Joseph!" Klin scolded, elbowing him in the ribs. Though, he really could not say he did not feel the same. He was boiling with rage. "Coronian, leave us." Misha ordered. "No." Beppo growled. "If you do not," Misha threatened, "I will consider it outside interference and influence." Beppo stood up, his face stormy as he gave her a bow and said, "As you wish bitora." Misha nodded as he left. "Now, shall we talk?"

"Not sure I want to hear anything you have to say." Klin growled, crossing his arms. "Especially not after our last encounter." Misha let out a sigh, "Yes, that does make sense. I do apologize for how I handled our last meeting. Your uncle releases the dark part of me I normally have under control."

"Even so," Joseph muttered angrily, "you better have a damn good reason for all this! Especially after the destruction of Cleana!" A distraught look came over Misha. "That was *not* my doing!" She said vehemently. "I was neither in charge nor ordering any who where there that did that!" Klin raised an eyebrow, "Yeah, sure. Like we would believe that. We've talked to one of the survivors." Misha frowned, looking confused, "Then they are either presuming or lying." Now it was Klin's turn to actually feel disturbed. It felt like she was telling the truth here. He looked over to Joseph who nodded. Damn. "Okay, fine, we'll leave that one alone for now." Klin said, "But if you knew Monastrath was lying, why are you after us?"

"Because you two are the key to restoring our kingdom!" Misha explained excitedly. "We need your unique powers!" Klin frowned. "What do you mean?"

"Oh, come on!" Misha sighed, "Your home is a prime example! The fat nobles who abuse their power, untouched by the king's reach. They sit around, indulging and abusing their power, neglecting their people." Joseph nodded, "I mean yeah, that's all true but I still fail to see how we factor into this."

"You two have extraordinary abilities." Misha said softly, "Those should be used for the betterment of our kingdom, your nation! You two nearly single-handedly took down one of the largest cities in the kingdom! And with little training! Fight for the king! Restore the fractured vestiges of Ardaven!"

"But we came to get away from war and violence." Klin protested, "We don't want to fight, even for this."

"Hahaha! Are you serious?" Misha barked derisively, "You cannot say that truthfully! I saw the hesitation in your eyes. You don't believe what you just said. Your journey has been rife with violence! You think you can escape on some tropical island?" Klin stayed silent. She was right. He *did* enjoy the fighting, the power it gave him over others. The ability to decide their fates. "Yeah, our journey's been pretty hectic." Joseph replied quietly, "But how would *you* know that? You've barely seen half of our journey. Something's always seemed off about this whole thing, so there are two options. Someone's either been watching us from a distance, or we have a traitor among us." Misha fell silent, a brief look of panic flashing across her face before she hid it. Yet that was all they needed. "This conversation's over." Klin said. "Wait." Misha commanded, "If you do not give up and come with us, you will be responsible for all the deaths that follow." Klin stopped, hand hovering over the stone, inches from turning it off. "Ah, so you *do* have inordinate respect for life. Maybe too much."

"Shut up bitch." Joseph growled, "You can't pin any deaths on us. We tried to get away peacefully, *you're* the one who keeps on insisting and threatening death!"

"Maybe," Misha replied causally, "But you two are in positions of power now. If there is a battle, you are the cause of it. I take no pleasure killing these men, but I will do what I must to make Ardaven great once more." Klin frowned, "I think you also haven't figured out the whole situation. You can't get on this island." Misha just smiled, "We are working on that problem currently. It will not be a problem for much longer." Klin felt a chill run through him. She...was too confident. That was no bluff. "Can-can you give us sometime to think this over?" Klin asked, rattled. Misha tilted her head in assent. "One hour. I expect the right choice to be made." She disappeared, golden light dancing in the air as the figure faded.

Celeste and Sasha walked to the Temple, Celeste practically dragging Sasha along. "Celeste, what in Threa are you doing?" Sasha cried. "What I said earlier." Celeste sighed, "Helping those idiots."

"But we're not allowed—"

"Oh, just shut up till we get in!" Celeste cried exasperated. Sheesh. She thought Sasha would be more eager to help. Seemed like rules had never bothered her before. "Ander's in danger you know. This will help."

"I-I know that!" Sasha stammered, "But I care about the others just as much you know!" *Highly doubtful.* Celeste thought. Celeste paused, expecting the inevitable comment from Yatta. When none came though, she felt that same spike of pain she had this whole past week. It felt like she was missing a part of herself. They made it to the doors of the Temple, unguarded. Just as she thought. Everyone was preparing for an attack that would never come. Those ships were merely an illusion created by Viscious. No army could make it through that storm. Celeste threw open the doors, still impressed by her own genius. It seemed one of her skills was betrayal. "What are we—wait, what's that?" Sasha asked, pointing at the sphere of water. "That girl, is our ticket to helping everyone." Celeste explained triumphantly. "I need you to undo the spell around the item in there." Sasha slowly began to walk towards the altar. "Are you sure I can do this?" She asked, her voice full of uncertainty. "How will this even help us?"

"It's a powerful magic item." Celeste explained hurriedly, "We take it and use it to frighten the Seekers away with a massive show of power."

Sasha frowned, "How do you even know about this? That we can even use it?"

"Yatta told me." Celeste lied nonchalantly, "She can sense and figure out that kind of stuff. She's got some weird knowledge." Sasha nodded, "I suppose that makes sense. I can feel the massive amounts of magic from it. And…I feel *pulled* to it. There's something unique about it. So, let's do this!" Celeste clapped her on the back. "That's the spirit!" Of course, as soon as she got hold of the orb, she would give it to Viscious who would then disperse the illusion and leave. After resurrecting Selene of course. Everyone would get want they want, and no one needed to get hurt to fulfill it. "Alright, I'm going to begin." Sasha told her, "And considering some of the spells that I can see from it, you might want to stand back." Celeste took a big step back, "You got!" She replied cheerily. Yeah, no one would be hurt right?

Ander stood on the beach, looking out at the line of thirty ships on the horizon. Erok stood a bit way off, chatting with some soldiers. Joshua had been with them but had run off ten minutes ago. Back to headquarters to tell Beppo the fact that these ships had made it through the storm somehow. Ander felt queasy as he looked at each ship. Supposedly, each one carried seventy-five Seekers. This was the most soldiers he had ever seen gathered in one place. *War is brimming.* Lupis mused. *I hope you are ready.* "Not really." Ander gulped, "I'm scared witless at this!" *Well, at least you have sense.* Sean said cheerily, *We honestly prefer our bearers to not have bloodlust.* Ander smiled at that. It was rare to hear the "virtues" of a warrior disparaged. "I should do something though." Ander said, feeling restless. "I'm tired of waiting around, doing nothing to help." *How about transforming and scouting the enemy?* Adamer suggested, *It's not like a normal sized animal would look odd.* "Oh, good idea!" Ander exclaimed. "Hold on, I'll go let Erok know first." Ander ran over and tapped his friend on the shoulder. "What's up?" Erok asked. "I'm going to go get us an exact head count." Ander explained. Erok hesitated, he face stiff with worry. "Are you sure? They might see you." Ander waved his hand. "Don't worry! I've gotten a lot better a controlling what size my forms are. Plus, I can transform three times a day now." He leaned in and whispered, "That, and I just need to get within a mile of them. I'll use Life Force."

Erok rubbed his chin before nodding. "Alright. That would help us. Plus, it's not that big a risk. Try doing seal though. It'll look less suspicious than a falcon." Ander nodded and pulled out his coin, flipping it up into the air. Falcon side. Oh well. Ander transformed and soared up into the air, darting like a bullet. "I just told you not to be a falcon you ass!" Erok shouted at him. Ander turned and squawked an apology at him. He still did not understand that it was kinda luck which form he took on. In no time though, Ander was circling the ships. Dark clouds were above them, but the storm stayed. They were right on the precipice of it. Somehow, these ships had made it past the storm, but now anyone on shore could not see past the magical storm. Men moved down below in rhythmic patterns. Ander activated Life Sense, ready to make a mental note of the men per ship. He squawked in surprise though as everything below him remained blank! "Wait, did I not activate it?" He asked. *Herking—no you did!* Lupis growled, *Look, you can sense the fish bellow. Something is wrong here.* Ander quickly focused in. Lupis was right. He could sense the fish swimming bellow the ship as if it was not there. That…was odd behavior. Ander turned his falcon enhanced eyes to the men on the ship. Now that he was paying attention, the people aboard move *too* rhythmically and too stiffly.

The man washing a stain from his shirt was making no progress on it at all. Other soldiers went through a cycle of exact same actions, over and over again. *Oh dear. Not good.* Sean moaned softly. *This is not good at all.* "What?" Ander asked, "What's going on?" *Dive bomb.* Lupis ordered. Ander hesitated, but he trusted them to know what they were doing. He dove down, aiming for one of the soldier's faces. He extended his talons to rake the face but passed clean through the entire body. He was so surprised, that he stopped flying and tried landing on the ship but went through it and fell in the water. "GAH!" He cried as the icy water shook his system. He quickly burst out, still shivering. *They're all illusions.* Adamer explained softly, *Natharian magic.* "That's a lot a weavers then." Ander replied, feeling terrified. *Or a massively powerful one.* Sean whispered worriedly. *And I would bet money on the later. Quick, extend the range to see if they are all fake!* Ander obeyed, struggling to keep in the air as he did. He gasped at what he discovered though. *Herking—this is much worse!* Adamer exclaimed. *Come! You must report this to the others!* Ander nodded as he darted back to shore, as fast as lighting, feeling terrified at what he had found.

All the ships were fake, which explained how they had made it past the storm. Yet, past the storm was the real army, and it was twice the size of the fake one. What in the world was going on?! He made it back to the island, and transformed back as he landed, immediately dashing over to Erok. "Oh, good your back." Erok said, letting out a sigh of relief. "No! Not good!" Ander exclaimed, "That army out there is a fake! Illusions made from Natharian magic! And even worse, the real army is on the other side of the storm, and twice the size!" Erok just laughed, "Why are you all freaked out then? This *is* good news. It just means that the paradox is still in place! We're safe!" At that moment, there was a thunderclap so loud that it left Ander dazed, his ears ringing. He fell down, head spinning. After a solid five minutes, his hearing returned and he found himself being pulled to his feet. "You okay?" Erok asked with a grimace. Ander nodded. Everyone looked around in confusion. What had done that? Suddenly one of the soldiers let out a wail. "NOOOOOO! THE STORM! IT'S GONE!" Ander looked out in dismay. The illusionary ships had disappeared, but so had the storm that protected Solanthis. "What was that about being safe?" Ander asked quietly. Battle was upon them it seemed as the sixty Ardaven ships sailed closer.

"Alright, we have ten minutes to get some sort of plan." Beppo said as he and his officers began to talk rapidly. Klin's heart was deep in a pit, freshly dug by the news Ander had brought with him. "Well then someone needs to start spitting ideas!" Beppo shouted angrily. Klin sighed, looking over at Celeste and Sasha. Both women had their heads hung low, rightfully ashamed after the tongue lashing Beppo had unleashed. He was not truly mad at them, just mad that they had played right into Misha's hands. That strange orb lay on the table. Beppo was refusing to let anyone touch it, saying they would die if they tried to use it. "How about Lorelei?" One of the officers asked. Klin snapped his attention back to their conversation. "We know she has both the skill and power for it." They turned to look at her, her face grave and solemn. "I'm not happy about killing, but I'll do it."

"Sis, you don't have ta—"

"Don't patronize me, Joshua." Lorelei said calmly. "I'm doing this to protect my sons." Joshua was silent, then looked at her. "I can't lose you too." Lorelei's eyes held pity as she looked at her brother. "Excuse us for a moment." Beppo nodded, "Of course mamater. We will fill you in on the rest of the plan later." Klin walked over to Sasha and Celeste as Lorelei walked away with his uncle. "Hey, listen." He said, "You guys messed up, but you can't let that hold you back! Especially not now! We need you guys at full force. Besides, you had no way of knowing that would have happened. None of us blame you for this."

"Yeah, well maybe you should." Celeste croaked. Klin's heart went out to her, but he placed a hand on her shoulder. "Maybe, maybe not. I've chosen not to blame you, so deal with it." He nodded to them and turned back to the war table but stopped. Sasha had grabbed his arm. "Klin?"

"Hmm?" Sasha's eyes had life returning to them, shimmering with their usual hope, but also a fire was lit. "Thank you." Klin smiled as she let go. One more hope before giving in. "Good, we have a plan now." Beppo proclaimed, arms crossed. "Let us hope this works. Klin! Joseph! It is time." The brothers nodded as everyone cleared away from the table. The Visual Com was flashing. Klin activated it. Misha leapt into sight, arms behind her back. "So, what is your answer?"

"Go rot in Heshtanus!" Joseph spat. "Along with those Natharian weavers you have!" Klin added. A dark cloud fell over Misha's face. "I will give you one more chance. Will you use your talents for the greater good, or not?"

"Your vision has become clouded Misha Varden." Klin answered, barely able to keep his hands from shaking. "How can you speak of greater good when using Natharian magic? This 'greater good' you speak of is nothing more than a sham that will not last. We'll use our powers. We'll use them to purge the world of true evil. Starting with you." Misha was silent for a bit, then declared. "I see. You may do that *after* you are done serving *me*! Remember, I offered peace. Any blood is on your hands." Misha vanished as a silence fell over the room. "Well, what are you waiting for?!" Beppo roared, "We have a bitora to get rid off! Prepare for battle!"

End of Act III

Chapter 35

The Battle of Solanthis

Klin and Nathaniel accompanied Beppo as they made their way to the docks. Klin's palms were slick with a cold sweat, his heart beating rapidly. "So, uh Beppo?" Klin pried, "What was it that you called Misha?" Beppo let out a small chuckle, "Ah, bitora. It means: one lower than a pig." Beppo continued to chuckle softly. Nathaniel simply nodded, "I like that. I think it is true, especially after what she did to Cleana." Klin remained silent, not sure how to react. He had not gotten a chance to ask Nathaniel about Misha's claim, and now hardly seemed the appropriate time. "Now, you two will stay with me." Beppo said, going over the plan once more. "Nathaniel, you protect Klin. Klin, you keep my vesua safe." Klin nodded and said with some sarcasm, "So, vesua mean ship? Or does it mean more?" Beppo grinned at him, "It is a more endearing term for a ship." Klin laughed and felt some of his nerves calm. He had this. Nathaniel had been instructing him in counter spells over the past month. Mainly in light, but the biggest thing was he had learned how to absorb a spell of the same element. According to Nathaniel, this was not a very well known spell, and only Misha was likely to know it out of everyone on the opposing side.

They made it to the docks just in time to see everyone lining up and boarding their ships. "How many we got?" Klin asked quietly. "Seven hundred men." Beppo replied, "And only enough ships for three hundred. Thirteen ships against sixty" A wry smile crossed the man's face, "They will soon realize their mistake. They should have brought a hundred-twenty ships if they wanted to stand a chance!" Klin grinned back. The Coronians were well known to have the best warriors in the world. The three climbed aboard the *Water's Maiden*, the Seeker fleet slowly approaching Solanthis. Either they had no Air Weavers, or they wanted to give them time to panic. Once aboard, Klin and Nathaniel went near the prow, but Beppo motioned them over to the railing overlooking the dock. Beppo then climbed the rigging, looking at his men. He nodded to one of his men, and Klin watched a spell placed over Beppo's throat. His voiced boomed, enhanced by the spell. "Gentlemen, ladies! Today is a historic day. A day which we never conceived could come. The Island of Paradox is now paradox-less! Eighty percent of our fleet is gone, out doing their duty, but these fools realize how little that helps them! These waters are ours! For some, we have sailed them since birth! For others, we made it as if we were born on them! We live upon the sea! We shall protect our home! Now, as many of you know, they are here for some tredos. Klin and Joseph Markus, nephews of Joshua Rickstone. Many of you respect him, and you know he is my bruela. You are all my fatima, so consider them to be so as well. They have more than earned it. Now, board! SAIL! FIGHT!"

The men let out a raucous cheer and had their ships sea-worthy in a matter of five minutes. "Holy—now that's *fast!*" Klin cried. Beppo grinned, "Well, we do this almost every day tredo! Misha is about to learn a grave lesson. Never mess with the C.L.S." Klin nodded, "By the way, I think I can gather based on context clues, but bruela and fatima?" Beppo gave him a warm smile. "Brother and family." Klin's heart felt warm, despite the approaching bloodshed. Suddenly, Nathaniel tapped him on the shoulder. "Are you prepared to kill?" He asked. Klin drew his swords, gripping them tightly. "Yeah, unfortunately I don't have that kind of skill. I can't spare them in a battle of this scale, at least not yet. We have to kill." Nathaniel gave him a grim smile and was about to say something when suddenly the wind kicked up, and they burst out of port. At the same time, from all the ships, there was a loud drumming. It was slightly sinister, but also energetic and...hopeful? Klin looked over to see three men beating on drums, ominous grins on their faces. Suddenly, the mean on all the ships began to sing. "Let the drums beat/ Let the waves sing! You have just found/ your fate is owned by we/ We the warriors of the sea!/ We the men who shall sing!/ Run! Run!/ The gate of Heshtanus open and we are the keepers!/ Flee! Flee! For the

C.L.S. approaches!" Klin felt chills run down his spine. He was glad they were on his side.

As they neared the enemy, Beppo began to call out orders. "Cannons at the ready! Weavers, get to your positions!" Klin ran to the prow, one foot atop it, gripping a rope, sword in the other hand. The wind billowed his coat in front of him as he stared down the fleet. The *Water's Maiden* took point, the other C.L.S ships forming a V-shape behind them. The Seeker fleet was lined up next to one another, ten ships side by side in rows of six. The head flag of the Seekers flapped in the wind, proudly hoisted high in the back of the fleet. "There you are." Klin growled. "Won't even lead the charge you bitora." They were sixty feet away from the enemy fleet when suddenly, a line of fireballs shot out, all of them at their ship. "Klin!" Beppo warned. "I know! I see them!" Klin retorted. Time to try out some new moves, and hopefully intimidate them. Klin held out his hands, Fire Threads forming. He snaked them out to the fireballs, and forced them all into one giant ball. He cut off the spell, and jumped off the ship, blasts of fire shotting from his feet. He was launched forward, right next to the giant fireball. He unsheathed his other sword and crossed his arms, slashing the thing. He destroyed it, sparks and embers flying through the air. He twisted around, shooting a bolt of lighting at the sails of the ship in front right before he began to plumet.

Before he could fall too far though, a tendril of water had wrapped around his waist, putting him back on the ship safely. "Excellent Klin!" Beppo whooped. "Now! Fire!" There was a loud blast as the air smelled of smoke as *The Water's Maiden* unleashed a barrage of cannon fire. There were loud cries of panic as the Seeker ship began to sink. "They placed too much hope in that one attack it seems." Nathaniel observed. "How odd for an elite group." Suddenly, the other nine ships burst forward, shooting past them. Three of the ships made is past the C.L.S, but the rest were engaged with their men, and they were losing. "Looks like they have Air weavers." Nathaniel muttered. "No shit." Klin retorted, spinning his swords anxiously. The second fleet was upon them now. Two Seeker ships approached them, stopping on either side of them. A man on the port side shouted at them. "Surrender now and we won't—" He never got to finish as a nail drilled into his skull. The man plopped to the ground. Klin spun to see Beppo with his hammer, tossing a few nails in his palm. "And what? You won't rape our women and kill our families?" Beppo finished. "Shouldn't be doing that anyway you scoundrels! FOR CORONUS!"

"FOR CORONUS!" The men roared. Seekers began to board their ship. Klin dodged as one tried to kick him while swinging over. He cut the man's torso off. Blood splattered the deck and Klin froze as a sickening feeling overtook him. There was a loud cry behind him. He spun around to see a Seeker's blade coming down at him. He had no time to react. The man stopped though as a rapier blade protruded from his jaw. Nathaniel withdrew it and kicked the man away. "Don't freeze!" He shouted. Klin merely nodded as he spun around to engage the enemy. Both swords ran red as killed. Men kept coming, but Klin's skill had increased since last time. He swung at one man, his speed too fast for the man to block. He took of his head, before spinning and lighting three approaching him on fire. The men screamed as the turned to leap into the sea. Beppo ran up to him, firing nails with exact precision. Klin ducked as he fired one over his head, right into one of their captains. Klin placed one sword under his arm, the other over his back as seven men surrounded them. He spun around, slicing into at least four. Their heads rolled across the deck. Beppo closed the remaining distance between them, bones and armor crunching as he smashed a skull with his hammer. The final two leapt at Klin, swords raised high. Klin blocked both and then swept their feet out from under them, stabbing them in the chest as they fell. "That's all." Beppo said, looking around. "Get these nasty vessels out of our way!" The men nodded as they fired the cannons on both sides, sinking both ships. The battle was in full force now.

Ander leapt from roof to roof, prowling about in his tiger form. He had been given three animana potions before the battle, and so had two transformations before he needed to take one of the remaining two. Erok and Sasha rode close behind him in the street atop Debo. The Seekers had managed to land three ships, and the north-east front needed help. Ander led the way, his higher vantage point allowing him to make sense of the maze of streets. When they finally reached the battle, Sasha let out a gasp of horror. The beach was stained as red as the Seeker's uniforms. The hasty barricades that had been made were up in flames, and of the hundred men stationed here, about thirty remained. "Stop gawking!" Erok snapped, his bolts clicking into place as he readied his crossbow. "We're here to help! Now, remember, we have to kill! Now move!"

Ander growled in assent. He didn't like it, but as Sean said, he shouldn't. Ander leapt down upon the nearest soldier, the man crying in surprise as a tiger tore open his throat. Feeling sick, his tongue and fangs wet with blood, Ander let him and killed another. The five Seekers across from him began to tremble as he spat out gore, but they did not run. Props to them, but their hesitation meant death. As quick as a snake, Ander pounced, slitting two of their throats with a swipe of his paws. Then using his jaws, he grabbed a third by the throat and threw him onto the remaining two soldiers, pinning them down. Ten more soldiers rushed him, so he leapt atop the nearby roof. The soldiers aimed some bows at him, but that was fine. Erok now had his chance. There was a loud whish as a line was flung by. Erok zipped across, flying along a circumfixal path. He let lose ten bolts, each one finding their target in a fatal blow.

Erok landed on a roof, and then shouted as loud as he could. "FALL BACK! GET TO THE STREETS!" Ander turned him and then quickly flipped the coin. Falcon. Awesome. He began to fly around, raking and pecking enemy eyes, or overall just being a nuisance. He was not doing much lasting damage to most, but he *was* giving their allies a chance to retreat. Slowly but surely, the C.L.S was able to retreat into the city. They would know what path to take, where they would find Sasha waiting for them with instructions. Erok continued to zip across roofs with his grappling hook, sniping soldiers as we did. When the last C.L.S. member got in the city, Erok shouted. "Alright, let's go!" Ander zipped back into the city, barley avoiding a spear thrown at him as he did. They had a surprisingly low number of archers with them. That was going to cost the Seekers.

They found their way back to Sasha, landing behind her. A few minutes later, the Seekers came charging up at them, but stopped as they realized Erok had been leading them on. Hundreds of icicles hung in the air before them, and before they could warn the others, Sasha and the Water Weavers with her fired. Blood mixed with the crystals upon the pavement as the C.L.S. let out a savage cheer, charging in to pick off those who have survived the attack. Ander returned to human, catching his breath. "Nice. That worked perfectly." Erok nodded with a small grin. "Right? For once it actually went well. Now, who's in charge here?" The men reassembled, the Seekers either fleeing or lying dead. "You are sir." One said. Erok paused, "Uh, what?" The man shrugged, "Our commanding officer died on the beach. That's half the reason we started to lose." Erok shook his head, "Damn, is there not anyone else?" One of the men shouted, "Well, you did save our lives back there!"

"Herk you all!" Erok yelled, "Fine! Get back here! We're going to set up some more traps! This city is a maze, so let's make it a little more deadly." The men nodded and set to work as Erok shouted out orders. "Damn it!" Ander cried suddenly, "We've got three more ships approaching shore!" Erok looked to where he was pointing, squinting at them. "Ah, they're idiots!" Erok laughed, "How are these guys elite warriors? They're approaching at normal speed, so we've got half an hour before they make shore! That'll cost them their lives." Erok chuckled menacingly as he continued laying out defenses. Ander shook his head. Erok's confidence made sense, but the Seekers; they were acting way too confident in their strategy. They were hiding something. Something dangerous. "Still, we should be wary." Ander said. "Something about their strategies seem strange. Like they know they have some ace up their sleeve." *Hmmm, good observation.* Lupis hummed. Erok paused, then cursed under his breath. "Shit, you're right. I'm getting overconfident myself. We need to be on the lookout. In the meantime, help a guy out!" Ander nodded as he hopped over to help with defenses.

Joseph stood by Celeste on the North Gate, watching the five ships approaching them. "Stay close by me, okay?" Joseph ordered softly. "I'm more skilled than you." Celeste grumbled, "You need to stick close to *me*." Joseph chuckled at that. "You got it Miss Aristocrat."

"Shut up idiot." But a smile was playing across her lips now. Joseph could not help but smile. Her confidence was almost back. Or, at least that false show of confidence she normally had. Something was broken in her. He couldn't figure out what, but any shadow of her former self was a good thing, especially before battle. As the wind blew across them, their hair flying in the wind, her look of love and fierce protection on her face; well, Joseph had never seen her look more beautiful. "Hey Celeste?" Celeste glanced at him, then frowned, noticing the seriousness in his face. "Yeah?"

"Do-don't die on me, okay?" Joseph said, looking out at the horizon. "I gotta tell you something after this, so you can't die on me, got it?" He looked down in surprise as Celeste squeezed his hand. "I won't, and I promise that none of us will die either." Joseph smiled as the conch horn blew, letting them all know to prepare. "All touching things." Joshua slurred, putting his arms around them and leaning over them. "But can it."

"Come one Uncle—"

"I said shut it!"

"Technically you said can it." Celeste retorted. Joshua just let out a groan. "Youngins, may the sharks take a large bite out of yer egos." At that moment, the ships made shore and Seekers began to pile off with a roaring charge. The C.L.S soldiers on the dock beat back three waves before being overwhelmed. Their ranks as it suddenly became a free for all fight to survive. "Aight! Looks like ya kids are up!" Joshua shouted. Then with a whoop, the crazy old man leapt from roof to roof, leaping into the fray. Celeste and Joseph looked each other in the eye, then nodded. Celeste slid down the ladder behind them, while Joseph waited. Some allied soldiers with bows made a show of shotting the men trying to breach the gate, but they were just a distraction.

"Markus." One of the archers called. Joseph walked over to the edge. The soldiers below had placed all their men with shields by the gate. They formed wall of iron shields, keeping them safe from the arrows above. Joseph let out a low whistle as he ignited his hand, purple energy swirling around it. "That's quite the number." He said. The archer nodded. "Good luck." Joseph flashed him a smile. "Thanks. Don't think I'll need it though." He leaned over and shouted, "Hey!" A few of the soldiers lowered their shields to look at him in confusion. "Screw you guys!" Joseph leapt down right in the opening, bracing his legs with dark magic energy, and punched the ground with his enhanced hand. The Seekers in a twenty-foot radius all flew into the air, suspended there. Joseph stood up and spun in a circle before punching the solider most in the middle. A great blast of purple energy emitted out in a cone behind the soldier for twenty feet. Anyone engulfed in was killed, leaving only corpses to hit the ground as his spell wore off.

Joseph then dance to the side before the soldiers he had not killed recovered. The gate doors flew open, revealing six cannons lining the entrance. Joseph gave them a dainty wave and said in a mockingly high-pitched voice. "Bye-bye!" A few Seekers turned to give him glares before they were cut down by the cannons. That was fair. He was making them seem like absolute fools. But fools were not able to kill as efficiently as they did. Joseph let out a ferocious roar as he leapt into battle, the gates shutting tight. He cut down an enemy who was about to kill an ally. He fought furiously, a whirlwind of black death as he danced across the battlefield. He used a mixture of magic infused brawling and heavy sword strikes. As he got surrounded, he spun in a circle, the Black Rose slashing through torsos and chests. A man in front of him had the sense to leap back, but Joseph jolted forward at the end of his spin, punching the man in the head. The helmet crumpled under his fist like aluminum foil.

As he fought, deflecting blows and counterattacking, he kept an eye out for Celeste. Where was she? Finally, he spotted her fighting a Lighting Weaver. She had just dodge a bolt of lightning, using Yatta to destroy it before it could run wild into their allies. Then killed the man who had cast it. Joseph quickly cut off the head of the woman he was fighting and began to make his way over to Celeste. It was hard. Seekers were everywhere. Yet, he was able to fight he was to her. They were on soldi ground now, the fighting moving off the dock pier. As soon as he reached her though, a all of stone leapt up around them. "Heh, well at least it's not fire." Joseph remarked. Celeste smirked at that. "Yeah, that's too cliché." They went back to back, muscles tensing and ready to strike. "Shut up!" A Seeker squealed, tossing a ball of fire at Celeste.

Joseph cut it down, and then glared at the man as more Seekers began to approach them. "Okay, you die first!" The man's eyes brimmed with fear, but he charged at Joseph. A wall of flame appeared and rushed him. Joseph cloaked his body in dark energy, forming a dome. He stabbed forward as the wall of fire was on him and heard a loud gurgle. Just like he'd thought. The man slumped as he removed the sword from his throat and the fire dissipated. "Come on!" Joseph screamed, "Who else wants some?!" There were about fifteen more Seekers, and they accepted his challenge. Joseph stopped thinking and just acted. He blocked three blades coming down at his head and pushed them off. He leaned back, avoiding two blades from either side trying to get his throat. The first three were off balance, so he crouched, the two trying to behead him and spun. Celeste had moved forward, so she was out of reach. He cut off the two's legs, then stood up, forming a shield of solid purple as a blast of light came at him. He grunted as he was pushed back a bit. Those first three were responsible for that. He ignored the screams of the legless soldiers and spun his shield to his back. He heard two blades bounce off of it, which were followed by two screams as Celeste dispatched them.

He quickly cut through three more blasts of golden light, then held out his hand, pushing the shield at some Seekers who were trying to circle around and sneak up on Celeste. He then detonated it, killing one in a small explosion while knocking the other two to the ground. He let Celeste take care of them while he kept blocking the attacks of Light magic. The three Weavers were obviously getting frustrated with him. They had never trained against someone who could simply destroy or block a spell with a sword. He finally rushed them, destroying their panic blasts. He brought his sword in a diagonal slash, nearly hitting one as he stumbled back. The other two threw up shields of light, but he shattered those with his strike. They cried out in dismay as all three were off balance. Before they could react, Joseph backhand the one who had not summoned a shield. The man flew at the earth wall with furious force, and slumped to the ground a corpse. He blocked a dual strike from the remaining two, then kicked one in the genitals, and slid up along the other, the blades scraping against one another. He grabbed the man by the throat, stabbing the other in the chest. He drew his sword out and hefted it with one hand, the one in his grip, eyes going wide with fear.

He dropped them, cutting off the head quickly before turning around. Five bodies lay dead and Celeste dueling the last one. The woman was twice her size and could give Joseph a run for muscle weight. She and Celeste had their blades locked, and the Seeker was pressing in on her. "Damn you!" Joseph roared as he charged forward. The woman glanced at him, which was all that Celeste needed to be able to pull out safely. They eyed one another before the woman lifted her sword with both hands, fire erupting around it. The sword only fell halfway as Celeste moved faster than Joseph had thought she was capable of. In a blur, she shot forward slicing the stomach, before spinning behind the cut both Achille's tendons. The woman fell to her knees, unable to stand, before being beheaded. Celeste had done it so quick, the woman had never had time to scream.

The earth resumed its normal formations as the stone sank back down, sand flying up as it did. Celeste quickly shook the blood from Yatta and nodded to him. They prepared to re-enter the fray when a massive wind knocked them over. There was a deafening roar of wind above them, and the wind whipped about so violently that he was forced to close his eyes. Went it ended, Joseph got to his feet, looking around. Besides a few moans of pain, the battlefield was silent. All the Seekers lay dead. "What just happened?" He asked bewildered. "Look out to sea kid." His uncle grunted as he approached them. He pointed a bloody finger towards the Seeker fleet. Approaching the fleet was not just one, or two, but *five* tornadoes. Four tornadoes circled around the fifth like some sort of barrier, and the fifth was enormous. "HAHAHA! We got this now!" Joseph cheered deliriously, "Who is that by the way?"

"Yer mother." Joshua answered solemnly. "She won't be able to do anything else after casting a spell like that, but that's how powerful she truly is." Joseph looked out in awe as four ships fell to his mother's fury. "Can you believe this Celeste? Who knew she had been hiding that kind of power!" He remarked turning to her, but she was gone. "Celeste?" He called, panic creeping in. "Where'd that bugger go?" Joshua growled. "I don't kno—wait." Dread crept into Joseph's heart. "Oh no. I think I do know." Suddenly her brokenness made sense. Her words to protect everyone came back to him. *Everyone.* "Shit." He muttered as he ran off towards the headquarters, where Celeste had gone.

Chapter 36

Choices & Consequences

Celeste's feet bounced and thudded against the pavement as she ran, blowing by the empty houses and cheering soldiers. She had to get the Water Seed before the battle was over. Before more people died. She rushed into the courtyard and ran face first into a guard. She fell on her rear and looked up panting as she recovered her breath. "Whoa! You okay there miss?" The guard exclaimed, then paused frowning. "Wait, what are you doing here?" Celeste began to panic. Beppo must have planned this, expecting her to try this! Damn him! What should she do?!

Lorelei watched in satisfaction as Seeker boat number twenty-one was torn apart. That would teach them to go after her sons. Various Weavers uselessly hurled spells at her, somehow expecting there weak power to break through a tornado. It had been summoned by magic, but it was now a natural force, barley needing her little remaining animana to be directed and controlled. The spells they shot at her only added to the power of her tornado. The idiots were just making it increasingly more difficult to defeat her. She shook her head as another ship sank under her wrath. No wonder the Ardaven king held so little power; his elite forces were laughable compared to the Coronus Elite Guard. Now *they* could destroy her spell. Suddenly a flurry of air slices shot at her smaller tornadoes. She let them hit, but her eyes went wide as they destroyed them. Guess they did have some in their ranks with actual power.

"Well, well that bastard didn't marry a weakling after all." Lorelei's blood ran cold at the sound of the voice. She would forever have his voice ingrained in her mind, even though she had only ever met him once before. Viscious hovered in the air before her, arms crossed smugly. "You!" Lorelei snarled as she threw one of her daggers, "You're supposed to be dead!" Viscious somehow made his dodge seem disdainful. "I could say the same about you. Better calm down or I won't make my offer." Lorelei kept her array of air blades around Visicious, having him surrounded in every way possible. "And what would that be?" Lorelei growled. Viscious smiled; sinister smile that made her heart drop and fear fill her chest. She might have already lost this battle. "A chance." He explained "Your only chance to win to be honest. I'm sure you've noticed some oddities across this adventure. How does Misha know so much about your sons? How did she find you again?" Lorelei waved her hand, "Yes, yes, there's a traitor. We've known that." Lorelei took a small amount of satisfaction at the surprise in the ugly creatures face.

"My brother and I have known for a long time and kept an eye out. It's Nathaniel obviously." Viscious actually had the audacity to laugh at that, which made Lorelei almost attack right then. But shed held. Barely. "No, but good guess!" Viscious sneered. Drat! She and Joshua had been so sure...oh no. "It's Celeste." Lorelei whispered, the poor girl's inner battle suddenly making much more sense. Viscious applauded, "Very good! Excellent job, really! Only took you two guesses! Now, for my offer, for I do love a good wager! Celeste is on her way to get me the Seed. Stop her, and I will get Misha to disappear, as well as myself, conceding defeat."

"And if I fail?" Lorelei asked. Viscious smiled ominously, folding his wings in, showing off a terrible scorch mark on his right wing. "I exact my revenge on those arrogant sons of yours. Master wants them on his side, but well...he won't be too bothered if they are dead." Lorelei hesitated before dropping all the spells around him. She dispersed her tornado, knowing well what it meant. As she turned away Viscious called, "Oh, and you must kill her for it to count. She's probably already hurt that loaf with the black hair." Lorelei felt her stomach sink, as she flew away with a boom, leaving Viscious laughing maniacally.

Ander wiped the blood from his mouth, seriously debating going vegan after this. The last of the Seekers that had made it to land were dead, with half the street gone too as their price. He had been dropping explosive barrels on the enemy and was exhausted. Dire forms turned

411

out to take a lot of effort when it wasn't the default form. He collapsed into Debo's side and let out a relieved sigh. "We done know?" He asked drearily. He leapt up though as he heard a scream. Heshtisi Gruntlets were pouring out of the ships and into the city. "ARE YOU HERKING KIDDING ME?!" Erok yelled from the rooftop. "WHERE THE HERK WERE THEY EVEN KEEPING THEM???!"

"Language!" Sasha scolded. Ander chugged his last animana restoring potion and threw it on the gournd. "Not herking now Sasha!" He exclaimed. He was sore, tired, and starving, yet he still flipped his coin, transforming a tiger. Sasha drank a potion herself and formed a whip of water, screaming, "I am *so* done with this!" as a Gruntlet leapt at her. The Heshtisi was ripped apart by her whip and their army let out a tired war cry as they met the new army.

Joseph burst onto the training grounds, his breathing ragged from running at his limit the whole way. His side ached, and chest hurt a little, but he ignored it as he quickly scanned around. The three men who had been guarding the entrance were lying on the ground. He ran over and checked their them out. They were just unconscious with no wounds. The doors to the headquarters were flung wide open though. He ran in and found more unconscious guards littering the halls. *Damn you Celeste.* He thought, *What in Heshtanus is driving you so much?*

He burst into Beppo's office and found her, hands inches from the water thingy. "STOP!" He cried. "Joseph…" Celeste said, her voice full of conflicted emotions. Anger, determination, insecurity, sadness. "Wh—how—why are you here?"

"That's my question!" Joseph snapped. "What are you doing? Beppo told us quite clearly if we use it, you die!" She shook her head shakily, "I-I'm not going to use it." Joseph threw up his hands, "Then what are you doing?!" Tears began to form at the edges of her beautiful blue eyes. "I-I-I have to give it to him!" She wailed, "Or I'll fail her again!" Joseph felt dread creeping up his spine like a spider. "To who?" He asked carefully, "Who's this 'her'?"

"Selene!" Celeste cried, tears coming down fast now. Joseph froze, "What? That doesn't make sense." She was shaking hard now. "Viscious. He—he told me that he can bring her back if I get this for him. Please, don't stop me. I know it's wrong. But I failed her and only she can save me. Ple-" She stopped and shrieked as Joseph approached her. She drew Yatta, which made him freeze, his heart aching. Joseph then decided to do what he knew must be done. He stepped forward, grabbing her wrist and twisting it. She yelped as she dropped Yatta, but it was muffled as he wrapped her into a hug. "I know. She's gone." Joseph whispered, "And I know how much it hurts to lose family, but she wouldn't want to be brought back! Not at the cost you're giving! Not like this!" Celeste looked at him, eyes full of wonder, confusion, and most of all, terror. She needed a reminder of how much she was loved.

So, Joseph did what he had been wanting to do for weeks now. He kissed her. He felt her surprise and hesitation, but she quickly melted into it and returned the kiss. They pulled away gently, Celeste looking up at him, her eyes shimmering. "I love you, Celeste." Joseph said softly, "So, I'm not going to let you make a deal with a demon! Got it?" She nodded, obviously at a loss for words. "Good, now let's get out of here." He let go off her and turned around to leave. Suddenly, there was a loud crack as something smacked him in the back of the head. Hard. He slumped to the ground, stunned and dazed, already feeling consciousness slipping out of his grasp. "Sorry." Celeste croaked, "But I've already made the deal." There was another loud bang, and all faded to black.

Lorelei burst through the window of Beppo's office, glass spraying the ground. She quickly surveyed the room. Celeste was looking at her in shock, her sword in hand and Joseph lying on the floor beside her, blood dripping from the sword's pommel. Lorelei let out a scream as she unleashed a flurry of air slices at her. Celeste somehow noticed them coming and dodged or sliced through them. Lorelei was somewhat impressed. No wonder the girl had made it this far. But she was now a threat and was no match for a mother's fury. Lorelei battered the traitor's defenses, wearing her down little by little.

Soon, the girl was covered in cuts along her arms and legs. Celeste wavered, so Lorelei threw out her daggers, guiding them as she spun them around her. Celeste let out a wail of pain as her face and wrists were cut. Nothing lethal or deep, but enough to force her to drop her sword. With a twirl of her wrists, Lorelei had Celeste bound and strung up in the air. "So, you *are* the traitor." Lorelei said contemptuously.

"You're a threat to us now. If you had not harmed anyone, I might have been willing to talk things out. Now though, I'm going to have to kill you. Anything to say for yourself?" Celeste stayed silent. As Lorelei held her daggers out in the air behind her, she looked Celeste in the eyes. If she was going to kill her, she needed to do that. Her face was red, wet, and puffy from crying. Some snot trickled down her blotched face, and her eyes...oh Genus her eyes. Those deep blue eyes shone with nothing but sadness, despair, and regret.

She was still a child. A child lost and in need of guidance and love. Lorelei's heart went to as she felt her anger abate and released the poor girl and hugged her. "Wha-?"

"Shh, it's okay." Lorelei soothed and stroked her head. "It's okay. I forgive you. You can explain this all later." She pulled back and looked Celeste in the eyes and smiled, "I'm a mother after all." That did it. Celeste's final wall crumbled as she fell to her knees. Covered in blood, snot, and tears, Celeste began to bawl like a newborn, clutching to Lorelei. "I'm sorry! I'm so sorry!" Celeste wailed, over and over again. Lorelei got down on her knees and simply hugged her, softly whispering to her. "It's okay. It will be all okay." They stayed like that for nearly ten minutes. Lorelei let out a small smile as she heard Joseph groan. Good, that meant he had not been hurt badly. She wiped the tears from Celeste's eyes. "Now, take some deep breaths." Celeste obeyed, as Lorelei did the same, using the last of her animana as she healed Joseph and Celeste. Celeste let out a small gasp as all her wounds closed. "Better?" Celeste nodded. "Good" Viscious snarled, "Time's up, and I'm tired of waiting!"

Lorelei spun around to see Viscious standing in the doorway. "And it looks like you lose!" He spat, "Even worse, no one followed any of the rules! None of the deals made were followed through on!" Lorelei was suddenly flung into the air. She struggled uselessly, the last of her magic spent. "The only thing I hate more than self-righteous pricks is cheaters!" Viscious growled. "No!" Celeste screamed, "Don't hurt her! We had a deal!" Viscsious gave her a triumphant smile as he scooped up the Seed. "Yes, we did. Yet how is any of this fulfilling our deal? *You* had to hand it to me. Are you giving it to me now? No? So be quiet." Celeste fell to her knees, the little hope Lorelei had been restoring squashed like a bug. Viscisous turned his attention back to Lorelei and let out a soft purr. "Ohhh, how I've longed for this! Do you have any idea how much I have wanted to kill you? It is more than those sons of yours, I can assure you of that!"

Joseph slowly stood up at that moment, finally recovered. "Mom? What's going on?" He asked. He froze, as he took in the sights. Frozen spikes appeared in the air all around him suddenly. "Don't move." Viscious said calmly, "I'm technically not allowed to kill you, at least not in this circumstance, but I *can* make you very immobile." A dark, fierce look spread across Joseph's face, but he stayed where he was. "Now, where was I? Oh yes!" Viscious grabbed Lorelei's face, his claws sinking into her cheeks. He forced her to look at his wing; at that garish black scorch mark. "Do you see this?" He asked quietly, "DO YOU?! *Your sons* did this! If you had controlled your lust better, then they would never have been born, you pig! You share in their crime! And since I can't kill them, I will *gladly* settle for the one who birthed them!"

"NO!" Joseph cried. At that moment, Celeste let out a soul-piercing scream as she leapt at Viscious, raking his face with her nails. Viscious grunted as he backhanded her off of him, sending her sprawled across the floor. "Attack me again, and I'll kill you." He hissed, "Consider this second chance your reward for serving me." Celeste weakly lifted her head off the ground staring at Lorelei, nothing but apologetic sorrow in her eyes. Viscious flashed a triumphant smile at Lorelei, "I will give you the honor of some last words." Lorelei looked at Joseph and Celeste and gave them a loving smile. "I don't blame you Celeste, and neither of you should. I love you." Then, Lorelei died smiling. As the Air Threads forced her throat open and went down into her lungs her lasts thoughts were of her husband. *I hope I did well Jethro. I'll see you soon enough to ask.* Her lungs expanded, exploding along with her body in a bloody mess.

Chapter 36

Reconciliation

Celeste threw up, her puke splattering all across the floor. "Damn Markuses." Viscious growled. "Even in death, they never beg or grovel." With that, he turned, grabbed the Water Seed, and strode out the door. Celeste looked at the pile of gore that had been Lorelei and screamed. She screamed and screamed until she could not muster the strength any longer. She rolled over and lay down, wishing it was her who had died there. Just like Selene, she had killed Lorelei. "Celeste." Joseph said hoarsely. "Just go away!: Celeste sobbed, "Go away or just kill me!"

She heard him get him and he loomed over her. "No." He said simply, some force returning to his voice and eyes. "Mom's final words were of love, and she didn't blame you, so neither will I!" Celeste sat up, curling up and shaking her head. "B-b-but it's still my fault!"

"NO! It's not." Joseph growled forcefully, "Viscious is completely responsible. Mom said to not blame yourself! So, damn you, don't do this! Get up!" Joseph yanked her to her feet, but she still protested. "What are we doing? She's dead—"

"I KNOW!" Joseph roared, "Damn it! I know." He whispered, barely holding back tears. "But we still have a job to do, so we can't fall apart and mourn her. Not yet." Joseph picked up Yatta and thrust her into her hands. Celeste almost did not keep hold of the blade out of surprise. *Celeste?* Yatta whispered, seeming scared. *I'm here.* Celeste replied gently. *I'm so sorry for everything.* She placed all her sorrow, regret, and love towards her friend. She could feel Yatta mulling over it and accepting it. These feelings were true and from love now, so while it was a bitter taste for Yatta, she would not be hurt. *I'm sorry too.* Yatta replied, *I wish there was something that could help. WAIT!* Joseph yelped,

416

clutching his head. "Ow! Yatta watch it! That hurt!" Yatta gave him a sheepish smiled as she appeared to the both of them. "Sorry." She chimed, "But I just remembered something. Something locked away until she was ready. I have a message for you. From Selene."

"What?" Celeste asked incredulously, "How—" She stopped though as Selene appeared in front of them. She was a flickering projection of light, but while see through, she still had all the colors she would have in the flesh. She...she was wearing the outfit Celeste had bought her for her birthday. Selene gave her a small smile. "Hey Celeste. If you're hearing this, then the best of the worst-case scenarios came to pass. The Heshtisi attacked at some point today, and you survived, but I'm dead. I've kept quiet about this to keep you safe, but the Heshtisi are real. They are those monsters you saw. Anyway, a leader of theirs has been in contact with me over the past few months. His name is Viscious."

"He wants me to join them. He makes all these promises, but I can see the evil lurking in his eyes. I would never trust a monster like him. But, if I don't they'll kill you. I will never serve them, but I refuse to let you die. I know you try so hard to do the right thing, but constantly feel like you have no skills in anything. I have to say sis, that's really vain of you to think that your sins are unique. Which means though you'll probably blame yourself for my death. Don't. At this point and time, there was nothing you could have done to prevent it. You're talented, even more than me, but you need more time before you can face these monsters head on. You'll be the one that can stand up to them, not me. Deep down, you're a much better person than me. But you need to start acknowledging you virtues as well as your sins Celeste. Otherwise, you'll never truly grow, and if you are going to take down Viscisous, which after this message I'm sure you're going to want to do, you'll need to grow before you are ready. Don't sweat it though, I know you'll surpass me in all things one day. I love you Celeste, never forget that."

The image of Selene vanished as Celeste stood there quietly, letting Selene's words rest in her heart. "Why now?" Celeste asked quietly, anger creeping into her voice. "Why after all *this*, did you finally show me that message?" Yatta reappeared, sitting on Joseph's shoulder. He looked over at her, and tried to touch her, his hand going through. She swatted him and said sadly, "Because you weren't ready to hear it. That

last of your walls are finally down and you can accept the truth again."
Celeste wanted to argue, but she knew Yatta was right. Years ago, that
message from Selene would not have changed anything. "Alright, no
more then." She declared. Joseph tried to say something, but she cut him
off. "No more doubt, self-pity, and lies" Celeste held out Yatta, other
hand on her waist. "I am Celeste Elizabeth Farvor'Coal! I am skilled
in swordplay, beautiful, and will be the death of that maggot Viscious!"

"Herk yeah!" Joseph whooped, "Let's kill that bastard rat with
wings!" Celeste sheathed Yatta and gave one final look at Lorelei's
corpse. *I swear I'll do my best to make you proud Ms. Lorelei.* With that
they let the room, breaking into a run. "Where do you think he's at?"
Joseph asked.

"The Temple."

"Why there?"

"The look he gave the Seed." Celeste explained, "I think it's still
locked or sealed somehow. He's going to want to unlock it." Joseph
nodded, "Alright, makes sense. But more importantly, how do we kill
him? Klin and I barely hurt him, remember?"

"I think I can help!" Yatta piped. The two skidded to a halt and
listened to Yatta explain. "Hmmm, yeah maybe." Joseph mused, stroking
his chin. He smiled evilly. "Let's do this."

Klin sliced a Gruntlet in two, watching it turn to ash. Just as they
had victory in their grasp, these damn things had started crawling out
of portals! Nathaniel stood at his back, slashing at one. "Can't really say
I missed these things." He chuckled. Klin blocked at blade as it went for
his head, stabbing the creature with his other sword. "Yeah, me either."
He remarked, "However, if they are coming from Seeker ships, they
must have been summoned by someone in the fleet." A cannon from
any enemy ship suddenly fired. Klin threw up his hands, a light shield
almost finished when a pillar of water shot up.

He flinched as salt water sprayed into a wound on his cheek. "That's
all of them sir!" One of the men shouted. "Someone blow off all these
ashes then!" Beppo commanded. "And sink that ship that just fired!"
A wind kicked up as the ashes were scattered to the sea, while *The
Ocean's Maiden* unleashed a volley of cannon fire at the enemy ship in
the distance. Beppo leapt down from some rigging and took the helm.

418

"What now?" Klin shouted. Beppo gave him a grim look as he pointed to the flagship. "We got for the head of the viper. How many enemy ships?"

"They only have twelve left Commander!" A soldier informed, "But, we only have three ships left, including us." Klin looked out to sea. It was a swamp of broken ship parts. "And there are seven ships ashore." Nathaniel cried out, lowering a spy glass. "If they have Heshtisi on their ships too, then they may need help also." Beppo cursed under his breath, "They most certainly have them. We need a plan, and fast." Klin raised his hand, "Commander, if I may?" Beppo nodded, "Speak freely." Klin climbed up next to the helm with him. "These last twelve Seeker ships, they refuse to advance on us. Why?" Beppo frowned. "Perhaps they have a trap in store." Klin shook his head. "I don't think so. I think they are afraid. Out of sixty ships, all of the thirty-eight we destroyed had weavers on them. About twenty per ship. That's an absurdly high number of Weavers, even for Ardaven. What is most likely going on then, is that if there *are* any Weavers left, they are only on Misha's ship."

Beppo nodded, "Hmm, yes that seems likely. So, what is it that you are proposing?" Klin held out his palm, "Nathaniel has been teaching me lots of different spells. Let me take out those eleven ships all at once!"

"No!" Beppo answered sharply, "You may be talented, but you are still human. A spell of that caliber would most likely kill you!"

"But—"

"I said no!" Beppo barked. Klin cast his head down. He could end this pointless battle so easily though! He looked up though as Beppo placed a hand on his shoulder and squeezed gently. "I would not be able to face your mother if you died." Beppo said gently, "Besides, *it is* still a good plan. We shall merely tweak it." Beppo turned around and shouted, "Send this out to the ships! We have a plan to win!"

Sasha hit the ground hard, her shoulder screaming out in pain. She paid it no head though as she rolled away from a gruntlet's blade. Debo let out a roar as he killed the monster. The owlbear stood in front of her protectively, squawking at the demons approaching them. She patted Debo with her good arm. Drat, the other might just be broken. "Herk, they just keep coming!" Sasha cried as she shot an ice shard at a gruntlet.

"Language!" Erok yelled as he saved her from a pagom with a well-placed shot between the eyes. "Shut up!" She shot back wearily. She was running low on animana. All those large-scale attacks had really pushed her to her limit. Ander was slowing down also. She gritted her teeth as she formed a water whip. That was another fifteen animana gone. She estimated she had about tweny left before she was spent.

She swung the whip in a wide arc in front of her, knocking the five pagom rushing her back with a crack. Sasha really could not afford to drop this spell. Suddenly Erok zipped down next to her, twin daggers in hand. "I'm all out of bolts." He said, "And our archers are spent too." There numbers were dwindling. The streets looked like rivers of blood. "We need a new plan. Now!" Erok snarled as he cut down three gruntlest in succent. "We need a miracle." Sasha whispered.

At that moment, three things happened. All of the Heshtis froze, a confused look to their expressions. Then they turned and began to flee as there was a large roar behind Sasha. She turned to see a whole battalion of C.L.S soldiers charging down the street, Joshua at their head. "Leave my kids alone!" He roared. The soldiers washed over the demons, overwhelming them in an instant. Sasha was about the cheer when there was a large explosion. "What was *that*? Sasha asked fearfully. Ander landed next to her, transforming back to human from his falcon from. "It's Beppo!" He explained, eyes wide. "He—he just blew up two of our ships!"

"What?!" Erok cried, "Is the man *insane?!*" Ander slumped forward. Sasha was barely able to catch him, her right arm screaming in pain as she caught him. "I saw their crew members being escorted back via water and air magic." Ander said, "They sent their ships into the Seeker fleet and blew them up!" At that moment Joshua walked over. "Heshtisi are dead. Everyone okay?" They all nodded. "Good 'casue—" *Boom!* The ground shook violently, knocking everyone to the ground. "Oh now what?!" Erok complained. Sasha got back to her feet, coughing and checked on the others. Joshua was standing, eyes wide and a manic look of alarm on his face. "Joshua?" Ander asked tentatively. "You two." Joshua ordered, pointing at Erok and Sasha, "Get to the Temple. Now!"

"Wha—"

"No time ta explain!" Joshua shouted, "Lives are in danger! Now move! Ander, you and me! Beach. Now!" He scooped up and Ander took off running. "Ahhhh!" Ander screamed as they disappeared. "What is he doing?" Sasha asked shrilly, "He's acting even more insane than usual!!!" Erok shook his head, "Yeah, but he has had uncanny insight during those bouts of insanity. Let's do as he says."

Klin watched in satisfaction as the ships exploded. The crews were back on land after prepping all the gunpowder barrels. The wind spells that fanned the flames helped a lot though also. He drew his swords as they sailed for the final ship left, the one that had lurked behind the those eleven, just watching them die. The flames around Misha's ship swerved away as the ship cut through the waves. Klin spotted Misha standing atop the prow. "Surrender bitora!" Beppo called cheerfully, "I might just let you live! It's over!"

"Not. Yet!" Misha snarled. Suddenly, hundreds of red threads appeared. A chill ran through Klin's spine as he warned. "Beppo! Shields up now!" He ran to the head of the ship and leapt off, blasting high into the air. Misha was weaving a fireball as large as their ship! Even worse, she looked on mildly strained from the effort. Klin heard the now familiar whoosh of wind as Beppo got their wind barrier up. Klin spun in the air, high enough now, that he dived down. The wind rushed in his ears, drowning out all but the rapid beating of his heart. Just as Misha's fireball appeared, he flipped, feet-first, and stabbed the fireball.

He saw the aftereffects of the spell only seconds before they went into effect. Just enough time to throw a protective sphere of light around himself. The fireball, instead of disappearing, exploded, throwing out a force so powerful that Klin was shot rocketing skyward. He bounced around in his little ball, getting extremely dizzy. Thankfully, the bouncing was painless. *Thanks Nathaniel.* He grunted, before realizing he was now falling. He had touched the clouds; he had been thrown so high! He reoriented himself, looking down. *The Ocean's Maiden* had been blown back to Solanthis's shore very unceremoniously. Yet, Misha's ship was completely undamaged! Klin made a split-second decision and roared, dropping his shield as he began to carefully blast his way to the ship.

He countered his speed with blasts of fire, slowing himself as needed. When he was thirty feet from the ship, a swirling storm of fire shot towards him. Klin narrowly avoided it by blasting to the side but cried out in pain as his backed slammed into a mast. As he fell, he stabbed his swords into the mast, sliding down with it. With a shout, he wove small blasts of fire under his feet. It slowed him, but not enough to land painlessly. He hit the ground and fell in a tumble. He heard the clatter of metal as he let go of his swords. Klin moaned as he finally came to a stop. His whole body hurt, and he felt dazed. He almost certainly had a concussion from that. At least nothing was broken though.

Suddenly, someone grabbed him by the collar of his coat and lifted him up. "You." Misha snarled, blood dripping from her forehead as she glared at him, eyes full of fury. "I bet you thought that was terribly clever of you, huh?" Klin smirked, "I mean, yeah it was." He got punched in the face as an answer. "All of my men are dead because of you!" She hissed. "I barely had time to save myself and then the ship!" Klin just now noticed the burned bodies across the ship. For most, even the bones were gone. "Shouldn't have tried to kill mine then." Klin growled. Misha hoisted him higher, choking him. "I may lost this battle," Misha whispered triumphantly, "But at least I get to take you back!" Klin grabbed her hands and gasped, "No thanks!" He spat in her eyes before kicking off her stomach. Misha squealed in anger as she lost her grip on him and wiped her eyes. "Why must you fight this every inch of the way!" She shrieked. Klin summoned a golden ball of energy. "I'm not the one who refused peace!" He snapped as he tossed it. Misha wove a small wall of fire in the air between her arms, blocking the attack.

"I'm not the one refusing a citizen's duty!" She screamed, her voicing reaching high pitches only dogs could probably hear. Klin tossed a bolt of lighting at her, but she intercepted it with a bolt of fire. "That the best you got?" She smirked, "First thing I'll do is teach you better spells!" Klin growled as he quickly wove a series of light spears around him. Misha's eyes widened as they launched at her. She already had a dome of fire up around though. Klin did not care since she had blinded herself. The true attack was being woven now. All three elements wove together in the air above them. It took all of the animana he had left, but it would be worth it. As Misha dropped her shield, Klin activated

the first part of the spell. Four flames snaked from the air above him and shout out, setting the ship aflame. The flames continued to circle around the ship, swooping down every few seconds.

Misha laughed as she extinguished the flames. "You do know I can put these out?"

"I know bitora." Klin replied as he dodged a blast from her. "Ugh! What does that even mean?!" Klin began scouring the ship for his swords, "It means one less than a pig."

"I'm going to kill that Zalecathian!" Misha sneered as she wove a whip of fire and lashed out. Klin barely dodged, finally spotting his swords. They were behind Misha. He gulped. He had never been particularly good at jump rope. Klin charged at Misha, who seemed somewhat surprised, and leapt over a strike from the whip. He hit the ground rolling, feeling the heat of the flames pass over his head. He then danced to the side, barely avoiding the whip as it broke the wooden boards of the deck. He then ran and leapt into a dive, just barely avoiding getting his face burned. As he hit the ground, he rolled back up and activated the final two parts of his spell. A dark thunder cloud appeared, and lightning began to lash out from hit, striking the ship. Misha glared at him as she shot fire at the lightning bolts. They were still magic, so she would be seeing the threads coming. Unfortunately, though, she decided to keep attacking him.

Klin kept avoiding the flames from her whip and blasts of fire, and swirling vortexes of it. He had to wait for the perfect opening. Even though she had barely managed to land a few hits on him. Even though the spell had left him so exhausted that his muscles screamed out in pain and his palms and knuckles were burned. He had to wait. "Why do you keep struggling?" Misha asked, "These attacks are pointless!" There! She was panting a little now. Klin screamed though. He had lost focus and so Misha had landed an attack from the whip on his face. His right side, from the bottom of his eye to jaw, were left with a searing burn. Suddenly, he found Misha looming over him. "Done now?" Klin grimaced, his face cracking and screaming out in pain. He was lucky that had not hit his eye. He still gave her a cocky smile though. "You should have let the ship burn. Misha frowned as he pointed up, then her eyes went wide as the final part of his spell went into effect. Misha screamed in anger and from effort as a golden beam of light shot down at her.

She held out her hands, a beam of flame as large as his golden one, bursting from them. Klin quickly got to his feet and moved as fast as he could, grabbing his swords. As soon as that spell was over, he would be tapped out of magic. He turned just in time to see Misha destroy the beam. Pity, as that had been the hardest part of the spell. He felt the immediate drain on his strength though, and almost fell over. Klin stumbled over to Misha, who had fallen to her knees, her own animana more than spent. Klin stood over her, looking her in the eyes. She was so exhausted that she could not even move, let alone cast a spell. Good, his plan had worked then. "For all the people who died today," Klin growled, "your screams will serve as their comfort. So, scream loud and hope the heavens accept them." He stabbed her legs, letting her scream. Then, with a sickening churn in his stomach, Klin realized what he was doing. This was torture. "I'm sorry." He whispered, tears in his eyes. "I'll end this quickly." With that, he beheaded Misha.

As her head rolled, he fell down. Finally, the battle was over. *I hope everyone's okay.* Klin thought as the ship still burned. The sparks danced beautifully above him. He lay there, not sure what to do. He would drown before he made it back to shore, but burn to death if he stayed here. There were no lifeboats, so that was not an option. He had destroyed them all unfortunately. A small spark of fear alit in him as he found the strength to stand. He was not going to die. He would figure something out. "KLIN!" His uncle shouted. Klin looked over, dumbfounded as Uncle Joshua ran over to him. Joshua scooped him up and jumped into the water. Klin gasped as the cold water shocked him to his senses. "Uncle what is—?" Joshua just grinned as he held onto him and they began to jet across the waves. Klin blinked a few times, very confused until he realized that Joshua was holding onto a very large seal. Ander? Oh well, at least they were safe. Klin closed his eyes. Thank the Eight they had won. It was finally over.

Chapter 37

Viscious

With a casual fling of his hand, Viscisous destroyed the Water Temple's doors. He took a deep breath. He had let his temper get away. It would be best to place the blame on Misha for Lorelei's death. She was already deviating from their plans anyway. She was of no use anymore. Viscious examined Sasara's Temple. It was by far more beautiful than anything that lout Straiman could come up with it. When this was over, maybe he would use the layout as a base for his Air Temple. It really *was* beautiful. He would of course have to destroy those windows though. He hated seeing any of the Sculptors; hated remembering their faces. Especially this one. Whoever had made this image had seen Sasara in person. It was far too accurate. Viscious was tempted to destroy the stained glass window then and there, but the beauty…he would wait. There might be a clue to unlocking the Seed.

With that, he turned back to his true purpose for being there. Unlocking the Water Seed, all that remained of Sasara's power. Or more accurately, the physical manifestation of where she had drawn all her power from. Viscious could use the thing right now, and wipe out that annoying army of Coronus, but it the power in the Water Seed would still pale in comparison if he could unlock it! He examined the blue crystal, looking over every inch of it before walking around the Temple. There was nothing here! *Viscisous. Report.* Viscious nearly dropped the Seed out of shock as Romevan's voice reverberated in his mind. *Ah, master! I have the Water Seed.* He replied quickly. *Hmm, good.* Romevan hummed pleased, *I assume you are on your way back then?*

Well, uh not yet. Viscisous answered, beginning to sweat despite his constant temperature control. *And why is that?* Romevan inquired

425

coolly. *I decided to look for clues on how to unseal the power within my Lord.* Viscious explained hastily, *All so that I may present it to you in a form more fitting for you!* He began to sweat and tremble as his master remained silent. Finally he replied, *I see. However generous your intentions are Viscisous, those were not your orders. I will allow this change, but pray I am not required to again.* Viscious bowed, unsure if Romevan would be able to see it. *Thank you my Lord! You are most generous! I understand!*

Good. Romevan said satisfied, *I will be making my move soon though. Do not interfere.* With that, Viscisous felt the overwhelming presence leave. He let out a sigh of relief. He better be careful. It seemed that Romevan might be catching on to him.

Celeste and Joseph stopped as they saw the rubble of the Temple doors. "Really?" Joseph muttered with a snort, "That's just rude." Celeste nodded, drawing her blade. "Agreed. Let's kick his ass." Joseph drew his sword. "Yeah, let's." They walked in and found the Archeshtis standing by the altar, completely unaware of them. Joseph pointed the Black Rose at him and shouted, "Hey, you flying rat!" The flying rat spun around. "Who dares--!" He stopped, his anger flashing to surprise before he plastered a smug smile across his face. "Really?" He asked, "You two cleaned up that mess already?" Joseph tightened his grip on his sword. "Shut it maggot." Viscisous held up his hands defensively, "Oh, sorry. Touch a nerve there? And you my dear, how can you stand there next to him after practically killing his mother? I'm shocked at the arrogance and vanity in you."

"That was all you!" Celeste snapped. Viscious tapped his chin with a finger. "Mmm, yes, but you made it possible. I mean, none of this would have been possible without you, so I'm not sure how you can spin it on me. Really though, thank you for that."

Ignore him. Yatta whispered to both Joseph and Celeste. *Remember the tales? He is the weakest in combat out of all Arctisisi. He uses words and manipulates to win.* Celeste gripped Yatta and took a strong stance and yelled. "That may be true, but all the more reason for me to work to atone for it, and I'll start by killing you, you dirty sister-killer!" Celeste took satisfaction at the utter stupefied shock of Viscisous right before she charged. She cut off Viscious's arm, then cut the tendons in his ankles. Visicosus fell to his knees with a half snarl, half cry of pain.

Then, Joseph moved in, stabbing him in the chest before kicking him back over to Celeste who beheaded him. They stayed there, breathing hard as they waited with bated breath. Then, Visciosus slowly got to his feet, his head regrowing and wounds closing. Celeste almost missed the scythe of air that shot towards her and Joseph. They leapt in opposite directions, standing a few feet apart from each other.

"Amusing." Viscious snarled, "But annoying! I hope you have more planned because that won't be nearly enough." *Wear him down.* Yatta reminded them, *Then I can turn those special emotions into magic, but you only get one strike.* Joseph and Celeste exchanged a brief nod, as they took up a fighting stance, warily staring at Viscisous as the air around him began to swirl. "Seriously, *you're* playing defensive?" Joseph complained. Viscious just gave him a smirk. "Well, I do enjoy my games. I could kill you like I killed Lorelei though if you prefer. Why aren't you overcome with grief by the way? Did you not love her?" Violet energy erupted in an arura around Joseph. "KEEP HER NAME OUT OF YOUR FILTHY MOUTH!" He roared, swinging the Black Rose, sending dark magic forward in a from the same as a sword slice. It hit the vortex, disrupting it for a bit. "Joseph, keep that up!" Celeste yelled. Joseph just screamed but attacked once more. Celeste dashed forward through the opening Joseph was creating and leapt at Viscious. The Archtisis caught her blade between his hands and tossed her behind him. Celeste barely managed to flip around and land on her feet.

She skidded back, almost stumbling into the vortex. There was a loud tearing sound as she almost fell into the vortex. As she righted herself, she saw that the bottom of her jacket had been torn to shreds. She looked back to Viscious and saw seven icicles headed towards her. She cartwheeled to the left, pushing off her hand and flying through the air. She landed as lithely as a bird next to Joseph, who had just broken through the barrier. Viscious merely raised an eyebrow at them, before slashing a claw through the air. Razor winds leapt off the claws, flying at them. "Behind!" Joseph barked. Celeste obeyed and stood behind him as he braced his sword, blocking the attack. Yet it was not a perfect block. Drops of blood dripped onto the stone tile, symmetrical diagonal cuts on Joseph's cheeks.

"You, okay?" Joseph asked. Celeste nodded, "Yeah, are you?" Joseph grinned at her as his coat flared back from a new surge of magic. "Merely a flesh wound." He then shot a blast of Dark magic at Viscious, who batted it aside with ease. "I thought I told you to up your game!" Visicious snorted, "I'm growing tired of this. Spice it up or I am ending this!" Suddenly, Celeste noticed hundreds of distorted slivers hanging in the air around them. The two went back to back, and began to deflect and slice through the incoming razors of air. For some reason, Visicous did not launch all of them at once, but sent them in groups. Celeste struggled to keep up as razor after razor was launched at them. For every ten that Celeste destroyed, two would hit her. Luckily, none of them were lethal, but the cuts along her arms and legs blazed with pain. Joseph fared no better. His coat was tattered, stains of red where red did not belong. "You see how helpless you feeble humans are before me?" Viscious hissed, "You destroy Gruntlets with ease, somehow thinking that makes you great, but they are only on the level of a human! All other Heshtisi are superior, and I am an Arctisi! One destined to take the place of the Sculptor Celerious! You are fighting a god! You really think that *you* could defeat *me*?!"

"I'm so sick of your voice." Joseph snapped in between labored breaths, "How about we remove that tongue?" Joseph rushed Vicsious, swinging at the head. There was an ear-piercing scrape as claws met metal as Viscious blocked. Celeste ran in, specks of blood flying in the air behind her. She slid under Joseph, coming up and slicing open Viscious's stomach. Viscious merely grunted as he kept his guard against Joseph. Celeste was taken off guard by the demon's stoicism, so she failed to make a follow-up attack. This allowed Viscious to finally push Joseph off of him, flinging air razors at him. Joseph destroyed a few before rolling to the side. Celeste was behind Viscious now though, having recovered her senses. As she rushed him, the air around whipped up and she found herself suddenly flung into the air. She barely avoiding hitting the city, but she clutched to Yatta tightly, despite losing her bearings. Suddenly, she found herself sitting on something plush and cool. Celeste looked down to see that she was sitting on a platform of solidified shadow.

428

Below, Joseph stood with arms held out, visible strain on his face. "Gotcha!" He exclaimed, "Just go for it now! In our state, wearing down this monster is impo—gah!"

"Joseph!" Celeste cried. Both his arms had been impaled by icicles. "I'm fine!" He snarled, "Just go for it!" Viscious flew up to Celeste, his crystal wings flapping softly. "My, he's as stubborn as his father." Viscious mused. A beam of darkness shot at him. Viscious sighed as he blocked it. "I'll take that as a comment!" Joseph yelled cockily. Celeste ignored Joseph for the moment and leapt at Viscious. He wasn't fast enough this time. She lodged Yatta in his shoulder, then using the hilt for support, she swung around behind him, removing the blade at the last second. Celeste then cut off his wings and stabbed the center of the spine. Viscious let out a horrible screech as they plummeted to the ground. Placing her trust in Joseph, she kicked off the monster, hearing a loud crash as Viscious hit the stone floor. Celeste's trust was not misplaced as a shadow tendril grabbed her and placed her on the ground safely. "Stop. Falling." Joseph begged, breathing shallowly. "Those spells are damn hard."

"Aww, I'm just going you a chance to be my hero." Celeste teased. Joseph just shook his head. Suddenly, Viscious began to laugh. He rose to his feet, the floor around him a small crater. "That was good." He giggled, "But now you die." Celeste saw the air distorting too late. She cried out in pain as the air around her arms and legs tightened, forcing her to drop Yatta. She was lifted into the air, helpless and unable to move. With a panicked thought, she realized that she was going to die like Lorelei. Viscious wet his lips, his eyes full of ravenous glee. "Ahahahaha! You see! You see it! Diearghgh!" Celeste watched as Viscious was consumed in a simultaneous blast of purple flames and energy, the two intertwining in a weird flame and liquid motion, being both at once. As her bonds were released, Joseph caught her. He spared her a quick glance before he said with an icy cold voice. "Hey fucker, forgetting about me?" Joseph gingerly set Celeste down and handed her Yatta. Viscious's screams had finally faded as the spell wore off. "You're deluded if you think I'm going to let you kill another!" Joseph growled, "Now, fuck off!" Joseph reignited the spell from before, and Viscious screams began anew. Celeste looked over at Joseph.

There was hatred shining in those eyes, but even more, like a beacon in a stormy night, was love and determination. Celeste felt a warm feeling spread through her. *You okay?* Yatta asked. Celeste smiled, *Yeah. Hey, you want this emotion?* Yatta appeared next to her and placed her hand on her rib. Celeste could feel the new emotion being absorbed by Yatta. *Wow Celeste! I have enough for* three *strikes now! You must really love—*. "We got a fight right now!" Celeste squeaked, earning a confused look from Joseph. "I'LL KILL HER!" Viscious screeched, hysterically, "NO! Wait.. I'Ll kiLL you BOTH!" Viscious had been writhing on the ground, but slowly got to his feet, his burned body slowly flaking as it healed. He stood hunched over, arms hung loosely when he suddenly rushed forward. Celeste leapt in front of Joseph, blocking the claw strike from him. Viscious let out a screech of anger as he began to attack Celeste instead. Celeste blocked two more strikes from the Arctisis before he was blown back by a solid punch from Joseph. His fist glowed purple as blood dribbled down his arms.

The two nodded at one another as they began a unified attack. They had noticed Viscious was now vulnerable. Consumed by hysterical rage, his strikes had become faster but much sloppier and predictable. Celeste swung down, hitting his shoulder before releasing three quick strikes on the torso. While Viscious was still recovering from that attack, Joseph jumped in and unleased a flurry of magic-infused punches before finishing it off with a roundhouse to the head. Viscisous was flung into the air, but stopped as he opened his wings. He then placed his arms above his head, and began to spin, flying at them. Joseph and Celeste leapt to opposite sides, and as Viscious passed by them, Celeste cut him in half. The monster screamed in agony as he fell to the floor. The two wasted no time as they rushed him. Viscious had just regrown his legs and swung at them. Celeste blocked the attack as Joseph pounded him. Celeste waited for an opening, but Joseph just kept punching. His punches became so fast it was like watching a hurricane hit the Archeshtisi. Each punch was so powerful that it left a brief imprint upon the body, forcing it back before he could heal. Joseph let out a roar as he ended with two solid punches to the face. There was a loud crack as Viscious's head snapped back at an unnatural angle. Joseph growled low, his knuckles bloody with both his and Viscious's blood.

Now! Yatta cried, *While he's dazed!* Celeste strode froward, her blade beginning to glow a bright white. Viscious's eyes widened in fear as he began to snap out of it. That was all the confirmation Celeste needed to know this would work. Before Viscious could move, she struck like a viper, moving behind him and cutting the stomach simultaneously. "That's for tricking me!" Celeste snapped. She then cut the tendons in the ankles as Viscious howled in pain. "That's for Lorelei!" She then moved back in front of him, forcing him to stare at her in the eyes. "AND THIS IS FOR SELENE!" She screamed as she beheaded Viscious, Archtisis of Wind. The head rolled off, clacking against the marble floor. As it stopped, the rest of the body crumbled to ash. Celeste watched as a mysterious wind blew away the pile. "It worked." Celeste said softly. "It actually worked!" She cried as she began to laugh. All those virtues emotions that Yatta had stored over the centuries actually hurt that monster! "I think we actually killed him." Joseph cried triumphantly. Celeste laughed, and then stopped feeling woozy. Her legs buckled and she fell forward. "Whoa!" Joseph cried softly as he caught her. "Guess we better get you back. We both need medics, huh?" Celeste gave him a weak smile and tried to walk but could not. Joseph grinned as he scooped her up and began to carry her out. "Good job Celeste." Joseph whispered, a proud smile on his face. "Both mom and your sister would be proud." Celeste simply nodded as she snuggled up against Joseph's chest. It was finally over.

Chapter 38

Revelations

Four Days Later

Celeste, Klin, Joseph, and Uncle Joshua carried Lorelei's open casket with dark and heavy faces. Flowers lay beautifully in her hair, the smile she had died with still there, even after the Life Weavers had put her corpse back into a humane form. They had walked to the edge of the city, right next to the Water Temple. A fresh grave had been dug in the ground behind the great window of Sasara, and many chairs had been brought out for the service. Erok, Sasha, Kyoko and Beppo stood in the front row. Over half the surviving members of the island had shown up. Klin blinked away tears as he placed down the casket next to the grave.

Beppo walked up to the podium that had been brought out, a wind stone to amplify his voice attached to it. "Friends, thank you for coming." Beppo began. "I know how many of you have lost loved ones, and that this service is the last of a long series of sad farewells." Klin took a deep breath, feeling his body sink under the weight of death and sadness he had seen the past three days. He and Joseph had attended each and every funeral. It was crushing. "But," Beppo continued, "None of you had to be here, and so the amount of you that have shown is a great testament to impact Lorelei had upon our lives. As her sons discovered while they were here, this was not her first visit to us. We all remember clearly her visits, rare and far between they may have been. Every visit, without fail, she would first visit our sick ward, healing with a near miraculous ability. Her love and joy that she spread to all, ignoring none and caring for all. She cared for all that she gave her life for us. I crowned her with my people's highest title, mamater. A

432

mother who goes beyond blood. Yet, those who knew her better than I can attest to her life."

Beppo gestured to Klin as he stepped down. Klin walked over, looked over the great crowd and took a deep breath. "My mother was ever loving. Not always perfect at it, as we all are. Oh, we got her to yell at us, and sometimes her protective care brought her to actions she always regretted. But the key was she was always repentant, something we could all learn from her life. I think the biggest thing we can learn from her is her capacity for forgiveness. You all know the full story of her death now. We made now effort to hide it. How Celeste Farvor'Coal betrayed us, even though it did not play out how she wished. I know many of you are calling for her punishment, a cry that seems unheard by Beppo. However, take it from me and my brother, whose mother died as consequence for her actions." Klin paused to look at Celeste, who had her head hung in shame, and smiled at her, "We've already forgiven her. We *all* lost loved ones, and she will always live with that guilt. But she killed Viscious, who orchestrated and betrayed her, his betrayal resulting in the death of our friends and family. We all commit great sins, and so allowing her to live her live in recompense is the greatest act of forgiveness we can give, for as my mom liked to remind me and my brother, we all mess up. Let us honor Lorelei, and show love to even our enemies." Klin stepped down from the podium and returned to his spot by Celeste and Joseph.

Celeste tackled him in a hug, sobbing. Klin returned the hug and began to sob himself. Joseph walked over, and the three embraced crying together. Soon enough, the rest of the mourners began to cry themselves, even Erok had tears rolling down his face. Klin, Joseph and Celeste stopped and watched the priest come over and begin to say the prayers over her. Once he was finished, he nodded and allowed the four pallet bears to lower Lorelei Markus into her final resting place.

Klin awoke the next day, his eyes and throat still raw from crying. Everything around him seemed dull and numb, even the bright colors of Solanthis seemed to lose their vigor. He wanted to lie in bed and never get up and never do anything ever again. Yet, he knew what Lorelei would say if she saw him now. She would scold him, saying that death is never as bad as we think. She would say, "Oh Klin, it is sad. But remember, death is never the end. We know that. What is it you would do if I died? I hope pray for me." Klin slowly rose and began to dress. He had a duty still, and while he knew his mom would be gentle, she would still be firm that he did it. He packed all of his things up, saying a silent prayer for his mom's soul as he did. *Whatever happens after we did, I hope Genus takes you to a happier place.*

Once he was finished, he left the room and found Joseph out there, leaning against the wall and his things slung in a pack over his shoulder. "Ready?" Klin nodded and walked with his brother as they left. "So, did you really forgive her?" Joseph asked. Klin shrugged, "I'm not really sure. I want to, I really do. But, I get these bursts of anger at what was taken from us. We'll never get her back. I'm not letting it affect how I treat Celeste, but the anger is there, lurking underneath it all." Joseph just chuckled. "What?" Klin asked annoyed. "Oh, nothing." Joseph replied, "Just that I'm the more virtuous one for once." Klin snorted as he elbowed his brother. "Don't brag about virtue bonehead. That's the exact opposite. Besides, I'm sure your new lover will find it unattractive." Joseph went bright red and looked away mumbling something. Klin just chuckled.

"That's nice." Joseph said. Klin frowned, "What is?"

"You're laughing. That's got to be the most genuine laugh I have heard from you in two months at least." Klin turned away, perturbed. Had it been that long since he had enjoyed himself? Two moths now though…two months ago he had been in Horst's basement. At that moment they reached the docks. Joshua waved them to a ship. "Slowpokes." He growled, "It's nearly eight. Yer the last one's here." He stomped off, swaying side to side a bit as he did. Beppo shook his head before turning to give them a small smile. "Tredos, I wish you safe and swift journey."

"Thank you." Joseph said, "We really appreciate all that you have done for us. Are you sure you don't want to come with?" Beppo gave them a fond smile. "It warms my hear that you want me on your adventure. Unfortunately, my duties are here for now, and yours are elsewhere. We must part ways, but, if you are still in the company of Emperor Gabriel in three months' time, I am sure we will meet again. Something tells me our stories are not done yet."

"Will it really be safer for us there?" Klin asked. Beppo nodded, "Until four days ago, the palace of Coronus was the second safest place for you. Now, it will be the first. Ardaven seems desperate to have you two for some reason, but they would not dare bring an army to the capital. Plus, Gabriel is quite good a weeding out corruption in his court, so you shall be safe with him." Klin nodded, "Alright then. Thank you again for everything Beppo." Beppo smiled and gave them both a hug. "It was my pleasure and honor tredos." He said tearily. He then clapped them on the shoulders. "Now, we must go. There are no weavers on this ship, other than Sasha and the little one. It will be a bit before you reach the mainland then. At least a day and a half. Take care my friends, and safe journey." Klin and Joseph climbed aboard the small ship. The whole crew lined up and waved farewell as they left the first home they had had since their journey had begun.

Ander leaned against the railing, golden sunlight intermingling with pink and purple as the lights danced off the water as the sun set. Kyoko stood next to him, silent and reserved. She really had not been herself since Lorelei had died. Ander was not sure he could fully blame her. He had to admit, he had come to love Lorelei trying to mother them. She was also still battling with a sense of guilt after not being allowed to fight. Kyoko was skilled, but she was still only a child, and war was no place for a child. "Do you think the king is a nice man?" Kyoko asked suddenly.

Ander looked down at in her in some surprise. "Not sure." He replied with a shrug. "Celeste says he is." Kyoko looked out over the water and mumbled, "Yeah, but how true is what *she* says." Ander opened his mouth, intending to scold, but closed it. He could not in good conscious scold his sister over something he himself agreed with. How trustworthy was Celeste now? Sure, she had sided with Joseph in killing Viscious, but they would never had needed to do that if it had not been for her. So many had died as a result of her actions. Not to mention Ander still had no idea what Joshua thought about this. He had spent most of the past four days utterly wasted. Klin and Joseph were the only ones who could get anything close to sensible to come from the man's mouth. Finally, Ander said, "Well, Beppo had nothing but good things to say about the Emperor, so he's probably a good guy." Kyoko nodded, "Yeah, but didn't people say similar things about dad?"

Ander grimaced, "Yeah. I guess they did. We'll just have to wait and see. If he's a bad dude, we got Klin, Joseph, Erok, and Sasha to protect us, right?" Kyoko let out a small smile at that and giggled softly, "I think Klin and Erok are the only ones who really count though." Ander raised an eyebrow, "Seriously? Not even Joseph? He took on Viscious!" Kyoko smiled mischievously and leapt up into the air, floating. "Yeah, but he doesn't have good judge of character. He's dating Celeste." Ander let out a soft snort, but a small spike of pain pierced his heart at that reminder. "Alright, fair enough." Kyoko tilted her head and frowned. "You're uspet that they are dating, aren't you? It's because you think Joseph is too good for her!" Ander plastered a smile on his face. "Okay, fair enough you got me." Kyoko nodded in satisfaction and landed back on the ground. "You should really tell him that if you are that bothered by it Ander. Celeste doesn't deserve to be happy!"

"Hey!" Ander scolded, "Never say that! Everyone should be happy Kyoko, regardless of what they have done." Kyoko tilted her head up at him, "Even dad and mom?" Ander froze, unsure what to say. Logically, with what he just said, yeah, even dad and mom. But, those scars cried out for justice. "I—I don't know." Ander admitted. Kyoko remained next to him quietly, the solemness from before overtaking them once more. "Ander?" Kyoko asked quietly. "Yeah Kyo?"

"Something's been bothering me." Kyoko whispered, "And it's starting to scare." Ander frowned, looking at her concernedly. "What's that? Are you worried Celeste will betray us again?" He knew Erok was worried about that. His friend was at this moment inconspicuously observing Celeste. Kyoko shook her head. "No. Can—can we talk about it somewhere else?" Now Ander was truly worried. "Yeah, sure." What had her so spooked that she felt the need to force them to talk somewhere else? They went to her and Sasha's room. The whole time they walked, Kyoko was jittery and jumpy. When they got in, Kyoko got a intense look of concentration on her face. When she stopped, she exclaimed, "There! Just placed a spell so that no one can hear us!" Ander looked around nervously, "Okay, you're starting to really scare me Kyo. What is going on?"

"It's Nathaniel!" She blurted out. "I keep getting scary feelings when I'm around him! I've also noticed he's been spending a lot of time with Klin!" Ander crossed his arms, feeling annoyed. "Oh, come Kyoko, those two are the most trustworthy of all of us! Besides, the two are good friends. Nothing odd about them spending time together." Kyoko shook her head vehemently, "I know, but there's something weird about him! Miss Lorelei thought so too! I told her that it seems really weird that he *always* shows up at really important moments for us! Is that not weird?" Ander felt a cold hand caress his heart, "Huh, I mean yeah, I did think that. But it was just coincidence. He's proven his loyalties lie with us."

"Are we *really sure*?" Kyoko whispered, "Miss Lorelei and Mr. Joshua were going to confront him after the battle, but then Celeste betrayed us. I—I keep catching him giving weird looks to everyone. A-an-and when Sasha was given the Water Seed before we left…his eyes. They changed Ander. They were purple and yellowish, and looked like a snake's." Kyoko shivered violently. "What are you implying?" Ander asked slowly. Kyoko sat down, wrapping her arms around her legs. "I—I don't know. Just that something is off about him." Ander knelt down next to her and gave her a hug before tousling her hair. "Don't worry about it Kyo. I'll go talk to Joshua about it. It'll all be okay, you'll see." Kyoko shook her head and remained on the ground. Ander sighed and left her there. It would be fine. It had to be. Ander walked around and asked after Joshua when he was not on the deck or in his room. No one really knew. Ander thought about where he might be and checked the kitchen. Sure enough, Joshua at the table, ten empty bottles of beer scattered across the table.

"Joshua?" He asked tentatively. Joshua spun around, his hair a tangled mess and his eyes wide. "Oh, it's just you. I thought a centipede had finally come for me." Ander opened his mouth to ask why he would be a centipede, but said, "You know what? I don't want to know." Joshua let out a snort, "Damn right you don't. Centipede bounty hunters are nasty business. They go after ones who know about them! Might want to sleep with one eye open now kid." Ander sighed and sat down next to Joshua. The crazy adventurer eyed him suspiciously. "You aren't here to drink with me, are ya?" He slurred. Ander shook his head. "Good!"

Joshua exclaimed, swinging his hands out and almost falling out of his seat. "You kids should never drink when sad!" Ander frowned, "But aren't you?" Joshua let out a coarse laugh. "Oh yes I am!" He giggled, "Ain't that a funny act of hyp-o-crisy!" Ander sighed and stood up, "You're in no state to talk to. I'll come back later." Joshua grabbed his wrist and forced him to sit back down. "Stop right there young man." He growled, "If you got something serious to say, say it." Joshua let out a small smirk, "I think more clearly when the ghosts are constantly whispering in my ear. What's up?"

"It's Kyoko." Ander explained. "She's scared of Nathaniel." Joshua froze in the middle of trying to take of drink of beer. "Scared? What she scared of him for?" Ander shrugged, "Well, she says she gets scary vibes from him. That he keeps giving all of us weird looks when he thinks no one is looking. Oh, and she said his eyes have changed before." Joshua gingerly placed the beer bottle down. "The eyes specifically?" Ander nodded, "Yeah. She said they were looked like a snake's and were a weird combo of yellow and purple." Joshua froze, all signs of drunkenness disappearing as he turned pale. "Kid, are ya sure she said those colors specifically?" Ander nodded, frowning apprehensively. "Yeah, why?"

"Herking Heshtanus!" Joshua exclaimed, "Things make way more sense now. The Seekers didn't track the magic! They had a herking spy among us the entire herking time!" Ander frowned, "Hold on, I thought you and Lorelei had already thought this? Besides, isn't this a bit of a jump? There isn't really much proof that Kyoko is telling the truth." Joshua leapt up, "We don't got time for this!"

"Joshua!" Ander barked, "Sit! Down!" Joshua froze, looking at Ander in amazement. "Did you just yell at me?" Joshua asked quietly. Ander froze, ice his heart. "Uh, yeah." Joshua laughed and sat back down. "Danm kid! You are just full of pleasant surprises!"

"Uh, thanks?" Ander replied tentatively. He was felling really confused. Joshua was *happy* he had yelled at him? *It is because you stood up for yourself.* Lupis mused, *I am not as surprised as he is, but still, good job young one.* "Anyway," Joshua chuckled, "Give me yer reasonings before I march up there and cut off the lying blue-blood's head."

"Well, um okay yeah don't do that." Ander fumbled, "But, here's the thing. We really don't know if he is a traitor. If we accuse him it's not as if he will just come on out and say it. We need some proof. So I say, we confront him after we make camp." Joshua nodded, "Alright, we'll do it yer way. But kid, do you know what yellow and purple mix signifies?" Ander tiled his head, "No, but now that you mention it, it sounds familiar." A very grim and serious look came across Joshua's face as he leaned froward. "Kid, that means—" *Dong. Dong. Dong.* Suddenly the bell rang, and Klin ran by the door, stopped and yelled at them, "Hey guys, we've made it to shore! Come on!" Joshua stood up, "Later. Come on." The two left the kitchen and parted, gathering their belongings. Once they were on deck, the crew was lowering the board to let them off. "This is where we part." The captain said. "We wish we could take you all the way to the port city, but we must get back to patrolling. Who knows how Ardaven will respond to our actions. I'm sorry we could not do more." Klin shook his head, "No worries. We appreciate what you did do. Thank you, and safe travels." The crew saluted them as one. "And to you as well friends." The captain responded, "May the hopes of Threa go with you!" They waved as the ship sailed away and began to walk. Night had nearly fallen.

"What did he mean by, 'the hopes of Threa?'" Ander asked. Erok shrugged, "It's a good-luck blessing type thing in Coronus." Ander smiled and let out a sigh of relief. "Oh good. I was worried he meant something like, 'You carry the hopes of all the world on you!' Or something like that." Erok snorted, "Oh Genus no! That sounds horrible!" They made their way into the woods nearby and after going about a mile in, Joshua stopped and declared, "Alright, let's make camp here. It's late now." The group let out a sigh of relief as they began to make camp. "Celeste, you and Erok get the fire going." Erok cast Celeste a nasty look. "You sure? She might decide to burn us all instead." Celeste cast her head away. "HEY!" Joshua snapped. "Shut the herk up! Alright, everyone stop what yer doing! Gather around!" Everyone obeyed, although everyone was also confused and hesitant. "So, seems Klin's speech weren't enough." Joshua growled. "Nor is my sis's late wishes enough for ya'll to dig your heads out of yer asses! Listen up you selfish pricks! None of us here are innocent! All of us got wrongs we done, and all of us have hurt others! So stop acting like Celeste is special in this regard! My nephews are the only other ones with more authority to say she's okay than me!"

"So what?" Erok snapped, "You've decided to move on and forget about your sister?" Joshua gave Erok a steely look. Ice and fire incarnate was in that stare. Erok gulped, and actually showed fear. "Watch it Erok." Joshua said icily, "I like you, but I won't hesitate to remove all yer teeth and tongue to stop more idiocy sprouting from that mouth of yours. Understood?" Erok nodded hastily, "Yes. Sorry. I'm really sorry about that."

Joshua gave him a nod of satisfaction. "Good. Now, see what I mean? Erok just said something incredibly stupid and insensitive and just plain nasty. All of us are guilty of a large sin or another. Celeste just happens to be the first to have done it on a large scale. Now, do I not hate her? Oh, I am full of detest for her. But, her plan was to stop a battle before it began. Misha went rouge though. All death was Misha's fault, not Celeste's. Emotions are always in response to rationality or goodness or what have you. But I know this, I'm going to let Celeste prove herself, and you idiots need to let her also. If you keep walking this path, each and everyone one of you will come to a situation where you'll mess up just a colossally. Celeste just happened to be the first, and so it would be good to get in the habit of allowing repairs to wrongs. Cause one day, it'll be yer turn." Joshua looked over each and everyone of them, staring them in the eye. "You don't have to like it. But you should. Get used to this. Tragedy will follow you like a bad smell from now on. You all need a shoulder to lean on, and Celeste needs all of us. She ain't special. So, will you give her yours?"

Everyone remained quiet as Joshua finished. After a long silence, Kyoko piped, "I will." She flew over to Celeste and smiled at her. "I never really wanted to hate you. I thought I had to." Tears brimmed at the corners of Celeste's eyes at the girls embraced. "Thanks Kyo." Ander smiled said, "I'll also give you chance. So will Erok." Erok sputterd, "Hey! I never said that! At least let me say it jerk." Sasha remained quiet as Erok and Ander started at her. "Fine." She huffed, "I don't like and don't expect me to be warm to you! But, I'll give you a chance." Celeste smiled and nodded. "Oh, come on." Nathaniel said testily, "You don't actually believe she's capable of being forgiven, do you?" Klin frowned, "Nathaniel, what—"

"I mean, no matter how you spin it or rationalize it, she started a battle of armies!" He sneered, "A battle that cost hundreds of lives on both sides! Do you think that the lives of the Seekers are worth less simply because they were led by Misha? She caused a *massacre*." Ander frowned. Something about Nathaniel's tone seemed familiar. "Shut it blue-blood." Joshua snarled, "No one is incapable of being forgiven." Nathaniel raised an eyebrow. "Really? Such ideal words from the one who said they detest the one they claim to forgive! Doesn't forgiveness involve a lack of hate? You seem quite incapable of forgiving her to me! And Joseph only has 'forgiven' her due to his lust."

"That's not true!" Joseph snapped, "Our relationship has nothing to do with that!"

"Oh, so you don't love her then?" Nathaniel inquired. Joseph, Nathaniel, and Joshua quickly devolved into a shouting match. Sasha and Klin began to try and clam them down. *Ander, have you remembered what the color of eyes means yet?* Sean asked. Ander shook his head. "No. I almost forgot." *Think young one. Who is the one who has been our common enemy through the ages?* Lupis whispered. Ander froze as the revelation hit him like punch to the gut. "Oh herk." He said quietly, "That's the color of the Eye of Romevan!" *Yes.* Adamar replied, *You know what you must do. We* must *know. Now!* Ander nodded and removed the limiter on Life Force and screamed. Everyone fell silent as they looked at him. "Ander?" Sasha asked worriedly, "What's wrong?"

"Na-Nathaniel!" He shrieked, "H-h-he doesn't have a human soul!" Where the thing that claimed to be Nathaniel was, was a black void. It had a very faint glow, and like other souls, but this one seemed to be trying to destroy itself. Everyone froze as they looked at Nathaniel. Klin laughed nervously, "Come on Ander, how could you know something like that? Right Nathaniel? Nathaniel?" The man, creature, thing, had started to laugh. He continued to laugh in a manic frenzy. Joshua and Erok whipped out their gun and crossbow. Joseph and Celeste drew their swords while Kyoko leapt behind Ander. "Oh my!" Nathaniel said as he wiped a tear, "I have not laughed like that in a long time! Thank you, Ander! I *was* hoping to stay hidden at least until we reached Coronus, however. I am *not* pleased at that." Ander felt his stomach churn as terror began to creep into him. "What in Hestanus are you?!"

441

Joshua roared. Nathaniel's eyes changed, the pupils becoming slits as the eyes turned to a yellow and purple mix. "Don't make demands of me *human*." Nathaniel sneered. "As for who I am? Well, my last name was your clue."

Klin's eyes went wide. "Hold on. Aradoth. Aradoth was the first human... of herk. No. No way. You could not possibly—" Nathaniel smiled, "Ah my dear Klin! I knew you would piece it together. For the rest of you? Our world's history should never be lost! I was once the first human. The First of the Scorned, father of Malanus, and the Heir to Nath. Who am I?" A death grip fell upon them. "Oh, herking Sculptors above." Joshua whispered, "You're Romevan himself." Romevan clapped his hands, "Bravo! I was wondering if you could ever connect any rational threads. Now, what will you all do I wonder?"

"RUN!" Joshua screamed. Ander transformed, into a giant bird and flew off with Kyoko. As everyone scattered, he could hear Romevan's evil laugh below. "Well, how predictable. I will give you all a head start to make it fair. Good luck!"

Chapter 39

The Wide Path

Darkness covered the land like a thick blanket as Klin dashed through the woods. No moonlight guided him as sprinted. Twigs and dead leaves crunched under his feet while branches scratched his face and hands. "Joseph! Celeste! Uncle!" He shouted. They had all just scattered, the terror making them flee like sheep from the wolf. But, they needed to regroup. No! They needed to get away! Wh-what in Hesh—Romevan! Klin's barely coherent thoughts ran amok as panic and hysteria fought to take full control in him. "Oh Klin." Romevan's voice seemed to echo all around him. "Why do you run? Did all our conversations mean nothing? What has changed that you feel like you must flee?" Klin ignored him, running even faster. Romevan chuckled, "Oh come now. You must know that running is pointless." The voice was not far behind him now.

Suddenly, a wall of black flame appeared in front of him. Klin let out a yelp as he barely managed to stop before running into it. Klin spun around to see Natha-no, Romevan walking towards him. He had his hands clasped behind his back and carried himself with all the grace and majesty of a king. "Understand I have no wish to harm you." Romevan said benevolently. Without thinking, Klin wove a light orb and tossed it at Romevan. The Heshtisi did not even move a muscle as the orb was batted by a slice of black energy. Klin felt his heart skip a beat. Even Viscious had needed to perform a physical movement for a spell like that. "Klin." Romevan tucked, "I'm disappointed. I thought you better than to do something so pointless." Romevan's entire voice had changed compared to when he had spoken as Nathaniel. His voice was far richer and more honeyed. It felt almost like a divine being was speaking to him. "Klin, you are an extraordinary human." The Heshtisi King continued, "A human born with no one or two, but *three* Connections! Not even I had that! In fact, I'm not even sure if there has *ever* been a human born with such power!"

Klin's palms were sweaty, but as he let Romevan talk, he began to reach for his swords. "I would not do that if I were you." Romevan said causally. "I do have the ability to heal you, but I would rather not use it." Klin stopped and lowered his hands. "Why do you want to talk?"

"There we go!" Romevan hummed, spreading out his hands in excitement. "Now we can get somewhere. You see Klin Markus, people are either born great, or they make themselves great. I was both, and so are you. Only a fool would think otherwise. You have incredible power, and you were born with it for a reason. You have a destiny, and it is one that you cannot refuse. Look at all the humans that you draw to yourself. Each one extraordinary in their own right." Klin crossed his arms and held Fire Threads underneath, hoping they would be hidden from Romevan's sight. "So, what is my destiny then?" He asked sarcastically. Before he could get an answer, there was a gunshot and Romevan was thrown to the ground as a bullet pierced his skull. "Get out of here!" Joshua ordered as he emerged from behind a tree. Romevan was already getting to his feet, but Joshua knocked him back down. "Damn it Klin! GO!" Klin debated for a brief second before he took off running. He could hear Joshua unloading his revolver and unleashing a string of curses. He spared a glance behind him and saw Joshua running, his massive sword on his back. "Damn monster destroyed my gun!" Joshua complained as he caught up to his nephew. "I'm charging him for that!"

Suddenly, they came to a clearing. Faint moonlight emerging from a cloud, the tan light barely casting enough to see by now. The others were in the center, gathered in a circle. "What in the Hestanus are you kids doing?!" Joshua yelled, "You need to keep moving!" At that moment a large, wavy barrier covered the whole clearing in a dome. "Fuck." Joshua said, "It's over." They ran over to the others and went back to back. "Glad you guys are okay." Joseph muttered. "You won't be after this." Joshua growled, "Ya should've kept moving!"

"Wow, great thank you for staying behind to help." Erok snapped. Joshua just glared. "Not now." Celeste said, "Where is he?"

"Oh, right above you." Romevan answered. They looked up to seem him floating down. "Really, I must thank you. I did not expect you all to regroup like this. This made my job much easier." Klin snarled as he wove seven Light Bombs. They were not complete though when a loud snap filled the air. Klin screamed and fell to the ground as a sharp pain pierced his chest. "I taught you that spell." Romevan sneered, "You really thought I would not know how to dismantle it?"

"Klin!" Celeste screamed. He felt a hand on his shoulder and glanced up to see Ander there. A fierce snarl was on his face. "You aren't coming near him!" Ander spat. Ander helped Klin to his feet, black spots rushing across his vision, but at that moment Celeste dashed forward with an infuriated scream. "Celeste don't!" Joshua barked. But Celeste ignored him as she leapt at Romevan. The King of Heshtanus gracefully dodged her strike before backhanding her. There was a crack as Celeste flew across the air and landed on the ground in an unconscious heap. "CELESTE!" Joseph screamed. "NO!" Klin warned, but his brother was overtaken by rage and charged Romvean also. Romevan avoided Jospeh's strikes before landing a spinning kick to Joseph's stomach. Joseph flew back, hitting the ground and not getting back up. "Idiots!" Joshua growled as he readied his sword. Ander had transformed into his wolf form, and his humanoid one. Erok and Sasha stood in a battle ready stance while Debo guarded the Kyoko and Joseph and Celeste.

"What have I done to earn such hate?" Romevan asked shaking his head. "Did I not just act in self-defense? Tell me, where did I make the first move?"

"How about when you attacked Solanthis!" Ander growled, his beastly voice booming. "Or when you sent Viscious after us!" Romevan nodded, "Ah, yes. Viscious. To be fair, I ordered both him and Misha to make sure that no actual battel ensued. However, both took that into their own hands it seems. I will make sure to properly punish him later."

"That bastard is *still* alive?!" Klin asked incredulously. Romevan rolled his eyes, "Oh come now. Did you really think you humans would be capable of killing him? Not even Threa, whom you all so revere could do it."

"Okay, so we buy this horsehit?" Erok asked, "What then?" Romevan let out an exasperated sigh. "We do what I have been trying to do this whole time. We talk." Sasha summoned a water whip and cracked it. "We won't listen to a single word you say!" She declared. "You are the ultimate deceiver and liar! Every word that comes from you mouth is a lie!" Romevan shook his head. "Really, you children are so naïve. Did I lie when I said I wished to see those slavers brought to justice? Did I lie when I said I would fight by your side? How can I be the ultimate deceiver when I follow through on my word?" Sasha looked uncertain and shaken. Romevan held out a hand. "So, can we talk then?"

"Never." Ander snarled and as one, he and Erok attacked. "Damn it!" Joshua cursed as he and Sasha followed close behind. Klin fell back to the ground as he lost his support, his chest still burning from a pain he did not understand. He watched as his friends and uncle attacked as one with such coordination and skill that he had not seen from them. Yet, he felt a pit of despair as Romevan dodged their well-coordinated assaulted with all the effort one gives to walking. How little their attack mattered to him was apparent. Erok's bolts were snapped in the air as soon as they were fired with inhuman speed. "Amusing. But enough you close minded fools." Romevan declared. He leapt into the air and hung there. Suddenly, the others were frozen and tossed back by Joseph and Celeste. They did not get up. "NO!" Klin screamed. He stood up, pushing through the pain and drew his swords. Kyoko screamed suddenly as she and Debo slumped over. "What did you do?" Klin snarled.

"Relax." Romevan said softly, "They are all merely unconscious. None of them have been harmed. Now put those down." Klin yelped as his swords were torn from his hands, landing at Romevan's feet. "Now, let us talk?" Klin kept a fighting stance, the pain in his chest finally going away. "About what?" He growled. "About you!" Romvean exclaimed, "This has always been about you! You Klin, are an extraordinary individual! One that I have taken quite the interest in."

"I'm so flattered." Klin replied dryly, "Why?" Romevan dramatically spread out his hands. "Why, is it not obvious? You have an incredible gift! Three elements! There is only one other human being that has gotten close to this, and I have been here since the beginning. You are meant for something great!" Klin crossed his arms staring at the Heshtisi coldly. "So? Could just be coincidence." Romevan gave him a silky and disarming smile. "I do not believe in such things Klin. Remember, I have spoken with Sculptors, with gods! Destiny is real. It is a force that drives the cosmos and we cannot escape it."

"So now you're going to claim you know my destiny. Is that it?"

"Correct!" Romevan clapped. "Your destiny, Klin Markus, is to stand by my side and aid me." Klin laughed derisively, "You can't be serious! We started this whole journey to escape you!" Romevan looked at him with dead serious eyes. "Yes and look at how much death and tragedy have followed you since. Those who run from destiny only find tragedy. Your Uncle and mother knew your destiny is by my side. Did he not warn you that continuing on the path you are only will only lead to more suffering?" Klin froze. The old stories with prophecies told a similar story. Those who run from fate only make it worse. "No. My fate cannot be to help you!" Klin retorted, "You want this world destroyed! That's why you killed those who made it!" But his voice trembled with uncertainty, the seed of doubt now planted in his mind. "Oh, is that what you think?" Romevan asked. "No, I killed the Sculptors for their evils and sins! They were unjust, inferior rulers! I proved to be the destined and superior God! When I rule, I will remake this world! One in which it will be perfect! Yet, as has been proven, I cannot do this alone. Join me Klin! Join me and help make the world perfect! Only you can help me! Only you are capable of bringing about such a world!"

Klin's heart pounded furiously against his chest. "No. No I can't! The death you bring is unacceptable!"

"Sacrifice must be made in the pursuit of perfection!" Romevan declared. "You know this. Virtue is formed amidst suffering. It is incapable of being otherwise. So too must the world suffer if it is to be reborn as something better! It must die to become perfect!" Each word struck against Klin, his heart trembling and feeling on the brink of a cliff. He sounded so *right*. What was true? Suddenly, is if by some grace, he remembered something and it filled him with determination. "No." Klin said softly. Romevan's smile faltered. "What?"

"I said no!" Klin growled, "I am the son of Jethro Markus, who spent the last three thousand years standing against you! I am his heir and his legacy and mission lives on in me! Besides, my friends would never accept my decision if I joined you!" Romevan's smiled disappeared completely. "Are you sure this is your answer?" Klin nodded. "Yes." Romevan let out a sad sigh and snapped his fingers. Suddenly, a massive ball of black energy appeared high in the air above his friends. "Wait, what are you doing?" Klin asked.

"I did not want to do this." Romevan explained with regret, "But, well sacrifices must be made for a better you." Fear gripped Klin's heart, latching onto it and chasing away any light within. "What are you doing?!" Romevan just ignored him. "Any last words to them? I can wake them if you wish."

"No! Nononononono!" Klin screamed, "You aren't taking anyone else away from me!"

"You have two choices then!" Romevan boomed, "Join me! Or somehow destroy my spell! But you are weak and cannot possibly—" He was cut off thought as a black bolt of energy hit him in the face. "Shut. Up." Klin said quietly, ice cold dripping from his voice. Hate, rage, the desire to win flowed through his entire being. He needed the power to win. So, he *would* gain power that he needed, that he *deserved*. But most of all...he wanted this disgusting creature gone. "First you praise me, then you mock me." Klin snarled, both hands full of pure black energy. "I'll show you which of us is the truly powerful one!" Romevan smiled. "I expected no less Klin Markus." With that, he tossed the let the sphere fall. Klin dashed forward and placed both of his hands together, pouring all of his might into the spell. A black beam leapt off of his hands, meeting the sphere head on. The spells collided, neither one giving in or breaking apart. *No! I* will *save them!* Klin screamed as he poured more of himself into the spell, feeling almost as if he was tapping into his very soul to fuel the spell. His feet dug into the dirt, sliding back as he sustained his beam of black energy.

Then, suddenly he felt the sphere give way. It shattered, fragmenting into thousands of ugly black splinters. Klin released his own spell and punched the earth, stabilizing himself. Breathing heavily, he looked up at Romevan and smirked. "HA! How's that for weak?!" Romevan though began to laugh. Klin snarled at him. "Why are you laughing?"

"I got what I wanted!" Romevan cackled, "And it happened just as I thought it would. Look down at your chest!" Klin cried out in pain as a thousand needles pricked his chest, burning the skin. When he stopped, he looked down his shirt to see, right over his heart, the Eye of Romevan tattooed on the skin. "All who use my power shall be marked by my sign." Romevan recited, "You used Natharian magic there Klin. You are now mine!" A chill went down Klin's spine, and he felt as if his heart had come to a stop. "No." He whispered, "No." Romevan walked over to his friends. "Now, they will wonder why I left you all alive. I must make whatever lie you come up with seem believable." Klin tried to move, but was so weak he collapsed onto the ground. Romevan clucked his tongue. "Careful my child. You have spent far too much energy. Here, I will help." Klin saw a Life Thread snake around his body. He could feel his animana being restored, but at the same time his lids grew heavy. "I shall see you again Klin. Rest well till then."

EPILOGUE

Klin awoke to a well-made camp, the others huddled around him. "Oh, thank the Eight!" Celeste cried as she hugged him. Klin was startled, but returned the hug. "It's alright. I'm okay." He soothed. "How's everyone else?" Ander, Celeste, and Sasha looked away morosely. "Other than the fact that we all almost died and lost the Seed?" Erok said crudely, "Fine. Just herking fantastic!" Joseph let out a sigh, "Drop it dude. Just be glad none of us died." Erok gave him a glare before sitting down crossly. "Kid, what happened?" Joshua asked. Klin stayed silent for a moment as he prepared his lie. He...was very shaken by the fact Romevan had stolen the Water Seed. He had not seen that. Finally, he began to weave his lie. "After you were all knocked out, he gave a spiel about how he wanted me to hand over the Seed. When I refused and fought back, he took it and left."

"Makes sense." Joseph grunted. "Yeah." Sasha put int, "But why did he not kill us for opposing him. Klin had prepared for that question. The best lies had truth sprinkled in. "Because, I think he wants us to join him at some point. Before he left, he made an allusion to that." The camp fell silent. "Holy herking Hestahnus." Erok whispered breathlessly, "I—herk." Celeste shook her head. "I'm not sure what's worse. That he has a Seed, or that we are only alive because he needs us." Joshua crossed his arms, brow furrowed, "Well, whatever the reason, we can worry about it later. For now, we need to move on." Ander stood up, the golden sky framed brilliantly behind him. "Joshua's right. Whatever just happened, we can discuss it more when we are safe in the palace of Coronus. Whatever happens, we are now all a part of it."

"Great. Just great." Erok moaned. "This is *way* more than I signed up for." Klin nodded, "Same for us. But we're in this together now. We've been through too much to separate now." Celeste smiled, "Agreed. So, shall we move on to Coronus?" Kyoko leapt up into the air and flew around them. "Yes please! I want to be a princess."

451

"Uh Kyo, being in a palace doesn't make you one." Ander replied. "Awww, damn it!" Everyone laughed and they set about packing everything up. As they set off, Klin could not help but wonder, as he started at the morning sky, what darkness lurked in it? He was now marked forever by a choice, a sin. What was his destiny? Joseph hit him on the shoulder, knocking his out of his reverie. "You good?" His brother asked. Klin looked around seeming his friends, no, his family, walking and talking. They had suffered a defeat, but marching forward still was the choice they had made. "Yeah, I'm good."

Romevan stepped from his portal into his palace in Heshtanus. He had always been amused at the artistic depictions humans gave of this place. Always seen as dark, black, and horrific. That was nowhere near what it really was like. Oh, he did have the obsidian throne with the skulls of the Eight Sculptors in it, but beside that nothing else humans thought about his home was right. Gold, marble, and precious gems decorated pillars and walls. Stained glass windows commemorating his victories were in the hall. But his favorite shone light on his throne. It was not a historical event, at least not yet. The window had Romevan, in his true form, with an extravagant crown on, the world under his feet and a scepter with all the Seeds inlaid in it. This was the world's destiny.

Romevan smiled to himself as he sat in his throne. "Manisma!"

"Yes, my lord?" The Archtisis of Life asked.

"Why is Viscious not here before me?" Romevan asked. Manisima prostrated herself before him. He smiled. That was what he liked to see. "I believe he said that he needed to heal my lord. Shall I fetch him for you?"

"Please do my daughter." Romevan said, "I must hear his report before I…make my judgement." Manisima's wings bristled, but rose and flew off, her pink butterfly wings flapping softly. Romevan awaited patiently, but his cold justice burned fiercely inside. Manisima came back, Viscious trailing behind her. Good. He had not dared to try an illusion. "Leave us." Romevan commanded. Manisima bowed and left. "M-my lord wished to see me?" Viscious stammered. He was still covered in wounds and his body was blackened and burned. "Yes. I believe you owe me a report?"

"O-of course my lord!" Viscious exclaimed. Romevan narrowed his eyes. "On your knees servant." Viscious prostrated himself and said, "I did as you ordered. I made an opening for the Seed. You saw the rest yourself!"

"And in the process killed Lorelei!" Romevan roared. "That alone could have cost us his allegiance and it certainly did not make it any easier! You fool! You nearly ruined the whole thing! He was nearly there, but *you* sent in more of our soldiers! The Seekers were the only ones who were supposed to be there and fight! So, tell me *worm. What made you think that was prudent?*" Viscious swallowed, "W-w-well the Seed was needed. I know you need it and they had nearly won! So—"

"Quiet insect!" Romevan barked. "I have heard enough. They were *supposed* to win, remember? It is clear to me that you wanted the Seed for yourself. Yet, when that failed, you came crawling back here, hoping I would not notice your obvious treachery." Viscious's eyes widened in fear. "No master! I would *never*—" Romevan said nothing as he a small ball of crackling black energy appeared over his pointer finger, no larger than his thumb. "Okay, yes I did!" Viscious wailed, "Please forgive me master! I am sorry I ever dared to think such things! Please, give me another chance! I promise I will not disappoint you!"

"Very well." Romevan said. Viscious looked up, "Really?" Romevan smiled benevolently. "Yes. For your next self will be more loyal." Viscious never even had time to scream as he was obliterated, the small orb absorbing and storing Viscious's matter for a latter use. Romevan took the spell and put it away. This was the tenth time Viscious had to needed to be reborn. At least it was only the third time for treachery. "Manisima!" He smiled as she flew in, not even sparing a look at the scorched marble floor. She had never needed to be reborn, but she had seen it happen enough. "Yes my lord?"

"Send word to Morgan." Romevan ordered, "We must move up our plans. Tell her that Lavina will be joining her. That should make her happy." Manisima bowed, "It shall be done." She flew off to carry out his orders. He leaned back in his throne and let out a satisfied smiled. All would end as he wished. It was destiny.

End of Book One

Klin's Notes: Thoughts and Recordings of the Adventures We Have Had

Spells and Magic: Terms and Names of Spells

After all that has happened, I decided to keep a list of the spells and different terms that are used in regard to magic. Joseph called me a nerd for this but I'm doing it anyway! One day this will be helpful for us, I'm sure.

Animana: This is the energy which magic comes from in humans. It is still mysterious and as of now, I do not fully understand it. Best way to describe it is the spiritual energy in which one draws from to be able to cast a spell. The more one expends their energy, the greater your pool of animana is.

Weavers: Those who can use magic. Different Weavers will receive titles based on their skill level in accordance with their element.

Threads: Threads are the semi-material structure of spells. They are color-coordinated to each type of element. The ability to "see" Threads is not limited to one being able to cast that element though. You can eventually see more than your own Threads. (Still not really sure if the reason I can see them so early is the due to the fact I can use three elements or not.) Anyway, the way threads are arranged determines what type of spell will be cast. As a general rule of thumb, you need to create an outline with the threads of what you want to create. The thickness and length of the Threads determine the power and strength of the spell. Mom explained it heavily, but I'll need a refresher. I need to study the Threads overall more, along with magic itself.

Magic: What is magic? How does it work? Where does it come from? Ancient questions that are answered by either myth or history. Today it's pretty heavily argued whether or not the Sculptors were real. For some reason though, we're pretty ready to say that Romevan is. But, we continued to have historical documentation of encounters with Heshtisisi, so I guess it's not too far a stretch. But the answer to the question is that we really do not know for sure what magic is. I think the best way to describe magic is as the ability to tap into the primal matter of reality and shape it. It is a fraction of what the Sculptors did, but in a less divine way. We create something with magic or alter the fabric of the world in a way that is somehow still in line with the workings of the universe. It is not unnatural nor contrary to nature, but above it while being with it. I think.

Connections: I heard this term from Romevan. I think it is an old term, or one used by high level Weavers. It is a human's ability to be "connected" to an elemental source. The attribute that allows us one to use magic.

Source: That from which a Weaver draws magic. It's unclear whether or not each Weaver has their own Source, or if all Weavers are Connected to the same Source. Mom seemed to think the later, however I'm a bit more inclined to say we each have our own Source, since based on experience that seems how it goes.

The Elements: There are Eight Elements, each attributed to a Sculptor whom we are believed to have gotten the abilities from. Light, Dark, Water, Earth, Fire, Life, Lightning, and Air.

Seeds: We are not sure what these are, except they are powerful vestiges of magic. They are rumored to be the physical manifestations of the last remains of the Sculptor's power, left behind after they were killed. There is one for each element.

Tredo: Translates to "my friend."

Meardo: "Young Miss"

Peartra: "Young man"

www.ingramcontent.com/pod-product-compliance
Lightning Source LLC
Chambersburg PA
CBHW020837030726
47493CB00028B/122